MICHAEL CRICHTON

TWO COMPLETE NOVELS

MICHAEL CRICHTON

TWO COMPLETE NOVELS

DISCLOSURE

RISING SUN

WINGS BOOKS
NEW YORK • AVENEL, NEW JERSEY

This edition contains the complete and unabridged texts of the original editions. They have been completely reset for this volume. This omnibus was originally published in separate volumes under the titles:

Disclosure, copyright © 1993 by Michael Crichton
Rising Sun, copyright © 1992 by Michael Crichton

For *Rising Sun:*
Grateful acknowledgment is made to Warner/Chappell Music, Inc. for permission to reprint excerpts from "Great Balls of Fire" by Otis Blackwell and Jack Hammer. Copyright © 1957 by Unichappell Music, Inc. & Chapell & Co. All rights reserved. Used by permission.

This 1996 edition is published by Wings Book,
a division of Random House Value Publishing, Inc.,
40 Engelhard Avenue, Avenel, New Jersey 07001,
by arrangement with Alfred A. Knopf, Inc.

Wings Books and colophon are trademarks of Random House Value Publishing, Inc.

Random House
New York • Toronto • London • Sydney • Auckland
http://www.randomhouse.com/

Printed and bound in the United States of America

Library of Congress Cataloging-in-Publication Data

Crichton, Michael, 1942–
  [Novels. Selections]
  Two complete novels / Michael Crichton
    p.   cm.
  Contents: Disclosure — Rising sun.
  ISBN 0–517–18245–9
  1. Detective and mystery stories, American. 2. Legal stories, American. I. Title.
PS3553.R48A61996   96–28387
813'.54—dc20   CIP

8 7 6 5 4 3 2 1

Contents

DISCLOSURE

For Douglas Crichton

It shall be an unlawful employment practice for an employer: (1) to fail or refuse to hire or to discharge any individual, or otherwise to discriminate against any individual with respect to his compensation, terms, conditions or privileges of employment because of such individual's race, color, religion, sex, or national origin or (2) to limit, segregate, or classify his employees or applicants for employment in any way which would deprive or tend to deprive any individual of employment opportunities or otherwise adversely affect his status as an employee, because of such individual's race, color, religion, sex, or national origin.

Title VII, Civil Rights Act of 1964

Power is neither male nor female.

Katharine Graham

MONDAY

FROM: DC/M
ARTHUR KAHN
TWINKLE/KUALA LUMPUR/MALAYSIA

TO: DC/S
TOM SANDERS
SEATTLE (AT HOME)

TOM:
   CONSIDERING THE MERGER, I THOUGHT YOU SHOULD GET
THIS AT HOME AND NOT THE OFFICE:

   TWINKLE PRODUCTION LINES RUNNING AT 29% CAPACITY
DESPITE ALL EFFORTS TO INCREASE. SPOT CHECKS ON DRIVES
SHOW AVG SEEK TIMES IN 120–140 MILLISECOND RANGE WITH
NO CLEAR INDICATION WHY WE ARE NOT STABLE AT SPECS.
ALSO, WE STILL HAVE POWER FLICKER IN SCREENS WHICH
APPEARS TO COME FROM HINGE DESIGN DESPITE IMPLEMEN-
TATION OF DC/S FIX LAST WEEK. I DON'T THINK IT'S SOLVED YET.

   HOW'S THE MERGER COMING? ARE WE GOING TO BE RICH
AND FAMOUS?

   CONGRATULATIONS IN ADVANCE ON YOUR PROMOTION.

ARTHUR

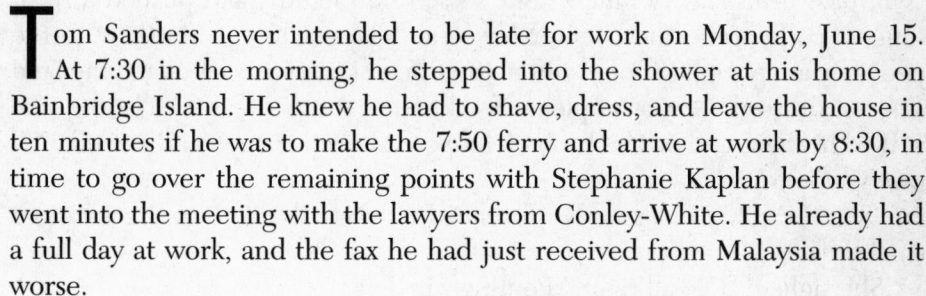

Tom Sanders never intended to be late for work on Monday, June 15. At 7:30 in the morning, he stepped into the shower at his home on Bainbridge Island. He knew he had to shave, dress, and leave the house in ten minutes if he was to make the 7:50 ferry and arrive at work by 8:30, in time to go over the remaining points with Stephanie Kaplan before they went into the meeting with the lawyers from Conley-White. He already had a full day at work, and the fax he had just received from Malaysia made it worse.

Sanders was a division manager at Digital Communications Technology in Seattle. Events at work had been hectic for a week, because DigiCom was being acquired by Conley-White, a publishing conglomerate in New York. The merger would allow Conley to acquire technology important to publishing in the next century.

But this latest news from Malaysia was not good, and Arthur had been right to send it to him at home. He was going to have a problem explaining it to the Conley-White people because they just didn't—

"Tom? Where are you? Tom?"

His wife, Susan, was calling from the bedroom. He ducked his head out of the spray.

"I'm in the shower!"

She said something in reply, but he didn't hear it. He stepped out, reaching for a towel. "What?"

"I said, Can you feed the kids?"

His wife was an attorney who worked four days a week at a downtown firm. She took Mondays off, to spend more time with the kids, but she was not good at managing the routine at home. As a result, there was often a crisis on Monday mornings.

"Tom? Can you feed them for me?"

"I can't, Sue," he called to her. The clock on the sink said 7:34. "I'm already late." He ran water in the basin to shave, and lathered his face. He was a handsome man, with the easy manner of an athlete. He touched the

11

dark bruise on his side from the company touch football game on Saturday. Mark Lewyn had taken him down; Lewyn was fast but clumsy. And Sanders was getting too old for touch football. He was still in good shape—still within five pounds of his varsity weight—but as he ran his hand through his wet hair, he saw streaks of gray. It was time to admit his age, he thought, and switch to tennis.

Susan came into the room, still in her bathrobe. His wife always looked beautiful in the morning, right out of bed. She had the kind of fresh beauty that required no makeup. "Are you sure you can't feed them?" she said. "Oh, nice bruise. Very butch." She kissed him lightly, and pushed a fresh mug of coffee onto the counter for him. "I've got to get Matthew to the pediatrician by eight-fifteen, and neither one of them has eaten a thing, and I'm not dressed. Can't you please feed them? Pretty please?" Teasing, she ruffled his hair, and her bathrobe fell open. She left it open and smiled. "I'll owe you one . . ."

"Sue, I can't." He kissed her forehead distractedly. "I've got a meeting, I can't be late."

She sighed. "Oh, all right." Pouting, she left.

Sanders began shaving.

A moment later he heard his wife say, "Okay, kids, let's go! Eliza, put your shoes on." This was followed by whining from Eliza, who was four, and didn't like to wear shoes. Sanders had almost finished shaving when he heard, "Eliza, you put on those shoes and take your brother downstairs right now!" Eliza's reply was indistinct, and then Susan said, "Eliza Ann, I'm talking to you!" Then Susan began slamming drawers in the hall linen closet. Both kids started to cry.

Eliza, who was upset by any display of tension, came into the bathroom, her face scrunched up, tears in her eyes. "Daddy . . . ," she sobbed. He put his hand down to hug her, still shaving with his other hand.

"She's old enough to help out," Susan called, from the hallway.

"Mommy," she wailed, clutching Sanders's leg.

"Eliza, will you *cut it out.*"

At this, Eliza cried more loudly. Susan stamped her foot in the hallway. Sanders hated to see his daughter cry. "Okay, Sue, I'll feed them." He turned off the water in the sink and scooped up his daughter. "Come on, Lize," he said, wiping away her tears. "Let's get you some breakfast."

He went out into the hallway. Susan looked relieved. "I just need ten minutes, that's all," she said. "Consuela is late again. I don't know what's the matter with her."

Sanders didn't answer her. His son, Matt, who was nine months old, sat in the middle of the hallway banging his rattle and crying. Sanders scooped him up in his other arm.

"Come on, kids," he said. "Let's go eat."

When he picked up Matt, his towel slipped off, and he clutched at it. Eliza giggled. "I see your penis, Dad." She swung her foot, kicking it.

"We don't kick Daddy there," Sanders said. Awkwardly, he wrapped the towel around himself again, and headed downstairs.

Susan called after him: "Don't forget Matt needs vitamins in his cereal. One dropperful. And don't give him any more of the rice cereal, he spits it out. He likes wheat now." She went into the bathroom, slamming the door behind her.

His daughter looked at him with serious eyes. "Is this going to be one of those days, Daddy?"

"Yeah, it looks like it." He walked down the stairs, thinking he would miss the ferry and that he would be late for the first meeting of the day. Not very late, just a few minutes, but it meant he wouldn't be able to go over things with Stephanie before they started, but perhaps he could call her from the ferry, and then—

"Do I have a penis, Dad?"

"No, Lize."

"Why, Dad?"

"That's just the way it is, honey."

"Boys have penises, and girls have vaginas," she said solemnly.

"That's right."

"Why, Dad?"

"Because." He dropped his daughter on a chair at the kitchen table, dragged the high chair from the corner, and placed Matt in it. "What do you want for breakfast, Lize? Rice Krispies or Chex?"

"Chex."

Matt began to bang on his high chair with his spoon. Sanders got the Chex and a bowl out of the cupboard, then the box of wheat cereal and a smaller bowl for Matt. Eliza watched him as he opened the refrigerator to get the milk.

"Dad?"

"What."

"I want Mommy to be happy."

"Me too, honey."

He mixed the wheat cereal for Matt, and put it in front of his son. Then he set Eliza's bowl on the table, poured in the Chex, glanced at her. "Enough?"

"Yes."

He poured the milk for her.

"No, Dad!" his daughter howled, bursting into tears. *"I wanted to pour the milk!"*

"Sorry, Lize—"

"Take it out—take the milk out—" She was shrieking, completely hysterical.

"I'm sorry, Lize, but this is—"

"I wanted to pour the milk!" She slid off her seat to the ground, where she lay kicking her heels on the floor. "Take it out, take the milk out!"

His daughter did this kind of thing several times a day. It was, he was assured, just a phase. Parents were advised to treat it with firmness.

"I'm sorry," Sanders said. "You'll just have to eat it, Lize." He sat down at the table beside Matt to feed him. Matt stuck his hand in his cereal and smeared it across his eyes. He, too, began to cry.

Sanders got a dish towel to wipe Matt's face. He noticed that the kitchen clock now said five to eight. He thought that he'd better call the office, to warn them he would be late. But he'd have to quiet Eliza first: she was still on the floor, kicking and screaming about the milk. "All right, Eliza, take it easy. Take it easy." He got a fresh bowl, poured more cereal, and gave her the carton of milk to pour herself. "Here."

She crossed her arms and pouted. "I don't want it."

"Eliza, you pour that milk *this minute.*"

His daughter scrambled up to her chair. "Okay, Dad."

Sanders sat down, wiped Matt's face, and began to feed his son. The boy immediately stopped crying, and swallowed the cereal in big gulps. The poor kid was hungry. Eliza stood on her chair, lifted the milk carton, and splashed it all over the table. "Uh-oh."

"Never mind." With one hand, he wiped the table with the dish towel, while with the other he continued to feed Matt.

Eliza pulled the cereal box right up to her bowl, stared fixedly at the picture of Goofy on the back, and began to eat. Alongside her, Matt ate steadily. For a moment, it was calm in the kitchen.

Sanders glanced over his shoulder: almost eight o'clock. He should call the office.

Susan came in, wearing jeans and a beige sweater. Her face was relaxed. "I'm sorry I lost it," she said. "Thanks for taking over." She kissed him on the cheek.

"Are you happy, Mom?" Eliza said.

"Yes, sweetie." Susan smiled at her daughter, and turned back to Tom.

"I'll take over now. You don't want to be late. Isn't today the big day? When they announce your promotion?"

"I hope so."

"Call me as soon as you hear."

"I will." Sanders got up, cinched the towel around his waist, and headed upstairs to get dressed. There was always traffic in town before the 8:20 ferry. He would have to hurry to make it.

He parked in his spot behind Ricky's Shell station, and strode quickly down the covered walkway to the ferry. He stepped aboard moments before they pulled up the ramp. Feeling the throb of the engines beneath his feet, he went through the doors onto the main deck.

"Hey, Tom."

He looked over his shoulder. Dave Benedict was coming up behind him. Benedict was a lawyer with a firm that handled a lot of high-tech companies. "Missed the seven-fifty, too, huh?" Benedict said.

"Yeah. Crazy morning."

"Tell me. I wanted to be in the office an hour ago. But now that school's out, Jenny doesn't know what to do with the kids until camp starts."

"Uh-huh."

"Madness at my house," Benedict said, shaking his head.

There was a pause. Sanders sensed that he and Benedict had had a similar morning. But the two men did not discuss it further. Sanders often wondered why it was that women discussed the most intimate details of their marriages with their friends, while men maintained a discreet silence with one another.

"Anyway," Benedict said. "How's Susan?"

"She's fine. She's great."

Benedict grinned. "So why are you limping?"

"Company touch football game on Saturday. Got a little out of hand."

"That's what you get for playing with children," Benedict said. DigiCom was famous for its young employees.

"Hey," Sanders said. "I scored."

"Is that right?"

"Damn right. Winning touchdown. Crossed the end zone in glory. And then I got creamed."

At the main-deck cafeteria, they stood in line for coffee. "Actually, I would've thought you'd be in bright and early today," Benedict said. "Isn't this the big day at DigiCom?"

Sanders got his coffee, and stirred in sweetener. "How's that?"

"Isn't the merger being announced today?"

"What merger?" Sanders said blandly. The merger was secret; only a handful of DigiCom executives knew anything about it. He gave Benedict a blank stare.

"Come on," Benedict said. "I heard it was pretty much wrapped up. And that Bob Garvin was announcing the restructuring today, including a bunch of new promotions." Benedict sipped his coffee. "Garvin is stepping down, isn't he?"

Sanders shrugged. "We'll see." Of course Benedict was imposing on him, but Susan did a lot of work with attorneys in Benedict's firm; Sanders couldn't afford to be rude. It was one of the new complexities of business relations at a time when everybody had a working spouse.

The two men went out on the deck and stood by the port rail, watching the houses of Bainbridge Island slip away. Sanders nodded toward the house on Wing Point, which for years had been Warren Magnuson's summer house when he was senator.

"I hear it just sold again," Sanders said.

"Oh yes? Who bought it?"

"Some California asshole."

Bainbridge slid to the stern. They looked out at the gray water of the Sound. The coffee steamed in the morning sunlight. "So," Benedict said. "You think maybe Garvin won't step down?"

"Nobody knows," Sanders said. "Bob built the company from nothing, fifteen years ago. When he started, he was selling knockoff modems from Korea. Back when nobody knew what a modem was. Now the company's got three buildings downtown, and big facilities in California, Texas, Ireland, and Malaysia. He builds fax modems the size of a dime, he markets fax and E-mail software, he's gone into CD-ROMs, and he's developed proprietary algorithms that should make him a leading provider in education markets for the next century. Bob's come a long way from some guy hustling three hundred baud modems. I don't know if he can give it up."

"Don't the terms of the merger require it?"

Sanders smiled. "If you know about a merger, Dave, you should tell me," he said. "Because I haven't heard anything." The truth was that Sanders didn't really know the terms of the impending merger. His work involved the development of CD-ROMs and electronic databases. Although these were areas vital to the future of the company—they were the main reason Conley-White was acquiring DigiCom—they were essentially technical areas. And Sanders was essentially a technical manager. He was not informed about decisions at the highest levels.

For Sanders, there was some irony in this. In earlier years, when he was based in California, he had been closely involved in management decisions. But since coming to Seattle eight years ago, he had been more removed from the centers of power.

Benedict sipped his coffee. "Well, I hear Bob's definitely stepping down, and he's going to promote a woman as chairman."

Sanders said, "Who told you that?"

"He's already got a woman as CFO, doesn't he?"

"Yes, sure. For a long time, now." Stephanie Kaplan was DigiCom's chief financial officer. But it seemed unlikely she would ever run the company. Silent and intense, Kaplan was competent, but disliked by many in the company. Garvin wasn't especially fond of her.

"Well," Benedict said, "the rumor I've heard is he's going to name a woman to take over within five years."

"Does the rumor mention a name?"

Benedict shook his head. "I thought you'd know. I mean, it's your company."

On the deck in the sunshine, he took out his cellular phone and called in. His assistant, Cindy Wolfe, answered. "Mr. Sanders's office."

"Hi. It's me."

"Hi, Tom. You on the ferry?"

"Yes. I'll be in a little before nine."

"Okay, I'll tell them." She paused, and he had the sense that she was choosing her words carefully. "It's pretty busy this morning. Mr. Garvin was just here, looking for you."

Sanders frowned. "Looking for me?"

"Yes." Another pause. "Uh, he seemed kind of surprised that you weren't in."

"Did he say what he wanted?"

"No, but he's going into a lot of offices on the floor, one after another, talking to people. Something's up, Tom."

"What?"

"Nobody's telling me anything," she said.

"What about Stephanie?"

"Stephanie called, and I told her you weren't in yet."

"Anything else?"

"Arthur Kahn called from KL to ask if you got his fax."

"I did. I'll call him. Anything else?"

"No, that's about it, Tom."

"Thanks, Cindy." He pushed the END button to terminate the call.

Standing beside him, Benedict pointed to Sanders's phone. "Those things are amazing. They just get smaller and smaller, don't they? You guys make that one?"

Sanders nodded. "I'd be lost without it. Especially these days. Who can remember all the numbers? This is more than a telephone: it's my telephone book. See, look." He began to demonstrate the features for Benedict. "It's got a memory for two hundred numbers. You store them by the first three letters of the name." Sanders punched in K-A-H to bring up the international number for Arthur Kahn in Malaysia. He pushed SEND, and heard a long string of electronic beeps. With the country code and area code, it was thirteen beeps.

"Jesus," Benedict said. "Where are you calling, Mars?"

"Just about. Malaysia. We've got a factory there."

DigiCom's Malaysia operation was only a year old, and it was manufacturing the company's new CD-ROM players—units rather like an audio CD player, but intended for computers. It was widely agreed in the business that all information was soon going to be digital, and much of it was going to be stored on these compact disks. Computer programs, databases, even books and magazines—everything was going to be on disk.

The reason it hadn't already happened was that CD-ROMs were notoriously slow. Users were obliged to wait in front of blank screens while the drives whirred and clicked—and computer users didn't like waiting. In an industry where speeds reliably doubled every eighteen months, CD-ROMs had improved much less in the last five years. DigiCom's SpeedStar technology addressed that problem, with a new generation of drives codenamed Twinkle (for "Twinkle, twinkle, little SpeedStar"). Twinkle drives were twice as fast as any in the world. Twinkle was packaged as a small, stand-alone multimedia player with its own screen. You could carry it in your hand, and use it on a bus or a train. It was going to be revolutionary. But now the Malaysia plant was having trouble manufacturing the new fast drives.

Benedict sipped his coffee. "Is it true you're the only division manager who isn't an engineer?"

Sanders smiled. "That's right. I'm originally from marketing."

"Isn't that pretty unusual?" Benedict said.

"Not really. In marketing, we used to spend a lot of time figuring out what the features of the new products were, and most of us couldn't talk to the engineers. I could. I don't know why. I don't have a technical background, but I could talk to the guys. I knew just enough so they couldn't bullshit me. So pretty soon, I was the one who talked to the engineers. Then eight years ago, Garvin asked me if I'd run a division for him. And here I am."

The call rang through. Sanders glanced at his watch. It was almost midnight in Kuala Lumpur. He hoped Arthur Kahn would still be awake. A moment later there was a click, and a groggy voice said, "Uh. Hello."

"Arthur, it's Tom."

Arthur Kahn gave a gravelly cough. "Oh, Tom. Good." Another cough. "You got my fax?"

"Yes, I got it."

"Then you know. I don't understand what's going on," Kahn said. "And I spent all day on the line. I had to, with Jafar gone."

Mohammed Jafar was the line foreman of the Malaysia plant, a very capable young man. "Jafar is gone? Why?"

There was a crackle of static. "He was cursed."

"I didn't get that."

"Jafar was cursed by his cousin, so he left."

"What?"

"Yeah, if you can believe that. He says his cousin's sister in Johore hired a sorcerer to cast a spell on him, and he ran off to the Orang Asli witch doctors for a counter-spell. The aborigines run a hospital at Kuala Tingit, in the jungle about three hours outside of KL. It's very famous. A lot of politicians go out there when they get sick. Jafar went out there for a cure."

"How long will that take?"

"Beats me. The other workers tell me it'll probably be a week."

"And what's wrong with the line, Arthur?"

"I don't know," Kahn said. "I'm not sure anything's wrong with the line.

But the units coming off are very slow. When we pull units for IP checks, we consistently get seek times above the hundred-millisecond specs. We don't know why they're slow, and we don't know why there's a variation. But the engineers here are guessing that there's a compatibility problem with the controller chip that positions the split optics, and the CD-driver software."

"You think the controller chips are bad?" The controller chips were made in Singapore and trucked across the border to the factory in Malaysia.

"Don't know. Either they're bad, or there's a bug in the driver code."

"What about the screen flicker?"

Kahn coughed. "I think it's a design problem, Tom. We just can't build it. The hinge connectors that carry current to the screen are mounted inside the plastic housing. They're supposed to maintain electrical contact no matter how you move the screen. But the current cuts in and out. You move the hinge, and the screen flashes on and off."

Sanders frowned as he listened. "This is a pretty standard design, Arthur. Every damn laptop in the world has the same hinge design. It's been that way for the last ten years."

"I know it," Kahn said. "But ours isn't working. It's making me crazy."

"You better send me some units."

"I already have, DHL. You'll get them late today, tomorrow at the latest."

"Okay," Sanders said. He paused. "What's your best guess, Arthur?"

"About the run? Well, at the moment we can't make our production quotas, and we're turning out a product thirty to fifty percent slower than specs. Not good news. This isn't a hot CD player, Tom. It's only incrementally better than what Toshiba and Sony already have on the market. They're making theirs a lot cheaper. So we have major problems."

"We talking a week, a month, what?"

"A month, if it's not a redesign. If it's a redesign, say four months. If it's a chip, it could be a year."

Sanders sighed. "Great."

"That's the situation. It isn't working, and we don't know why."

Sanders said, "Who else have you told?"

"Nobody. This one's all yours, my friend."

"Thanks a lot."

Kahn coughed. "You going to bury this until after the merger, or what?"

"I don't know. I'm not sure I can."

"Well, I'll be quiet at this end. I can tell you that. Anybody asks me, I don't have a clue. Because I don't."

"Okay. Thanks, Arthur. I'll talk to you later."

Sanders hung up. Twinkle definitely presented a political problem for the impending merger with Conley-White. Sanders wasn't sure how to handle it. But he would have to deal with it soon enough; the ferry whistle blew, and up ahead, he saw the black pilings of Colman Dock and the sky-scrapers of downtown Seattle.

DigiCom was located in three different buildings around historic Pio-neer Square, in downtown Seattle. Pioneer Square was actually shaped like a triangle, and had at its center a small park, dominated by a wrought-iron pergola, with antique clocks mounted above. Around Pioneer Square were low-rise red-brick buildings built in the early years of the century, with sculpted façades and chiseled dates; these buildings now housed trendy architects, graphic design firms, and a cluster of high-tech companies that included Aldus, Advance Holo-Graphics, and DigiCom. Originally, Digi-Com had occupied the Hazzard Building, on the south side of the square. As the company grew, it expanded into three floors of the adjacent Western Building, and later, to the Gorham Tower on James Street. But the execu-tive offices were still on the top three floors of the Hazzard Building, over-looking the square. Sanders's office was on the fourth floor, though he expected later in the week to move up to the fifth.

He got to the fourth floor at nine in the morning, and immediately sensed that something was wrong. There was a buzz in the hallways, an elec-tric tension in the air. Staff people clustered at the laser printers and whis-pered at the coffee machines; they turned away or stopped talking when he walked by.

He thought, Uh-oh.

But as a division head, he could hardly stop to ask an assistant what was happening. Sanders walked on, swearing under his breath, angry with him-self that he had arrived late on this important day.

Through the glass walls of the fourth-floor conference room, he saw Mark Lewyn, the thirty-three-year-old head of Product Design, brief-ing some of the Conley-White people. It made a striking scene: Lewyn, young, handsome, and imperious, wearing black jeans and a black Armani T-shirt, pacing back and forth and talking animatedly to the blue-suited

Conley-White staffers, who sat rigidly before the product mock-ups on the table, and took notes.

When Lewyn saw Sanders he waved, and came over to the door of the conference room and stuck his head out.

"Hey, guy," Lewyn said.

"Hi, Mark. Listen—"

"I have just one thing to say to you," Lewyn said, interrupting. "Fuck 'em. Fuck Garvin. Fuck Phil. Fuck the merger. Fuck 'em all. This reorg sucks. I'm with you on this one, guy."

"Listen, Mark, can you—"

"I'm in the middle of something here." Lewyn jerked his head toward the Conley people in the room. "But I wanted you to know how I feel. It's not right, what they're doing. We'll talk later, okay? Chin up, guy," Lewyn said. "Keep your powder dry." And he went back into the conference room.

The Conley-White people were all staring at Sanders through the glass. He turned away and walked quickly toward his office, with a sense of deepening unease. Lewyn was notorious for his tendency to exaggerate, but even so, the—

It's not right, what they're doing.

There didn't seem to be much doubt what that meant. Sanders wasn't going to get a promotion. He broke into a light sweat and felt suddenly dizzy as he walked along the corridor. He leaned against the wall for a moment. He wiped his forehead with his hand and blinked his eyes rapidly. He took a deep breath and shook his head to clear it.

No promotion. Christ. He took another deep breath, and walked on.

Instead of the promotion he expected, there was apparently going to be some kind of reorganization. And apparently it was related to the merger.

The technical divisions had just gone through a major reorganization nine months earlier, which had revised all the lines of authority, upsetting the hell out of everybody in Seattle. Staff people didn't know who to requisition for laser-printer paper, or to degauss a monitor. There had been months of uproar; only in the last few weeks had the tech groups settled down into some semblance of good working routines. Now . . . to reorganize again? It didn't make any sense at all.

Yet it was last year's reorganization that placed Sanders in line to assume leadership of the tech divisions now. That reorganization had structured the Advanced Products Group into four subdivisions—Product Design, Programming, Data Telecommunications, and Manufacturing—all under the direction of a division general manager, not yet appointed. In recent months, Tom Sanders had informally taken over as DGM, largely because as head of manufacturing, he was the person most concerned with coordinating the work of all the other divisions.

But now, with still another reorganization ... who knew what might happen? Sanders might be broken back to simply managing DigiCom's production lines around the world. Or worse—for weeks, there had been persistent rumors that company headquarters in Cupertino was going to take back all control of manufacturing from Seattle, turning it over to the individual product managers in California. Sanders hadn't paid any attention to those rumors, because they didn't make a lot of sense; the product managers had enough to do just pushing the products, without also worrying about their manufacture.

But now he was obliged to consider the possibility that the rumors were true. Because if they were true, Sanders might be facing more than a demotion. He might be out of a job.

Christ: out of a job?

He found himself thinking of some of the things Dave Benedict had said to him on the ferry earlier that morning. Benedict chased rumors, and he had seemed to know a lot. Maybe even more than he had been saying.

Is it true you're the only division manager who isn't an engineer?

And then, pointedly:

Isn't that pretty unusual?

Christ, he thought. He began to sweat again. He forced himself to take another deep breath. He reached the end of the fourth-floor corridor and came to his office, expecting to find Stephanie Kaplan, the CFO, waiting there for him. Kaplan could tell him what was going on. But his office was empty. He turned to his assistant, Cindy Wolfe, who was busy at the filing cabinets. "Where's Stephanie?"

"She's not coming."

"Why not?"

"They canceled your nine-thirty meeting because of all the personnel changes," Cindy said.

"What changes?" Sanders said. "What's going on?"

"There's been some kind of reorganization," Cindy said. She avoided meeting his eyes, and looked down at the call book on her desk. "They just scheduled a private lunch with all the division heads in the main conference room for twelve-thirty today, and Phil Blackburn is on his way down to talk to you. He should be here any minute. Let's see, what else? DHL is delivering drives from Kuala Lumpur this afternoon. Gary Bosak wants to meet with you at ten-thirty." She ran her finger down the call book. "Don

Cherry called twice about the Corridor, and you just got a rush call from Eddie in Austin."

"Call him back." Eddie Larson was the production supervisor in the Austin plant, which made cellular telephones. Cindy placed the call; a moment later he heard the familiar voice with the Texas twang.

"Hey there, Tommy boy."

"Hi, Eddie. What's up?"

"Little problem on the line. You got a minute?"

"Yes, sure."

"Are congratulations on a new job in order?"

"I haven't heard anything yet," Sanders said.

"Uh-huh. But it's going to happen?"

"I haven't heard anything, Eddie."

"Is it true they're going to shut down the Austin plant?"

Sanders was so startled, he burst out laughing. *"What?"*

"Hey, that's what they're saying down here, Tommy boy. Conley-White is going to buy the company and then shut us down."

"Hell," Sanders said. "Nobody's buying anything, and nobody's selling anything, Eddie. The Austin line is an industry standard. And it's very profitable."

He paused. "You'd tell me if you knew, wouldn't you, Tommy boy?"

"Yes, I would," Sanders said. "But it's just a rumor, Eddie. So forget it. Now, what's the line problem?"

"Diddly stuff. The women on the production line are demanding that we clean out the pinups in the men's locker room. They say it's offensive to them. You ask me, I think it's bull," Larson said. "Because women never go into the men's locker room."

"Then how do they know about the pinups?"

"The night cleanup crews have women on 'em. So now the women working the line want the pinups removed."

Sanders sighed. "We don't need any complaints about being unresponsive on sex issues. Get the pinups out."

"Even if the women have pinups in *their* locker room?"

"Just do it, Eddie."

"You ask me, it's caving in to a lot of feminist bullshit."

There was a knock on the door. Sanders looked up and saw Phil Blackburn, the company lawyer, standing there.

"Eddie, I have to go."

"Okay," Eddie said, "but I'm telling you—"

"Eddie, I'm sorry. I have to go. Call me if anything changes."

Sanders hung up the phone, and Blackburn came into the room.

Sanders's first impression was that the lawyer was smiling too broadly, behaving too cheerfully.

It was a bad sign.

Philip Blackburn, the chief legal counsel for DigiCom, was a slender man of forty-six wearing a dark green Hugo Boss suit. Like Sanders, Blackburn had been with DigiCom for over a decade, which meant that he was one of the "old guys," one of those who had "gotten in at the beginning." When Sanders first met him, Blackburn was a brash, bearded young civil rights lawyer from Berkeley. But Blackburn had long since abandoned protest for profits, which he pursued with singleminded intensity—while carefully emphasizing the new corporate issues of diversity and equal opportunity. Blackburn's embrace of the latest fashions in clothing and correctness made "PC Phil" a figure of fun in some quarters of the company. As one executive put it, "Phil's finger is chapped from wetting it and holding it to the wind." He was the first with Birkenstocks, the first with bell-bottoms, the first with sideburns off, and the first with diversity.

Many of the jokes focused on his mannerisms. Fussy, preoccupied with appearances, Blackburn was always running his hands over himself, touching his hair, his face, his suit, seeming to caress himself, to smooth out the wrinkles in his suit. This, combined with his unfortunate tendency to rub, touch, and pick his nose, was the source of much humor. But it was humor with an edge: Blackburn was mistrusted as a moralistic hatchet man.

Blackburn could be charismatic in his speeches, and in private could convey a convincing impression of intellectual honesty for short periods. But within the company he was seen for what he was: a gun for hire, a man with no convictions of his own, and hence the perfect person to be Garvin's executioner.

In earlier years, Sanders and Blackburn had been close friends; not only had they grown up with the company, but their lives were intertwined personally as well: when Blackburn went through his bitter divorce in 1982, he lived for a while in Sanders's bachelor apartment in Sunnyvale. A few years later, Blackburn had been best man at Sanders's own wedding to a young Seattle attorney, Susan Handler.

But when Blackburn remarried in 1989, Sanders was not invited to the wedding, for by then, their relationship had become strained. Some in the company saw it as inevitable. Blackburn was a part of the inner power circle in Cupertino, to which Sanders, based in Seattle, no longer belonged. In addition, the two men had had sharp disputes about setting up the production lines in Ireland and Malaysia. Sanders felt that Blackburn ignored the inevitable realities of production in foreign countries.

Typical was Blackburn's demand that half the workers on the new line in Kuala Lumpur should be women, and that they should be intermingled with the men; the Malay managers wanted the women segregated, allowed to work only on certain parts of the line, away from the men. Phil strenuously objected. Sanders kept telling him, "It's a Muslim country, Phil."

"I don't give a damn," Phil said. "DigiCom stands for equality."

"Phil, it's their country. They're Muslim."

"So what? It's our factory."

Their disagreements went on and on. The Malaysian government didn't want local Chinese hired as supervisors, although they were the best-qualified; it was the policy of the Malaysian government to train Malays for supervisory jobs. Sanders disagreed with this blatantly discriminatory policy, because he wanted the best supervisors he could get for the plant. But Phil, an outspoken opponent of discrimination in America, immediately acquiesced to the Malay government's discriminatory policy, saying that DigiCom should embrace a true multicultural perspective. At the last minute, Sanders had had to fly to Kuala Lumpur and meet with the Sultans of Selangor and Pahang, to agree to their demands. Phil then announced that Sanders had "toadied up to the extremists."

It was just one of the many controversies that surrounded Sanders's handling of the new Malaysia factory.

Now, Sanders and Blackburn greeted each other with the wariness of former friends who had long since ceased to be anything but superficially cordial. Sanders shook Blackburn's hand as the company lawyer stepped into the office. "What's going on, Phil?"

"Big day," Blackburn said, slipping into the chair facing Sanders's desk. "Lot of surprises. I don't know what you've heard."

"I've heard Garvin has made a decision about the restructuring."

"Yes, he has. Several decisions."

There was a pause. Blackburn shifted in his chair and looked at his hands. "I know that Bob wanted to fill you in himself about all this. He came by earlier this morning to talk to everyone in the division."

"I wasn't here."

"Uh-huh. We were all kind of surprised that you were late today."

Sanders let that pass without comment. He stared at Blackburn, waiting.

"Anyway, Tom," Blackburn said, "the bottom line is this. As part of the overall merger, Bob has decided to go outside the Advanced Products Group for leadership of the division."

So there it was. Finally, out in the open. Sanders took a deep breath, felt the bands of tightness in his chest. His whole body was tense. But he tried not to show it.

"I know this is something of a shock," Blackburn said.

"Well," Sanders shrugged. "I've heard rumors." Even as he spoke, his mind was racing ahead. It was clear now that there would not be a promotion, there would not be a raise, he would not have a new opportunity to—

"Yes. Well," Blackburn said, clearing his throat. "Bob has decided that Meredith Johnson is going to head up the division."

Sanders frowned. "Meredith *Johnson*?"

"Right. She's in the Cupertino office. I think you know her."

"Yes, I do, but . . ." Sanders shook his head. It didn't make any sense. "Meredith's from sales. Her background is in sales."

"Originally, yes. But as you know, Meredith's been in Operations the last couple of years."

"Even so, Phil. The APG is a technical division."

"You're not technical. You've done just fine."

"But I've been involved in this for years, when I was in Marketing. Look, the APG is basically programming teams and hardware fabrication lines. How can she run it?"

"Bob doesn't expect her to run it directly. She'll oversee the APG division managers, who will report to her. Meredith's official title will be Vice President for Advanced Operations and Planning. Under the new structure, that will include the entire APG Division, the Marketing Division, and the TelCom Division."

"Jesus," Sanders said, sitting back in his chair. "That's pretty much everything."

Blackburn nodded slowly.

Sanders paused, thinking it over. "It sounds," he said finally, "like Meredith Johnson's going to be running this company."

"I wouldn't go *that* far," Blackburn said. "She won't have direct control over sales or finance or distribution in this new scheme. But I think there is no question Bob has placed her in direct line for succession, when he steps down as CEO sometime in the next two years." Blackburn shifted in his chair. "But that's the future. For the present—"

"Just a minute. She'll have four APG division managers reporting to her?" Sanders said.

"Yes."

"And who are those managers going to be? Has that been decided?"

"Well." Phil coughed. He ran his hands over his chest, and plucked at the handkerchief in his breast pocket. "Of course, the actual decision to name the division managers will be Meredith's."

"Meaning I might not have a job."

"Oh hell, Tom," Blackburn said. "Nothing of the sort. Bob wants everyone in the divisions to stay. Including you. He'd hate very much to lose you."

"But it's Meredith Johnson's decision whether I keep my job."

"Technically," Blackburn said, spreading his hands, "it has to be. But I think it's pretty much pro forma."

Sanders did not see it that way at all. Garvin could easily have named all the division managers at the same time he named Meredith Johnson to run the APG. If Garvin decided to turn the company over to some woman from Sales, that was certainly his choice. But Garvin could still make sure he kept his division heads in place—the heads who had served him and the company so well.

"Jesus," Sanders said. "I've been with this company twelve years."

"And I expect you will be with us many more," Blackburn said smoothly. "Look: it's in everybody's interest to keep the teams in place. Because as I said, she can't run them directly."

"Uh-huh."

Blackburn shot his cuffs and ran his hand through his hair. "Listen, Tom. I know you're disappointed that this appointment didn't come to you. But let's not make too much of Meredith appointing the division heads. Realistically speaking, she isn't going to make any changes. Your situation is secure." He paused. "You know the way Meredith is, Tom."

"I used to," Sanders said, nodding. "Hell, I lived with her for a while. But I haven't seen her in years."

Blackburn looked surprised. "You two haven't kept in contact?"

"Not really, no. By the time Meredith joined the company, I was up here in Seattle, and she was based in Cupertino. I ran into her once, on a trip down there. Said hello. That's about it."

"Then you only know her from the old days," Blackburn said, as if it all suddenly made sense. "From six or seven years ago."

"It's longer than that," Sanders said. "I've been in Seattle eight years. So it must be . . ." Sanders thought back. "When I was going out with her, she worked for Novell in Mountain View. Selling Ethernet cards to small businesses for local area networks. When was that?" Although he remembered the relationship with Meredith Johnson vividly, Sanders was hazy about exactly when it had occurred. He tried to recall some memorable event—a birthday, a promotion, an apartment move—that would mark the date. Finally he remembered watching election returns with her on television: balloons rising up toward the ceiling, people cheering. She was drinking beer. That had been early in their relationship. "Jesus, Phil. It must be almost ten years ago."

"That long," Blackburn said.

When Sanders first met Meredith Johnson, she was one of the thousands of pretty saleswomen working in San Jose—young women in their twenties, not long out of college, who started out doing the product demos on the computer while a senior man stood beside her and did all the talking to the customer. Eventually, a lot of those women learned enough to do the selling themselves. At the time Sanders first knew Meredith, she had acquired enough jargon to rattle on about token rings and 10BaseT hubs. She didn't really have any deep knowledge, but she didn't need to. She was good-looking, sexy, and smart, and she had a kind of uncanny self-possession that carried her through awkward moments. Sanders had admired her, back in those days. But he never imagined that she had the ability to hold a major corporate position.

Blackburn shrugged. "A lot's happened in ten years, Tom," he said. "Meredith isn't just a sales exec. She went back to school, got an MBA. She worked at Symantec, then Conrad, and then she came to work with us. The last couple of years, she's been working very closely with Garvin. Sort of his protégé. He's been pleased with her work on a number of assignments."

Sanders shook his head. "And now she's my boss . . ."

"Is that a problem for you?"

"No. It just seems funny. An old girlfriend as my boss."

"The worm turns," Blackburn said. He was smiling, but Sanders sensed he was watching him closely. "You seem a little uneasy about this, Tom."

"It takes some getting used to."

"Is there a problem? Reporting to a woman?"

"Not at all. I worked for Eileen when she was head of HRI, and we got along great. It's not that. It's just funny to think of Meredith Johnson as my boss."

"She's an impressive and accomplished manager," Phil said. He stood up, smoothed his tie. "I think when you've had an opportunity to become reacquainted, you'll be very impressed. Give her a chance, Tom."

"Of course," Sanders said.

"I'm sure everything will work out. And keep your eye on the future. After all, you should be rich in a year or so."

"Does that mean we're still spinning off the APG Division?"

"Oh yes. Absolutely."

It was a much-discussed part of the merger plan that after Conley-White bought DigiCom, it would spin off the Advanced Products Division and take it public, as a separate company. That would mean enormous profits for everyone in the division. Because everyone would have the chance to buy cheap options before the stock was publicly sold.

"We're working out the final details now," Blackburn said. "But I expect that division managers like yourself will start with twenty thousand shares vested, and an initial option of fifty thousand shares at twenty-five cents a share, with the right to purchase another fifty thousand shares each year for the next five years."

"And the spin-off will go forward, even with Meredith running the divisions?"

"Trust me. The spin-off will happen within eighteen months. It's a formal part of the merger plan."

"There's no chance that she may decide to change her mind?"

"None at all, Tom," Blackburn smiled. "I'll tell you a little secret. Originally, this spin-off was Meredith's idea."

Blackburn left Sanders's office and went down the hall to an empty office and called Garvin. He heard the familiar sharp bark: "Garvin here."

"I talked to Tom Sanders."

"And?"

"I'd say he took it well. He was disappointed, of course. I think he'd already heard a rumor. But he took it well."

Garvin said, "And the new structure? How did he respond?"

"He's concerned," Blackburn said. "He expressed reservations."

"Why?"

"He doesn't feel she has the technical expertise to run the division."

Garvin snorted. "Technical expertise? That's the last goddamn thing I care about. Technical expertise is not an issue here."

"Of course not. But I think there was some uneasiness on the personal level. You know, they once had a relationship."

"Yes," Garvin said. "I know that. Have they talked?"

"He says, not for several years."

"Bad blood?"

"There didn't seem to be."

"Then what's he concerned about?"

"I think he's just getting used to the idea."

"He'll come around."

"I think so."

"Tell me if you hear otherwise," Garvin said, and hung up.

Alone in the office, Blackburn frowned. The conversation with Sanders left him vaguely uneasy. It had seemed to go well enough, and yet . . . Sanders, he felt sure, was not going to take this reorganization lying down. Sanders was popular in the Seattle division, and he could easily cause trouble. Sanders was too independent, he was not a team player, and the company needed team players now. The more Blackburn thought about it, the more certain he was that Sanders was going to be a problem.

Tom Sanders sat at his desk, staring forward, lost in thought. He was trying to put together his memory of a pretty young saleswoman in Silicon Valley with this new image of a corporate officer running company divisions, executing the complex groundwork required to take a division public. But his thoughts kept being interrupted by random images from the past: Meredith smiling, wearing one of his shirts, naked beneath it. An opened suitcase on the bed. White stockings and white garter belt. A bowl of popcorn on the blue couch in the living room. The television with the sound turned off.

And for some reason, the image of a flower, a purple iris, in stained glass. It was one of those hackneyed Northern California hippie images. Sanders knew where it came from: it was on the glass of the front door to the apartment where he had lived, back in Sunnyvale. Back in the days when he had known Meredith. He wasn't sure why he should keep thinking of it now, and he—

"Tom?"

He glanced up. Cindy was standing in the doorway, looking concerned.

"Tom, do you want coffee?"

"No, thanks."

"Don Cherry called again while you were with Phil. He wants you to come and look at the Corridor."

"They having problems?"

"I don't know. He sounded excited. You want to call him back?"

"Not right now. I'll go down and see him in a minute."

She lingered at the door. "You want a bagel? Have you had breakfast?"

"I'm fine."

"Sure?"

"I'm fine, Cindy. Really."

She went away. He turned to look at his monitor, and saw that the icon for his E-mail was blinking. But he was thinking again about Meredith Johnson.

Sanders had more or less lived with her for about six months. It had been quite an intense relationship for a while. And yet, although he kept having isolated, vivid images, he realized that in general his memories from that time were surprisingly vague. Had he really lived with Meredith for six months? When exactly had they first met, and when had they broken up? Sanders was surprised at how difficult it was for him to fix the chronology in his mind. Hoping for clarity, he considered other aspects of his life: what had been his position at DigiCom in those days? Was he still working in Marketing, or had he already moved to the technical division? He wasn't sure, now. He would have to look it up in the files.

He thought about Blackburn. Blackburn had left his wife and moved in with Sanders around the time Sanders was involved with Meredith. Or was it afterward, when things had gone bad? Maybe Phil had moved into his apartment around the time he was breaking up with Meredith. Sanders wasn't sure. As he considered it, he realized he wasn't sure about anything from that time. These events had all happened a decade ago, in another city, at another period in his life, and his memories were in disarray. Again, he was surprised at how confused he was.

He pushed the intercom. "Cindy? I've got a question for you."

"Sure, Tom."

"This is the third week of June. What were you doing the third week of June, ten years ago?"

She didn't even hesitate. "That's easy: graduating from college."

Of course that would be true. "Okay," he said. "Then how about June, nine years ago."

"Nine years ago?" Her voice sounded suddenly cautious, less certain. "Gee . . . Let's see, June . . . Nine years ago? . . . June . . . Uh . . . I think I was with my boyfriend in Europe."

"Not your present boyfriend?"

"No . . . This guy was a real jerk."

Sanders said, "How long did that last?"

"We were there for a month."

"I mean the relationship."

"With him? Oh, let's see, we broke up . . . oh, it must have been . . . uh, December . . . I think it was December, or maybe January, after the holidays . . . Why?"

"Just trying to figure something out," Sanders said. Already he was relieved to hear the uncertain tone of her voice, as she tried to piece together the past. "By the way, how far back do we have office records? Correspondence, and call books?"

"I'd have to check. I know I have about three years."

"And what about earlier?"

"Earlier? How much earlier?"

"Ten years ago," he said.

"Gee, that'd be when you were in Cupertino. Do they have that stuff in storage down there? Did they put it on fiche, or was it just thrown out?"

"I don't know."

"You want me to check?"

"Not now," he said, and clicked off. He didn't want her making any inquiries in Cupertino now. Not right now.

Sanders rubbed his eyes with his fingertips. His thoughts drifting back over time. Again, he saw the stained-glass flower. It was oversize, bright, banal. Sanders had always been embarrassed by the banality of it. In those days, he had lived in one of the apartment complexes on Merano Drive. Twenty units clustered around a chilly little swimming pool. Everybody in the building worked for a high-tech company. Nobody ever went in the pool. And Sanders wasn't around much. Those were the days when he flew with Garvin to Korea twice a month. The days when they all flew coach. They couldn't even afford business class.

And he remembered how he would come home, exhausted from the long flight, and the first thing he would see when he got to his apartment was that damned stained-glass flower on the door.

And Meredith, in those days, was partial to white stockings, a white garter belt, little white flowers on the snaps with—

"Tom?" He looked up. Cindy was at the doorway. She said, "If you want to see Don Cherry, you'd better go now because you have a ten-thirty with Gary Bosak."

He felt as if she was treating him like an invalid. "Cindy, I'm fine."

"I know. Just a reminder."

"Okay, I'll go now."

As he hurried down the stairs to the third floor, he felt relieved at the distraction. Cindy was right to get him out of the office. And he was curious to see what Cherry's team had done with the Corridor.

The Corridor was what everyone at DigiCom called VIE: the Virtual Information Environment. VIE was the companion piece to Twinkle, the second major element in the emerging future of digital information as envisioned by DigiCom. In the future, information was going to be stored on disks, or made available in large databases that users would dial into over telephone lines. At the moment, users saw information displayed on flat screens—either televisions or computer screens. That had been the traditional way of handling information for the last thirty years. But soon, there would be new ways to present information. The most radical, and the most exciting, was virtual environments. Users wore special glasses to see computer-generated, three-dimensional environments which allowed them to feel as though they were literally moving through another world. Dozens of high-tech companies were racing to develop virtual environments. It was exciting, but very difficult, technology. At DigiCom, VIE was one of Garvin's pet projects; he had thrown a lot of money at it; he had had Don Cherry's programmers working on it around the clock for two years.

And so far, it had been nothing but trouble.

The sign on the door said "VIE" and underneath, "When Reality Is Not Enough." Sanders inserted his card in the slot, and the door clicked open. He passed through an anteroom, hearing a half-dozen voices shouting from the main equipment room beyond. Even in the anteroom, he noticed a distinctly nauseating odor in the air.

Entering the main room, he came upon a scene of utter chaos. The windows were thrown wide; there was the astringent smell of cleaning fluid. Most of the programmers were on the floor, working with disassembled equipment. The VIE units lay scattered in pieces, amid a tangle of multicolored cables. Even the black circular walker pads had been taken apart, the rubber bearings being cleaned one by one. Still more wires descended from the ceiling to the laser scanners which were broken open, their circuit boards exposed. Everyone seemed to be talking at once. And in the center of the room, looking like a teenage Buddha in an electric blue T-shirt that said "Reality Sucks," was Don Cherry, the head of Programming. Cherry was twenty-two years old, widely acknowledged to be indispensable, and famous for his impertinence.

When he saw Sanders he shouted: "Out! Out! Damned management! Out!"

"Why?" Sanders said. "I thought you wanted to see me."

"Too late! You had your chance!" Cherry said. "Now it's over!"

For a moment, Sanders thought Cherry was referring to the promotion he hadn't gotten. But Cherry was the most apolitical of the DigiCom division heads, and he was grinning cheerfully as he walked toward Sanders, stepping over his prostrate programmers. "Sorry, Tom. You're too late. We're fine-tuning now."

"Fine-tuning? It looks like ground zero here. And what's that terrible smell?"

"I know." Cherry threw up his hands. "I ask the boys to wash every day, but what can I say. They're programmers. No better than dogs."

"Cindy said you called me several times."

"I did," Cherry said. "We had the Corridor up and running, and I wanted you to see it. But maybe it's just as well you didn't."

Sanders looked at the complex equipment scattered all around him. "You had it *up*?"

"That was then. This is now. Now, we're fine-tuning." Cherry nodded to the programmers on the floor, working on the walker pads. "We finally got the bug out of the main loop, last night at midnight. The refresh rate doubled. The system really rips now. So we have to adjust the walkers and the servos to update responsiveness. It's a *mechanical* problem," he said disdainfully. "But we'll take care of it anyway."

The programmers were always annoyed when they had to deal with mechanical problems. Living almost entirely in an abstract world of computer code, they felt that physical machinery was beneath them.

Sanders said, "What is the problem, exactly?"

"Well, look," Cherry said. "Here's our latest implementation. The user wears this headset," he said, pointing to what looked like thick silver sunglasses. "And he gets on the walker pad, here."

The walker pad was one of Cherry's innovations. The size of a small round trampoline, its surface was composed of tightly packed rubber balls. It functioned like a multidirectional treadmill; walking on the balls, users could move in any direction. "Once he's on the walker," Cherry said, "the user dials into a database. Then the computer, over there—" Cherry pointed to a stack of boxes in the corner, "takes the information coming from the database and constructs a virtual environment which is projected inside the headset. When the user walks on the pad, the projection changes, so you feel like you're walking down a corridor lined with drawers of data on all sides. The user can stop anywhere, open any file drawer with his hand, and thumb through data. Completely realistic simulation."

"How many users?"

"At the moment, the system can handle five at one time."

"And the Corridor looks like what?" Sanders said. "Wire-frame?" In the earlier versions, the Corridor was outlined in skeletal black-and-white outlines. Fewer lines made it faster for the computer to draw.

"Wire-frame?" Cherry sniffed. "*Please*. We dumped that two weeks ago. Now we are talking 3-D surfaces fully modeled in 24-bit color, with anti-alias texture maps. We're rendering true curved surfaces—no polygons. Looks completely real."

"And what're the laser scanners for? I thought you did position by infrared." The headsets had infrared sensors mounted above them, so that the system could detect where the user was looking and adjust the projected image inside the headset to match the direction of looking.

"We still do," Cherry said. "The scanners are for body representation."

"Body representation?"

"Yeah. Now, if you're walking down the Corridor with somebody else, you can turn and look at them and you'll see them. Because the scanners are capturing a three-dimensional texture map in real time: they read body and expression, and draw the virtual face of the virtual person standing beside you in the virtual room. You can't see the person's eyes, of course, because they're hidden by the headset they're wearing. But the system generates a face from the stored texture map. Pretty slick, huh?"

"You mean you can see other users?"

"That's right. See their faces, see their expressions. And that's not all. If other users in the system aren't wearing a headset, you can still see them, too. The program identifies other users, pulls their photo out of the personnel file, and pastes it onto a virtual body image. A little kludgey, but not bad." Cherry waved his hand in the air. "And that's not all. We've also built in virtual help."

"Virtual help?"

"Sure, users always need online help. So we've made an angel to help you. Floats alongside you, answers your questions." Cherry was grinning. "We thought of making it a blue fairy, but we didn't want to offend anybody."

Sanders stared thoughtfully at the room. Cherry was telling him about his successes. But something else was happening here: it was impossible to miss the tension, the frantic energy of the people as they worked.

"Hey, Don," one of the programmers shouted. "What's the Z-count supposed to be?"

"Over five," Cherry said.

"I got it to four-three."

"Four-three sucks. Get it above five, or you're fired." He turned to Sanders. "You've got to encourage the troops."

Sanders looked at Cherry. "All right," he said finally. "Now what's the *real* problem?"

Cherry shrugged. "Nothing. I told you: fine-tuning."

"Don."

Cherry sighed. "Well, when we jumped the refresh rate, we trashed the builder module. You see, the room is being built in real time by the box. With a faster refresh off the sensors, we have to build objects much faster. Otherwise the room seems to lag behind you. You feel like you're drunk. You move your head, and the room swooshes behind you, catching up."

"And?"

"And, it makes the users throw up."

Sanders sighed. "Great."

"We had to take the walker pads apart because Teddy barfed all over everything."

"Great, Don."

"What's the matter? It's no big deal. It cleans up." He shook his head. "Although I do wish Teddy hadn't eaten huevos rancheros for breakfast. That was unfortunate. Little bits of tortilla everywhere in the bearings."

"You know we have a demo tomorrow for the C-W people."

"No problem. We'll be ready."

"Don, I can't have their top executives throwing up."

"Trust me," Cherry said. "We'll be ready. They're going to love it. Whatever problems this company has, the Corridor is not one of them."

"That's a promise?"

"That," Cherry said, "is a guarantee."

Sanders was back in his office by ten-twenty, and was seated at his desk when Gary Bosak came in. Bosak was a tall man in his twenties, wearing jeans, running shoes, and a Terminator T-shirt. He carried a large fold-over leather briefcase, the kind that trial attorneys used.

"You look pale," Bosak said. "But everybody in the building is pale today. It's tense as hell around here, you know that?"

"I've noticed."

"Yeah, I bet. Okay to start?"

"Sure."

"Cindy? Mr. Sanders is going to be unavailable for a few minutes."

Bosak closed the office door and locked it. Whistling cheerfully, he unplugged Sanders's desk phone, and the phone beside the couch in the corner. From there, he went to the window and closed the blinds. There was a small television in the corner; he turned it on. He snapped the latches on his briefcase, took out a small plastic box, and flipped the switch on the side. The box began to blink, and emitted a low white noise hiss. Bosak set it in the middle of Sanders's desk. Bosak never gave information until the white noise scrambler was in place, since most of what he had to say implied illegal behavior.

"I have good news for you," Bosak said. "Your boy is clean." He pulled out a manila file, opened it up, and started handing over pages. "Peter John Nealy, twenty-three, DigiCom employee for sixteen months. Now working as a programmer in APG. Okay, here we go. His high school and college transcripts . . . Employment file from Data General, his last employer. All in order. Now, the recent stuff . . . Credit rating from TRW . . . Phone bills from his apartment . . . Phone bills for his cellular line . . . Bank statement . . . Savings account . . . Last two 1040s . . . Twelve months of credit charges, VISA and Master . . . Travel records . . . E-mail messages inside the company, and off the Internet . . . Parking tickets . . . And this is the clincher . . . Ramada Inn in Sunnyvale, last three visits, his phone charges there, the numbers he called . . . Last three car rentals with mileage . . . Rental car cellular phone, the numbers called . . . That's everything."

"And?"

"I ran down the numbers he called. Here's the breakdown. A lot of calls to Seattle Silicon, but Nealy's seeing a girl there. She's a secretary, works in sales, no conflict. He also calls his brother, a programmer at Boeing, does parallel processing stuff for wing design, no conflict. His other calls are to suppliers and code vendors, and they're all appropriate. No calls after hours. No calls to pay phones. No overseas calls. No suspicious pattern in the calls. No unexplained bank transfers, no sudden new purchases. No reason to think he's looking for a move. I'd say he's not talking to anybody you care about."

"Good," Sanders said. He glanced down at the sheets of paper, and paused. "Gary . . . Some of this stuff is from our company. Some of these reports."

"Yeah. So?"

"How'd you get them?"

Bosak grinned. "Hey. You don't ask and I don't tell you."

"How'd you get the Data General file?"

Bosak shook his head. "Isn't this why you pay me?"

"Yes it is, but—"

"Hey. You wanted a check on an employee, you got it. Your kid's clean. He's working only for you. Anything else you want to know about him?"

"No." Sanders shook his head.

"Great. I got to get some sleep." Bosak collected all the files and placed them back in his folder. "By the way, you're going to get a call from my parole officer."

"Uh-huh."

"Can I count on you?"

"Sure, Gary."

"I told him I was doing consulting for you. On telecommunications security."

"And so you are."

Bosak switched off the blinking box, put it in his briefcase, and reconnected the telephones. "Always a pleasure. Do I leave the bill with you, or Cindy?"

"I'll take it. See you, Gary."

"Hey. Anytime. You need more, you know where I am."

Sanders glanced at the bill, from NE Professional Services, Inc., of Bellevue, Washington. The name was Bosak's private joke: the letters NE stood for "Necessary Evil." Ordinarily, high-tech companies employed retired police officers and private investigators to do background checks, but occasionally they used hackers like Gary Bosak, who could gain access to electronic data banks, to get information on suspect employees. The advantage of using Bosak was that he could work quickly, often making a report in a matter of hours, or overnight. Bosak's methods were of course illegal; simply by hiring him, Sanders himself had broken a half-dozen laws. But background checks on employees were accepted as standard practice in high-tech firms, where a single document or product development plan might be worth hundreds of thousands of dollars to competitors.

And in the case of Pete Nealy, a check was particularly crucial. Nealy was developing hot new compression algorithms to pack and unpack video images onto CD-ROM laser disks. His work was vital to the new Twinkle technology. High-speed digital images coming off the disk were going to transform a sluggish technology and produce a revolution in education. But if Twinkle's algorithms became available to a competitor, then DigiCom's advantage would be greatly reduced, and that meant—

The intercom buzzed. "Tom," Cindy said. "It's eleven o'clock. Time for the APG meeting. You want the agenda on your way down?"

"Not today," he said. "I think I know what we'll be talking about."

I n the third-floor conference room, the Advanced Products Group was already meeting. This was a weekly meeting in which the division heads discussed problems and brought everyone up to date. It was a meeting that Sanders ordinarily led. Around the table were Don Cherry, the chief of Programming; Mark Lewyn, the temperamental head of Product Design, all in black Armani; and Mary Anne Hunter, the head of Data Telecommunications. Petite and intense, Hunter was dressed in a sweatshirt, shorts, and Nike running tights, she never ate lunch, but ordinarily went on a five-mile run after each meeting.

Lewyn was in the middle of one of his storming rages: "It's insulting to everybody in the division. I have no idea why she got this position. I don't know what her qualifications could be for a job like this, and—"

Lewyn broke off as Sanders came into the room. There was an awkward moment. Everyone was silent, glancing at him, then looking away.

"I had a feeling," Sanders said, smiling, "you'd be talking about this."

The room remained silent. "Come on," he said, as he slipped into a chair. "It's not a funeral."

Mark Lewyn cleared his throat. "I'm sorry, Tom. I think it's an outrage."

Mary Anne Hunter said, "Everybody knows it should have been you."

Lewyn said, "It's a shock to all of us, Tom."

"Yeah," Cherry said, grinning. "We've been trying like hell to get you sacked, but we never really thought it would work."

"I appreciate all this," Sanders said, "but it's Garvin's company, and he can do what he wants with it. He's been right more often than not. And I'm a big boy. Nobody ever promised me anything."

Lewyn said, "You're really okay with this?"

"Believe me. I'm fine."

"You talked with Garvin?"

"I talked with Phil."

Lewyn shook his head. "That sanctimonious asshole."

"Listen," Cherry said, "did Phil say anything about the spin-off?"

"Yes," Sanders said. "The spin-off is still happening. Eighteen months after the merger, they'll structure the IPO, and take the division public."

There were little shrugs around the table. Sanders could see they were relieved. Going public meant a lot of money to all the people sitting in the room.

"And what did Phil say about Ms. Johnson?"

"Not much. Just that she's Garvin's choice to head up the technical side."

At that moment Stephanie Kaplan, DigiCom's Chief Financial Officer, came into the room. A tall woman with prematurely gray hair and a notably silent manner, she was known as Stephanie Stealth, or the Stealth Bomber—the latter a reference to her habit of quietly killing projects she did not consider profitable enough. Kaplan was based in Cupertino, but she generally sat in once a month on the Seattle division meetings. Lately, she had been up more often.

Lewyn said, "We're trying to cheer up Tom, Stephanie."

Kaplan took a seat, and gave Sanders a sympathetic smile. She didn't speak.

Lewyn said, "Did *you* know this Meredith Johnson appointment was coming?"

"No," Kaplan said. "It was a surprise to everybody. And not everybody's happy about it." Then, as if she had said too much, she opened her briefcase, and busied herself with her notes. As usual, she slid into the background; the others quickly ignored her.

"Well," Cherry said, "I hear Garvin's got a real thing for her. Johnson's only been with the company four years, and she hasn't been especially outstanding. But Garvin took her under his wing. Two years ago, he began moving her up, fast. For some reason, he just thinks Meredith Johnson is *great*."

Lewyn said, "Is Garvin fucking her?"

"No, he just likes her."

"She must be fucking somebody."

"Wait a minute," Mary Anne Hunter said, sitting up. "What's this? If Garvin brought in some guy from Microsoft to run this division, nobody'd say he must be fucking somebody."

Cherry laughed. "It'd depend on who he was."

"I'm serious. Why is it when a woman gets a promotion, she must be fucking somebody?"

Lewyn said, "Look: if they brought in Ellen Howard from Microsoft, we wouldn't be having this conversation because we all know Ellen's very competent. We wouldn't like it, but we'd accept it. But nobody even *knows* Meredith Johnson. I mean, does anybody here know her?"

"Actually," Sanders said, "I know her."

There was silence.

"I used to go out with her."

Cherry laughed. "So *you're* the one she's fucking."

Sanders shook his head. "It was years ago."

Hunter said, "What's she like?"

"Yeah," Cherry said, grinning lasciviously. "What's she like?"

"Shut up, Don."

"Lighten up, Mary Anne."

"She worked for Novell when I knew her," Sanders said. "She was about twenty-five. Smart and ambitious."

"Smart and ambitious," Lewyn said. "That's fine. The world's full of smart and ambitious. The question is, can she run a technical division? Or have we got another Screamer Freeling on our hands?"

Two years earlier, Garvin had put a sales manager named Howard Freeling in charge of the division. The idea was to bring product development in contact with customers at an earlier point, to develop new products more in line with the emerging market. Freeling instituted focus groups, and they all spent a lot of time watching potential customers play with new products behind one-way glass.

But Freeling was completely unfamiliar with technical issues. So when confronted with a problem, he screamed. He was like a tourist in a foreign country who didn't speak the language and thought he could make the locals understand by shouting at them. Freeling's tenure at APG was a disaster. The programmers loathed him; the designers rebelled at his idea for neon-colored product boxes; the manufacturing glitches at factories in Ireland and Texas didn't get solved. Finally, when the production line in Cork went down for eleven days, Freeling flew over and screamed. The Irish managers all quit, and Garvin fired him.

"So: is that what we have? Another Screamer?"

Stephanie Kaplan cleared her throat. "I think Garvin learned his lesson. He wouldn't make the same mistake twice."

"So you think Meredith Johnson is up to the job?"

"I couldn't say," Kaplan replied, speaking very deliberately.

"Not much of an endorsement," Lewyn said.

"But I think she'll be better than Freeling," Kaplan said.

Lewyn snorted. "This is the Taller Than Mickey Rooney Award. You can still be very short and win."

"No," Kaplan said, "I think she'll be better."

Cherry said, "Better-looking, at least, from what I hear."

"Sexist," Mary Anne Hunter said.

"What: I can't say she's good-looking?"

"We're talking about her competence, not her appearance."

"Wait a minute," Cherry said. "Coming over here to this meeting, I pass the women at the espresso bar, and what are they talking about? Whether Richard Gere has better buns than Mel Gibson. They're talking about the crack in the ass, lift and separate, all that stuff. I don't see why they can talk about—"

"We're drifting afield," Sanders said.

"It doesn't matter what you guys say," Hunter said, "the fact is, this company is dominated by males; there are almost no women except Stephanie in high executive positions. I think it's great that Bob has appointed a woman to run this division, and I for one think we should support her." She looked at Sanders. "We all love you, Tom, but you know what I mean."

"Yeah, we all love you," Cherry said. "At least, we did until we got our cute new boss."

Lewyn said, "I'll support Johnson—if she's any good."

"No you won't," Hunter said. "You'll sabotage her. You'll find a reason to get rid of her."

"Wait a minute—"

"No. What is this conversation *really* about? It's about the fact that you're all pissed off because now you have to report to a woman."

"Mary Anne . . ."

"I mean it."

Lewyn said, "I think Tom's pissed off because he didn't get the job."

"I'm not pissed off," Sanders said.

"Well, I'm pissed off," Cherry said, "because Meredith used to be Tom's girlfriend, so now he has a special in with the new boss."

"Maybe." Sanders frowned.

Lewyn said, "On the other hand, maybe she hates you. All my old girlfriends hate me."

"With good reason, I hear," Cherry said, laughing.

Sanders said, "Let's get back to the agenda, shall we?"

"What agenda?"

"Twinkle."

There were groans around the table. "Not again."

"Goddamn Twinkle."

"How bad is it?" Cherry said.

"They still can't get the seek times down, and they can't solve the hinge problems. The line's running at twenty-nine percent."

Lewyn said, "They better send us some units."

"We should have them today."

"Okay. Table it till then?"

"It's okay with me." Sanders looked around the table. "Anybody else have a problem? Mary Anne?"

"No, we're fine. We still expect prototype card-phones off our test line within two months."

The new generation of cellular telephones were not much larger than a credit card. They folded open for use. "How's the weight?"

"The weight's now four ounces, which is not great, but okay. The problem is power. The batteries only run 180 minutes in talk mode. And the keypad sticks when you dial. But that's Mark's headache. We're on schedule with the line."

"Good." He turned to Don Cherry. "And how's the Corridor?"

Cherry sat back in his chair, beaming. He crossed his hands over his belly. "I am pleased to report," he said, "that as of half an hour ago, the Corridor is fan-fucking-*tastic*."

"Really?"

"That's great news."

"Nobody's throwing up?"

"*Please*. Ancient history."

Mark Lewyn said, "Wait a minute. Somebody threw up?"

"A vile rumor. That was then. This is now. We got the last delay bug out half an hour ago, and all functions are now fully implemented. We can take any database and convert it into a 3-D 24-bit color environment that you can navigate in real time. You can walk through any database in the world."

"And it's stable?"

"It's a rock."

"You've tried it with naïve users?"

"Bulletproof."

"So you're ready to demo for Conley?"

"We'll blow 'em away," Cherry said. "They won't fucking believe their eyes."

Coming out of the conference room, Sanders ran into a group of Conley-White executives being taken on a tour by Bob Garvin. Robert T. Garvin looked the way every CEO wanted to look in the pages of *Fortune* magazine. He was fifty-nine years old and handsome, with a craggy face and salt-and-pepper hair that always looked windblown, as if he'd just come in from a fly-fishing trip in Montana, or a weekend sailing in the San Juans. In the old days, like everyone else, he had worn jeans and denim work shirts in the office. But in recent years, he favored dark blue Caraceni suits. It was one of the many changes that people in the company had noticed since the death of his daughter, three years before.

Brusque and profane in private, Garvin was all charm in public. Leading the Conley-White executives, he said, "Here on the third floor, you have our tech divisions and advanced product laboratories. Oh, Tom. Good." He threw his arm around Sanders. "Meet Tom Sanders, our division manager for advanced products. One of the brilliant young men who's made our company what it is. Tom, say hello to Ed Nichols, the CFO for Conley-White . . ."

A thin, hawk-faced man in his late fifties, Nichols carried his head tilted back, so that he seemed to be pulling away from everything, as if there were a bad smell. He looked down his nose through half-frame glasses at Sanders, regarding him with a vaguely disapproving air, and shook hands formally.

"Mr. Sanders. How do you do?"

"Mr. Nichols."

". . . and John Conley, nephew of the founder, and vice president of the firm . . ."

Sanders turned to a stocky, athletic man in his late twenties. Wire-frame spectacles. Armani suit. Firm handshake. Serious expression. Sanders had the impression of a wealthy and very determined man.

"Hi there, Tom."

"Hi, John."

". . . and Jim Daly, from Goldman, Sachs . . ."

A balding, thin, storklike man in a pinstripe suit. Daly seemed distracted, befuddled, and shook hands with a brief nod.

". . . and of course, Meredith Johnson, from Cupertino."

She was more beautiful than he had remembered. And different in some subtle way. Older, of course, crow's-feet at the corners of her eyes, and faint creases in her forehead. But she stood straighter now, and she had a vibrancy, a confidence, that he associated with power. Dark blue suit, blond hair, large eyes. Those incredibly long eyelashes. He had forgotten.

"Hello, Tom, nice to see you again." A warm smile. Her perfume.

"Meredith, nice to see you."

She released his hand, and the group swept on, as Garvin led them down the hall. "Now, just ahead is the VIE Unit. You'll be seeing that work tomorrow."

Mark Lewyn came out of the conference room and said, "You met the rogues' gallery?"

"I guess so."

Lewyn watched them go. "Hard to believe those guys are going to be running this company," he said. "I did a briefing this morning, and let me tell you, they don't know *anything*. It's scary."

As the group reached the end of the hallway, Meredith Johnson looked back over her shoulder at Sanders. She mouthed, "I'll call you." And she smiled radiantly. Then she was gone.

Lewyn sighed. "I'd say," he said, "that you have an in with top management there, Tom."

"Maybe so."

"I just wish I knew why Garvin thinks she's so great."

Sanders said, "Well, she certainly looks great."

Lewyn turned away. "We'll see," he said. "We'll see."

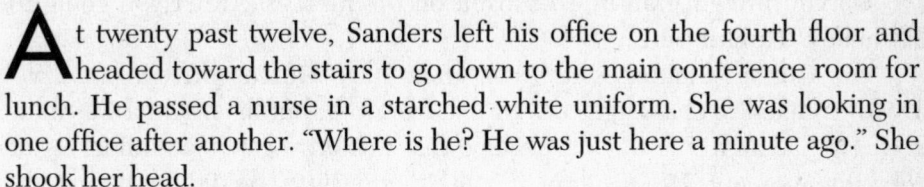

At twenty past twelve, Sanders left his office on the fourth floor and headed toward the stairs to go down to the main conference room for lunch. He passed a nurse in a starched white uniform. She was looking in one office after another. "Where is he? He was just here a minute ago." She shook her head.

"Who?" Sanders said.

"The professor," she replied, blowing a strand of hair out of her eyes. "I can't leave him alone for a minute."

"What professor?" Sanders said. But by then he heard the female giggles coming from a room farther down the hall, and he already knew the answer. "Professor Dorfman?"

"Yes. Professor Dorfman," the nurse said, nodding grimly, and she headed toward the source of the giggles.

Sanders trailed after her. Max Dorfman was a German management consultant, now very elderly. At one time or another, he had been a visiting professor at every major business school in America, and he had gained a particular reputation as a guru to high-tech companies. During most of the 1980s, he had served on the board of directors of DigiCom, lending prestige to Garvin's upstart company. And during that time, he had been a mentor to Sanders. In fact, it was Dorfman who had convinced Sanders to leave Cupertino eight years earlier and take the job in Seattle.

Sanders said, "I didn't know he was still alive."

"Very much so," the nurse said.

"He must be ninety."

"Well, he doesn't act a day over eighty-five."

As they approached the room, he saw Mary Anne Hunter coming out. She had changed into a skirt and blouse, and she was smiling broadly, as if she had just left her lover. "Tom, you'll never guess who's here."

"Max," he said.

"That's right. Oh, Tom, you should see him: he's exactly the same."

"I'll bet he is," Sanders said. Even from outside the room, he could smell the cigarette smoke.

The nurse said, "Now, Professor," in a severe tone, and strode into the room. Sanders looked in; it was one of the employee lounges. Max Dorfman's wheelchair was pulled up to the table in the center of the room. He was surrounded by pretty assistants. The women were making a fuss over him, and in their midst Dorfman, with his shock of white hair, was grinning happily, smoking a cigarette in a long holder.

"What's he doing here?" Sanders said.

"Garvin brought him in, to consult on the merger. Aren't you going to say hello?" Hunter said.

"Oh, Christ," Sanders said. "You know Max. He can drive you crazy." Dorfman liked to challenge conventional wisdom, but his method was indirect. He had an ironic way of speaking that was provocative and mocking at the same moment. He was fond of contradictions, and he did not hesitate to lie. If you caught him in a lie, he would immediately say, "Yes, that's true. I don't know what I was thinking of," and then resume talking in the same maddening, elliptical way. He never really said what he meant; he left it for you to put it together. His rambling sessions left executives confused and exhausted.

"But you were such friends," Hunter said, looking at him. "I'm sure he'd like you to say hello."

"He's busy now. Maybe later." Sanders looked at his watch. "Anyway, we're going to be late for lunch."

He started back down the hallway. Hunter fell into step with him, frowning. "He always got under your skin, didn't he?"

"He got under everybody's skin. It was what he did best."

She looked at him in a puzzled way, and seemed about to say more, then shrugged. "It's okay with me."

"I'm just not in the mood for one of those conversations," Sanders said. "Maybe later. But not right now." They headed down the stairs to the ground floor.

In keeping with the stripped-down functionality of modern high-tech firms, DigiCom maintained no corporate dining room. Instead, lunches and dinners were held at local restaurants, most often at the nearby Il Terrazzo. But the need for secrecy about the merger obliged DigiCom to cater a lunch in the large, wood-paneled conference room on the ground floor. At twelve-thirty, with the principal managers of the DigiCom technical divisions, the Conley-White executives, and the Goldman, Sachs bankers all present, the room was crowded. The egalitarian ethos of the company meant that there was no assigned seating, but the principal C-W executives ended up at one side of the table near the front of the room, clustered around Garvin. The power end of the table.

Sanders took a seat farther down on the opposite side, and was surprised when Stephanie Kaplan slid into the chair to his right. Kaplan usually sat much closer to Garvin; Sanders was distinctly further down the pecking order. To Sander's left was Bill Everts, the head of Human Resources—a nice, slightly dull guy. As white-coated waiters served the meal, Sanders talked about fishing on Orcas Island, which was Everts's passion. As usual, Kaplan was quiet during most of the lunch, seeming to withdraw into herself.

Sanders began to feel he was neglecting her. Toward the end of the meal, he turned to her and said, "I notice you've been up here in Seattle more often the last few months, Stephanie. Is that because of the merger?"

"No." She smiled. "My son's a freshman at the university, so I like to come up because I get to see him."

"What's he studying?"

"Chemistry. He wants to go into materials chemistry. Apparently it's going to be a big field."

"I've heard that."

"Half the time I don't know what he's talking about. It's funny, when your child knows more than you do."

He nodded, trying to think of something else to ask her. It wasn't easy: although he had sat in meetings with Kaplan for years, he knew little about her personally. She was married to a professor at San Jose State, a jovial chubby man with a mustache, who taught economics. When they were together, he did all the talking while Stephanie stood silently by. She was a tall, bony, awkward woman who seemed resigned to her lack of social graces. She was said to be a very good golfer—at least, good enough that Garvin wouldn't play her anymore. No one who knew her was surprised that she had made the error of beating Garvin too often; wags said that she wasn't enough of a loser to be promoted.

Garvin didn't really like her, but he would never think of letting her go. Colorless, humorless, and tireless, her dedication to the company was legendary; she worked late every night and came in most weekends. When she had had a bout of cancer a few years back, she refused to take even a single day off. Apparently she was cured of the cancer; at least, Sanders hadn't heard anything more about it. But the episode seemed to have increased Kaplan's relentless focus on her impersonal domain, figures and spreadsheets, and heightened her natural inclination to work behind the scenes. More than one manager had come to work in the morning, only to find a pet project killed by the Stealth Bomber, with no lingering trace of how or why it had happened. Thus her tendency to remain aloof in social situations was more than a reflection of her own discomfort; it was also a reminder of the power she wielded within the company, and how she wielded it. In her own way, she was mysterious—and potentially dangerous.

While he was trying to think of something to say, Kaplan leaned toward him confidentially and lowered her voice. "In the meeting this morning, Tom, I didn't really feel I could say anything. But I hope you're okay. About this new reorganization."

Sanders concealed his surprise. In twelve years, Kaplan had never said anything so directly personal to him. He wondered why she would do so now. He was instantly wary, unsure of how to respond.

"Well, it was a shock," he said.

She looked at him with a steady gaze. "It was a shock to many of us," she said quietly. "There was an uproar in Cupertino. A lot of people questioned Garvin's judgment."

Sanders frowned. Kaplan never said anything even obliquely critical of Garvin. Never. But now this. Was she testing him? He said nothing, and poked at his food.

"I can imagine you're uneasy about the new appointment."

"Only because it was so unexpected. It seemed to come out of the blue."

Kaplan looked at him oddly for a moment, as if he had disappointed her. Then she nodded. "It's always that way with mergers," she said. Her tone was more open, less confidential. "I was at CompuSoft when it merged with

Symantec, and it was exactly the same: last-minute announcements, switches in the organization charts. Jobs promised, jobs lost. Everybody up in the air for weeks. It's not easy to bring two organizations together—— especially these two. There are big differences in corporate cultures. Garvin has to make them comfortable." She gestured toward the end of the table where Garvin was sitting. "Just look at them," she said. "All the Conley people are wearing suits. Nobody in our company wears suits, except lawyers."

"They're East Coast," Sanders said.

"But it goes deeper than that. Conley-White likes to present itself as a diversified communications company, but it's really not so grand. Its primary business is textbooks. That's a lucrative business, but you're selling to school boards in Texas and Ohio and Tennessee. Many of them are deeply conservative. So Conley's conservative, by instinct and experience. They want this merger because they need to acquire a high-tech capacity going into the next century. But they can't get used to the idea of a very young company, where the employees work in T-shirts and jeans, and everybody goes by first names. They're in shock. Besides," Kaplan added, lowering her voice again, "there are internal divisions within Conley-White. Garvin has to deal with that, too."

"What internal divisions?"

She nodded toward the head of the table. "You may have noticed that their CEO isn't here. The big man hasn't honored us with his presence. He won't show up until the end of the week. For now, he's only sent his minions. Their highest-ranking officer is Ed Nichols, the CFO."

Sanders glanced over at the suspicious, sharp-faced man he had met earlier. Kaplan said, "Nichols doesn't want to buy this company. He thinks we're overpriced and underpowered. Last year, he tried to form a strategic alliance with Microsoft, but Gates blew him off. Then Nichols tried to buy InterDisk, but that fell through: too many problems, and InterDisk had that bad publicity about the fired employee. So they ended up with us. But Ed isn't happy about where he landed."

"He certainly doesn't look happy," Sanders said.

"The main reason is he hates the Conley kid."

Seated beside Nichols was John Conley, the bespectacled young lawyer in his twenties. Distinctly younger than anyone around him, Conley was speaking energetically, jabbing his fork in the air as he made a point to Nichols.

"Ed Nichols thinks Conley's an asshole."

"But Conley's only a vice president," Sanders said. "He can't have that much power."

Kaplan shook her head. "He's the heir, remember?"

"So? What does that mean? His grandfather's picture is on some board-room wall?"

"Conley owns four percent of C-W stock, and controls another twenty-six percent still held by the family or vested in trusts controlled by the family. John Conley has the largest voting block of Conley-White stock."

"And John Conley wants the deal?"

"Yes." Kaplan nodded. "Conley handpicked our company to acquire. And he's going forward fast, with the help of his friends like Jim Daly at Goldman, Sachs. Daly's very smart, but investment bankers always have big fees riding on a merger. They'll do their due diligence, I'm not saying they won't. But it'd take a lot to get them to back out of the deal now."

"Uh-huh."

"So Nichols feels he's lost control of the acquisition, and he's being rushed into a deal that's a lot richer than it should be. Nichols doesn't see why C-W should make us all wealthy. He'd pull out of this deal if he could—if only to screw Conley."

"But Conley's driving this deal."

"Yes. And Conley's abrasive. He likes to make little speeches about youth versus age, the coming digital era, a young vision for the future. It enrages Nichols. Ed Nichols feels he's doubled the net worth of the com-pany in a decade, and now this little twerp is giving him lectures."

"And how does Meredith fit in?"

Kaplan hesitated. "Meredith is suitable."

"Meaning what?"

"She's Eastern. She grew up in Connecticut and went to Vassar. The Conley people like that. They're comfortable with that."

"That's all? She has the right accent?"

"You didn't hear it from me," Kaplan said. "But I think they also see her as weak. They think they can control her once the merger is completed."

"And Garvin's going along with that?"

Kaplan shrugged. "Bob's a realist," she said. "He needs capitalization. He's built his company skillfully, but we're going to require massive infu-sions of cash for the next phase, when we go head-to-head with Sony and Philips in product development. Conley-White's textbook operation is a cash cow. Bob looks at them and sees green—and he's inclined to do what they want, to get their money."

"And of course, Bob likes Meredith."

"Yes. That's true. Bob likes her."

Sanders waited while she poked at her food for a while. "And you, Stephanie? What do you think?"

Kaplan shrugged. "She's able."

"Able but weak?"

"No." Kaplan shook her head. "Meredith has ability. That's not in question. But I'm concerned about her experience. She's not as seasoned as she
might be. She's being put in charge of four major technical units that are
expected to grow rapidly. I just hope she's up to it."

There was the clink of a spoon on a glass, and Garvin stepped to the
front of the room. "Even though you're still eating dessert, let's get started,
so we can finish by two o'clock," he said. "Let me remind you of the new
timetable. Assuming everything continues as planned, we expect to make
the formal announcement of the acquisition at a press conference here on
Friday noon. And now, let me introduce our new associates from Conley-
White . . ."

As Garvin named the C-W people, and they stood up around the table,
Kaplan leaned over and whispered to Tom, "This is all fluff and feathers.
The real reason for this lunch is you-know-who."

". . . and finally," Garvin said, "let me introduce someone that many of
you know, but some of you do not, the new Vice President for Advanced
Operations and Planning, Meredith Johnson."

There was scattered, brief applause as Johnson got up from her seat and
walked to a podium at the front of the room. In her dark blue suit, she
looked the model of corporate correctness, but she was strikingly beautiful.
At the podium, she put on horn-rimmed glasses and lowered the conference room lights.

"Bob has asked me to review the way the new structure will work," she
said, "and to say something about what we see happening in the coming
months." She bent over the podium, where a computer was set up for pre-
sentations. "Now, if I can just work this thing . . . let me see . . ."

In the darkened room, Don Cherry caught Sanders's eye and shook his
head slowly.

"Ah, okay, here we are," Johnson said, at the podium. The screen behind
her came to life. Animated images generated by the computer were projected onto the screen. The first image showed a red heart, which broke into
four pieces. "The heart of DigiCom has always been its Advanced Products
Group, which consists of four separate divisions as you see here. But as all
information throughout the world becomes digital, these divisions will
inevitably merge." On the screen, the pieces of the heart slid back together,
and the heart transformed itself into a spinning globe. It began to throw off
products. "For the customer in the near future, armed with cellular phone,
built-in fax modem, and hand-held computer or PDA, it will be increasingly
irrelevant where in the world he or she is and where the information is

coming from. We are talking about the true globalization of information, and this implies an array of new products for our major markets in business and education." The globe expanded and dissolved, became classrooms on all continents, students at desks. "In particular, education will be a growing focus of this company as technology moves from print to digital displays to virtual environments. Now, let's review exactly what this means, and where I see it taking us."

And she proceeded to do it all—hypermedia, embedded video, authoring systems, work-group structures, academic sourcing, customer acceptance. She moved on to the cost structures—projected research outlays and revenues, five-year goals, offshore variables. Then to major product challenges—quality control, user feedback, shorter development cycles.

Meredith Johnson's presentation was flawless, the images blending and flowing across the screen, her voice confident, no hesitation, no pauses. As she continued, the room became quiet, the atmosphere distinctly respectful.

"Although this is not the time to go into technical matters," she said, "I want to mention that new CD-drive seek times under a hundred milliseconds, combined with new compression algorithms, should shift the industry standard for CD to full-res digitized video at sixty fields per second. And we are talking about platform-independent RISC processors supported by 32-bit color active-matrix displays and portable hard copy at 1200 DPI and wireless networking in both LAN and WAN configurations. Combine that with an autonomously generated virtual database—especially when ROM-based software agents for object definition and classification are in place—and I think we can agree we are looking at prospects for a very exciting future."

Sanders saw that Don Cherry's mouth was hanging open. Sanders leaned over to Kaplan. "Sounds like she knows her stuff."

"Yes," Kaplan said, nodding. "The demo queen. She started out doing demos. Appearance has always been her strongest point." Sanders glanced at Kaplan; she looked away.

But then the speech ended. There was applause as the lights came up, and Johnson went back to her seat. The room broke up, people heading back to work. Johnson left Garvin, and went directly to Don Cherry, said a few words to him. Cherry smiled: the charmed geek. Then Meredith went across the room to Mary Anne, spoke briefly to her, and then to Mark Lewyn.

"She's smart," Kaplan said, watching her, "touching base with all the division heads—especially since she didn't name them in her speech."

Sanders frowned. "You think that's significant?"

"Only if she's planning to make changes."

"Phil said she wasn't going to."

"But you never know, do you?" Kaplan said, standing up, dropping her napkin on the table. "I've got to go—and it looks like you're next on her list."

Kaplan moved discreetly away as Meredith came up to Sanders. She was smiling. "I wanted to apologize, Tom," Meredith said, "for not mentioning your name and the names of the other division heads in my presentation. I don't want anybody to get the wrong idea. It's just that Bob asked me to keep it short."

"Well," Sanders said, "it looks like you won everybody over. The reaction was very favorable."

"I hope so. Listen," she said, putting her hand on his arm, "we've got a slew of due diligence sessions tomorrow. I've been asking all the heads to meet with me today, if they can. I wonder if you're free to come to my office at the end of the day for a drink. We can go over things, and maybe catch up on old times, too."

"Sure," he said. He felt the warmth of her hand on his arm. She didn't take it away.

"They've given me an office on the fifth floor, and with any luck there should be furniture in by later today. Six o'clock work for you?"

"Fine," he said.

She smiled. "You still partial to dry chardonnay?"

Despite himself, he was flattered that she remembered. He smiled, "Yes, I still am."

"I'll see if I can get one. And we'll go over some of the immediate problems, like that hundred-millisecond drive."

"Okay, fine. About that drive—"

"I know," she said, her voice lower. "We'll deal with it." Behind her, the Conley-White executives were coming up. "Let's talk tonight."

"Good."

"See you then, Tom."

"See you then."

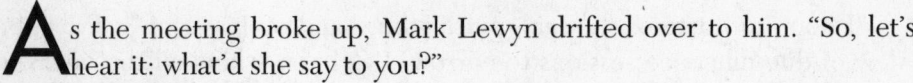

As the meeting broke up, Mark Lewyn drifted over to him. "So, let's hear it: what'd she say to you?"

"Meredith?"

"No, the Stealthy One. Kaplan was bending your ear all during lunch. What's up?"

Sanders shrugged. "Oh, you know. Just small talk."

"Come on. Stephanie doesn't do small talk. She doesn't know how. And Stephanie talked more to you than I've seen her talk in years."

Sanders was surprised to see how anxious Lewyn was. "Actually," he said, "we talked mostly about her son. He's a freshman at the university."

But Lewyn wasn't buying it. He frowned and said, "She's up to something, isn't she. She never talks without a reason. Is it about me? I know she's critical of the design team. She thinks we're wasteful. I've told her many times that it's not true—"

"Mark," Sanders said. "Your name didn't even come up. Honest."

To change the subject, Sanders asked, "What'd you think of Johnson? Pretty strong presentation, I thought."

"Yes. She's impressive. There was only one thing that bothered me," Lewyn said. He was still frowning, still uneasy. "Isn't she supposed to be a late-breaking curve, forced on us by management at Conley?"

"That's what I heard. Why?"

"Her presentation. To put together a graphic presentation like that takes two weeks, at a minimum," Lewyn said. "In my design group, I get the designers on it a month in advance, then we run it through for timing, then say a week for revisions and re-do's, then another week while they transfer to a drive. And that's my own in-house group, working fast. For an executive, it'd take longer. They pawn it off on some assistant, who tries to make it for them. Then the executive looks at it, wants it all done over again. And it takes more time. So if this was her presentation, I'd say she's known about her new job for a while. Months."

Sanders frowned.

"As usual," Lewyn said, "the poor bastards in the trenches are the last to know. I just wonder what *else* we don't know."

Sanders was back at his office by 2:15. He called his wife to tell her he would be home late, that he had a meeting at six.

"What's happening over there?" Susan said. "I got a call from Adele Lewyn. She says Garvin's screwing everybody, and they're changing the organization around."

"I don't know yet," he said cautiously. Cindy had just walked in the room.

"Are you still getting a promotion?"

"Basically," he said, "the answer is no."

"I can't believe it," Susan said. "Tom, I'm sorry. Are you okay? Are you upset?"

"I would say so, yes."

"Can't talk?"

"That's right."

"Okay. I'll leave soup on. I'll see you when you get here."

Cindy placed a stack of files on his desk. When Sanders hung up, she said, "She already knew?"

"She suspected."

Cindy nodded. "She called at lunchtime," she said. "I had the sense. The spouses are talking, I imagine."

"I'm sure everybody's talking."

Cindy went to the door, then paused. Cautiously, she said, "And how was the lunch meeting?"

"Meredith was introduced as the new head of all the tech divisions. She gave a presentation. She says she's going to keep all the division heads in place, all reporting to her."

"Then there's no change for us? Just another layer on top?"

"So far. That's what they're telling me. Why? What do you hear?"

"I hear the same."

He smiled. "Then it must be true."

"Should I go ahead and buy the condo?" She had been planning this for some time, a condo in Queen Anne's Hill for herself and her young daughter.

Sanders said, "When do you have to decide?"

"I have another fifteen days. End of the month."

"Then wait. You know, just to be safe."

She nodded, and went out. A moment later, she came back. "I almost forgot. Mark Lewyn's office just called. The Twinkle drives have arrived from KL. His designers are looking at them now. Do you want to see them?"

"I'm on my way."

The Design Group occupied the entire second floor of the Western Building. As always, the atmosphere there was chaotic; all the phones were ringing, but there was no receptionist in the little waiting area by the elevators, which was decorated with faded, taped-up posters for a 1929 Bauhaus Exhibition in Berlin and an old science-fiction movie called *The Forbin Project*. Two Japanese visitors sat at a corner table, speaking rapidly, beside the battered Coke machine and the junk food dispenser. Sanders nodded to them, used his card to open the locked door, and went inside.

The floor was a large open space, partitioned at unexpected angles by slanted walls painted to look like pastel-veined stone. Uncomfortable-looking wire chairs and tables were scattered in odd places. Rock-and-roll music blared. Everybody was casually dressed; most of the designers wore shorts and T-shirts. It was clearly A Creative Area.

Sanders went through to Foamland, the little display of the latest product designs the group had made. There were models of tiny CD-ROM drives and miniature cellular phones. Lewyn's teams were charged with creating product designs for the future, and many of these seemed absurdly small: a cellular phone no larger than a pencil, and another that looked like a postmodern version of Dick Tracy's wrist radio, in pale green and gray; a pager the size of a cigarette lighter; and a micro-CD player with a flip-up screen that could fit easily in the palm of the hand.

Although these devices looked outrageously tiny, Sanders had long since become accustomed to the idea that the designs were at most two years in the future. The hardware was shrinking fast; it was difficult for Sanders to remember that when he began working at DigiCom, a "portable" computer was a thirty-pound box the size of a carry-on suitcase—and cellular telephones didn't exist at all. The first cellular phones that DigiCom manufactured were fifteen-pound wonders that you lugged around on a shoulder strap. At the time, people thought they were a miracle. Now, customers complained if their phones weighed more than a few ounces.

Sanders walked past the big foam-cutting machine, all twisted tubes and knives behind Plexiglas shields, and found Mark Lewyn and his team bent over three dark blue CD-ROM players from Malaysia. One of the players already lay in pieces on the table; under bright halogen lights, the team was poking at its innards with tiny screwdrivers, glancing up from time to time to the scope screens.

"What've you found?" Sanders said.

"Ah, hell," Lewyn said, throwing up his hands in artistic exasperation. "Not good, Tom. Not good."

"Talk to me."

Lewyn pointed to the table. "There's a metal rod inside the hinge. These clips maintain contact with the rod as the case is opened; that's how you maintain power to the screen."

"Yes . . ."

"But power is intermittent. It looks like the rods are too small. They're supposed to be fifty-four millimeters. These seem to be fifty-two, fifty-three millimeters."

Lewyn was grim, his entire manner suggesting unspeakable consequences. The bars were a millimeter off, and the world was coming to an end. Sanders understood that he would have to calm Lewyn down. He'd done it many times before.

He said, "We can fix that, Mark. It'll mean opening all the cases and replacing the bars, but we can do that."

"Oh sure," Lewyn said. "But that still leaves the clips. Our specs call for $16/10$ stainless, which has requisite tension to keep the clips springy and maintain contact with the bar. These clips seem to be something else, maybe $16/4$. They're too stiff. So when you open the cases the clips bend, but they don't spring back."

"So we have to replace the clips, too. We can do that when we switch the bars."

"Unfortunately, it's not that easy. The clips are heat-pressed into the cases."

"Ah, hell."

"Right. They are integral to the case unit."

"You're telling me we have to build new housings just because we have bad clips?"

"Exactly."

Sanders shook his head. "We've run off thousands so far. Something like four thousand."

"Well, we've got to do 'em again."

"And what about the drive itself?"

"It's slow," Lewyn said. "No doubt about it. But I'm not sure why. It might be power problems. Or it might be the controller chip."

"If it's the controller chip . . ."

"We're in deep shit. If it's a primary design problem, we have to go back to the drawing board. If it's only a fabrication problem, we have to change the production lines, maybe remake the stencils. But it's months, either way."

"When will we know?"

"I've sent a drive and power supply to the Diagnostics guys," Lewyn said. "They should have a report by five. I'll get it to you. Does Meredith know about this yet?"

"I'm briefing her at six."

"Okay. Call me after you talk to her?"

"Sure."

"In a way, this is good," Lewyn said.

"How do you mean?"

"We're throwing her a big problem right away," Lewyn said. "We'll see how she handles it."

Sanders turned to go. Lewyn followed him out. "By the way," Lewyn said. "*Are* you pissed off that you didn't get the job?"

"Disappointed," Sanders said. "Not pissed. There's no point being pissed."

"Because if you ask me, Garvin screwed you. You put in the time, you've demonstrated you can run the division, and he put in someone else instead."

Sanders shrugged. "It's his company."

Lewyn threw his arm over Sanders's shoulder, and gave him a rough hug. "You know, Tom, sometimes you're too reasonable for your own good."

"I didn't know being reasonable was a defect," Sanders said.

"Being *too* reasonable is a defect," Lewyn said. "You end up getting pushed around."

"I'm just trying to get along," Sanders said. "I want to be here when the division goes public."

"Yeah, true. You got to stay." They came to the elevator. Lewyn said, "You think she got it because she's a woman?"

Sanders shook his head. "Who knows?"

"Pale males eat it again. I tell you. Sometimes I get so sick of the constant pressure to appoint women," Lewyn said. "I mean, look at this design group. We've got forty percent women here, better than any other division, but they always say, why don't you have more? More women, more—"

"Mark," he said, interrupting. "It's a different world now."

"And not a better one," Lewyn said. "It's hurting everybody. Look: when I started in DigiCom, there was only one question. Are you good? If you were good, you got hired. If you could cut it, you stayed. No more. Now, ability is only one of the priorities. There's also the question of whether you're the right sex and skin color to fill out the company's HR profiles. And if you turn out to be incompetent, we can't fire you. Pretty soon, we start to get junk like this Twinkle drive. Because no one's accountable anymore. No one is responsible. You can't build products on a *theory*. Because the product you're making is real. And if it stinks, it stinks. And no one will buy it."

Coming back to his office, Sanders used his electronic passcard to open the door to the fourth floor. Then he slipped the card in his trouser pocket, and headed down the hallway. He was moving quickly, thinking about the meeting with Lewyn. He was especially bothered by one thing that Lewyn had said: that he was allowing himself to be pushed around by Garvin—that he was being too passive, too understanding.

But Sanders didn't see it that way. When Sanders had said it was Garvin's company, he meant it. Bob was the boss, and Bob could do what he wanted. Sanders was disappointed not to get the job, but no one had promised it to him. Ever. He and others in the Seattle divisions had come, over a period of weeks, to assume that Sanders would get the job. But Garvin had never mentioned it. Nor had Phil Blackburn.

As a result, Sanders felt he had no reason to gripe. If he was disappointed, it was only because he had done it to himself. It was classic: counting your chickens before they hatched.

And as for being too passive—what did Lewyn expect him to do? Make a fuss? Yell and scream? That wouldn't do any good. Because clearly Meredith Johnson had this job, whether Sanders liked it or not. Resign? That *really* wouldn't do any good. Because if he quit, he would lose the profits pending when the company went public. That would be a real disaster.

So on reflection, all he could do was accept Meredith Johnson in the new job, and get on with it. And he suspected that if the situation were reversed, Lewyn, for all his bluster, would do exactly the same thing: grin and bear it.

But the bigger problem, as he thought it over, was the Twinkle drive. Lewyn's team had torn up three drives that afternoon, and they still didn't have any idea why they were malfunctioning. They had found some non-spec components in the hinge, which Sanders could track down. He'd find out soon enough why they were getting non-spec materials. But the real problem—the slowness of the drives—remained a mystery to which they had no clue, and that meant that he was going to—

"Tom? You dropped your card."

"What?" He looked up absently. An area assistant was frowning, pointing back down the hall.

"You dropped your card."

"Oh." He saw the passcard lying there, white against the gray carpet. "Thanks."

He went back to retrieve it. Obviously, he must be more upset than he realized. You couldn't get anywhere in the DigiCom buildings without a passcard. Sanders bent over, picked it up, and slipped it in his pocket.

Then he felt the second card, already there. Frowning, he took both cards out and looked at them.

The card on the floor wasn't his card, it was someone else's. He paused for a moment, trying to decide which was his. By design, the passcards were featureless: just the blue DigiCom logo, a stamped serial number, and a magstripe on the back.

He ought to be able to remember his card number, but he couldn't. He hurried back to his office, to look it up on his computer. He glanced at his watch. It was four o'clock, two hours before his meeting with Meredith Johnson. He still had a lot to do to prepare for that meeting. He frowned as he walked along, staring at the carpet. He would have to get the production reports, and perhaps also the design detail specs. He wasn't sure she would understand them, but he should be prepared with them, anyway. And what else? He did not want to go into this first meeting having forgotten something.

Once again, his thoughts were disrupted by images from his past. An opened suitcase. The bowl of popcorn. The stained-glass window.

"So?" said a familiar voice. "You don't say hello to your old friends anymore?"

Sanders looked up. He was outside the glass-walled conference room. Inside the room, he saw a solitary figure hunched over in a wheelchair, staring at the Seattle skyline, his back to Sanders.

"Hello, Max," Sanders said.

Max Dorfman continued to stare out the window. "Hello, Thomas."

"How did you know it was me?"

Dorfman snorted. "It must be magic. What do you think? Magic?" His voice was sarcastic. "Thomas: I can *see* you."

"How? You have eyes in the back of your head?"

"No, Thomas. I have a reflection in *front* of my head. I see you in the glass, of course. Walking with your head down, like a defeated *putz*." Dorfman snorted again, and then wheeled his chair around. His eyes were bright, intense, mocking. "You were such a promising man. And now you are hanging your head?"

Sanders wasn't in the mood. "Let's just say this hasn't been one of my better days, Max."

"And you want everybody to know about it? You want sympathy?"

"No, Max." He remembered how Dorfman had ridiculed the idea of sympathy. Dorfman used to say that an executive who wanted sympathy was not an executive. He was a sponge, soaking up something useless.

Sanders said, "No, Max. I was thinking."

"Ah. *Thinking*. Oh, I like thinking. Thinking is good. And what were you thinking about, Thomas: the stained glass in your apartment?"

Despite himself, Sanders was startled: "How did you know that?"

"Maybe it's magic," Dorfman said, with a rasping laugh. "Or perhaps I can read minds. You think I can read minds, Thomas? Are you stupid enough to believe that?"

"Max, I'm not in the mood."

"Oh well, then I must stop. If you're not in the mood, I must stop. We must at all costs preserve your mood." He slapped the arm of his wheelchair irritably. "*You told me, Thomas*. That's how I knew what you were thinking."

"I told you? When?"

"Nine or ten years ago, it must have been."

"What did I tell you?"

"Oh, you don't remember? No wonder you have problems. Better stare at the floor some more. It may do you good. Yes. I think so. Keep staring at the floor, Thomas."

"Max, for Christ's sake."

Dorfman grinned at him. "Do I irritate you?"

"You always irritate me."

"Ah. Well. Then perhaps there is hope. Not for you, of course—for me. I am old, Thomas. Hope has a different meaning, at my age. You wouldn't understand. These days, I cannot even get around by myself. I must have someone *push* me. Preferably a pretty woman, but as a rule they do not like to do such things. So here I am, with no pretty woman to push me. *Unlike you.*"

Sanders sighed. "Max, do you suppose we can just have an ordinary conversation?"

"What a good idea," Dorfman said. "I would like that very much. What is an ordinary conversation?"

"I mean, can we just talk like normal people?"

"If it will not bore you, Thomas, yes. But I am worried. You know how old people are worried about being boring."

"Max. What did you mean about the stained glass?"

He shrugged. "I meant Meredith, of course. What else?"

"What about Meredith?"

"How am I to know?" Dorfman said irritably. "All I know of this is what you told me. And all you told me is that you used to take trips, to Korea or Japan, and when you came back, Meredith would—"

"Tom, I'm sorry to interrupt," Cindy said, leaning in the door to the conference room.

"Oh, don't be sorry," Max said. "Who is this beautiful creature, Thomas?"

"I'm Cindy Wolfe, Professor Dorfman," she said. "I work for Tom."

"Oh, what a lucky man he is!"

Cindy turned to Sanders. "I'm really sorry, Tom, but one of the executives from Conley-White is in your office, and I thought you would want to—"

"Yes, yes," Dorfman said immediately. "He must go. Conley-White, it sounds *very* important."

"In a minute," Sanders said. He turned to Cindy. "Max and I were in the middle of something."

"No, no, Thomas," Dorfman said. "We were just talking about old times. You better go."

"Max—"

"You want to talk more, you think it's important, you come visit me. I am at the Four Seasons. You know that hotel. It has a *wonderful* lobby, such high ceilings. Very grand, especially for an old man. So, you go right along, Thomas." His eyes narrowed. "And leave the beautiful Cindy with me."

Sanders hesitated. "Watch out for him," he said. "He's a dirty old man."

"As dirty as possible," Dorfman cackled.

Sanders headed down the hallway to his office. As he left, he heard Dorfman say, "Now beautiful Cindy, please take me to the lobby where I have a car waiting. And on the way, if you don't mind indulging an old man, I have a few little questions. So many *interesting* things are happening in this company. And the secretaries always know everything, don't they?"

M r. Sanders." Jim Daly stood quickly, as Sanders came into the room. "I'm glad they found you."

They shook hands. Sanders gestured for Daly to sit down, and slid behind his own desk. Sanders was not surprised; he had been expecting a visit from Daly or one of the other investment bankers for several days. Members of the Goldman, Sachs team had been speaking individually with people in various departments, going over aspects of the merger. Most of the time they wanted background information; although high technology was central to the acquisition, none of the bankers understood it very well. Sanders expected Daly to ask about progress on the Twinkle drive, and perhaps the Corridor.

"I appreciate your taking the time," Daly said, rubbing his bald head. He was a very tall, thin man, and he seemed even taller sitting down, all knees and elbows. "I wanted to ask you some things, ah, off the record."

"Sure," Sanders said.

"It's to do with Meredith Johnson," Daly said, in an apologetic voice. "If you, ah, don't mind, I'd prefer we just keep this conversation between us."

"All right," Sanders said.

"I understand that you have been closely involved with setting up the plants in Ireland and Malaysia. And that there has been a little controversy inside the company about how that was carried out."

"Well." Sanders shrugged. "Phil Blackburn and I haven't always seen eye to eye."

"Showing your good sense, in my view," Daly said dryly. "But I gather that in these disputes you represent technical expertise, and others in the company represent, ah, various other concerns. Would that be fair?"

"Yes, I'd say so." What was he getting at?

"Well, it's along those lines that I'd like to hear your thoughts. Bob Garvin has just appointed Ms. Johnson to a position of considerable authority, a step which many in Conley-White applaud. And certainly it would be unfair to prejudge how she will carry out her new duties within the company. But by the same token, it would be derelict of me not to inquire about her past duties. Do you get my drift?"

"Not exactly," Sanders said.

"I'm wondering," Daly said, "what you feel about Ms. Johnson's past performance with regard to the technical operations of the company. Specifically, her involvement in the foreign operations of DigiCom."

Sanders frowned, thinking back. "I'm not aware that she's had much involvement," he said. "We had a labor dispute two years ago in Cork. She was part of the team that went over to negotiate a settlement. She lobbied in Washington about flat-panel display tariffs. And I know she headed the Ops Review Team in Cupertino, which approved the plans for the new plant at Kuala Lumpur."

"Yes, exactly."

"But I don't know that her involvement goes beyond that."

"Ah. Well. Perhaps I was given wrong information," Daly said, shifting in his chair.

"What did you hear?"

"Without going into specifics, let me say a question of judgment was raised."

"I see," Sanders said. Who would have said anything to Daly about Meredith? Certainly not Garvin or Blackburn. Kaplan? It was impossible to know for sure. But Daly would be talking only to highly placed officers.

"I was wondering," Daly said, "if you had any thoughts on her technical judgment. Speaking privately, of course."

At that moment, Sanders's computer screen beeped three times. A message flashed:

ONE MINUTE TO DIRECT VIDEO LINKUP: DC/M-DC/S
SEN: A. KAHN
REC: T. SANDERS

Daly said, "Is something wrong?"

"No," Sanders said. "It looks like I have a video feed coming in from Malaysia."

"Then I'll be brief and leave you to it," Daly said. "Let me put it to you directly. Within your division, is there any concern whether Meredith Johnson is qualified for this post?"

Sanders shrugged. "She's the new boss. You know how organizations are. There's always concern with a new boss."

"You're very diplomatic. I mean to say, is there concern about her expertise? She's relatively young, after all. Geographic move, uprooting. New faces, new staffing, new problems. And up here, she won't be so directly under Bob Garvin's, ah, wing."

"I don't know what to say," Sanders said. "We'll all have to wait and see."

"And I gather that there was trouble in the past when a non-technical person headed the division . . . a man named, ah, Screamer Freeling?"

"Yes. He didn't work out."

"And there are similar concerns about Johnson?"

Sanders said, "I've heard them expressed."

"And her fiscal measures? These cost-containment plans of hers? That's the crux, isn't it?"

Sanders thought: what cost-containment plans?

The screen beeped again:

30 SECONDS TO DIRECT VIDEO LINKUP: DC/ M-DC/S

"There goes your machine again," Daly said, unfolding himself from the chair. "I'll let you go. Thank you for your time, Mr. Sanders."

"Not at all."

They shook hands. Daly turned and walked out of the room. Sanders's computer beeped three times in rapid succession:

15 SECONDS TO DIRECT VIDEO LINKUP: DC/M-DC/S

He sat down in front of the monitor and twisted his desk lamp so that the light shone on his face. The numbers on the computer were counting backward. Sanders looked at his watch. It was five o'clock—eight o'clock in Malaysia. Arthur would probably be calling from the plant.

A small rectangle appeared in the center of the screen and grew outward in progressive jumps. He saw Arthur's face, and behind him, the brightly lit assembly line. Brand-new, it was the epitome of modern manufacturing: clean and quiet, the workers in street clothes, arranged on both sides of the green conveyor belt. At each workstation there was a bank of fluorescent lights, which flared a little in the camera.

Kahn coughed and rubbed his chin. "Hello, Tom. How are you?" When he spoke, his image blurred slightly. And his voice was out of sync, since the bounce to the satellite caused a slight delay in the video, but the voice was transmitted immediately. This unsynchronized quality was very distracting for the first few seconds; it gave the linkup a dreamy quality. It was a little like talking to someone under water. Then you got used to it.

"I'm fine, Arthur," he said.

"Well, good. I'm sorry about the new organization. You know how I feel personally."

"Thank you, Arthur." He wondered vaguely how Kahn in Malaysia would have heard already. But in any company, gossip traveled fast.

"Yeah. Well. Anyway, Tom, I'm standing here on the floor," Kahn said, gesturing behind him. "And as you can see, we're still running very slow. And the spot checks are unimproved. What do the designers say? Have they gotten the units yet?"

"They came today. I don't have any news yet. They're still working on it."

"Uh-huh. Okay. And have the units gone to Diagnostics?" Kahn asked.

"I think so. Just went."

"Yeah. Okay. Because we got a request from Diagnostics for ten more drive units to be sent in heat-sealed plastic bags. And they specified that they wanted them sealed inside the factory. Right as they came off the line. You know anything about that?"

"No, this is the first I heard of it. Let me find out, and I'll get back to you."

"Okay, because I have to tell you, it seemed strange to me. I mean, ten units is a lot. Customs is going to query it if we send them all together. And I don't know what this sealing is about. We send them wrapped in plastic anyway. But not sealed. Why do they want them sealed, Tom?" Kahn sounded worried.

"I don't know," Sanders said. "I'll get into it. All I can think is that it's a full-court press around here. People really want to know why the hell those drives don't work."

"Hey, us too," Kahn said. "Believe me. It's making us crazy."

"When will you send the drives?"

"Well, I've got to get a heat-sealer first. I hope I can ship Wednesday, you can have them Thursday."

"Not good enough," Sanders said. "You should ship today, or tomorrow at the latest. You want me to run down a sealer for you? I can probably get one from Apple." Apple had a factory in Kuala Lumpur.

"No. That's a good idea. I'll call over there and see if Ron can loan me one."

"Fine. Now what about Jafar?"

"Hell of a thing," Kahn said. "I just talked to the hospital, and apparently he's got cramps and vomiting. Won't eat anything. The abo doctors say they can't figure out anything except, you know, a spell."

"They believe in spells?"

"Damn right," Kahn said. "They've got laws against sorcery here. You can take people to court."

"So you don't know when he'll be back?"

"Nobody's saying. Apparently he's really sick."

"Okay, Arthur. Anything else?"

"No. I'll get the sealer. And let me know what you find out."

"I will," Sanders said, and the transmission ended. Kahn gave a final wave, and the screen went blank.

SAVE THIS TRANSMISSION TO DISK OR DAT?

He clicked DAT, and it was saved to digital tape. He got up from the desk. Whatever all this was about, he'd better be informed before he had his meeting with Johnson at six. He went to the outer area, to Cindy's desk.

Cindy was turned away, laughing on the phone. She looked back and saw Sanders, and stopped laughing. "Listen, I got to go."

Sanders said, "Would you mind pulling the production reports on Twinkle for the last two months? Better yet, just pull everything since they opened the line."

"Sure."

"And call Don Cherry for me. I need to know what his Diagnostics group is doing with the drives."

He went back into his office. He noticed his E-mail cursor was blinking, and pushed the key to read them. While he waited, he looked at the three faxes on his desk. Two were from Ireland, routine weekly production reports. The third was a requisition for a roof repair at the Austin plant; it had been held up in Operations in Cupertino, and Eddie had forwarded it to Sanders to try and get action.

The screen blinked. He looked up at the first of his E-mail messages:

OUT OF NOWHERE WE GOT A BEAN COUNTER FROM OPERA-
TIONS DOWN HERE IN AUSTIN. HE'S GOING OVER ALL THE
BOOKS, DRIVING PEOPLE MAD. AND THE WORD IS WE GOT MORE
COMING DOWN TOMORROW. WHAT GIVES? THE RUMORS ARE

FLYING, AND SLOWING HELL OUT OF THE LINE. TELL ME WHAT
TO SAY. IS THIS COMPANY FOR SALE OR NOT?

EDDIE

Sanders did not hesitate. He couldn't tell Eddie what was going on.
Quickly, he typed his reply:

THE BEAN COUNTERS WERE IN IRELAND LAST WEEK, TOO.
GARVIN'S ORDERED A COMPANY-WIDE REVIEW, AND THEY'RE
LOOKING AT EVERYTHING. TELL EVERYBODY DOWN THERE TO
FORGET IT AND GO BACK TO WORK.

TOM

He pushed the SEND button. The message disappeared.
"You called?" Don Cherry walked into the room without knocking, and
dropped into the chair. He put his hands behind his head. "Jesus, what a
day. I've been putting out fires all afternoon."
"Tell me."
"I got some dweebs from Conley down there, asking my guys what the
difference is between RAM and ROM. Like they have time for this. Pretty
soon, one of the dweebs hears 'flash memory' and he goes, 'How often does
it flash?' Like it was a flashlight or something. And my guys have to put up
with this. I mean, this is high-priced talent. They shouldn't be doing reme-
dial classes for lawyers. Can't you stop it?"
"Nobody can stop it," Sander said.
"Maybe Meredith can stop it," Cherry said, grinning.
Sanders shrugged. "She's the boss."
"Yeah. So—what's on your mind?"
"Your Diagnostics group is working on the Twinkle drives."
"True. That is, we're working on the bits and pieces that're left after
Lewyn's nimble-fingered *artistes* tore the hell out of them. Why did they go
to Design first? Never, *ever*, let a designer near an actual piece of electronic
equipment, Tom. Designers should only be allowed to draw pictures on
pieces of paper. And only give them one piece of paper at a time."
"What have you found?" Sanders said. "About the drives."

"Nothing yet," Cherry said. "But we got a few ideas we're kicking around."

"Is that why you asked Arthur Kahn to send you ten drives, heat-sealed from the factory?"

"You bet your ass."

"Kahn was wondering about that."

"So?" Cherry said. "Let him wonder. It'll do him good. Keep him from playing with himself."

"I'd like to know, too."

"Well look," Cherry said. "Maybe our ideas won't amount to anything. At the moment, all we have is one suspicious chip. That's all Lewyn's clowns left us. It's not very much to go on."

"The chip is bad?"

"No, the chip is fine."

"What's suspicious about it?"

"Look," Cherry said. "We've got enough rumors flying around as it is. I can report that we're working on it, and we don't know yet. That's all. We'll get the sealed drives tomorrow or Wednesday, and we should know within an hour. Okay?"

"You thinking big problem, or little problem? I've got to know," Sanders said. "It's going to come up in the meetings tomorrow."

"Well, at the moment, the answer is we don't know. It could be anything. We're working on it."

"Arthur thinks it might be serious."

"Arthur might be right. But we'll solve it. That's all I can tell you."

"Don . . ."

"I understand you want an answer," Cherry said. "Do you understand that I don't have one?"

Sanders stared at him. "You could have called. Why'd you come up in person?"

"Since you asked," Cherry said, "I've got a small problem. It's delicate. Sexual harassment thing."

"*Another* one? It seems like that's all we have around here."

"Us and everybody else," Cherry said. "I hear UniCom's got fourteen suits going right now. Digital Graphics has even more. And MicroSym, look out. They're all pigs over there, anyway. But I'd like your read on this."

Sanders sighed. "Okay."

"In one of my programming groups, the remote DB access group. The group's all pretty old: twenty-five to twenty-nine years old. The supervisor for the fax modem team, a woman, has been asking one of the guys out. She thinks he's cute. He keeps turning her down. Today she asks him again in the parking lot at lunch; he says no. She gets in her car, rams his car, drives off. Nobody hurt, and he doesn't want to make a complaint. But he's worried, thinks it's a little out of hand. Comes to me for advice. What should I do?"

Sanders frowned. "You think that's the whole story? She's just mad at him because he turned her down? Or did he do something to provoke this?"

"He says no. He's a pretty straight guy. A little geeky, not real sophisticated."

"And the woman?"

"She's got a temper, no question. She blows at the team sometimes. I've had to talk to her about that."

"What does she say about the incident in the parking lot?"

"Don't know. The guy's asked me not to talk to her. Says he's embarrassed and doesn't want to make it worse."

Sanders shrugged. "What can you do? People are upset but nobody will talk . . . I don't know, Don. If a woman rammed his car, I'd guess he must have done something. Chances are he slept with her once, and won't see her again, and now she's pissed. That's my guess."

"That would be my guess, too," Cherry said, "but of course, maybe not."

"Damage to the car?"

"Nothing serious. Broken taillight. He just doesn't want it to get any worse. So, do I drop it?"

"If he won't file charges, I'd drop it."

"Do I speak to her informally?"

"I wouldn't. You go accusing her of impropriety—even informally—and you're asking for trouble. Nobody's going to support you. Because the chances are, your guy *did* do something to provoke her."

"Even though he says he didn't."

Sanders sighed. "Listen, Don, they always say they didn't. I never heard of one who said, 'You know, I deserve this.' Never happens."

"So, drop it?"

"Put a note in the file that he told you the story, be sure you characterize the story as alleged, and forget it."

Cherry nodded, turned to leave. At the door, he stopped and looked back. "So tell me this. How come we're both so convinced this guy must have done something?"

"Just playing the odds," Sanders said. "Now fix that damned drive for me."

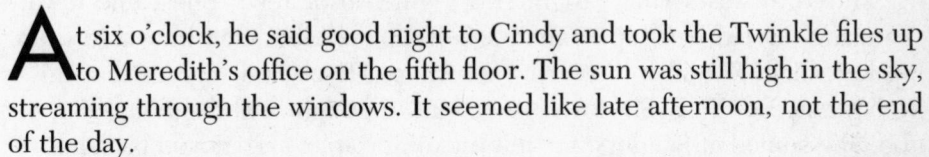

At six o'clock, he said good night to Cindy and took the Twinkle files up to Meredith's office on the fifth floor. The sun was still high in the sky, streaming through the windows. It seemed like late afternoon, not the end of the day.

Meredith had been given the big corner office, where Ron Goldman used to be. Meredith had a new assistant, too, a woman. Sanders guessed she had followed her boss up from Cupertino.

"I'm Tom Sanders," he said. "I have an appointment with Ms. Johnson."

"Betsy Ross, from Cupertino, Mr. Sanders," she said. She looked at him. "Don't say anything."

"Okay."

"Everybody says something. Something about the flag. I get really sick of it."

"Okay."

"My whole life."

"Okay. Fine."

"I'll tell Miss Johnson you're here."

"Tom." Meredith Johnson waved from behind her desk, her other hand holding the phone. "Come in, sit down."

Her office had a view north toward downtown Seattle: the Space Needle, the Arly towers, the SODO building. The city looked glorious in the afternoon sun.

"I'll just finish this up." She turned back to the phone. "Yes, Ed, I'm with

Tom now, we'll go over all of that. Yes. He's brought the documentation with him."

Sanders held up the manila folder containing the drive data. She pointed to her briefcase, which was lying open on the corner of the desk, and gestured for him to put it inside.

She turned back to the phone. "Yes, Ed, I think the due diligence will go smoothly, and there certainly isn't any impulse to hold anything back . . . No, no . . . Well, we can do it first thing in the morning if you like."

Sanders put the folder in her briefcase.

Meredith was saying, "Right, Ed, right. Absolutely." She came toward Tom and sat with one hip on the edge of the desk, her navy blue skirt riding up her thigh. She wasn't wearing stockings. "Everybody agrees that this is important, Ed. Yes." She swung her foot, the high heel dangling from her toe. She smiled at Sanders. He felt uncomfortable, and moved back a little. "I promise you, Ed. Yes. Absolutely."

Meredith hung up the phone on the cradle behind her, leaning back across the desk, twisting her body, revealing her breasts beneath the silk blouse. "Well, that's done." She sat forward again, and sighed. "The Conley people heard there's trouble with Twinkle. That was Ed Nichols, flipping out. Actually, it's the third call I've had about Twinkle this afternoon. You'd think that was all there was to this company. How do you like the office?"

"Pretty good," he said. "Great view."

"Yes, the city's beautiful." She leaned on one arm and crossed her legs. She saw that he noticed, and said, "In the summer, I'd rather not wear stockings. I like the bare feeling. So much cooler on a hot day."

Sanders said, "From now to the end of summer, it will be pretty much this way."

"I have to tell you, I dread the weather," she said. "I mean, after California . . ." She uncrossed her legs again, and smiled. "But you like it here, don't you? You seem happy here."

"Yes." He shrugged. "You get used to rain." He pointed to her briefcase. "Do you want to go over the Twinkle stuff?"

"Absolutely," she said, sliding off the desk, coming close to him. She looked him directly in the eyes. "But I hope you don't mind if I impose on you first. Just a little?"

"Sure."

She stepped aside. "Pour the wine for us."

"Okay."

"See if it's chilled long enough." He went over to the bottle on the side table. "I remember you always liked it cold."

"That's true," he said, spinning the bottle in the ice. He didn't like it so cold anymore, but he did in those days.

"We had a lot of fun back then," she said.

"Yes," he said. "We did."

"I swear," she said. "Sometimes I think that back when we were both young and trying to make it, I think that was the best it ever was."

He hesitated, not sure how to answer her, what tone to take. He poured the wine.

"Yes," she said. "We had a good time. I think about it often."

Sanders thought: I never do.

She said, "What about you, Tom? Do you think about it?"

"Of course." He crossed the room carrying the glasses of wine to her, gave her one, clinked them. "Sure I do. All us married guys think of the old days. You know I'm married now."

"Yes," she said, nodding. "Very married, I hear. With how many kids? Three?"

"No, just two." He smiled. "Sometimes it seems like three."

"And your wife is an attorney?"

"Yes." He felt safer now. The talk of his wife and children made him feel safer somehow.

"I don't know how somebody can be married," Meredith said. "I tried it." She held up her hand. "Four more alimony payments to the son of a bitch and I'm free."

"Who did you marry?"

"Some account executive at CoStar. He was cute. Amusing. But it turned out he was a typical gold digger. I've been paying him off for three years. *And* he was a lousy lay." She waved her hand, dismissing the subject. She looked at her watch. "Now come and sit down, and tell me how bad it is with the Twinkle drive."

"You want the file? I put it in your briefcase."

"No." She patted the couch beside her. "You just tell me yourself."

He sat down beside her.

"You look good, Tom." She leaned back and kicked off her heels, wiggled her bare toes. "God, what a day."

"Lot of pressure?"

She sipped her wine and blew a strand of hair from her face. "A lot to keep track of. I'm glad we're working together, Tom. I feel as though you're the one friend I can count on in all this."

"Thanks. I'll try."

"So: how bad is it?"

"Well. It's hard to say."

"Just tell me."

He felt he had no choice but to lay it all out for her. "We've built very successful prototypes, but the drives coming off the line in KL are running nowhere near a hundred milliseconds."

Meredith sighed, and shook her head. "Do we know why?"

"Not yet. We're working on some ideas."

"That line's a start-up, isn't it?"

"Two months ago."

She shrugged. "Then we have problems on a new line. That's not so bad."

"But the thing is," he said, "Conley-White is buying this company for our technology, and especially for the CD-ROM drive. As of today, we may not be able to deliver as promised."

"You want to tell them *that*?"

"I'm concerned they'll pick it up in due diligence."

"Maybe, maybe not." She leaned back in the couch. "We have to remember what we're really looking at. Tom, we've all seen production problems loom large, only to vanish overnight. This may be one of those situations. We're shaking out the Twinkle line. We've identified some early problems. No big deal."

"Maybe. But we don't know that. In reality, there may be a problem with controller chips, which means changing our supplier in Singapore. Or there may be a more fundamental problem. A design problem, originating here."

"Perhaps," Meredith said, "but as you say, we don't know that. And I don't see any reason for us to speculate. At this critical time."

"But to be honest—"

"It's not a matter of honesty," she said. "It's a matter of the underlying reality. Let's go over it, point by point. We've told them we have a Twinkle drive."

"Yes."

"We've built a prototype and tested the hell out of it."

"Yes."

"And the prototype works like gangbusters. It's twice as fast as the most advanced drives coming out of Japan."

"Yes."

"We've told them we're in production on the drive."

"Yes."

"Well, then," Meredith said, "we've told them all that anybody knows for sure, at this point. I'd say we are acting in good faith."

"Well, maybe, but I don't know if we can—"

"Tom." Meredith placed her hand on his arm. "I always liked your directness. I want you to know how much I appreciate your expertise and your frank approach to problems. All the more reason why I'm sure the Twinkle drive will get ironed out. We know that fundamentally it's a good product that performs as we say it does. Personally, I have complete confidence in it, and in your ability to make it work as planned. And I have no problem saying that at the meeting tomorrow." She paused, and looked intently at him. "Do you?"

Her face was very close to him, her lips half-parted. "Do I what?"

"Have a problem saying that at the meeting?"

Her eyes were light blue, almost gray. He had forgotten that, as he had forgotten how long her lashes were. Her hair fell softly around her face. Her lips were full. She had a dreamy look in her eyes. "No," he said. "I don't have a problem."

"Good. Then at least *that's* settled." She smiled and held out her glass. "Do the honors again?"

"Sure."

He got up from the couch and went over to the wine. She watched him. "I'm glad you haven't let yourself go, Tom. You work out?"

"Twice a week. How about you?"

"You always had a nice tush. Nice hard tush."

He turned. "Meredith . . ."

She giggled. "I'm sorry. I can't help it. We're old friends." She looked concerned. "I didn't offend you, did I?"

"No."

"I can't imagine you ever getting prudish, Tom."

"No, no."

"Not you." She laughed. "Remember the night we broke the bed?"

He poured the wine. "We didn't exactly break it."

"Sure we did. You had me bent over the bottom of the footboard and—"

"I remember—"

"And first we broke the footboard, and then the bottom of the bed crashed down—but you didn't want to stop so we moved up and then when I was grabbing the headboard it all came—"

"I remember," he said, wanting to interrupt her, to stop this. "Those days were great. Listen, Meredith—"

"And then the woman from downstairs called up? Remember her? The old Lithuanian lady? She vanted ta know if somebody had died or vhat?"

"Yeah. Listen. Going back to the drive . . ."

She took the wineglass. "I *am* making you uncomfortable. What—did you think I was coming on to you?"

"No, no. Nothing like that."

"Good, because I really wasn't. I promise." She gave him an amused glance, then tilted her head back, exposing her long neck, and sipped the wine. "In fact, I—ah! Ah!" She winced suddenly.

"What is it?" he said, leaning forward, concerned.

"My neck, it goes into spasm, it's right there . . ." With her eyes still squeezed shut in pain, she pointed to her shoulder, near the neck.

"What should I—"

"Just rub it, squeeze—there—"

He put down his wineglass and rubbed her shoulder. "There?"

"Yes, ah, harder—squeeze—"

He felt the muscles of her shoulder relax, and she sighed. Meredith turned her head back and forth slowly, then opened her eyes. "Oh . . . Much better . . . Don't stop rubbing."

He continued rubbing.

"Oh, thanks. That feels good. I get this nerve thing. Pinched something, but when it hits, it's really . . ." She turned her head back and forth. Testing. "You did that very well. But you were always good with your hands, Tom."

He kept rubbing. He wanted to stop. He felt everything was wrong, that he was sitting too close, that he didn't want to be touching her. But it also felt good to touch her. He was curious about it.

"Good hands," she said. "God, when I was married, I thought about you all the time."

"You did?"

"Sure," she said. "I told you, he was terrible in bed. I hate a man who doesn't know what he's doing." She closed her eyes. "That was never your problem, was it."

She sighed, relaxing more, and then she seemed to lean into him, melting toward his body, toward his hands. It was an unmistakable sensation. Immediately, he gave her shoulder a final friendly squeeze, and took his hands away.

She opened her eyes. She smiled knowingly. "Listen," she said, "don't worry."

He turned and sipped his wine. "I'm not worried."

"I mean, about the drive. If it turns out we really have problems and need agreement from higher management, we'll get it. But let's not jump the gun now."

"Okay, fine. I think that makes sense." He felt secretly relieved to be talking once again about the drive. Back on safe ground. "Who would you take it to? Directly to Garvin?"

"I think so. I prefer to deal informally." She looked at him. "You've changed, haven't you."

"No . . . I'm still the same."

"I think you've changed." She smiled. "You never would have stopped rubbing me before."

"Meredith," he said, "it's different. You run the division now. I work for you."

"Oh, don't be silly."

"It's true."

"We're colleagues." She pouted. "Nobody around here really believes I'm superior to you. They just gave me the administrative work, that's all. We're colleagues, Tom. And I just want us to have an open, friendly relationship."

"So do I."

"Good. I'm glad we agree on that." Quickly, she leaned forward and kissed him lightly on the lips. "There. Was that so terrible?"

"It wasn't terrible at all."

"Who knows? Maybe we'll have to go to Malaysia together, to check on the assembly lines. They have very nice beaches in Malaysia. You ever been to Kuantan?"

"No."

"You'd love it."

"I'm sure."

"I'll show it to you. We could take an extra day or two. Stop over. Get some sun."

"Meredith—"

"Nobody needs to know, Tom."

"I'm married."

"You're also a man."

"What does that mean?"

"Oh Tom," she said, with mock severity, "don't ask me to believe you never have a little adventure on the side. I *know* you, remember?"

"You knew me a long time ago, Meredith."

"People don't change. Not *that* way."

"Well, I think they do."

"Oh, come on. We're going to be working together, we might as well enjoy ourselves."

He didn't like the way any of this was going. He felt pushed into an awkward position. He felt stuffy and puritanical when he said: "I'm married now."

"Oh, I don't care about your personal life," she said lightly. "I'm only responsible for your on-the-job performance. All work and no play, Tom. It can be bad for you. Got to stay playful." She leaned forward. "Come on. Just one little kiss . . ."

The intercom buzzed. "Meredith," the assistant's voice said.

She looked up in annoyance. "I told you, no calls."

"I'm sorry. It's Mr. Garvin, Meredith."

"All right." She got off the couch and walked across the room to her desk, saying loudly, "But after this, Betsy, no more calls."

"All right, Meredith. I wanted to ask you, is it okay if I leave in about ten minutes? I have to see the landlord about my new apartment."

"Yes. Did you get me that package?"

"I have it right here."

"Bring it in, and then you can leave."

"Thank you, Meredith. Mr. Garvin is on two."

Meredith picked up the phone and poured more wine. "Bob," she said. "Hi. What's up?" It was impossible to miss the easy familiarity in her voice.

She spoke to Garvin, her back turned to Sanders. He sat on the couch, feeling stranded, foolishly passive and idle. The assistant entered the room carrying a small package in a brown paper bag. She gave the package to Meredith.

"Of course, Bob," Meredith was saying. "I couldn't agree more. We'll certainly deal with that."

The assistant, waiting for Meredith to dismiss her, smiled at Sanders. He felt uncomfortable just sitting there on the couch, so he got up, walked to the window, pulled his cellular phone out of his pocket, and dialed Mark Lewyn's number. He had promised to call Lewyn anyway.

Meredith was saying, "That's a very good thought, Bob. I think we should act on it."

Sanders heard his call dial, and then an answering machine picked up. A male voice said, "Leave your message at the beep." Then an electronic tone.

"Mark," he said, "it's Tom Sanders. I've talked about Twinkle with Meredith. Her view is that we're in early production and we are shaking out the lines. She takes the position that we can't say for sure that there are any significant problems to be flagged, and that we should treat the situation as standard procedure for the bankers and C-W people tomorrow . . ."

The assistant walked out of the room, smiling at Sanders as she passed him.

". . . and that if we have problems with the drive later on that we have to get management involved with, we'll face that later. I've given her your thoughts, and she's talking to Bob now, so presumably we'll go into the meeting tomorrow taking that position . . ."

The assistant came to the door to the office. She paused briefly to twist the lock in the doorknob, then left, closing the door behind her.

Sanders frowned. *She had locked the door on her way out.* It wasn't so much the fact that she had done it, but the fact that he seemed to be in the middle of an arrangement, a planned event in which everyone else understood what was going on and he did not.

". . . Well, anyway, Mark, if there is a significant change in all this, I'll contact you before the meeting tomorrow, and—"

"Forget that phone," Meredith said coming up suddenly, very close to him, pushing his hand down, and pressing her body against his. Her lips mashed against his mouth. He was vaguely aware of dropping the phone on the windowsill as they kissed and she twisted, turning away, and they tumbled over onto the couch.

"Meredith, wait—"

"Oh God, I've wanted you all day," she said intensely. She kissed him again, rolling on top of him, lifting one leg to hold him down. His position was awkward but he felt himself responding to her. His immediate thought was that someone might come in. He had a vision of himself, lying on his back on the couch with his boss half-straddling him in her businesslike navy suit, and he was anxious about what the person seeing them would think, and then he was truly responding.

She felt it too, and it aroused her more. She pulled back for a breath. "Oh God, you feel so *good*, I can't stand the bastard touching me. Those stupid glasses. Oh! I'm so *hot*, I haven't had a decent fuck—" and then she threw herself back on him, kissing him again, her mouth mashed on him. Her tongue was in his mouth and he thought, *Jesus, she's pushing it.* He smelled her perfume, and it immediately brought back memories.

She shifted her body so she could reach down and touch him, and she moaned when she felt him through his trousers. She fumbled at the zipper. He had suddenly conflicting images, his desire for her, his wife and his kids, memories of the past, of being with her in the apartment in Sunnyvale, of breaking the bed. Images of his wife.

"Meredith—"

"*Oooh.* Don't talk. No! No . . ." She was gasping in little breaths, her mouth puckering rhythmically like a goldfish. He remembered that she got that way. He had forgotten until now. He felt her hot panting breath on his face, saw her flushed cheeks. She got his trousers open. Her hot hand on him.

"Oh, Jesus," she said, squeezing him, and she slid down his body, running her hands over his shirt.

"Listen, Meredith."

"Just let me," she said hoarsely. "Just for a minute." And then her mouth was on him. She was always good at this. Images flooding back to him. The way she liked to do it in dangerous places. While he was driving on the freeway. In the men's room at a sales conference. On the beach at Napili at night. The secret impulsive nature, the secret heat. When he was first introduced to her, the exec at ConTech had said, *She's one of the great cocksuckers.*

Feeling her mouth on him, feeling his back arch as the tension ran through his body, he had the uneasy sense of pleasure and danger at once. So much had happened during the day, so many changes, everything was so sudden. He felt dominated, controlled, and at risk. He had the feeling as he lay on his back that he was somehow agreeing to a situation that he did not understand fully, that was not fully recognized. There would be trouble later. He did not want to go to Malaysia with her. He did not want an affair with his boss. He did not even want a one-night stand. Because what always happened was that people found out, gossip at the water cooler, meaningful looks in the hallway. And sooner or later the spouses found out. It always happened. Slammed doors, divorce lawyers, child custody.

And he didn't want any of that. His life was arranged now, he had things in place. He had commitments. This woman from his past understood none of that. She was free. He was not. He shifted his body.

"Meredith—"

"God, you taste good."

"Meredith—"

She reached up, and pressed her fingers over his lips. "Ssshhh. I know you like it."

"I do like it," he said, "but I—"

"Then let me."

As she sucked him, she was unbuttoning his shirt, pinching his nipples. He looked down and saw her straddling his legs, her head bent over him. Her blouse was open. Her breasts swung free. She reached up, took his hands, and pulled them down, placing them on her breasts.

She still had perfect breasts, the nipples hard under his touch. She moaned. Her body squirming as she straddled him. He felt her warmth. He began to hear a buzzing in his ears, a suffusing intoxicated flush in his face as sounds went dull, the room seemed distant, and there was nothing but this woman and her body and his desire for her.

In that moment he felt a burst of anger, a kind of male fury that he was pinned down, that she was dominating him, and he wanted to be in control, to take her. He sat up and grabbed her hair roughly, lifting her head and twisting his body. She looked in his eyes and saw instantly.

"Yes!" she said, and she moved sideways, so he could sit up beside her. He slipped his hand between her legs. He felt warmth, and lacy underpants. He tugged at them. She wriggled, helping him, and he slid them down to her knees; then she kicked them away. Her hands were caressing his hair, her lips at his ear. "Yes," she whispered fiercely. "Yes!"

Her blue skirt was bunched up around her waist. He kissed her hard, pulling her blouse wide, pressing her breasts to his bare chest. He felt her heat all along his body. He moved his fingers, probing between her lips. She gasped as they kissed, nodding her head *yes*. Then his fingers were in her.

For a moment he was startled: she was not very wet, and then he remembered that, too. The way she would start, her words and body immediately passionate, but this central part of her slower to respond, taking her eventual arousal from his. She was always turned on most by his desire for her, and always came after he did—sometimes within a few seconds, but sometimes he struggled to stay hard while she rocked against him, pushing to her own completion, lost in her own private world while he was fading. He always felt alone, always felt as if she were using him. Those memories gave him pause, and she sensed his hesitation and grabbed him fiercely, fumbling at his belt, moaning, sticking her hot tongue in his ear.

But reluctance was seeping back into him now, his angry heat was fading, and unbidden the thought flashed through his mind: *It's not worth it.*

All his feelings shifted again, and now he had a familiar sensation. Going back to see an old lover, being attracted over dinner, then getting involved again, feeling desire and, suddenly, in the heat of the moment, in the press of flesh, being reminded of all the things that had been wrong with the relationship, feeling old conflicts and angers and irritations rise up again, and wishing that he had never started. Suddenly thinking of how to get out of it, how to stop what was started. But usually there was no way to get out of it.

Still his fingers were inside her, and she was moving her body against his hand, shifting to be sure he would touch the right place. She was wetter, her lips were swelling. She opened her legs wider for him. She was breathing very hard, stroking him with her fingers. "Oh God, I love the way you feel," she said.

Usually there was no way to get out of it.

His body was tense and ready. Her hard nipples brushed against his chest. Her fingers caressed him. She licked the bottom of his earlobe with a quick dart of her tongue and instantly there was nothing but his desire, hot and angry, more intense for the fact that he didn't really want to be there, that he felt she had manipulated him to this place. Now he would fuck her. He wanted to fuck her. Hard.

She sensed his change and moaned, no longer kissing him, leaning back on the couch, waiting. She watched him through half-closed eyes, nodding her head. His fingers still touched her, rapidly, repeatedly, making her gasp, and he turned, pushed her down on her back on the couch. She hiked up her skirt and spread her legs for him. He crouched over her and she smiled at him, a knowing, victorious smile. It made him furious to see this sense that she had somehow won, this watchful detachment, and he wanted to catch her, to make her feel as out of control as he felt, to make her part of this, to wipe that smug detachment from her face. He spread her lips but did not enter her, he held back, his fingers moving, teasing her.

She arched her back, waiting for him. "No, no . . . please . . ."

Still he waited, looking at her. His anger was fading as quickly as it had come, his mind drifting away, the old reservations returning. In an instant of harsh clarity, he saw himself in the room, a panting middle-aged, married man with his trousers down around his knees, bent over a woman on an office couch that was too small. What the hell was he doing?

He looked at her face, saw the way the makeup cracked at the corners of her eyes. Around her mouth.

She had her hands on his shoulders, tugging him toward her. "Oh please . . . No . . . No . . ." And then she turned her head aside and coughed.

Something snapped in him. He sat back coldly. "You're right." He got off the couch, and pulled up his trousers. "We shouldn't do this."

She sat up. "What are you doing?" She seemed puzzled. "You want this as much as I do. You know you do."

"No," he said. "We shouldn't do this, Meredith." He was buckling his belt. Stepping back.

She stared at him in dazed disbelief, like someone awakened from sleep. "You're not serious . . ."

"This isn't a good idea. I don't feel good about it."

And then her eyes were suddenly furious. "You fucking *son of a bitch*."

She got off the couch fast, rushing at him, hitting him hard with bunched fists. "You bastard! You prick! You fucking bastard!" he was trying to button his shirt, turning away from her blows. "You shit! You bastard!"

She moved around him as he turned away, grabbing his hands, tearing at his shirt to keep him from buttoning it.

"You can't! You can't do this to me!"

Buttons popped. She scratched him, long red welts running down his chest. He turned again, avoiding her, wanting only to get out of there. To get dressed and get out of there. She pounded his back.

"You fucker, you can't leave me like this!"

"Cut it out, Meredith," he said. "It's over."

"*Fuck* you!" She grabbed a handful of his hair, pulling him down with surprising strength, and she bit his ear hard. He felt an intense shooting pain and he pushed her away roughly. She toppled backward, off balance, crashing against the glass coffee table, sprawling on the ground.

She sat there, panting. "You fucking son of a bitch."

"Meredith, just leave me alone." He was buttoning his shirt again. All he could think was: *Get out of here.* Get your stuff and get out of here. He reached for his jacket, then saw his cellular phone on the windowsill.

He moved around the couch and picked up the phone. The wineglass crashed against the window near his head. He looked over and saw her standing in the middle of the room, reaching for something else to throw.

"I'll kill you!" she said. "I'll fucking kill you."

"That's enough, Meredith," he said.

"The hell." She threw a small paper bag at him. It thunked against the glass and dropped to the floor. A box of condoms fell out.

"I'm going home." He moved toward the door.

"That's right," she said. "You go home to your wife and your little fucking family."

Alarms went off in his head. He hesitated for a moment.

"Oh yes," she said, seeing him pause. "I know *all* about you, you asshole. Your wife isn't fucking you, so you come in here and lead me on, you set me up and then you walk out on me, you hostile violent fucking asshole. You think you can treat women this way? You asshole."

He reached for the doorknob.

"You walk out on me, you're dead!"

He looked back and saw her leaning unsteadily on the desk, and he thought, *She's drunk.*

"Good night, Meredith," he said. He twisted the knob, them remembered that the door had been locked. He unlocked the door and walked out, without looking back.

In the outer room, a cleaning woman was emptying trash baskets from the assistants' desks.

"I'll fucking kill you for this!" Meredith called after him.

The cleaning woman heard it, and stared at Sanders. He looked away from her, and walked straight to the elevator. He pushed the button. A moment later, he decided to take the stairs.

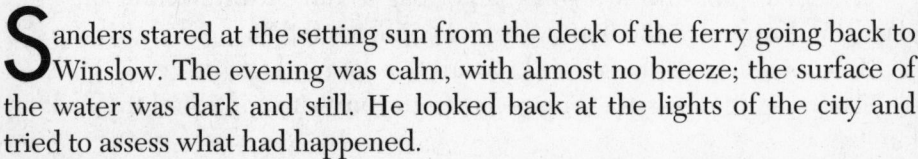

Sanders stared at the setting sun from the deck of the ferry going back to Winslow. The evening was calm, with almost no breeze; the surface of the water was dark and still. He looked back at the lights of the city and tried to assess what had happened.

From the ferry, he could see the upper floors of the DigiCom buildings, rising behind the horizontal gray concrete of the viaduct that ran along the water's edge. He tried to pick out Meredith's office window, but he was already too far away.

Out here on the water, heading home to his family, slipping back into his familiar daily routine, the events of the previous hour had already begun to take on an unreal quality. He found it hard to believe that it had happened. He reviewed the events in his mind, trying to see just where he had gone wrong. He felt certain that it was all his fault, that he had misled Meredith in some important way. Otherwise, she would never have come on to him. The whole episode was an embarrassment for him, and probably for her, too. He felt guilty and miserable—and deeply uneasy about the future. What would happen now? What would she do?

He couldn't even guess. He realized then that he didn't really know her at all. They had once been lovers, but that was a long time ago. Now she was a new person, with new responsibilities. She was a stranger to him.

Although the evening was mild, he felt chilled. He went back inside the ferry. He sat in a booth and took out his phone to call Susan. He pushed the buttons, but the light didn't come on. The battery was dead. For a moment he was confused; the battery should last all day. But it was dead.

The perfect end to his day.

Feeling the throb of the ferry engines, he stood in the bathroom and stared at himself in the mirror. His hair was messed; there was a faint smear of lip-stick on his lips, and another on his neck; two buttons of his shirt were missing, and his clothes were rumpled. He looked as if he had just gotten laid. He turned his head to see his ear. A tiny bruise marked where she had bitten him. He unbuttoned the shirt and looked at the deep red scratches running in parallel rows down his chest.

Christ.

How was he going to keep Susan from seeing this?

He dampened paper towels and scrubbed away the lipstick. He patted down his hair, and buttoned his sport coat, hiding most of his shirt. Then he went back outside, sat down at a booth by the window, and stared into space.

"Hey, Tom."

He looked up and saw John Perry, his neighbor on Bainbridge. Perry was a lawyer with Marlin, Howard, one of the oldest firms in Seattle. He was one of those irrepressibly enthusiastic people, and Sanders didn't much feel like talking to him. But Perry slipped into the seat opposite him.

"How's it going?" Perry asked cheerfully.

"Pretty good," Sanders said.

"I had a *great* day."

"Glad to hear it."

"Just *great*," Perry said. "We tried a case, and I tell you, we kicked ass."

"Great," Sanders said. He stared fixedly out the window, hoping Perry would take the hint and go away.

Perry didn't. "Yeah, and it was a damned tough case, too. Uphill all the way for us," he said. "Title VII, Federal Court. Client's a woman who worked at MicroTech, claimed she wasn't promoted because she was a female. Not a very strong case, to tell the truth. Because she drank, and so on. There were problems. But we have a gal in our firm, Louise Fernandez, a Hispanic gal, and she is just *lethal* on these discrimination cases. Lethal. Got the jury to award our client nearly half a million. That Fernandez can work the case law like nothing you've ever seen. She's won fourteen of her last sixteen cases. She acts so sweet and demure, and inside, she's just *ice*. I tell you, sometimes women scare the hell out of me."

Sanders said nothing.

He came home to a silent house, the kids already asleep. Susan always put the kids to bed early. He went upstairs. His wife was sitting up in bed, reading, with legal files and papers scattered across the bedcovers. When she saw him, she got out of bed and came over to hug him. Involuntarily, his body tensed.

"I'm really sorry, Tom," she said. "I'm sorry about this morning. And I'm sorry about what happened at work." She turned her face up and kissed him lightly on the lips. Awkwardly, he turned away. He was afraid she would smell Meredith's perfume, or—

"You mad about this morning?" she asked.

"No," he said. "Really, I'm not. It was just a long day."

"Lot of meetings on the merger?"

"Yes," he said. "And more tomorrow. It's pretty crazy."

Susan nodded. "It must be. You just got a call from the office. From a Meredith Johnson."

He tried to keep his voice casual. "Oh yes?"

"Uh-huh. About ten minutes ago." She got back in bed. "Who is she, anyway?" Susan was always suspicious when women from the office called.

Sanders said, "She's the new veep. They just brought her up from Cupertino."

"I wondered . . . She acted like she knew me."

"I don't think you've ever met." He waited, hoping he wouldn't have to say more.

"Well," she said, "she sounded very friendly. She said to tell you everything is fine for the due diligence meeting tomorrow morning at eight-thirty, and she'll see you then."

"Okay. Fine."

He kicked off his shoes, and started to unbutton his shirt, then stopped. He bent over and picked his shoes up.

"How old is she?" Susan asked.

"Meredith? I don't know. Thirty-five, something like that. Why?"

"Just wondered."

"I'm going to take a shower," he said.

"Okay." She picked up her legal briefs, and settled back in bed, adjusting the reading light.

He started to leave.

"Do you know her?" Susan asked.

"I've met her before. In Cupertino."

"What's she doing up here?"

"She's my new boss."

"*She's* the one."

"Yeah," he said. "She's the one."

"She's the woman that's close to Garvin?"

"Yeah. Who told you? Adele?" Adele Lewyn, Mark's wife, was one of Susan's best friends.

She nodded. "Mary Anne called, too. The phone never stopped ringing."

"I'll bet."

"So is Garvin fucking her or what?"

"Nobody knows," he said. "The general belief is that he's not."

"Why'd he bring her in, instead of giving the job to you?"

"I don't know, Sue."

"You didn't talk to Garvin?"

"He came around to see me in the morning, but I wasn't there."

She nodded. "You must be pissed. Or are you being your usual understanding self?"

"Well." He shrugged. "What can I do?"

"You can quit," she said.

"Not a chance."

"They passed over you. Don't you *have* to quit?"

"This isn't the best economy to find another job. And I'm forty-one. I don't feel like starting over. Besides, Phil insists they're going to spin off the technical division and take it public in a year. Even if I'm not running it, I'd still be a principal in that new company."

"And did he have details?"

He nodded. "They'll vest us each twenty thousand shares, and options for fifty thousand more. Then options for another fifty thousand shares each additional year."

"At?"

"Usually it's twenty-five cents a share."

"And the stock will be offered at what? Five dollars?"

"At least. The IPO market is getting stronger. Then, say it goes to ten. Maybe twenty, if we're hot."

There was a brief silence. He knew she was good with figures. "No," she said finally. "You can't possibly quit."

He had done the calculations many times. At a minimum, Sanders would realize enough on his stock options to pay off his mortgage in a single payment. But if the stock went through the roof, it could be truly fantastic— somewhere between five and fourteen million dollars. That was why going public was the dream of anyone who worked in a technical company.

He said, "As far as I'm concerned, they can bring in Godzilla to manage that division, and I'll stay at least two more years."

"And is that what they've done? Brought in Godzilla?"

He shrugged. "I don't know."

"Do you get along with her?"

He hesitated. "I'm not sure. I'm going to take a shower."

"Okay," she said. He glanced back at her: she was reading her notes again.

After his shower, he plugged his phone into the charger unit on the sink, and put on a T-shirt and boxer shorts. He looked at himself in the mirror; the shirt covered his scratches. But he was still worried about the smell of Meredith's perfume. He splashed after-shave on his cheeks.

Then he went into his son's room to check on him. Matthew was snoring loudly, his thumb in his mouth. He had kicked down the covers. Sanders pulled them back up gently and kissed his forehead.

Then he went into Eliza's room. At first he could not see her; his daughter had lately taken to burrowing under a barricade of covers and pillows when she slept. He tiptoed in, and saw a small hand reach up, and wave to him. He came forward.

"Why aren't you asleep, Lize?" he whispered.

"I was having a dream," she said. But she didn't seem frightened.

He sat on the edge of the bed, and stroked her hair. "What kind of a dream?"

"About the beast."

"Uh-huh . . ."

"The beast was really a prince, but he was placed under a powerful spell by a 'chantress."

"That's right . . ." He stroked her hair.

"Who turned him into a hideous beast."

She was quoting the movie almost verbatim.

"That's right," he said.

"Why?"

"I don't know, Lize. That's the story."

"Because he didn't give her shelter from the bitter cold?" She was quoting again. "Why didn't he, Dad?"

"I don't know," he said.

"Because he had no love in his heart," she said.

"Lize, it's time for sleep."

"Give me a dream first, Dad."

"Okay. There's a beautiful silver cloud hanging over your bed, and—"

"That dream's no good, Dad." She was frowning at him.

"Okay. What kind of dream do you want?"

"With Kermit."

"Okay. Kermit is sitting right here by your head, and he is going to watch over you all night."

"And you, too."

"Yes. And me, too." He kissed her forehead, and she rolled away to face the wall. As he left the room he could hear her sucking her thumb loudly.

He went back to the bedroom and pushed aside his wife's legal briefs to get into bed.

"Was she still awake?" Susan asked.

"I think she'll go to sleep. She wanted a dream. About Kermit."

His wife nodded. "Kermit is a very big deal now."

She didn't comment on his T-shirt. He slipped under the covers and felt suddenly exhausted. He lay back against the pillow and closed his eyes. He felt Susan picking up the briefs on the bed, and a moment later she turned off the light.

"Mmm," she said. "You smell good."

She snuggled up against him, pressing her face against his neck, and threw her leg over his side. This was her invariable overture, and it always annoyed him. He felt pinned down by her heavy leg.

She stroked his cheek. "Is that after-shave for me?"

"Oh, Susan . . ." He sighed, exaggerating his fatigue.

"Because it works," she said, giggling. Beneath the covers, she put her hand on his chest. He felt it slide down, and slip under the T-shirt.

He had a burst of sudden anger. What was the matter with her? She never had any sense about these things. She was always coming on to him at inappropriate times and places. He reached down and grabbed her hand.

"Something wrong?"

"I'm really tired, Sue."

She stopped. "Bad day, huh?" she said sympathetically.

"Yeah. Pretty bad."

She got up on one elbow, and leaned over him. She stroked his lower lip with one finger. "You don't want me to cheer you up?"

"I really don't."

"Not even a little?"

He sighed again.

"You sure?" she asked, teasingly. "Really, *really* sure?" And then she started to slide beneath the covers.

He reached down and held her head with both hands. "Susan. Please. Come on."

She giggled. "It's only eight-thirty. You can't be *that* tired."

"I am."

"I bet you're not."

"Susan, damn it. I'm not in the mood."

"Okay, okay." She pulled away from him. "But I don't know why you put on the after-shave, if you're not interested."

"For Christ's sake."

"We hardly ever have sex anymore, as it is."

"That's because you're always traveling." It just slipped out.

"I'm not 'always traveling.'"

"You're gone a couple of nights a week."

"That's not 'always traveling.' And besides, it's my job. I thought you were going to be more supportive of my job."

"I am supportive."

"Complaining is not supportive."

"Look, for Christ's sake," he said, "I come home early whenever you're out of town, I feed the kids, I take care of things so you don't have to worry—"

"*Sometimes,*" she said. "And sometimes you stay late at the office, and the kids are with Consuela until all hours—"

"Well, I have a job, too—"

"So don't give me this 'take care of things' crap," she said. "You're not home anywhere near as much as I am, I'm the one who has two jobs, and mostly you do exactly what you want, just like every other fucking man in the world."

"Susan . . ."

"Jesus, you come home early once in a while, and you act like a fucking martyr." She sat up, and turned on her bedside light. "Every woman I know works harder than any man."

"Susan, I don't want to fight."

"Sure, make it *my* fault. I'm the one with the problem. Fucking *men.*"

He was tired, but he felt suddenly energized by anger. He felt suddenly strong, and got out of bed and started pacing. "What does being a man have to do with it? Am I going to hear how oppressed you are again now?"

"Listen," she said, sitting straighter. "Women are oppressed. It's a fact."

"Is it? How are you oppressed? You never wash a load of clothes. You never cook a meal. You never sweep a floor. Somebody does all that for you. You have somebody to do everything for you. You have somebody to take the kids to school and somebody to pick them up. You're a partner in a law firm, for Christ's sake. You're about as oppressed as Leona Helmsley."

She was staring at him in astonishment. He knew why: Susan had made her oppression speech many times before, and he had never contradicted her. Over time, with repetition it had become an accepted idea in their marriage. Now he was disagreeing. He was changing the rules.

"I can't believe you. I thought you were different." She squinted at him, her judicious look. "This is because a woman got your job, isn't it?"

"What're we going to now, the fragile male ego?"

"It's true, isn't it? You're threatened."

"No it's not. It's crap. Who's got the fragile ego around here? Your ego's so fucking fragile, you can't even take a rejection in bed without picking a fight."

That stopped her. He saw it instantly: she had no comeback. She sat there frowning at him, her face tight.

"Jesus," he said, and turned to leave the room.

"You picked this fight," she said.

He turned back. "I did not."

"Yes, you did. You were the one who started in with the traveling."

"No. You were complaining about no sex."

"I was *commenting*."

"Christ. Never marry a lawyer."

"And your ego *is* fragile."

"Susan, you want to talk fragile? I mean, you're so fucking self-involved that you had a shitfit this morning because you wanted to look pretty for the *pediatrician*."

"Oh, there it is. Finally. You *are* still mad because I made you late. What is it? You think you didn't get the job because you were late?"

"No," he said, "I didn't—"

"You didn't get the job," she said, "because Garvin didn't give it to you. You didn't play the game well enough, and somebody else played it better. That's why. A woman played it better."

Furious, shaking, unable to speak, he turned on his heel and left the room.

"That's right, leave," she said. "Walk away. That's what you always do. Walk away. Don't stand up for yourself. You don't want to hear it, Tom. But it's the truth. If you didn't get the job, you have nobody to blame but yourself."

He slammed the door.

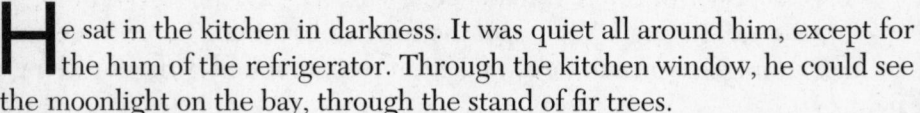

He sat in the kitchen in darkness. It was quiet all around him, except for the hum of the refrigerator. Through the kitchen window, he could see the moonlight on the bay, through the stand of fir trees.

He wondered if Susan would come down, but she didn't. He got up and walked around, pacing. After a while, it occurred to him that he hadn't eaten. He opened the refrigerator door, squinting in the light. It was stacked with baby food, juice containers, baby vitamins, bottles of formula. He poked among the stuff, looking for some cheese, or maybe a beer. He couldn't find anything except a can of Susan's Diet Coke.

Christ, he thought, not like the old days. When his refrigerator was full of frozen food and chips and salsa and lots of beer. His bachelor days.

He took out the Diet Coke. Now Eliza was starting to drink it, too. He'd told Susan a dozen times he didn't want the kids to get diet drinks. They ought to be getting healthy food. Real food. But Susan was busy, and Consuela indifferent. The kids ate all kinds of crap. It wasn't right. It wasn't the way he had been brought up.

Nothing to eat. Nothing in his own damned refrigerator. Hopeful, he lifted the lid of a Tupperware container and found a partially eaten peanut butter and jelly sandwich, with Eliza's small toothmarks in one side. He picked the sandwich up and turned it over, wondering how old it was. He didn't see any mold.

What the hell, he thought, and he ate the rest of Eliza's sandwich, standing there in his T-shirt, in the light of the refrigerator door. He was startled by his own reflection in the glass of the oven. "Another privileged member of the patriarchy, lording it over the manor."

Christ, he thought, where did women come up with this crap?

He finished the sandwich and rubbed the crumbs off his hands. The wall clock said 9:15. Susan went to sleep early. Apparently she wasn't coming down to make up. She usually didn't. It was his job to make up. He was the peacemaker. He opened a carton of milk and drank from it, then put it back on the wire shelf. He closed the door. Darkness again.

He walked over to the sink, washed his hands, and dried them on a dish towel. Having eaten a little, he wasn't so angry anymore. Fatigue crept over him. He looked out the window and through the trees and saw the lights of a ferry, heading west toward Bremerton. One of the things he liked about this house was that it was relatively isolated. It had some land around it. It was good for the kids. Kids should grow up with a place to run and play.

He yawned. She definitely wasn't coming down. It'd have to wait until morning. He knew how it would go: he'd get up first, fix her a cup of coffee, and take it to her in bed. Then he'd say he was sorry, and she would reply that she was sorry, too. They'd hug, and he would go get dressed for work. And that would be it.

He went back up the dark stairs to the second floor, and opened the door to the bedroom. He could hear the quiet rhythms of Susan's breathing.

He slipped into bed, and rolled over on his side. And then he went to sleep.

TUESDAY

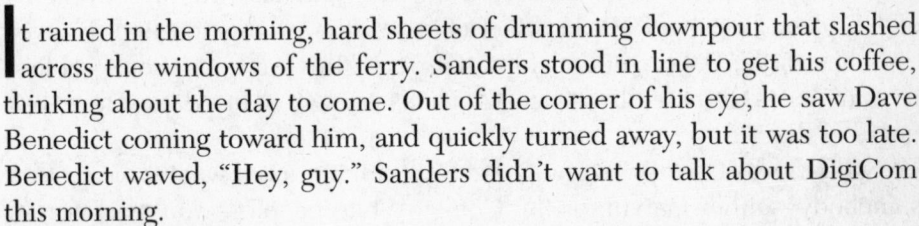

It rained in the morning, hard sheets of drumming downpour that slashed across the windows of the ferry. Sanders stood in line to get his coffee, thinking about the day to come. Out of the corner of his eye, he saw Dave Benedict coming toward him, and quickly turned away, but it was too late. Benedict waved, "Hey, guy." Sanders didn't want to talk about DigiCom this morning.

At the last moment, he was saved by a call: the phone in his pocket went off. He turned away to answer it.

"Fucking A, Tommy boy." It was Eddie Larson in Austin.

"What is it, Eddie?"

"You know that bean counter Cupertino sent down? Well, get this: there's *eight* of 'em here now. Independent accounting firm of Jenkins, McKay, out of Dallas. They're going over all the books, like a swarm of roaches. And I mean everything: receivables, payables, A and L's, year to date, *everything*. And now they're going back through every year to 'eighty-nine."

"Yeah? Disrupting everything?"

"Better believe it. The gals don't even have a place to sit down and answer the phone. Plus, everything from 'ninety-one back is in storage, downtown. We've got it on fiche here, but they say they want original documents. They want the damned paper. And they get all squinty and paranoid when they order us around. Treating us like we're thieves or something trying to pull a fast one. It's insulting."

"Well," Sanders said, "hang in there. You've got to do what they ask."

"The only thing that really bothers me," Eddie said, "is they got another seven more coming in this afternoon. Because they're also doing a complete inventory of the plant. Everything from the furniture in the offices to the air handlers and the heat stampers out on the line. We got a guy there now, making his way down the line, stopping at each work station. Says, 'What's this thing called? How do you spell it? Who makes it? What's the model number? How old is it? Where's the serial number? You ask me, we might as well shut the line down for the rest of the day."

Sanders frowned. "They're doing an *inventory*?"

"Well, that's what they call it. But it's beyond any damn inventory I ever heard of. These guys have worked over at Texas Instruments or someplace, and I'll give 'em one thing: they know what they're talking about. This morning, one of the Jenkins guys came up and asked me what kind of glass we got in the ceiling skylights. I said, 'What kind of glass?' I thought he was shitting me. He says, 'Yeah, is it Corning two-forty-seven, or two-forty-seven slash nine.' Or some damned thing like that. They're different kinds of UV glass, because UV can affect chips on the production line. I never even heard that UV can affect chips. 'Oh yeah,' this guy says. 'Real problem if your ASDs get over two-twenty.' That's annual sunny days. Have you heard of that?"

Sanders wasn't really listening. He was thinking about what it meant that somebody—either Garvin, or the Conley-White people—would ask for an inventory of the plant. Ordinarily, you called for an inventory only if you were planning to sell a facility. Then you had to do it, to figure your write-downs at the time of transfer of assets, and—

"Tom, you there?"

"I'm here."

"So I say to this guy, I never heard that. About the UV and the chips. And we been putting chips in the phones for years, never any trouble. And then the guy says, 'Oh, not for installing chips. UV affects it if you're *manufacturing* chips.' And I say, we don't do that here. And he says, 'I know.' So, I'm wondering: what the hell does he care what kind of glass we have? Tommy boy? You with me? What's the story?" Larson said. "We're going to have fifteen guys crawling all over us by the end of the day. Now don't tell me this is *routine*."

"It doesn't sound like it's routine, no."

"It sounds like they're going to sell the plant to somebody who makes chips, is what it sounds like. And that ain't us."

"I agree. That's what it sounds like."

"Fucking A," Eddie said. "I thought you told me this wasn't going to happen. Tom: people here are getting upset. And I'm one of 'em."

"I understand."

"I mean, I got people asking me. They just bought a house, their wife's pregnant, they got a baby coming, and they want to know. What do I tell 'em?"

"Eddie, I don't have any information."

"Jesus, Tom, you're the division head."

"I know. Let me check with Cork, see what the accountants did there. They were out there last week."

"I already talked to Colin an hour ago. Operations sent two people out there. For one day. Very polite. Not like this at all."

"No inventory?"

"No inventory."

"Okay," Sanders said. He sighed. "Let me get into it."

"Tommy boy," Eddie said. "I got to tell you right out. I'm concerned you don't already know."

"Me, too," Sanders said. "Me, too."

He hung up the phone. Sanders pushed K-A-P for Stephanie Kaplan. She would know what was going on in Austin, and he thought she would tell him. But her assistant said Kaplan was out of the office for the rest of the morning. He called Mary Anne, but she was gone, too. Then he dialed the Four Seasons Hotel, and asked for Max Dorfman. The operator said Mr. Dorfman's lines were busy. He made a mental note to see Max later in the day. Because if Eddie was right, then Sanders was out of the loop. And that wasn't good.

In the meantime, he could bring up the plant closing with Meredith at the conclusion of the morning meeting with Conley-White. That was the best he could do, for the moment. The prospect of talking to her made him uneasy. But he'd get through it somehow. He didn't really have a choice.

When he got to the fourth-floor conference room, nobody was there. At the far end, a wall board showed a cutaway of the Twinkle drive and a schematic for the Malaysia assembly line. There were notes scribbled on some of the pads, open briefcases beside some of the chairs.

The meeting was already under way.

Sanders had a sense of panic. He started to sweat.

At the far end of the room, an assistant came in, and began moving around the table, setting out glasses and water.

"Where is everybody?" he asked.

"Oh, they left about fifteen minutes ago," she said.

"Fifteen minutes ago? When did they start?"

"The meeting started at eight."

"Eight?" Sanders said. "I thought it was supposed to be eight-thirty."

"No, the meeting started at eight."

Damn.

"Where are they now?"

"Meredith took everybody down to VIE, to demo the Corridor."

Entering VIE, the first thing Sanders heard was laughter. When he walked into the equipment room, he saw that Don Cherry's team had two of the Conley-White executives up on the system. John Conley, the young lawyer, and Jim Daly, the investment banker, were both wearing headsets while they walked on the rolling walker pads. The two men were grinning wildly. Everyone else in the room was laughing too, including the normally sour-faced CFO of Conley-White, Ed Nichols, who was standing beside a monitor which showed an image of the virtual corridor that the users were seeing. Nichols had red marks on his forehead from wearing the headset.

Nichols looked over as Sanders came up. "This is *fantastic.*"

Sanders said, "Yes, it's pretty spectacular."

"Simply fantastic. It's going to wipe out all the criticism in New York, once they see this. We've been asking Don if he can run this on our own corporate database."

"No problem," Cherry said. "Just get us the programming hooks for your DB, and we'll plug you right in. Take us about an hour."

Nichols pointed to the headset. "And we can get one of these contraptions in New York?"

"Easy," Cherry said. "We can ship it out later today. It'll be there Thursday. I'll send one of our people to set it up for you."

"This is going to be a *great* selling point," Nichols said. "Just great." He took out his half-frame glasses. They were a complicated kind of glasses that folded up very small. Nichols unfolded them carefully and put them on his nose.

On the walker pad, John Conley was laughing. "Angel," he said. "How do I open this drawer?" Then he cocked his head, listening.

"He's talking to the help angel," Cherry said. "He hears the angel through his earphones."

"What's the angel telling him?" Nichols said.

"That's between him and his angel," Cherry laughed.

On the walker pad, Conley nodded as he listened, then reached forward into the air with his hand. He closed his fingers, as if gripping something, and pulled back, pantomiming someone opening a file drawer.

On the monitor, Sanders saw a virtual file drawer slide out from the wall of the corridor. Inside the drawer he saw neatly arranged files.

"Wow," Conley said. "This is amazing. Angel: can I see a file? . . . Oh. Okay."

Conley reached out and touched one of the file labels with his fingertip. Immediately the file popped out of the drawer and opened up, apparently hanging in midair.

"We have to break the physical metaphor sometimes," Cherry said. "Because users have only one hand. And you can't open a regular file with one hand."

Standing on the black walker pad, Conley moved his hand through the air in short arcs, mimicking someone turning pages with his hand. On the monitor, Sanders saw Conley was actually looking at a series of spreadsheets. "Hey," Conley said, "you people ought to be more careful. I have all your financial records here."

"Let me see that," Daly said, turning around on the walker pad to look.

"You guys look all you want," Cherry laughed. "Enjoy it while you can. In the final system, we'll have safeguards built in to control access. But for now, we bypass the entire system. Do you notice that some of the numbers are red? That means they have more detail stored away. Touch one."

Conley touched a red number. The number zoomed out, creating a new plane of information that hung in the air above the previous spreadsheet.

"Wow!"

"Kind of a hypertext thing," Cherry said, with a shrug. "Sort of neat, if I say so myself."

Conley and Daly were giggling, poking rapidly at numbers on the spreadsheet, zooming out dozens of detail sheets that now hung in the air all around them. "Hey, how do you get rid of all this stuff?"

"Can you find the original spreadsheet?"

"It's hidden behind all this other stuff."

"Bend over, and look. See if you can get it."

Conley bent at the waist, and appeared to look under something. He reached out and pinched air. "I got it."

"Okay, now you see a green arrow in the right corner. Touch it."

Conley touched it. All the papers zoomed back into the original spreadsheet.

"Fabulous!"

"I want to do it," Daly said.

"No, you can't. I'm going to do it."

"No, me!"

"Me!"

They were laughing like delighted kids.

Blackburn came up. "I know this is enjoyable for everyone," he said to Nichols, "but we're falling behind our schedule and perhaps we ought to go back to the conference room."

"All right," Nichols said, with obvious reluctance. He turned to Cherry. "You sure you can get us one of these things?"

"Count on it," Cherry said. "Count on it."

Walking back to the conference room, the Conley-White executives were in a giddy mood; they talked rapidly, laughing about the experience. The DigiCom people walked quietly beside them, not wanting to disrupt the good mood. It was at that point that Mark Lewyn fell into step alongside Sanders and whispered, "Hey, why didn't you call me last night?"

"I did," Sanders said.

Lewyn shook his head. "There wasn't any message when I got home," he said.

"I talked to your answering machine, about six-fifteen."

"I never got a message," Lewyn said. "And then when I came in this morning, you weren't here." He lowered his voice. "Christ. What a mess. I had to go into the meeting on Twinkle with no idea what the approach was going to be."

"I'm sorry," Sanders said. "I don't know what happened."

"Fortunately, Meredith took over the discussion," Lewyn said. "Otherwise I would have been in deepest shit. In fact, I—We'll do this later," he said, seeing Johnson drop back to talk to Sanders. Lewyn stepped away.

"Where the hell were you?" Johnson said.

"I thought the meeting was for eight-thirty."

"I called your house last night, specifically because it was changed to eight. They're trying to catch a plane to Austin for the afternoon. So we moved everything up."

"I didn't get that message."

"I talked to your wife. Didn't she tell you?"

"I thought it was eight-thirty."

Johnson shook her head, as if dismissing the whole thing. "Anyway," she said, "in the eight o'clock session, I had to take another approach to Twinkle, and it's very important that we have some coordination in the light of—"

"Meredith?" Up at the front of the group, Garvin was looking back at her. "Meredith, John has a question for you."

"Be right there," she said. With a final angry frown at Sanders, she hurried up to the head of the group.

Back in the conference room the mood was light. They were all still joking as they took their seats. Ed Nichols began the meeting by turning to Sanders. "Meredith's been bringing us up to date on the Twinkle drive. Now that you're here, we'd like your assessment as well."

I had to take another approach to Twinkle, Meredith had said. Sanders hesitated. "My assessment?"

"Yes," Nichols said. "You're in charge of Twinkle, aren't you?"

Sanders looked at the faces around the table, turned expectantly toward him. He glanced at Johnson, but she had opened her briefcase and was rummaging through her papers, taking out several bulging manila envelopes.

"Well," Sanders said. "We built several prototypes and tested them thoroughly. There's no doubt that the prototypes performed flawlessly. They're the best drives in the world."

"I understand that," Nichols said. "But now you are in production, isn't that right?"

"That's right."

"I think we're more interested in your assessment of the production."

Sanders hesitated. What had she told them? At the other end of the room, Meredith Johnson closed her briefcase, folded her hands under her chin, and stared steadily at him. He could not read her expression.

What had she told them?

"Mr. Sanders?"

"Well," Sanders began, "we've been shaking out the lines, dealing with the problems as they arise. It's a pretty standard start-up experience for us. We're still in the early stages."

"I'm sorry," Nichols said. "I thought you've been in production for two months."

"Yes, that's true."

"Two months doesn't sound like 'the early stages' to me."

"Well—"

"Some of your product cycles are as short as nine months, isn't that right?"

"Nine to eighteen months, yes."

"Then after two months, you must be in full production. How do you assess that, as the principal person in charge?"

"Well, I'd say the problems are of the order of magnitude we generally experience at this point."

"I'm interested to hear that," Nichols said, "because earlier today, Meredith indicated to us that the problems were actually quite serious. She said you might even have to go back to the drawing board."

Shit.

How should he play it now? He'd already said that the problems were not so bad. He couldn't back down. Sanders took a breath and said, "I hope I haven't conveyed the wrong impression to Meredith. Because I have full confidence in our ability to manufacture the Twinkle drive."

"I'm sure you do," Nichols said. "But we're looking down the barrel at competition from Sony and Philips, and I'm not sure that a simple expression of your confidence is adequate. How many of the drives coming off the line meet specifications?"

"I don't have that information."

"Just approximately."

"I wouldn't want to say, without precise figures."

"Are precise figures available?"

"Yes. I just don't have them at hand."

Nichols frowned. His expression said: why don't you have them when you knew this is what the meeting was about?

Conley cleared his throat. "Meredith indicated that the line is running at twenty-nine percent capacity, and that only five percent of the drives meet specifications. Is that your understanding?"

"That's more or less how it has been. Yes."

There was a brief silence around the table. Abruptly, Nichols sat forward. "I'm afraid I need some help here," he said. "With figures like that, on what do you base your confidence in the Twinkle drive?"

"The reason is that we've seen all this before," Sanders replied. "We've seen production problems that look insurmountable but then get resolved quickly."

"I see. So you think your past experience will hold true here."

"Yes, I do."

Nichols sat back in his seat and crossed his arms over his chest. He looked extremely dissatisfied.

Jim Daly, the thin investment banker, sat forward and said, "Please don't misunderstand, Tom. We're not trying to put you on the spot," he said. "We have long ago identified several reasons for acquisition of this company, irrespective of any specific problem with Twinkle. So I don't think Twinkle is a critical issue today. We just want to know where we stand on it. And we'd like you to be as frank as possible."

"Well, there *are* problems," Sanders said. "We're in the midst of assessing them now. We have some ideas. But some of the problems may go back to design."

Daly said, "Give us worst case."

"Worst case? We pull the line, rework the housings and perhaps the controller chips, and then go back on."

"Causing a delay of?"

Nine to twelve months. "Up to six months," Sanders said.

"Jesus," somebody whispered.

Daly said, "Johnson suggested that the maximum delay would be six *weeks*."

"I hope that's right. But you asked for worse case."

"Do you really think it will take six months?"

"You asked for worst case. I think it's unlikely."

"But possible?"

"Yes, possible."

Nichols sat forward again and gave a big sigh. "Let me see if I understand this right. If there *are* design problems with the drive, they occurred under your stewardship, is that correct?"

"Yes, it is."

Nichols shook his head. "Well. Having gotten us into this mess, do you really think you're the person to clean it up?"

Sanders suppressed a surge of anger. "Yes I do," he said. "In fact, I think I'm the best possible person to do it. As I said, we've seen this kind of situation before. And we've handled it before. I'm close to all the people involved. And I am sure we can resolve it." He wondered how he could explain to these people in suits the reality of how products were made. "When you're working the cycles," he said, "it's sometimes not so serious to go back to the boards. Nobody likes to do it, but it may have advantages. In the old days, we made a complete generation of new products every year or so. Now, more and more, we also make incremental changes within generations. If we have to redo the chips, we may be able to code in the video compression algorithms, which weren't available when we started. That will enhance the end-user perception of speed by more than the simple drive specs. We won't go back to build a hundred-millisecond drive. We'll go back to build an eighty-millisecond drive."

"But," Nichols said, "in the meantime, you won't have entered the market."

"No, that's true."

"You won't have established your brand name, or established market share for your product stream. You won't have your dealerships, or your OEMs or your ad campaign, because you won't have a product line to support it. You may have a better drive, but it'll be an unknown drive. You'll be starting from scratch."

"All true. But the market responds fast."

"And so does the competition. Where will Sony be by the time you get to market? Will they be at eighty milliseconds, too?"

"I don't know," Sanders said.

Nichols sighed. "I wish I had more confidence about where we are on this thing. To say nothing of whether we're properly staffed to fix it."

Meredith spoke for the first time. "I may be a little bit at fault here," she said. "When you and I spoke about Twinkle, Tom, I understood you to say that the problems were quite serious."

"They are, yes."

"Well, I don't think we want to be covering anything up here."

He said quickly, "I'm not covering anything up." The words came out almost before he realized it. He heard his voice, high-pitched, tight.

"No, no," Meredith said soothingly. "I didn't mean to suggest you were. It's just that these technical issues are hard for some of us to grasp. We're looking for a translation into layman's terms of just where we are. If you can do that for us."

"I've been trying to do that," he said. He knew he sounded defensive. But he couldn't help it.

"Yes, Tom, I know you have," Meredith said, her voice still soothing. "But for example: if the laser read-write heads are out of sync with the m-subset instructions off the controller chip, what is that going to mean for us, in terms of down time?"

She was just grandstanding, demonstrating her facility with tech-talk, but her words threw him off balance anyway. Because the laser heads were read-only, not read-write, and they had nothing to do with the m-subset off the controller chip. The position controls all came off the x-subset. And the x-subset was licensed code from Sony, part of the driver code that every company used in their CD drives.

To answer without embarrassing her, he had to move into fantasy, where nothing he could say was true. "Well," he said, "you raise a good point, Meredith. But I think the m-subset should be a relatively simple problem, assuming the laser heads are tracking to tolerance. Perhaps three or four days to fix."

He glanced quickly at Cherry and Lewyn, the only people in the room who would know that Sanders had just spoken gibberish. Both men nodded sagely as they listened. Cherry even rubbed his chin.

Johnson said, "And do you anticipate a problem with the asynchronous tracking signals from the mother board?"

Again, she was mixing everything up. The tracking signals came from the power source, and were regulated by the controller chip. There wasn't a mother board in the drive units. But by now he was in the swing. He answered quickly: "That's certainly a consideration, Meredith, and we should check it thoroughly. I expect we'll find that the asynchronous signals may be phase-shifted, but nothing more than that."

"A phase-shift is easy to repair?"

"Yes, I think so."

Nichols cleared his throat. "I feel this is an in-house technical issue," he said. "Perhaps we should move on to other matters. What's next on the agenda?"

Garvin said, "We've scheduled a demo of the video compression just down the hall."

"Fine. Let's do that."

Chairs scraped back. Everyone stood up, and they filed out of the room. Meredith was slower to close up her files. Sanders stayed behind for a moment, too.

W hen they were alone he said, "What the hell was all that about?"
"All what?"

"All that gobbledygook about controller chips and read heads. You don't know what you were talking about."

"Oh yes I do," she said angrily. "I was fixing the mess that you made." She leaned over the table and glared at him. "Look, Tom. I decided to take your advice last night, and tell the truth about the drive. This morning I said there were severe problems with it, that you were very knowledgeable, and you would tell them what the problems were. I set it up, for you to say what you told me you wanted to say. But then you came in and announced there were no problems of significance."

"But I thought we agreed last night—"

"These men aren't fools, and we're not going to be able to fool them." She snapped her briefcase shut. "I reported in good faith what you told me. And then you said I didn't know what I was talking about."

He bit his lip, trying to control his anger.

"I don't know what you think is going on here," she said. "These men don't care about technical details. They wouldn't know a drive head from a dildo. They're just looking to see if anybody's in charge, if anybody has a handle on the problems. They want reassurance. And you didn't reassure them. So I had to jump in and fix it with a lot of techno-bullshit. I had to clean up after you. I did the best I could. But let's face it, you didn't inspire confidence today, Tom. Not at all."

"Goddamn it," he said. "You're just talking about appearances. Corporate appearances in a corporate meeting. But in the end somebody has to actually build the damn drive—"

"I'll say—"

"And I've been running this division for eight years, and running it damn well—"

"Meredith." Garvin stuck his head in the door. They both stopped talking.

"We're waiting, Meredith," he said. He turned and looked coldly at Sanders.

She picked up her briefcase and swept out of the room.

Sanders went immediately downstairs to Blackburn's office. "I need to see Phil."

Sandra, his assistant, sighed. "He's pretty busy today."

"I need to see him now."

"Let me check, Tom." She buzzed the inner office. "Phil? It's Tom Sanders." She listened a moment. "He says go right in."

Sanders went into Blackburn's office and closed the door. Blackburn stood up behind his desk and ran his hands down his chest. "Tom. I'm glad you came down."

They shook hands briefly. "It isn't working out with Meredith," Sanders said at once. He was still angry from his encounter with her.

"Yes, I know."

"I don't think I can work with her."

Blackburn nodded. "I know. She already told me."

"Oh? What'd she tell you?"

"She told me about the meeting last night, Tom."

Sanders frowned. He couldn't imagine that she had discussed that meeting. "Last night?"

"She told me that you sexually harassed her."

"I *what*?"

"Now, Tom, don't get excited. Meredith's assured me she's not going to press charges. We can handle it quietly, in house. That will be best for everyone. In fact, I've just been going over the organization charts, and—"

"Wait a minute," Sanders said. "She's saying *I* harassed *her*?"

Blackburn stared at him. "Tom. We've been friends a long time. I can assure you, this doesn't have to be a problem. It doesn't have to get around the company. Your wife doesn't need to know. As I said, we can handle this quietly. To the satisfaction of everyone involved."

"Wait a minute, it's not true—"

"Tom, just give me a minute here, please. The most important thing now is for us to separate the two of you. So you aren't reporting to her. I think a lateral promotion for you would be ideal."

"Lateral promotion?"

"Yes. There's an opening for technical vice president in the Cellular Division in Austin. I want to transfer you there. You'll go with the same seniority, salary, and benefit package. Everything the same, except you'll be in Austin and you won't have to have any direct contact with her. How does that sound?"

"Austin."

"Yes."

"Cellular."

"Yes. Beautiful weather, nice working conditions . . . university town . . . chance to get your family out of this rain . . ."

Sanders said, "But Conley's going to sell off Austin."

Blackburn sat down behind his desk. "I can't imagine where you heard that, Tom," he said calmly. "It's completely untrue."

"You sure about that?"

"Absolutely. Believe me, selling Austin is the last thing they'd do. Why, it makes no sense at all."

"Then why are they inventorying the plant?"

"I'm sure they're going over the whole operation with a fine-tooth comb. Look, Tom. Conley's worried about cash flow after the acquisition, and the Austin plant is, as you know, very profitable. We've given them the figures. Now they're verifying them, making sure they're real. But there's no chance they would sell it. Cellular is only going to grow, Tom. You know that. And that's why I think a vice presidency there in Austin is an excellent career opportunity for you to consider."

"But I'd be leaving the Advanced Products Division?"

"Well, yes. The whole point would be to move you out of this division."

"And then I wouldn't be in the new company when it spins off."

"That's true."

Sanders paced back and forth. "That's completely unacceptable."

"Well, let's not be hasty," Blackburn said. "Let's consider all the ramifications."

"Phil," he said. "I don't know what she told you, but—"

"She told me the whole story—"

"But I think you should know—"

"And I want you to know, Tom," Blackburn said, "that I don't have any judgment about what may have happened. That's not my concern or my interest. I'm just trying to solve a difficult problem for the company."

"Phil. Listen. I didn't do it."

"I understand that's probably how you feel, but—"

"I didn't harass her. She harassed me."

"I'm sure," Blackburn said, "it may have *seemed* like that to you at the time, but—"

"Phil, I'm telling you. She did everything but rape me." He paced angrily. "Phil: *she* harassed *me*."

Blackburn sighed and sat back in his chair. He tapped his pencil on the corner of his desk. "I have to tell you frankly, Tom. I find that difficult to believe."

"It's what happened."

"Meredith's a beautiful woman, Tom. A very vital, sexy woman. I think it's natural for a man to, uh, lose control."

"Phil, you aren't hearing me. She harassed me."

Blackburn gave a helpless shrug. "I hear you, Tom. I just . . . I find that difficult to picture."

"Well, she did. You want to hear what really happened last night?"

"Well." Blackburn shifted in his chair. "Of course I want to hear your version. But the thing is, Tom, Meredith Johnson is very well connected in this company. She has impressed a lot of extremely important people."

"You mean Garvin."

"Not only Garvin. Meredith has built a power base in several areas."

"Conley-White?"

Blackburn nodded. "Yes. There, too."

"You don't want to hear what I say happened?"

"Of course I do," Blackburn said, running his hands through his hair. "Absolutely, I do. And I want to be scrupulously fair. But I'm trying to tell you that no matter what, we're going to have to make some transfers here. And Meredith has important allies."

"So it doesn't matter what I say."

Blackburn frowned, watching him pace. "I understand that you are upset. I can see that. And you're a valued person in this company. But what I'm trying to do here, Tom, is to get you to look at the situation."

"What situation?" Sanders said.

Blackburn sighed. "Were there any witnesses, last night?"

"No."

"So it's your word against hers."

"I guess so."

"In other words, it's a pissing match."

"So? That's no reason to assume I'm wrong, and she's right."

"Of course not," Blackburn said. "But look at the situation. A man claiming sexual harassment against a woman is, well, pretty unlikely. I don't think there's ever been a case in this company. It doesn't mean it couldn't happen. But it does mean that it'd be very uphill for you—even if Meredith wasn't so well connected." He paused. "I just don't want to see you get hurt in this."

"I've already been hurt."

"Again, we're talking about feelings here. Conflicting claims. And unfortunately, Tom, no witnesses." He rubbed his nose, tugged at his lapels.

"You move me out of the APD, and I'm hurt. Because I won't get to be part of the new company. The company I worked on for twelve years."

"That's an interesting legal position," Blackburn said.

"I'm not talking about a legal position. I'm talking about—"

"Look. Tom. Let me review this with Garvin. Meanwhile, why don't you go off and think this Austin offer over. Think about it carefully. Because no one wins in a pissing match. You may hurt Meredith, but you'll hurt yourself much more. That's my concern here, as your friend."

"If you were my friend—" Sanders began.

"I *am* your friend," Blackburn said. "Whether you know it at this moment, or not." He stood up behind his desk. "You don't need this splashed all over the papers. Your wife doesn't need to hear about this, or your kids. You don't need to be the gossip of Bainbridge for the rest of the summer. That isn't going to do you any good at all."

"I understand that, but—"

"But we have to face reality, Tom," Blackburn said. "The company is faced with conflicting claims. What's happened has happened. We have to go on from here. And all I'm saying is, I'd like to resolve this quickly. So think it over. Please. And get back to me."

After Sanders left, Blackburn called Garvin. "I just talked with him," he told Garvin.

"And?"

"He says it was the other way around. That she harassed him."

"Christ," Garvin said. "What a mess."

"Yes. But on the other hand, it's what you'd expect him to say," Blackburn said. "It's the usual response in these cases. The man always denies it."

"Yeah. Well. This is dangerous, Phil."

"I understand."

"I don't want this thing to blow up on us."

"No, no."

"There's nothing more important right now than getting this thing resolved."

"I understand, Bob."

"You made him the Austin offer?"

"Yes. He's thinking it over."

"Will he take it?"

"My guess is no."

"And did you push it?"

"Well, I tried to convey to him that we weren't going to back down on Meredith. That we were going to support her through this."

"Damn right we are," Garvin said.

"I think he was clear about that. So let's see what he says when he comes back to us."

"He wouldn't go off and file, would he?"

"He's too smart for that."

"We hope," Garvin said irritably, and hung up.

L *ook at the situation.*

Sanders stood in Pioneer Park and leaned against a pillar, staring at the light drizzle. He was replaying the meeting with Blackburn.

Blackburn hadn't even been willing to listen to Sanders's version. He hadn't let Sanders tell him. Blackburn already knew what had happened.

She's a very sexy woman. It's natural for a man to lose control.

That was what everyone at DigiCom would think. Every single person in the company would have that view of what had happened. Blackburn had said he found it difficult to believe that Sanders had been harassed. Others would find it difficult, too.

Blackburn had told him it didn't matter what happened. Blackburn was telling him that Johnson was well connected, and that nobody would believe a man had been harassed by a woman.

Look at the situation.

They were asking him to leave Seattle, leave the APG. No options, no big payoff. No return for his twelve long years of work. All that was gone.

Austin. Baking hot, dry, brand-new.

Susan would never accept it. Her practice in Seattle was successful; she had spent many years building it. They had just finished remodeling the house. The kids liked it here. If Sanders even suggested a move, Susan would be suspicious. She'd want to know what was behind it. And sooner or later, she would find out. If he accepted the transfer, he would be confirming his guilt to his wife.

No matter how he thought about it, how he tried to put it together in his mind, Sanders could see no good outcome. He was being screwed.

I'm your friend, Tom. Whether you know it right now or not.

He recalled the moment at his wedding when Blackburn, his best man, said he wanted to dip Susan's ring in olive oil because there was always a problem about getting it on the finger. Blackburn in a panic, in case some little moment in the ceremony went wrong. That was Phil: always worried about appearances.

Your wife doesn't need to hear about this.

But Phil was screwing him. Phil, and Garvin behind him. They were both screwing him. Sanders had worked hard for the company for many years, but now they didn't give a damn about him. They were taking Meredith's side, without any question. They didn't even want to hear his version of what had happened.

As Sanders stood in the rain, his sense of shock slowly faded. And with it, his sense of loyalty. He started to get angry.

He took out his phone and placed a call.

"Mr. Perry's office."

"It's Tom Sanders calling."

"I'm sorry, Mr. Perry is in court. Can I give him a message?"

"Maybe you could help me. The other day he mentioned that you have a woman there who handles sexual harassment cases."

"We have several attorneys who do that, Mr. Sanders."

"He mentioned a Hispanic woman." He was trying to remember what else Perry had said about her. Something about being sweet and demure? He couldn't recall for sure.

"That would be Ms. Fernandez."

"I wonder if you could connect me," Sanders said.

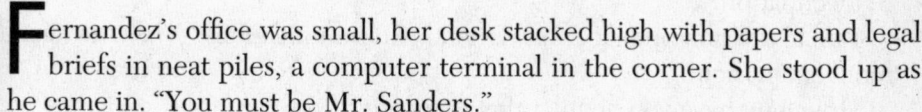

Fernandez's office was small, her desk stacked high with papers and legal briefs in neat piles, a computer terminal in the corner. She stood up as he came in. "You must be Mr. Sanders."

She was a tall woman in her thirties, with straight blond hair and a handsome, aquiline face. She was dressed in a pale, cream-colored suit. She had a direct manner and a firm handshake. "I'm Louise Fernandez. How can I help you?"

She wasn't at all what he had expected. She wasn't sweet and demure at all. And certainly not Hispanic. He was so startled that without thinking he said, "You're not what I—"

"Expected?" She raised an eyebrow. "My father's from Cuba. We left there when I was a child. Please sit down, Mr. Sanders." She turned and walked back around her desk.

He sat down, feeling embarrassed. "Anyway, thank you for seeing me so quickly."

"Not at all. You're John Perry's friend?"

"Yes. He mentioned the other day that you, uh, specialized in these cases."

"I do labor law, primarily constructive termination and Title VII suits."

"I see." He felt foolish that he had come. He was taken aback by her brisk manner and elegant appearance. In fact, she reminded him very much of Meredith. He felt certain that she would not be sympathetic to his case.

She put on horn-rimmed glasses and peered at him across the desk. "Have you eaten? I can get you a sandwich if you like."

"I'm not hungry, thanks."

She pushed a half-eaten sandwich to the side of her desk. "I'm afraid I have a court appearance in an hour. Sometimes things get a bit rushed." She got out a yellow legal pad and set it before her. Her movements were quick, decisive.

Sanders watched her, sure she was the wrong person. He should never have come here. It was all a mistake. He looked around the office. There was a neat stack of bar charts for a courtroom appearance.

Fernandez looked up from the pad, her pen poised. It was one of those expensive fountain pens. "Would you like to tell me the situation?"

"Uh . . . I'm not sure where to begin."

"We could start with your full name and address, and your age."

"Thomas Robert Sanders." He gave his address.

"And your age?"

"Forty-one."

"Occupation?"

"I'm a division manager at Digital Communications. The Advanced Products Division."

"How long have you been at that company?"

"Twelve years."

"Uh-huh. And in your present capacity?"

"Eight years."

"And why are you here today, Mr. Sanders?"

"I've been sexually harassed."

"Uh-huh." She showed no surprise. Her expression was completely neutral. "You want to tell me the circumstances?"

"My boss, ah, came on to me."

"And the name of your boss?"

"Meredith Johnson."

"Is that a man or a woman?"

"A woman."

"Uh-huh." Again, no sign of surprise. She continued making notes steadily, the pen scratching. "When did this happen?"

"Last night."

"What were the exact circumstances?"

He decided not to mention the merger. "She has just been appointed my new boss, and we had several things to go over. She asked if we could meet at the end of the day."

"She requested this meeting?"

"Yes."

"And where did the meeting take place?"

"In her office. At six o'clock."

"Anybody else present?"

"No. Her assistant came in briefly, at the start of the meeting, then left. Before anything happened."

"I see. Go on."

"We talked for a while, about business, and we had some wine. She had gotten some wine. And then she came on to me. I was over by the window and suddenly she started kissing me. Then pretty soon we were sitting on the couch. And then she started, uh . . ." He hesitated. "How much detail do you want?"

"Just the broad strokes for now." She bit her sandwich. "You say you were kissing."

"Yes."

"And she initiated this?"

"Yes."

"What was your reaction when she did that?"

"I was uncomfortable. I'm married."

"Uh-huh. What was the general atmosphere in the meeting, prior to this kiss?"

"It was a regular business meeting. We were talking about business. But all the time, she was making, uh, suggestive remarks."

"Like what."

"Oh, about how good I looked. How I was in shape. How glad she was to see me."

"How glad she was to see you," Fernandez repeated, with a puzzled look.

"Yes. We knew each other before."

"You had a prior relationship?"

"Yes."

"When was that?"

"Ten years ago."

"And were you married then?"

"No."

"Did you both work for the same company at that time?"

"No. I did, but she worked for another company."

"And how long did your relationship last?"

"About six months."

"And have you kept up contact?"

"No. Not really."

"Any contact at all?"

"Once."

"Intimate?"

"No. Just, you know, hello in the hallway. At the office."

"I see. In the last eight years, have you ever been to her house or apartment?"

"No."

"Dinners, drinks after work, anything?"

"No. I really haven't seen her at all. When she joined the company, she was in Cupertino, in Operations. I was in Seattle, in Advanced Products. We didn't have much contact."

"So during this time, she wasn't your superior?"

"No."

"Give me a picture of Ms. Johnson. How old?"

"Thirty-five."

"Would you characterize her as attractive."

"Yes."

"Very attractive?"

"She was a Miss Teenage something as a kid."

"So you would say she's very attractive." The pen scratched on the legal pad.

"Yes."

"And how about other men—would you say they find her very attractive?"

"Yes."

"What about her manner with regard to sexual matters? Does she make jokes? Sexual jokes, innuendoes, ribald comments?"

"No, never."

"Body language? Flirtatious? Does she touch people?"

"Not really. She certainly knows she's good-looking, and she can play on that. But her manner is . . . kind of cool. She's the Grace Kelly type."

"They say Grace Kelly was very sexually active, that she had affairs with most of her leading men."

"I wouldn't know."

"Uh-huh. What about Ms. Johnson, does she have affairs inside the company?"

"I wouldn't know. I haven't heard anything."

Fernandez flipped to a new page on her pad. "All right. And how long has she been your supervisor? Or is she your supervisor?"

"Yes, she is. One day."

For the first time, Fernandez looked surprised. She glanced at him, and took another bite of her sandwich. "One day?"

"Yes. Yesterday was the first day of a new company organization. She had just been appointed."

"So the day she is appointed, she meets with you, in the evening."

"Yes."

"All right. You were telling me, you were sitting on the couch and she was kissing you. And what happened then?"

"She unzipped—well, first of all, she started rubbing me."

"Your genitals."

"Yes. And kissing me." He found himself sweating. He wiped his forehead with his hand.

"I understand this is difficult. I'll try to make this as brief as possible," Fernandez said. "And then?"

"Then, she unzipped my pants, and started rubbing me with her hand."

"Was your penis exposed?"

"Yes."

"Who exposed it?"

"She took it out."

"So she took your penis out of your pants, and then rubbed it with her hand, is that right?" She peered at him over her glasses, and for a moment he glanced away in embarrassment. But when he looked back at her, he saw that she was not the least embarrassed, that her manner was more than clinical, more than professional—that she was in some deep way detached, and very cold.

"Yes," he said. "That's what happened."

"And what was your reaction?"

"Well." He gave an embarrassed shrug. "It worked."

"You were sexually aroused."

"Yes."

"Did you say anything to her?"

"Like what?"

"I'm just asking whether you said anything to her."

"Like what? I don't know."

"Did you say anything at all?"

"I said something, I don't know. I was feeling very uncomfortable."

"Do you remember what you said?"

"I think I just kept saying 'Meredith,' trying to get her to stop, you know, but she kept interrupting me, or kissing me."

"Did you say anything else besides 'Meredith'?"

"I don't remember."

"How did you feel about what she was doing?"

"I felt uncomfortable."

"Why?"

"I was afraid of getting involved with her, because she was my boss now, and because I was married now and I didn't want any complications in my life. You know, an office affair."

"Why not?" Fernandez asked.

The question took him aback. "Why *not*?"

"Yes." She looked at him directly, her eyes cool, appraising. "After all, you're alone with a beautiful woman. Why not have an affair?"

"Jesus."

"It's a question most people would ask."

"I'm married."

"So what? Married people have affairs all the time."

"Well," he said. "For one thing, my wife is a lawyer and very suspicious."

"Do I know her?"

"Her name is Susan Handler. She's with Lyman, King."

Fernandez nodded. "I've heard of her. So. You were afraid that she would find out."

"Sure. I mean, you have an affair in the office, and everybody's going to know. There isn't any way to keep it quiet."

"So you were concerned about this becoming known."

"Yes. But that wasn't the main reason."

"What was the main reason?"

"She was my boss. I didn't like the position I was in. She was, you know . . . well, she had the right to fire me. If she wanted to. So it was like I *had* to do it. I was very uncomfortable."

"Did you tell her that?"

"I tried."

"How did you try?"

"Well, I just tried."

"Would you say that you indicated to her that her advances were not welcome?"

"Eventually, yes."

"How is that?"

"Well, eventually, we continued this . . . whatever you call it, foreplay or whatever, and she had her panties off, and—"

"I'm sorry. How did she come to have her panties off?"

"I took them off."

"Did she ask you to do that?"

"No. But I got pretty worked up at one point, I was going to do it, or at least I was thinking about doing it."

"You were going to have intercourse." Her voice again cool. The pen scratching.

"Yes."

"You were a willing participant."

"For a while there. Yes."

"In what way were you a willing participant?" she asked. "What I mean is, did you initiate touching her body or breast or genitals without her encouragement?"

"I don't know. She was pretty much encouraging everything."

"I am asking, did you volunteer. Did you do it on your own. Or did she, for example, take your hand and place it on her—"

"No. I did it on my own."

"What about your earlier reservations?"

"I was worked up. Excited. I didn't care at that point."

"All right. Go on."

He wiped his forehead. "I'm being very honest with you."

"That's exactly what you should be. It's the best thing all around. Please go on."

"And she was lying on the couch with her skirt pulled up, and she wanted me to enter her, to . . . and she was sort of moaning, you know, saying, 'No, no,' and suddenly I had this feeling again that I didn't want to do this, so I said, 'Okay, let's not,' and I got off the couch and started getting dressed."

"You broke off from the encounter yourself."

"Yes."

"Because she had said, 'no'?"

"No, that was just an excuse. Because I was feeling uneasy at that point."

"Uh-huh. So you got off the couch and started to get dressed . . ."

"Yes."

"And did you say anything at that time? To explain your actions?"

"Yes. I said that I didn't think this was a good idea, and I didn't feel good about it."

"And how did she respond?"

"She got very angry. She started throwing things at me. Then she started hitting me. And scratching me."

"Do you have any marks?"

"Yes."

"Where are they?"

"On my neck and chest."

"Have they been photographed yet?"

"No."

"All right. Now when she scratched you, how did you respond?"

"I just tried to get dressed and get out of there."

"You didn't respond directly to her attack?"

"Well, at one point I pushed her back, to get her away from me, and she tripped on a table and fell on the floor."

"You make it sound like pushing her was self-defense on your part."

"It was. She was ripping the buttons off my shirt. I had to go home, and I didn't want my wife to see my shirt, so I pushed her away."

"Did you ever do anything that was *not* self-defense?"

"No."

"Did you hit her at any time?"

"No."

"You're sure about that?"

"Yes."

"All right. What happened then?"

"She threw a wineglass at me. But by then I was pretty much dressed. I went and got my phone from her windowsill, and then I went—"

"I'm sorry. You got your phone? What phone is that?"

"I had a cellular phone." He took it out of his pocket and showed her. "We all carry them in the company, because we make them. And I had been using the phone to make a call from her office, when she started kissing me."

"Were you in the middle of a call when she started kissing you?"

"Yes."

"Whom were you talking to?"

"An answering machine."

"I see." She was clearly disappointed. "Go on, please."

"So I went and got my phone and got the hell out of there. She was screaming that I couldn't do this to her, that she would kill me."

"And you responded how?"

"Nothing. I just left."

"And this was at what time."

"About six forty-five."

"Did anybody see you leave."

"The cleaning lady."

"Do you happen to know her name?"

"No."

"Ever seen her before?"

"No."

"Do you think she worked for your company?"

"She had a company uniform on. You know, for the maintenance firm that cleans up our offices."

"Uh-huh. And then?"

He shrugged. "I went home."

"Did you tell your wife what happened?"

"No."

"Did you tell anybody what happened?"

"No."

"Why not?"

"I guess I was in shock."

She paused and looked back over her notes. "All right. You say you were sexually harassed. And you have described a very direct overture by this woman. Since she was your boss, I would have thought you'd feel yourself at some risk in turning her down."

"Well. I was concerned. Sure. But I mean, don't I have the right to turn her down? Isn't that what this is about?"

"Certainly you have that right. I'm asking about your state of mind."

"I was very upset."

"Yet you did not want to tell anybody what had happened? You did not want to share this upsetting experience with a colleague? A friend? A family member, perhaps a brother? Anybody at all?"

"No. It didn't even occur to me. I didn't know how to deal with what—I guess I was in shock. I just wanted it to go away. I wanted to think it had never happened."

"Did you make any notes?"

"No."

"All right. Now, you mentioned that you didn't tell your wife. Would you say you concealed it from your wife?"

He hesitated. "Yes."

"Do you often conceal things from her?"

"No. But in this instance, you know, involving an old girlfriend, I didn't think she would be sympathetic. I didn't want to deal with her about this."

"Have you had other affairs?"

"This wasn't an affair."

"I'm asking a general question. In terms of your relationship to your wife."

"No. I haven't had affairs."

"All right. I advise you to tell your wife at once. Make a full and complete disclosure. Because I promise you that she will find out, if she hasn't done so already. However difficult it may be to tell her, your best chance to pre-serve your relationship is to be completely honest with her."

"Okay."

"Now, going back to last night. What happened next?"

"Meredith Johnson called the house and spoke to my wife."

Fernandez's eyebrows went up. "I see. Did you expect that to happen?"

"God, no. It scared the hell out of me. But apparently she was friendly, and just called to say that the morning meeting was rescheduled for eight-thirty. Today."

"I see."

"But when I got to work today, I found that the meeting had actually been scheduled for eight."

"So you arrived late, and were embarrassed, and so on."

"Yes."

"And you believe that it was a setup."

"Yes."

Fernandez glanced at her watch. "I'm afraid I'm running out of time. Bring me up to date about what happened today quickly, if you can."

Without mentioning Conley-White, he described the morning meeting briefly and his subsequent humiliation. His argument with Meredith. His conversation with Phil Blackburn. The offer of a lateral transfer. The fact that the transfer would deny him the benefits of a possible spin-off. His decision to seek advice.

Fernandez asked few questions and wrote steadily. Finally, she pushed the yellow pad aside.

"All right. I think I have enough to get the picture. You're feeling slighted and ignored. And your question is, do you have a harassment case?"

"Yes," he said, nodding.

"Well. Arguably you do. It's a jury case, and we don't know what would happen if we went to trial. But based on what you have told me here, I have to advise you that your case is not strong."

Sanders felt stunned. "Jesus."

"I don't make the laws. I'm just telling you frankly, so you can arrive at an informed decision. Your situation is not good, Mr. Sanders."

Fernandez pushed back from her desk and began to stuff papers into her briefcase. "I have five minutes, but let me review for you what sexual harassment actually is, under the law, because many clients aren't clear about it. Title VII of the Civil Rights Act of 1964 made sex discrimination in the workplace illegal, but as a practical matter what we call sexual harassment was not defined for many years. Since the middle nineteen-eighties, the Equal Employment Opportunities Commission has, under Title VII, produced guidelines to define sexual harassment. In the last few years, these EEOC guidelines have been further clarified by case law. So the definitions are quite explicit. According to the law, for a complaint to qualify as sexual harassment, the behavior must contain three elements. First, it must be sexual. That means, for example, that making a profane or scatological joke is not sexual harassment, even though a listener may find it offensive. The conduct must be sexual in nature. In your case, there's no doubt about the explicitly sexual element, from what you have told me."

"Okay."

"Second, the behavior must be unwelcome. The courts distinguish between behavior that is voluntary and behavior that is welcome. For example, a person may be having a sexual relationship with a superior and it's obviously voluntary—no one's holding a gun to the person's head. But the courts understand that the employee may feel that they have no choice but to comply, and therefore the sexual relationship was not freely entered into—it's not welcome.

"To determine if behavior is really unwelcome, the courts look at the surrounding behavior in broad terms. Did the employee make sexual jokes in the workplace, and thus indicate that such jokes from others were welcome? Did the employee routinely engage in sexual banter, or sexual teasing with other employees? If the employee engaged in an actual affair, did they allow the supervisor into their apartment, did they visit the supervisor in the hospital, or see them at times when they didn't strictly have to, or engage in other actions that would suggest that they were actively and willingly participating in the relationship. In addition, the courts look to see if the employee ever told the supervisor the behavior was unwelcome, if the employee complained to anyone else about the relationship or tried to take any action to evade the unwelcome situation. That consideration becomes more significant when the employee is highly placed, and presumably more free to act."

"But I didn't tell anybody."

"No. And you didn't tell her, either. At least, not explicitly, so far as I can determine."

"I didn't feel I could."

"I understand you didn't. But it's a problem for your case. Now, the third element in sexual harassment is discrimination on the basis of gender. The most common is quid pro quo—the exchange of sexual favors in return for keeping your job or getting a promotion. The threat of that may be explicit or implied. I believe you said it was your understanding that Ms. Johnson had the ability to fire you?"

"Yes."

"How did you gain that understanding?"

"Phil Blackburn told me."

"Explicitly?"

"Yes."

"And what about Ms. Johnson? Did she make any offer contingent on sex? Did she make any reference to her ability to fire you, in the course of the evening?"

"Not exactly, but it was there. It was always in the air."

"How did you know?"

"She said things like 'As long as we're working together, we might as well have a little fun.' And she talked about wanting to have an affair during company trips we would make together to Malaysia, and so on."

"You interpreted this as an implied threat to your job?"

"I interpreted it to mean that if I wanted to get along with her, I had better go along with her."

"And you didn't want to do that?"

"No."

"Did you say so?"

"I said I was married, and that things had changed between us."

"Well, under most circumstances, that exchange alone would probably serve to establish your case. If there were witnesses."

"But there weren't."

"No. Now, there is a final consideration, which we call hostile working environment. This is ordinarily invoked in situations where an individual is harassed in a pattern of incidents that may not in themselves be sexual but that cumulatively amount to harassment based on gender. I don't believe you can claim hostile work environment on this single incident."

"I see."

"Unfortunately, the incident you describe is simply not as clear-cut as it might be. We would then turn to ancillary evidence of harassment. For example, if you were fired."

"I think in effect I have been fired," Sanders said. "Because I'm being pulled out of the division, and I won't get to participate in the spin-off."

"I understand. But the company's offer to transfer you laterally makes things complicated. Because the company can argue—very successfully, I think—that it does not owe you anything more than a lateral transfer. That it has never promised you the golden egg of a spin-off. That such a spin-off is in any case speculative, intended to occur at some future time, and it might never happen. That the company is not required to compensate you for your hopes—for some vague expectation of a future that might never occur. And therefore the company will claim that a lateral transfer is fully acceptable, and that you are being unreasonable if you turn it down. That you are in effect quitting, not being fired. It will place the burden back on you."

"That's ridiculous."

"Actually, it's not. Suppose, for example, you found out that you had terminal cancer and were going to die in six months. Would the company be required to pay the proceeds of the spin-off to your survivors? Clearly, no. If you're working in the company when it spins off, you participate. If you're not, you don't. The company has no broader obligation."

"You're saying I might as well have cancer."

"No, I'm saying that you're angry and you feel the company owes you something that the court will not agree it does. In my experience, sexual harassment claims often have this quality. People come in feeling angry and wronged, and they think they have rights that they simply don't have."

He sighed. "Would it be different if I were a woman?"

"Basically, no. Even in the most clear-cut situations—the most extreme and outrageous situations—sexual harassment is notoriously difficult to prove. Most cases occur as yours has: behind closed doors, with no witnesses. It's one person's word against another's. In that circumstance, where there is no clear-cut corroborating evidence, there is often a prejudice against the man."

"Uh-huh."

"Even so, one-fourth of all sexual harassment cases are brought by men. Most of those are brought against male bosses, but one-fifth are brought against women. And the number is increasing all the time, as we have more women bosses in the workplace."

"I didn't know that."

"It isn't much discussed," she said, peering over her glasses. "But it's happening. And from my point of view, it's to be expected."

"Why do you say that?"

"Harassment is about power—the undue exercise of power by a superior over a subordinate. I know there's a fashionable point of view that says women are fundamentally different from men, and that women would never harass an employee. But from where I sit, I've seen it all. I've seen and heard everything that you can imagine—and a lot that you wouldn't believe if I told you. That gives me another perspective. Personally, I don't deal much in theory. I have to deal with the facts. And on the basis of facts, I don't see much difference in the behavior of men and women. At least, nothing that you can rely on."

"Then you believe my story?"

"Whether I believe you is not at issue. What's at issue is whether you realistically have a case, and therefore what you should do in your circumstances. I can tell you that I've heard it all before. You're not the first man I've been asked to represent, you know."

"What do you advise me to do?"

"I can't advise you," Fernandez said briskly. "The decision you face is much too difficult. I can only lay out the situation." She pushed her intercom button. "Bob, tell Richard and Eileen to bring the car around. I'll meet them in front of the building." She turned back to Sanders.

"Let me review your problems," she said. She ticked them off on her fingers. "One: you claim that you got into an intimate situation with a younger, very attractive woman but you turned her down. In the absence of witnesses or corroborating evidence, that isn't going to be an easy story to sell to a jury.

"Two: if you bring a lawsuit, the company will fire you. You're looking at three years before you come to trial. You have to think about how you'll support yourself during that time, about how you'll make your house payments, and your other expenses. I might take you on a contingency basis, but you'll still have to pay all direct costs throughout the trial. That will be a minimum of one hundred thousand dollars. I don't know whether you'll want to mortgage your house to pay for it. But it has to be dealt with.

"Three: a lawsuit will bring all this out into the open. It'll be in the papers and on the evening news for years before the trial begins. I can't adequately describe how destructive an experience that is—for you, and for your wife and family. Many families don't survive the pre-trial period intact. There are divorces, suicides, illnesses. It's *very* difficult.

"Four: because of the offer of lateral transfer, it's not clear what we can claim as damages. The company will claim that you have no case, and we'll have to fight it. But even with a stunning victory, you may end up with only a couple of hundred thousand dollars after expenses and fees and three years of your life. And of course the company can appeal, delaying payment further.

"Five: if you bring a lawsuit, you'll never work in this industry again. I know it's not supposed to work that way, but as a practical matter, you'll never be hired for another job. That's just how it goes. It would be one thing if you were fifty-five. But you're only forty-one. I don't know if you want to make that choice, at this point in your life."

"Jesus." He slumped back in the chair.

"I'm sorry, but these are the facts of litigation."

"But it's so unjust."

She put on her raincoat. "Unfortunately, the law has nothing to do with justice, Mr. Sanders," she said. "It's merely a method for dispute resolution." She snapped her briefcase shut and extended her hand. "I'm sorry, Mr. Sanders. I wish it were different. Please feel free to call me again if you have any further questions."

She hurried out of the office, leaving him sitting there. After a moment the assistant came in. "Can I do anything for you?"

"No," Sanders said, shaking his head slowly. "No, I was just leaving."

In the car, driving to the courthouse, Louise Fernandez recounted Sanders's story to the two junior lawyers traveling with her. One lawyer, a woman, said, "You don't really believe him?"

"Who knows?" Fernandez said. "It was behind closed doors. There's never a way to know."

The young woman shook her head. "I just can't believe a woman would act that way. So aggressively."

"Why not?" Fernandez said. "Suppose this wasn't a case of harassment. Suppose this was a question of implied promise between a man and a woman. The man claims that behind closed doors he was promised a big bonus, but the woman denies it. Would you assume that the man was lying because a woman wouldn't act that way?"

"Not about that, no."

"In that situation, you'd think that anything was possible."

"But this isn't a contract," the woman said. "This is sexual behavior."

"So you think women are unpredictable in their contractual arrangements, but stereotypical in their sexual arrangements?"

The woman said, "I don't know if *stereotypical* is the word I'd use."

"You just said that you can't believe a woman would act aggressively in sex. Isn't that a stereotype?"

"Well, no," The woman said. "It's not a stereotype, because it's true. Women are different from men when it comes to sex."

"And black people have rhythm," Fernandez said. "Asians are workaholics. And Hispanics don't confront . . ."

"But this is different. I mean, there are studies about this. Men and woman don't even talk to each other the same way."

"Oh, you mean like the studies that show that women are less good at business and strategic thinking?"

"No. Those studies are wrong."

"I see. Those studies are wrong. But the studies about sexual differences are right?"

"Well, sure. Because sex is fundamental. It's a primal drive."

"I don't see why. It's used for all sorts of purposes. As a way of relating, a way of placating, a way of provoking, as an offer, as a weapon, as a threat. It can be quite complicated, the ways sex is used. Haven't you found that to be true?"

The woman crossed her arms. "I don't think so."

Speaking for the first time, the young man said, "So what'd you tell this guy? Not to litigate?"

"No. But I told him his problems."

"What do you think he should do?"

"I don't know," Fernandez said. "But I know what he should have done."

"What?"

"It's terrible to say it," she said. "But in the real world? With no witnesses? Alone in the office with his boss? He probably should have shut up and fucked her. Because right now, that poor bastard has no options at all. If he's not careful, his life is over."

Sanders walked slowly back down the hill toward Pioneer Square. The rain had stopped, but the afternoon was still damp and gray. The wet pavement beneath his feet sloped steeply downward. Around him the tops of the skyscrapers disappeared into the low-hanging, chilly mist.

He was not sure what he had expected to hear from Louise Fernandez, but it was certainly not a detailed account of the possibility of his being fired, mortgaging his house, and never working again.

Sanders felt overwhelmed by the sudden turn that his life had taken, and by a realization of the precariousness of his existence. Two days ago, he was an established executive with a stable position and a promising future. Now he faced disgrace, humiliation, loss of his job. All sense of security had vanished.

He thought of all the questions Fernandez had asked him—questions that had never occurred to him before. Why hadn't he told anyone? Why hadn't he made notes? Why hadn't he told Meredith explicitly that her advances were unwelcome? Fernandez operated in a world of rules and distinctions that he did not understand, that had never crossed his mind. And now those distinctions turned out to be vitally important.

Your situation is not good, Mr. Sanders.

And yet . . . how could he have prevented this? What should he have done instead? He considered the possibilities.

Suppose he had called Blackburn right after the meeting with Meredith, and had told him in detail that Meredith had harassed him. He could have called from the ferry, lodged his complaint before she lodged hers. Would it have made a difference? What would Blackburn have done?

He shook his head, thinking about it. It seemed unlikely that anything would make a difference. Because in the end, Meredith was tied in to the power structure of the company in a way that Sanders was not. Meredith was a corporate player; she had power, allies. That was the message—the final message—of this situation. Sanders didn't count. He was just a technical guy, a cog in the corporate wheels. His job was to get along with his new boss, and he had failed to do that. Whatever he did now was just whining. Or worse: ratting on the boss. Whistle-blowing. And nobody liked a whistle-blower.

So what could he have done?

As he thought about it, he realized that he couldn't have called Blackburn right after the meeting because his cellular phone had gone dead, its power drained.

He had a sudden image of a car—*a man and a woman in a car, driving to a party.* Somebody had told him something once . . . a story about some people in a car.

It teased him. He couldn't quite get it.

There were plenty of reasons why the phone might be dead. The most likely explanation was nicad memory. The new phones used rechargeable nickel-cadmium batteries, and if they didn't completely discharge between uses, the batteries could reset themselves at a shorter duration. You never knew when it was going to show up. Sanders had had to throw out batteries before because they developed a short memory.

He took out his phone, turned it on. It glowed brightly. The battery was holding up fine today.

But there was something . . .

Driving in a car.

Something he wasn't thinking about.

Going to a party.

He frowned. He couldn't get it. It hung at the back of his memory, too dim to recover.

But it started him thinking: what else wasn't he getting? Because as he considered the whole situation, he began to have the nagging sense that there was something else that he was overlooking. And he had the feeling that Fernandez had overlooked it, too. Something hadn't come up in her questions to him. Something that everybody was taking for granted, even though—

Meredith.

Something about Meredith.

She had accused him of harassment. She had gone to Blackburn and accused him the next morning. Why would she do that? No doubt she felt guilty about what had happened at the meeting. And perhaps she was afraid Sanders would accuse her, so she decided to accuse him first. Her accusation was understandable in that light.

But if Meredith really had power, it didn't make sense to raise the sexual issue at all. She could just as easily have gone to Blackburn and said, Listen, it isn't working out with Tom. I can't deal with him. We have to make a change. And Blackburn would have done it.

Instead, she had accused him of harassment. And that must have been embarrassing to her. Because harassment implied a loss of control. It meant that she had not been able to control her subordinate in a meeting. Even if something unpleasant did happen, a boss would never mention it.

Harassment is about power.

It was one thing if you were a lowly female assistant fondled by a stronger, powerful man. But in this case Meredith was the boss. She had all the power. Why would she claim harassment by Sanders? Because the fact was, subordinates didn't harass their bosses. It just didn't happen. You'd have to be crazy to harass your boss.

Harassment is about power—the undue exercise of power by a superior over a subordinate.

For her to claim sexual harassment was, in an odd way, to admit that she was subordinate to Sanders. And she would never do that. Quite the contrary: Meredith was new to her job, eager to prove that she was in control of the situation. So her accusation made no sense—unless she was using it as a convenient way to destroy him. Sexual harassment had the advantage of being a charge that was difficult to recover from. You were presumed guilty until proven innocent—and it was hard to prove innocence. It tarnished any man, no matter how frivolous the accusation. In that sense, harassment was a very powerful accusation. The most powerful accusation she could make.

But then, she said that she wasn't going to press charges. And the question was—

Why not?

Sanders stopped on the street.

That was it.

She's assured me, she's not going to press charges.

Why wasn't Meredith going to press charges?

At the time that Blackburn said that, Sanders had never questioned it. Louise Fernandez had never questioned it. But the fact was, Meredith's refusal to press charges made no sense at all. She had already accused him. Why not press it? Why not carry it to its conclusion?

Maybe Blackburn had talked her out of it. Blackburn was always so concerned about appearances.

But Sanders didn't think that was what had happened. Because a formal accusation could still be handled quietly. It could be processed inside the company.

And from Meredith's standpoint, there were real advantages to a formal accusation. Sanders was popular at DigiCom. He had been with the company a long time. If her goal was to get rid of him, to banish him to Texas, why not defuse the inevitable corporate grumbling by letting the accusation work its way through the company grapevine? Why not make it official?

The more Sanders thought about it, the more it seemed that there was only one explanation: Meredith wasn't going to press charges because she couldn't.

She couldn't, because she had some other problem.

Some other consideration.

Something else was going on.

We can handle it quietly.

Slowly, Sanders began to see everything differently. In the meeting earlier that day, Blackburn hadn't been ignoring him or slighting him. Not at all: Blackburn was scrambling.

Blackburn was scared.

We can handle it quietly. It's best for everyone.

What did he mean, best for everyone?

What problem did Meredith have?

What problem *could* she have?

The more Sanders thought about it, the more it seemed that there could be only one possible reason why she wasn't pressing charges against him.

He took out his phone, called United Airlines, and booked three round-trip tickets to Phoenix.

And then he called his wife.

"You goddamn son of a bitch," Susan said.

They were sitting at a corner table at Il Terrazzo. It was two o'clock; the restaurant was nearly deserted. Susan had listened to him for half an hour, without interruption or comment. He told her everything that had happened in his meeting with Meredith, and everything that had happened that morning. The Conley-White meeting. The conversation with Phil. The conversation with Fernandez. Now he had finished. She stared at him.

"I could really learn to despise you, you know that? You son of a bitch, why didn't you tell me she was your ex-girlfriend?"

"I don't know," he said. "I didn't want to go into it."

"You didn't want to go into it? Adele and Mary Anne are talking to me on the phone all day, and they know, but I don't? It's humiliating, Tom."

"Well," he said, "you know you've been upset a lot lately, and—"

"Cut the crap, Tom," she said. "This has nothing to do with me. You didn't tell me because you didn't want to."

"Susan, that's not—"

"Yes it is, Tom. I was asking you about her, last night. You could have told me if you wanted to. But you didn't." She shook her head. "Son of a bitch. I can't believe what an asshole you are. You've made a real mess of this. Do you realize what a mess this is?"

"Yes," he said, hanging his head.

"Don't act contrite with me, you asshole."

"I'm sorry," he said.

"You're sorry? Fuck you, you're sorry. Jesus Christ. I can't believe you. What an asshole. You spent the night with your goddamned *girlfriend.*"

"I didn't spend the night. And she's not my girlfriend."

"What do you mean? She was your big heartthrob."

"She wasn't my 'big heartthrob.' "

"Oh yeah? Then why wouldn't you tell me?" She shook her head. "Just answer one question. Did you fuck her or not?"

"No. I didn't."

She stared at him intently, stirring her coffee. "You're telling me the truth?"

"Yes."

"Nothing left out? No inconvenient parts skipped?"

"No. Nothing."

"Then why would she accuse you?"

"What do you mean?" he said.

"I mean, there must be a reason she accused you. You must have done something."

"Well, I didn't. I turned her down."

"Uh-huh. Sure." She frowned at him. "You know, this is not just about you, Tom. This involves your whole family: me and the kids."

"I understand that."

"Why didn't you tell me? If you told me last night, I could have helped you."

"Then help me now."

"Well, there isn't much we can do now," Susan said, with heavy sarcasm. "Not after she's gone to Blackburn and made an accusation first. Now you're finished."

"I'm not so sure."

"Trust me, you haven't got a move," she said. "If you go to trial, it'll be living hell for at least three years, and I personally don't think you can win. You're a man bringing a charge of harassment against a woman. They'll laugh you out of court."

"Maybe."

"Trust me, they will. So you can't go to trial. What can you do? Move to Austin. Jesus."

"I keep thinking," Sanders said. "She accused me of harassment, but now she isn't pressing charges. And I keep thinking, Why isn't she pressing charges?"

"Who *cares*?" Susan said, with an irritable wave of the hand. "It could be any of a million reasons. Corporate politics. Or Phil talked her out of it. Or Garvin. It doesn't matter why. Tom, face the facts: *you have no move*. Not now, you stupid son of a bitch."

"Susan, will you settle down?"

"Fuck you, Tom. You're dishonest and irresponsible."

"Susan—"

"We've been married five years. I deserve better than this."

"Will you take it easy? I'm trying to tell you: I think I *do* have a move."

"Tom. You *don't*."

"I think I do. Because this is a very dangerous situation," Sanders said. "It's dangerous for everybody."

"What does that mean?"

"Let's assume that Louise Fernandez told me the truth about my lawsuit."

"She did. She's a good lawyer."

"But she wasn't looking at it from the company's standpoint. She was looking at it from the plaintiff's standpoint."

"Yeah, well, you're a plaintiff."

"No, I'm not," he said. "I'm a *potential* plaintiff."

There was a moment of silence.

Susan stared at him. Her eyes scanned his face. She frowned. He watched her put it together. "You're kidding."

"No."

"You must be out of your mind."

"No. Look at the situation. DigiCom's in the middle of a merger with a very conservative East Coast company. A company that's already pulled out of one merger because an employee had a little bad publicity. Supposedly this employee used some rough language while firing a temp secretary, and then Conley-White pulled out. They're very skittish about publicity. Which means the last thing anybody at DigiCom wants is a sexual harassment suit against the new female vice president."

"Tom. Do you realize what you're saying?"

"Yes," he said.

"If you do this, they're going to go *crazy*. They're going to try to destroy you."

"I know."

"Have you talked to Max about this? Maybe you should."

"The hell with Max. He's a crazy old man."

"I'd ask him. Because this isn't really your thing, Tom. You were never a corporate infighter. I don't know if you can pull this off."

"I think I can."

"It'll be nasty. In a day or so, you're going to wish you had taken the Austin job."

"Fuck it."

"It'll get really mean, Tom. You'll lose your friends."

"Fuck it."

"Just so you're ready."

"I am." Sanders looked at his watch. "Susan, I want you to take the kids and visit your mother for a few days." Her mother lived in Phoenix. "If you go home now and pack, you can make the eight o'clock flight at Sea-Tac. I've booked three seats for you."

She stared at him, as if she were seeing a stranger. "You're really going to do this . . . ," she said slowly.

"Yes. I am."

"Oh boy." She bent over, picked up her purse from the floor, and pulled out her day organizer.

He said, "I don't want you or the kids to be involved. I don't want anybody pushing a news camera in their faces, Susan."

"Well, just a minute . . ." She ran her finger down her appointments. "I can move that . . . And . . . conference call . . . Yes." She looked up. "Yes. I can leave for a few days." She glanced at her watch. "I guess I better hurry and pack."

He stood up and walked outside the restaurant with her. It was raining; the light on the street was gray and bleak. She looked up at him and kissed him on the cheek. "Good luck, Tom. Be careful."

He could see that she was frightened. It made him frightened, too.

"I'll be okay."

"I love you," she said. And then she walked quickly away in the rain. He waited for a moment to see if she looked back at him, but she never did.

Walking back to his office, he suddenly realized how alone he felt. Susan was leaving with the kids. He was on his own now. He had imagined he would feel relieved, free to act without restraint, but instead he felt abandoned and at risk. Chilled, he thrust his hands into the pockets of his raincoat.

He hadn't handled the lunch with Susan well. And she would be going off, mulling over his answers.

Why didn't you tell me?

He hadn't answered that well. He hadn't been able to express the conflicting feelings he had experienced last night. The unclean feeling, and the guilt, and the sense that he had somehow done something wrong, even though he hadn't done anything wrong.

You could have told me.

He hadn't done anything wrong, he told himself. But then why hadn't he told her? He had no answer to that. He passed a graphics shop, and a plumbing supply store with white porcelain fixtures in a window display.

You didn't tell me because you didn't want to.

But that made no sense. Why wouldn't he want to tell her? Once again, his thoughts were interrupted by images from the past: the white garter belt . . . a bowl of popcorn . . . the stained-glass flower on the door to his apartment.

Cut the crap, Tom. This has nothing to do with me.

Blood in the white bathroom sink, and Meredith laughing about it. Why was she laughing? He couldn't remember now; it was just an isolated image. A stewardess putting a tray of airline food in front of him. A suitcase on the bed. The television sound turned off. The stained-glass flower, in gaudy orange and purple.

Have you talked to Max?

She was right about that, he thought. He should talk to Max. And he would, right after he gave Blackburn the bad news.

Sanders was back at his office at two-thirty. He was surprised to find Blackburn there, standing behind Sanders's desk, talking on his phone. Blackburn hung up, looking a little guilty. "Oh, Tom. Good. I'm glad you're back." He walked back around Sanders's desk. "What have you decided?"

"I've thought this over very carefully," Sanders said, closing the door to the hallway.

"And?"

"I've decided to retain Louise Fernandez of Marin, Howard to represent me."

Blackburn looked puzzled. "To represent you?"

"Yes. In the event it becomes necessary to litigate."

"Litigate," Blackburn said. "On what basis would you litigate, Tom?"

"Sexual harassment under Title VII," Sanders said.

"Oh, Tom," Blackburn said, making a mournful face. "That would be unwise. That would be very unwise. I urge you to reconsider."

"I've reconsidered all day," Sanders said. "But the fact is, Meredith Johnson harassed me, she made advances to me and I turned her down. Now she's a woman scorned, and she is being vindictive toward me. I'm prepared to sue if it comes to that."

"Tom . . ."

"That's it, Phil. That's what'll happen if you transfer me out of the division."

Blackburn threw up his hands. "But what do you expect us to do? Transfer Meredith?"

"Yes," Sanders said. "Or fire her. That's the usual thing one does with a harassing supervisor."

"But you forget: she's accused you of harassment, too."

"She's lying," Sanders said.

"But there are no witnesses, Tom. No evidence either way. You and she are both our trusted employees. How do you expect us to decide who to believe?"

"That's your problem, Phil. All I have to say is, I'm innocent. And I'm prepared to sue."

Blackburn stood in the middle of the room, frowning. "Louise Fernandez is a smart attorney. I can't believe she recommended this course of action to you."

"No. This is my decision."

"Then it's very unwise," Blackburn said. "You are putting the company in a very difficult position."

"The company is putting me in a difficult position."

"I don't know what to say," Phil said. "I hope this doesn't force us to terminate you."

Sanders stared at him, meeting his gaze evenly. "I hope not, too," he said. "But I don't have confidence that the company has taken my complaint seriously. I'll fill out a formal charge of sexual harassment with Bill Everts in HRC later today. And I'm asking Louise to draw up the necessary papers to file with the state Human Rights Commission."

"Christ."

"She should file first thing tomorrow morning."

"I don't see what the rush is."

"There's no rush. It's just a filing. To get the complaint on record. I'm required to do that."

"But this is very serious, Tom."

"I know it, Phil."

"I'd like to ask you to do me a favor, as your friend."

"What's that?"

"Hold off the formal complaint. At least, with the HRC. Give us a chance to conduct an in-house investigation before you take this outside."

"But you aren't conducting an in-house investigation, Phil."

"Yes, we are."

"You didn't even want to hear my side of the story this morning. You told me it didn't matter."

"That's not true," Blackburn said. "You misunderstood me entirely. Of course it matters. And I assure you, we will hear your story in detail as part of our investigation."

"I don't know, Phil," Sanders said. "I don't see how the company can be neutral on this issue. It seems everything is stacked against me. Everybody believes Meredith and not me."

"I assure you that is not the case."

"It certainly seems like it. You told me this morning how well connected she is. How many allies she has. You mentioned that several times."

"Our investigation will be scrupulous and impartial. But in any case it seems reasonable to ask you to wait for the outcome before filing with a state agency."

"How long do you want me to wait?"

"Thirty days."

Sanders laughed.

"But that's the standard time for a harassment investigation."

"You could do it in a day, if you wanted to."

"But you must agree, Tom, that we're very busy right now, with all the merger meetings."

"That's your problem, Phil. I have a different problem. I've been unjustly treated by my superior, and I feel I have a right, as a long-standing senior employee, to see my complaint resolved promptly."

Blackburn sighed. "All right. Let me get back to you," he said. He hurried out of the room.

Sanders slumped in his chair and stared into space.

It had begun.

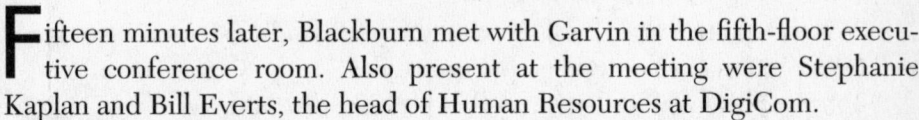

Fifteen minutes later, Blackburn met with Garvin in the fifth-floor executive conference room. Also present at the meeting were Stephanie Kaplan and Bill Everts, the head of Human Resources at DigiCom.

Blackburn began the meeting by saying, "Tom Sanders has retained outside counsel and is threatening litigation over Meredith Johnson."

"Oh, Christ," Garvin said.

"He's claiming sexual harassment."

Garvin kicked the leg of the table. "That son of a bitch."

Kaplan said, "What does he say happened?"

"I don't have all the details yet," Blackburn said. "But in essence he claims that Meredith made sexual overtures to him in her office last night, that he turned her down, and that now she is being vindictive."

Garvin gave a long sigh. "Shit," he said. "This is just what I didn't want to happen. This could be a *disaster*."

"I know, Bob."

Stephanie Kaplan said, "Did she do it?"

"Christ," Garvin said. "Who knows in these situations? That's always the question." He turned to Everts. "Has Sanders come to you about this?"

"Not yet, no. I imagine he will."

"We have to keep it in-house," Garvin said. "That's essential."

"Essential," Kaplan said, nodding. "Phil has to make sure it stays in-house."

"I'm trying," Blackburn said. "But Sanders is talking about filing tomorrow with the HRC."

"That's a public filing?"

"Yes."

"How soon is it made public?"

"Probably within forty-eight hours. Depending on how fast HRC does the paperwork."

"Christ," Garvin said. "Forty-eight hours? What's the matter with him? Doesn't he realize what he's doing?"

Blackburn said, "I think he does. I think he knows exactly."

"Blackmail?"

"Well. Pressure."

Garvin said, "Have you talked to Meredith?"

"Not since this morning."

"Somebody's got to talk to her. I'll talk to her. But how are we going to stop Sanders?"

Blackburn said, "I asked him to hold off the HRC filing, pending our investigation, for thirty days. He said no. He said we should be able to conduct our investigation in one day."

"Well, he got that right," Garvin said. "For all kinds of reasons, we damn well better conduct the investigation in one day."

"Bob, I don't know if that's possible," Blackburn said. "We have significant exposure here. The corporation is required by law to conduct a thorough and impartial investigation. We can't appear to be rushed or—"

"Oh, for Christ's sake," Garvin said. "I don't want to hear this legal pissing and moaning. What are we talking about? Two people, right? And no witnesses, right? So there's just two people. How long does it take to interview two people?"

"Well, it may not be that simple," Blackburn said, with a significant look.

"I'll tell you what's simple," Garvin said. "This is what's simple. Conley-White is a company obsessed with its public image. They sell textbooks to school boards that believe in Noah's ark. They sell magazines for kids. They have a vitamin company. They have a health-food company that markets baby foods. Rainbow Mush or something. Now Conley-White's buying our company, and in the middle of the acquisition a high-profile female executive, the woman in line to become CEO within two years, is accused of seeking sexual favors from a married man. You know what they're going to do if that gets out? They're going to *bail*. You know that Nichols is looking for any excuse to weasel out of this thing. This is perfect for him. Christ."

"But Sanders has already questioned our impartiality," Blackburn said. "And I'm not sure how many people know about the, ah, prior questions that we—"

"Quite a few," Kaplan said. "And didn't it come up at an officers' meeting last year?"

"Check the minutes," Garvin said. "We have no legal problem with current corporate officers, is that right?"

"That's right," Blackburn said. "Current corporate officers cannot be questioned or deposed on these matters."

"And we haven't lost any corporate officers in the last year? Nobody retired or moved?"

"No."

"Okay. So fuck him." Garvin turned to Everts. "Bill, I want you to go back through the HR records, and look carefully at Sanders. See if he's dotted every *i* and crossed every *t*. If he hasn't, I want to know."

"Right," Everts said. "But my guess is he's clean."

"All right," Garvin said, "let's assume that he is. What's it going to take to make Sanders go away? What does he want?"

Blackburn said, "I think he wants his job, Bob."

"He can't have his job."

"Well, that's the problem," Blackburn said.

Garvin snorted. "What's our liability, assuming he ever got to trial?"

"I don't think he has a case, based on what happened in that office. Our biggest liability would come from any perceived failure to respect due process and conduct a thorough investigation. Sanders could win on that alone, if we're not careful. That's my point."

"So we'll be careful. Fine."

"Now, guys," Blackburn said. "I feel strongly obliged to insert a note of caution. The extreme delicacy of this situation means that we have to be mindful of the details. As Pascal once said, 'God is in the details.' And in this case, the competing balance of legitimate legal claims forces me to admit it's unclear precisely what our best—"

"Phil," Garvin said. "Cut the crap."

Kaplan said, "Mies."

Blackburn said, "What?"

"Mies van der Rohe said, 'God is in the details.' "

"Who gives a shit?" Garvin said, pounding the table. "The point is, Sanders has no case—he just has us by the balls. And he knows it."

Blackburn winced. "I wouldn't phrase it exactly that way, but—"

"But that's the fucking situation."

"Yes."

Kaplan said, "Tom's smart, you know. A little naïve, but smart."

"Very smart," Garvin said. "Remember, I trained him. Taught him all he knows. He's going to be a big problem." He turned to Blackburn. "Get to the bottom line. What're we dealing with? Impartiality, right?"

"Yes . . ."

"And we want to move him out."

"Right."

"Okay. Will he accept mediation?"

"I don't know. I doubt it."

"Why not?"

"Ordinarily, we only use mediation to resolve settlement packages for employees who are leaving."

"So?"

"I think that's how he'll view it."

"Let's try, anyway. Tell him it's nonbinding, and see if we can get him to accept it on that basis. Give him three names and let him pick one. Mediate it tomorrow. Do I need to talk to him?"

"Probably. Let me try first, and you back up."

"Okay."

Kaplan said, "Of course, if we go to an outside mediator, we introduce an unpredictable element."

"You mean the mediator could find against us? I'll take the risk," Garvin said. "The important thing is to get the thing resolved. Quietly—and fast. I don't want Ed Nichols backpedaling on me. We have a press conference scheduled for Friday noon. I want this issue dead and buried by then, and I want Meredith Johnson announced as the new head of the division on Friday. Everybody clear on what's going to happen?"

They said they were.

"Then do it," Garvin said, and walked out of the room. Blackburn hurried after him.

In the hallway outside, Garvin said to Blackburn, "Christ, what a mess. Let me tell you. I'm very unhappy."

"I know," Blackburn said mournfully. He was shaking his head sadly.

"You really screwed the pooch on this one, Phil. Christ. You could have handled this one better. A *lot* better."

"How? What could I have done? He says that she hustled him, Bob. It's a serious matter."

"Meredith Johnson is vital to the success of this merger," Garvin said flatly.

"Yes, Bob. Of course."

"We must keep her."

"Yes, Bob. But we both know that in the past she has—"

"She has proven herself an outstanding piece of executive talent," Garvin said, interrupting him. "I won't allow these ridiculous allegations to jeopardize her career."

Blackburn was aware of Garvin's unswerving support of Meredith. For years, Garvin had had a blind spot for Johnson. Whenever criticisms of Johnson arose, Garvin would somehow change the subject, shift to something else. There was no reasoning with him. But now Blackburn felt he had to try. "Bob," he said. "Meredith's only human. We know she has her limitations."

"Yes," Garvin said. "She has youth. Enthusiasm. Honesty. Unwillingness to play corporate games. And of course, she's a woman. That's a real limitation, being a woman."

"But Bob—"

"I tell you, I can't stomach the excuses anymore," Garvin said. "We don't have women in high corporate positions here. Nobody does. Corporate America is rooms full of men. And whenever I talk about putting a woman in, there's always a 'But Bob' that comes up. The hell with it, Phil. We've got to break the glass ceiling sometime."

Blackburn sighed. Garvin was shifting the subject again. He said, "Bob, nobody's disagreeing with—"

"Yes, they are. You're disagreeing, Phil. You're giving me excuses why Meredith isn't suitable. And I'm telling you that if I had named some other woman, there'd be other excuses why that other woman isn't suitable. And I tell you, I'm tired of it."

Blackburn said, "We've got Stephanie. We've got Mary Anne."

"Tokens," Garvin said, with a dismissing wave. "Sure, let the CFO be a woman. Let a couple of the midrange execs be women. Throw the broads a bone. The fact remains. You can't tell me that a bright, able young woman starting out in business isn't held back by a hundred little *reasons*, oh such good *reasons*, why she shouldn't be advanced, why she shouldn't attain a major position of power. But in the end, it's just prejudice. And it has to stop. We have to give these bright young women a decent opportunity."

Blackburn said, "Well, Bob. I just think it would be prudent for you to get Meredith's view of this situation."

"I will. I'll find out what the hell happened. I know she'll tell me. But this thing still has to be resolved."

"Yes, it does, Bob."

"And I want you to be clear. I expect you to do whatever is necessary to get it resolved."

"Okay, Bob."

"*Whatever* is necessary," Garvin said. "Put the pressure on Sanders. Make sure he feels it. Rattle his cage, Phil."

"Okay, Bob."

"I'll deal with Meredith. You just take care of Sanders. I want you to rattle his fucking cage until he's black and blue."

Bob." Meredith Johnson stood at one of the center tables in the Design Group laboratory, going over the torn-apart Twinkle drives with Mark Lewyn. She came over when she saw Garvin standing to one side. "I can't tell you how sorry I am about all this business with Sanders."

"We're having some problems with it," Garvin said.

"I keep going over what happened," she said. "Wondering what I should have done. But he was angry and out of control. He had too much to drink, and he behaved badly. Not that we all haven't done that at some time in our lives, but . . ." She shrugged. "Anyway, I'm sorry."

"Apparently, he's going to file a harassment charge."

"That's unfortunate," she said. "But I suppose it's part of the pattern—trying to humiliate me, to discredit me with the people in the division."

"I won't let that happen," Garvin said.

"He resented my getting the job, and he couldn't deal with having me as his superior. He had to try and put me in my place. Some men are like that." She shook her head sadly. "For all the talk about the new male sensibility, I'm afraid very few men are like you, Bob."

Garvin said, "My concern now, Meredith, is that his filing may interfere with the acquisition."

"I can't see why that would be a problem," she said. "I think we can keep it under control."

"It's a problem, if he files with the state HRC."

"You mean he's going to go *outside*?" she asked.

"Yes. That's exactly what I mean."

Meredith stared off into space. For the first time, she seemed to lose her composure. She bit her lip. "That could be very awkward."

"I'll say. I've sent Phil to see him, to ask if we can mediate. With an experienced outside person. Someone like Judge Murphy. I'm trying to arrange it for tomorrow."

"Fine," Meredith said. "I can clear my schedule for a couple of hours tomorrow. But I don't know what we can expect to come out of it. He won't admit what happened, I'm sure. And there isn't any record, or any witnesses."

"I wanted you to fill me in," Garvin said, "on exactly what did happen, last night."

"Oh, Bob," she sighed. "I blame myself, every time I go over it."

"You shouldn't."

"I know, but I do. If my assistant hadn't gone off to rent her apartment, I could have buzzed her in, and none of this would have happened."

"I think you better tell me, Meredith."

"Of course, Bob." She leaned toward him and spoke quietly, steadily, for the next several minutes. Garvin stood beside her, shaking his head angrily as he listened.

Don Cherry put his Nikes up on Lewyn's desk. "Yeah? So Garvin came in. Then what happened?"

"So Garvin's standing over there in the corner, hopping up and down from one foot to the other, the way he does. Waiting to be noticed. He won't come over, he's waiting to be noticed. And Meredith's talking to me about the Twinkle drive that I have spread all over the table, and I'm showing her what we've found is wrong with the laser heads—"

"She gets all that?"

"Yeah, she seems okay. She's not Sanders, but she's okay. Fast learner."

"And better perfume than Sanders," Cherry said.

"Yeah, I like her perfume," Lewyn said. "Anyway—"

"Sanders's perfume leaves a lot to be desired."

"Yeah. Anyway, pretty soon Garvin gets tired of hopping, and he gives a discreet little cough, and Meredith notices Garvin and she goes 'Oh,' with a little thrill in her voice, you know that little sharp intake of breath."

"Uh-oh," Cherry said. "Are we talking humparoonie here or what?"

"Well, that's the *thing*," Lewyn said. "She goes running over to him, and he holds out his arms to her, and I tell you it looks like that ad where the two lovers run toward each other in slow motion."

"Uh-oh," Cherry said. "Garvin's wife is going to be pissed."

"But that's the thing," Lewyn said. "When they finally get together, standing there side by side, it isn't that way at all. They're talking, and she's sort of cooing and batting her eyes at him, and he's such a tough guy he doesn't acknowledge it, but it's working on him."

"She's seriously cute, that's why," Cherry said. "I mean face it, she's got an outstanding molded case, with superior fit and finish."

"But the thing is, it's not like lovers at all. I'm staring, trying not to stare, and I tell you, it's not lovers. It's something else. It's almost like father-daughter, Don."

"Hey. You can fuck your daughter. Millions do."

"No, you know what I think? I think Bob sees himself in her. He sees something that reminds him of himself when he was younger. Some kind of energy or something. And I tell you, she plays it, Don. He crosses his arms, she crosses hers. He leans against the wall, she leans against the wall. She matches him exactly. And from a distance, I'm telling you: *she looks like him,* Don."

"No . . ."

"Yes. Think about it."

"It'd have to be from a *very* long distance," Cherry said. He took his feet off the table, and got up to leave. "So what're we saying here? Nepotism in disguise?"

"I don't know. But Meredith's got some kind of rapport with him. It isn't pure business."

"Hey," Cherry said. "Nothing's pure business. I learned that one a long time ago."

Louise Fernandez came into her office, and dropped her briefcase on the floor. She thumbed through a stack of phone messages and turned to Sanders. "What's going on? I have three calls this afternoon from Phil Blackburn."

"That's because I told him I had retained you as my attorney, that I was prepared to litigate my claim. And I, uh, suggested that you were filing with the HRC in the morning."

"I couldn't possibly file tomorrow," she said. "And I wouldn't recommend that we do so now, in any event. Mr. Sanders, I take false statements very seriously. Don't ever characterize my actions again."

"I'm sorry," he said. "But things are happening very fast."

"Just so we are clear. I don't like it, and if it happens again, you'll be looking for new counsel." That coldness again, the sudden coldness. "Now. So you told Blackburn. What was his response?"

"He asked me if I would mediate."

"Absolutely not," Fernandez said.

"Why not?"

"Mediation is invariably to the benefit of the company."

"He said it would be nonbinding."

"Even so. It amounts to free discovery on their part. There's no reason to give it to them."

"And he said you could be present," he said.

"Of course I can be present, Mr. Sanders. That's no concession. You must have an attorney present at all times or the mediation will be invalid."

"Here are the three names he gave me, as possible mediators." Sanders passed her the list.

She glanced at it briefly. "The usual suspects. One of them is better than the other two. But I still don't—"

"He wants to do the mediation tomorrow."

"Tomorrow?" Fernandez stared at him, and sat back in her chair. "Mr. Sanders, I'm all for a timely resolution, but this is ridiculous. We can't be ready by tomorrow. And as I said, I don't recommend that you agree to mediate under any circumstances. Is there something here I don't know?"

"Yes," he said.

"Let's have it."

He hesitated.

She said, "Any communication you make to me is privileged and confidential."

"All right. DigiCom is about to be acquired by a New York company called Conley-White."

"So the rumors are true."

"Yes," he said. "They intend to announce the merger at a press conference on Friday. And they intend to announce Meredith Johnson as the new vice president of the company, on Friday."

"I see," she said. "So that's Phil's urgency."

"Yes."

"And your complaint presents an immediate and serious problem for him."

He nodded. "Let's say it comes at a very sensitive time."

She was silent for a moment, peering at him over her reading glasses. "Mr. Sanders, I misjudged you. I had the impression you were a timid man."

"They're forcing me to do this."

"Are they." She gave him an appraising look. Then she pushed the intercom button. "Bob, let me see my calendar. I have to clear some things. And ask Herb and Alan to come in. Tell them to drop whatever they're doing. This is more important." She pushed the papers aside. "Are all the mediators on this list available?"

"I assume so."

"I'm going to request Barbara Murphy. Judge Murphy. You won't like her, but she'll do a better job than the others. I'll try and set it up for the afternoon if I can. We need the time. Otherwise, late morning. You realize the risk you're taking? I assume you do. This is a very dangerous game you've decided to play." She pushed the intercom. "Bob? Cancel Roger Rosenberg. Cancel Ellen at six. Remind me to call my husband and tell him I won't be home for dinner." She looked at Sanders. "Neither will you. Do you need to call home?"

"My wife and kids are leaving town tonight."

She raised her eyebrows. "You told her everything?"

"Yes."

"You *are* serious."

"Yes," he said. "I'm serious."

"Good," she said. "You're going to need to be. Let's be frank, Mr. Sanders. What you have embarked upon is not strictly a legal procedure. In essence, you're playing the pressure points."

"That's right."

"Between now and Friday, you're in a position to exert considerable pressure on your company."

"That's right."

"And they on you, Mr. Sanders. They on you."

He found himself in a conference room, facing five people, all taking notes. Seated on either side of Fernandez were two young lawyers, a woman named Eileen and a man named Richard. Then there were two investigators, Alan and Herb: one tall and handsome; the other chubby, with a pockmarked face and a camera hanging around his neck.

Fernandez made Sanders go over his story again, in greater detail. She paused frequently to ask questions, noting down times, names, and specific details. The two lawyers never said anything, although Sanders had the strong impression that the young woman was unsympathetic to him. The two investigators were also silent, except at specific points. After Sanders mentioned Meredith's assistant, Alan, the handsome one, said, "Her name again?"

"Betsy Ross. Like in the flag."

"She's on the fifth floor?"

"Yes."

"What time does she go home?"

"Last night, she left at six-fifteen."

"I may want to meet her casually. Can I go up to the fifth floor?"

"No. All visitors are stopped at reception in the downstairs lobby."

"What if I'm delivering a package? Would Betsy take delivery of a package?"

"No. Packages go to central receiving."

"Okay. What about flowers? Would they be delivered directly?"

"Yes, I guess so. You mean, like flowers for Meredith?"

"Yes," Alan said.

"I guess you could deliver those in person."

"Fine," Alan said, and made a note.

They stopped him a second time when he mentioned the cleaning woman he had seen on leaving Meredith's office.

"DigiCom uses a cleaning service?"

"Yes. AMS—American Management Services. They're over on—"

"We know them. On Boyle. What time do the cleaning crews enter the building?"

"Usually around seven."

"And this woman you didn't recognize. Describe her."

"About forty. Black. Very slender, gray hair, sort of curly."

"Tall? Short? What?"

He shrugged. "Medium."

Herb said, "That's not much. Can you give us anything else?"

Sanders hesitated. He thought about it. "No. I didn't really see her."

"Close your eyes," Fernandez said.

He closed them.

"Now take a deep breath, and put yourself back. It's yesterday evening. You have been in Meredith's office, the door has been closed for almost an hour, you have had your experience with her, now you are leaving the room, you are going out . . . How does the door open, in or out?"

"It opens in."

"So you pull the door open. . . . you walk out . . . Fast or slow?"

"I'm walking fast."

"And you go into the outer room . . . What do you see?"

Through the door. Into the outer room, elevators directly ahead. Feeling disheveled, off balance, hoping there is no one to see him. Looking to the right at Betsy Ross's desk: clean, bare, chair pulled up to the edge of the desk. Notepad. Plastic cover on the computer. Desk light still burning.

Eyes swinging left, a cleaning woman at the other assistant's desk. Her big gray cleaning cart stands alongside her. The cleaning woman is lifting a trash basket to empty it into the plastic sack that hangs open from one end of the cart. The woman pauses in mid-lift, stares at him curiously. He is wondering how long she has been there, what she has heard from inside the room. A tinny radio on the cart is playing music.

"I'll fucking kill you for this!" Meredith calls after him.

The cleaning woman hears it. He looks away from her, embarrassed, and hurries toward the elevator. Feeling almost panic. He pushes the button.

"Do you see the woman?" Fernandez said.

"Yes. But it was so fast . . . And I didn't want to look at her." Sanders shook his head.

"Where are you now? At the elevator?"

"Yes."

"Can you see the woman?"

"No. I didn't want to look at her again."

"All right. Let's go back. No, no, keep your eyes closed. We'll do it again. Take a deep breath, and let it out slowly . . . Good . . . This time you're going to see everything in slow motion, like a movie. Now . . . come out through the door . . . and tell me when you see her for the first time."

Coming through the door. Everything slow. His head moving gently up and down with each footstep. Into the outer room. The desk to the right, tidy, lamp on. To the left, the other desk, the cleaning woman raising the—

"I see her."

"All right, now freeze what you see. Freeze it like a photograph."

"Okay."

"Now look at her. You can look at her now."

Standing with the trash basket in her hand. Staring at him, a bland expression. She's about forty. Short hair, curls, blue uniform, like a hotel maid. A silver chain around her neck—no, hanging eyeglasses.

"She wears glasses around her neck, on a metal chain."

"Good. Just take your time. There's no rush. Look her up and down."

"I keep seeing her face . . ." *Staring at him. A bland expression.*

"Look away from her face. Look her up and down."

The uniform. Spray bottle clipped to her waist. Knee-length blue skirt. White shoes. Like a nurse. No. Sneakers. No. Thicker—running shoes. Thick soles. Dark laces. Something about the laces.

"She's got . . . sort of running shoes. Little old lady running shoes."

"Good."

"There's something funny about the laces."

"Can you see what's funny?"

"No. They're dark. Something funny. I . . . can't tell."

"All right. Open your eyes."

He looked at the five of them. He was back in the room. "That was weird," he said.

"If there was time," Fernandez said, "I would have a professional hypnotist take you through the entire evening. I've found it can be very useful. But there's no time. Boys? It's five o'clock. You better get started."

The two investigators collected their notes and left.

"What are they going to do?"

"If we were litigating this," Fernandez said, "we would have the right to depose potential witnesses—to question individuals within the company who might have knowledge bearing on the case. Under the present circumstances, we have no right to interrogate anybody, because you're entering into private mediation. But if one of the DigiCom assistants chooses to have a drink with a handsome delivery man after work, and if the conversation happens to turn to gossip about sex in the office, well, that's the way the cookie crumbles."

"We can use that information?"

Fernandez smiled. "Let's see what we find out first," she said. "Now, I want to go back over several points in your story, particularly starting at the time you decided not to have intercourse with Ms. Johnson."

"Again?"

"Yes. But I have a few things to do first. I need to call Phil Blackburn and arrange tomorrow's sessions. And I have some other things to check on. Let's break now and meet again in two hours. Meanwhile, have you cleaned out your office?"

"No," he said.

"You better clean it out. Anything personal or incriminating, get it out. From now on, expect your desk drawers to be gone through, your files to be searched, your mail to be read, your phone messages checked. Every aspect of your life is now public."

"Okay."

"So, go through your desk and your files. Remove anything of a personal nature."

"Okay."

"On your office computer, if you have any passwords, change them. Anything in electronic data files of a personal nature, get it out."

"Okay."

"Don't just remove it. Make sure you erase it, so it's unrecoverable."

"Okay."

"It's not a bad idea to do the same thing at home. Your drawers and files and computer."

"Okay." He was thinking: at home? Would they really break into his home?

"If you have any sensitive materials that you want to store, bring them to Richard here," she said, pointing to the young lawyer. "He'll have them taken to a safe-deposit box where they'll be kept for you. Don't tell me. I don't want to know anything about it."

"Okay."

"Now. Let's discuss the telephone. From now on, if you have any sensitive calls to make, don't use your office phone, your cellular phone, or your phone at home. Use a pay phone, and don't put it on a charge card, even your personal charge card. Get a roll of quarters and use them instead."

"You really think this is necessary?"

"I know it is necessary. Now. Is there anything in your past conduct with this company which might be said to be out of order?" She was peering at him over her glasses.

He shrugged. "I don't think so."

"Anything at all? Did you overstate your qualifications on your original job application? Did you abruptly terminate any employee? Have you had any kind of inquiry about your behavior or decisions? Were you ever the subject of an internal company investigation? And even if you weren't, did you ever, to your knowledge, do anything improper, however small or apparently minor?"

"Jesus," he said. "It's been twelve years."

"While you are cleaning out, think about it. I need to know anything that the company might drag up about you. Because if they can, they will."

"Okay."

"And one other point. I gather from what you've told me that nobody at your company is entirely clear why Johnson has enjoyed such a rapid rise among the executives."

"That's right."

"Find out."

"It won't be easy," Sanders said. "Everybody's talking about it, and nobody seems to know."

"But for everybody else," Fernandez said, "it's just gossip. For you, it's vital. We need to know where her connections are and why they exist. If we know that, we have a chance of pulling this thing off. But if we don't, Mr. Sanders, they're probably going to tear us apart."

He was back at DigiCom at six. Cindy was cleaning up her desk and was about to leave.

"Any calls?" he said, as he went into his office.

"Just one," she said. Her voice was tight.

"Who was that?"

"John Levin. He said it was important." Levin was an executive with a hard drive supplier. Whatever Levin wanted, it could wait.

Sanders looked at Cindy. She seemed tense, almost on the verge of tears.

"Something wrong?"

"No. Just a long day." A shrug: elaborate indifference.

"Anything I should know about?"

"No. It's been quiet. You didn't have any other calls." She hesitated. "Tom, I just want you to know, I don't believe what they are saying."

"What are they saying?" he asked.

"About Meredith Johnson."

"What about her?"

"That you sexually harassed her."

She blurted it out, and then waited. Watching him, her eyes moving across his face. He could see her uncertainty. Sanders felt uneasy in turn that this woman he had worked alongside for so many years would now be so openly unsure of him.

He said firmly, "It's not true, Cindy."

"Okay. I didn't think it was. It's just that everybody is—"

"There's no truth to it at all."

"Okay. Good." She nodded, put the call book in the desk drawer. She seemed eager to leave. "Did you need me to stay?"

"No."

"Good night, Tom."

"Good night, Cindy."

He went into his office and closed the door behind him. He sat behind his desk and looked at it a moment. Nothing seemed to have been touched. He flicked on his monitor, and began going through the drawers, rummaging through, trying to decide what to take out. He glanced up at the monitor, and saw that his E-mail icon was blinking. Idly, he clicked it on.

NUMBER OF PERSONAL MESSAGES: 3. DO YOU WANT TO READ THEM NOW?

He pressed the key. A moment later, the first message came up:

SEALED TWINKLE DRIVES ARE ON THEIR WAY TO YOU TODAY DHL. YOU SHOULD HAVE THEM TOMORROW. HOPE YOU FIND SOMETHING ... JAFAR IS STILL SEVERELY ILL. THEY SAY HE MAY DIE.

ARTHUR KAHN

He pressed the key, and another message came up:

THE WEENIES ARE STILL SWARMING DOWN HERE. ANY NEWS
YET?

EDDIE

Sanders couldn't worry about Eddie now. He pushed the key, and the
third message came up.

I GUESS YOU HAVEN'T BEEN READING BACK ISSUES OF COMLINE.
STARTING FOUR YEARS AGO.

AFRIEND

Sanders stared at the screen. ComLine was DigiCom's in-house
newsletter—an eight-page monthly, filled with chatty accounts of hiring and
promotions and babies born. The summer schedule for the softball team,
things like that. Sanders never paid any attention to it and couldn't imagine
why he should now.
And who was "Afriend?"
He clicked the REPLY button on the screen.

CAN'T REPLY—SENDER ADDRESS NOT AVAILABLE

He clicked the SENDER INFO button. It should give him the name and
address of the person sending the E-mail message. But instead he saw
dense rows of type:

FROM UU5.PSI.COM!UWA.PCM.COM. EDU!CHARON TUE JUN 16
04:43:31 REMOTE FROM DCCSYS
RECEIVED: FROM UUPS15 BY DCCSYS.DCC.COM ID AA02599; TUE,
16 JUN 4:42:19 PST
RECEIVED: FROM   UWA.PCM.COM.EDU   BY   UU5.PSI.COM
(5.65B/4.0.071791-PSI/PSINET)

ID AA28153; TUE, 16 JUN 04:24:58 -0500
RECEIVED: FROM RIVERSTYX.PCM.COM.EDU BY UWA.PCM.
COM.EDU (4.1/SMI-4.1)
ID AA15969; TUE, 16 JUN 04:24:56 PST
RECEIVED: BY RIVERSTYX.PCM.COM.EDU (920330.SGI/5.6)
ID AA00448; TUE, 16 JUN 04:24:56 -0500
DATE: TUE, 16 JUN 04:24:56 -0500
FROM: CHARON@UWA.PCM.COM.EDU
(AFRIEND)
MESSAGE-ID: <9212220924.AA90448@RIVERSTYX.PCM.
COM.EDU>
TO: TSANDERS@DCC.COM

Sanders stared. The message hadn't come to him from inside the company at all. He was looking at an Internet routing. Internet was the vast worldwide computer network connecting universities, corporations, government agencies, and private users. Sanders wasn't knowledgeable about the Internet, but it appeared that the message from "Afriend," network name CHARON, had originated from UWA.PCM.COM.EDU, wherever that was. Apparently some kind of educational institution. He pushed the PRINT SCREEN button, and made a mental note to turn this one over to Bosak. He needed to talk to Bosak anyway.

He went down the hall and got the sheet as it came out of the printer. Then he went back to his office and stared at the screen. He decided to try a reply to this person.

FROM: TSANDERS@DCC.COM
TO: CHARON@UWA.PCM.COM.EDU
ANY HELP GREATLY APPRECIATED.

SANDERS

He pushed the SEND button. Then he deleted both the original message and his own reply.

SORRY, YOU CANNOT DELETE THIS MAIL.

Sometimes E-mail was protected with a flag that prevented it from being deleted.

He typed: UNPROTECT MAIL.

THE MAIL IS UNPROTECTED.

He typed: DELETE MAIL.

SORRY, YOU CANNOT DELETE THIS MAIL.

What the hell is this? he thought. The system must be hanging up. Maybe it had been stymied by the Internet address. He decided to delete the message from the system at the control level.

He typed: SYSTEM.

WHAT LEVEL?

He typed: SYSOP.

SORRY, YOUR PRIVILEGES DO NOT INCLUDE SYSOP CON-TROL.

"Christ," he said. They'd gone in and taken away his privileges. He couldn't believe it.

He typed: SHOW PRIVILEGES.

SANDERS, THOMAS L.
PRIOR USER LEVEL: 5 (SYSOP)
USER LEVEL CHANGE: TUE JUNE 16 4:50 PM PST
CURRENT USER LEVEL: 0 (ENTRY)
NO FURTHER MODIFICATIONS

There it was: they had locked him out of the system. User level zero was the level that assistants in the company were given.

Sanders slumped back in the chair. He felt as if he had been fired. For the first time, he began to realize what this was going to be like.

Clearly, there was no time to waste. He opened his desk drawer, and saw at once that the pens and pencils were neatly arranged. Someone had already been there. He pulled open the file drawer below. Only a half-dozen files were there; the others were all missing.

They had already gone through his desk.

Quickly, he got up and went out to the big filing cabinets behind Cindy's desk. These cabinets were locked, but he knew Cindy kept the key in her desk. He found the key, and unlocked the current year's files.

The cabinet was empty. There were no files there at all. They had taken everything.

He opened the cabinet for the previous year: empty.

The year before: empty.

All the others: empty.

Jesus, he thought. No wonder Cindy had been so cool. They must have had a gang of workmen up there with trolleys, cleaning everything out during the afternoon.

Sanders locked the cabinets again, replaced the key in Cindy's desk, and headed downstairs.

The press office was on the third floor. It was deserted now except for a single assistant, who was closing up. "Oh. Mr. Sanders. I was just getting ready to leave."

"You don't have to stay. I just wanted to check some things. Where do you keep the back issues of ComLine?"

"They're all on that shelf over there." She pointed to a row of stacked issues. "Was there anything in particular?"

"No. You go ahead home."

The assistant seemed reluctant, but she picked up her purse and headed out the door. Sanders went to the shelf. The issues were arranged in six-month stacks. Just to be safe, he started ten stacks back—five years ago.

He began flipping through the pages, scanning the endless details of game scores and press releases on production figures. After a few minutes, he found it hard to pay attention. And of course he didn't know what he was looking for, although he assumed it was something about Meredith Johnson. He went through two stacks before he found the first article.

NEW MARKETING ASSISTANT NAMED

Cupertino, May 10: DigiCom President Bob Garvin today announced the appointment of Meredith Johnson as Assistant Director of Marketing and Promotion for Telecommunications. She will report to Howard Gottfried in M and P. Ms. Johnson, 30, came to us from her position as Vice President for Marketing at Conrad Computer Systems of Sunnyvale. Before that, she was a senior administrative assistant at the Novell Network Division in Mountain View.

Ms. Johnson, who has degrees from Vassar College and Stanford Business School, was recently married to Gary Henley, a marketing executive at CoStar. Congratulations! As a new arrival to DigiCom, Ms. Johnson . . .

He skipped the rest of the article; it was all PR fluff. The accompanying photo was standard B-school graduate: against a gray background with light coming from behind one shoulder, it showed a young woman with shoulder-length hair in a pageboy style, a direct businesslike stare just shy of harsh, and a firm mouth. But she looked considerably younger than she did now.

Sanders continued to thumb through the issues. He glanced at his watch. It was almost seven, and he wanted to call Bosak. He came to the end of the year, and the pages were nothing but Christmas stuff. A picture of Garvin and his family ("Merry Christmas from the Boss! Ho Ho Ho!") caught his attention because it showed Bob with his former wife, along with his three college-age kids, standing around a big tree.

Had Garvin been going out with Emily yet? Nobody ever knew. Garvin was cagey. You never knew what he was up to.

Sanders went to the next stack, for the following year. January sales predictions. ("Let's get out and make it happen!") Opening of the Austin plant to manufacture cellular phones; a photo of Garvin in harsh sunlight, cutting the ribbon. A profile of Mary Anne Hunter that began, "Spunky, athletic Mary Anne Hunter knows what she wants out of life . . ." They had called her "Spunky" for weeks afterward, until she begged them to give it up.

Sanders flipped pages. Contract with the Irish government to break ground in Cork. Second-quarter sales figures. Basketball team scores against Aldus. Then a black box:

JENNIFER GARVIN

Jennifer Garvin, a third-year student at Boalt Hall School of Law in Berkeley, died on March 5 in an automobile accident in San Francisco. She was twenty-four years old. Jennifer had been accepted to the firm of Harley, Wayne and Myers following her graduation. A memorial service was held at the Presbyterian Church of Palo Alto for friends of the family and her many classmates. Those wishing to make memorial donations should send contributions to Mothers Against Drunk Drivers. All of us at Digital Communications extend our deepest sympathy to the Garvin family.

Sanders remembered that time as difficult for everyone. Garvin was snappish and withdrawn, drinking too much, and frequently absent from work. Not long afterward, his marital difficulties became public; within two years, he was divorced, and soon after that he married Emily Chen, a young executive in her twenties. But there were other changes, too. Everyone agreed: Garvin was no longer the same boss after the death of his daughter.

Garvin had always been a scrapper, but now he became protective, less ruthless. Some said that Garvin was stopping to smell the roses, but that wasn't it at all. He was newly aware of the arbitrariness of life, and it led him to control things, in a way that hadn't been true before. Garvin had always been Mr. Evolution: put it on the shore and see if it eats or dies. It made him a heartless administrator but a remarkably fair boss. If you did a good job, you were recognized. If you couldn't cut it, you were gone. Everybody understood the rules. But after Jennifer died, all that changed. Now he had overt favorites among staff and programs, and he nurtured those favorites and neglected others, despite the evidence in front of his face. More and more, he made business decisions arbitrarily. Garvin wanted events to turn out the way he intended them to. It gave him a new kind of fervor, a new sense of what the company should be. But it was also a more difficult place to work. A more political place.

It was a trend that Sanders had ignored. He continued to act as if he still worked at the old DigiCom—the company where all that mattered were results. But clearly, that company was gone.

Sanders continued thumbing through the magazines. Articles about early negotiations for a plant in Malaysia. A photo of Phil Blackburn in Ireland, signing an agreement with the city of Cork. New production figures for the Austin plant. Start of production of the A22 cellular model. Births and deaths and promotions. More DigiCom baseball scores.

JOHNSON TO TAKE OPERATIONS POST

Cupertino, October 20: Meredith Johnson has been named new Assistant Manager for Division Operations in Cupertino, replacing the very popular Harry Warner, who retired after fifteen years of service. The shift to Ops Manager takes Johnson out of marketing, where she has been very effective for the last year, since joining the company. In her new position, she will work closely with Bob Garvin on international operations for DigiCom.

But it was the accompanying picture that caught Sanders's attention. Once again, it was a formal head shot, but Johnson now looked completely different. Her hair was light blond. Gone was the neat business-school pageboy. She wore her hair short, in a curly, informal style. She was wearing much less makeup and smiling cheerfully. Overall, the effect was to make her appear much more youthful, open, innocent.

Sanders frowned. Quickly, he flipped back through the issues he had already looked at. Then he went back to the previous stack, with its year-end Christmas pictures: "Merry Christmas from the Boss! Ho Ho Ho!"

He looked at the family portrait. Garvin standing behind his three children, two sons and a daughter. That must be Jennifer. His wife, Harriet, stood to one side. In the picture, Garvin was smiling, his hand resting lightly on his daughter's shoulder, and she was tall and athletic-looking, with short, light blond, curly hair.

"I'll be damned," he said aloud.

He thumbed back quickly to the first article, to look at the original picture of Johnson. He compared it to the later one. There was no doubt about what she had done. He read the rest of the first article:

> As a new arrival to DigiCom, Ms. Johnson brings her considerable business acumen, her sparkling humor, and her sizzling softball pitch. She's a major addition to the DigiCom team! Welcome, Meredith!
>
> Her admiring friends are never surprised to learn that Meredith was once a finalist in the Miss Teen Connecticut contest. In her student days at Vassar, Meredith was a valued member of both the tennis team and the debating society. A member of Phi Beta Kappa, she took her major in psychology, with a minor in abnormal psych. Hope you won't be needing that around here, Meredith! At Stanford, she obtained her MBA with honors, graduating near the top of her class. Meredith told us, "I am delighted to join DigiCom and I look forward to an exciting career with this forward-looking company." We couldn't have said it better, Ms. Johnson!

"No shit," Sanders said. He had known almost none of this. From the start, Meredith had been based in Cupertino; Sanders never saw her. The one time he had run into her was soon after her arrival, before she changed her hair. Her hair—and what else?

He looked carefully at the two pictures. Something else was subtly different. Had she had plastic surgery? It was impossible to know. But her appearance was definitely changed between the two portraits.

He moved through the remaining issues of the magazine quickly now, convinced that he had learned what there was to know. Now he skimmed only the headlines:

**GARVIN SENDS JOHNSON TO TEXAS
FOR AUSTIN PLANT OVERSIGHT**

**JOHNSON WILL HEAD NEW
OPERATIONS REVIEW UNIT**

**JOHNSON NAMED OPERATOR VEEP
TO WORK DIRECTLY UNDER GARVIN**

**JOHNSON: TRIUMPH IN MALAYSIA
LABOR CONFLICT NOW RESOLVED**

**MEREDITH JOHNSON OUR RISING STAR
A SUPERB MANAGER; HER SKILL IN
TECHNICAL AREAS VERY STRONG**

This final headline ran above a lengthy profile of Johnson, well placed on the second page of the magazine. It had appeared in ComLine only two issues ago. Seeing it now, Sanders realized that the article was intended for internal consumption—softening up the beachhead before the June landing. This article was a trial balloon that Cupertino had floated, to see if Meredith would be acceptable to run the technical divisions in Seattle. The only trouble was, Sanders never saw it. And nobody had ever mentioned it to him.

The article stressed the technical savvy that Johnson had acquired during her years with the company. She was quoted as saying, "I began my career working in technical areas, back with Novell. The technical fields have always been my first love; I'd love to go back to it. After all, strong technical innovation lies at the heart of a forward-looking company like DigiCom. Any good manager here must be able to run the technical divisions."

There it was.

He looked at the date: May 2. Published six weeks ago. Which meant that the article had been written at least two weeks before that.

As Mark Lewyn had suspected, Meredith Johnson knew she was going to be the head of the Advanced Products Division at least two months ago. Which meant, in turn, that Sanders had never been under consideration to become division head. He had never had a chance.

It was a done deal.

Months ago.

Sanders swore, took the articles over to the Xerox machine and copied them, then put the stacks back on the shelf, and left the press office.

He got on the elevator. Mark Lewyn was there. Sanders said, "Hi, Mark." Lewyn didn't answer. Sanders pushed the button for the ground floor.

The doors closed.

"I just hope you know what the fuck you're doing," Lewyn said angrily.

"I think I do."

"Because you could fuck this thing up for everybody. You know that?"

"Fuck what up?"

"Just because you got your ass in the sling, it's not our problem."

"Nobody said it was."

"I don't know what's the matter with you," Lewyn said. "You're late for work, you don't call me when you say you will . . . What is it, trouble at home? More shit with Susan?"

"This has nothing to do with Susan."

"Yeah? I think it does. You've been late two days running and even when you're here, you walk around like you're dreaming. You're in fucking dreamland, Tom. I mean, what the hell were you doing, going to Meredith's office at night, anyway?"

"She asked me to come to her office. She's the boss. You're saying I shouldn't have gone?"

Lewyn shook his head in disgust. "This innocent act is a lot of crap. Don't you take any responsibility for anything?"

"What—"

"Look, Tom, everybody in the company knows that Meredith is a shark. Meredith Manmuncher, they call her. The Great White. Everybody knows she's protected by Garvin, that she can do what she wants. And what she wants is to play grabass with cute guys who show up in her office at the end of the day. She has a couple of glasses of wine, she gets a little flushed, and she wants service. A delivery boy, a trainee, a young account guy. Whatever. And nobody can say a word because Garvin thinks she walks on water. So, how come everybody else in the company knows it but you?"

Sanders was stunned. He did not know how to answer. He stared at Lewyn, who stood very close to him, his body hunched, hands in his pockets. He could feel Lewyn's breath on his face. But he could hardly hear Lewyn's words. It was as if they came to him from a great distance.

"Hey, Tom. You walk the same halls, you breathe the same air as the rest of us. You know who's doing what. You go marching up there to her office . . . and you know damned well what's coming. Meredith's done everything but announce to the world that she wants to suck your dick. All day long, she's touching your arm, giving you those *meaningful* little looks and squeezes. Oh, *Tom*. So *nice* to see you again. And now you tell me you didn't know what was coming in that office? *Fuck* you, Tom. You're an asshole."

The elevator doors opened. Before them, the ground floor lobby was deserted, growing dark in the fading light of the June evening. A soft rain fell outside. Lewyn started toward the exit, then turned back. His voice echoed in the lobby.

"You realize," he said, "that you're acting like one of those women in all this. The way they always go, 'Who, me? I never intended that.' The way they go, 'Oh, it's not *my* responsibility. I never thought if I got drunk and kissed him and went to his room and lay down on his bed that he'd fuck me. Oh dear me no.' It's bullshit, Tom. Irresponsible bullshit. And you better think about what I'm saying, because there's a lot of us who have worked every bit as hard as you have in this company, and we don't want to see you screw up this merger and this spin-off for the rest of us. You want to pretend you can't tell when a woman's coming on to you, that's fine. You want to screw up your own life, it's your decision. But you screw up mine, and I'm going to fucking put you away."

Lewyn stalked off. The elevator doors started to close. Sanders stuck his hand out; the doors closed on his fingers. He jerked his hand, and the doors opened again. He hurried out into the lobby after Lewyn.

He grabbed Lewyn on the shoulder. "Mark, wait, listen—"

"I got nothing to say to you. I got kids, I got responsibilities. You're an asshole."

Lewyn shrugged Sanders's arm off, pushed open the door, and walked out. He strode quickly away, down the street.

As the glass doors closed, Sanders saw a flash of blond in the moving reflection. He turned.

"I thought that was a little unfair," Meredith Johnson said. She was standing about twenty feet behind him, near the elevators. She was wearing gym clothes—navy tights, and a sweatshirt—and she carried a gym bag in her hand. She looked beautiful, overtly sexual in a certain way. Sanders felt tense: there was no one else in the lobby. They were alone.

"Yes," Sanders said. "I thought it was unfair."

"I meant, to women," Meredith said. She swung the gym bag over her shoulder, the movement raising her sweatshirt and exposing her bare abdomen above her tights. She shook her head and pushed her hair back from her face. She paused a moment, and then she began to speak. "I want to tell you I'm sorry about all this," she said. She moved toward him in a steady, confident way, almost stalking. Her voice was low. "I never wanted any of this, Tom." She came a little closer, approaching slowly, as if he were an animal that might be frightened away. "I have only the warmest feelings for you." Still closer. "Only the warmest." Closer. "I can't help it, Tom, if I still want you." Closer. "If I did anything to offend you, I apologize." She was very close now, her body almost touching his, her breasts inches from his arm. "I'm truly sorry, Tom," she said softly. She seemed filled with emotion, her breasts rising and falling, her eyes moist and pleading as she looked up at him. "Can you forgive me? Please? You know how I feel about you."

He felt all the old sensations, the old stirrings. He clenched his jaw. "Meredith. The past is past. Cut it out, will you?"

She immediately changed her tone and gestured to the street. "Listen, I have a car here. Can I drop you somewhere?"

"No, thanks."

"It's raining. I thought you might want a lift."

"I don't think it's a good idea."

"Only because it's raining."

"This is Seattle," he said. "It rains all the time here."

She shrugged, walked to the door, and leaned her weight against it, thrusting out her hip. Then she looked back at him and smiled. "Remind me never to wear tights around you. It's embarrassing: you make me wet."

Then she turned away, pushed through the door, and walked quickly to the waiting car, getting in the back. She closed the door, looked back at him, and waved cheerfully. The car drove off.

Sanders unclenched his hands. He took a deep breath and let it out slowly. His whole body was tense. He waited until the car was gone, then went outside. He felt the rain on his face, the cool evening breeze.

He hailed a taxi. "The Four Seasons Hotel," he said to the driver.

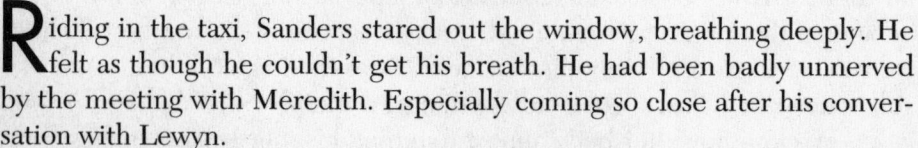

Riding in the taxi, Sanders stared out the window, breathing deeply. He felt as though he couldn't get his breath. He had been badly unnerved by the meeting with Meredith. Especially coming so close after his conversation with Lewyn.

Sanders was distressed by what Lewyn had said, but you could never take Mark too seriously. Lewyn was an artistic hothead who handled his creative tensions by getting angry. He was angry about something most of the time. Lewyn liked being angry. Sanders had known him a long time. Personally, he had never understood how Adele, Mark's wife, put up with it.. Adele was one of those wonderfully calm, almost phlegmatic women who could talk on the phone while her two kids crawled all over her, tugging at her, asking her questions. In a similar fashion, Adele just let Lewyn rage while she went on about her business. In fact, everyone just let Lewyn rage, because everyone knew that, in the end, it didn't mean anything.

Yet, it was also true that Lewyn had a kind of instinct for public perceptions and trends. That was the secret of his success as a designer. Lewyn would say, "Pastel colors," and everybody would groan and say that the new design colors looked like hell. But two years later, when the products were coming off the line, pastel colors would be just what everybody wanted. So Sanders was forced to admit that what Lewyn had said about him, others would soon be saying. Lewyn had said the company line: that Sanders was screwing up the chances for everybody else.

Well, screw them, he thought.

As for Meredith—he had had the distinct feeling that she had been toying with him in the lobby. Teasing him, playing with him. He could not understand why she was so confident. Sanders was making a very serious allegation against her. Yet she behaved as if there was no threat at all. She had a kind of imperviousness, an indifference, that made him deeply uneasy. It could only mean she knew that she had Garvin's backing.

The taxi pulled into the turnaround of the hotel. He saw Meredith's car up ahead. She was talking to the driver. She looked back and saw him.

There was nothing to do but get out and walk toward the entrance.

"Are you following me?" she said, smiling.

"No."

"Sure?"

"Yes, Meredith. I'm sure."

They went up the escalator from the street to the lobby. He stood behind her on the escalator. She looked back at him. "I wish you were."

"Yeah. Well, I'm not."

"It would have been nice," she said. She smiled invitingly.

He didn't know what to say; he just shook his head. They rode the rest of the way in silence until they came to the high ornate lobby. She said, "I'm in room 423. Come and see me anytime." She headed toward the elevators.

He waited until she was gone, then crossed the lobby and turned left to the dining room. Standing at the entrance, he saw Dorfman at a corner table, eating dinner with Garvin and Stephanie Kaplan. Max was holding forth, gesturing sharply as he spoke. Garvin and Kaplan both leaned forward, listening. Sanders was reminded that Dorfman had once been a director of the company—according to the stories, a very powerful director. It was Dorfman who had persuaded Garvin to expand beyond modems into cellular telephony and wireless communications, back in the days when nobody could see any link between computers and telephones. The link was obvious now but obscure in the early 1980s, when Dorfman had said, "Your business is not hardware. Your business is communications. Your business is access to information."

Dorfman had shaped company personnel as well. Supposedly, Kaplan owed her position to his glowing endorsement. Sanders had come to Seattle on Dorfman's recommendation. Mark Lewyn had been hired because of Dorfman. And any number of vice presidents had vanished over the years because Dorfman found them lacking in vision or stamina. He was a powerful ally or a lethal opponent.

And his position at the time of the merger was equally strong. Although Dorfman had resigned as a director years before, he still owned a good deal of DigiCom stock. He still had Garvin's ear. And he still had the contacts and prestige within the business and financial community that made a merger like this much simpler. If Dorfman approved the terms of the merger, his admirers at Goldman, Sachs and at First Boston would raise the money easily. But if Dorfman was dissatisfied, if he hinted that the merger of the two companies did not make sense, then the acquisition might unravel. Everyone knew it. Everyone understood very well the power he wielded—especially Dorfman himself.

Sanders hung back at the entrance to the restaurant, reluctant to come forward. After a while, Max glanced up and saw him. Still talking, he shook his head fractionally: *no*. Then, as he continued to talk, he made a subtle motion with his hand, tapping his watch. Sanders nodded, and went back into the lobby and sat down. He had the stack of ComLine photocopies on his lap. He browsed through them, studying again the way Meredith had changed her appearance.

A few minutes later, Dorfman rolled out in his wheelchair. "So, Thomas. I am glad you are not bored with your life."

"What does that mean?"

Dorfman laughed and gestured to the dining room. "They're talking of nothing else in there. The only topic this evening is you and Meredith. Everyone is so excited. So *worried*."

"Including Bob?"

"Yes, of course. Including Bob." He wheeled closer to Sanders. "I cannot really speak to you now. Was there something in particular?"

"I think you ought to look at this," Sanders said, handing Dorfman the photocopies. He was thinking that Dorfman could take these pictures to Garvin. Dorfman could make Garvin understand what was really going on.

Dorfman examined them in silence a moment. "Such a lovely woman," he said. "So beautiful . . ."

"Look at the differences, Max. Look at what she did to herself."

Dorfman shrugged. "She changed her hair. Very flattering. So?"

"I think she had plastic surgery as well."

"It wouldn't surprise me," Dorfman said. "So many women do, these days. It is like brushing their teeth, to them."

"It gives me the creeps."

"Why?" Dorfman said.

"Because it's underhanded, that's why."

"What's underhanded?" Dorfman said, shrugging. "She is resourceful. Good for her."

"I'll bet Garvin has no idea what she's doing to him," Sanders said.

Dorfman shook his head. "I'm not concerned about Garvin," he said. "I'm concerned about you, Thomas, and this outrage of yours—hmm?"

"I'll tell you why I'm outraged," Sanders said. "Because this is the kind of sneaky shit that a woman can pull but a man can't. She changes her appearance, she dresses and acts like Garvin's daughter, and that gives her an advantage. Because I sure as hell can't act like his daughter."

Dorfman sighed, shaking his head. "Thomas. Thomas."

"Well, I can't. Can I?"

"Are you enjoying this? You seem to be enjoying this outrage."

"I'm not."

"Then give it up," Dorfman said. He turned his wheelchair to face Sanders. "Stop talking this nonsense, and face what is true. Young people in organizations advance by alliances with powerful, senior people. True?"

"Yes."

"And it is always so. At one time, the alliance was formal—an apprentice and master, or a pupil and tutor. It was arranged, yes? But today, it is not formal. Today, we speak of mentors. Young people in business have mentors. True?"

"Okay . . ."

"So. How do young people attach themselves to a mentor? What is the process? First, by being agreeable, by being helpful to the senior person, doing jobs that need to be done. Second, by being attractive to the older person—imitating their attitudes and tastes. Third, by advocacy—adopting their agenda within the company."

"That's all fine," Sanders said. "What does it have to do with plastic surgery?"

"Do you remember when you joined DigiCom in Cupertino?"

"Yes, I remember."

"You came over from DEC. In 1980?"

"Yes."

"At DEC, you wore a coat and tie every day. But when you joined DigiCom, you saw that Garvin wore jeans. And soon, you wore jeans, too."

"Sure. That was the style of the company."

"Garvin liked the Giants. You began to go to games in Candlestick Park."

"He was the boss, for Christ's sake."

"And Garvin liked golf. So you took up golf, even though you hated it. I remember you complained to me about how much you hated it. Chasing the stupid little white ball."

"Listen. I didn't have plastic surgery to make myself look like his kid."

"Because you didn't have to, Thomas," Dorfman said. He threw up his hands in exasperation. "Can you not see this point? Garvin liked brash, aggressive young men who drank beer, who swore, who chased women. And you did all those things in those days."

"I was young. That's what young men do."

"No, Thomas. That's what Garvin liked young men to do." Dorfman shook his head. "So much of this is unconscious. Rapport is unconscious, Thomas. But the task of building rapport is different, depending on whether you are the same sex as that person, or not. If your mentor is a man, you may act like his son, or brother, or father. Or you may act like that man when he was younger—you may remind him of himself. True? Yes, you see that. Good.

"But if you are a woman, everything is different. Now you must be your mentor's daughter, or lover, or wife. Or perhaps sister. In any case, very different."

Sanders frowned.

"I see this often, now that men are starting to work for women. Many times men cannot structure the relationship because they do not know how to act as the subordinate to a woman. Not with comfort. But in other cases, men slip easily into a role with a woman. They are the dutiful son, or the substitute lover or husband. And if they do it well, the women in the organization become angry, because they feel that they cannot compete as son or lover or husband to the boss. So they feel that the man has an advantage."

Sanders was silent.

"Do you understand?" Dorfman said.

"You're saying it happens both ways."

"Yes, Thomas. It is inevitable. It is the process."

"Come on, Max. There's nothing inevitable about it. When Garvin's daughter died, it was a personal tragedy. He was upset, and Meredith took advantage of—"

"*Stop,*" Dorfman said, annoyed. "Now you want to change human nature? There are always tragedies. And people always take advantage. This is nothing new. Meredith is intelligent. It is delightful to see such an intelligent, resourceful woman who is also beautiful. She is a gift from God. She is delightful. This is your trouble, Thomas. And it has been a long time coming."

"What does that—"

"And instead of dealing with your trouble, you waste your time with these . . . *trivialities.*" He handed back the pictures. "These are not important, Thomas."

"Max, will you—"

"You were never a good corporate player, Thomas. It was not your strength. Your strength was that you could take a technical problem and grind it down, push the technicians, encourage them and bully them, and finally get it solved. You could make it work. Is that not so?"

Sanders nodded.

"But now you abandon your strengths for a game that does not suit you."

"Meaning what?"

"You think that by threatening a lawsuit, you put pressure on her and on the company. In fact, you played into her hands. You have let her define the game, Thomas."

"I had to do something. She broke the law."

"She broke the law," Dorfman mimicked him, with a sarcastic whine. "Oh me, oh my. And you are so defenseless. I am filled with sorrow for your plight."

"It's not easy. She's well connected. She has strong supporters."

"Is that so? Every executive with strong supporters has also strong detractors. And Meredith has her share of detractors."

"I tell you, Max," Sanders said, "she's dangerous. She's one of those MBA image people, focused on image, everything image, never substance."

"Yes," Dorfman said, nodding approvingly. "Like so many young executives today. Very skilled with images. Very interested in manipulating that reality. A fascinating trend."

"I don't think she's competent to run this division."

"And what if she is not?" Dorfman snapped. "What difference does it make to you? If she's incompetent, Garvin will eventually acknowledge it and replace her. But by then, you will be long gone. Because you will lose this game with her, Thomas. She is better at politics than you. She always was."

Sanders nodded. "She's ruthless."

"Ruthless, schmoothless. She is *skilled*. She has an instinct. You lack it. You will lose everything if you persist this way. And you will deserve the fate that befalls you because you have behaved like a fool."

Sanders was silent. "What do you recommend I do?"

"Ah. So now you want advice?"

"Yes."

"Really?" He smiled. "I doubt it."

"Yes, Max. I do."

"All right. Here is my advice. Go back, apologize to Meredith, apologize to Garvin, and resume your job."

"I can't."

"Then you don't want advice."

"I can't do that, Max."

"Too much pride?"

"No, but—"

"You are infatuated with the anger. How dare this woman act this way? She has broken the law, she must be brought to justice. She is dangerous, she must be stopped. You are filled with *delicious*, righteous indignation. True?"

"Oh, hell, Max. I just can't do it, that's all."

"Of course you can do it. You mean you *won't*."

"All right. I won't."

Dorfman shrugged. "Then what do you want from me? You come to ask my advice in order not to take it? This is nothing special." He grinned. "I have a lot of other advice you won't take, either."

"Like what?"

"What do you care, since you won't take it?"

"Come on, Max."

"I'm serious. You won't take it. We are wasting our time here. Go away."

"Just tell me, will you?"

Dorfman sighed. "Only because I remember you from the days when you had sense. First point. Are you listening?"

"Yes, Max. I am."

"First point: you know everything you need to know about Meredith Johnson. So forget her now. She is not your concern."

"What does that mean?"

"Don't interrupt. Second point. Play your own game, not hers."

"Meaning what?"

"Meaning, solve the problem."

"Solve what problem? The lawsuit?"

Dorfman snorted and threw up his hands. "You are impossible. I am wasting my time."

"You mean drop the lawsuit?"

"Can you understand English? *Solve the problem.* Do what you do well. Do your job. Now go away."

"But Max—"

"Oh, I can't do anything for you," Dorfman said. "It's your life. You have your own mistakes to make. And I must return to my guests. But try to pay attention, Thomas. Do not sleep through this. And remember, all human behavior has a reason. All behavior is solving a problem. Even *your* behavior, Thomas."

And he spun in his wheelchair and went back to the dining room.

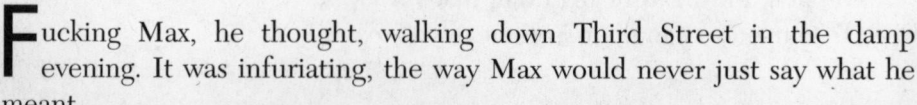

Fucking Max, he thought, walking down Third Street in the damp evening. It was infuriating, the way Max would never just say what he meant.

This is your trouble, Thomas. And it has been a long time coming.

What the hell was that supposed to mean?

Fucking Max. Infuriating and frustrating and exhausting, too. That was what Sanders remembered most about the sessions he used to have, when Max was on the DigiCom board. Sanders would come away exhausted. In those days, back in Cupertino, the junior execs had called Dorfman "The Riddler."

All human behavior is solving a problem. Even your behavior, Thomas.

Sanders shook his head. It made no sense at all. Meanwhile, he had things to do. At the end of the street, he stepped into a phone booth and dialed Gary Bosak's number. It was eight o'clock. Bosak would be home, just getting out of bed and having coffee, starting his working day. Right now, he would be yawning in front of a half-dozen modems and computer screens as he began to dial into all sorts of databases.

The phone rang, and a machine said, "You have reached NE Professional Services. Leave a message." And a beep.

"Gary, this is Tom Sanders. I know you're there, pick up."

A click, and then Bosak said, "Hey. The last person I thought I'd hear from. Where're you calling from?"

"Pay phone."

"Good. How's it going with you, Tom?"

"Gary, I need some things done. Some data looked up."

"Uh . . . Are we talking things for the company, or private things?"

"Private."

"Uh . . . Tom. I'm pretty busy these days. Can we talk about this next week?"

"That's too late."

"But the thing is, I'm pretty busy now."

"Gary, what is this?"

"Tom, come on. You know what this is."

"I need help, Gary."

"Hey. And I'd love to help you. But I just got a call from Blackburn who told me that if I had anything to do with you, anything at all, I could expect the FBI going through my apartment at six a.m. tomorrow morning."

"Christ. When was this?"

"About two hours ago."

Two hours ago. Blackburn was way ahead of him. "Gary . . ."

"Hey. You know I always liked you, Tom. But not this time. Okay? I got to go."

Click.

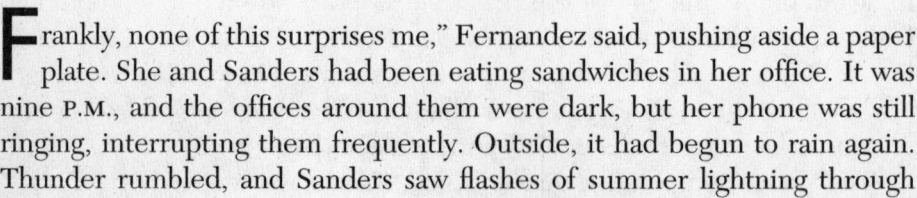

"Frankly, none of this surprises me," Fernandez said, pushing aside a paper plate. She and Sanders had been eating sandwiches in her office. It was nine P.M., and the offices around them were dark, but her phone was still ringing, interrupting them frequently. Outside, it had begun to rain again. Thunder rumbled, and Sanders saw flashes of summer lightning through the windows.

Sitting in the deserted law offices, Sanders had the feeling that he was all alone in the world, with nobody but Fernandez and the encroaching darkness. Things were happening quickly; this person he had never met before today was fast becoming a kind of lifeline for him. He found himself hanging on every word she said.

"Before we go on, I want to emphasize one thing," Fernandez said. "You were right not to get in the car with Johnson. You are not to be alone with her ever again. Not even for a few moments. Not ever, under any circumstances. Is that clear?"

"Yes."

"If you do, it will destroy your case."

"I won't."

"All right," she said. "Now. I had a long talk with Blackburn. As you guessed, he's under tremendous pressure to get this matter resolved. I tried to move the mediation session to the afternoon. He implied that the company was ready to deal and wanted to get started right away. He's concerned about how long the negotiations will take. So we'll start at nine tomorrow."

"Okay."

"Herb and Alan have been making progress. I think they'll be able to help us tomorrow. And these articles about Johnson may be useful, too," she said, glancing at the photocopies of the ComLine pieces.

"Why? Dorfman says they're irrelevant."

"Yes, but they document her history in the company, and that gives us leads. It's something to work on. So is this E-mail from your friend." She frowned at the sheet of printout. "This is an Internet address."

"Yes," he said, surprised that she knew.

"We do a lot of work with high-technology companies. I'll have somebody check it out." She put it aside. "Now let's review where we are. You couldn't clean out your desk because they were already there."

"Right."

"And you would have cleaned out your computer files, but you've been shut out of the system."

"Yes."

"Which means that you can't change anything."

"That's right. I can't do anything. It's like I'm an assistant."

She said, "Were you going to change any files?"

He hesitated. "No. But I would have, you know, looked around."

"Nothing in particular you were aware of?"

"No."

"Mr. Sanders," she said, "I want to emphasize that I have no judgment here. I'm simply trying to prepare for what may happen tomorrow. I want to know what surprises they'll have for us."

He shook his head. "There isn't anything in the files that's embarrassing to me."

"You've thought it over carefully?"

"Yes."

"Okay," she said. "Then considering the early start, I think you better get some sleep. I want you sharp tomorrow. Will you be able to sleep?"

"Jeez, I don't know."

"Take a sleeping pill if you need to."

"I'll be okay."

"Then go home and go to bed, Mr. Sanders. I'll see you in the morning. Wear a coat and tie tomorrow. Do you have some kind of a blue coat?"

"A blazer."

"Fine. Wear a conservative tie and a white shirt. No after-shave."

"I never dress like that at the office."

"This is not the office, Mr. Sanders. That's just the point." She stood up and shook his hand. "Get some sleep. And try not to worry. I think everything is going to be fine."

"I bet you say that to all your clients."

"Yes, I do," she said. "But I'm usually right. Get some sleep, Tom. I'll see you tomorrow."

He came home to a dark, empty house. Eliza's Barbie dolls lay in an untidy heap on the kitchen counter. One of his son's bibs, streaked with green baby food, was on the counter beside the sink. He set up the coffeemaker for the morning and went upstairs. He walked past the answering machine but neglected to look at it, and failed to notice the blinking light.

Upstairs, when he undressed in the bathroom, he saw that Susan had taped a note to the mirror. "Sorry about lunch. I believe you. I love you. S."

It was just like Susan to be angry and then to apologize. But he was glad for the note and considered calling her now. But it was nearly midnight in Phoenix, which meant it was too late. She'd be asleep.

Anyway, as he thought about it, he realized that he didn't want to call her. As she had said at the restaurant, this had nothing to do with her. He was alone in this. He'd stay alone.

Wearing just shorts, he padded into his little office. There were no faxes. He switched on his computer and waited while it came up.

The E-mail icon was blinking. He clicked it.

TRUST NOBODY.

AFRIEND

Sanders shut off the computer and went to bed.

WEDNESDAY

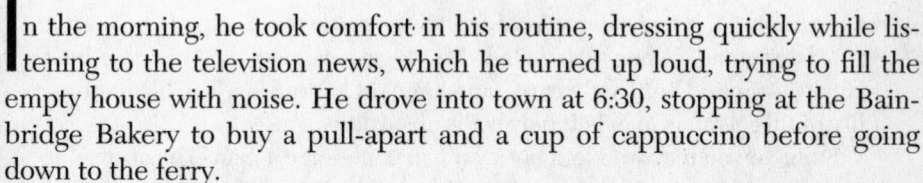

In the morning, he took comfort in his routine, dressing quickly while listening to the television news, which he turned up loud, trying to fill the empty house with noise. He drove into town at 6:30, stopping at the Bainbridge Bakery to buy a pull-apart and a cup of cappuccino before going down to the ferry.

As the ferry pulled away from Winslow, he sat toward the stern, so he would not have to look at Seattle as it approached. Lost in his thoughts, he stared out the window at the gray clouds hanging low over the dark water of the bay. It looked like it would rain again today.

"Bad day, huh?" a woman said.

He looked up and saw Mary Anne Hunter, pretty and petite, standing with her hands on her hips, looking at him with concern. Mary Anne lived on Bainbridge, too. Her husband was a marine biologist at the university. She and Susan were good friends, and often jogged together. But he didn't often see Mary Anne on the ferry because she usually went in early.

"Morning, Mary Anne."

"What I can't understand is how they got it," she said.

"Got what?" Sanders said.

"You mean you haven't seen it? Jesus. You're in the papers, Tom." She handed him the newspaper under her arm.

"You're kidding."

"No. Connie Walsh strikes again."

Sanders looked at the front page, but saw nothing. He began flipping through quickly.

"It's in the Metro section," she said. "The first opinion column on the second page. Read it and weep. I'll get more coffee." She walked away.

Sanders opened the paper to the Metro section.

AS I SEE IT

by Constance Walsh

MR. PIGGY AT WORK

The power of the patriarchy has revealed itself again, this time in a local high-tech firm I'll call Company X. This company has appointed a brilliant, highly competent woman to a major executive position. But many men in the company are doing their damnedest to get rid of her.

One man in particular, let's call him Mr. Piggy, has been especially vindictive. Mr. Piggy can't tolerate a woman supervisor, and for weeks he has been running a bitter campaign of innuendo inside the company to keep it from happening. When that failed, Mr. Piggy claimed that his new boss sexually assaulted him, and nearly raped him, in her offices. The blatant hostility of this claim is matched only by its absurdity.

Some of you may wonder how a woman could rape a man. The answer is, of course, she can't. Rape is a crime of violence. It is exclusively a crime of males, who use rape with appalling frequency to keep women in their place. That is the deep truth of our society, and of all other societies before ours.

For their part, women simply do not oppress men. Women are powerless in the hands of men. And to claim that a woman committed rape is absurd. But that didn't stop Mr. Piggy, who is interested only in smearing his new supervisor. He's even bringing a formal charge of sexual harassment against her!

In short, Mr. Piggy has the nasty habits of a typical patriarch. As you might expect, they appear everywhere in his life. Although Mr. Piggy's wife is an outstanding attorney, he pressures her to give up her job and stay home with the kids. After all, Mr. Piggy doesn't want his wife out in the business world, where she might hear about his affairs with young women and his excessive drinking. He probably figures his new female supervisor wouldn't approve of that, either. Maybe she won't allow him to be late to work, as he so often is.

So Mr. Piggy has made his underhanded move, and another talented businesswoman sees her career unfairly jeopardized. Will she be able to keep the pigs in the pen at Company X? Stay tuned for updates.

"Christ," Sanders said. He read it through again.

Hunter came back with two cappuccinos in paper cups. She pushed one toward him. "Here. Looks like you need it."

"How did they get the story?" he said.

Hunter shook her head. "I don't know. It looks to me like there's a leak inside the company."

"But who?" Sanders was thinking that if the story made the paper, it must have been leaked by three or four p.m. the day before. Who in the company even knew that he was considering a harassment charge at that time?

"I can't imagine who it could be," Hunter said. "I'll ask around."

"And who's Constance Walsh?"

"You never read her? She's a regular columnist at the *Post-Intelligencer*," Hunter said. "Feminist perspectives, that kind of thing." She shook her head. "How is Susan? I tried to call her this morning, and there's no answer at your house."

"Susan's gone away for a few days. With the kids."

Hunter nodded slowly. "That's probably a good idea."

"We thought so."

"She knows about this?"

"Yes."

"And is it true? Are you charging harassment?"

"Yes."

"Jesus."

"Yes," he said, nodding.

She sat with him for a long time, not speaking. She just sat with him. Finally she said, "I've known you for a long time. I hope this turns out okay."

"Me, too."

There was another long silence. Finally, she pushed away from the table and got up.

"See you later, Tom."

"See you, Mary Anne."

He knew what she was feeling. He had felt it himself, when others in the company had been accused of harassment. There was suddenly a distance. It didn't matter how long you had known the person. It didn't matter if you were friends. Once an accusation was made, everybody pulled away. Because the truth was, you never knew what had happened. You couldn't afford to take sides—even with your friends.

He watched her walk away, a slender, compact figure in exercise clothes, carrying a leather briefcase. She was barely five feet tall. The men on the ferry were so much larger. He remembered that she had once told Susan that she took up running because of her fear of rape. "I'll just outrun them," she had said. Men didn't know anything about that. They didn't understand that fear.

But there was another kind of fear that only men felt. He looked at the newspaper column with deep and growing unease. Key words and phrases jumped out at him:

Vindictive . . . bitter . . . can't tolerate a woman . . . blatant hostility . . . rape . . . crime of males . . . smearing his supervisor . . . affairs with young

*women . . . excessive drinking . . . late to work . . . unfairly jeopardized . . .
pigs in the pen.*

These characterizations were more than inaccurate, more than
unpleasant. They were dangerous. And it was exemplified by what happened to John Masters—a story that had reverberated among many senior
men in Seattle.

Masters was fifty, a marketing manager at MicroSym. A stable guy, solid
citizen, married twenty-five years, two kids—the older girl in college, the
younger girl a junior in high school. The younger girl starts to have trouble
with school, her grades go down, so the parents send her to a child psychologist. The child psychologist listens to the daughter and then says, You
know, this is the typical story of an abused child. Do you have anything like
that in your past?

Gee, the girl says, I don't think so.

Think back, the psychologist says.

At first the girl resists, but the psychologist keeps at her: Think back. Try
to remember. And after a while, the girl starts to recall some vague memories. Nothing specific, but now she thinks it's possible. Maybe Daddy did do
something wrong, way back when.

The psychologist tells the wife what is suspected. After twenty-five years
together, the wife and Masters have some anger between them. The wife
goes to Masters and says, Admit what you did.

Masters is thunderstruck. He can't believe it. He denies everything. The
wife says, You're lying, I don't want you around here. She makes him move
out of the house.

The older daughter flies home from college. She says, What is this madness? You know Daddy didn't do anything. Come to your senses. But the
wife is angry. The daughter is angry. And the process, once set in motion,
can't be stopped.

The psychologist is required by state law to report any suspected abuse.
She reports Masters to the state. The state is required by law to conduct an
investigation. Now a social worker is talking to the daughter, the wife, and
Masters. Then to the family doctor. The school nurse. Pretty soon, everybody knows.

Word of the accusation gets to MicroSym. The company suspends
him from his job, pending the outcome. They say they don't want negative
publicity.

Masters is seeing his life dissolve. His younger daughter won't talk to
him. His wife won't talk to him. He's living alone in an apartment. He has
money problems. Business associates avoid him. Everywhere he turns, he

sees accusing faces. He is advised to get a lawyer. And he is so shattered, so uncertain, he starts going to a shrink himself.

His lawyer makes inquiries; disturbing details emerge. It turns out that the particular psychologist who made the accusation uncovers abuse in a high percentage of her cases. She has reported so many cases that the state agency has begun to suspect bias. But the agency can do nothing; the law requires that all cases be investigated. The social worker assigned to the case has been previously disciplined for her excessive zeal in pursuing questionable cases and is widely thought to be incompetent, but the state cannot fire her for the usual reasons.

The specific accusation—never formally presented—turns out to be that Masters molested his daughter in the summer of her third grade. Masters thinks back, has an idea. He gets his old canceled checks out of storage, digs up his old business calendars. It turns out that his daughter was at a camp in Montana that whole summer. When she came home in August, Masters was on a business trip in Germany. He did not return from Germany until after school had started again.

He had never even seen his daughter that summer.

Masters's shrink finds it significant that his daughter would locate the abuse at the one time when abuse was impossible. The shrink concludes that the daughter felt abandoned and has translated that into a memory of abuse. Masters confronts the wife and daughter. They listen to the evidence and admit that they must have the date wrong, but remain adamant that the abuse occurred.

Nevertheless, the facts about the summer schedule lead the state to drop its investigation, and MicroSym reinstates Masters. But Masters has missed a round of promotions, and a vague cloud of prejudice hangs over him. His career has been irrevocably damaged. His wife never reconciles, eventually filing for divorce. He never again sees his younger daughter. His older daughter, caught between warring family factions, sees less of him as time goes on. Masters lives alone, struggles to rebuild his life, and suffers a near-fatal heart attack. After his recovery, he sees a few friends, but now he is morose and drinks too much, a poor companion. Other men avoid him. No one has an answer to his constant question: What did I do wrong? What should I have done instead? How could I have prevented this?

Because, of course, he could not have prevented it. Not in a contemporary climate where men were assumed to be guilty of anything they were accused of.

Among themselves, men sometimes talked of suing women for false accusations. They talked of penalties for damage caused by those accusations. But that was just talk. Meanwhile, they all changed their behavior. There were new rules now, and every man knew them:

Don't smile at a child on the street, unless you're with your wife. Don't ever touch a strange child. Don't ever be alone with someone else's child, even for a moment. If a child invites you into his or her room, don't go unless another adult, preferably a woman, is also present. At a party, don't let a little girl sit on your lap. If she tries, gently push her aside. If you ever have occasion to see a naked boy or girl, look quickly away. Better yet, leave.

And it was prudent to be careful around your own children, too, because if your marriage went sour, your wife might accuse you. And then your past conduct would be reviewed in an unfavorable light: "Well, he was such an affectionate father—perhaps a little *too* affectionate." Or, "He spent so much time with the kids. He was always hanging around the house . . ."

This was a world of regulations and penalties entirely unknown to women. If Susan saw a child crying on the street, she picked the kid up. She did it automatically, without thinking. Sanders would never dare. Not these days.

And of course there were new rules for business, as well. Sanders knew men who would not take a business trip with a woman, who would not sit next to a female colleague on an airplane, who would not meet a woman for a drink in a bar unless someone else was also present. Sanders had always thought such caution was extreme, even paranoid. But now, he was not so sure.

The sound of the ferry horn roused Sanders from his thoughts. He looked up and saw the black pilings of the Colman Dock. The clouds were still dark, still threatening rain. He stood, belted his raincoat, and headed downstairs to his car.

On his way to the mediation center, he stopped by his office for a few minutes to pick up background documentation on the Twinkle drive. He thought it might be necessary in the morning's work. But he was surprised to see John Conley in his office, talking with Cindy. It was 8:15 in the morning.

"Oh, Tom," Conley said. "I was just trying to arrange an appointment with you. Cindy tells me that you have a very busy schedule and may be out of the office most of the day."

Sanders looked at Cindy. Her face was tight. "Yes," he said, "at least for the morning."

"Well, I only need a few minutes."

Sanders waved him into the office. Conley went in, and Sanders closed the door.

"I'm looking forward to the briefing tomorrow for John Marden, our CEO," Conley said. "I gather you'll be speaking then."

Sanders nodded vaguely. He had heard nothing about a briefing. And tomorrow seemed very far away. He was having trouble concentrating on what Conley was saying.

"But of course we'll all be asked to take a position on some of these agenda items," Conley said. "And I'm particularly concerned about Austin."

"Austin?"

"I mean, the sale of the Austin facility."

"I see," Sanders said. So it was true.

"As you know, Meredith Johnson has taken an early and strong position in favor of the sale," Conley said. "It was one of the first recommendations she gave us, in the early stages of shaping this deal. Marden's worried about cash flow after the acquisition; the deal's going to add debt, and he's worried about funding high-tech development. Johnson thought we could ease the debt load by selling off Austin. But I don't feel myself competent to judge the pros and cons on this. I was wondering what your view was."

"On a sale of the Austin plant?"

"Yes. Apparently there's tentative interest from both Hitachi and Motorola. So it's quite possible that it could be liquidated quickly. I think that's what Meredith has in mind. Has she discussed it with you?"

"No," Sanders said.

"She probably has a lot of ground to cover, settling in to her new job," Conley said. He was watching Sanders carefully as he spoke. "What do you think about a sale?"

Sanders said, "I don't see a compelling reason for it."

"Apart from cash-flow issues, I think her argument is that manufacturing cellular phones has become a mature business," Conley said. "As a technology, it's gone through its exponential growth phase, and it's now approaching a commodity. The high profits are gone. From now on, there will be only incremental sales increases, against increasing severe foreign competition. So, telephones aren't likely to represent a major income source in the future. And of course there's the question of whether we should be manufacturing in the States at all. A lot of DigiCom's manufacturing is already offshore."

"That's all true," Sanders said. "But it's beside the point. First of all, cellular phones may be reaching market saturation, but the general field of wireless communications is still in its infancy. We're going to see more and more wireless office nets and wireless field links in the future. So the market is still expanding, even if telephony is not. Second, I would argue that wireless is a major part of our company's future interest, and one way to stay competitive is to continue to make products and sell them. That forces you to maintain contact with your customer base, to keep knowledgeable about their future interests. I wouldn't opt out now. If Motorola and Hitachi see a business there, why don't we? Third, I think that we have an obligation—a social obligation, if you will—to keep high-paying skilled jobs in the U.S. Other countries don't export good jobs. Why should we? Each of our offshore manufacturing decisions has been made for a specific reason, and, personally, I hope we start to move them back here. Because there are many hidden costs in offshore fabrication. But most important of all, even though we are primarily a development unit here— making new products—we need manufacturing. If there's anything that the last twenty years has shown us, it's that design and manufacturing are all one process. You start splitting off the design engineers from the manufacturing guys and you'll end up with bad design. You'll end up with General Motors."

He paused. There was a brief silence. Sanders hadn't intended to speak so strongly; it just came out. But Conley just nodded thoughtfully. "So you believe selling Austin would hurt the development unit."

"No question about it. In the end, manufacturing is a discipline."

Conley shifted in his seat. "How do you think Meredith Johnson feels on these issues?"

"I don't know."

"Because you see, all this raises a related question," Conley said. "Having to do with executive judgment. To be frank, I've heard some rumblings in the division about her appointment. In terms of whether she really has a good enough grasp of the issues to run a technical division."

Sanders spread his hands. "I don't feel I can say anything."

"I'm not asking you to," Conley said. "I gather she has Garvin's support."

"Yes, she does."

"And that's fine with us. But you know what I'm driving at," Conley said. "The classic problem in acquisitions is that the acquiring company doesn't really understand what they are buying, and they kill the goose that lays the golden egg. They don't intend to; but they do. They destroy the very thing they want to acquire. I'm concerned that Conley-White not make a mistake like that."

"Uh-huh."

"Just between us. If this issue comes up in the meeting tomorrow, would you take the position you just took?"

"Against Johnson?" Sanders shrugged. "That could be difficult." He was thinking that he probably wouldn't be at the meeting tomorrow. But he couldn't say that to Conley.

"Well." Conley extended his hand. "Thanks for your candor. I appreciate it." He turned to go. "One last thing. It'd be very helpful if we had a handle on the Twinkle drive problem by tomorrow."

"I know it," Sanders said. "Believe me, we're working on it."

"Good."

Conley turned, and left. Cindy came in. "How are you today?"

"Nervous."

"What do you need me to do?"

"Pull the data on the Twinkle drives. I want copies of everything I took Meredith Monday night."

"It's on your desk."

He scooped up a stack of folders. On top was a small DAT cartridge. "What's this?"

"That's your video link with Arthur from Monday."

He shrugged, and dropped it in his briefcase.

Cindy said, "Anything else?"

"No." He glanced at his watch. "I'm late."

"Good luck, Tom," she said.

He thanked her and left the office.

Driving in morning rush-hour traffic, Sanders realized that the only surprise in his encounter with Conley was how sharp the young lawyer was. As for Meredith, her behavior didn't surprise him at all. For years, Sanders had fought the B-school mentality that she exemplified. After watching these graduates come and go, Sanders had finally concluded that there was a fundamental flaw in their education. They had been trained to believe that they were equipped to manage anything. But there was no such thing as general managerial skills and tools. In the end, there were only specific problems, involving specific industries and specific workers. To apply general tools to specific problems was to fail. You needed to know the market, you needed to know the customers, you needed to know the limits of manufacturing and the limits of your own creative people. None of that was obvious. Meredith couldn't see that Don Cherry and Mark Lewyn needed a link to manufacturing. Yet time and again, Sanders had been shown a prototype and had asked the one significant question: It looks fine, but can you make it on a production line? Can you build it, reliably and quickly, for a price? Sometimes they could, and sometimes they couldn't. If you took away that question, you changed the entire organization. And not for the better.

Conley was smart enough to see that. And smart enough to keep his ear to the ground. Sanders wondered how much Conley knew of what he hadn't said in their meeting. Did he also know about the harassment suit? It was certainly possible.

Christ, Meredith wanted to sell Austin. Eddie had been right all along. He considered telling him, but he really couldn't. And in any case, he had more pressing things to worry about. He saw the sign for the Magnuson Mediation Center and turned right. Sanders tugged at the knot on his tie, and pulled into a space in the parking lot.

The Magnuson Mediation Center was located just outside Seattle, on a hill overlooking the city. It consisted of three low buildings arranged around a central courtyard where water splashed in fountains and pools. The entire atmosphere was designed to be peaceful and relaxing, but Sanders was tense when he walked up from the parking lot and found Fernandez pacing.

"You see the paper today?" she said.

"Yeah, I saw it."

"Don't let it upset you. This is a very bad tactical move on their part," she said. "You know Connie Walsh?"

"No."

"She's a bitch," Fernandez said briskly. "Very unpleasant and very capable. But I expect Judge Murphy to take a strong position on it in the sessions. Now, this is what I worked out with Phil Blackburn. We'll begin with your version of the events of Monday night. Then Johnson will tell hers."

"Wait a minute. Why should I go first?" Sanders said. "If I go first, she'll have the advantage of hearing—"

"You are the one bringing the claim so you are obligated to present your case first. I think it will be to our advantage," Fernandez said. "This way Johnson will testify last, before lunch." They started toward the center building. "Now, there are just two things you have to remember. First, always tell the truth. No matter what happens, just tell the truth. Exactly as you remember it even if you think it hurts your case. Okay?"

"Okay."

"Second, don't get mad. Her lawyer will try to make you angry and trap you. Don't fall for it. If you feel insulted or start to get mad, request a five-minute break to consult with me. You're entitled to that, whenever you want. We'll go outside and cool off. But whatever you do, keep cool, Mr. Sanders."

"Okay."

"Good." She swung open the door. "Now let's go do it."

The mediation room was wood-paneled and spare. He saw a polished wooden table with a pitcher of water and glasses and some notepads; in the corner, a sideboard with coffee and a plate of pastries. Windows opened out on a small atrium with a fountain. He heard the sound of soft gurgling water.

The DigiCom legal team was already there, ranged along one side of the table. Phil Blackburn, Meredith Johnson, an attorney named Ben Heller, and two other grim-faced female attorneys. Each woman had an imposing stack of Xeroxed papers before her on the table.

Fernandez introduced herself to Meredith Johnson, and the two women shook hands. Then Ben Heller shook hands with Sanders. Heller was a florid, beefy man with silver hair, and a deep voice. Well connected in

Seattle, he reminded Sanders of a politician. Heller introduced the other women, but Sanders immediately forgot their names.

Meredith said, "Hello, Tom."

"Meredith."

He was struck by how beautiful she looked. She wore a blue suit with a cream-colored blouse. With her glasses and her blond hair pulled back, she looked like a lovely but studious schoolgirl. Heller patted her hand reassuringly, as if speaking to Sanders had been a terrible ordeal.

Sanders and Fernandez sat down opposite Johnson and Heller. Everybody got out papers and notes. Then there was an awkward silence, until Heller said to Fernandez, "How'd that King Power thing turn out?"

"We were pleased," Fernandez said.

"They fixed an award yet?"

"Next week, Ben."

"What are you asking?"

"Two million."

"Two *million*?"

"Sexual harassment's serious business, Ben. Awards are going up fast. Right now the average verdict is over a million dollars. Especially when the company behaves that badly."

At the far end of the room, a door opened and a woman in her mid-fifties entered. She was brisk and erect, and wore a dark blue suit not very different from Meredith's.

"Good morning," she said. "I'm Barbara Murphy. Please refer to me as Judge Murphy, or Ms. Murphy." She moved around the room, shaking hands with everyone, then took a seat at the head of the table. She opened her briefcase and took out her notes.

"Let me tell you the ground rules for our sessions here," Judge Murphy said. "This is not a court of law, and our proceedings won't be recorded. I encourage everyone to maintain a civil and courteous tone. We're not here to make wild accusations or to fix blame. Our goal is to define the nature of the dispute between the parties, and to determine how best to resolve that dispute.

"I want to remind everyone that the allegations made on both sides are extremely serious and may have legal consequences for all parties. I urge you to treat these sessions confidentially. I particularly caution you against discussing what is said here with any outside person or with the press. I have taken the liberty of speaking privately to Mr. Donadio, the editor of the *Post-Intelligencer*, about the article that appeared today by Ms. Walsh. I reminded Mr. Donadio that all parties in 'Company X' are private individuals and that Ms. Walsh is a paid employee of the paper. The risk of a defamation suit against the *P-I* is very real. Mr. Donadio seemed to take my point."

She leaned forward, resting her elbows on the table. "Now then. The parties have agreed that Mr. Sanders will speak first, and he will then be questioned by Mr. Heller. Ms. Johnson will speak next, and will be questioned by Ms. Fernandez. In the interest of time, I alone will have the right to ask questions during the testimony of the principals, and I will set limits on the questions of opposing attorneys. I'm open to some discussion, but I ask your cooperation in letting me exercise judgment and keep things moving. Before we begin, does anybody have any questions?"

Nobody did.

"All right. Then let's get started. Mr. Sanders, why don't you tell us what happened, from your point of view."

Sanders talked quietly for the next half hour. He began with his meeting with Blackburn, where he learned that Meredith was going to be the new vice president. He reported the conversation with Meredith after her speech, in which she suggested a meeting about the Twinkle drive. He told what happened in the six o'clock meeting in detail.

As he spoke, he realized why Fernandez had insisted he tell this story over and over, the day before. The flow of events came easily to him now; he found that he could talk about penises and vaginas without hesitation. Even so, it was an ordeal. He felt exhausted by the time he described leaving the room and seeing the cleaning woman outside.

He then told about the phone call to his wife, and the early meeting the next morning, his subsequent conversation with Blackburn, and his decision to press charges.

"That's about it," he finished.

Judge Murphy said, "I have some questions before we go on. Mr. Sanders, you mentioned that wine was drunk during the meeting."

"Yes."

"How much wine would you say you had?"

"Less than a glass."

"And Ms. Johnson? How much would you say?"

"At least three glasses."

"All right." She made a note. "Mr. Sanders, do you have an employment contract with the company?"

"Yes."

"What is your understanding of what the contract says about transferring you or firing you?"

"They can't fire me without cause," Sanders said. "I don't know what it says about transfers. But my point is that by transferring me, they might as well be firing me—"

"I understand your point," Murphy said, interrupting him. "I'm asking about your contract. Mr. Blackburn?"

Blackburn said, "The relevant clause refers to 'equivalent transfer.' "

"I see. So it is arguable. Fine. Let's go on. Mr. Heller? Your questions for Mr. Sanders, please."

Ben Heller shuffled his papers and cleared his throat. "Mr. Sanders, would you like a break?"

"No, I'm fine."

"All right. Now, Mr. Sanders. You mentioned that when Mr. Blackburn told you on Monday morning that Ms. Johnson was going to be the new head of the division, you were surprised."

"Yes."

"Who did you think the new head would be?"

"I didn't know. Actually, I thought I might be in line for it."

"Why did you think that?"

"I just assumed it."

"Did anybody in the company, Mr. Blackburn or anybody else, lead you to think you were going to get the job?"

"No."

"Was there anything in writing to suggest you would get the job?"

"No."

"So when you say you assumed it, you were drawing a conclusion based on the general situation at the company, as you saw it."

"Yes."

"But not based on any real evidence?"

"No."

"All right. Now, you've said that when Mr. Blackburn told you that Ms. Johnson was going to get the job, he also told you that she could choose new division heads if she wanted, and you told him you interpreted that to mean Ms. Johnson had the power to fire you?"

"Yes, that's what he said."

"Did he characterize it in any way? For example, did he say it was likely or unlikely?"

"He said it was unlikely."

"And did you believe him?"

"I wasn't sure what to believe, at that point."

"Is Mr. Blackburn's judgment on company matters reliable?"

"Ordinarily, yes."

"But in any case, Mr. Blackburn did say that Ms. Johnson had the right to fire you."

"Yes."

"Did Ms. Johnson ever say anything like that to you?"

"No."

"She never made any statement that could be interpreted as an offer contingent upon your performance, including sexual performance?"

"No."

"So when you say that during your meeting with her you felt that your job was at risk, that was not because of anything Ms. Johnson actually said or did?"

"No," Sanders said. "But it was in the situation."

"You *perceived* it as being in the situation."

"Yes."

"As you had earlier perceived that you were in line for a promotion, when in fact you were not? The very promotion that Ms. Johnson ended up getting?"

"I don't follow you."

"I'm merely observing," Heller said, "that perceptions are subjective, and do not have the weight of fact."

"Objection," Fernandez said. "Employee perceptions have been held valid in contexts where the reasonable expectation—"

"Ms. Fernandez," Murphy said, "Mr. Heller hasn't challenged the validity of your client's perceptions. He has questioned their accuracy."

"But surely they are accurate. Because Ms. Johnson was his superior, and she could fire him if she wanted to."

"That's not in dispute. But Mr. Heller is asking whether Mr. Sanders has a tendency to build up unjustified expectations. And that seems to me entirely relevant."

"But with all due respect, Your Honor—"

"Ms. Fernandez," Murphy said, "we're here to clarify this dispute. I'm going to let Mr. Heller continue. Mr. Heller?"

"Thank you, Your Honor. So to summarize, Mr. Sanders: Although you felt your job was on the line, you never got that sense from Ms. Johnson?"

"No, I didn't."

"Or from Mr. Blackburn?"

"No."

"Or, in fact, from anyone else?"

"No."

"All right. Let's turn to something else. How did it happen that there was wine at the six o'clock meeting?"

"Ms. Johnson said that she would get a bottle of wine."

"You didn't ask her to do that?"

"No. She volunteered to do it."

"And what was your reaction?"

"I don't know." He shrugged. "Nothing in particular."

"Were you pleased?"

"I didn't think about it one way or the other."

"Let me put it a different way, Mr. Sanders. When you heard that an attractive woman like Ms. Johnson was planning to have a drink with you after work, what went through your head?"

"I thought I better do it. She's my boss."

"That's all you thought?"

"Yes."

"Did you mention to anyone that you wanted to be alone with Ms. Johnson in a romantic setting?"

Sanders sat forward, surprised. "No."

"Are you sure about that?"

"Yes." Sanders shook his head. "I don't know what you're driving at."

"Isn't Ms. Johnson your former lover?"

"Yes."

"And didn't you want to resume your intimate relationship?"

"No, I did not. I was just hoping we would be able to find some way to be able to work together."

"Is that difficult? I would have thought it'd be quite easy to work together, since you knew each other so well in the past."

"Well, it's not. It's quite awkward."

"Is it? Why is that?"

"Well. It just is. I had never actually worked with her. I knew her in a totally different context, and I just felt awkward."

"How did your prior relationship with Ms. Johnson end, Mr. Sanders?"

"We just sort of . . . drifted apart."

"You had been living together at the time?"

"Yes. And we had our normal ups and downs. And finally, it just didn't work out. So we split up."

"No hard feelings?"

"No."

"Who left whom?"

"It was sort of mutual, as I recall."

"Whose idea was it to move out?"

"I guess . . . I don't really remember. I guess it was mine."

"So there was no awkwardness or tension about how the affair ended, ten years ago."

"No."

"And yet you felt there was awkwardness now?"

"Sure," Sanders said. "Because we had one kind of relationship in the past, and now we were going to have another kind of relationship."

"You mean, now Ms. Johnson was going to be your superior."

"Yes."

"Weren't you angry about that? About her appointment?"

"A little. I guess."

"Only a little? Or perhaps more than a little?"

Fernandez sat forward and started to protest. Murphy shot her a warning look. Fernandez put her fists under her chin and said nothing.

"I was a lot of things," Sanders said. "I was angry and disappointed and confused and worried."

"So in your mind, although you were feeling many different and confusing feelings, you're certain that you did not, under any circumstances, contemplate having sex with Ms. Johnson that night."

"No."

"It never crossed your mind?"

"No."

There was a pause. Heller shuffled his notes, then looked up. "You're married, are you not, Mr. Sanders?"

"Yes, I am."

"Did you call your wife to tell her you had a late meeting?"

"Yes."

"Did you tell her with whom?"

"No."

"Why not?"

"My wife is sometimes jealous about my past relationships. I didn't see any reason to cause her anxiety or make her upset."

"You mean, if you told her you were having a late meeting with Ms. Johnson, your wife might think that you would renew your sexual acquaintance."

"I don't know what she would think," Sanders said.

"But in any case, you didn't tell her about Ms. Johnson."

"No."

"What did you tell her?"

"I told her I had a meeting and I would be home late."

"How late?"

"I told her it might run to dinner or after."

"I see. Had Ms. Johnson suggested dinner to you?"

"No."

"So you presumed, when you called your wife, that your meeting with Ms. Johnson might be a long one?"

"No," Sanders said. "I didn't. But I didn't know exactly how long it would be. And my wife doesn't like me to call once and say I'll be an hour late, and then call again to say it'll be two hours. That annoys her. So it's easier for her if I just tell her I may be home after dinner. That way, she doesn't expect me and doesn't wait for me; and if I get home early, it's great."

"So this is your usual policy with your wife."

"Yes."

"Nothing unusual."

"No."

"In other words, your usual procedure is to lie to your wife about events at the office because in your view she can't take the truth."

"Objection," Fernandez said. "What's the relevance?"

"That's not it at all," Sanders continued, angrily.

"How is it, Mr. Sanders?"

"Look. Every marriage has its own way to work things out. This is ours. It makes things smoother, that's all. It's about scheduling at home, not about lying."

"But wouldn't you say that you lied when you failed to tell your wife you were seeing Ms. Johnson that night?"

"Objection," Fernandez said.

Murphy said, "I think this is *quite* enough, Mr. Heller."

"Your Honor, I'm trying to show that Mr. Sanders intended to consummate an encounter with Ms. Johnson, and that all his behavior is consistent with that. And in addition, to show that he routinely treats women with contempt."

"You haven't shown that, you haven't even laid a groundwork for that," Murphy said. "Mr. Sanders has explained his reasons, and in the absence of contrary evidence I accept them. Do you have contrary evidence?"

"No, Your Honor."

"Very well. Bear in mind that inflammatory and unsubstantiated characterizations do not assist our mutual efforts at resolution."

"Yes, Your Honor."

"I want everyone here to be clear: these proceedings are potentially damaging to all parties—not only in their outcome, but in the conduct of the proceedings themselves. Depending on the outcome, Ms. Johnson and Mr. Sanders may find themselves working together in some capacity in the future. I will not permit these proceedings to unnecessarily poison such future relationships. Any further unwarranted accusations will cause me to halt these proceedings. Does anyone have any questions about what I've just said?"

No one did.

"All right. Mr. Heller?"

Heller sat back. "No further questions, Your Honor."

"All right," Judge Murphy said. "We'll break for five minutes, and return to hear Ms. Johnson's version."

"Y ou're doing fine," Fernandez said. "You're doing very well. Your voice was strong. You were clear and even. Murphy was impressed. You're doing fine." They were standing outside, by the fountains in the courtyard. Sanders felt like a boxer between rounds, being worked over by his trainer. "How do you feel?" she asked. "Tired?"

"A little. Not too bad."

"You want coffee?"

"No, I'm okay."

"Good. Because the hard part is coming up. You're going to have to be very strong when she gives her version. You won't like what she says. But it's important that you stay calm."

"Okay."

She put her hand on his shoulder. "By the way, just between us: How *did* the relationship end?"

"To tell the truth, I can't remember exactly."

Fernandez looked skeptical. "But this was important, surely . . ."

"It was almost ten years ago," Sanders said. "To me, it feels like another lifetime."

She was still skeptical.

"Look," Sanders said. "This is the third week in June. What was going on in your love life the third week of June, ten years ago? Can you tell me?"

Fernandez was silent, frowning.

"Were you married?" Sanders prompted.

"No."

"Met your husband yet?"

"Uh, let's see . . . no . . . not until . . . I must have met my husband . . . about a year later."

"Okay. Do you remember who you were seeing before him?"

Fernandez was silent. Thinking.

"How about *anything* that happened between you and a lover in June, ten years ago?"

She was still silent.

"See what I mean?" Sanders said. "Ten years is a long time. I remember the affair with Meredith, but I'm not clear about the last few weeks of it. I don't remember the details of how it ended."

"What do you remember?"

He shrugged. "We had more fights, more yelling. We were still living together, but somehow, we began to arrange our schedules so that we never saw each other. You know how that happens. Because when we did run into each other, we fought.

"And finally one night, we had a big argument while we were getting dressed to go to a party. Some formal party for DigiCom. I remember I had to wear a tux. I threw my cuff links at her and then I couldn't find them. I had to get down on the floor and look. But once we were driving to the party, we sort of calmed down, and we started talking about breaking up. In this very ordinary way. Very reasonable way. It just came out. Both of us. Nobody shouted. And in the end, we decided it was best if we broke it off."

Fernandez was looking at him thoughtfully. "That's it?"

"Yeah." He shrugged. "Except we never got to the party."

Something at the back of his mind. *A couple in a car, going to a party. Something about a cellular phone. All dressed up, going to the party and they make a call, and—*

He couldn't get it. It hung in his memory, just beyond recollection.

The woman made a call on the cellular phone, and then . . . Something embarrassing afterward . . .

"Tom?" Fernandez said, shaking his shoulder. "Looks like our time is about up. Ready to go back?"

"I'm ready," he said.

As they were heading back to the mediation room, Heller came over. He gave Sanders an oily smile, then turned to Fernandez. "Counselor," he said. "I wonder if this is the time to talk about settlement."

"Settlement?" Fernandez said, showing elaborate surprise. "Why?"

"Well, things aren't going so well for your client, and—"

"Things are going fine for my client—"

"And this whole inquiry will only get more embarrassing and awkward for him, the longer it continues—"

"My client isn't embarrassed at all—"

"And perhaps it is to everyone's advantage to end it now."

Fernandez smiled. "I don't think that's my client's wish, Ben, but if you have an offer to make, we will of course entertain it."

"Yes. I have an offer."

"All right."

Heller cleared his throat. "Considering Tom's current compensation base and associated benefits package, and taking into consideration his lengthy service with the company, we're prepared to settle for an amount equal to several years of compensation. We'll add an allowance for your fees and other miscellaneous expenses of termination, the cost of a headhunter to relocate to a new position, and all direct costs that may be associated with moving his household, and all together make it four hundred thousand dollars. I think that's very generous."

"I'll see what my client says," Fernandez said. She took Sanders by the arm, and walked a short distance away. "Well?"

"No," Sanders said.

"Not so fast," she said. "That's a pretty reasonable offer. It's as much as you're likely to get in court, without the delay and expenses."

"No."

"Want to counter?"

"No. Fuck him."

"I think we should counter."

"Fuck him."

Fernandez shook her head. "Let's be smart, not angry. What do you hope to gain from all this, Tom? There must be a figure you would accept."

"I want what I'll get when they take the company public," Sanders said. "And that's somewhere between five and twelve million."

"You *think*. It's a speculative estimate for a future event."

"That's what it'll be, believe me."

Fernandez looked at him. "Would you take five million now?"

"Yes."

"Alternatively, would you take the compensation package he outlined, plus the stock options you would get at the time of the offering?"

Sanders considered that. "Yes."

"All right. I'll tell him."

She walked back across the courtyard to Heller. The two spoke briefly. After a moment, Heller turned on his heel and stalked away.

Fernandez came back, grinning. "He didn't go for it." They headed back inside. "But I'll tell you one thing: this is a good sign."

"It is?"

"Yes. If they want to settle before Johnson gives her testimony, it's a very good sign."

In view of the acquisition," Meredith Johnson said, "I felt it was important that I meet with all the division heads on Monday." She spoke calmly and slowly, looking at everyone seated around the table in turn. Sanders had the sense of an executive giving a presentation. "I met with Don Cherry, Mark Lewyn, and Mary Anne Hunter during the afternoon. But Tom Sanders said he had a very busy schedule, and asked if we could meet at the end of the day. At his request, I scheduled the meeting with Tom at six o'clock."

He was amazed at the cool way that she lied. He had expected her to be effective, but he was still astonished to see her in action.

"Tom suggested that we could have a drink as well, and go over old times. That wasn't really my style, but I agreed. I was especially concerned to establish good relations with Tom, because I knew he was disappointed he had not gotten the job, and because we had a past history. I wanted our working relationship to be cordial. For me to refuse a drink with him seemed . . . I don't know—standoffish, or stiff. So I said yes.

"Tom came to the office at six o'clock. We had a glass of wine, and talked about the problems with the Twinkle drive. However, from the outset he kept making comments of a personal nature that I considered inappropriate—for example, comments about my appearance, and about how often he thought about our past relationship. Reference to sexual incidents in the past, and so on."

Son of a bitch. Sanders's whole body was tense. His hands were clenched. His jaw was tight.

Fernandez leaned over and put her hand on his wrist.

Meredith Johnson was saying, ". . . had some calls from Garvin and others. I took them at my desk. Then my assistant came in and asked if she could leave early, to deal with some personal matters. I said she could. She left the room. That was when Tom came over and suddenly started kissing me."

She paused for a moment, looking around the room. She met Sanders's eyes with a steady gaze.

"I was taken aback by his sudden and unexpected overture," she said, staring evenly at him. "At first, I tried to protest, and to defuse the situation. But Tom is much larger than I am. Much stronger. He pulled me over onto the couch and started to disrobe, and to take my clothes off as well. As you can imagine, I was horrified and frightened. The situation was out of control, and the fact that it was happening made our future working relationship very difficult. To say nothing of how I felt personally, as a woman. I mean, to be assaulted in this way."

Sanders stared at her, trying desperately to control his anger. He heard Fernandez, at his ear. *"Breathe."* He took a deep breath and let it out slowly. He had not been aware until then that he was holding his breath.

"I kept trying to make light of it," Meredith continued, "to make jokes, to get free. I was trying to say to him, Oh, come on Tom, let's not do this. But he was determined. And when he tore my underwear off, when I heard the sound of the cloth ripping, I realized that I could not get out of this situation in any diplomatic way. I had to acknowledge that Mr. Sanders was raping me and I became very scared and very angry. When he moved away from me on the couch, to free his penis from his trousers, prior to penetration, I kneed him in the groin. He rolled off the couch, onto the floor. Then he got to his feet, and I got to my feet.

"Mr. Sanders was angry that I had refused his advances. He started shouting at me, and then he hit me, knocking me down onto the floor. But by then I was angry, too. I remember saying, 'You can't do this to me,' and swearing at him. But I can't say I remember everything that he said or that I said. He came back at me one more time, but by then I had my shoes in my hand, and I hit him in the chest with my high heels, trying to drive him away. I think I tore his shirt. I'm not sure. I was so angry by then, I wanted to kill him. I'm sure I scratched him. I remember I said I wanted to kill him. I was so angry. Here it was my first day in this new job, I was under so much pressure, I was trying to do a good job and this . . . this *thing* had happened that ruined our relationship and was going to cause a lot of trouble for everybody in the company. He went off in an angry rage. After he left, the question for me was how to handle it."

She paused, shaking her head, apparently lost in the emotions of that moment.

Heller said gently, "How did you decide to handle it?"

"Well, it's a problem. Tom's an important employee, and he is not an easy person to replace. Furthermore, in my judgment it would not be wise to make a replacement in the middle of the acquisition. My first impulse was to see if we could forget the whole thing. After all, we're both adults. I was personally embarrassed, but I thought that Tom would probably be embarrassed, too; when he sobered up and had a chance to think it over. And I thought that maybe we could just go on from there. After all, awkward things happen sometimes. People can overlook them.

"So when the meeting time changed, I called his house to tell him. He wasn't there, but I had a very pleasant conversation with his wife. It was clear from our conversation that she did not know that Tom had been meeting me, or that Tom and I knew each other from the past. Anyway, I gave his wife the new meeting time, and asked her to tell Tom.

"The next day, at the meeting, things did not go well. Tom showed up late, and changed his story about the Twinkle drive, minimizing the problems and contradicting me. He was clearly undercutting my authority in a corporate meeting and I could not permit that. I went directly to Phil Blackburn and told him everything that had happened. I said I did not want to press formal charges, but I made it clear that I could not work with Tom and that a change would have to be made. Phil said he would talk to Tom. And eventually it was decided that we would try to mediate a resolution."

She sat back, and placed her hands flat on the table. "That's all, I think. That's everything." She looked around at everyone, meeting their eyes in turn. Very cool, very controlled.

It was a spectacular performance, and in Sanders it produced a quite unexpected effect: he felt guilty. He felt as if he had done the things that she said he had done. He felt sudden shame, and looked down at the table, hanging his head.

Fernandez kicked him in the ankle, hard. He jerked his head up, wincing. She was frowning at him. He sat up.

Judge Murphy cleared her throat. "Evidently," she said, "we are presented with two entirely incompatible reports. Ms. Johnson, I have only a few questions before we go on."

"Yes, Your Honor?"

"You're an attractive woman. I'm sure you've had to fend off your share of unwanted approaches in the course of your business career."

Meredith smiled. "Yes, Your Honor."

"And I'm sure you have developed some skill at it."

"Yes, Your Honor."

"You've said you were aware of tensions from your past relationship with Mr. Sanders. Considering those tensions, I would have thought that a meeting held in the middle of the day, without wine, would have been more professional—would have set a better tone."

"I'm sure that's correct in hindsight," Meredith said. "But at the time, this was all in the context of the acquisition meetings. Everybody was busy. I was just trying to fit the meeting with Mr. Sanders in before the Conley-White sessions the next day. That's all I was thinking about. Schedules."

"I see. And after Mr. Sanders left your office, why didn't you call Mr. Blackburn, or someone else in the company, to report what had happened?"

"As I said, I was hoping it could all be overlooked."

"Yet the episode you describe," Murphy said, "is a serious breach of normal business behavior. As an experienced manager, you must have known the chance of a good working relationship with Mr. Sanders was nil. I would have thought you'd feel obliged to report what happened to a superior at once. And from a practical standpoint, I would have thought you'd want to go on record as soon as possible."

"As I said, I was still hoping." She frowned, thinking. "You know, I guess . . . I felt responsible for Tom. As an old friend, I didn't want to be the reason why he lost his job."

"On the other hand, you are the reason why he lost his job."

"Yes. Again, in hindsight."

"I see. All right. Ms. Fernandez?"

"Thank you, Your Honor." Fernandez turned in her chair to face Johnson. "Ms. Johnson, in a situation like this, when private behavior occurs behind closed doors, we need to look at surrounding events where we can. So I'll ask you a few questions about surrounding events."

"Fine."

"You've said that when you made the appointment with Mr. Sanders, he requested wine."

"Yes."

"Where did the wine come from, that you drank that night?"

"I asked my assistant to get it."

"This is Ms. Ross?"

"Yes."

"She's been with you a long time?"

"Yes."

"She came up with you from Cupertino?"

"Yes."

"She is a trusted employee?"

"Yes."

"How many bottles did you ask Ms. Ross to buy?"

"I don't remember if I specified a particular number."

"All right. How many bottles did she get?"

"Three, I think."

"Three. And did you ask your assistant to buy anything else?"

"Like what?"

"Did you ask her to buy condoms?"

"No."

"Do you know if she bought condoms?"

"No, I don't."

"In fact, she did. She bought condoms from the Second Avenue Drugstore."

"Well, if she bought condoms," Johnson said, "it must have been for herself."

"Do you know of any reason why your assistant would say she bought condoms for you?"

"No," Johnson said, speaking slowly. She was thinking it over. "I can't imagine she would do that."

"Just a moment," Murphy said, interrupting. "Ms. Fernandez, are you alleging that the assistant *did* say that she bought the condoms for Ms. Johnson?"

"Yes, Your Honor. We are."

"You have a witness to that effect?"

"Yes, we do."

Sitting beside Johnson, Heller rubbed the bottom of his lip with one finger. Johnson showed no reaction at all. She didn't even blink. She just continued to gaze calmly at Fernandez, waiting for the next question.

"Ms. Johnson, did you instruct your assistant to lock the door to your office when Mr. Sanders was with you?"

"I most certainly did not."

"Do you know if she locked the door?"

"No, I don't."

"Do you know why she would tell someone that you ordered her to lock the door?"

"No."

"Ms. Johnson. Your meeting with Mr. Sanders was at six o'clock. Did you have any appointments later that day?"

"No. His was the last."

"Isn't it true that you had a seven o'clock appointment that you canceled?"

"Oh. Yes, that's true. I had one with Stephanie Kaplan. But I canceled it because I wasn't going to have the figures ready for her to go over. There wasn't time to prepare."

"Are you aware that your assistant told Ms. Kaplan that you were canceling because you had another meeting that was going to run late?"

"I don't know what my assistant said to her," Meredith replied, showing impatience for the first time. "We seem to be talking a great deal about my assistant. Perhaps you should be asking her these questions."

"Perhaps we should. I'm sure it can be arranged. All right. Let's turn to something else. Mr. Sanders said he saw a cleaning woman when he left your office. Did you also see her?"

"No. I stayed in my office after he had gone."

"The cleaning woman, Marian Walden, says she overheard a loud argument prior to Mr. Sanders's departure. She says she heard a man say, 'This isn't a good idea, I don't want to do this,' and she heard a woman say, 'You fucking bastard, you can't leave me like this.' Do you recall saying anything like that?"

"No. I recall saying, 'You can't do this to me.' "

"But you don't recall saying, 'You can't leave me like this.' "

"No, I do not."

"Ms. Walden is quite clear that was what you said."

"I don't know what Ms. Walden thought she heard," Johnson said. "The doors were closed the entire time."

"Weren't you speaking quite loudly?"

"I don't know. Possibly."

"Ms. Walden said you were shouting. And Mr. Sanders has said you were shouting."

"I don't know."

"All right. Now, Ms. Johnson, you said that you informed Mr. Blackburn that you could not work with Mr. Sanders after the unfortunate Tuesday morning meeting, is that right?"

"Yes. That's right."

Sanders sat forward. He suddenly realized that he had overlooked that, while Meredith was making her original statement. He had been so upset, he hadn't realized that she had lied about when she saw Blackburn. Because Sanders had gone to Blackburn's office right after the meeting—and Blackburn already knew.

"Ms. Johnson, what time would you say you went to see Mr. Blackburn?"

"I don't know. After the meeting."

"About what time?"

"Ten o'clock."

"Not earlier?"

"No."

Sanders glanced over at Blackburn, who sat rigidly at the end of the table. He looked tense, and bit his lip.

Fernandez said, "Shall I ask Mr. Blackburn to confirm that? I imagine his assistant has a log, if he has difficulty with exact memory."

There was a short silence. She looked over at Blackburn. "No," Meredith said. "No. I was confused. What I meant to say was I talked to Phil after the initial meeting, and before the second meeting."

"The initial meeting being the one at which Sanders was absent? The eight o'clock meeting."

"Yes."

"So Mr. Sanders's behavior at the second meeting, where he contradicted you, could not have been relevant to your decision to speak to Mr. Blackburn. Because you had already spoken to Mr. Blackburn by the time that meeting took place."

"As I say, I was confused."

"I have no more questions of this witness, Your Honor."

Judge Murphy closed her notepad. Her expression was bland and unreadable. She looked at her watch. "It's now eleven-thirty. We will break for lunch for two hours. I'm allowing extra time so that counsel can meet to review the situation and to decide how the parties wish to proceed." She stood up. "I am also available if counsel wish to meet with me for any reason. Otherwise, I'll see you all back here at one-thirty sharp. Have a pleasant and productive lunch." She turned and walked out of the room.

Blackburn stood and said, "Personally, I'd like to meet with opposing counsel, right now."

Sanders glanced over at Fernandez.

Fernandez gave the faintest of smiles. "I'm amenable to that, Mr. Blackburn," she said.

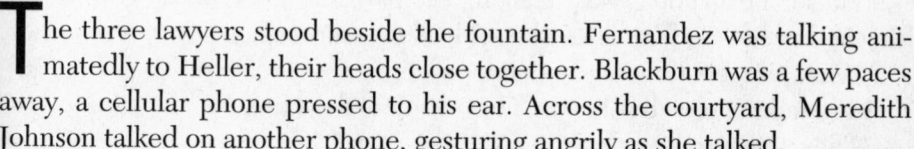

The three lawyers stood beside the fountain. Fernandez was talking animatedly to Heller, their heads close together. Blackburn was a few paces away, a cellular phone pressed to his ear. Across the courtyard, Meredith Johnson talked on another phone, gesturing angrily as she talked.

Sanders stood off to one side by himself, and watched. There was no question in his mind that Blackburn would seek a settlement. Piece by piece, Fernandez had torn Meredith Johnson's version apart: demonstrating that she had ordered her assistant to buy wine, to buy condoms, to lock the door when Sanders was there, and to cancel later appointments. Clearly, Meredith Johnson was not a supervisor surprised by a sexual overture. She had been planning it all afternoon. Her crucial reaction—her angry statement that "You can't leave me"—had been overheard by the cleaning woman. And she had lied about the timing and motivation of her report to Blackburn.

There could be no doubt in anyone's mind that Meredith was lying. The only question now was what Blackburn and DigiCom would do about it. Sanders had sat through enough management sensitivity seminars on sexual harassment to know what the company's obligation was. They really had no choice.

They would have to fire her.

But what would they do about Sanders? That was another question entirely. He had the strong intuition that by bringing this accusation, he had burned his bridges at the company; he would never be welcomed back. Sanders had shot down Garvin's pet bird, and Garvin would not forgive him for it.

So: they wouldn't let him back. They would have to pay him off.

"They're calling it quits already, huh?"

Sanders turned and saw Alan, one of the investigators, coming up from the parking lot. Alan had glanced over at the lawyers and quickly appraised the situation.

"I think so," Sanders said.

Alan squinted at the lawyers. "They should. Johnson has a problem. And a lot of people in the company know about it. Especially her assistant."

Sanders said, "You talked to her last night?"

"Yeah," he said. "Herb found the cleaning woman and got her taped. And I had a late night with Betsy Ross. She's a lonely lady, here in a new town. She drinks too much, and I taped it all."

"Did she know that?"

"She doesn't have to," Alan said. "It's still admissible." He watched the lawyers for a moment. "Blackburn must be shitting staples about now."

Louise Fernandez was stalking across the courtyard, grim-faced, hunched over. "God*damn* it," she said, as she came up.

"What happened?" Sanders said.

Fernandez shook her head. "They won't make a deal."

"They won't make a deal?"

"That's right. They just deny every point. Her assistant bought wine? That was for Sanders. Her assistant bought condoms? That was for the assistant. The assistant says she bought them for Johnson? The assistant is an unreliable drunk. The cleaning lady's report? She couldn't know what she heard, she had the radio on. And always the constant refrain, 'You know, Louise, this won't stand up in court.' And Bullet-proof Betty is on the phone, running the whole thing. Telling everybody what to do." Fernandez swore. "I have to tell you. This is the kind of shit male executives pull. They look you right in the eye and say, 'It never happened. It just isn't there. You have no case.' It burns my ass. *Damn* it!"

"Better get some lunch, Louise," Alan said. To Sanders he said, "She sometimes forgets to eat."

"Yeah, fine. Sure. Eat." They started toward the parking lot. She was walking fast, shaking her head. "I can't understand how they can take this position," she said. "Because I know—I could see it in Judge Murphy's eyes—that she didn't think there'd be an afternoon session at all. Judge Murphy heard the evidence and concluded it's all over. So did I. But it's not over. Blackburn and Heller aren't moving *one inch*. They're not going to settle. They're basically inviting us to sue."

"So we'll sue," Sanders said, shrugging.

"Not if we're smart," Fernandez said. "Not *now*. This is exactly what I was afraid would happen. They got a lot of free discovery, and we got nothing. We're back to square one. And they have the next three years to work on that assistant, and that cleaning lady, and anything else we come up with. And let me tell you: in three years we won't even be able to *find* that assistant."

"But we have her on tape . . ."

"She still has to appear in court. And believe me, she never will. Look, DigiCom has huge exposure. If we show that DigiCom didn't respond in a timely and adequate fashion to what they knew about Johnson, they could be liable for extremely large damages. There was a case in point last month in California: nineteen point four million dollars, found for the plaintiff. With exposure like that, take my word for it: the assistant will be unavailable. She'll be on vacation in Costa Rica for the rest of her life."

"So what do we do?" Sanders said.

"For better or worse, we're committed now. We've taken this line and we have to continue it. Somehow, we have to force them to come to terms," he said. "But we're going to need something else to do that. You got anything else?"

Sanders shook his head. "No, nothing."

"Hell," Fernandez said. "What's going on? I thought DigiCom was worried about this allegation becoming public before they finished the acquisition. I thought they had a publicity problem."

Sanders nodded. "I thought they did, too."

"Then there's something we don't understand. Because Heller and Blackburn both act like they couldn't care less what we do. Now why is that?"

A heavyset man with a mustache walked past them, carrying a sheaf of papers. He looked like a cop.

"Who's he?" Fernandez said.

"Never seen him before."

"They were calling on the phone for somebody. Trying to locate somebody. That's why I ask."

Sanders shrugged. "What do we do now?"

"We eat," Alan said.

"Right. Let's go eat," Fernandez said, "and forget it for a while."

In the same moment, a thought popped into his mind: *Forget that phone.* It seemed to come from nowhere, like a command:

Forget that phone.

Walking beside him, Fernandez sighed. "We still have things we can develop. It's not over yet. You've still got things, right, Alan?"

"Absolutely," Alan said. "We've hardly begun. We haven't gotten to Johnson's husband yet, or to her previous employer. There's lots of stones left to turn over and see what crawls out."

Forget that phone.

"I better check in with my office," Sanders said, and took out his cellular phone to dial Cindy.

A light rain began to fall. They came to the cars in the parking lot. Fernandez said, "Who's going to drive?"

"I will," Alan said.

They went to his car, a plain Ford sedan. Alan unlocked the doors, and Fernandez started to get in. "And I thought that at lunch today we would be going to have a party," she said.

Going to a party . . .

Sanders looked at Fernandez sitting in the front seat, behind the rain-spattered windshield. He held the phone up to his ear and waited while the call went through to Cindy. He was relieved that his phone was working correctly. Ever since Monday night when it went dead, he hadn't trusted it completely. But it seemed to be fine. Nothing wrong with it at all.

The couple was going to a party and she made a call on a cellular phone. From the car . . .

Forget that phone.

Cindy said, "Mr. Sanders's office."

And when she called, she got an answering machine. She left a message on the answering machine. And then she hung up.

"Hello? Mr. Sanders's office. Hello?"

"Cindy, it's me."

"Oh, hi, Tom." Still reserved.

"Any messages?" he said.

"Uh, yes, let me look at the book. You had a call from Arthur in KL, he wanted to know if the drives arrived. I checked with Don Cherry's team; they got them. They're working on them now. And you had a call from Eddie in Austin; he sounded worried. And you had another call from John Levin. He called you yesterday, too. And he said it was important."

Levin was the executive with a hard drive supplier. Whatever was on his mind, it could wait.

"Okay. Thanks, Cindy."

"Are you going to be back in the office today? A lot of people are asking."

"I don't know."

"John Conley from Conley-White called. He wanted to meet with you at four."

"I don't know. I'll see. I'll call you later."

"Okay." She hung up.

He heard a dial tone.

And then she had hung up.

The story tugged at the back of his mind. The two people in the car. Going to the party. Who had told him that story? How did it go?

On her way to the party, Adele had made a call from the car and then she had hung up.

Sanders snapped his fingers. Of course! Adele! The couple in the car had been Mark and Adele Lewyn. And they had had an embarrassing incident. It was starting to come back to him now.

Adele had called somebody and gotten the answering machine. She left a message, and hung up the phone. Then she and Mark talked in the car about the person Adele had just called. They made jokes and unflattering comments for about fifteen minutes. And later they were very embarrassed . . .

Fernandez said, "Are you just going to stand there in the rain?"

Sanders didn't answer. He took the cellular phone down from his ear. The keypad and screen glowed bright green. Plenty of power. He looked at the phone and waited. After five seconds, it clicked itself off; the screen went blank. That was because the new generation of phones had an auto-shutdown feature to conserve battery power. If you didn't use the phone or press the keypad for fifteen seconds, the phone shut itself off. So it wouldn't go dead.

But his phone had gone dead in Meredith's office.

Why?

Forget that phone.

Why had his cellular phone failed to shut itself off? What possible explanation could there be? Mechanical problems: one of the keys stuck, keeping the phone on. It had been damaged when he dropped it, when Meredith first kissed him. The battery was low because he forgot to charge it the night before.

No, he thought. The phone was reliable. There was no mechanical fault. And it was fully charged.

No.

The phone had worked correctly.

They made jokes and unflattering comments for about fifteen minutes.

His mind began to race, with scattered fragments of conversation coming back to him.

"Listen, why didn't you call me last night?"

"I did, Mark."

Sanders was certain that he had called Mark Lewyn from Meredith's office. Standing in the parking lot in the rain, he again pressed L-E-W on his keypad: The phone turned itself back on, the little screen flashing LEWYN and Mark's home number.

"There wasn't any message when I got home."

"I talked to your answering machine, about six-fifteen."

"I never got a message."

Sanders was sure that he had called Lewyn and had talked to his answering machine. He remembered a man's voice saying the standard message, "Leave a message when you hear the tone."

Standing there with the phone in his hand, staring at Lewyn's phone number, he pressed the SEND button. A moment later, the answering machine picked up. A woman's voice said, "Hi, you've reached Mark and Adele at home. We're not able to come to the phone right now, but if you leave a message, we'll call you back." *Beep.*

That was a different message.

He *hadn't* called Mark Lewyn that night.

Which could only mean he hadn't pressed L-E-W that night. Nervous in Meredith's office, he must have pressed something else. He had gotten somebody else's answering machine.

And his phone had gone dead.

Because . . .

Forget that phone.

"Jesus Christ," he said. He suddenly put it together. He knew exactly what had happened. And it meant that there was the chance that—

"Tom, are you all right?" Fernandez said.

"I'm fine," he said. "Just give me a minute. I think I've got something important."

He hadn't pressed L-E-W.

He had pressed something else. Something very close, probably one letter off. With fumbling fingers, Sanders pushed L-E-L. The screen stayed blank: he had no number stored for that combination. L-E-M. No number stored. L-E-S. No number stored. L-E-V.

Bingo.

Printed across the little screen was:

LEVIN

And a phone number for John Levin.

Sanders had called John Levin's answering machine that night.

John Levin called. He said it was important.

I'll bet he did, Sanders thought.

He remembered now, with sudden clarity, the exact sequence of events in Meredith's office. He had been talking on the phone and she said, "Forget that phone," and pushed his hand down as she started kissing him. He had dropped the phone on the windowsill as they kissed, and left it there.

Later on, when he left Meredith's office, buttoning his shirt, he had picked up the cellular phone from the sill, but by then it was dead. Which could only mean that it had remained constantly on for almost an hour. It had remained on during the entire incident with Meredith.

In the car, when Adele finished the call, she hung the phone back in the cradle, She didn't press the END *button, so the phone line stayed open, and their entire conversation was recorded on the person's answering machine. Fifteen minutes of jokes and personal commentary, all recorded on his answering machine.*

And Sanders's phone had been dead because the line stayed open. The whole conversation had been recorded.

Standing in the parking lot, he quickly dialed John Levin's number. Fernandez got out of the car and came over to him. "What's going on?" Fernandez said. "Are we going to lunch, or what?"

"Just a minute."

The call went through. A click of the pickup, then a man's voice: "John Levin."

"John, it's Tom Sanders."

"Well, hey there, Tom boy!" Levin burst out laughing. "My *man*! Are you having a red-hot sex life these days, or what? I tell you, Tom, my ears were burning."

Sanders said, "Was it recorded?"

"Jesus Christ, Tom, you better believe it. I came in Tuesday morning to check my messages, and I tell you, it went on for half an hour, I mean—"

"John—"

"Whoever said married life was dull—"

"John. Listen. *Did you keep it*?"

There was a pause. Levin stopped laughing. "Tom, what do you think I am, a *pervert*? Of *course* I kept it. I played it for the whole office. They loved it!"

"John. Seriously."

Levin sighed. "Yeah. I kept it. It sounded like you might be having a little trouble, and . . . I don't know. Anyway, I kept it."

"Good. Where is it?"

"Right here on my desk," Levin said.

"John, I want that tape. Now listen to me: this is what I want you to do."

Driving in the car, Fernandez said, "I'm waiting."

Sanders said, "There's a tape of the whole meeting with Meredith. It was all recorded."

"How?"

"It was an accident. I was talking to an answering machine," he said, "and when Meredith started kissing me, I put the phone down but didn't end the call. So the phone stayed connected to the answering machine. And everything we said went right onto the answering machine."

"Hot damn," Alan said, slapping the steering wheel as he drove.

"This is an audio tape?" Fernandez said.

"Yes."

"Good quality?"

"I don't know. We'll see. John's bringing it to lunch."

Fernandez rubbed her hands together. "I feel better already."

"Yes?"

"Yes," she said. "Because if it's any good at all, we can really draw blood."

John Levin, florid and jovial, pushed away his plate and drained the last of his beer. "Now that's what I call a meal. *Excellent* halibut." Levin weighed nearly three hundred pounds, and his belly pressed up against the edge of the table.

They were sitting in a booth in the back room of McCormick and Schmick's on First Avenue. The restaurant was noisy, filled with the lunchtime business crowd. Fernandez pressed the headphones to her ears as she listened to the tape on a Walkman. She had been listening intently for more than half an hour, making notes on a yellow legal pad, her food still uneaten. Finally she got up. "I have to make a call."

Levin glanced at Fernandez's plate. "Uh . . . do you want that?"

Fernandez shook her head, and walked away.

Levin grinned. "Waste not, want not," he said, and pulled the plate in front of him. He began to eat. "So Tom, are you in shit or what?"

"Deep shit," Sanders said. He stirred a cappuccino. He hadn't been able to eat lunch. He watched Levin wolf down great bites of mashed potatoes.

"I figured that," Levin said. "Jack Kerry over at Aldus called me this morning and said you were suing the company because you refused to jump some woman."

"Kerry is an asshole."

"The worst," Levin nodded. "The absolute worst. But what can you do? After Connie Walsh's column this morning, everybody's been trying to figure out who Mr. Piggy is." Levin took another huge bite of food. "But how'd she get the story in the first place? I mean, she's the one who broke it."

Sanders said, "Maybe you told her, John."

"Are you kidding?" Levin said.

"You had the tape."

Levin frowned. "You keep this up, Tom, you're going to piss me off." He shook his head. "No, you ask me, it was a woman who told her."

"What woman knew? Only Meredith, and she wouldn't tell."

"I'll bet you anything it'll turn out to be a woman," Levin said. "If you ever find out—which I doubt." He chewed thoughtfully. "Swordfish is a little rubbery. I think we should tell the waiter." He looked around the room. "Uh, Tom."

"Yes?"

"There's a guy standing over there, hopping from one foot to the other. I think maybe you know him."

Sanders looked over his shoulder. Bob Garvin was standing by the bar, looking at him expectantly. Phil Blackburn stood a few paces behind.

"Excuse me," Sanders said, and he got up from the table.

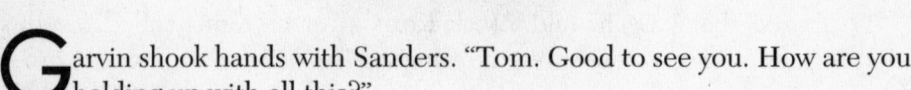

Garvin shook hands with Sanders. "Tom. Good to see you. How are you holding up with all this?"

"I'm okay," Sanders said.

"Good, good." Garvin placed his hand in a fatherly way on Sanders's shoulder. "It's nice to see you again."

"Nice to see you too, Bob."

Garvin said, "There's a quiet place in the corner over there. I asked them for a couple of cappuccinos. We can talk for a minute. Is that okay?"

"That's fine," Sanders said. He was well acquainted with the profane, angry Garvin. This cautious, polite Garvin made him uneasy.

They sat in the corner of the bar. Garvin settled into his chair and faced him.

"Well, Tom. We go way back, you and I."

"Yes, we do."

"Those damn trips to Seoul, eating that crappy food, and your ass hurting like hell. You remember all that."

"Yes, I do."

"Yeah, those were the days," Garvin said. He was watching Sanders carefully. "Anyway, Tom, we know each other, so I'm not going to bullshit you. Let me just put all the cards on the table," Garvin said. "We've got a problem here, and it's got to be solved before it turns into a real mess for everybody. I want to appeal to your better judgment about how we proceed from here."

"My better judgment?" Sanders said.

"Yes," Garvin said. "I'd like to look at this thing from all sides."

"How many sides are there?"

"There are at least two," Garvin said, with a smile. "Look, Tom. I'm sure it's no secret that I've supported Meredith inside our company. I've always believed that she's got talent and the kind of executive vision that we want for the future. I've never seen her do anything before that would suggest otherwise. I know she's only human, but she's very talented and I support her."

"Uh-huh . . ."

"Now perhaps in this case . . . perhaps it is true that she's made a mistake. I don't know."

Sanders said nothing. He just waited, staring at Garvin's face. Garvin was doing a convincing impression of an open-minded man. Sanders didn't buy it.

"In fact, let's say she has," Garvin said. "Let's say she did make a mistake."

"She did, Bob," Sanders said, firmly.

"All right. Let's say she did. An error of judgment, let's call it. An overstepping of bounds. The point is, Tom, faced with a situation like this, I still strongly support her."

"Why?"

"Because she's a woman."

"What does that have to do with it?"

"Well, women in business have traditionally been excluded from executive positions, Tom."

"Meredith hasn't been excluded," Sanders said.

"And after all," Garvin said, "she's young."

"She's not that young," Sanders said.

"Sure she is. She's practically a college kid. She just got her MBA a couple of years ago."

"Bob," Sanders said. "Meredith Johnson's thirty-five. She's not a kid at all."

Garvin did not seem to hear that. He looked at Sanders sympathetically. "Tom, I can understand that you were disappointed about the job," he said. "And I can understand that in your eyes, Meredith made a mistake in the way she approached you."

"She didn't approach me, Bob. She jumped me."

Garvin showed a flash of irritation. "You're no kid either, you know."

"That's right, I'm not," Sanders said. "But I *am* her employee."

"And I know she holds you in the highest regard," Garvin said, settling back in his chair. "As does everybody in the company, Tom. You're vital to our future. You know it, I know it. I want to keep our team together. And I keep coming back to the idea that we have to make allowances for women. We have to cut them a little slack."

"But we're not talking about women," Sanders said. "We're talking about one particular woman."

"Tom—"

"And if a man had done what she did, you wouldn't be talking about cutting him slack. You'd fire him, and throw him out on his ass."

"Possibly so."

"Well, that's the problem," Sanders said.

Garvin said, "I'm not sure I follow you there, Tom." His tone carried a warning: Garvin didn't like being disagreed with. Over the years, as his company grew in wealth and success, Garvin had grown accustomed to deference. Now, approaching retirement, he expected obedience and agreement. "We have an obligation to attain equality," Garvin said.

"Fine. But equality *means* no special breaks," Sanders said. "Equality means treating people the same. You're asking for *in*equality toward Meredith, because you won't do what you would do to a man—fire him."

Garvin sighed. "If it was a clear case, Tom, I would. But I understand this particular situation isn't so clear."

Sanders considered telling him about the tape. Something made him hold back. He said, "I think it is."

"But there are always differences of opinion on these matters," Garvin said, leaning across the bar. "That's a fact, isn't it? Always a difference of opinion. Tom. Look: what did she do that was so bad? I mean, really. She made a pass? Fine. You could have decided it was flattering. She's a beautiful woman, after all. There are worse things that could happen. A beautiful woman puts her hand on your knee. Or you could have just said, no thank you. You could have handled it any number of ways. You're a grown-up. But this . . . *vindictiveness*. Tom. I have to tell you. I'm surprised at you."

Sanders said, "Bob, she broke the law."

"That really remains to be seen, doesn't it?" Garvin said. "You can throw open your personal life for a jury to inspect, if that's what you want to do. I wouldn't want to do it, myself. And I don't see that it helps anybody to take this into court. It's a no-win situation, all around."

"What're you saying?"

"You don't want to go to court, Tom." Garvin's eyes were narrow, dangerous.

"Why not?"

"You just don't." Garvin took a deep breath. "Look. Let's stay on track here. I've talked to Meredith. She feels as I do, that this thing has gotten out of hand."

"Uh-huh . . ."

"And I'm talking to you now, too. Because my hope, Tom, is that we can put this to rest, and go back to the way things were—now hear me out, please—go back to the way things were, before this unfortunate misunderstanding happened. You stay at your job, Meredith stays at hers. You two continue to work together like civilized adults. You move forward and build the company, take it public, and everybody makes a pile of money a year down the line. What's wrong with that?"

Sanders felt something like relief, and a sense of normalcy returning. He longed to escape from the lawyers and from the tension of the last three days. To sink back into the way things were seemed as appealing as a warm bath.

"I mean, look at it this way, Tom. Right after this thing happened on Monday night, nobody blew the whistle. You didn't call anybody. Meredith didn't call anybody. I think you both wanted this thing to go away. Then there was an unfortunate mix-up the next day, and an argument that needn't have happened. If you'd been on time for the meeting, if you and Meredith had been in sync on the story, none of this would have happened. You two would still be working together, and whatever happened between you would remain your private business. Instead, we have this. It's all a big mistake, really. So why not just forget it and go forward? And get rich. Tom? What's wrong with that?"

"Nothing," Sanders said, finally.

"Good."

"Except it won't work," Sanders said.

"Why not?"

A dozen answers flashed through his mind: Because she's not competent. Because she's a snake. Because she's a corporate player, all image, and this is a technical division that has to get out the product. Because she's a liar. Because I have no respect for her. Because she'll do it again. Because she has no respect for me. Because you're not treating me fairly. Because she's your pet. Because you chose her over me. Because . . .

"Things have gone too far," he said.

Garvin stared at him. "Things can go back."

"No, Bob. They can't."

Garvin leaned forward. His voice dropped. "Listen you little *feringi* pissant. I know exactly what's going on here. I took you in when you didn't know *bulkogi* from bullshit. I gave you your start, I gave you help, I gave you opportunities, all along the line. Now you want to play rough? Fine. You want to see the shit come down? Just fucking wait, Tom." He stood up.

Sanders said, "Bob, you've never been willing to listen to reason on the subject of Meredith Johnson."

"Oh, you think *I* have a problem with Meredith?" Garvin laughed harshly. "Listen, Tom: she was your girlfriend, but she was smart and independent, and you couldn't handle her. You were pissed when she dropped you. And now, all these years later, you're going to pay her back. That's what this is about. It has nothing to do with business ethics or breaking the law or sexual harassment or any other damned thing. It's personal, and it's petty. And you're so full of shit your eyes are brown."

And he stalked out of the restaurant, pushing angrily past Blackburn. Blackburn remained behind for a moment, staring at Sanders, and then hurried after his boss.

As Sanders walked back to his table, he passed a booth with several guys from Microsoft, including two major assholes from systems programming. Someone made a snorting pig sound.

"Hey Mr. Piggy," said a low voice.

"Suwee! Suwee!"

"Couldn't get it up, huh?"

Sanders walked on a few paces, then turned back. "Hey, guys," he said. "At least I'm not bending over and grabbing my ankles in late-night meetings with—" and he named a Programming head at Microsoft.

They all roared with laughter.

"Whoa ho!"

"Mr. Piggy speaks!"

"Oink oink."

Sanders said, "What're you guys doing in town, anyway? They run short on K-Y jelly in Redmond?"

"Whoa!"

"The Piggy is pissed!"

They were doubled over, laughing like college kids. They had a big pitcher of beer on the table. One of them said, "If Meredith Johnson pulled off her pants for me, I sure wouldn't call the police about it."

"No way, Jose!"

"Service with a smile!"

"Hard charger!"

"Ladies *first*!"

"Ka-jung! Ka-jung!"

They pounded the table, laughing.

Sanders walked away.

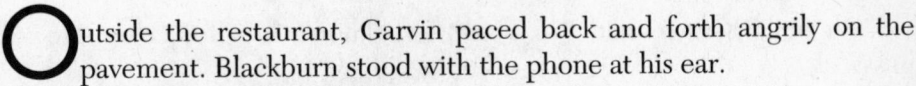

Outside the restaurant, Garvin paced back and forth angrily on the pavement. Blackburn stood with the phone at his ear.

"Where is that fucking car?" Garvin said.

"I don't know, Bob."

"I told him to *wait*."

"'I know, Bob. I'm trying to get him."

"Christ Almighty, the simplest things. Can't even get the fucking cars to work right."

"Maybe he had to go to the bathroom."

"So? How long does that take? Goddamn Sanders. Could you believe him?"

"No, I couldn't, Bob."

"I just don't understand. He won't deal with me on this. And I'm bending over backward here. I offer him his job back, I offer him his stock back, I offer him everything. And what does he do? Jesus."

"He's not a team player, Bob."

"You got that right. And he's not willing to meet us. We've got to get him to come to the table."

"Yes we do, Bob."

"He's not feeling it," Garvin said. "That's the problem."

"The story ran this morning. It can't have made him happy."

"Well, he's not feeling it."

Garvin paced again.

"There's the car," Blackburn said, pointing down the street. The Lincoln sedan was driving toward them.

"Finally," Garvin said. "Now look, Phil. I'm tired of wasting time on Sanders. We tried being nice, and it didn't work. That's the long and the short of it. So what are we going to do, to make him feel it?"

"I've been thinking about that," Phil said. "What's Sanders doing? I mean really doing? He's smearing Meredith, right?"

"Goddamn right."

"He didn't hesitate to smear her."

"He sure as hell didn't."

"And it's not true, what he's saying about her. But the thing about a smear is that it doesn't have to be true. It just has to be something people are willing to believe is true."

"So?"

"So maybe Sanders needs to see what that feels like."

"Like what feels like? What're you talking about?"

Blackburn stared thoughtfully at the approaching car. "I think that Tom's a violent man."

"Oh hell," Garvin said, "he's not. I've known him for years. He's a pussycat."

"No," Blackburn said, rubbing his nose. "I disagree. I think he's violent. He was a football player in college, he's a rough-and-tumble sort of guy. Plays football on the company team, knocks people around. He has a violent streak. Most men do, after all. Men are violent."

"What kind of shit is this?"

"And you have to admit, he was violent to Meredith," Blackburn continued. "Shouting. Yelling. Pushing her. Knocking her over. Sex and violence. A man out of control. He's much bigger than she is. Just stand them side by side, anybody can see the difference. He's much bigger. Much stronger. All you have to do is look, and you see he is a violent abusive man. That nice exterior is just a cover. Sanders is one of those men who take out their hostility by beating up defenseless women."

Garvin was silent. He squinted at Blackburn. "You'll never make this fly."

"I think I can."

"Nobody in their right mind'll buy it."

Blackburn said, "I think somebody will."

"Yeah? Who?"

"Somebody," Blackburn said.

The car pulled up to the curb. Garvin opened the door. "Well, all I know," he said, "is that we need to get him to negotiate. We need to apply pressure to bring him to the table."

Blackburn said, "I think that can be arranged."

Garvin nodded. "It's in your hands, Phil. Just make sure it happens." He got in the car. Blackburn got in the car after Garvin. Garvin said to the driver, "Where the fuck have you been?"

The door slammed shut. The car drove off.

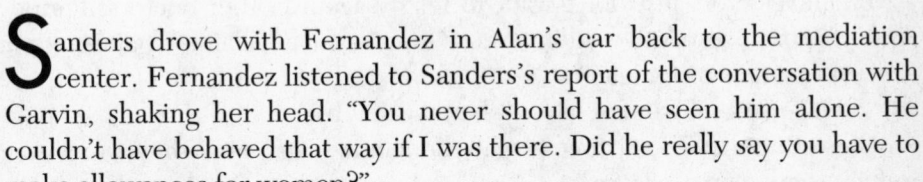

Sanders drove with Fernandez in Alan's car back to the mediation center. Fernandez listened to Sanders's report of the conversation with Garvin, shaking her head. "You never should have seen him alone. He couldn't have behaved that way if I was there. Did he really say you have to make allowances for women?"

"Yes."

"That's noble of him. He's found a virtuous reason why we should protect a harasser. It's a nice touch. Everyone should sit back and allow her to break the law because she's a woman. Very nice."

Sanders felt stronger hearing her words. The conversation with Garvin had rattled him. He knew that Fernandez was working on him, building him back up, but it worked anyway.

"The whole conversation is ridiculous," Fernandez said. "And then he threatened you?"

Sanders nodded.

"Forget it. It's just bluster."

"You're sure?"

"Absolutely," she said. "Just talk. But at least now you know why they say men just don't get it. Garvin gave you the same lines that every corporate guy has been giving for years: Look at it from the harasser's point of view. What did they do that was so wrong. Let bygones be bygones. Everybody just go back to work. We'll be one big happy family again."

"Incredible," Alan said, driving the car.

"It is, in this day and age," Fernandez said. "You can't pull that stuff anymore. How old is Garvin, anyway?"

"Almost sixty."

"That helps explain it. But Blackburn should have told him it's completely unacceptable. According to the law, Garvin really doesn't have any choice. At a minimum, he has to transfer Johnson, not you. And almost certainly, he should fire her."

"I don't think he will," Sanders said.

"No, of course he won't."

"She's his favorite," Sanders said.

"More to the point, she's his vice president," Fernandez said. She stared out the window as they went up the hill toward the mediation center. "You have to realize, all these decisions are about power. Sexual harassment is about power, and so is the company's resistance to dealing with it. Power protects power. And once a woman gets up in the power structure, she'll be protected by the structure, the same as a man. It's like the way doctors won't testify against other doctors. It doesn't matter if the doctor is a man or a woman. Doctors just don't want to testify against other doctors. Period. And corporate executives don't want to investigate claims against other executives, male or female."

"So it's just that women haven't had these jobs?"

"Yes. But they're starting to get them now. And now they can be as unfair as any man ever was."

"Female chauvinist sows," Alan said.

"Don't you start," Fernandez said.

"Tell him the figures," Alan said.

"What figures?" Sanders said.

"About five percent of sexual harassment claims are brought by men against women. It's a relatively small figure. But then, only five percent of corporate supervisors are women. So the figures suggest that women executives harass men in the same proportion as men harass women. And as more women get corporate jobs, the percentage of claims by men is going up. Because the fact is, harassment is a power issue. And power is neither male nor female. Whoever is behind the desk has the opportunity to abuse power. And women will take advantage as often as men. A case in point being the delightful Ms. Johnson. And her boss isn't firing her."

"Garvin says it's because the situation isn't clear."

"I'd say that tape is pretty damn clear," Fernandez said. She frowned. "Did you tell him about the tape?"

"No."

"Good. Then I think we can wrap this case up in the next two hours."

Alan pulled into the parking lot and parked the car. They all got out.

"All right," Fernandez said. "Let's see where we are with her significant others. Alan. We've still got her previous employer—"

"Conrad Computer. Right. We're on it."

"And also the one before that."

"Symantec."

"Yes. And we have her husband—"

"I've got a call into CoStar for him."

"And the Internet business? 'Afriend'?"

"Working on it."

"And we have her B-school, and Vassar."

"Right."

"Recent history is the most important. Focus on Conrad and the husband."

"Okay," Alan said. "Conrad's a problem, because they supply systems to the government and the CIA. They gave me some song and dance about neutral reference policy and nondisclosure of prior employees."

"Then get Harry to call them. He's good on negligent referral. He can shake them up if they continue to stonewall."

"Okay. He may have to."

Alan got back in the car. Fernandez and Sanders started walking up to the mediation center. Sanders said, "You're checking her past companies?"

"Yes. Other companies don't like to give damaging information on prior employees. For years, they would never give anything at all except the dates of employment. But now there's something called compelled self-publication, and something called negligent referral. A company can be liable now for failing to reveal a problem with a past employee. So we can try to scare them. But in the end, they may not give us the damaging information we want."

"How do you know they have damaging information to give?"

Fernandez smiled. "Because Johnson is a harasser. And with harassers, there's always a pattern. It's never the first time."

"You think she's done this before?"

"Don't sound so disappointed," Fernandez said. "What did you think? That she did all this because she thought you were so cute? I guarantee you she has done it before." They walked past the fountains in the courtyard toward the door to the center building. "And now," Fernandez said, "let's go cut Ms. Johnson to shreds."

Precisely at one-thirty, Judge Murphy entered the mediation room. She looked at the seven silent people sitting around the table and frowned. "Has opposing counsel met?"

"We have," Heller said.

"With what result?" Murphy said.

"We have failed to reach a settlement," Heller said.

"Very well. Let's resume." She sat down and opened her notepad. "Is there further discussion relating to the morning session?"

"Yes, Your Honor," Fernandez said. "I have some additional questions for Ms. Johnson."

"Very well. Ms. Johnson?"

Meredith Johnson put on her glasses. "Actually, Your Honor, I would like to make a statement first."

"All right."

"I've been thinking about the morning session," Johnson said, speaking slowly and deliberately, "and Mr. Sanders's account of the events of Monday night. And I've begun to feel that there may be a genuine misunderstanding here."

"I see." Judge Murphy spoke absolutely without inflection. She stared at Meredith. "All right."

"When Tom first suggested a meeting at the end of the day, and when he suggested that we have some wine, and talk over old times, I'm afraid I may have unconsciously responded to him in a way that he might not have intended."

Judge Murphy didn't move. Nobody was moving. The room was completely still.

"I believe it is correct to say that I took him at his word, and began to imagine a, uh, romantic interlude. And to be frank, I was not opposed to that possibility. Mr. Sanders and I had a very special relationship some years ago, and I remembered it as a very exciting relationship. So I believe it is fair to say that I was looking forward to our meeting, and that perhaps I

230

presumed that it would lead to an encounter. Which I was, unconsciously, quite willing to have occur."

Alongside Meredith, Heller and Blackburn sat completely stonefaced, showing no reaction at all. The two female attorneys showed no reaction. This had all been worked out in advance, Sanders realized. What was going on? Why was she changing her story?

Johnson cleared her throat, then continued in the same deliberate way. "I believe it is correct to say that I was a willing participant in all the events of the evening. And it may be that I was too forward, at one point, for Mr. Sanders's taste. In the heat of the moment, I may have overstepped the bounds of propriety and my position in the company. I think that's possible. After serious reflection, I find myself concluding that my own recollection of events and Mr. Sanders's recollection of events are in much closer agreement than I had earlier recognized."

There was a long silence. Judge Murphy said nothing. Meredith Johnson shifted in her chair, took her glasses off, then put them back on again.

"Ms. Johnson," Murphy said finally, "do I understand you to say that you are now agreeing to Mr. Sanders's version of the events on Monday night?"

"In many respects, yes. Perhaps in most respects."

Sanders suddenly realized what had happened: *they knew about the tape.*

But how could they know? Sanders himself had learned of it only two hours ago. And Levin had been out of his office, having lunch with them. So Levin couldn't have told them. How could they know?

"And, Ms. Johnson," Murphy said, "are you also agreeing to the charge of harassment by Mr. Sanders?"

"Not at all, Your Honor. No."

"Then I'm not sure I understand. You've changed your story. You say you now agree that Mr. Sanders's version of the events is correct in most respects. But you do not agree that he has a claim against you?"

"No, Your Honor. As I said, I think it was all a misunderstanding."

"A *misunderstanding*," Murphy repeated, with an incredulous look on her face.

"Yes, Your Honor. And one in which Mr. Sanders played a very active role."

"Ms. Johnson. According to Mr. Sanders, you initiated kissing over his protests; you pushed him down on the couch over his protests; you unzipped his trousers and removed his penis over his protests; and you removed your own clothing over his protests. Since Mr. Sanders is your employee, and dependent on you for employment, it is difficult for me to comprehend why this is not a clear-cut and indisputable case of sexual harassment on your part."

"I understand, Your Honor," Meredith Johnson said calmly. "And I realize I have changed my story. But the reason I say it is a misunderstanding is that from the beginning, I genuinely believed that Mr. Sanders was seeking a sexual encounter with me, and that belief guided my actions."

"You do not agree that you harassed him."

"No, Your Honor. Because I thought I had clear *physical* indications that Mr. Sanders was a willing participant. At times he certainly took the lead. So now, I have to ask myself why he would take the lead—and then so suddenly withdraw. I don't know why he did that. But I believe he shares responsibility for what happened. That is why I feel that, at the very least, we had a genuine misunderstanding. And I want to say that I am sorry— truly, deeply sorry—for my part in this misunderstanding."

"You're sorry." Murphy looked around the room in exasperation. "Can anyone explain to me what is going on? Mr. Heller?"

Heller spread his hands. "Your Honor, my client told me what she intended to do here. I consider it a very brave act. She is a true seeker after truth."

"Oh, spare me," Fernandez said.

Judge Murphy said, "Ms. Fernandez, considering this radically different statement from Ms. Johnson, would you like a recess before you proceed with your questions?"

"No, Your Honor. I am prepared to go forward now," Fernandez said.

"I see," Murphy said, puzzled. "All right. Fine." Judge Murphy clearly felt that there was something everyone else in the room knew that she didn't.

Sanders was still wondering how Meredith knew about the tape. He looked over at Phil Blackburn, who sat at one end of the table, his cellular phone before him. He was rubbing the phone nervously.

Phone records, Sanders thought. That must be it.

DigiCom would have had somebody—most probably Gary Bosak— going through all of Sanders's records, looking for things to use against him. Bosak would have checked all the calls made on Sanders's cellular phone. When he did that, he would have discovered a call that lasted forty-five minutes on Monday night. It would stand out: a whopping big duration and charge. And Bosak must have looked at the time of the call and figured out what had happened. He'd realize that Sanders hadn't been talking on the phone during that particular forty-five minutes on Monday night. Therefore, there could only be one explanation. The call was running to an answering machine, which meant there was a tape. And Johnson knew it, and had adjusted her story accordingly. That was what had made her change.

"Ms. Johnson," Fernandez said. "Let's clear up a few factual points first. Are you now saying that you *did* send your assistant to buy wine and condoms, that you *did* tell her to lock the door, and that you *did* cancel your seven o'clock appointment in anticipation of a sexual encounter with Mr. Sanders?"

"Yes, I did."

"In other words, you lied earlier."

"I presented my point of view."

"But we are not talking about a point of view. We are talking about facts. And given this set of facts, I'm curious to know why you feel that Mr. Sanders shares responsibility for what happened in that room Monday night."

"Because I felt . . . I felt that Mr. Sanders had come to my office with the clear intention of having sex with me, and he later denied any such intention. I felt he had set me up. He led me on, and then accused me, when I had done nothing more than simply respond to him."

"You feel he set you up?"

"Yes."

"And that's why you feel he shares responsibility?"

"Yes."

"In what way did he set you up?"

"Well, I think it's obvious. Things had gone very far along, when he suddenly got off the couch and said he was not going to proceed. I'd say that was a setup."

"Why?"

"Because you can't go so far and then just stop. That's obviously a hostile act, intended to embarrass and humiliate me. I mean . . . anyone can see that."

"All right. Let's review that particular moment in detail," Fernandez said. "As I understand it, we're talking about the time when you were on the couch with Mr. Sanders, with both of you in a state of partial undress. Mr. Sanders was crouched on his knees on the couch, his penis was exposed, and you were lying on your back with your panties removed and your legs spread, is that correct?"

"Basically. Yes." She shook her head. "You make it sound so . . . crude."

"But that was the situation at that moment, was it not?"

"Yes. It was."

"Now, at that moment, did you say, 'No, no, please,' and did Mr. Sanders reply, 'You're right, we shouldn't be doing this,' and then get off the couch?"

"Yes," she said. "That's what he said."

"Then what was the misunderstanding?"

"When I said, 'No, no,' I meant, 'No, don't wait.' Because he was waiting, sort of teasing me, and I wanted him to go ahead. Instead, he got off the couch, which made me very angry."

"Why?"

"Because I wanted him to do it."

"But Ms. Johnson, you said, 'No, no.' "

"I know what I said," she replied irritably, "but in that situation, it's perfectly clear what I was really saying to him."

"Is it?"

"Of course. He knew exactly what I was saying to him, but he chose to ignore it."

"Ms. Johnson, have you ever heard the phrase, 'No means no'?"

"Of course, but in this situation—"

"I'm sorry, Ms. Johnson. Does no mean no, or not?"

"Not in this case. Because at that time, lying on that couch, it was absolutely clear what I was really saying to him."

"You mean it was clear to you."

Johnson became openly angry. "It was clear to him, too," she snapped.

"Ms. Johnson. When men are told that 'no means no,' what does that mean?"

"I don't know." She threw up her hands in irritation. "I don't know what you're trying to say."

"I'm trying to say that men are being told that they must take women at their literal word. That no means no. That men cannot assume that no means maybe or yes."

"But in this particular situation, with all our clothes off, when things had gone so far—"

"What does that have to do with it?" Fernandez said.

"Oh, come off it," Johnson said. "When people are getting together, they begin with little touches, then little kisses, then a little petting, then some more petting. Then the clothes come off, and you're touching various private parts, and so on. And pretty soon you have an expectation about what's going to happen. And you don't turn back. To turn back is a hostile act. That's what he did. He set me up."

"Ms. Johnson. Isn't it true that women claim the right to turn back at any point, up to the moment of actual penetration? Don't women claim the unequivocal right to change their minds?"

"Yes, but in this instance—"

"Ms. Johnson. If women have the right to change their minds, don't men as well? Can't Mr. Sanders change his mind?"

"It was a hostile act." Her face had a fixed, stubborn look. "He set me up."

"I'm asking whether Mr. Sanders has the same rights as a woman in this situation. Whether he has the right to withdraw, even at the last moment."

"No."

"Why?"

"Because men are different."

"How are they different?"

"Oh, for Christ's sake," Johnson said angrily. "What are we talking about here? This is Alice in Wonderland. Men and women are *different*. Everybody knows that. Men can't control their impulses."

"Apparently Mr. Sanders could."

"Yes. As a hostile act. Out of his desire to humiliate me."

"But what Mr. Sanders actually said at the time was, 'I don't feel good about this.' Isn't that true?"

"I don't remember his exact words. But his behavior was very hostile and degrading toward me as a woman."

"Let's consider," Fernandez said, "who was hostile and degrading toward whom. Didn't Mr. Sanders protest the way things were going earlier in the evening?"

"Not really. No."

"I thought he had." Fernandez looked at her notes. "Early on, did you say to Mr. Sanders, 'You look good,' and 'You always had a nice hard tush'?"

"I don't know. I might have. I don't remember."

"And what did he reply?"

"I don't remember."

Fernandez said, "Now, when Mr. Sanders was talking on the phone, did you come up, push it out of his hand, and say, 'Forget that phone'?"

"I might have. I don't really remember."

"And did you initiate kissing at that point?"

"I'm not really sure. I don't think so."

"Well, let's see. How else could it have occurred? Mr. Sanders was talking on his cellular phone, over by the window. You were on another phone at your desk. Did he interrupt his call, set down his phone, come over, and start kissing you?"

She paused for a moment. "No."

"Then who initiated the kissing?"

"I guess I did."

"And when he protested and said, 'Meredith,' did you ignore him, press on, and say, 'God, I've wanted you all day. I'm so hot, I haven't had a decent fuck'?" Fernandez repeated these statements in a flat uninflected monotone, as if reading from a transcript.

"I may have . . . I think that might be accurate. Yes."

Fernandez looked again at her notes. "And then, when he said, 'Meredith, wait,' again clearly speaking in a tone of protest, did you say, 'Oh, don't talk, no, no, oh Jesus'?"

"I think . . . possibly I did."

"On reflection, would you say these comments by Mr. Sanders were protests that you ignored?"

"If they were, they were not very clear protests. No."

"Ms. Johnson. Would you characterize Mr. Sanders as fully enthusiastic throughout the encounter?"

Johnson hesitated a moment. Sanders could almost see her thinking, trying to decide how much the tape would reveal. Finally she said, "He was enthusiastic sometimes, not so much at other times. That's my point."

"Would you say he was ambivalent?"

"Possibly. Somewhat."

"Is that a yes or a no, Ms. Johnson?"

"Yes."

"All right. So Mr. Sanders was ambivalent throughout the session. He's told us why: because he was being asked to embark on an office affair with an old girlfriend who was now his boss. And because he was now married. Would you consider those valid reasons for ambivalence?"

"I suppose so."

"And in this state of ambivalence, Mr. Sanders was overwhelmed at the last moment with the feeling that he didn't want to go forward. And he told you how he felt, simply and directly. So, why would you characterize that as a 'setup'? I think we have ample evidence that it is just the opposite—an uncalculated, rather desperate human response to a situation which you entirely controlled. This was not a reunion of old lovers, Ms. Johnson, though you prefer to think it was. This was not a meeting of equals at all. The fact is, you are his superior and you controlled every aspect of the meeting. You arranged the time, bought the wine, bought the condoms, locked the door—and then you blamed your employee when he failed to please you. That is how you continue to behave now."

"And you're trying to put his behavior in a good light," Johnson said. "But what I'm saying is that as a practical matter, waiting to the last minute to stop makes people very angry."

"Yes," Fernandez said. "That's how many men feel, when women withdraw at the last minute. But women say a man has no right to be angry, because a woman can withdraw at any time. Isn't that true?"

Johnson rapped her fingers on the table irritably. "Look," she said. "You're trying to make some kind of federal case here, by trying to obscure basic facts. What did I do that was so wrong? I made him an offer, that's all.

If Mr. Sanders wasn't interested, all he had to do was say, 'No.' But he never said that. Not once. Because he intended to *set me up*. He's angry he didn't get the job and he's retaliating the only way he can—by smearing me. This is nothing but guerrilla warfare and character assassination. I'm a successful woman in business, and he resents my success and he's out to get me. You're saying all kinds of things to avoid that central and unavoidable fact"

"Ms. Johnson. The central and unavoidable fact is that you're Mr. Sanders's superior. And your behavior toward him was illegal. And it *is* in fact a federal case."

There was a short silence.

Blackburn's assistant came into the room and handed him a note. Blackburn read the note and passed it to Heller.

Murphy said, "Ms. Fernandez? Are you ready to explain what's going on to me now?"

"Yes, Your Honor. It turns out there is an audio tape of the meeting."

"Really? Have you heard it?"

"I have, Your Honor. It confirms Mr. Sanders's story."

"Are you aware of this tape, Ms. Johnson?"

"No, I am not."

"Perhaps Ms. Johnson and her attorney would like to hear it, too. Perhaps we should all hear it," Murphy said, looking directly at Blackburn.

Heller put the note in his pocket and said, "Your Honor, I'd like to request a ten-minute recess."

"Very well, Mr. Heller. I'd say this development warrants it."

Outside in the courtyard, black clouds hung low. It was threatening to rain again. Over by the fountains, Johnson huddled with Heller and Blackburn. Fernandez watched them. "I just don't understand this," she said. "There they all are, talking again. What is there to talk about? Their client lied, and then changed her story. There's no question that Johnson's guilty of sexual harassment. We have it recorded on tape. So what are they talking about?"

Fernandez stared for a moment, frowning. "You know, I have to admit it. Johnson's a hell of a smart woman," she said.

"Yes," Sanders said.

"She's quick and she's cool."

"Uh-huh."

"Moved up the corporate ladder fast."

"Yes."

"So . . . how'd she let herself get into this situation?"

"What do you mean?" Sanders said.

"I mean, what's she doing coming on to you the very first day at work? And coming on so strongly? Leaving herself open to all these problems? She's too smart for that."

Sanders shrugged.

"You think it's just because you're irresistible?" Fernandez said. "With all due respect, I doubt it."

He found himself thinking of the time he first knew Meredith, when she was doing demos, and the way she used to cross her legs whenever she was asked a question she couldn't answer. "She could always use sex to distract people. She's good at that."

"I believe it," Fernandez said. "So what is she distracting us from now?"

Sanders had no answer. But his instinct was that something else was going on. "Who knows how people really are in private?" he said. "I once knew this woman, she looked like an angel, but she liked bikers to beat her up."

"Uh-huh," Fernandez said. "That's fine. I'm not buying it for Johnson. Because Johnson strikes me as very controlled, and her behavior with you was not controlled."

"You said it yourself, there's a pattern."

"Yeah. Maybe. But why the first day? Why right away? I think she had another reason."

Sanders said, "And what about me? Do you think I had another reason?"

"I assume you did," she said, looking at him seriously. "But we'll talk about that later."

Alan came up from the parking lot, shaking his head.

"What've you got?" Fernandez said.

"Nothing good. We're striking out everywhere," he said. He flipped open his notepad. "Okay. Now, we've checked out that Internet address. The message originated in the 'U District.' And 'Afriend' turns out to be Dr. Arthur A. Friend. He's a professor of inorganic chemistry at the University of Washington. That name mean anything to you?"

"No," Sanders said.

"I'm not surprised. At the moment, Professor Friend is in northern Nepal on a consulting job for the Nepalese government. He's been there for three weeks. He's not expected back until late July. So it probably isn't him sending the messages anyway."

"Somebody's using his Internet address?"

"His assistant says that's impossible. His office is locked while he's away, and nobody goes in there except her. So nobody has access to his computer terminal. The assistant says she goes in once a day and answers Dr. Friend's E-mail, but otherwise the computer is off. And nobody knows the password but her. So I don't know."

"It's a message coming out of a locked office?" Sanders said, frowning.

"I don't know. We're still working on it. But for the moment, it's a mystery."

"All right, fine," Fernandez said. "What about Conrad Computer?"

"Conrad has taken a very hard position. They will only release information to the hiring company, meaning DigiCom. Nothing to us. And they say that the hiring company has not requested it. When we pushed, Conrad called DigiCom themselves, and DigiCom told them they weren't interested in any information Conrad might have."

"Hmmm."

"Next, the husband," Alan said. "I talked to someone who worked in his company, CoStar. Says the husband hates her, has lots of bad things to say about her. But he's in Mexico on vacation with his new girlfriend until next week."

"Too bad."

"Novell," Alan said. "They keep only the last five years current. Prior to that, records are in cold storage at headquarters in Utah. They have no idea what they'll show, but they're willing to get them out if we'll pay for it. It'll take two weeks."

Fernandez shook her head. "Not good."

"No."

"I have a strong feeling that Conrad Computer is sitting on something," Fernandez said.

"Maybe, but we'll have to sue to get it. And there's no time," Alan looked across the courtyard at the others. "What's happening now?"

"Nothing. They're hanging tough."

"Still?"

"Yeah."

"Jesus," Alan said. "Who's she got behind her?"

"I'd love to know," Fernandez said.

Sanders flipped open his cellular phone and checked in with his office. "Cindy, any messages?"

"Just two, Tom. Stephanie Kaplan asked if she could meet with you today."

"She say why?"

"No. But she said it wasn't important. And Mary Anne has come by twice, looking for you."

"Probably wants to skin me," Sanders said.

"I don't think so, Tom. She's about the only one who— she's very concerned about you, I think."

"Okay. I'll call her."

He started to dial Mary Anne's number when Fernandez nudged him in the ribs. He looked over and saw a slender, middle-aged woman walking up from the parking lot toward them.

"Buckle up," Fernandez said.

"Why? Who's that?"

"That," Fernandez said, "is Connie Walsh."

Connie Walsh was about forty-five years old, with gray hair and a sour expression. "Are you Tom Sanders?"

"That's right."

She pulled out a tape recorder. "Connie Walsh, from the *Post-Intelligencer*. Can we talk for a moment?"

"Absolutely not," Fernandez said.

Walsh looked over at her.

"I'm Mr. Sanders's attorney."

"I know who you are," Walsh said, and turned back to Sanders. "Mr. Sanders, our paper's going with a story on this discrimination suit at DigiCom. My sources tell me that you are accusing Meredith Johnson of sex discrimination, is that correct?

"He has no comment," Fernandez said, stepping between Walsh and Sanders.

Walsh looked past her shoulder and said, "Mr. Sanders, is it also true that you and she are old lovers, and that your accusation is a way to even the score?"

"He has no comment," Fernandez said.

"It looks to me like he does," Walsh said. "Mr. Sanders, you don't have to listen to her. You can say something if you want to. And I really think you should take this opportunity to defend yourself. Because my sources are also saying that you physically abused Ms. Johnson in the course of your meeting. These are very serious charges people are making against you, and I imagine you'll want to respond. What do you have to say to her allegations? Did you physically abuse her?"

Sanders started to speak, but Fernandez shot him a warning glance, and put her hand on his chest. She said to Walsh, "Has Ms. Johnson made these allegations to you? Because she was the only other one besides Mr. Sanders who was there."

"I'm not free to say. I have the story from very well-informed sources."

"Inside or outside the company?"

"I really can't say."

"Ms. Walsh," Fernandez said, "I am going to forbid Mr. Sanders to talk to you. And you better check with the *P-I* counsel before you run any of these unsubstantiated allegations."

"They're not unsubstantiated, I have very reliable—"

"If there is any question in your counsel's mind, you might have her call Mr. Blackburn and he will explain what your legal position is in this matter."

Walsh smiled bleakly. "Mr. Sanders, do you want to make a comment?"

Fernandez said, "Just check with your counsel, Ms. Walsh."

"I will, but it won't matter. You can't squash this. Mr. Blackburn can't squash this. And speaking personally, I have to say I don't know how you can defend a case like this."

Fernandez leaned close to her, smiled, and said, "Why don't you step over here with me, and I'll explain something to you."

She walked with Walsh a few yards away, across the courtyard.

Alan and Sanders remained where they were. Alan sighed. He said, "Wouldn't you give anything to know what they were saying right now?"

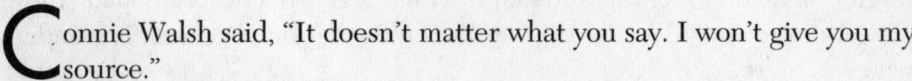

Connie Walsh said, "It doesn't matter what you say. I won't give you my source."

"I'm not asking for your source. I'm simply informing you that your story is wrong—"

"Of course you'd say that—"

"And that there's documentary evidence that it's wrong."

Connie Walsh paused. She frowned. "Documentary evidence?"

Fernandez nodded slowly. "That's right."

Walsh thought it over. "But there can't be," she said. "You said it yourself. They were alone in the room. It's his word against hers. There's no documentary evidence."

Fernandez shook her head, and said nothing.

"What is it? A tape?"

Fernandez smiled thinly. "I really can't say."

"Even if there is, what can it show? That she pinched his butt a little? She made a couple of jokes? What's the big deal? Men have been doing that for hundreds of years."

"That's not the issue in this—"

"Give me a break. So this guy gets a little pinch, and he starts screaming bloody murder. That's not normal behavior in a man. This guy obviously hates and demeans women. That's clear, just to look at him. And there's no question: he hit her, in that meeting. The company had to call a doctor to examine her for a concussion. And I have several reliable sources that tell me he's known to be physically abusive. He and his wife have had trouble for years. In fact, she's left town with the kids and is going to file for divorce." Walsh was watching Fernandez carefully as she said it.

Fernandez just shrugged.

"It's a fact. The wife has left town," Walsh said flatly. "Unexpectedly. She took the kids. And nobody knows where she went. Now, you tell me what that means."

Fernandez said, "Connie, all I can do is advise you in my capacity as Mr.

Sanders's attorney that documentary evidence contradicts your sources about this harassment charge."

"Are you going to show me this evidence?"

"Absolutely not."

"Then how do I know it exists?"

"You don't. You only know I have informed you of its existence."

"And what if I don't believe you."

Fernandez smiled. "These are the decisions a journalist must make."

"You're saying it'd be reckless disregard."

"If you go with your story, yes."

Walsh stepped back. "Look. Maybe you've got some kind of a technical legal case here, and maybe you don't. But as far as I'm concerned, you're just another minority woman trying to get ahead with the patriarchy by getting down on her knees. If you had any self-respect you wouldn't be doing their dirty work for them."

"Actually, Connie, the person who seems to be caught in the grip of the patriarchy is you."

"That's a lot of crap," Walsh said. "And let me tell you, you're not going to evade the facts here. He led her on, and then he beat her up. He's an ex-lover, he's resentful, and he's violent. He's a typical man. And let me tell you, before I'm through, he'll wish he had never been born."

Sanders said, "Is she going to run the story?"

"No," Fernandez said. She stared across the courtyard at Johnson, Heller, and Blackburn. Connie Walsh had gone over to Blackburn and was talking to him. "Don't get distracted by this," Fernandez said. "It's not important. The main issue is: what're they going to do about Johnson."

A moment later, Heller came toward them. He said, "We've been going over things on our side, Louise."

"And?"

"We've concluded that we see no purpose to further mediation and are withdrawing, as of now. I've informed Judge Murphy that we will not continue."

"Really. And what about the tape?"

"Neither Ms. Johnson nor Mr. Sanders knew they were being taped. Under law, one party must know the interaction is being recorded. Therefore the tape is inadmissible."

"But Ben—"

"We argue that the tape should be disallowed, both from this mediation and from any subsequent legal proceeding. We argue that Ms. Johnson's characterization of the meeting as a misunderstanding between consenting adults is the correct one, and that Mr. Sanders bears a responsibility for that misunderstanding. He was an active participant, Louise, no way around it. He took her panties off. Nobody held a gun to his head. But since there was fault on both sides, the proper thing is for the two parties to shake hands, let go of all animosity, and return to work. Apparently Mr. Garvin has already proposed this to Mr. Sanders, and Mr. Sanders has refused. We believe that under the circumstances Mr. Sanders is acting unreasonably and that if he does not reconsider in a timely manner, he should be fired for his refusal to show up for work."

"Son of a bitch," Sanders said.

Fernandez laid a restraining hand on his arm. "Ben," she said calmly. "Is this a formal offer of reconciliation and return to the company?"

"Yes, Louise."

"And what are the sweeteners?"

"No sweeteners. Everybody just goes back to work."

"The reason I ask," Fernandez said, "is that I believe I can successfully argue that Mr. Sanders was aware the tape was being made, and thus it is indeed admissible. I will argue further that it is admissible under discovery of public records over common carriers as defined in *Waller* v. *Herbst*. I will argue further that the company knew of Ms. Johnson's long history of harassment, and has failed to take proper steps to investigate her behavior, either prior to this incident, or now. And I will argue that the company was derelict in protecting Mr. Sanders's reputation when it leaked the story to Connie Walsh."

"Wait a minute here—"

"I will argue that the company had a clear reason for leaking it: they desired to cheat Mr. Sanders out of his well-deserved reward for more than a decade of service to the company. And you've got an employee in Ms. Johnson who has had some trouble before. I will claim defamation and ask for punitive damages of sufficient magnitude to send a message to corporate America. I'll ask for sixty million dollars, Ben. And you'll settle for forty million—the minute I get the judge to allow the jury to hear this tape. Because we both know that when the jury hears that tape, they will take about five seconds to find against Ms. Johnson and the company."

Heller shook his head. "You've got a lot of long shots there, Louise. I don't think they'll ever let that tape be played in court. And you're talking bout three years from now."

Fernandez nodded slowly. "Yes," she said. "Three years is a long time."

"You're telling me, Louise. Anything can happen."

"Yes, and frankly, I'm worried about that tape. So many untoward things an happen with evidence that is so scandalous. I can't guarantee somebody hasn't made a copy already. It'd be terrible if one fell into the hands of KQEM, and they started playing it over the radio."

"Christ," Heller said. "Louise, I can't believe you said that."

"Said what? I'm merely expressing my legitimate fears," Fernandez said. "I'd be derelict if I did not let you know my concerns. Let's face facts here, Ben. The cat's out of the bag. The press already has this story. Somebody eaked it to Connie Walsh. And she printed a story that's very damaging to Mr. Sanders's reputation. And it seems that somebody is still leaking, because now Connie is planning to write some unfounded speculation bout physical violence by my client. It's unfortunate that someone on your ide should have chosen to talk about this case. But we both know how it is vith a hot story in the press—you never know where the next leak will come rom."

Heller was uneasy. He glanced back at the others by the fountain. "Louise, I don't think there's any movement over there."

"Well, just talk to them."

Heller shrugged, and walked back.

"What do we do now?" Sanders said.

"We go back to your office."

"We?"

"Yes," Fernandez said. "This isn't the end. More is going to happen oday, and I want to be there when it does."

riving back, Blackburn talked on the car phone with Garvin. "The mediation's over. We called it off."

"And?"

"We're pushing Sanders hard to go back to work. But he's not responding so far. He's hanging tough. Now he's threatening punitive damages of sixty million dollars."

"Christ," Garvin said. "Punitive damages on what basis?"

"Defamation from corporate negligence dealing with the fact that we supposedly knew that Johnson had a history of harassment."

"I never knew of any history," Garvin said. "Did you know of any history Phil?"

"No," Blackburn said.

"Is there any documentary evidence of such a history?"

"No," Blackburn said. "I'm sure there isn't."

"Good. Then let him threaten. Where did you leave it with Sanders?"

"We gave him until tomorrow morning to rejoin the company at his old job or get out."

"All right," Garvin said. "Now let's get serious. What have we got on him?"

"We're working on that felony charge," Blackburn said. "It's early, but think it's promising."

"What about women?"

"There isn't any record on women. I know Sanders was screwing one o his assistants a couple of years back. But we can't find the records in the computer. I think he went in and erased them."

"How could he? We blocked his access."

"He must have done it some time ago. He's a cagey guy."

"Why the hell would he do it some time ago, Phil? He had no reason to expect any of this."

"I know, but we can't find the records now." Blackburn paused. "Bob, think we should move up the press conference."

"To when?"

"Late tomorrow."

"Good idea," Garvin said. "I'll arrange it. We could even do it noon tomorrow. John Marden is flying in in the morning," he said, referring to Conley-White's CEO. "That'll work out fine."

"Sanders is planning to string this out until Friday," Blackburn said "Let's just beat him to the punch. We've got him blocked as it is. He can' get into the company files. He can't get access to Conrad or anything else He's isolated. He can't possibly come up with anything damaging between now and tomorrow."

"Fine," Garvin said. "What about the reporter?"

"I think she'll break the story on Friday," Blackburn said. "She already has it, I don't know where from. But she won't be able to resist trashing

Sanders. It's too good a story; she'll go with it. And he'll be dead meat when she does."

"That's fine," Garvin said.

Meredith Johnson came off the fifth-floor elevator at DigiCom and ran into Ed Nichols. "We missed you at the morning meetings," Nichols said.

"Yeah, I had some things to take care of," she said.

"Anything I should know?"

"No," she said. "It's boring. Just some technical matters about tax exemptions in Ireland. The Irish government wants to expand local content at the Cork plant and we're not sure we can. This has been going on for more than a year."

"You look a little tired," Nichols said, with concern. "A little pale."

"I'm okay. I'll be happy when this is all over."

"We all will," Nichols said. "You have time for dinner?"

"Maybe Friday night, if you're still in town," she said. She smiled. "But really, Ed. It's just tax stuff."

"Okay, I believe you."

He waved and went down the hallway. Johnson went into her office.

She found Stephanie Kaplan there, working at the computer terminal on Johnson's desk. Kaplan looked embarrassed. "Sorry to use your computer. I was just running over some accounts while I waited for you."

Johnson threw her purse on the couch. "Listen, Stephanie," she said. "Let's get something straight right now. I'm running this division, and nobody's going to change that. And as far as I'm concerned, this is the time when a new vice president decides who's on their side, and who isn't. Somebody supports me, I'll remember. Somebody doesn't, I'll deal with that, too. Do we understand each other?"

Kaplan came around the desk. "Yes, sure, Meredith."

"Don't fuck with me."

"Never entered my mind, Meredith."

"Good. Thank you, Stephanie."

"No problem, Meredith."

Kaplan left the office. Johnson closed the door behind her and went directly to her computer terminal and stared intently at the screen.

S anders walked through the corridors of DigiCom with a sense of un-reality. He felt like a stranger. The people who passed him in the halls looked away and brushed past him, saying nothing.

"I don't exist," he said to Fernandez.

"Never mind," she said.

They passed the main part of the floor, where people worked in chest-high cubicles. Several pig grunts were heard. One person sang softly, "Be-cause I used to fuck her, but it's all over now. . ."

Sanders stopped and turned toward the singing. Fernandez grabbed his arm.

"Never mind," she said.

"But Christ. . ."

"Don't make it worse than it is."

They passed the coffee machine. Beside it, someone had taped up a pic-ture of Sanders. They had used it for a dartboard.

"Jesus."

"Keep going."

As he came to the corridor leading to his office, he saw Don Cherry coming the other way.

"Hi, Don."

"You screwed up bad on this one, Tom." He shook his head and walked on.

Even Don Cherry.

Sanders sighed.

"You knew this was going to happen," Fernandez said.

"Maybe."

"You did. This is the way it works."

Outside his office, Cindy stood up when she saw him. She said, "Tom, Mary Anne asked you to call her as soon as you got in."

"Okay."

"And Stephanie said to say never mind, she found out whatever she needed to know. She said, uh, not to call her."

"Okay."

He went in the office and closed the door. He sat down behind his desk and Fernandez sat opposite him. She took her cellular phone out of her briefcase, and dialed. "Let's get one thing squared away—Ms. Vries's office please . . . Louise Fernandez calling."

She cupped her hand over the phone. "This shouldn't take—Oh, Eleanor? Hi, Louise Fernandez. I'm calling you about Connie Walsh. Uh-huh . . . I'm sure you've been going over it with her. Yes, I know she feels strongly. Eleanor, I just wanted to confirm to you that there is a tape of the event, and it substantiates Mr. Sanders's version rather than Ms. Johnson's. Actually, yes, I could do that. Entirely off the record? Yes, I could. Well, the problem with Walsh's source is that the company now has huge liability and if you print a story that's wrong—even if you got it from a source—I think they have an action against you. Oh yes, I think absolutely Mr. Blackburn would sue. He wouldn't have any choice. Why don't you—I see. Uh-huh. Well, that could change, Eleanor. Uh-huh. And don't forget that Mr. Sanders is considering defamation right now, based on the Mr. Piggy piece. Yes, why don't you do that. Thank you."

She hung up and turned to Sanders. "We went to law school together. Eleanor is very competent and very conservative. She'd never have allowed the story in the first place, and would never have considered it now, if she didn't place a lot of reliance on Connie's source."

"Meaning?"

"I'm pretty sure I know who gave her the story," Fernandez said. She was dialing again.

"Who?" Sanders said.

"Right now, the important thing is Meredith Johnson. We've got to document the pattern, to demonstrate that she has harassed employees before. Somehow we've got to break this deadlock with Conrad Computer." She turned away. "Harry? Louise. Did you talk to Conrad? Uh-huh. And?" A pause. She shook her head irritably. "Did you explain to them about their liabilities? Uh-huh. Hell. So what's our next move? Because we've got a time problem here, Harry, that's what I'm concerned about."

While she was talking, Sanders turned to his monitor. The E-mail light was flashing. He clicked it.

YOU HAVE 17 MESSAGES WAITING.

Christ. He could only imagine. He clicked the READ button. They flashed up in order.

FROM: DON CHERRY, CORRIDOR
PROGRAMMING TEAM
TO: ALL SUBJECTS

WE HAVE DELIVERED THE VIE UNIT TO CONLEY–WHITE'S PEOPLE. THE UNIT IS NOW ACTIVE INTO THEIR COMPANY DB SINCE THEY GAVE US THE HOOKS TODAY. JOHN CONLEY ASKED THAT IT BE DELIVERED TO A SUITE AT THE FOUR SEASONS HOTEL BECAUSE THEIR CEO IS ARRIVING THURSDAY MORNING AND WILL SEE IT THEN. ANOTHER PROGRAMMING TRIUMPH BROUGHT TO YOU BY THE SWELL FOLKS AT VIE.

DON THE MAGNIFICENT

Sanders flipped to the next one.

FROM: DIAGNOSTICS GROUP
TO: APG TEAM

ANALYSIS OF TWINKLE DRIVES. THE PROBLEM WITH THE CONTROLLER TIMING LOOP DOES NOT SEEM TO COME FROM THE CHIP ITSELF. WE VERIFIED MICRO-FLUCTUATIONS IN CURRENT FROM THE POWER UNIT WHICH WAS APPARENTLY ETCHED WITH SUBSTANDARD OR INADEQUATE RESISTANCES ON THE BOARD BUT THIS IS MINOR AND DOES NOT EXPLAIN OUR FAILURE TO MEET SPECS. ANALYSIS IS CONTINUING.

Sanders viewed the message with a sense of detachment. It didn't really tell him anything. Just words that concealed the underlying truth: they still didn't know what the problem was. At another time, he'd be on his way down to the Diagnostics team, to ride them hard to get to the bottom of it. But now . . . He shrugged and went to the next message.

FROM: BASEBALL CENTRAL
TO: ALL PLAYERS
RE: NEW SUMMER SOFTBALL SCHEDULE

DOWNLOAD FILE BB.72 TO GET THE NEW REVISED SUMMER SCHEDULE. SEE YOU ON THE FIELD!

He heard Fernandez say on the phone, "Harry, we've got to crack this one somehow. What time do they close their offices in Sunnyvale?" Sanders went to the next message.

NO MORE GROUP MESSAGES. DO YOU WANT TO READ PERSONAL MESSAGES?

He clicked the icon.

WHY DON'T YOU JUST ADMIT YOU ARE GAY?
(UNSIGNED)

He didn't bother to see where it had come from. They would probably have manually entered it as coming from Garvin's address, or something like that. He could check the real address inside the system, but not without the access privileges they had taken away. He went to the next message.

SHE'S BETTER LOOKING THAN YOUR ASSISTANT, AND YOU DIDN'T SEEM TO MIND SCREWING HER.
(UNSIGNED)

Sanders clicked to the next one.

YOU SLIMY WEASEL-GET OUT OF THIS COMPANY.
YOUR BEST ADVICE

Christ, he thought. The next one:

LITTLE TOMMY HAD A PECKER
HE PLAYED WITH EVERY DAY
BUT WHEN A LADY TRIED TO TOUCH IT
LITTLE TOMMY SAID GO AWAY.

The verses ran on, down to the bottom of the screen, but Sanders didn't read the rest. He clicked and went on.

IF YOU WEREN'T FUCKING YOUR DAUGHTER SO MUCH YOU
MIGHT BE ABLE TO

He clicked again. He was clicking faster and faster, going through the
messages.

GUYS LIKE YOU GIVE MEN A BAD NAME YOU ASSHOLE.
                    BORIS

Click.

YOU FILTHY LYING MALE PIG

Click.

HIGH TIME SOMEBODY STUCK IT TO THE WHINING BITCHES. I'M
TIRED OF THE WAY THEY BLAME EVERYBODY BUT THEIRSELVES.
TITS AND BLAME ARE SEX-LINKED TRAITS. THEY'RE BOTH ON
THE X-CHROMOSOME.
                    KEEP ON TRUCKIN'

He went through them, no longer reading. Eventually he was going so
fast he almost missed one of the later ones:

JUST RECEIVED WORD THAT MOHAMMED JAFAR IS DYING. HE'S
STILL IN THE HOSPITAL, AND NOT EXPECTED TO SURVIVE UNTIL
MORNING. I GUESS MAYBE THERE'S SOMETHING TO THIS SOR-
CERY BUSINESS, AFTER ALL.
                    ARTHUR KAHN

Sanders stared at the screen. A man dying of sorcery? He couldn't begin
to imagine what had really happened. The very idea seemed to belong to
another world, not his. He heard Fernandez say, "I don't care, Harry, but
Conrad has information relevant to the pattern, and somehow we have to
get it out of them."
Sanders clicked to the final message.

YOU'RE CHECKING THE WRONG COMPANY.
                    AFRIEND

Sanders twisted the monitor around so Fernandez could see it. She frowned as she talked on the phone. "Harry, I got to go. Do what you can." She hung up. "What does it mean, we're checking the wrong company? How does this friend even know what we're doing? When did this come in?"

Sanders looked at the message headers. "One-twenty this afternoon."

Fernandez made a note on her legal pad. "That was about the time Alan was talking to Conrad. And Conrad called DigiCom, remember? So this message has to be coming from inside DigiCom."

"But it's on the Internet."

"Wherever it appears to be coming from, it's actually from somebody inside the company trying to help you."

His immediate thought, out of nowhere, was *Max*. But that didn't make any sense. Dorfman was tricky, but not in this way. Besides, Max wasn't knowledgeable about the minute-to-minute workings of the company.

No, this was somebody who wanted to help Sanders but who didn't want the help to be traced back.

"You're checking the wrong company. . ." he repeated aloud.

Could it be someone at Conley-White? Hell, he thought, it could be anybody.

"What does it mean, we're checking the wrong company?" he said. "We're checking all her past employers, and we're having a very difficult—"

He stopped.

You're checking the wrong company.

"I must be an idiot," he said. He started typing at his computer.

"What is it?" Fernandez said.

"They've restricted my access, but I still should be able to get this," he said, typing quickly.

"Get what?" she said, puzzled.

"You say harassers have a pattern, right?"

"Right."

"It shows up again and again, right?"

"Right."

"And we're checking her past employers, to get information about past episodes of harassment."

"Right. And failing."

"Yes. But the thing is," Sanders said, "she's worked here for the last four years, Louise. We're checking the wrong company."

He watched as the computer terminal flashed:

SEARCHING DATABASE

And then, after a moment, he turned the screen so Fernandez could see:

Digital Communications Data Reference Search Report

DB 4: Human Resources (Sub 5/Employee Records)
Search Criteria:
1. Disposition: Terminated a/o Transferred a/o Resigned
2. Supervisor: Johnson, Meredith
3. Other Criteria: males only

Summary Search Results:

Michael Tate	5/9/89	Terminate	Drug Use	HR RefMed
Edwin Sheen	7/5/89	Resign	Alt Employment	D-Silicon
William Rogin	11/9/89	Transfer	Own Request	Austin
Frederic Cohen	4/2/90	Resign	Alt Employment	Squire Sx
Robert Ely	6/1/90	Transfer	Own Request	Seattle
Michael Backes	8/11/90	Transfer	Own Request	Malaysia
Peter Saltz	1/4/91	Resign	Alt Employment	Novell
Ross Wald	8/5/91	Transfer	Own Request	Cork
Richard Jackson	11/14/91	Resign	Alt Employment	Aldus
James French	2/2/92	Transfer	Own Request	Austin

Fernandez scanned the list. "Looks like working for Meredith Johnson can be hazardous to your job. You're looking at the classic pattern: people last only a few months, and then resign or ask to be transferred elsewhere. Everything voluntary. Nobody ever fired, because that might trigger a wrongful termination suit. Classic. You know any of these people?"

"No," Sanders said, shaking his head. "But three of them are in Seattle," he said.

"I only see one."

"No, Aldus is here. And Squire Systems is out in Bellevue. So Richard Jackson and Frederic Cohen are up here, too."

"You have any way to get details of termination packages on these people?" she said. "That would be helpful. Because if the company paid anybody off, then we have a de facto case."

"No." Sanders shook his head. "Financial data is beyond minimal access."

"Try anyway."

"But what's the point? The system won't let me."

"Do it," Fernandez said.

He frowned. "You think they're monitoring me?"

"I guarantee it."

"Okay." He typed in the parameters and pressed the search key. The answer came back:

FINANCIAL DATABASE SEARCH IS BEYOND LEVEL (0) ACCESS

He shrugged. "Just as I thought. No cigar."

"But the point is, we asked the question," Fernandez said. "It'll wake them right up."

Sanders was heading toward the bank of elevators when he saw Meredith coming toward him with three Conley-White executives. He turned quickly, then went to the stairwell and started walking down the four flights to the street level. The stairwell was deserted.

One flight below, the door opened and Stephanie Kaplan appeared and started coming up the stairs. Sanders was reluctant to speak to her; Kaplan was, after all, the chief financial officer and close to both Garvin and Blackburn. In the end, he said casually, "How's it going, Stephanie."

"Hello, Tom." Her nod to him was cool, reserved.

Sanders continued past her, going down a few more steps, when he heard her say, "I'm sorry this is so difficult for you."

He paused. Kaplan was one flight above him, looking down. There was no one else in the stairwell.

He said, "I'm managing."

"I know you are. But still, it must be hard. So much going on at once, and nobody giving you information. It must be confusing to try to figure everything out."

Nobody giving you information?

"Well, yes," he said, speaking slowly. "It is hard to figure things out, Stephanie."

She nodded. "I remember when I first started out in business," she said. "I had a woman friend who got a very good job in a company that didn't usually hire women executives. In her new position, she had a lot of stress and crises. She was proud of the way she was dealing with the problems. But it turned out she'd only been hired because there was a financial scandal in her division, and from the beginning they were setting her up to take the fall. Her job was never about any of the things she thought it was. She was a patsy. And she was looking the wrong way when they fired her."

Sanders stared at her. Why was she telling him this? He said, "That's an interesting story."

Kaplan nodded. "I've never forgotten it," she said.

On the stairs above, a door clanged open, and they heard footsteps descending. Without another word, Kaplan turned and continued up.

Shaking his head, Sanders continued down.

In the newsroom of the Seattle *Post-Intelligencer,* Connie Walsh looked up from her computer terminal and said, "You've got to be kidding."

"No, I'm not," Eleanor Vries said, standing over her. "I'm killing this story." She dropped the printout back on Walsh's desk.

"But you know who my source is," Walsh said. "And you know Jake was listening in to the entire conversation. We have very good notes, Eleanor. Very complete notes."

"I know."

"So, given the source, how can the company possibly sue?" Walsh said. "Eleanor: *I have the fucking story.*"

"You have *a* story. And the paper faces a substantial exposure already."

"Already? From what?"

"The Mr. Piggy column."

"Oh, for Christ's sake. There's no way to claim identification from that column."

Vries pulled out a xerox of the column. She had marked several passages in yellow highlighter. "Company X is said to be a high-tech company in Seattle that just named a woman to a high position. Mr. Piggy is said to be her subordinate. He is said to have brought a sexual harassment action. Mr. Piggy's wife is an attorney with young children. You say Mr. Piggy's charge is without merit, that he is a drunk and a womanizer. I think Sanders can absolutely claim identification and sue for defamation."

"But this is a column. An opinion piece."

"This column alleges facts. And it alleges them in a sarcastic and wildly overstated manner."

"It's an opinion piece. Opinion is protected."

"I don't think that's certain in this case at all. I'm disturbed that I allowed this column to run in the first place. But the point is, we cannot claim to be absent malice if we allow further articles to go out."

Walsh said, "You have no guts."

"And you're very free with other people's guts," Vries said. "The story's killed and that's final. I'm putting it in writing, with copies to you, Marge, and Tom Donadio."

"Fucking lawyers. What a world we live in. This story needs to be told."

"Don't screw around with this, Connie. I'm telling you. Don't."

And she walked away.

Walsh thumbed through the pages of the story. She had been working on it all afternoon, polishing it, refining it. Getting it exactly right. And now she wanted the story to run. She had no patience with legal thinking. This whole idea of protecting rights was just a convenient fiction. Because when you got right down to it, legal thinking was just narrow-minded, petty, self-protective—the kind of thinking that kept the power structure firmly in place. And in the end, fear served the power structure. Fear served men in power. And if there was anything that Connie Walsh believed to be true of herself, it was that she was not afraid.

After a long time, she picked up the phone and dialed a number. "KSEA-TV, good afternoon."

"Ms. Henley, please."

Jean Henley was a bright young reporter at Seattle's newest independent TV station. Walsh had spent many evenings with Henley, discussing the problems of working in the male-dominated mass media. Henley knew the value of a hot story in building a reporter's career.

This story, Walsh told herself, would be told. One way or another, it would be told.

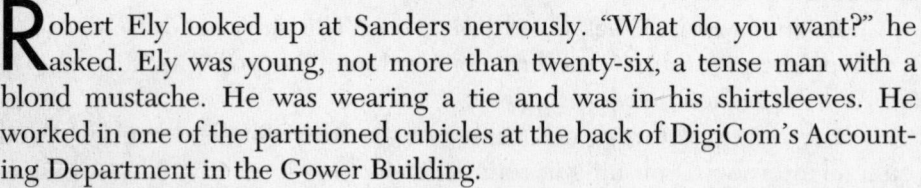

Robert Ely looked up at Sanders nervously. "What do you want?" he asked. Ely was young, not more than twenty-six, a tense man with a blond mustache. He was wearing a tie and was in his shirtsleeves. He worked in one of the partitioned cubicles at the back of DigiCom's Accounting Department in the Gower Building.

"I want to talk about Meredith," Sanders said. Ely was one of the three Seattle residents on his list.

"Oh God," Ely said. He glanced around nervously. His Adam's apple bobbed. "I don't—I don't have anything to say."

"I just want to talk," Sanders said.

"Not *here*," Ely said.

"Then let's go to the conference room," Sanders said. They walked down the hall to a small conference room, but a meeting was being held there. Sanders suggested they go to the little cafeteria in the corner of Accounting, but Ely told him that wouldn't be private. He was growing more nervous by the minute.

"Really, I have nothing to tell you," he kept saying. "There's nothing, really nothing."

Sanders knew he had better find a quiet place at once, before Ely bolted and ran. They ended up in the men's room—white tile, spotlessly clean. Ely leaned against a sink. "I don't know why you are talking to me. I don't have anything I can tell you."

"You worked for Meredith, in Cupertino."

"Yes."

"And you left there two years ago?"

"Yes."

"Why did you leave?"

"Why do you think?" Ely said, in a burst of anger. His voice echoed off the tiles. "You know why, for Christ's sake. Everybody knows why. She made my life hell."

"What happened?" Sanders asked.

258

"What happened." Ely shook his head, remembering. "Every day, everyday. 'Robert, would you stay late, we have some things to go over.' After a while, I tried to make excuses. Then she would say, 'Robert, I'm not sure you're showing the proper dedication to this company.' And she would put little comments in my performance review. Subtle little negative things. Nothing that I could complain about. But they were there. Piling up. 'Robert, I think you need my help here. Why don't you see me after work.' 'Robert, why don't you drop by my apartment and we'll discuss it. I really think you should.' I was—it was terrible. The, uh, person I was living with did not, uh . . . I was in a real bind."

"Did you report her?"

Ely laughed harshly. "Are you kidding? She's practically a member of Garvin's *family*."

"So you just put up with it. . ."

Ely shrugged. "Finally, the person I was living with got another job. When he came up here, I transferred, too. I mean, of course I wanted to go. It just worked out all around."

"Would you make a statement about Meredith now?"

"Not a chance."

"You realize," Sanders said, "that the reason she gets away with it is that nobody reports her."

Ely pushed away from the sink. "I have enough problems in my life without going public on this." He went to the door, paused, and turned back. "Just so you're clear: I've got nothing to say on the subject of Meredith Johnson. If anybody asks, I'll say our working relationship was correct at all times. And I'll also say that I never met you."

Meredith Johnson? Of course I remember her," Richard Jackson said. "I worked for her for more than a year." Sanders was in Jackson's office on the second floor of the Aldus Building, on the south side of Pioneer Square. Jackson was a good-looking man of thirty, with the hearty manner of an ex-athlete. He was a marketing manager at Aldus; his office was friendly, cluttered with product boxes for graphics programs: Intellidraw, Freehand, SuperPaint, and Pagemaker.

"Beautiful and charming woman," Jackson said. "Very intelligent. Always a pleasure."

Sanders said, "I was wondering why you left."

"I was offered this job, that's why. And I've never regretted it. Wonderful job. Wonderful company. I've had a great experience here."

"Is that the only reason you left?"

Jackson laughed. "You mean, did Meredith Manmuncher come on to me?" he said. "Hey, is the Pope Catholic? Is Bill Gates rich? Of *course* she came on to me."

"Did that have anything to do with your leaving?"

"No, no," Jackson said. "Meredith came on to everybody. She's sort of an equal opportunity employer, in that respect. She chased *everybody*. When I first started in Cupertino, she had this little gay guy she used to chase around the table. Terrorized the poor bastard. Little skinny nervous guy. Christ, she used to make him tremble."

"And you?"

Jackson shrugged. "I was a single guy, just starting out. She was beautiful. It was okay with me."

"You never had any difficulties?"

"Never. Meredith was fabulous. Shitty lay, of course. But you can't have everything. She's a very intelligent, very beautiful woman. Always dressed great. And she liked me, so she took me to all these functions. I met people, made contacts. It was great."

"So you saw nothing wrong?"

"Not a damn thing," Jackson said. "She could get a little bossy. That got old. There were a couple of other women I was seeing, but I always had to be on call for her. Even at the last minute. That could be irritating sometimes. You begin to think your life is not your own. And she's got a mean temper sometimes. But what the hell. You do what you have to do. Now I'm assistant manager here at thirty. I'm doing great. Great company. Great town. Great future. And I owe it to her. She's great."

Sanders said, "You were an employee of the company at the time that you were having your relationship, isn't that right?"

"Yeah, sure."

"Isn't she required by company policy to report any relationship with an employee? Did she report her relationship with you?"

"Christ, no," Jackson said. He leaned across his desk. "Let's get one thing straight, just between you and me. I think Meredith is great. If you have a problem with her, it's your problem. I don't know what it could be. You used to live with her, for Christ's sake. So there can't be any surprises. Meredith likes to fuck guys. She likes to tell them to do this, do that. She likes to order them around. That's who she is. And I don't see anything wrong with it."

Sanders said, "I don't supposed you'd—"

"Make a statement?" Jackson said. "Get serious. Listen, there's a lot of bullshit around now. I hear things like, 'You can't go out with the people you work with.' Christ, if I couldn't go out with the people I worked with, I'd still be a virgin. That's all anybody can go out with—the people you work with. That's the only people you get to know. And sometimes those people are your superiors. Big deal. Women screw men and get ahead. Men screw women and get ahead. Everybody's going to screw everybody else anyway, if they can. Because they want to. I mean, women are just as hot as men. They want it just like we do. That's real life. But you get some people who are pissed off, so they file a complaint, and say, 'Oh no, you can't do that to me.' I'm telling you, it's all bullshit. Like these sensitivity training seminars we all have to go to. Everybody sits there with their hands in their laps like a fucking Red Guard meeting, learning the correct way to address your fellow workers. But afterward everybody goes out and fucks around, the same as they always did. The assistants go, 'Oh, Mr. Jackson, have *you* been to the *gym*? You look so *strong*.' Batting their eyelashes. So what am I supposed to do? You can't make rules about this. People get hungry, they eat. Doesn't matter how many meetings they attend. This is all a gigantic jerk off. And anybody who buys into it is an asshole."

"I guess you answered my question," Sanders said. He got up to leave. Obviously, Jackson wasn't going to help him.

"Look," Jackson said. "I'm sorry you've got a problem here. But everyone's too damned sensitive these days. I see people now, kids right out of college, and they really think they should never experience an unpleasant moment. Nobody should ever say anything they don't like, or tell a joke they don't like. But the thing is, nobody can make the world be the way they want it to be all the time. Things always happen that embarrass you or piss you off. That's life. I hear women telling jokes about men every day. Offensive jokes. Dirty jokes. I don't get bent out of shape. Life is great. Who has time for this crap? Not me."

Sanders came out of the Aldus Building at five o'clock. Tired and discouraged, he trudged back toward the Hazzard Building. The streets were wet, but the rain had stopped, and the afternoon sunlight was trying to break through the clouds.

He was back in his office ten minutes later. Cindy was not at her desk, and Fernandez was gone. He felt deserted and alone and hopeless. He sat down and dialed the final number on his list.

"Squire Electronic Data Systems, good evening."

Sanders said, "Frederic Cohen's office, please."

"I'm sorry, Mr. Cohen has gone for the day."

"Do you know how I could reach him?"

"I'm afraid I don't. Do you want to leave voice mail?"

Damn, he thought. What was the point? But he said, "Yes, please."

There was a click. Then, "Hi, this is Fred Cohen. Leave a message at the tone. If it's after hours, you can try me on my car phone at 502-8804 or my home at 505-9943."

Sanders jotted the numbers down. He dialed the car phone first. He heard a crackle of static, then:

"I know, honey, I'm sorry I'm late, but I'm on my way. I just got tied up."

"Mr. Cohen?"

"Oh." A pause. "Yes. This is Fred Cohen."

"My name is Tom Sanders. I work over at DigiCom, and—"

"I know who you are." The voice sounded tense.

"I understand you used to work for Meredith Johnson."

"Yes. I did."

"I wonder if I could talk to you."

"What about?"

"About your experiences. Working for her."

There was a long pause. Finally, Cohen said, "What would be the point of that?"

"Well, I'm in a sort of a dispute with Meredith now, and—"

"I know you are."

"Yes, and you see, I would like to—"

"Look. Tom. I left DigiCom two years ago. Whatever happened is ancient history now."

"Well, actually," Sanders said, "it's not, because I'm trying to establish a pattern of behavior and—"

"I know what you're trying to do. But this is very touchy stuff, Tom. I don't want to get into it."

"If we could just talk," Sanders said. "Just for a few minutes."

"Tom." Cohen's voice was flat. "Tom, I'm married now. I have a wife. She's pregnant. I don't have anything to say about Meredith Johnson. Nothing at all."

"But—"

"I'm sorry. I've got to go."

Click.

Cindy came back in as he was hanging up the phone. She pushed a cup of coffee in front of him. "Everything okay?"

"No," he said. "Everything is terrible." He was reluctant to admit, even to himself, that he had no more moves left. He had approached three men, and they had each refused to establish a pattern of behavior for him. He doubted that the other men on the list would behave differently. He found himself thinking of what his wife, Susan, had said two days before. *You have no moves.* Now, after all this effort, it turned out to be true. He was finished. "Where's Fernandez?"

"She's meeting with Blackburn."

"What?"

Cindy nodded. "In the small conference room. They've been there about fifteen minutes now."

"Oh, Christ."

He got up from his desk and went down the hall. He saw Fernandez sitting with Blackburn in the conference room. Fernandez was making notes on her legal pad, head bent deferentially. Blackburn was running his hands down his lapels and looking upward as he spoke. He seemed to be dictating to her.

Then Blackburn saw him, and waved him over. Sanders went into the conference room. "Tom," Blackburn said, with a smile. "I was just coming to see you. Good news: I think we've been able to resolve this situation. I mean, really resolve it. Once and for all."

"Uh-huh," Sanders said. He didn't believe a word of it. He turned to Fernandez.

Fernandez looked up from her legal pad slowly. She appeared dazed. "That's the way it looks."

Blackburn stood and faced Sanders. "I can't tell you how pleased I am, Tom. I've been working on Bob all afternoon. And he's finally come to face reality. The plain fact is, the company has a problem, Tom. And we owe you a debt of gratitude for bringing it so clearly to our attention. This can't go on. Bob knows he has to deal with it. And he will."

Sanders just stared. He couldn't believe what he was hearing. But there was Fernandez, nodding and smiling.

Blackburn smoothed his tie. "But as Frank Lloyd Wright once said, 'God is in the details.' You know, Tom, we have one small immediate problem, a political problem, having to do with the merger. We're asking your help with the briefing tomorrow for Marden, Conley's CEO. But after that . . . well, you've been badly wronged, Tom. This company has wronged you. And we recognized that we have an obligation to make it up to you, whatever way we can."

Still disbelieving it, Sanders said harshly, "What exactly are we talking about?"

Blackburn's voice was soothing. "Well, Tom, at this point, that's really up to you," he said. "I've given Louise the parameters of a potential deal, and all the options that we would agree to. You can discuss it with her and get back to us. We'll sign any interim papers you require, of course. All that we ask in return is that you attend the meeting tomorrow and help us to get through the merger. Fair enough?"

Blackburn extended his hand and held it there.

Sanders stared.

"From the bottom of my heart, Tom, I'm sorry for all that has happened."

Sanders shook his hand.

"Thank you, Tom," Blackburn said. "Thank you for your patience, and thank you on behalf of this company. Now, sit down and talk with Louise, and let us know what you decide."

And Blackburn left the room, closing the door softly behind him.

He turned to Fernandez. "What the hell is this all about?"

Fernandez gave a long sigh. "It's called capitulation," she said. "Total and complete capitulation. DigiCom just folded."

S anders watched Blackburn walk down the hallway away from the conference room. He was filled with confused feelings. Suddenly, he was being told it was all over, and over without a fight. Without blood being spilled.

Watching Blackburn, he had a sudden image of blood in the bathroom sink of his old apartment. And this time, he remembered where it came from. A part of the chronology fell into place.

Blackburn was staying at his apartment during his divorce. He was on edge, and drinking too much. One day he cut himself so badly while shaving that the sink was spattered with blood. Later on, Meredith saw the blood in the sink and on the towels, and she said, "Did one of you guys fuck her while she was having her period?" Meredith was always blunt that way. She liked to startle people, to shock them.

And then, one Saturday afternoon, she walked around the apartment in white stockings and a garter belt and a bra while Phil was watching television. Sanders said to her, "What are you doing that for?"

"Just cheering him up," Meredith replied. She threw herself back on the bed. "Now why don't you cheer me up?" she said. And she pulled her legs back, opening—

"Tom? Are you listening to me?" Fernandez was saying. "Hello? Tom? Are you there?"

"I'm here," Sanders said.

But he was still watching Blackburn, thinking about Blackburn. Now he remembered another time, a few years later. Sanders had started dating Susan, and Phil had dinner with the two of them one night. Susan went to the bathroom. "She's great," Blackburn said. "She's terrific. She's beautiful and she's great."

"But?"

"But. . ." Blackburn had shrugged. "She's a lawyer."

"So?"

"You can never trust a lawyer," Blackburn had said, and laughed. One of his rueful, wise laughs.

You can never trust a lawyer.

Now, standing in the DigiCom conference room, Sanders watched as Blackburn disappeared around a corner. He turned back to Fernandez.

". . .really had no choice," Fernandez was saying. "The whole situation finally became untenable. The fact situation with Johnson is bad. And the tape is dangerous— they don't want it played, and they're afraid it will get out. They have a problem about prior sexual harassment by Johnson; she's done it before, and they know it. Even though none of the men you talked to has agreed to talk, one of them might in the future, and they know it. And of course they've got their chief counsel revealing company information to a reporter."

Sanders said, "What?"

She nodded. "Blackburn was the one who gave the story to Connie Walsh. He acted in flagrant violation of all rules of conduct for an employee of the company. He's a major problem for them. And it all just became too much. These things could bring down the entire company. Looking at it rationally, they had to make a deal with you."

"Yeah," Sanders said. "But none of this is rational, you know?"

"You're acting like you don't believe it," Fernandez said. "Believe it. It just got too big. They couldn't sit on it anymore."

"So what's the deal?"

Fernandez looked at her notes. "You got your whole shopping list. They'll fire Johnson. They'll give you her job, if you want that. Or they'll reinstate you at your present position. Or they'll give you another position in the company. They'll pay you a hundred thousand in pain and suffering and they'll pay my fees. Or they'll negotiate a termination agreement, if you want that. In any case, they'll give you full stock options if and when the division goes public. Whether you choose to remain with the company or not."

"Jesus Christ."

She nodded. "Total capitulation."

"You really believe Blackburn means it?"

You can never trust a lawyer.

"Yes," she said. "Frankly, it's the first thing that has made any sense to me all day. They had to do this, Tom. Their exposure is too great, and the stakes are too high."

"And what about this briefing?"

"They're worried about the merger—as you suspected when all this began. They don't want to blow it with any sudden changes now. So they want you to participate in the briefing tomorrow with Johnson, as if everything was normal. Then early next week, Johnson will have a physical exam as part of her insurance for the new job. The exam will uncover serious health problems, maybe even cancer, which will force a regrettable change in management."

"I see."

He went to the window and looked out at the city. The clouds were higher, and the evening sun was breaking through. He took a deep breath.

"And if I don't participate in the briefing?"

"It's up to you, but I would, if I were you," Fernandez said. "At this point, you really are in a position to bring down the company. And what good is that?"

He took another deep breath. He was feeling better all the time.

"You're saying this is over," he said, finally.

"Yes. It's over, and you've won. You pulled it off. Congratulations, Tom." She shook his hand.

"Jesus Christ," he said.

She stood up. "I'm going to draw up an instrument outlining my conversation with Blackburn, specifying these options, and send it to him for his signature in an hour. I'll call you when I have it signed. Meanwhile, I recommend you do whatever preparation you need for this meeting tomorrow, and get some much deserved rest. I'll see you tomorrow."

"Okay."

It was slowly seeping into him, the realization that it was over. Really over. It had happened so suddenly and so completely, he was a little dazed.

"Congratulations again," Fernandez said. She folded her briefcase and left.

He was back in his office at about six. Cindy was leaving; she asked if he needed her, and he said he didn't. Sanders sat at his desk and stared out the window for a while, savoring the conclusion of the day. Through his open door, he watched as people left for the night, heading down the hall. Finally he called his wife in Phoenix to tell her the news, but her line was busy.

There was a knock at his door. He looked up and saw Blackburn standing there, looking apologetic. "Got a minute?"

"Sure."

"I just wanted to repeat to you, on a personal level, how sorry I am about all this. In the press of complex corporate problems like this, human values may get lost, despite the best of intentions. While we intend to be fair to everyone, sometimes we fail. And what is a corporation if not a human group, a group of human beings? We're all people, underneath it all. As Alexander Pope once said, 'We're all just human.' So recognizing your own graciousness through all this, I want to say to you. . . ."

Sanders wasn't listening. He was tired; all he really heard was that Phil realized he had screwed up, and now was trying to repair things in his usual manner, by sucking up to someone he had earlier bullied.

Sanders interrupted, saying, "What about Bob?" Now that it was over, Sanders was having a lot of feelings about Garvin. Memories going back to his earliest days with the company. Garvin had been a kind of father to Sanders, and he wanted to hear from Garvin now. He wanted an apology. Or something.

"I imagine Bob's going to take a couple of days to come around," Blackburn said. "This was a very difficult decision for him to arrive at. I had to work very hard on him, on your behalf. And now he's got to figure out how to break it to Meredith. All that."

"Uh-huh."

"But he'll eventually talk to you. I know he will. Meanwhile, I wanted to go over a few things about the meeting tomorrow," Blackburn said. "It's for Marden, their CEO, and it's going to be a bit more formal than the way we usually do things. We'll be in the big conference room on the ground floor. It'll start at nine, and go to ten. Meredith will chair the meeting, and she'll call on all the division heads to give a summary of progress and problems in their divisions. Mary Anne first, then Don, then Mark, then you. Everyone will talk three to four minutes. Do it standing. Wear a jacket and tie. Use visuals if you have them, but stay away from technical details. Keep it an overview. In your case, they'll expect to hear mostly about Twinkle."

Sanders nodded. "All right. But there isn't really much new to report. We still haven't figured out what's wrong with the drives."

"That's fine. I don't think anybody expects a solution yet. Just emphasize the success of the prototypes, and the fact that we've overcome production problems before. Keep it upbeat, and keep it moving. If you have a prototype or a mock-up, you might want to bring it along."

"Okay."

"You know the stuff—bright rosy digital future, minor technical glitches won't stand in the way of progress."

"Meredith's okay with that?" he said. He was slightly disturbed to hear that she was chairing the meeting.

"Meredith is expecting all the heads to be upbeat and nontechnical. There won't be a problem."

"Okay," Sanders said.

"Call me tonight if you want to go over your presentation," Blackburn said. "Or in the morning, early. Let's just finesse this session, and then we can move on. Start making changes next week."

Sanders nodded.

"You're the kind of man this company needs," Blackburn said. "I appreciate your understanding. And again, Tom, I'm sorry."

He left.

Sanders called down to the Diagnostics Group, to see if they had any further word. But there was no answer. He went out to the closet behind Cindy's desk and took out the AV materials: the big schematic drawing of the Twinkle drive, and the schematic of the production line in Malaysia. He could prop these on easels while he talked.

But as he thought about it, it occurred to him that Blackburn was right. A mock-up or a prototype would be good to have. In fact, he should probably bring one of the drives that Arthur had sent from KL.

It reminded him that he should call Arthur in Malaysia. He dialed the number.

"Mr. Kahn's office."

"It's Tom Sanders calling."

The assistant sounded surprised. "Mr. Kahn is not here, Mr. Sanders."

"When is he expected back?"

"He's out of the office, Mr. Sanders. I don't know when he'll be back."

"I see." Sanders frowned. That was odd. With Mohammed Jafar missing, it was unlike Arthur to leave the plant without supervision.

The assistant said, "Can I give him a message?"

"No message, thanks."

He hung up, went down to the third floor to Cherry's programming group, and put his card in the slot to let himself in. The card popped back out, and the LED blinked oooo. It took him a moment to realize that they had cut off his access. Then he remembered the other card he had picked up earlier. He pushed it in the slot, and the door opened. Sanders went inside.

He was surprised to find the unit deserted. The programmers all kept strange hours; there was almost always somebody there, even at midnight.

He went to the Diagnostics room, where the drives were being studied. There were a series of benches, surrounded by electronic equipment and blackboards. The drives were set out on the benches, all covered in white cloth. The bright overhead quartz lights were off.

He heard rock-and-roll music from an adjacent room, and went there. A lone programmer in his early twenties was sitting at a console typing. Beside him, a portable radio blared.

Sanders said, "Where is everybody?"

The programmer looked up. "Third Wednesday of the month."

"So?"

"OOPS meets on the third Wednesday."

"Oh." The Object Oriented Programmer Support association, or OOPS, was an association of programmers in the Seattle area. It was started by Microsoft some years earlier, and was partly social and partly trade talk.

Sanders said, "You know anything about what the Diagnostics team found?"

"Sorry." The programmer shook his head. "I just came in."

Sanders went back to the Diagnostics room. He flicked on the lights and gently removed the white cloth that covered the drives. He saw that only three of the CD-ROM drives had been opened, their innards exposed to powerful magnifying glasses and electronic probes on the tables. The remaining seven drives were stacked to one side, still in plastic.

He looked up at the blackboards. One had a series of equations and hastily scribbled data points. The other had a flowchart list that read:

A. Contr. Incompat.
   VLSI?
   pwr?
B. Optic Dysfunct-? voltage reg?/arm?/servo?
C. Laser R/O (a,b,c)
D. Σ Mechanical √ √
E. Gremlins

It didn't mean much to Sanders. He turned his attention back to the tables, and peered at the test equipment. It looked fairly standard, except that there were a series of large-bore needles lying on the table, and several white circular wafers encased in plastic that looked like camera filters. There were also Polaroid pictures of the drives in various stages of disassembly; the team had documented their work. Three of the Polaroids were placed in a neat row, as if they might be significant, but Sanders couldn't see why. They just showed chips on a green circuit board.

He looked at the drives themselves, being careful not to disturb anything. Then he turned to the stack of drives that were still wrapped in plastic. But looking closely, he noticed fine, needle-point punctures in the plastic covering four of the drives.

Nearby was a medical syringe and an open notebook. The notebook showed a column of figures:

PPU
7
II (repeat II)
5
2

And at the bottom someone had scrawled, "Fucking Obvious!" But it wasn't obvious to Sanders. He decided that he'd better call Don Cherry later tonight, to have him explain it. In the meantime, he took one of the extra drives from the stack to use in the presentation the following morning.

He left the Diagnostics room carrying all his presentation materials, the easel boards flapping against his legs. He headed downstairs to the ground floor conference room, which had an AV closet where speakers stored visual material before a presentation. He could lock his material away there.

In the lobby, he passed the receptionist's desk, now manned by a black security guard, who watched a baseball game and nodded to Sanders. Sanders went back toward the rear of the floor, moving quietly on the plush carpeting. The hallway was dark, but the lights were on in the conference room; he could see them shining from around the corner.

As he came closer, he heard Meredith Johnson say, "And then what?" And a man's voice answered something indistinct.

Sanders paused.

He stood in the dark corridor and listened. From where he stood, he could see nothing of the room.

There was a moment of silence, and then Johnson said, "Okay, so will Mark talk about design?"

The man said, "Yes, he'll cover that."

"Okay," Johnson said. "Then what about the. . ."

Sanders couldn't hear the rest. He crept forward, moving silently on the carpet, and cautiously peered around the corner. He still could not see into the conference room itself, but there was a large chrome sculpture in the hallway outside the room, a sort of propeller shape, and in the reflection of its polished surface he saw Meredith moving in the room. The man with her was Blackburn.

Johnson said, "So what if Sanders doesn't bring it up?"

"He will," Blackburn said.

"You're sure he doesn't—that the—" Again, the rest was lost.

"No, he—no idea."

Sanders held his breath. Meredith was pacing, her image in the reflection, twisting and distorted. "So when he does—I will say that this is a—is that—you mean?"

"Exactly," Blackburn said.

"And if he—"

Blackburn put his hand on her shoulder. "Yes, you have to—"

"—So—want me to—"

Blackburn said something quiet in reply, and Sanders heard none of it, except the phrase "—must demolish him."

"—Can do that—"

"—Make sure—counting on you—"

There was the shrill sound of a telephone. Both Meredith and Blackburn reached for their pockets. Meredith answered the call, and the two began to move toward the exit. They were heading toward Sanders.

Panicked, Sanders looked around, and saw a men's room to his right. He slipped inside the door as they came out of the conference room and started down the hallway.

"Don't worry about this, Meredith," Blackburn said. "It'll go fine."

"I'm not worried," she said.

"It should be quite smooth and impersonal," Blackburn said. "There's no reason for rancor. After all, you have the facts on your side. He's clearly incompetent."

"He still can't get into the database?" she said.

"No. He's locked out of the system."

"And there's no way he can get into Conley-White's system?"

Blackburn laughed. "No way in hell, Meredith."

The voices faded, moving down the hallway. Sanders strained to listen, finally heard the click of a door closing. He stepped out of the bathroom into the hallway.

The hallway was deserted. He stared toward the far door.

His own telephone rang in his pocket, the sound so loud it made him jump. He answered it. "Sanders."

"Listen," Fernandez said. "I sent the draft of your contract to Blackburn's office, but it came back with a couple of added statements that I'm not sure about. I think we better meet to discuss them."

"In an hour," Sanders said.

"Why not now?"

"I have something to do first," he said.

"Ah, Thomas." Max Dorfman opened the door to his hotel room and immediately wheeled away, back toward the television set. "You have finally decided to come."

"You've heard?"

"Heard what?" Dorfman said. "I am an old man. No one bothers with me anymore. I'm cast by the wayside. By everyone—including you." He clicked off the television set and grinned.

Sanders said, "What have you heard?"

"Oh, just a few things. Rumors, idle talk. Why don't you tell me yourself?"

"I'm in trouble, Max."

"Of course you are in trouble," Dorfman snorted. "You have been in trouble all week. You only noticed now?"

"They're setting me up."

"They?"

"Blackburn and Meredith."

"Nonsense."

"It's true."

"You believe Blackburn can set you up? Philip Blackburn is a spineless fool. He has no principles and almost no brains. I told Garvin to fire him years ago. Blackburn is incapable of original thought."

"Then Meredith."

"Ah. Meredith. Yes. So beautiful. Such lovely breasts."

"Max, please."

"You thought so too, once."

"That was a long time ago," Sanders said.

Dorfman smiled. "Times have changed?" he said, with heavy irony.

"What does that mean?"

"You are looking pale, Thomas."

"I can't figure anything out. I'm scared."

"Oh, you're scared. A big man like you is scared of this beautiful woman with beautiful breasts."

"Max—"

"Of course, you are right to be scared. She has done all these many terrible things to you. She has tricked you and manipulated you and abused you, yes?"

"Yes," Sanders said.

"You have been victimized by her and Garvin."

"Yes."

"Then why were you mentioning to me the flower, hmm?"

He frowned. For a moment he didn't know what Dorfman was talking about. The old man was always so confusing and he liked to be—

"The *flower*," Dorfman said irritably, rapping his knuckles on the wheelchair arm. "The stained-glass flower in your apartment. We were speaking of it the other day. Don't tell me you have forgotten it?"

The truth was that he had, until that moment. Then he remembered the image of the stained-glass flower, the image that had come unbidden to his mind a few days earlier. "You're right. I forgot."

"You *forgot*." Dorfman's voice was heavy with sarcasm. "You expect me to believe that?"

"Max, I did, I—"

He snorted. "You are impossible. I cannot believe you will behave so transparently. You didn't forget, Thomas. You merely chose not to confront it."

"Confront what?"

In his mind, Sanders saw the stained-glass flower, in bright orange and purple and yellow. The flower mounted in the door of his apartment. Earlier in the week, he had been thinking about it constantly, almost obsessing about it, and yet today—

"I cannot bear this charade," Dorfman said. "Of course you remembered it all. But you are *determined* not to think of it."

Sanders shook his head, confused.

"Thomas. You told it all to me, ten years ago," Dorfman said, waving his hand. "You *confided* in me. Blubbering. You were very upset at the time. It was the most important thing in your life, at the time. Now you say it is all forgotten?" He shook his head. "You told me that you would take trips with Garvin to Japan and Korea. And when you returned, she would be waiting for you in the apartment. In some erotic costume, or whatever. Some erotic pose. And you told me that sometimes, when you got home, you would see her first through the stained glass. Isn't that what you told me, Thomas? Or do I have it wrong?"

He had it wrong.

It came back to Sanders in a rush then, like a picture zooming large and bright before his eyes. He saw everything, almost as if he were there once again: the steps leading up to his apartment on the second floor, and the sounds he heard as he went up the steps in the middle of the afternoon, sounds he could not identify at first, but then he realized what he was hearing as he came to the landing and looked in through the stained glass and he saw—

"I came back a day early," Sanders said.

"Yes, that's right. You came back *unexpectedly*."

The glass in patterns of yellow and orange and purple. And through it, her naked back, moving up and down. She was in the living room, on the couch, moving up and down.

"And what did you do?" Dorfman said. "When you saw her?"

"I rang the bell."

"That's right. Very civilized of you. Very nonconfrontational and polite. You rang the bell."

In his mind he saw Meredith turning, looking toward the door. Her tangled hair falling across her face. She brushed the hair away from her eyes. Her expression changed as she saw him. Her eyes widened.

Dorfman prodded: "And then what? What did you do?"

"I left," Sanders said. "I went back to the . . . I went to the garage and got in my car. I drove for a while. A couple of hours. Maybe more. It was dark when I got back."

"You were upset, naturally."

He came back up the stairs, and again looked in through the stained glass. The living room was empty. He unlocked the door and entered the living room. There was a bowl of popcorn on the couch. The couch was creased. The television was on, soundless. He looked away from the couch and went into the bedroom, calling her name. He found her packing, her open suitcase on the bed. He said, "What are you doing?"

"Leaving," she said. She turned to face him. Her body was rigid, tense. "Isn't that what you want me to do?"

"I don't know," he said.

And then she burst into tears. Sobbing, reaching for a Kleenex, blowing her nose loudly, awkwardly, like a child. And somehow in her distress he held his arms out, and she hugged him and said she was sorry, repeating the words, again and again, through her tears. Looking up at him. Touching his face.

And then somehow . . .

Dorfman cackled. "Right on the suitcase, yes? Right there on the suitcase, on her clothes that were being packed, you made your reconciliation."

"Yes," Sanders said, remembering.

"She aroused you. You wanted her back. She excited you. She challenged you. You wanted to possess her."

"Yes. . ."

"Love is wonderful," Dorfman sighed, sarcastic again. "So pure, so innocent. And then you were together again, is that right?"

"Yes. For a while. But it didn't work out."

It was odd, how it had finally ended. He had been so angry with her at first, but he had forgiven her, and he thought that they could go on. They had talked about their feelings, they had expressed their love, and he had tried to go on with the best will in the world. But in the end, neither of them could; the incident had fatally ruptured the relationship, and something vital had been torn from it. It didn't matter how often they told themselves that they could go on. Something else now ruled. The core was dead. They fought more often, managing in this way to sustain the old energy for a while. But finally, it just ended.

"And when it was over," Dorfman said, "that was when you came and talked to me."

"Yes," Sanders said.

"And what did you come to talk to me about?" Dorfman asked. "Or have you 'forgotten' that, too?"

"No. I remember. I wanted your advice."

He had gone to Dorfman because he was considering leaving Cupertino. He was breaking up with Meredith, his life was confused, everything was in disarray, and he wanted to make a fresh start, to go somewhere else. So he was considering moving to Seattle to head the Advanced Projects Division. Garvin had offered him the job in passing one day, and Sanders was thinking about taking it. He had asked Dorfman's advice.

"You were quite upset," Dorfman said. "It was an unhappy ending to a love affair."

"Yes."

"So you might say that Meredith Johnson is the reason you are here in Seattle," Dorfman said. "Because of her, you changed your career, your life. You made a new life here. And many people knew this fact of your past. Garvin knew. And Blackburn knew. That is why he was so careful to ask you if you could work with her. Everyone was so worried about how it would be. But you reassured them, Thomas, didn't you?"

"Yes."

"And your reassurances were false."

Sanders hesitated. "I don't know, Max."

"Come, now. You know *exactly*. It must have been like a bad dream, a nightmare from your past, to hear that this person you had run away from was now coming to Seattle, pursuing you up here, and that she would be your superior in the company. Taking the job that you wanted. That you thought you deserved."

"I don't know. . ."

"Don't you? In your place, I would be angry. I would want to be rid of her, yes? She hurt you once very badly, and you would not want to be hurt again. But what choice did you have? She had the job, and she was Garvin's protégé. She was protected by Garvin's power, and he would not hear a word against her. True?"

"True."

"And for many years you had not been close to Garvin, because Garvin didn't really want you to take the Seattle job in the first place. He had offered it to you, expecting you to turn it down. Garvin likes protégés. He likes admirers at his feet. He does not like his admirers to pack up and leave for another city. So Garvin was disappointed with you. Things were never the same. And now suddenly here was this woman out of your past, a woman with Garvin's backing. So, what choice did you have? What could you do with your anger?"

His mind was spinning, confused. When he thought back to the events of that first day—the rumors, the announcement by Blackburn, the first meeting with her—he did not remember feeling anger. His feelings had been so complicated on that day, but he had not felt anger, he was sure of it . . .

"Thomas, Thomas. Stop dreaming. There is no time for it."

Sanders was shaking his head. He couldn't think clearly.

"Thomas, *you arranged all this*. Whether you admit it or not, whether you are aware of it or not. On some level, what has happened is exactly what you intended. And you made sure it would happen."

He found himself remembering Susan. What had she said at the restaurant?

Why didn't you tell me? I could have helped you.

And she was right, of course. She was an attorney; she could have advised him if he had told her what happened the first night. She would have told him what to do. She could have gotten him out of it. But he hadn't told her.

There's not much we can do now.

"You wanted this confrontation, Thomas."

And then Garvin: *She was your girlfriend, and you didn't like it when she dropped you. So now you want to pay her back.*

"You worked all week to ensure this confrontation."

"Max—"

"So don't tell me you are a victim here. You're not a victim. You call yourself a victim because you don't want to take responsibility for your life. Because you are sentimental and lazy and naïve. You think other people should take care of you."

"Jesus, Max," Sanders said.

"You deny your part in this. You pretend to forget. You pretend to be unaware. And now you pretend to be confused."

"Max—"

"Oh! I don't know why I bother with you. How many hours do you have until this meeting? Twelve hours? Ten? Yet you waste your time talking to a crazy old man." He spun in his wheelchair. "If I were you, I would get to work."

"Meaning what?"

"Well, we know what your intentions are, Thomas. But what are *her* intentions, hmmm? She is solving a problem, too. She has a purpose here. So: what is the problem she is solving?"

"I don't know," Sanders said.

"Clearly. But how will you find out?"

ost in thought, he walked the five blocks to Il Terrazzo. Fernandez was waiting for him outside. They went in together.

"Oh Christ," Sanders said, as he looked around.

"All the usual suspects," Fernandez said.

In the far section straight ahead, Meredith Johnson was having dinner with Bob Garvin. Two tables away, Phil Blackburn was eating with his wife, Doris, a thin bespectacled woman who looked like an accountant. Near them, Stephanie Kaplan was having dinner with a young man in his twenties—probably her son at the university, Sanders thought. And over to the right, by the window, the Conley-White people were in the midst of a working dinner, their briefcases open at their feet, papers scattered all over the table. Ed Nichols sat with John Conley to his right, and Jim Daly to his left. Daly was speaking into a tiny dictating machine.

"Maybe we should go somewhere else," Sanders said.

"No," Fernandez said. "They've already seen us. We can sit in the corner over there."

Carmine came over. "Mr. Sanders," he said with a formal nod.

"We'd like a table in the corner, Carmine."

"Yes of course, Mr. Sanders."

They sat to one side. Fernandez was staring at Meredith and Garvin. "She could be his daughter," she said.

"Everybody says so."

"It's quite striking."

The waiter brought menus. Nothing on it appealed to Sanders, but they ordered anyway. Fernandez was looking steadily at Garvin. "He's a fighter, isn't he."

"Bob? Famous fighter. Famous tough guy."

"She knows how to play him." Fernandez turned away and pulled papers out of her briefcase. "This is the contract that Blackburn sent back. It is all in order, except for two clauses. First, they claim the right to terminate you if you are shown to have committed a felony on the job."

"Uh-huh." He wondered what they might mean.

"And this second clause claims the right to terminate you if you have 'failed to demonstrate satisfactory performance in the job as measured by industry standards.' What does that mean?"

He shook his head. "They must have something in mind." He told her about the conversation he had overheard in the conference room.

As usual, Fernandez showed no reaction. "Possible," she said.

"Possible? They're going to do it."

"I meant legally. It's possible that they intend something of this sort. And it would work."

"Why?"

"A harassment claim brings up the entire performance of an employee. If there is dereliction, even a very old or minor dereliction, it may be used to dismiss the claim. I had one client who worked for a company for ten years. But the company was able to demonstrate that the employee had lied on the original application form, and the case was dismissed. The employee was fired."

"So this comes down to my performance."

"It may. Yes."

He frowned. What did they have on him?

She is solving a problem, too. So: what is the problem she is solving?

Beside him, Fernandez pulled the tape recorder out of her pocket. "There's a couple of other things I want to go over," she said. "There's something that happens early on in the tape."

"Okay."

"I want you to listen."

She gave the player to him. He held it close to his ear.

He heard his own voice saying clearly, ". . .we'll face that later. I've given her your thoughts, and she's talking to Bob now, so presumably we'll go into the meeting tomorrow taking that position. Well, anyway, Mark, if there is a significant change in all this, I'll contact you before the meeting tomorrow, and—"

"Forget that phone," Meredith's voice said loudly, and then there was the sound of rustling, like fabric, and a sort of hissing sound, and a dull *thunk* as the phone was dropped. The momentary sharp crackle of static.

More rustling. Then silence.

A grunt. Rustling.

As he listened, he tried to imagine the action in the room. They must have moved over to the couch, because now the voices were lower, less distinct. He heard himself say, "Meredith, wait—"

"Oh God," she said, "I've wanted you all day."

More rustling. Heavy breathing. It was hard to be certain what was happening. A little moan from her. More rustling.

She said, "Oh God, you feel so *good,* I can't stand the bastard touching me. Those stupid glasses. Oh! I'm so *hot,* I haven't had a decent fuck—"

More rustling. Static crackle. Rustling. More rustling. Sanders listened with a sense of disappointment. He could not really create images for what was going on— and he had been there. This tape would not be persuasive to someone else. Most of it sounded like obscure noise. With long periods of silence.

"Meredith—"

"*Oooh.* Don't talk. No! No. . ." He heard her gasping, in little breaths.

Then more silence.

Fernandez said, "That's enough."

Sanders put the player down and shut it off. He shook his head.

"You can't tell anything from this. About what was really going on."

"You can tell enough," Fernandez said. "And don't you start worrying about the evidence. That's my job. But you heard her first statements?" She consulted her notepad. "Where she says, 'I've wanted you all day'? And then she says, 'Oh God you feel so good, I can't stand the bastard touching me. Those stupid glasses, oh I'm so hot, I haven't had a decent fuck.' You heard that part?"

"Yes. I heard it."

"Okay. Who is she talking about?"

"Talking about?"

"Yes. Who is the bastard she can't stand touching her?"

"I assume her husband," Sanders said. "We were talking about him earlier. Before the tape."

"Tell me what was said earlier."

"Well, Meredith was complaining about having to pay alimony to her husband, and then she said her husband was terrible in bed. She said, 'I hate a man who doesn't know what he's doing.' "

"So you think 'I can't stand the bastard touching me' refers to her husband?"

"Yes."

"I don't," Fernandez said. "They were divorced months ago. The divorce was bitter. The husband hates her. He has a girlfriend now; he's taken her to Mexico. I don't think she means her husband."

"Then who?"

"I don't know."

Sanders said, "I suppose it could be anybody."

"I don't think it's just anybody. Listen again. Listen to how she sounds."

He rewound the tape, held the player to his ear. After a moment, he put the player down. "She sounds almost angry."

Fernandez nodded. "Resentful is the term I'd use. She's in the midst of this episode with you, and she's talking about someone else. 'The bastard.' It's as if she wants to pay somebody back. Right at that moment, she's getting even."

Sanders said, "I don't know. Meredith's a talker. She always talked about other people. Old boyfriends, that stuff. She's not what you'd call a romantic."

He remembered one time when they were lying on the bed in the apartment in Sunnyvale, feeling a sort of relaxed glow. A Sunday afternoon. Listening to kids laughing in the street outside. His hand resting on her thigh, feeling the sweat. And in this thoughtful way she said, "You know, I once went out with this Norwegian guy, and he had a curved dick. Curved like a sword, sort of bent over to the side, and he—"

"Jesus, Meredith."

"What's the matter? It's true. He really did."

"Not now."

Whenever this sort of thing happened, she'd sigh, as if she was obliged to put up with his excessive sensitivity. "Why is it that guys always want to think they're the only ones?"

"We don't. We know we're not. Just not now, okay?"

And she'd sigh again . . .

Sitting in the restaurant, Fernandez said, "Even if it's not unusual for her to talk during sex—even if she is indiscreet or distancing—who is she talking about here?"

Sanders shook his head. "I don't know, Louise."

"And she says she can't stand him touching her . . . as if she has no choice. And she mentions his silly glasses." She looked over at Meredith, who was eating quietly with Garvin. "Him?"

"I don't think so."

"Why not?"

"Everybody says no. Everybody says Bob isn't screwing her."

"Everybody could be wrong."

Sanders shook his head. "It'd be incest."

"You're probably right."

The food came. Sanders poked at his pasta *puttanesca,* picking out the olives. He wasn't feeling hungry. Beside him, Fernandez ate heartily. They had ordered the same thing.

Sanders looked over at the Conley-White people. Nichols was holding up a clear plastic sheet of 35-millimeter transparencies. Slides. Of what? he wondered. His half-frame glasses were perched on his nose. He seemed to be taking a long time. Beside him, Conley glanced at his watch and said something about the time. The others nodded. Conley glanced over at Johnson, then turned back to his papers.

Daly said something. ". . .have that figure?"

"It's here," Conley said, pointing to the sheet.

"This is really very good," Fernandez said. "You shouldn't let it get cold."

"Okay." He took a bite. It had no taste. He put the fork down.

She wiped her chin with her napkin. "You know, you never really told me why you stopped. At the end."

"My friend Max Dorfman says I set it all up."

"Uh-huh," Fernandez said.

"Do you think that, too?"

"I don't know. I was just asking what you were feeling, at the time. At the time you pulled away."

He shrugged. "I just didn't want to."

"Uh-huh. Didn't feel like it when you got there, huh?"

"No, I didn't." Then he said, "You really want to know what it was? She coughed."

"She coughed?" Fernandez said.

Sanders saw himself again in the room, his trousers down around his knees, bent over Meredith on the office couch. He remembered thinking, What the hell am I doing? And she had her hands on his shoulders, tugging him toward her. "Oh please . . . No . . . No. . ."

And then she turned her head aside and coughed.

That cough was what did it. That was when he sat back, and said, "You're right," and got off the couch.

Fernandez frowned. "I have to say," Fernandez said. "A cough doesn't seem like a big deal."

"It was." He pushed his plate away. "I mean, you can't cough at a time like that."

"Why? Is this some etiquette I don't know about?" Fernandez said. "No coughing in the clinch?"

"It's not that at all," Sanders said. "It's just what it means."

"I'm sorry, you've lost me. What does a cough mean?"

He hesitated. "You know, women always think that men don't know what's going on. There's this whole idea that men can't find the place, they don't know what to do, all that stuff. How men are stupid about sex."

"I don't think you're stupid. What does a cough mean?"

"A cough means you're not involved."

She raised her eyebrows. "That seems a little extreme."

"It's just a fact."

"I don't know. My husband has bronchitis. He coughs all the time."

"Not at the last moment, he doesn't."

She paused, thinking about it. "Well, he certainly does right afterward. He breaks out in a fit of coughing. We always laugh about how he does that."

"Right after is different. But at the moment, right in the intense moment, I'm telling you—nobody coughs."

More images flashed through his mind. Her cheeks turn red. Her neck is blotchy, or her upper chest. Nipples no longer hard. They were hard at first, but not now. The eyes get dark, sometimes purple below. Lips swollen. Breathing changes. Sudden surging heat. Shift in the hips, shifting rhythm, tension but something else, something liquid. Forehead frowning. Wincing. Biting. So many different ways, but—

"Nobody coughs," he said again.

And then he felt a kind of sudden embarrassment, and pulled his plate back, and took a bite of pasta. He wanted a reason not to say more, because he had the feeling that he had overstepped the rules, that there was still this area, this kind of knowledge, this awareness that everyone pretended didn't exist . . .

Fernandez was staring at him curiously. "Did you read about this somewhere?"

He shook his head, chewing.

"Do men discuss it? Things like this?"

He shook his head, no.

"Women do."

"I know." He swallowed. "But anyway, she coughed, and that was why I stopped. She wasn't involved, and I was very—angry about it, I guess. I mean she was lying there panting and moaning, but she was really uninvolved. And I felt. . ."

"Exploited?"

"Something like that. Manipulated. Sometimes I think maybe if she hadn't coughed right then. . ." Sanders shrugged.

"Maybe I should ask her," Fernandez said, nodding her head in Meredith's direction.

Sanders looked up and saw that she was coming over to their table. "Oh, hell."

"Calmly, calmly. Everything's fine."

Meredith came over, a big smile on her face. "Hello, Louise. Hello, Tom." Sanders started to get up. "Don't get up, Tom, please." She rested her hand on his shoulder, gave it a little squeeze. "I just came by for a moment." She was smiling radiantly. She looked exactly like the confident boss, stopping to say hello to a couple of colleagues. Back at her table, Sanders saw Garvin paying the bill. He wondered if he would come over, too.

"Louise, I just wanted to say no hard feelings," Meredith said. "Everybody had a job to do. I understand that. And I think it served a purpose, clearing the air. I just hope we can go on productively from here."

Meredith was standing behind Sanders's chair as she talked. He had to twist his head and crane his neck to look at her.

Fernandez said, "Don't you want to sit down?"

"Well, maybe for a minute."

Sanders stood to get her a chair. He was thinking that to the Conley people, all this would look exactly right. The boss not wanting to intrude, waiting to be pressed by her co-workers to join them. As he brought the chair, he glanced over and saw that Nichols was looking at them, peering over his glasses. So was young Conley.

Meredith sat down. Sanders pushed the chair in for her. "You want anything?" Fernandez said solicitously.

"I just finished, thanks."

"Coffee? Anything?"

"I'm fine, thanks."

Sanders sat down. Meredith leaned forward. "Bob's been telling me about his plans to take this division public. It's very exciting. It looks like full speed ahead."

Sanders watched her with astonishment.

"Now, Bob has a list of names for the new company. When we spin it off next year. See how these sound to you: SpeedCore, SpeedStar, PrimeCore, Talisan, and Tensor. I think SpeedCore makes racing parts for stock cars. SpeedStar is right on the money—but maybe too right on. PrimeCore sounds like a mutual fund. How about Talisan or Tensor?"

"Tensor is a lamp," Fernandez said.

"Okay. But Talisan is pretty good, I think."

"The Apple-IBM joint venture is called Taligent," Sanders said.

"Oh. You're right. Too close. How about MicroDyne? That's not bad. Or ADG, for Advanced Data Graphics? Do either of those work, do you think?"

"MicroDyne is okay."

"I thought so, too. And there was one more . . . AnoDyne."

"That's a painkiller," Fernandez said.

"What is?"

"An anodyne is a painkiller. A narcotic."

"Oh. Forget that. Last one, SynStar."

"Sounds like a drug company."

"Yeah, it does. But we've got a year to come up with a better one. And MicroDyne isn't bad, to start. Sort of combining micro with dynamo. Good images, don't you think?"

Before they could answer, she pushed her chair back. "I've got to go. But I thought you'd like to hear the thinking. Thanks for your input. Good night, Louise. And Tom, I'll see you tomorrow." She shook hands with them both and crossed the room to Garvin. Together she and Garvin went over to the Conley table to say hello.

Sanders stared at her. " 'Good images,' " he repeated. "Christ. She's talking about names for a company, but she doesn't even know what the company is."

"It was quite a show."

"Sure," Sanders said. "She's all show. But it had nothing to do with us. It's for them." He nodded toward the Conley-White people, sitting across the restaurant. Garvin was shaking hands all around, and Meredith was talking to Jim Daly. Daly made a joke and she laughed, throwing her head back, showing her long neck.

"The only reason she talked to us was so that when I get fired tomorrow, she won't be seen as having planned it."

Fernandez was paying the bill. "You want to go?" she said. "I still have some things to check."

"Really? What do you have to check?"

"Alan may have gotten something more for us. There's a possibility."

At the Conley table, Garvin was saying good-bye. He gave a final wave, then crossed the room to talk to Carmine.

Meredith remained at the Conley-White table. She was standing behind John Conley, with her hands resting on his shoulders while she talked to Daly and Ed Nichols. Ed Nichols said something, peering over his glasses, and Meredith laughed, and came around to look over his shoulder at a sheet of figures he was holding. Her head was very close to Nichols. She nodded, talked, pointed to the sheet.

You're checking the wrong company.

Sanders stared at Meredith, smiling and joking with the three men from Conley-White. What had Phil Blackburn said to him yesterday?

The thing is, Tom, Meredith Johnson is very well connected in this company. She has impressed a lot of important people.

Like Garvin.

Not only Garvin. Meredith has built a power base in several areas.

Conley-White?

Yes. There, too.

Alongside him, Fernandez stood up. Sanders stood and said, "You know what, Louise?"

"What?"

"We've been checking the wrong company."

Fernandez frowned, then looked over at the Conley-White table. Meredith was nodding with Ed Nichols and pointing with one hand, her other hand flat on the table for balance. Her fingers were touching Ed Nichols. He was peering at the sheets of data over his glasses.

"Stupid glasses. . ." Sanders said.

No wonder Meredith wouldn't press harassment charges against him. It would have been too embarrassing for her relationship with Ed Nichols. And no wonder Garvin wouldn't fire her. It made perfect sense. Nichols was already uneasy about the merger—his affair with Meredith might be all that was holding it in place.

Fernandez sighed. "You think so? Nichols?"

"Yeah. Why not?"

Fernandez shook her head. "Even if it's true, it doesn't help us. They can argue paramour preference, they can argue lots of things—if there's even an argument that needs to be made. This isn't the first merger made in the sack, you know. I say, forget it."

"You mean to tell me," he said, "that there's nothing improper with her having an affair with someone at Conley-White and being promoted as a result?"

"Nothing at all. At least, not in the strict legal sense. So forget it."

Suddenly he remembered what Kaplan had said. *She was looking in the wrong direction when they fired her.*

"I'm tired," he said.

"We all are. They look tired, too."

Across the room, the meeting was breaking up. Papers were being put back into briefcases. Meredith and Garvin were chatting with them. They all started leaving. Garvin shook hands with Carmine, who opened the front door for his departing guests.

And then it happened.

There was the sudden harsh glare of quartz lights, shining in from the street outside. The group huddled together, trapped in the light. They cast long shadows back into the restaurant.

"What's going on?" Fernandez said.

Sanders turned to look, but already the group was ducking back inside, closing the door. There was a moment of sudden chaos. They heard Garvin say, "God*damn* it," and spin to Blackburn.

Blackburn stood, a stricken look on his face, and rushed over to Garvin. Garvin was shifting from foot to foot. He was simultaneously trying to reassure the Conley-White people and chew out Blackburn.

Sanders went over. "Everything okay?"

"It's the goddamned press," Garvin said. "KSEA-TV is out there."

"This is an outrage," Meredith said.

"They're asking about some harassment suit," Garvin said, looking darkly at Sanders.

Sanders shrugged.

"I'll speak to them," Blackburn said. "This is just ridiculous."

"I'll say it's ridiculous," Garvin said. "It's an outrage, is what it is."

Everyone seemed to be talking at once, agreeing that it was an outrage. But Sanders saw that Nichols looked shaken. Now Meredith was leading them out of the restaurant the back way, onto the terrace. Blackburn went out the front, into the harsh lights. He held up his hands, like a man being arrested. Then the door closed.

Nichols was saying, "Not good, not good."

"Don't worry, I know the news director over there," Garvin was saying. "I'll put this one away."

Jim Daly said something about how the merger ought to be confidential.

"Don't worry," Garvin said grimly. "It's going to be confidential as hell by the time I get through."

Then they were gone, out the back door, into the night. Sanders went back to the table, where Fernandez was waiting.

"A little excitement," Fernandez said calmly.

"More than a little," Sanders said. He glanced across the room at Stephanie Kaplan, still having dinner with her son. The young man was talking, gesturing with his hands, but Kaplan was staring fixedly at the back door, where the Conley-White people had departed. She had a curious expression on her face. Then, after a moment, she turned back and resumed her conversation with her son.

The evening was black, damp, and unpleasant. He shivered as he walked back to his office with Fernandez.

"How did a television crew get the story?"

"Probably from Walsh," Fernandez said. "But maybe another way. It's really a small town. Anyway, never mind that. You've got to prepare for the meeting tomorrow."

"I've been trying to forget that."

"Yeah. Well, don't."

Ahead they saw Pioneer Square, with windows in the buildings still brightly lit. Many of the companies here had business with Japan, and stayed open to overlap with the first hours of the day in Tokyo.

"You know," Fernandez said, "watching her with those men, I noticed how cool she was."

"Yes. Meredith is cool."

"Very controlled."

"Yes. She is."

"So why did she approach you so overtly—and on her first day? What was the rush?"

What is the problem she is trying to solve? Max had said. Now Fernandez was asking the same thing. Everyone seemed to understand except Sanders.

You're not a victim.

So, solve it, he thought.

Get to work.

He remembered the conversation when Meredith and Blackburn were leaving the conference room.

It should be quite smooth and impersonal. After all, you have the facts on your side. He's clearly incompetent.

He still can't get into the database?

No. He's locked out of the system.

And there's no way he can get into Conley-White's system?

No way in hell, Meredith.

They were right, of course. He couldn't get into the system. But what difference would it make if he could?

Solve the problem, Max had said. *Do what you do best.*

Solve the problem.

"Hell," Sanders said.

"It'll come," Fernandez said.

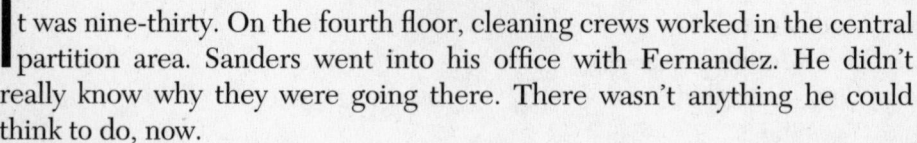

It was nine-thirty. On the fourth floor, cleaning crews worked in the central partition area. Sanders went into his office with Fernandez. He didn't really know why they were going there. There wasn't anything he could think to do, now.

Fernandez said, "Let me talk to Alan. He might have something." She sat down and began to dial.

Sanders sat behind his desk, and stared at the monitor. On the screen, his E-mail message read:

YOU'RE STILL CHECKING THE WRONG COMPANY.

AFRIEND

"I don't see how," he said, looking at the screen. He felt irritable, playing with a puzzle that everyone could solve except him.

Fernandez said, "Alan? Louise. What have you got? Uh-huh. Uh-huh. Is that . . . Well, that's very disappointing, Alan. No, I don't know, now. If you can, yes. When would you be seeing her? All right. Whatever you can." She hung up. "No luck tonight."

"But we've only got tonight."

"Yes."

Sanders stared at the message on the computer screen. Somebody inside the company was trying to help him. Telling him he was checking the wrong company. The message seemed to imply that there was a way for him to check the other company. And presumably, whoever knew enough to send this message also knew that Sanders had been cut out of the DigiCom system, his privileges revoked.

What could he do?

Nothing.

Fernandez said, "Who do you think this 'Afriend' is?"

"I don't know."

"Suppose you had to guess."

"I don't know."

"What comes into your mind?" she said.

He considered the possibility that 'Afriend' was Mary Anne Hunter. But Mary Anne wasn't really a technical person; her strength was marketing. She wasn't likely to be sending routed messages over the Internet. She probably didn't know what the Internet was. So: not Mary Anne.

And not Mark Lewyn. Lewyn was furious at him.

Don Cherry? Sanders paused, considering that. In a way, this was just like Cherry. But the only time that Sanders had seen him since this began, Cherry had been distinctly unfriendly.

Not Cherry.

Then who else could it be? Those were the only people with executive sysop access in Seattle. Hunter, Lewyn, Cherry. A short list.

Stephanie Kaplan? Unlikely. At heart, Kaplan was plodding and unimaginative. And she didn't know enough about computers to do this.

Was it somebody outside the company? It could be Gary Bosak, he thought. Gary probably felt guilty about having turned his back on Sanders. And Gary had a hacker's devious instincts—and a hacker's sense of humor.

It might very well be Gary.

But it still didn't do Sanders any good.

You were always good at technical problems. That was always your strength.

He pulled out the Twinkle CD-ROM drive, still in plastic. Why would they want it wrapped that way?

Never mind, he thought. Stay focused.

There was something wrong with the drive. If he knew what, he would have the answer. Who would know?

Wrapped in plastic.

It was something to do with the production line. It must be. He fumbled with the material on his desk and found the DAT cartridge. He inserted it into the machine.

It came up, showing his conversation with Arthur Kahn. Kahn was on one side of the screen, Sanders on the other.

Behind Arthur, the brightly lit assembly line beneath banks of fluorescent lights. Kahn coughed, and rubbed his chin. "Hello, Tom. How are you?"

"I'm fine, Arthur," he said.

"Well, good. I'm sorry about the new organization."

But Sanders wasn't listening to the conversation. He was looking at Kahn. He noticed now that Kahn was standing very close to the camera, so close that his features were slightly blurred, out of focus. His face was large, and blocked any clear view of the production line behind him. "You know how I feel personally," Kahn was saying, on the screen.

His face was blocking the line.

Sanders watched a moment more, then switched the tape off.

"Let's go downstairs," he said.

"You have an idea?"

"Call it a last-ditch hope," he said.

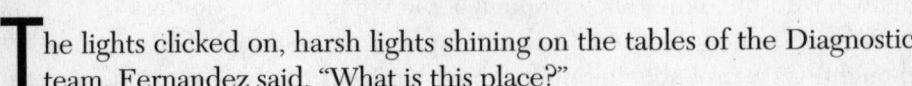

The lights clicked on, harsh lights shining on the tables of the Diagnostic team. Fernandez said, "What is this place?"

"This is where they check the drives."

"The drives that don't work?"

"Right."

Fernandez gave a little shrug. "I'm afraid I'm not—"

"Me neither," Sanders said. "I'm not a technical person. I can just read people."

She looked around the room. "Can you read this?"

He sighed. "No."

Fernandez said, "Are they finished?"

"I don't know," he said.

And then he saw it. They *were* finished. They had to be. Because otherwise the Diagnostics team would be working all night, trying to get ready for the meeting tomorrow. But they had covered the tables up and gone to their professional association meeting because they were finished.

The problem was solved.

Everybody knew it but him.

That was why they had only opened three drives. They didn't need to open the others. And they had asked for them to be sealed in plastic . . .

Because . . .

The punctures . . .

"Air," he said.

"Air?"

"They think it's the air."

"What air?" she said.

"The air in the plant."

"The plant in Malaysia?"

"Right."

"This is about air in Malaysia?"

"No. Air in the *plant*."

He looked again at the notebook on the table. "PPU" followed by a row of figures. PPU stood for "particulates per unit." It was the standard measure of air cleanliness in a plant. And these figures, ranging from two to eleven—they were way off. They should be running zero particulates . . . one, at most. These figures were unacceptable.

The air in the plant was bad.

That meant that they would be getting dirt in the split optics, dirt in the drive arms, dirt in the chip joins . . .

He looked at the chips attached to the board.

"Christ," he said.

"What is it?"

"Look."

"I don't see anything."

"There's a space between the chips and the boards. The chips aren't seated."

"It looks okay to me."

"It's not."

He turned to the stacked drives. He could see at a glance that all the chips were seated differently. Some were tight, some had a gap of a few millimeters, so you could see the metal contacts.

"This isn't right," Sanders said. "This should never happen." The fact was that the chips were inserted on the line by automated chip pressers. Every board, every chip should look exactly the same coming off the line. But they didn't. They were all different. Because of that, you could get voltage irregularities, memory allocation problems—all kinds of random stuff. Which was exactly what they were getting.

He looked at the blackboard, the list of the flowchart. One item caught his eye.

D. Σ Mechanical $\checkmark$ $\checkmark$

The Diagnostics team had put two checks beside "Mechanical." The problem with the CD-ROM drives was a mechanical problem. Which meant it was a problem in the production line.

And the production line was his responsibility.

He'd designed it, he'd set it up. He'd checked all the specs on that line, from beginning to end.

And now it wasn't working right.

He was sure that it wasn't his fault. Something must have happened after he had set up the line. Somehow it had been changed around, and it didn't work anymore. But what had happened?

To find out, he needed to get onto the databases.

But he was locked out.

There wasn't any way to get online.

Immediately, he thought of Bosak. Bosak could get him on. So, for that matter, could one of the programmers on Cherry's teams. These kids were hackers: they would break into a system for a moment of minor amusement the way ordinary people went out for coffee. But there weren't any programmers in the building now. And he didn't know when they would be back from their meeting. Those kids were so unreliable. Like the kid that had thrown up all over the walker pad. That was the problem. They were just kids, playing with toys like the walker pad. Bright creative kids, fooling around, no cares at all, and—

"Oh, Jesus." He sat forward. "Louise."

"Yes?"

"There's a way to do this."

"Do what?"

"Get into the database." He turned and hurried out of the room. He was rummaging through his pockets, looking for the second electronic passcard.

Fernandez said, "Are we going somewhere?"

"Yes, we are."

"Do you mind telling me where?"

"New York," Sanders said.

The lights flicked on one after another, in long banks. Fernandez stared at the room. "What is this? The exercise room from hell?"

"It's a virtual reality simulator," Sanders said.

She looked at the round walker pads, and all the wires, the cables hanging from the ceiling. "This is how you're going to get to New York?"

"That's right."

Sanders went over to the hardware cabinets. There were large hand-painted signs reading, "Do Not Touch" and "Hands Off, You Little Wonk." He hesitated, looking for the control console.

"I hope you know what you're doing," Fernandez said. She stood by one of the walker pads, looking at the silver headset. "Because I think somebody could get electrocuted with this."

"Yeah, I know." Sanders lifted covers off monitors and put them back on again, moving quickly. He found the master switch. A moment later, the equipment hummed. One after another, the monitors began to glow. Sanders said, "Get up on the pad."

He came over and helped her stand on the walker pad. Fernandez moved her feet experimentally, feeling the balls roll. Immediately, there was a green flash from the lasers. "What was that?"

"The scanner. Mapping you. Don't worry about it. Here's the headset." He brought the headset down from the ceiling and started to place it over her eyes.

"Just a minute." She pulled away. "What is this?"

"The headset has two small display screens. They project images right in front of your eyes. Put it on. And be careful. These things are expensive."

"How expensive?"

"A quarter of a million dollars apiece." He fitted the headset over her eyes and put the headphones over her ears.

"I don't see any images. It's dark in here."

"That's because you're not plugged in, Louise." He plugged in her cables.

"Oh," she said, in a surprised voice. "What do you know . . . I can see a big blue screen, like a movie screen. Right in front of me. At the bottom of the screen there are two boxes. One says 'ON' and one says 'OFF.' "

"Just don't touch anything. Keep your hands on this bar," he said, putting her fingers on the walker handhold. "I'm going to mount up."

"This thing on my head feels funny."

Sanders stepped up onto the second walker pad and brought the headset down from the ceiling. He plugged in the cable. "I'll be right with you," he said.

He put on the headset.

Sanders saw the blue screen, surrounded by blackness. He looked to his left and saw Fernandez standing beside him. She looked entirely normal, dressed in her street clothes. The video was recording her appearance, and the computer eliminated the walker pad and the headset.

"I can see you," she said, in a surprised voice. She smiled. The part of her face covered by the headset was computer animated, giving her a slightly unreal, cartoonlike quality.

"Walk up to the screen."

"How?"

"Just walk, Louise." Sanders started forward on the walker pad. The blue screen became larger and larger, until it filled his field of vision. He went over to the ON button, and pushed it with his finger.

The blue screen flashed. In huge lettering, stretching wide in front of them, it said:

DIGITAL COMMUNICATIONS DATA SYSTEMS

Beneath that was listed a column of oversize menu items. The screen looked exactly like an ordinary DigiCom monitor screen, the kind on everybody's office desk, now blown up to enormous size.

"A gigantic computer terminal," Fernandez said. "Wonderful. Just what everybody has been hoping for."

"Just wait." Sanders poked at the screen, selecting menu items. There was a kind of *whoosh* and the lettering on the screen curved inward, pulling back and deepening until it formed a sort of funnel that stretched away from them into the distance. Fernandez was silent.

That shut her up, he thought.

Now, as they watched, the blue funnel began to distort. It widened, became rectangular. The lettering and the blue color faded. Beneath his feet, a floor emerged. It looked like veined marble. The walls on both sides became wood paneling. The ceiling was white.

"It's a corridor," she said, in a soft voice.

The Corridor continued to build itself, progressively adding more detail. Drawers and cabinets appeared in the walls. Pillars formed along its length. Other hallways opened up, leading down to other corridors. Large light fixtures emerged from the walls and turned themselves on. Now the pillars cast shadows on the marble floors.

"It's like a library," she said. "An old-fashioned library."

"This part is, yes."

"How many parts are there?"

"I'm not sure." He started walking forward.

She hurried to catch up to him. Through his earphones, he heard the sound of their feet clicking on the marble floor. Cherry had added that—a nice touch.

Fernandez asked, "Have you been here before?"

"Not for several weeks. Not since it was finished."

"Where are we going?"

"I'm not exactly sure. But somewhere in here there's a way to get into the Conley-White database."

She said, "Where are we now?"

"We're in data, Louise. This is all just data."

"This corridor is data?"

"There is no corridor. Everything you see is just a bunch of numbers. It's the DigiCom company database, exactly the same database that people access every day through their computer terminals. Except it's being represented for us as a place."

She walked alongside him. "I wonder who did the decorating."

"It's modeled on a real library. In Oxford, I think."

They came to the junction, with other corridors stretching away. Big signs hung overhead. One said "Accounting." Another said "Human Resources." A third said "Marketing."

"I see," Fernandez said. "We're inside your company database."

"That's right."

"This is amazing."

"Yeah. Except we don't want to be here. Somehow, we have to get into Conley-White."

"How do we do that?"

"I don't know," Sanders said. "I need help."

"Help is here," said a soft voice nearby. Sanders looked over and saw an angel, about a foot high. It was white, and hovered in the air near his head. It held a flickering candle in its hands.

"Goddamn," Louise said.

"I am sorry," the angel said. "Is that a command? I do not recognize 'Goddamn.'"

"No," Sanders said quickly. "It's not a command." He was thinking that he would have to be careful or they would crash the system.

"Very well. I await your command."

"Angel: I need help."

"Help is here."

"How do I enter the Conley-White database?"

"I do not recognize 'the Conley-White database.'"

That made sense, Sanders thought. Cherry's team wouldn't have programmed anything about Conley-White into the Help system. He would have to phrase the question more generally. Sanders said, "Angel: I am looking for a database."

"Very well. Database gateways are accessed with the keypad."

"Where is the keypad?" Sanders said.

"Make a fist with your hand."

Sanders made a fist and a gray pad formed in the air so that he appeared to be holding it. He pulled it toward him and looked at it.

"Pretty neat," Fernandez said.

"I also know jokes," the angel said. "Would you like to hear one?"

"No," Sanders said.

"Very well. I await your command."

Sanders stared at the pad. It had a long list of operator commands, with arrows and push buttons. Fernandez said, "What is that, the world's most complicated TV remote?"

"Just about."

He found a push button marked OTHER DB. That seemed likely. He pressed it.

Nothing happened.

He pressed it again.

"The gateway is opening," the angel announced.

"Where? I don't see anything."

"The gateway is opening."

Sanders waited. Then he realized that the DigiCom system would have to connect to any remote database. The connection was going through; that was causing a delay.

"Connecting . . . now," the angel said.

The wall of the Corridor began to dissolve. They saw a large gaping black hole, and nothing beyond it.

"That's creepy," Fernandez said.

White wire-frame lines began to appear, outlining a new corridor. The spaces filled, one by one, creating the appearance of solid shapes.

"This one looks different," Fernandez said.

"We're connecting over a T-1 high-speed data line," Sanders said. "But even so, it's much slower."

The Corridor rebuilt itself as they watched. This time the walls were gray. They faced a black-and-white world.

"No color?"

"The system's trying to generate a simpler environment. Color means more data to push around. So this is black and white."

The new corridor added lights, a ceiling, a floor. After a moment, Sanders said, "Shall we go in?"

"You mean, the Conley-White database is in there?"

"That's right," Sanders said.

"I don't know," she said. She pointed: "What about this?"

Directly in front of them was a kind of flowing river of black-and-white static. It ran along the floor, and also along the walls. It made a loud hissing sound.

"I think that's just static off the phone lines."

"You think it's okay to cross?"

"We have to."

He started forward. Immediately, there was a growl. A large dog blocked their path. It had three heads that floated above its body, looking in all directions.

"What's that?"

"Probably a representation of their system's security." Cherry and his sense of humor, he thought.

"Can it hurt us?"

"For God's sake, Louise. It's just a cartoon." Somewhere, of course, there was an actual monitoring system running on the Conley-White database. Perhaps it was automatic, or perhaps there was a real person who actually watched users come and go on the system. But now it was nearly one o'clock in the morning in New York. The dog was most likely just an automatic device of some kind.

Sanders walked forward, stepping through the flowing river of static. The dog growled as he approached. The three heads swiveled, watching him as he passed with cartoon eyes. It was a strange sensation. But nothing happened.

He looked back at Fernandez. "Coming?"

She moved forward tentatively. The angel remained behind, hovering in the air.

"Angel, are you coming?"

It didn't answer.

"Probably can't cross a gateway," Sanders said. "Not programmed."

They walked down the gray corridor. It was lined with unmarked drawers on all sides.

"It looks like a morgue," Fernandez said.

"Well, at least we're here."

"This is their company database in New York?"

"Yes. I just hope we can find it."

"Find what?"

He didn't answer her. He walked over to one file cabinet at random and pulled it open. He scanned the folders.

"Building permits," he said. "For some warehouse in Maryland, looks like."

"Why aren't there labels?"

Even as she said it, Sanders saw that labels were slowly emerging out of the gray surfaces. "I guess it just takes time." Sanders turned and looked in all directions, scanning the other labels. "Okay. That's better. HR records are on this wall, over here."

He walked along the wall. He pulled open a drawer.

"Uh-oh," Fernandez said.

"What?"

"Somebody's coming," she said, in an odd voice.

At the far end of the corridor, a gray figure was approaching. It was still too distant to make out details. But it was striding directly toward them.

"What do we do?"

"I don't know," Sanders said.

"Can he see us?"

"I don't know. I don't think so."

"We can see him, but he can't see us?"

"I don't know." Sanders was trying to figure it out. Cherry had installed another virtual system in the hotel. If someone was on that system, then he or she could probably see them. But Cherry had said that his system represented other users as well, such as somebody accessing the database from a computer. And somebody using a computer wouldn't be able to see them. A computer user wouldn't know who else was in the system.

The figure continued to advance. It seemed to come forward in jerks, not smoothly. They saw more detail; they could start to see eyes, a nose, a mouth.

"This is really creepy," Fernandez said.

The figure was still closer. The details were filling in.

"No kidding," Sanders said.

It was Ed Nichols.

Up close, they saw that Nichols's face was represented by a black-and-white photograph wrapped crudely around an egg-shaped head, atop a gray moving body that had the appearance of a mannequin or a puppet. It was a computer-generated figure. Which meant that Nichols wasn't on the virtual system. He was probably using his notebook computer in his hotel room. Nichols walked up to them and continued steadily past them.

"He can't see us."

Fernandez said, "Why does his face look that way?"

"Cherry said that the system pulls a photo from the file and pastes it on users."

The Nichols-figure continued on walking down the corridor, away from them.

"What's he doing here?"

"Let's find out."

They followed him back down the corridor until Nichols stopped at one file cabinet. He pulled it open and began to go through the records. Sanders and Fernandez came up and stood by his shoulder, and watched what he was doing.

The computer-generated figure of Ed Nichols was thumbing through his notes and E-mail. He went back two months, then three months, then six months. Now he began to pull out sheets of paper, which seemed to hang in the air as he read them. Memos. Notations. Personal and Confidential. Copies to File.

Sanders said, "These are all about the acquisition."

More notes came out. Nichols was pulling them quickly, one after another.

"He's looking for something specific."

Nichols stopped. He had found what he was looking for. His gray computer image held it in his hand and looked at it. Sanders read it over his shoulder, and said certain phrases aloud to Fernandez: "Memo dated December 4, last year. 'Met yesterday and today with Garvin and Johnson in Cupertino re possible acquisition of DigiCom . . .' bla bla . . . 'Very favorable first impression . . . Excellent grounding in critical areas we seek to acquire . . .' bla bla . . . 'Highly capable and aggressive executive staff at all levels. Particularly impressed with competence of Ms. Johnson despite youth.' I'll bet you were impressed, Ed."

The computer-generated Nichols moved down the hall to another drawer and opened it. He didn't find what he wanted and closed it. He went on to another drawer.

Then he began reading again, and Sanders read this one, too: " 'Memo to John Marden. Cost issues re DigiCom acquisition' . . . bla bla . . . 'Concern for high technology development costs in new company' . . . bla bla . . . Here we are. 'Ms. Johnson has undertaken to demonstrate her fiscal responsibility in new Malaysia operation . . . Suggests savings can be made . . . Expected cost savings . . .' How the hell could she do that?"

"Do what?" Fernandez said.

"Demonstrate fiscal responsibility in the Malaysia operation? That was my operation."

"Uh-oh," Fernandez said. "You're not going to believe this."

Sanders glanced over at her. Fernandez was staring down the corridor. He turned to look.

Someone else was coming toward them.

"Busy night," he said.

But even from a distance, he could see that this figure was different. The head was more lifelike, and the body was fully detailed. The figure walked smoothly, naturally. "This could be trouble," he said. Sanders recognized him, even from a distance.

"It's John Conley," Fernandez said.

"Right. And he's on the walker pad."

"Which means?"

Conley abruptly stopped in the middle of the corridor, and stared.

"He can see us," Sanders said.

"He can? How?"

"He's on the system we installed in the hotel. That's why he's so detailed. He's on the other virtual system, so he can see us, and we can see him."

"Uh-oh."

"You said it."

Conley moved forward, slowly. He was frowning. He looked from Sanders to Fernandez to Nichols and back to Sanders. He seemed uncertain what to do.

Then he held his finger to his lips, a gesture for silence.

"Can he hear us?" Fernandez whispered.

"No," Sanders said, in a normal voice.

"Can we talk to him?"

"No."

Conley seemed to make a decision. He walked over to Sanders and Fernandez, until he was standing very close. He looked from one to the other. They could see his expression perfectly.

Then he smiled. He extended his hand.

Sanders reached out, and shook it. He didn't feel anything, but through the headset his saw what looked like his hand gripping Conley's.

Then Conley shook Fernandez's hand.

"This is extremely weird," Fernandez said.

Conley pointed toward Nichols. Then he pointed to his own eyes. Then to Nichols again.

Sanders nodded. They all went over to stand beside Nichols as he went through records.

"You mean Conley's watching him, too?"

"Yes."

"So we can all see Nichols . . ."

"Yes."

"But Nichols can't see any of us."

"Right."

The gray computer figure of Ed Nichols was pulling files hastily out of a drawer.

"What's he up to now?" Sanders said. "Ah. Going through expense records. Now he's found one: 'Sunset Shores Lodge, Carmel. December 5 and 6.' Two days after his memo. And look at these expenses. A hundred and ten dollars for breakfast? Somehow I don't think our Ed was alone there."

He looked over at Conley.

Conley shook his head, frowning.

Suddenly, the record Nichols was holding vanished.

"What happened?"

"I think he just deleted it."

Nichols thumbed through other records. He found four more for the Sunset Shores, and deleted them all. They vanished in midair. Then he closed the drawer, turned, and walked away.

Conley remained behind. He looked at Sanders and drew a finger quickly under his throat.

Sanders nodded.

Conley again put his finger to his lips.

Sanders nodded. He would keep quiet. "Come on," Sanders said to Fernandez. "We're done in here." He started back toward the DigiCom Corridor.

She walked alongside him, then said, "I think we have company."

Sanders looked back: Conley was following them.

"It's okay," he said. "Let him come."

They crossed the gateway, past the barking dog, and came back into the Victorian library. Fernandez sighed. "It feels good to be home again, doesn't it?"

Conley was walking along, showing no surprise. But then, he had seen the Corridor before. Sanders walked quickly. The angel floated alongside them.

"But you realize," Fernandez said, "that none of this makes any sense. Because Nichols is the one who's been opposed to the acquisition, and Conley is the one pushing for it."

"That's right," Sanders said. "It's perfect. Nichols is having it off with Meredith. He promotes her behind the scenes as the new head of the division. And how does he hide that fact? By continuously bitching and moaning to anybody who will listen."

"You mean, it's a cover."

"Sure. That's why Meredith never answered his complaints in any of the meetings. She knew he wasn't a real threat."

"And Conley?" she said.

Conley was still walking alongside them.

"Conley genuinely wants the acquisition. And he wants it to work well. Conley's smart, and I think he realizes that Meredith isn't competent for the job. But Conley sees Meredith as the price of Nichols's support. So Conley has gone along with the choice of Meredith—at least for the time being."

"And what are we doing now?"

"Finding out about the last missing piece."

"Which is?"

Sanders was looking down the hallway marked OPERATIONS. This wasn't really his area of the database, except in specific places of overlap. The files were marked alphabetically. He went down the row until he found DIGICOM/MALAYSIA SA.

He opened it up and searched the file section marked STARTUP. He found his own memos, feasibility studies, site reports, government negotia-tions, first set specifications, memos from their Singapore suppliers, more government negotiations, all stretching back two years.

"What are you looking for?"

"Building plans."

He expected to see the thick sheets of blueprints and inspection sum-maries, but instead there was just a thin file. He opened the first sheet, and a three-dimensional image of the factory floated in the air in front of him. It was just an outline at first, but it rapidly filled in and became solid-looking. Sanders, Fernandez, and Conley stood on three sides of it, looking at it. It was like a very large, detailed doll's house. They peered in through the windows.

Sanders pushed a button. The model became transparent, then turned into a cutaway; now they could see the assembly line, the physical plant. A green line—the conveyor belt—started moving, and the machines and workers assembled the CD-ROM drives as the parts came down the line.

"What are you looking for?"

"Revisions." He shook his head. "This is the first set of plans."

The second sheet was marked "Revisions I/First Set" with the date. He opened it up. The model of the plant seemed to shimmer for a moment, but it remained the same.

"Nothing happened."

The next sheet was marked "Revisions II/Detail Only." Again, when he opened it, the plant shimmered briefly but was unchanged.

"According to these records, the plant was never revised," Sanders said. "But we know it was."

"What's he doing?" Fernandez said. She was looking at Conley.

Sanders saw that Conley was slowly mouthing words, his facial movements exaggerated.

"He's trying to tell us something," she said to Sanders. "Can you see what it is?"

"No." Sanders watched a moment, but the cartoonlike quality of Conley's face made it impossible to read his lips. Finally Sanders shook his head.

Conley nodded, and took the keypad out of Sanders's hand. He pushed a button marked RELATED and Sanders saw a list of related databases flash up in the air. It was an extensive list, including the permits from the Malay government, the architect's notes, the contractor agreements, health and medical inspections, and more. All together, there were about eighty items on the list. Sanders felt sure he would have overlooked the one in the middle of the list that Conley was now pointing to:

OPERATIONS REVIEW UNIT

"What's that?" Fernandez said.

Sanders pressed the name and a new sheet fluttered up. He pushed a button marked SUMMARY and read the sheet aloud: " 'The Operations Review Unit was formed four years ago in Cupertino by Philip Blackburn to address problems not normally within Operations Management purview. The mission of the Review Unit was to improve management efficiency within DigiCom. Over the years, the Operations Review Unit has successfully resolved a number of management problems at DigiCom.' "

"Uh-huh," Fernandez said.

" 'Nine months ago, the Operations Review Unit, then headed by Meredith Johnson of Cupertino Operations, undertook a review of the proposed manufacturing facility in Kuala Lumpur, Malaysia. The immediate stimulus for the review was a conflict with the Malay government over the number and ethnic composition of workers employed at the proposed facility.' "

"Uh-oh," Fernandez said.

" 'Led by Ms. Johnson, with legal assistance from Mr. Blackburn, the Operations Review Unit had outstanding success in resolving the many problems facing DigiCom's Malaysian operation.' "

"What is this, a press release?" Fernandez said.

"Looks like it," Sanders said. He read on: " 'Specific issues concerned the number and ethnic composition of workers employed at the facility. The original plans called for seventy workers to be employed. Responding to the requests of the Malay government, Operations Review was able to increase the number of workers to eighty-five by reducing the amount of automation at the plant, thus making the facility more suitable to the economy of a developing country.' " Sanders looked over at Fernandez. "And screwing us completely," he said.

"Why?"

He continued: " 'In addition, a cost-savings review generated important fiscal benefits in a number of areas. Costs were reduced with no detriment to product quality at the plant. Air-handling capacity was revised to more appropriate levels, and outsourcing supplier contracts were reallocated, with substantial savings benefit to the company.' " Sanders shook his head. "That's it," he said. "That's the whole ball game."

"I don't understand," Fernandez said. "This makes sense to you?"

"You're damned right it does."

He pushed the DETAIL button for more pages.

"I am sorry," the angel said, "there is no more detail."

"Angel, where are the supporting memos and files?" Sanders knew that there had to be massive paperwork behind these summary changes. The renegotiations with the Malay government alone would fill drawers of files.

The angel said, "I am sorry. There is no more detail available."

"Angel, show me the files."

"Very well."

After a moment, a sheet of pink paper flashed up:

THE DETAIL FILES ON
OPERATIONS REVIEW UNIT/MALAYSIA
HAVE BEEN DELETED
SUNDAY 6/14 AUTHORIZATION DC/C/5905

"Hell," Sanders said.

"What does that mean?"

"Somebody cleaned up," Sanders said. "Just a few days ago. Who knew all this was going to happen? Angel, show me all communications between Malaysia and DC for the past two weeks."

"Do you wish telephone or video links?"

"Video."

"Press V."

He pushed a button, and a sheet uncurled in the air:

Date	Linking	To	Duration	Auth
6/1	A. Kahn > M. Johnson		0812-0814	ACSS
6/1	A. Kahn > M. Johnson		1343-1346	ADSS
6/2	A. Kahn > M. Johnson		1801-1804	DCSC
6/2	A. Kahn > T. Sanders		1822-1826	DCSE
6/3	A. Kahn > M. Johnson		0922-0924	ADSC
6/4	A. Kahn > M. Johnson		0902-0912	ADSC
6/5	A. Kahn > M. Johnson		0832-0832	ADSC
6/7	A. Kahn > M. Johnson		0904-0905	ACSS
6/11	A. Kahn > M. Johnson		2002-2004	ADSC
6/13	A. Kahn > M. Johnson		0902-0932	ADSC
6/14	A. Kahn > M. Johnson		1124-1125	ACSS
6/15	A. Kahn > T. Sanders		1132-1134	DCSE

"Burning up the satellite links," Sanders said, staring at the list. "Arthur Kahn and Meredith Johnson talked almost every day until June fourteenth. Angel, show me these video links."

"The links are not available for viewing except for 6/15."

That had been his own transmission to Kahn, two days earlier. "Where are the others?"

A message flashed up:

THE VIDEO FILES ON
OPERATIONS REVIEW UNIT/MALAYSIA
HAVE BEEN DELETED
SUNDAY 6/14 AUTHORIZATION DC/C/5905

Scrubbed again. He was pretty sure who had done it, but he had to be sure. "Angel, how do I check deletion authorization?"

"Press the data you desire," the angel said.

Sanders pressed the authorization number. A small sheet of paper came upward out of the top sheet and hung in the air:

AUTHORIZATION DC/C/5905 IS
DIGITAL COMMUNICATIONS
CUPERTINO/OPERATIONS EXECUTIVE
SPECIAL PRIVILEGES NOTED
(NO OPERATOR ID NECESSARY)

"It was done by somebody very high up in Operations in Cupertino a few days ago."

"Meredith?"

"Probably. And it means I'm screwed."

"Why?"

"Because now I know what was done at the Malaysia plant. I know exactly what happened: Meredith went in and changed the specs. But she's erased the data, right down to her voice transmissions to Kahn. Which means I can't prove any of it."

Standing in the corridor, Sanders poked the sheet, and it fluttered back down, dissolving into the top sheet. He closed the file, put it back in the drawer, and watched the model dissolve and disappear.

He looked over at Conley. Conley gave a little resigned shrug. He seemed to understand the situation. Sanders shook his hand, gripping air, and waved good-bye. Conley nodded and turned to leave.

"Now what?" Fernandez said.

"It's time to go," Sanders said.

The angel began to sing: "It's time to go, so long again till next week's show—"

"Angel, be quiet." The angel stopped singing. He shook his head. "Just like Don Cherry."

"Who's Don Cherry?" Fernandez asked.

"Don Cherry is a living god," the angel said.

They walked back to the entrance to the Corridor and then climbed out of the blue screen.

Back in Cherry's lab, Sanders took off the headset and, after a moment of disorientation, stepped off the walker pad. He helped Fernandez remove her equipment. "Oh," she said, looking around. "We're back in the real world."

"If that's what you call it," he said. "I'm not sure it's that much more real." He hung up her headset and helped her down from the walker pad. Then he turned off the power switches around the room.

Fernandez yawned and looked at her watch. "It's eleven o'clock. What are you going to do now?"

There was only one thing he could think of. He picked up the receiver on one of Cherry's data modem lines and dialed Gary Bosak's number. Sanders couldn't retrieve any data, but perhaps Bosak could—if he could talk him into it. It wasn't much of a hope. But it was all he could think to do.

An answering machine said, "Hi, this is NE Professional Services. I'm out of town for a few days, but leave a message." And then a beep.

Sanders sighed. "Gary, it's eleven o'clock on Wednesday. I'm sorry I missed you. I'm going home." He hung up.

His last hope.

Gone.

Out of town for a few days.

"Shit," he said.

"Now what?" Fernandez said, yawning.

"I don't know," he said. "I've got half an hour to make the last ferry. I guess I'll go home and try to get some sleep."

"And the meeting tomorrow?" she asked. "You said you need documentation."

Sanders shrugged. "Louise, I've done all that I can do. I know what I'm up against. I'll manage somehow."

"Then I'll see you tomorrow?"

"Yeah," he said. "See you tomorrow."

He felt less sanguine on the ferry going home, looking back at the lights of the city in the rippling black water. Fernandez was right; he ought to be getting the documentation he needed. Max would criticize him, if he knew. He could almost hear the old man's voice: "Oh, so you're *tired*? That's a good reason, Thomas."

He wondered if Max would be at the meeting tomorrow. But he found he couldn't really think about it. He couldn't imagine the meeting. He was too tired to concentrate. The loudspeaker announced that they were five minutes from Winslow, and he went belowdecks to get into his car.

He unlocked the door and slipped behind the wheel. He looked in the rearview mirror and saw a dark silhouette in the backseat.

"Hey," Gary Bosak said.

Sanders started to turn.

"Just keep looking forward," Bosak said. "I'll get out in a minute. Now listen carefully. They're going to screw you tomorrow. They're going to pin the Malaysia fiasco on you."

"I know."

"And if that doesn't work, they're going to hit you with employing me. Invasion of privacy. Felonious activity. All that crap. They've talked to my parole officer. Maybe you've seen him—a fat guy with a mustache?"

Sanders vaguely remembered the man walking up to the mediation center the day before. "I think so, yes. Gary, listen, I need some documents—"

"Don't talk. There's no time. They pulled all the documents relating to the plant off the system. Nothing's there anymore. It's gone. I can't help you." They heard the sound of the ferry horn. All around them, drivers were starting their engines. "But I'm not going down for this felony crap. And you're not, either. Take this." He reached forward, and handed Sanders an envelope.

"What's this?"

"Summary of some work I did for another officer of your company. Garvin. You might want to fax it to him in the morning."

"Why don't you?"

"I'm crossing the border tonight. I have a cousin in BC, I'll stay there for a while. You can leave a message on my machine if it turns out okay."

"All right."

"Stay cool, guy. The shit's really going to hit the fan tomorrow. Lots of changes coming."

Up ahead, the ramp went down with a metallic clang. The traffic officers were directing cars off the ferry.

"Gary. You've been monitoring me?"

"Yeah. Sorry about that. They told me I had to."

"Then who's 'Afriend'?"

Bosak laughed. He opened the door and got out. "I'm surprised at you, Tom. Don't you know who your friends are?"

The cars were beginning to pull out. Sanders saw brake lights on the car ahead of him flash red, and the car began to move.

"Gary—" he said, turning. But Bosak was gone.

He put the car in gear and drove off the ferry.

At the top of the driveway, he stopped to pick up his mail. There was a lot of it; he hadn't checked the mailbox for two days. He drove down to the house and left the car outside the garage. He unlocked the front door and went in. The house seemed empty and cold. It had a lemony odor. Then he remembered that Consuela had probably cleaned up.

He went into the kitchen and set up the coffeemaker for the morning. The kitchen was clean and the children's toys had been picked up; Consuela had definitely been there. He looked at the answering machine.

A red numeral was blinking: 14.

Sanders replayed the calls. The first was from John Levin, asking him to call, saying it was urgent. Then Sally, asking if the kids could arrange a play date. But then the rest were all hang-ups. And as he listened, they all seemed to sound exactly the same—the thin hissing background static of an overseas call and then the abrupt click of disconnection. Again and again.

Someone was trying to call him.

One of the later calls was apparently placed by an operator, because a woman's lilting voice said, "I'm sorry, there is no answer. Do you wish to leave a message?" And then a man's voice replied, "No." And then disconnection.

Sanders played it back, listening to that "No."

He thought it sounded familiar. Foreign, but still familiar.

"No."

He listened several times but could not identify the speaker.

"No."

One time, he thought the man sounded hesitant. Or was it hurried? He couldn't tell.

"Do you wish to leave a message?"

"No."

Finally he gave up, rewound the machine, and went upstairs to his office. He'd had no faxes. His computer screen was blank. No further help from "Afriend" tonight.

He read through the paper that Bosak had given him in the car. It was a single sheet, a memo addressed to Garvin, containing a report summary of a Cupertino employee whose name was blanked out. There was also a xerox of a check made out to NE Professional Services signed by Garvin.

It was after one when Sanders went into the bathroom and took a shower. He turned the water up hot, held his face close to the nozzle, and felt the stinging spray on his skin. With the sound of the shower roaring in his ears, he almost missed hearing the telephone ringing. He grabbed a towel and ran into the bedroom.

"Hello?"

He heard the static hiss of an overseas connection. A man's voice said, "Mr. Sanders, please."

"This is Mr. Sanders speaking."

"Mr. Sanders, sir," the voice said, "I do not know if you will remember me. This is Mohammad Jafar."

THURSDAY

The morning was clear. Sanders took an early ferry to work and got to his office at eight. He passed the downstairs receptionist and saw a sign that said "Main Conference Room in Use." For a horrified moment he thought that he had again mistaken the time for his meeting, and hurried to look in. But it was Garvin, addressing the Conley-White executives. Garvin was speaking calmly, and the executives were nodding as they listened. Then as he watched, Garvin finished and introduced Stephanie Kaplan, who immediately launched into a financial review with slides. Garvin left the conference room, and immediately his expression turned grim as he walked down the hallway toward the espresso bar at the end of the corridor, ignoring Sanders.

Sanders was about to head upstairs when he heard Phil Blackburn say, "I really feel I have a right to protest the way this matter has been handled."

"Well, you don't," Garvin said angrily. "You don't have any rights at all."

Sanders moved forward, toward the espresso bar. From his position across the hallway, he was able to see into the bar. Blackburn and Garvin were talking by the coffee machines.

"But this is extremely unfair," Blackburn said.

"Fuck unfair," Garvin said. "She named you as the source, you stupid asshole."

"But Bob, you told me—"

"I told you what?" Garvin said, eyes narrowing.

"You told me to handle it. To put pressure on Sanders."

"That's right, Phil. And you told *me* that you were going to take care of it."

"But you knew I talked to—"

"I knew you had done something," Garvin said. "But I didn't know what. Now she's named you as a source."

Blackburn hung his head. "I just think it's extremely unfair."

"Really? But what do you expect me to do? You're the fucking lawyer,

315

Phil. You're the one always sweating about how things look. You tell me. What do I do?"

Blackburn was silent for a moment. Finally he said, "I'll get John Robinson to represent me. He can work out the settlement agreement."

"Okay, fine." Garvin nodded. "That's fine."

"But I just want to say to you, on a personal level, Bob, that I feel my treatment in this matter has been very unfair."

"Goddamn it, Phil, don't talk to me about your feelings. Your feelings are for sale. Now listen with both ears: Don't go upstairs. Don't clean out your desk. Go right to the airport. I want you on a plane in the next half hour. I want you fucking out of here, right now. Is that clear?"

"I just think you should acknowledge my contribution to the company."

"I am, you asshole," Garvin said. "Now get the fuck out of here, before I lose my temper."

Sanders turned and hurried upstairs. It was hard for him to keep from cheering. Blackburn was fired! He wondered if he should tell anybody; perhaps Cindy, he thought.

But when he got to the fourth floor, the hallways were buzzing; everyone was out of their offices, talking in the corridors. Obviously, rumors of the firing had already leaked. Sanders was not surprised that staffers were in hallways. Even though Blackburn was disliked, his firing would cause widespread uneasiness. Such a sudden change, involving a person so close to Garvin, conveyed to everyone a sense of peril. Everything was at risk.

Outside his office, Cindy said, "Tom, can you believe it? They say Garvin is going to fire Phil."

"You're kidding," Sanders said.

Cindy nodded. "Nobody knows why, but apparently it had something to do with a news crew last night. Garvin's been downstairs explaining it to the Conley-White people."

Behind him, somebody shouted, "It's on the E-mail!" The hallway was instantly deserted; everyone vanished into their offices. Sanders stepped behind his desk and clicked the E-mail icon. But it was slow coming up, probably because every employee in the building was clicking at exactly the same time.

Fernandez came in and said, "Is it true about Blackburn?"

"I guess so," Sanders said. "It's just coming over the E-mail now."

FROM: ROBERT GARVIN, PRESIDENT AND CEO
TO: ALL THE DIGICOM FAMILY

IT IS WITH GREAT SADNESS AND A DEEP SENSE OF PERSONAL

LOSS THAT I TODAY ANNOUNCE THE RESIGNATION OF OUR
VALUED AND TRUSTED CHIEF CORPORATE COUNSEL, PHILIP A.
BLACKBURN. PHIL HAS BEEN AN OUTSTANDING OFFICER OF
THIS COMPANY FOR NEARLY FIFTEEN YEARS, A WONDERFUL
HUMAN BEING, AND A CLOSE PERSONAL FRIEND AND ADVISOR
AS WELL. I KNOW THAT LIKE ME, MANY OF YOU WILL MISS HIS
WISE COUNSEL AND GOOD HUMOR PROFOUNDLY IN THE DAYS
AND WEEKS TO COME. AND I AM SURE THAT YOU WILL ALL JOIN
ME IN WISHING HIM THE BEST OF GOOD FORTUNE IN HIS NEW
ENDEAVORS. A HEARTY THANK YOU, PHIL. AND GOOD LUCK.

THIS RESIGNATION IS EFFECTIVE IMMEDIATELY. HOWARD
EBERHARDT WILL SERVE AS ACTING COUNSEL UNTIL SUCH TIME
AS A NEW PERMANENT APPOINTMENT IS MADE.

ROBERT GARVIN

Fernandez said, "What does it say?"
"It says, 'I fired his sanctimonious ass.' "
"It had to happen," Fernandez said. "Especially since he was the source
on the Connie Walsh story."
Sanders said, "How did you know that?"
"Eleanor Vries."
"She told you?"
"No. But Eleanor Vries is a very cautious attorney. All those media attorneys are. The safest way to keep your job is to refuse to let things run. When
in doubt, throw it out. So I had to ask myself, why did she let the Mr. Piggy
story run, when it's clearly defamatory. The only possible reason is that she
felt Walsh had an unusually strong source inside the company—a source
that understood the legal implications. A source that, in giving the story, was
in essence also saying, we won't sue if you print it. Since high-ranking corporate officers never know anything about law, it means the source could
only be a high-ranking lawyer."
"Phil."
"Yes."
"Jesus."
"Does this change your plans?" Fernandez said.
Sanders had been considering that. "I don't think so," he said. "I think
Garvin would have fired him later in the day, anyway."
"You sound confident."
"Yeah. I got some ammunition last night. And I hope more today."

Cindy came in and said, "Are you expecting something from KL? A big file?"

"Yes."

"This one's been coming in since seven a.m. It must be a monster." She put a DAT cartridge on his desk. It was exactly like the DAT cartridge that had recorded his video link with Arthur Kahn.

Fernandez looked at him. He shrugged.

At eight-thirty, he transmitted Bosak's memo to Garvin's private fax machine. Then he asked Cindy to make copies of all the faxes that Mohammed Jafar had sent him the previous night. Sanders had been up most of the night, reading the material that Jafar had sent him. And it made interesting reading.

Jafar of course was not ill; he had never been ill. That had been a little story that Kahn had contrived with Meredith.

He pushed the DAT videocassette into the machine, and turned to Fernandez.

"You going to explain?" she said.

"I hope it'll be self-explanatory," Sanders said.

On the monitor, the following appeared:

5 SECONDS TO DIRECT VIDEO LINKUP: DC/M-DC/C
SEN: A. KAHN
REC: M. JOHNSON

On the screen, he saw Kahn at the factory, and then a moment later the screen split and he saw Meredith at her office in Cupertino.

"What is this?" Fernandez said.

"A recorded video communication. From last Sunday."

"I thought the communications were all erased."

"They were, here. But there was still a record in KL. A friend of mine sent it to me."

On the screen, Arthur Kahn coughed. "Uh, Meredith. I'm a little concerned."

"Don't be," Meredith said.

"But we still aren't able to manufacture to specs. We have to replace the air handlers, at the very least. Put in better ones."

"Not now."

"But we have to, Meredith."

"Not yet."

"But those handlers are inadequate, Meredith. We both thought they'd be okay, but they aren't."

"Never mind."

Kahn was sweating. He rubbed his chin nervously. "It's only a matter of time before Tom figures it out, Meredith. He's not stupid, you know."

"He'll be distracted."

"So you say."

"And besides, he's going to quit."

Kahn looked startled. "He is? I don't think he—"

"Trust me. He'll quit. He's going to hate working for me."

Sitting in Sanders's office, Fernandez leaned forward, staring at the screen. She said, "No shit."

Kahn said, "Why will he hate it?"

Meredith said, "Believe me. He will. Tom Sanders will be out in my first forty-eight hours."

"But how can you be sure—"

"What choice does he have? Tom and I have a history. Everybody in the company knows that. If any problem comes up, nobody will believe him. He's smart enough to understand that. If he ever wants to work again, he'll have no choice but to take whatever settlement he's offered and leave."

Kahn nodded, wiping the sweat from his cheek. "And then we say Sanders made the changes at the plant? He'll deny that he did."

"He won't even know. Remember. He'll be gone by then, Arthur."

"And if he isn't?"

"Trust me. He'll be gone. He's married, has a family. He'll go."

"But if he calls me about the production line—"

"Just evade it, Arthur. Be mystified. You can do that, I'm sure. Now, who else does Sanders talk to there?"

"The foreman, sometimes. Jafar. Jafar knows everything, of course. And he's one of those honest sorts. I'm afraid if—"

"Make him take a vacation."

"He just took one."

"Make him take another one, Arthur. I only need a week here."

"Jesus," Kahn said. "I'm not sure—"

She cut in: "Arthur."

"Yes, Meredith."

"This is the time when a new vice president counts favors that will be repaid in the future."

"Yes, Meredith."

"That's all."

The screen went blank. There were white streaking video lines, and then the screen was dark.

"Pretty cut and dried," Fernandez said.

Sanders nodded. "Meredith didn't think the changes would matter, because she didn't know anything about production. She was just cutting costs. But she knew that the changes at the plant would eventually be traced back to her, so she thought she had a way to get rid of me, to make me quit the company. And then she would be able to blame me for the problems at the plant."

"And Kahn went along with it."

Sanders nodded.

"And they got rid of Jafar."

Sanders nodded. "Kahn told Jafar to go visit his cousin in Johore for a week—to get out of town. To make it impossible for me to reach Jafar. But he never thought that Jafar would call me." He glanced at his watch. "Now, where is it?"

"What?"

On the screen, there was a series of tones, and they saw a handsome, dark-skinned newscaster at a desk, facing a camera and speaking rapidly in a foreign language.

"What's this?" Fernandez said.

"The Channel Three evening news, from last December." Sanders got up and pushed a button on the tape machine. The cassette popped out.

"What does it show?"

Cindy came back from the copying machine with wide eyes. She carried a dozen stacks of paper, each neatly clipped. "What're you going to do with this?"

"Don't worry about it," he said.

"But this is outrageous, Tom. What she's done."

"I know," he said.

"Everybody is talking," she said. "The word is that the merger is off."

"We'll see," Sanders said.

With Cindy's help, he began arranging the piles of paper in identical manila folders.

Fernandez said, "What exactly are you going to do?"

"Meredith's problem is that she lies," Sanders said. "She's smooth, and she gets away with it. She's gotten away with it her whole life. I'm going to see if I can get her to make a single, very big lie."

He looked at his watch. It was eight forty-five.

The meeting would start in fifteen minutes.

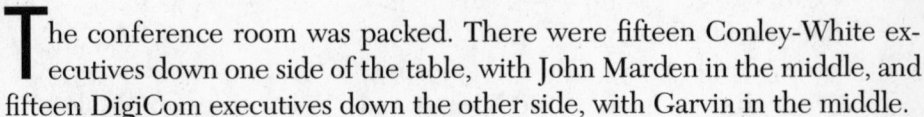

The conference room was packed. There were fifteen Conley-White executives down one side of the table, with John Marden in the middle, and fifteen DigiCom executives down the other side, with Garvin in the middle.

Meredith Johnson stood at the head of the table and said, "Next, we'll hear from Tom Sanders. Tom, I wonder if you could review for us where we stand with the Twinkle drive. What is the status of our production there."

"Of course, Meredith." Sanders stood, his heart pounding. He walked to the front of the room. "By way of background, Twinkle is our code name for a stand-alone CD-ROM drive player which we expect to be revolutionary." He turned to the first of his charts. "CD-ROM is a small laser disk used to store data. It is cheap to manufacture, and can hold an enormous amount of information in any form—words, images, sound, video, and so on. You can put the equivalent of six hundred books on a single small disk, or, thanks to our research here, an hour and a half of video. And any combination. For example, you could make a textbook that combines text, pictures, short movie sequences, animated cartoons, and so on. Production costs will soon be at ten cents a unit."

He looked down the table. The Conley-White people were interested. Garvin was frowning. Meredith looked tense.

"But for CD-ROM to be effective, two things need to happen. First, we need a portable player. Like this." He held up the player, and then passed it down the Conley-White side.

"A five-hour battery, and an excellent screen. You can use it on a train, a bus, or in a classroom—anywhere you can use a book."

The executives looked at it, turned it over in their hands. Then they looked back at Sanders.

"The other problem with CD-ROM technology," Sanders said, "is that it's slow. It's sluggish getting to all that wonderful data. But the Twinkle drives that we have successfully made in prototype are twice as fast as any other drive in the world. And with added memory for our packing and unpacking images, it is as quick as a small computer. We expect to get the unit cost for these drives down to the price of a video-game unit within a year. And we are manufacturing the drives now. We have had some early problems, but we are solving them."

Meredith said, "Can you tell us more about that? I gather from talking to Arthur Kahn that we're still not clear on why the drives have problems."

"Actually, we are," Sanders said. "It turns out that the problems aren't serious at all. I expect them to be entirely resolved in a matter of days."

"Really." She raised her eyebrows. "Then we've found what the trouble is?"

"Yes, we have."

"That's wonderful news."

"Yes, it is."

"Very good news indeed," Ed Nichols said. "Was it a design problem?"

"No," Sanders said. "There's nothing wrong with the design we made here, just as there was nothing wrong with the prototypes. What we have is a fabrication problem involving the production line in Malaysia."

"What sort of problems?"

"It turns out," Sanders said, "that we don't have the proper equipment on the line. We should be using automatic chip installers to lock the controller chips and the RAM cache on the board, but the Malays on the line have been installing chips by hand. Literally pushing them in with their thumbs. And it turns out that the assembly line is dirty, so we're getting particulate matter in the split optics. We should have level-seven air handlers, but we only have level-five handlers installed. And it turns out that we should be ordering components like hinge rods and clips from one very reliable Singapore supplier, but the components are actually coming from another supplier. Less expensive, less reliable."

Meredith looked uneasy, but only for a moment. "Improper equipment, improper conditions, improper components . . ." She shook her head. "I'm sorry. Correct me if I'm wrong, but didn't you set up that line, Tom?"

"Yes, I did," Sanders said. "I went out to Kuala Lumpur last fall and set it up with Arthur Kahn and the local foreman, Mohammed Jafar."

"Then how is it that we have so many problems?"

"Unfortunately, there was a series of bad judgment calls in setting up the line."

Meredith looked concerned. "Tom, we all know that you're extremely competent. How could this have happened?"

Sanders hesitated.

This was the moment.

"It happened because the line was changed," he said. "The specifications were altered."

"Altered? How?"

"I think that's something for you to explain to this group, Meredith," he said. "Since you ordered the changes."

"I ordered them?"

"That's right, Meredith."

"Tom, you must be mistaken," she said coolly. "I haven't had anything to do with that Malaysia line."

"Actually, you have," Sanders said. "You made two trips there, in November and December of last year."

"Two trips to Kuala Lumpur, yes. Because you mishandled a labor dispute with the Malaysian government. I went there and resolved the dispute. But I had nothing to do with the actual production line."

"I'd say you're mistaken, Meredith."

"I assure you," she said coldly. "I am not. I had nothing to do with the line, and any so-called changes."

"Actually, you went there and inspected the changes you ordered."

"I'm sorry, Tom. I didn't. I've never even seen the actual line."

On the screen behind her, the videotape of the newscast began to play silently with the sound off. The newscaster in coat and tie speaking to the camera.

Sanders said, "You never went to the plant itself?"

"Absolutely not, Tom. I don't know who could have told you such a thing—or why you would say it now."

The screen behind the newscaster showed the DigiCom building in Malaysia, then the interior of the plant. The camera showed the production lines and an official inspection tour taking place. They saw Phil Blackburn, and alongside him, Meredith Johnson. The camera moved in on her as she chatted with one of the workers.

There was a murmur in the room.

Meredith spun around and looked. "This is outrageous. This is out of context. I don't know where this could have come from—"

"Malaysia Channel Three. Their version of the BBC. I'm sorry, Meredith." The newscast segment finished and the screen went blank. Sanders made a gesture, and Cindy began moving around the table, handing a manila folder to each person.

Meredith said, "Wherever this so-called tape came from—"

Sanders said, "Ladies and gentlemen, if you will open your packets, you will find the first of a series of memos from the Operations Review Unit, which was under the direction of Ms. Johnson in the period in question. I direct your attention to the first memo, dated November eighteenth of last year. You will notice that it has been signed by Meredith Johnson, and it stipulates that the line will be changed to accommodate the labor demands of the Malay government. In particular, this first memo states that automated chip installers will not be included, but that this work will be done by hand. That made the Malay government happy, but it meant we couldn't manufacture the drives."

Johnson said, "But you see, what you are overlooking is that the Malays gave us no choice—"

"In that case, we should never have built the plant there," Sanders said, cutting her off. "Because we can't manufacture the intended product at those revised specifications. The tolerances are inadequate."

Johnson said, "Well, that may be your own opinion—"

"The second memo, dated December third, indicates that a cost-savings review diminished air-handling capacities on the line. Again, this is a variance in the specifications that I established. Again, it is critical—we can't manufacture high-performance drives under these conditions. The long and the short of it is that these decisions doomed the drives to failure."

"Now look," Johnson said. "If anybody believes that the failure of these drives is anything but your—"

"The third memo," Sanders said, "summarizes cost savings from the Operations Review Unit. You'll see that it claims an eleven percent reduction in operating costs. That savings has already been wiped out by fabrication delays, not counting our time-to-market delay costs. Even if we immediately restore the line, this eleven percent savings translates into a production cost increase, over the run, of nearly seventy percent. First year, it's a hundred and ninety percent increase.

"Now the next memo," Sanders said, "explains why this cost-cutting was adopted in the first place. During acquisition talks between Mr. Nichols and Ms. Johnson in the fall of last year, Ms. Johnson indicated she would demonstrate that it was possible to reduce high-technology development costs, which were a source of concern to Mr. Nichols when they were meeting at—"

"Oh *Christ*," Ed Nichols said, staring at the paper.

Meredith pushed forward, stepping in front of Sanders. "Excuse me, Tom," she said, speaking firmly, "but I really must interrupt you. I'm sorry to have to say this, but no one here is fooled by this little charade." She swept her arm wide, encompassing the room. "Or by your so-called evidence." She spoke more loudly. "You weren't present when these management decisions were carefully taken by the best minds in this company. You don't understand the thinking that lies behind them. And the false postures you are striking now, the so-called memos that you are holding up to convince us . . . No one here is persuaded." She gave him a pitying look. "It's all empty, Tom. Empty words, empty phrases. When it comes right down to it, you're all show and no substance. You think you can come in here and second-guess the management team? I'm here to tell you that you can't."

Garvin stood abruptly, and said, "Meredith—"

"Let me finish," Meredith said. She was flushed, angry. "Because this is important, Bob. This is the heart of what is wrong with this division. Yes, there were some decisions taken that may be questionable in retrospect. Yes, we tried innovative procedures which perhaps went too far. But that hardly excuses the behavior we see today. This calculated, manipulative attitude by an individual who will do anything—anything at all—to get ahead, to make a name for herself at the expense of others, who will savage the reputation of anyone who stands in her path—I mean, that stands in *his* path—this ruthless demeanor that we are seeing . . . No one is fooled by this, Tom. Not for a minute. We're being asked to accept the worst kind of fraudulence. And we simply won't do it. It's wrong. This is all wrong. And it is bound to catch up with you. I'm sorry. You can't come here and do this. It simply won't work—it hasn't worked. That's all."

She stopped to catch her breath and looked around the table. Everyone was silent, motionless. Garvin was still standing; he appeared to be in shock. Slowly, Meredith seemed to realize that something was wrong. When she spoke again, her voice was quieter.

"I hope that I have . . . that I have accurately expressed the sentiments of everyone here. That's all I intended to do."

There was another silence. Then Garvin said, "Meredith, I wonder if you would leave the room for a few minutes."

Stunned, she stared at Garvin for a long moment. Then she said, "Of course, Bob."

"Thank you, Meredith."

Walking very erect, she left the room. The door clicked shut behind her.

John Marden sat forward and said, "Mr. Sanders, please continue with your presentation. In your view, how long will it be until the line is repaired and fully functioning?"

It was noon. Sanders sat in his office with his feet on his desk and stared out the window. The sun was shining brightly on the buildings around Pioneer Square. The sky was clear and cloudless. Mary Anne Hunter, wearing a business suit, came in and said, "I don't get it."

"Get what?"

"That news tape. Meredith must have known about it. Because she was there when they were shooting it."

"Oh, she knew about it, all right. But she never thought I'd get it. And she never thought she'd appear in it. She thought they'd only show Phil. You know—a Muslim country. In a story about executives, they usually just show the men."

"Uh-huh. So?"

"But Channel Three is the government station," Sanders said. "And the story that night was that the government had been only partially successful in negotiating changes in the DigiCom plant—that the foreign executives had been intransigent and uncooperative. It was a story intended to protect the reputation of Mr. Sayad, the finance minister. So the cameras focused on her."

"Because . . ."

"Because she was a woman."

"Foreign she-devil in a business suit? Can't make a deal with a *feringi* woman?"

"Something like that. Anyway, the story focused on her."

"And you got the tape."

"Yeah."

Hunter nodded. "Well," she said, "it's fine with me." She left the room, and Sanders was alone again, staring out the window.

After a while, Cindy came in and said, "The latest word is the acquisition is off."

Sanders shrugged. He was flat, drained. He didn't care.

Cindy said, "Are you hungry? I can get you some lunch."

"I'm not hungry. What are they doing now?"

"Garvin and Marden are talking."

"Still? It's been more than an hour."

"They just brought in Conley."

"Only Conley? Nobody else?"

"No. And Nichols has left the building."

"What about Meredith?"

"Nobody's seen her."

He leaned back in his chair. He stared out the window. His computer gave three beeps.

```
30 SECONDS TO DIRECT VIDEO LINKUP: DC/M-DC/S
SEN: A. KAHN
REC: T. SANDERS
```

Kahn was calling. Sanders smiled grimly. Cindy came in and said, "Arthur's going to call."

"I see that."

```
15 SECONDS TO DIRECT VIDEO LINKUP: DC/M-DC/S
```

Sanders adjusted his desk lamp and sat back. The screen blossomed, and he saw the shimmering image resolve. It was Arthur, in the plant.

"Oh, Tom. Good. I hope it's not too late," Arthur said.

"Too late for what?" Sanders said.

"I know there's a meeting today. There's something I have to tell you."

"What's that, Arthur?"

"Well, I'm afraid I haven't been entirely straightforward with you, Tom. It's about Meredith. She made changes in the line six or seven months ago, and I'm afraid she intends to blame that on you. Probably in the meeting today."

"I see."

"I feel terrible about this, Tom," Arthur said, hanging his head. "I don't know what to say."

"Don't say anything, Arthur," Sanders said.

Kahn smiled apologetically. "I wanted to tell you earlier. I really did. But Meredith kept saying that you would be out. I didn't know what to do. She said there was a battle coming, and I had better pick the winner."

"You picked wrong, Arthur," Sanders said. "You're fired." He reached up and snapped off the television camera in front of him.

"What're you talking about?"

"You're fired, Arthur."

"But you can't do this to me . . . ," Kahn said. His image faded, began to shrink. "You can't—"

The screen was blank.

Fifteen minutes later, Mark Lewyn came by the office. He tugged at the neck of his black Armani T-shirt. "I think I'm an asshole," he said.

"Yeah. You are."

"It's just . . . I didn't understand the situation," he said.

"That's right, you didn't."

"What're you going to do now?"

"I just fired Arthur."

"Jesus. And what else?"

"I don't know. We'll see how it shakes out."

Lewyn nodded and went away nervously. Sanders decided to let him be nervous for a while. In the end, their friendship would be repaired. Adele and Susan were good friends. And Mark was too talented to replace in the company. But Lewyn could sweat for a while; it'd do him good.

At one o'clock, Cindy came in and said, "The word is Max Dorfman just went into the conference with Garvin and Marden."

"What about John Conley?"

"He's gone. He's with the accountants now."

"Then that's a good sign."

"And the word is Nichols was fired."

"Why do they think that?"

"He flew home an hour ago."

Fifteen minutes later, Sanders saw Ed Nichols walking down the hallway. Sanders got up and went out to Cindy's desk. "I thought you said Nichols went home."

"Well, that's what I heard," she said. "It's crazy. You know what they're saying about Meredith now?"

"What?"

"They say she's staying on."

"I don't believe it," Sanders said.

"Bill Everts told Stephanie Kaplan's assistant that Meredith Johnson is not going to be fired, that Garvin is backing her one hundred percent. Phil is going to take the rap for what happened in Malaysia but Garvin still believes Meredith is young and this shouldn't be held against her. So she's staying in her job."

"I don't believe it."

Cindy shrugged. "That's what they say," she said.

He went back to his office and stared out the window. He told himself it was just a rumor. After a while, the intercom buzzed. "Tom? Meredith Johnson just called. She wants to see you in her office right away."

Bright sunlight streamed in through the big windows on the fifth floor. The assistant outside Meredith's office was away from her desk. The door was ajar. He knocked.

"Come in," Meredith Johnson said.

She was standing, leaning back against the edge of her desk, her arms folded across her chest. Waiting.

"Hello, Tom," she said.

"Meredith."

"Come in. I won't bite."

He came in, leaving the door open.

"I must say that you outdid yourself this morning, Tom. I was surprised at how much you were able to learn in a short time. And it was really quite resourceful, the approach you took in the meeting."

He said nothing.

"Yes, it was a really excellent effort. You feeling proud of yourself?" she said, staring hard at him.

"Meredith . . ."

"You think you've finally paid me back? Well, I have news for you, Tom. You don't know *anything* about what's really going on."

She pushed away from the desk, and as she moved away, he saw a cardboard packing box on the desktop beside the telephone. She walked around behind the desk, and begun putting pictures and papers and a pen set into the box.

"This whole thing was Garvin's idea. For three years, Garvin's been looking for a buyer. He couldn't find one. Finally he sent me out, and I found him one. I went through twenty-seven different companies until I got to Conley-White. They were interested, and I sold them hard. I put in the hours. I did whatever I had to do to keep the deal moving forward. *Whatever* I had to do." She pushed more papers into the box angrily.

Sanders watched her.

"Garvin was happy as long as I was delivering Nichols to him on a platter," Johnson said. "He wasn't fussy about how I was doing it. He wasn't even interested. He just wanted it done. I busted my ass for him. Because the chance to get this job was a big break for me, a real career opportunity. Why shouldn't I have it? I did the work. I put the deal together. I *earned* this job. I beat you fairly."

Sanders said nothing.

"But that's not how it turns out, is it. Garvin won't support me when the going gets tough. Everybody said he was like a father to me. But he was just using me. He was just making a deal, any way he could. And that's all he's doing now. Just another fucking deal, and who cares who gets hurt. Everybody moves on. Now I've got to find an attorney to negotiate my severance package. Nobody gives a damn."

She closed the box and leaned on it. "But I beat you, fair and square, Tom. I don't deserve this. I've been screwed by the damned system."

"No you haven't," Sanders said, staring her straight in the eye. "You've been fucking your assistants for years. You've been taking every advantage of your position that you could. You've been cutting corners. You've been lazy. You've been living on image and every third word out of your mouth is a lie. Now you're feeling sorry for yourself. You think the system is what's wrong. But you know what, Meredith? The system didn't screw you. The system *revealed* you, and dumped you out. Because when you get right down to it, you're completely full of shit." He turned on his heel. "Have a nice trip. Wherever you're going."

He left the room, and slammed the door behind him.

He was back in his office five minutes later, still angry, pacing back and forth behind his desk.

Mary Anne Hunter came in, wearing a sweatshirt and exercise tights. She sat down, and put her running shoes up on Sanders's desk. "What're you all worked up about? The press conference?"

"What press conference?"

"They've scheduled a press conference for four o'clock."

"Who says?"

"Marian in PR. Swears it came from Garvin himself. And Marian's assistant has been calling the press and the stations."

Sanders shook his head. "It's too soon." Considering all that had happened, the press conference should not be held until the following day.

"I think so," Hunter said, nodding. "They must be going to announce that the merger has fallen through. You heard what they're saying about Blackburn?"

"No, what?"

"That Garvin made him a million-dollar settlement."

"I don't believe it."

"That's what they say."

"Ask Stephanie."

"Nobody's seen her. Supposedly she went back to Cupertino, to deal with finances now that the merger is off." Hunter got up and walked to the window. "At least it's a nice day."

"Yeah. Finally."

"I think I'll go for a run. I can't stand this waiting."

"I wouldn't leave the building."

She smiled. "Yeah, I guess not." She stood at the window for a while. Finally she said, "Well, what do you know . . ."

Sanders looked up. "What?"

Hunter pointed down toward the street. "Minivans. With antennas on the top. I guess there is going to be a press conference, after all."

They held the press conference at four, in the main downstairs conference room. Strobes flashed as Garvin stood before the microphone, at the end of the table.

"I have always believed," he said, "that women must be better represented in high corporate office. The women of America represent our nation's most important underutilized resource as we go into the twenty-first century. And this is true in high technology no less than in other industries. It is therefore with great pleasure that I announced, as part of our merger with Conley-White Communications, that the new Vice President at

Digital Communications Seattle is a woman of great talent, drawn from within the ranks in our Cupertino headquarters. She has been a resourceful and dedicated member of the DigiCom team for many years, and I am sure she will be even more resourceful in the future. I am pleased to introduce now the new Vice President for Advanced Planning, Ms. Stephanie Kaplan."

There was applause, and Kaplan stepped to the microphone and brushed back her shock of gray hair. She wore a dark maroon suit and smiled quietly. "Thank you, Bob. And thanks to everyone who has worked so hard to make this division so great. I want to say particularly that I look forward to working with the outstanding division heads we have here, Mary Anne Hunter, Mark Lewyn, Don Cherry, and, of course, Tom Sanders. These talented people stand at the center of our company, and I intend to work hand in hand with them as we move into the future. As for myself, I have personal as well as professional ties here in Seattle, and I can say no more than that I am delighted, just delighted, to be here. And I look forward to a long and happy time in this wonderful city."

Back in his office, Sanders got a call from Fernandez. "I finally heard from Alan. Are you ready for this? Arthur A. Friend is on sabbatical in Nepal. Nobody goes into his office except his assistant and a couple of his most trusted students. In fact, there's only one student who has been there during the time he is away. A freshman in the chemistry department named Jonathan—"

"Kaplan," Sanders said.

"That's right. You know who he is?" Fernandez said.

"He's the boss's son. Stephanie Kaplan's just been named the new head of the division."

Fernandez was silent for a moment. "She must be a very remarkable woman," she said.

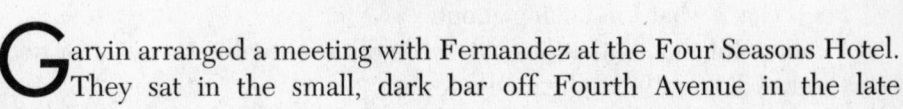

Garvin arranged a meeting with Fernandez at the Four Seasons Hotel. They sat in the small, dark bar off Fourth Avenue in the late afternoon.

"You did a hell of a job, Louise," he said. "But justice was not served, I can tell you that. An innocent woman took the fall for a clever, scheming man."

"Come on, Bob," she said. "Is that why you called me over here? To complain?"

"Honest to God, Louise, this harassment thing has gotten out of hand. Every company I know has at least a dozen of these cases now. Where will it end?"

"I'm not worried," she said. "It'll shake out."

"Eventually, maybe. But meanwhile innocent people—"

"I don't see many innocent people in my line of work," she said. "For example, it's come to my attention that DigiCom's board members were aware of Johnson's problem a year ago and did nothing to address it."

Garvin blinked. "Who told you that? It's completely untrue."

She said nothing.

"And you could never have proved it."

Fernandez raised her eyebrows and said nothing.

"Who said that?" Garvin said. "I want to know."

"Look, Bob," she said. "The fact is, there's a category of behavior that no one condones anymore. The supervisor who grabs genitals, who squeezes breasts in the elevator, who invites an assistant on a business trip but books only one hotel room. All that is ancient history. If you have an employee behaving like that, whether that employee is male or female, gay or straight, you are obliged to stop it."

"Okay, fine, but sometimes it's hard to know—"

"Yes," Fernandez said. "And there's the opposite extreme. An employee doesn't like a tasteless remark and files a complaint. Somebody has to tell her it's not harassment. By then, her boss has been accused, and everybody in the company knows. He won't work with her anymore; there's suspicion, and bad feelings, and it's all a big mess at the company. I see that a lot. That's unfortunate, too. You know, my husband works in the same firm I do."

"Uh-huh."

"After we first met, he asked me out five times. At first I said no, but finally I said yes. We're happily married now. And the other day he said to me that, given the climate now, if we met today, he probably wouldn't ask me out five times. He'd just drop it."

"See? That's what I'm talking about."

"I know. But those situations will settle out eventually. In a year or two, everybody will know what the new rules are."

"Yes, but—"

"But the problem is that there's that third category, somewhere in the middle, between the two extremes," Fernandez said. "Where the behavior is gray. It's not clear what happened. It's not clear who did what to whom. That's the largest category of complaints we see. So far, society's tended to focus on the problems of the victim, not the problems of the accused. But the accused has problems, too. A harassment claim is a weapon, Bob, and there are no good defenses against it. Anybody can use the weapon—and lots of good people have. It's going to continue for a while, I think."

Garvin sighed.

"It's like that virtual reality thing you have," Fernandez said. "Those environments that seem real but aren't really there. We all live every day in virtual environments, defined by our ideas. Those environments are changing. It's changed with regard to women, and it's going to start changing with regard to men. The men didn't like it when it changed before, and the women aren't going to like it changing now. And some people will take advantage. But in the final analysis, it'll all work out."

"When? When will it all end?" Garvin said, shaking his head.

"When women have fifty percent of the executive positions," she said. "That's when it will end."

"You know I favor that."

"Yes," Fernandez said, "and I gather you have just appointed an outstanding woman. Congratulations, Bob."

Mary Anne Hunter was assigned to drive Meredith Johnson to the airport, to take a plane back to Cupertino. The two women sat in silence for fifteen minutes, Meredith Johnson hunched down in her trench coat, staring out the window.

Finally, when they were driving past the Boeing plant, Johnson said, "I didn't like it here, anyway."

Choosing her words carefully, Hunter said, "It has its good and bad points."

There was another silence. Then Johnson asked, "Are you a friend of Sanders?"

"Yes."

"He's a nice guy," Johnson said. "Always was. You know, we used to have a relationship."

"I heard that," Hunter said.

"Tom didn't do anything wrong, really," Johnson said. "He just didn't know how to handle a passing remark."

"Uh-huh," Hunter said.

"Women in business have to be perfect all the time, or they just get murdered. One little slip and they're dead."

"Uh-huh."

"You know what I'm talking about."

"Yes," Hunter said. "I know."

There was another long silence. Johnson shifted in her seat.

She stared out the window.

"The system," Johnson said. "That's the problem. I was raped by the fucking system."

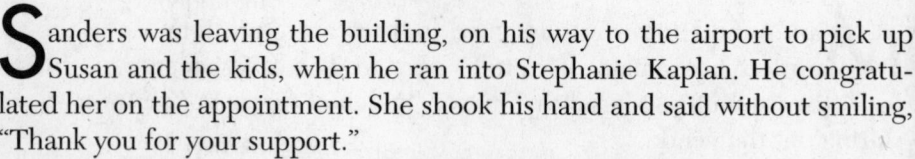

Sanders was leaving the building, on his way to the airport to pick up Susan and the kids, when he ran into Stephanie Kaplan. He congratulated her on the appointment. She shook his hand and said without smiling, "Thank you for your support."

He said, "Thank you for yours. It's nice to have a friend."

"Yes," she said. "Friendships are nice. So is competence. I'm not going to keep this job very long, Tom. Nichols is out as CFO of Conley, and their number-two man is a modest talent at best. They'll be looking for someone in a year or so. And when I go over there, someone will have to take over the new company here. I imagine it should be you."

Sanders bowed slightly.

"But that's in the future," Kaplan said crisply. "In the meantime, we have to get the work here back on track. The division is a mess. Everyone's been distracted by this merger, and the product lines have been compromised by Cupertino's ineptitude. We've got a lot to do to turn this around. I've set the first production meeting with all the division heads for seven a.m. tomorrow morning. I'll see you then, Tom."

And she turned away.

Sanders stood at the arrivals gate at Sea-Tac and watched the passengers come off the Phoenix plane. Eliza came running up to him, shouting "Daddy!" as she leapt into his arms. She had a suntan.

"Did you have a nice time in Phoenix?"

"It was great, Dad! We rode horses and ate tacos, and guess what?"

"What?"

"I saw a snake."

"A real snake?"

"Uh-huh. A green one. It was *this* big," she said, stretching her hands.

"That's pretty big, Eliza."

"But you know what? Green snakes don't hurt you."

Susan came up, carrying Matthew. She had a suntan, too. He kissed her, and Eliza said, "I told Daddy about the snake."

"How are you?" Susan said, looking at his face.

"I'm fine. Tired."

"Is it finished?"

"Yes. It's finished."

They walked on. Susan slipped her arm around his waist. "I've been thinking. Maybe I'm traveling too much. We ought to spend more time together."

"That'd be nice," he said.

They walked toward the baggage claim. Carrying his daughter, feeling her small hands on his shoulder, he glanced over and saw Meredith Johnson standing at the check-in counter of one of the departure gates. She was wearing a trench coat. Her hair was pulled back. She didn't turn and see him.

Susan said, "Somebody you know?"

"No," he said. "It's nobody."

Postscript

Constance Walsh was fired by the Seattle *Post-Intelligencer* and sued the paper for wrongful termination and sexual discrimination under Title VII of the Civil Rights Act of 1964. The paper settled out of court.

Philip Blackburn was named chief counsel at Silicon Holographics of Mountain View, California, a company twice as large as DigiCom. He was later elected Chairman of the Ethics Panel of the San Francisco Bar Association.

Edward Nichols took early retirement from Conley-White Communications and moved with his wife to Nassau, Bahamas, where he worked part-time as a consultant to offshore firms.

Elizabeth "Betsy" Ross was hired by Conrad Computers in Sunnyvale, California, and soon after joined Alcoholics Anonymous.

John Conley was named Vice President for Planning at Conley-White Communications. He died in an automobile accident in Patchogue, New York, six months later.

Mark Lewyn was charged with sexual harassment under Title VII by an employee of the Design Group. Although Lewyn was cleared of the charge, his wife filed for divorce not long after the investigation was concluded.

Arthur Kahn joined Bull Data Systems in Kuala Lumpur, Malaysia.

Richard Jackson of Aldus was charged with sexual harassment under Title VII by an employee of American DataHouse, a wholesale distributor for Aldus. After an investigation, Aldus fired Jackson.

Gary Bosak developed a data encryption algorithm, which he licensed to IBM, Microsoft, and Hitachi. He became a multi-millionaire.

Louise Fernandez was appointed to the federal bench. She delivered a lecture to the Seattle Bar Association in which she argued that sexual harassment suits had become increasingly used as a weapon to resolve corporate disputes. She suggested that in the future there might be a need to revise laws or to limit the involvement of attorneys in such matters. Her speech was received coolly.

Meredith Johnson was named Vice President for Operations and Planning at IBM's Paris office. She subsequently married the United States Ambassador to France, Edward Harmon, following his divorce. She has since retired from business.

Afterword

The episode related here is based on a true story. Its appearance in a novel is not intended to deny the fact that the great majority of harassment claims are brought by women against men. On the contrary: the advantage of a role-reversal story is that it may enable us to examine aspects concealed by traditional responses and conventional rhetoric. However readers respond to this story, it is important to recognize that the behavior of the two antagonists mirrors each other, like a Rorschach inkblot. The value of a Rorschach test lies in what it tells us about ourselves.

It is also important to emphasize that the story in its present form is fiction. Because allegations of sexual harassment in the workplace involve multiple, conflicting legal rights, and because such claims now create substantial risk not only for the individuals but for corporations, it has been necessary to disguise the real event with care. All the principals in this case agreed to be interviewed with the understanding that their identities would be concealed. I am grateful to them for their willingness to help clarify the difficult issues inherent in investigations of sexual harassment.

In addition, I am indebted to a number of attorneys, human relations officers, individual employees, and corporate officials who provided valuable perspectives on this evolving issue. It is characteristic of the extreme sensitivity surrounding any discussion of sexual harassment that everyone I talked to asked to remain anonymous.

RISING SUN

To my mother,

Zula Miller Crichton

We are entering a world where the old rules no longer apply.

Phillip Sanders

Business is war.

Japanese motto

LOS ANGELES POLICE DEPARTMENT
CONFIDENTIAL TRANSCRIPT
OF INTERNAL RECORDS

Contents: Transcript of Video Interrogation
Detective Peter J. Smith
March 13-15

re: "Nakamoto Murder" (A8895-404)

This transcript is the property of the
Los Angeles Police Department and is
for internal use only. Permission to copy,
quote from, or otherwise reproduce or
reveal the contents of this document is
limited by law. Unauthorized use carries
severe penalties.

Direct all inquiries to:

Commanding Officer
Internal Affairs Division
Los Angeles Police Department
PO Box 2029
Los Angeles, CA 92038-2029
Telephone: (213) 555-7600
Telefax: (213) 555-7812

Case: "<u>Nakamoto Murder</u>"

<u>Description of interrogation:</u> Subject (Lt. Smith) was inter-
rogated for 22 hours over 3 days from Monday, March 13 to
Wednesday, March 15. Interview was recorded on S-VHS/SD
videotape.

<u>Description of image:</u> Subject (Smith) seated at desk in
Video Room #4, LAPD HQ. Clock visible on the wall behind
subject. Image includes surface of desk, coffee cup, and Subject from the waist up. Subject wears coat and tie (day 1);
shirt and tie (day 2); and shirtsleeves only (day 3). Video
timecode in lower right corner.

<u>Purpose of interrogation:</u> Clarification of Subject role in
"Nakamoto Murder." (A8895-404) Officers in charge of the
interrogation were Det. T. Conway and Det. P. Hammond.
Subject waived his right to an attorney.

<u>Disposition of case:</u> Filed as "case unsolved."

INT: Okay. The tape is running. State your name for the record, please.

SUBJ: Peter James Smith.

INT: State your age and rank.

SUBJ: I'm thirty-four years old. Lieutenant, Special Services Division. Los Angeles Police Department.

INT: Lieutenant Smith, as you know, you are not being charged with a crime at this time.

SUBJ: I know.

INT: Nevertheless you have a right to be represented here by an attorney.

SUBJ: I waive that right.

INT: Okay. And have you been coerced to come here in any way?

SUBJ: (long pause) No. I have not been coerced in any way.

INT: Okay. Now we want to talk to you about the Nakamoto Murder. When did you first become involved in that case?

SUBJ: On Thursday night, February 9, about nine o'clock.

INT: What happened at that time?

SUBJ: I was at home. I got a phone call.

INT: And what were you doing at the time you got the call?

FIRST NIGHT

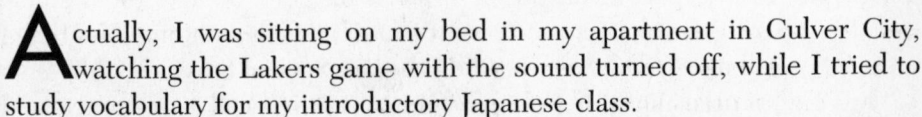

Actually, I was sitting on my bed in my apartment in Culver City, watching the Lakers game with the sound turned off, while I tried to study vocabulary for my introductory Japanese class.

It was a quiet evening; I had gotten my daughter to sleep about eight. Now I had the cassette player on the bed, and the cheerful woman's voice was saying things like, "Hello, I am a police officer. Can I be of assistance?" and "Please show me the menu." After each sentence, she paused for me to repeat it back, in Japanese. I stumbled along as best I could. Then she would say, "The vegetable store is closed. Where is the post office?" Things like that. Sometimes it was hard to concentrate, but I was trying. "Mr. Hayashi has two children."

I tried to answer. "*Hayashi-san wa kodomo ga fur . . . futur . . .*" I swore. But by then the woman was talking again.

"This drink is not very good at all."

I had my textbook open on the bed, alongside a Mr. Potato Head I'd put back together for my daughter. Next to that, a photo album, and the pictures from her second birthday party. It was four months after Michelle's party, but I still hadn't put the pictures in the album. You have to try and keep up with that stuff.

"There will be a meeting at two o'clock."

The pictures on my bed didn't reflect reality any more. Four months later, Michelle looked completely different. She was taller; she'd outgrown the expensive party dress my ex-wife had bought for her: black velvet with a white lace collar.

In the photos, my ex-wife plays a prominent role—holding the cake as Michelle blows out the candles, helping her unwrap the presents. She looks like a dedicated mom. Actually, my daughter lives with me, and my ex-wife doesn't see much of her. She doesn't show up for weekend visitation half the time, and she misses child-support payments.

But you'd never know from the birthday photos.

"Where is the toilet?"

"I have a car. We can go together."

I continued studying. Of course, officially I was on duty that night: I was the Special Services officer on call for division headquarters downtown. But February ninth was a quiet Thursday, and I didn't expect much action. Until nine o'clock, I only had three calls.

Special Services includes the diplomatic section of the police department; we handle problems with diplomats and celebrities, and provide translators and liaison for foreign nationals who come into contact with the police for one reason or another. It's varied work, but not stressful: when I'm on call I can expect a half-dozen requests for help, none of them emergencies. I hardly ever have to roll out. It's much less demanding than being a police press liaison, which is what I did before Special Services.

Anyway, on the night of February ninth, the first call I got concerned Fernando Conseca, the Chilean vice-consul. A patrol car had pulled him over; Ferny was too drunk to drive, but he was claiming diplomatic immunity. I told the patrolmen to drive him home, and I made a note to complain to the consulate again in the morning.

Then an hour later, I got a call from detectives in Gardena. They'd arrested a suspect in a restaurant shooting who spoke only Samoan, and they wanted a translator. I said I could get one, but that Samoans invariably spoke English; the country had been an American trust territory for years. The detectives said they'd handle it. Then I got a call that mobile television vans were blocking fire lanes at the Aerosmith concert; I told the officers to give it to the fire department. And it was quiet for the next hour. I went back to my textbook and my sing-song woman saying things like, "Yesterday's weather was rainy."

Then Tom Graham called.

"It's the fucking Japs," Graham said. "I can't believe they're pulling this shit. Better get over here, Petey-san. Eleven hundred Figueroa, corner of Seventh. It's the new Nakamoto building."

"What is the problem?" I had to ask. Graham is a good detective but he has a bad temper, and he tends to blow things out of proportion.

"The problem," Graham said, "is that the fucking Japs are demanding to see the fucking Special Services liaison. Which is you, buddy. They're saying the police can't proceed until the liaison gets here."

"Can't proceed? Why? What have you got?"

"Homicide," Graham said. "Caucasian female approximately twenty-five years old, apparent six-oh-one. Lying flat on her back, right in their damn boardroom. Quite a sight. You better get down here as soon as you can."

I said, "Is that music in the background?"

"Hell, yes," Graham said. "There's a big party going on. Tonight is the grand opening of the Nakamoto Tower, and they're having a reception. Just get down here, will you?"

I said I would. I called Mrs. Ascenio next door, and asked her if she would watch the baby while I was gone; she always needed extra money. While I waited for her to arrive I changed my shirt and put on my good suit. Then Fred Hoffmann called. He was watch commander at DHD downtown; a short, tough guy with gray hair. "Listen, Pete. I think you might want help on this one."

I said, "Why is that?"

"Sounds like we got a homicide involving Japanese nationals. It may be sticky. How long have you been a liaison?"

"About six months," I said.

"If I was you, I'd get some experienced help. Pick up Connor and take him downtown with you."

"Who?"

"John Connor. Ever heard of him?"

"Sure," I said. Everyone in the division had heard of Connor. He was a legend, the most knowledgeable of the Special Services officers. "But isn't he retired?"

"He's on indefinite leave, but he still works cases involving the Japanese. I think he could be helpful to you. Tell you what. I'll call him for you. You just go down and pick him up." Hoffmann gave me his address.

"Okay, fine. Thanks."

"And one other thing. Land lines on this one, okay, Pete?"

"Okay," I said. "Who requested that?"

"It's just better."

"Whatever you say, Fred."

Land lines meant to stay off the radios, so our transmissions wouldn't be picked up by the media monitoring police frequencies. It was standard procedure in certain situations. Whenever Elizabeth Taylor went to the hospital, we went to land lines. Or if the teenage son of somebody famous died in a car crash, we'd go to land lines to make sure the parents got the news before the TV crews started banging on their door. We used land lines for that kind of thing. I'd never heard it invoked in a homicide before.

But driving downtown, I stayed off the car phone, and listened to the radio. There was a report of a shooting of a three-year-old boy who was now paralyzed from the waist down. The child was a bystander during a 7-Eleven robbery. A stray bullet hit him in the spine and he was—

I switched to another station, got a talk show. Ahead, I could see the lights of the downtown skyscrapers, rising into mist. I got off the freeway at San Pedro, Connor's exit.

What I knew about John Connor was that he had lived for a time in Japan, where he acquired his knowledge of Japanese language and culture. At one point, back in the 1960s, he was the only officer who spoke fluent Japanese, even though Los Angeles then had the largest Japanese population outside the home islands.

Now, of course, the department has more than eighty officers who speak Japanese—and more, like me, who are trying to learn. Connor had retired several years before. But the liaison officers who worked with him agreed he was the best. He was said to work very fast, often solving cases in a few hours. He had a reputation as a skilled detective and an extraordinary interviewer, able to get information from witnesses like nobody else. But most of all, the other liaisons praised his even-handed approach. One said to me, "Working with the Japanese is like balancing on a tightrope. Sooner or later, everybody falls off on one side or the other. Some people decide the Japanese are fabulous and can do no wrong. Some people decide they're vicious pricks. But Connor always keeps his balance. He stays in the middle. He always knows exactly what he is doing."

John Connor lived in the industrial area off Seventh Street, in a large brick warehouse alongside a diesel truck depot. The freight elevator in the building was broken. I walked upstairs to the third floor and knocked on his door.

"It's open," a voice said.

I entered a small apartment. The living room was empty, and furnished in the Japanese style: tatami mats, shoji screens, and wood-paneled walls. A calligraphy scroll, a black lacquer table, a vase with a single splash of white orchid.

I saw two pairs of shoes set out beside the door. One was a man's brogues. The other was a pair of women's high heels.

I said, "Captain Connor?"

"Just a minute."

A shoji screen slid back and Connor appeared. He was surprisingly tall, maybe a hundred and ninety centimeters, well over six feet. He wore a *yukata,* a light Japanese robe of blue cotton. I estimated he was fifty-five years old. Broad-shouldered, balding, with a trim mustache, sharp features, piercing eyes. Deep voice. Calm.

"Good evening, Lieutenant."

We shook hands. Connor looked me up and down, and nodded approvingly. "Good. Very presentable."

I said, "I used to work press. You never knew when you might have to appear in front of cameras."

He nodded. "And now you're the SSO on call?"

"That's right."

"How long have you been a liaison?"

"Six months."

"You speak Japanese?"

"A little. I'm taking lessons."

"Give me a few minutes to change." He turned and disappeared behind the shoji screen. "This is a homicide?"

"Yes."

"Who notified you?"

"Tom Graham. He's the OIC at the crime scene. He said the Japanese were insisting on a liaison officer being present."

"I see." There was a pause. I heard running water. "Is that a common request?"

"No. In fact, I've never heard of it happening. Usually, officers call for a liaison because they have a language problem. I've never heard of the Japanese asking for a liaison."

"Neither have I," Connor said. "Did Graham ask you to bring me? Because Tom Graham and I don't always admire each other."

"No," I said. "Fred Hoffmann suggested I bring you in. He felt I didn't have enough experience. He said he was going to call you for me."

"Then you were called at home twice?" Connor said.

"Yes."

"I see." He reappeared, wearing a dark blue suit, knotting his tie. "It seems that time is critical." He glanced at his watch. "When did Graham call you?"

"About nine."

"Then forty minutes have already passed. Let's go, Lieutenant. Where's your car?"

We hurried downstairs.

I drove up San Pedro and turned left onto Second, heading toward the Nakamoto building. There was a light mist at street level. Connor stared out the window. He said, "How good is your memory?"

"Pretty good, I guess."

"I wonder if you could repeat for me the telephone conversations you had tonight," he said. "Give them to me in as much detail as possible. Word for word, if you can."

"I'll try."

I recounted my phone calls. Connor listened without interruption or comment. I didn't know why he was so interested, and he didn't tell me. When I finished, he said, "Hoffmann didn't tell you who called for land lines?"

"No."

"Well, it's a good idea in any case. I never use a car phone if I can help it. These days, too many people listen in."

I turned onto Figueroa. Up ahead I saw searchlights shining in front of the new Nakamoto Tower. The building itself was gray granite, rising up into the night. I got into the right lane and flipped open the glove box to grab a handful of business cards.

The cards said Detective Lieutenant Peter J. Smith, Special Services Liaison Officer, Los Angeles Police Department. Printed in English on one side, in Japanese on the back.

Connor looked at the cards. "How do you want to handle this situation, Lieutenant? Have you negotiated with the Japanese before?"

I said, "Not really, no. Couple of drunk driving arrests."

Connor said politely, "Then perhaps I can suggest a strategy for us to follow."

"That's fine with me," I said. "I'd be grateful for your help."

"All right. Since you're the liaison, it's probably best if you take charge of the scene when we arrive."

"Okay."

"Don't bother to introduce me, or refer to me in any way. Don't even look in my direction."

"Okay."

"I am a nonentity. You alone are in charge."

"Okay, fine."

"It'll help to be formal. Stand straight, and keep your suit jacket buttoned at all times. If they bow to you, don't bow back—just give a little head nod. A foreigner will never master the etiquette of bowing. Don't even try."

"Okay," I said.

"When you start to deal with the Japanese, remember that they don't like to negotiate. They find it too confrontational. In their own society they avoid it whenever possible."

"Okay."

"Control your gestures. Keep your hands at your sides. The Japanese find big arm movements threatening. Speak slowly. Keep your voice calm and even."

"Okay."

"If you can."

"Okay."

"It may be difficult to do. The Japanese can be irritating. You'll probably find them irritating tonight. Handle it as best you can. But whatever happens, don't lose your temper."

"All right."

"That's extremely bad form."

"All right," I said.

Connor smiled. "I'm sure you'll do well," he said. "You probably won't need my help at all. But if you get stuck, you'll hear me say 'Perhaps I can be of assistance.' That will be the signal that I'm taking over. From that point on, let me do the talking. I'd prefer you not speak again, even if you are spoken to directly by them. Okay?"

"Okay."

"You may want to speak, but don't be drawn out."

"I understand."

"Furthermore, whatever I do, show no surprise. *Whatever* I do."

"Okay."

"Once I take over, move so that you're standing slightly behind me and to my right. Never sit. Never look around. Never appear distracted. Remember that although you come from an MTV video culture, they do not. They are Japanese. Everything you do will have meaning to them. Every aspect of your appearance and behavior will reflect on you, on the police department, and on me as your superior and *sempai*."

"Okay, Captain."

"Any questions?"

"What's a *sempai*?"

Connor smiled.

We drove past the searchlights, down the ramp into the underground garage.

"In Japan," he said, "a *sempai* is a senior man who guides a junior man, known as a *kōhai*. The *sempai-kōhai* relationship is quite common. It's often assumed to exist whenever a younger man and an older man are working together. They will probably assume it of us."

I said, "Sort of a mentor and apprentice?"

"Not exactly," Connor said. "In Japan, *sempai-kōhai* has a different quality. More like a fond parent: the *sempai* is expected to indulge his *kōhai*, and put up with all sorts of youthful excesses and errors from the junior man." He smiled. "But I'm sure you won't do that to me."

We came to the bottom of the ramp, and saw the flat expanse of the parking garage ahead of us. Connor stared out the window and frowned. "Where is everybody?"

The garage of the Nakamoto Tower was full of limousines, the drivers leaning against their cars, talking and smoking. But I saw no police cars. Ordinarily, when there's a homicide, the place is lit up like Christmas, with lights flashing from a half-dozen black and whites, the medical examiner, paramedics, and all the rest.

But there was nothing tonight. It just looked like a garage where somebody was having a party: elegant people standing in clusters, waiting for their cars.

"Interesting," I said.

We came to a stop. The parking attendants opened the doors, and I stepped out onto plush carpet, and heard soft music. I walked with Connor toward the elevator. Well-dressed people were coming the other way: men in tuxedos, women in expensive gowns. And standing by the elevator, wearing a stained corduroy sport coat and furiously smoking a cigarette, was Tom Graham.

When Graham played halfback at U.S.C. he never made first string. That bit of history stuck like a character trait: all his life he seemed to miss the crucial promotion, the next step up a detective's career. He had transferred from one division to another, never finding a precinct that suited him, or a partner that worked well with him. Always too outspoken, Graham had made enemies in the chief's office, and at thirty-nine, further advancement was unlikely. Now he was bitter, gruff, and putting on weight—a big man who had become ponderous, and a pain in the ass: he just rubbed people the wrong way. His idea of personal integrity was to be a failure, and he was sarcastic about anybody who didn't share his views.

"Nice suit," he said to me, as I walked up. "You look fucking beautiful, Peter." He flicked imaginary dust off my lapel.

I ignored it. "How's it going, Tom?"

"You guys should be attending this party, not working it." He turned to Connor and shook his hand. "Hello, John. Whose idea was it to get you out of bed?"

"I'm just observing," Connor said mildly.

I said, "Fred Hoffmann asked me to bring him down."

"Hell," Graham said. "It's okay with me that you're here. I can use some help. It's pretty tense up there."

We followed him toward the elevator. I still saw no other police officers. I said, "Where is everybody?"

"Good question," Graham said. "They've managed to keep all of our people around back at the freight entrance. They claim the service elevator gives fastest access. And they keep talking about the importance of their grand opening, and how nothing must disrupt it."

By the elevators, a uniformed Japanese private security guard looked us over carefully. "These two are with me," Graham said. The security man nodded, but squinted at us suspiciously.

We got on the elevator.

"Fucking Japanese," Graham said, as the doors closed. "This is still our country. We're still the fucking police in our own country."

The elevator was glass walled and we looked out on downtown Los Angeles as it went up into the light mist. Directly across was the Arco building. All lit up at night.

"You know these elevators are illegal," Graham said. "According to code, no glass elevators past ninety floors, and this building is ninety-seven floors, the highest building in L.A. But then this whole building is one big special case. And they got it up in six months. You know how? They brought in prefab units from Nagasaki, and slapped them together here. Didn't use American construction workers. Got a special permit to bypass our unions because of a so-called technical problem that only Japanese workers could handle. You believe that shit?"

I shrugged. "They got it past the American unions."

"Hell, they got it past the *city council*," Graham said. "But of course that's just money. And if there's one thing we know, the Japanese have money. So they got variances on the zoning restrictions, the earthquake ordinances. They got everything they wanted."

I shrugged. "Politics."

"My ass. You know they don't even pay tax? That's right: they got an eight-year break on property taxes from the city. Shit: we're *giving* this country away."

We rode for a moment in silence. Graham stared out the windows. The elevators were high-speed Hitachis, using the latest technology. The fastest and smoothest elevators in the world. We moved higher into the mist.

I said to Graham, "You want to tell us about this homicide, or do you want it to be a surprise?"

"Fuck," Graham said. He flipped open his notebook. "Here you go. The original call was at eight thirty-two. Somebody saying there is a 'problem of disposition of a body.' Male with a thick Asian accent, doesn't speak good English. The operator couldn't get much out of him, except an address. The Nakamoto Tower. Black and white goes over, arrives at eight thirty-nine p.m., finds it's a homicide. Forty-sixth floor, which is an office floor in this building. Victim is Caucasian female, approximately twenty-five years old. Hell of a good-looking girl. You'll see.

"The blue suits stretch the tape and call the division. I go over with Merino, arriving at eight fifty-three. Crime scene IU and SID show up about the same time for PE, prints, and pics. Okay so far?"

"Yes," Connor said, nodding.

Graham said, "We're just getting started when some Jap from the Nakamoto Corporation comes up in a thousand-dollar blue suit and announces that he is entitled to a fucking conversation with the L.A.P.D. liaison officer before anything is done in their fucking building. And he's saying things like we got no probable cause.

"I go, what the fuck is this. We got an obvious homicide here. I think this guy should get back. But this Jap speaks excellent fucking English and he seems to know a lot of law. And everybody at the scene becomes, you know, concerned. I mean, there's no point in pushing to start an investigation if it's going to invalidate due process, right? And this Jap fucker is insisting the liaison must be present before we do anything. Since he speaks such fucking good English I don't know what the problem is. I thought the whole idea of a liaison was for people who don't speak the language and this fucking guy has Stanford law school written all over him. But anyway." He sighed.

"You called me," I said.

"Yeah."

I said, "Who is the man from Nakamoto?"

"Shit." Graham scowled at his notes. "Ishihara. Ishiguri. Something like that."

"You have his card? He must have given you his card."

"Yeah, he did. I gave it to Merino."

I said, "Any other Japanese there?"

"What are you, kidding?" Graham laughed. "The place is swarming with them. Fucking Disneyland up there."

"I mean the crime scene."

"So do I," Graham said. "We can't keep 'em out. They say it's their building, they have a right to be there. Tonight is the grand opening of the Nakamoto Tower. They have a right to be there. On and on."

I said, "Where is the opening taking place?"

"One floor below the murder, on the forty-fifth floor. They're having one hell of a bash. Must be eight hundred people there. Movie stars, senators, congressmen, you name it. I hear Madonna is there, and Tom Cruise. Senator Hammond. Senator Kennedy. Elton John. Senator Morton. Mayor Thomas's there. District Attorney Wyland's there. Hey, maybe your ex-wife is there, too, Pete. She still works for Wyland, doesn't she?"

"Last I heard."

Graham sighed. "Must be great to fuck a lawyer, instead of getting fucked by them. Must make for a nice change."

I didn't want to talk about my ex-wife. "We don't have a lot of contact any more," I said.

A little bell rang, then the elevator said, "*Yonjūsan kai.*"

Graham glanced at the glowing numbers above the door. "Can you believe that shit?"

"*Yonjūyon kai,*" the elevator said. "*Mōsugu de gozaimasu.*"

"What'd it say?"

" 'We're almost at the floor.' "

"Fuck," Graham said. "If an elevator's going to talk, it should be English. This is still America."

"Just barely," Connor said, staring out at the view.

"*Youjūgo kai,*" the elevator said.

The door opened.

Graham was right: it was a hell of a party. The whole floor had been made into a replica forties ballroom. Men in suits. Women in cocktail dresses. The band playing Glenn Miller swing music. Standing near the elevator door was a gray-haired, suntanned man who looked vaguely familiar. He had the broad shoulders of an athlete. He stepped onto the elevator and turned to me. "Ground floor, please." I smelled whiskey.

A second, younger man in a suit instantly appeared by his side. "This elevator is going up, Senator."

"What's that?" the gray-haired man said, turning to his aide.

"This elevator's going up, sir."

"Well. I *want* to go *down.*" He was speaking with the careful, over-articulated speech of the drunk.

"Yes, sir. I know that, sir," the aide replied cheerfully. "Let's take the next elevator, Senator." He gripped the gray-haired man firmly by the elbow and led him off the elevator.

The doors closed. The elevator continued up.

"Your tax dollars at work," Graham said. "Recognize him? Senator Stephen Rowe. Nice to find him partying here, considering he's on the Senate Finance Committee, which sets all Japanese import regulations. But like his pal Senator Kennedy, Rowe is one of the great pussy patrollers."

"Oh, yeah?"

"They say he can drink pretty good, too."

"I noticed that."

"That's why he's got that kid with him. To keep him out of trouble."

The elevator stopped at the forty-sixth floor. There was a soft electronic ping. *"Yonjūroku kai. Goriyō arigatō gozaimashita."*

"Finally," Graham said. "Now maybe we can get to work."

The doors opened. We faced a solid wall of blue business suits, backs turned to us. There must have been twenty men jammed in the area just beyond the elevator. The air was thick with cigarette smoke.

"Coming through, coming through," Graham said, pushing his way roughly past the men. I followed, Connor behind me, silent and inconspicuous.

The forty-sixth floor had been designed to house the chief executive offices of Nakamoto Industries, and it was impressive. Standing in the carpeted reception area just beyond the elevators, I could see the entire floor—it was a gigantic open space. It was about sixty by forty meters, half the size of a football field. Everything added to the sense of spaciousness and elegance. The ceilings were high, paneled in wood. The furnishings were all wood and fabric, black and gray, and the carpet was thick. Sound was muted and lights were low, adding to the soft, rich quality. It looked more like a bank than a business office.

The richest bank you ever saw.

And it made you stop and look. I stood by the yellow crime-scene tape, which blocked access to the floor itself, and got my bearings. Directly ahead was the large atrium, a kind of open bullpen for secretaries and lower-level people. There were desks in clusters, and trees to break up the space. In the center of the atrium stood a large model of the Nakamoto Tower, and the complex of surrounding buildings still under construction. A spotlight shone on the model, but the rest of the atrium was relatively dark, with night lights.

Private offices for the executives were arranged around the perimeter of the atrium. The offices had glass walls facing the atrium, and glass walls on the outside walls as well, so that from where I was standing you could look straight out to the surrounding skyscrapers of Los Angeles. It made you think the floor was floating in midair.

There were two glass-walled conference rooms, on the left and right. The room on the right was smaller, and there I saw the body of the girl, lying on a long black table. She was wearing a black dress. One leg dangled down toward the floor. I didn't see any blood. But I was pretty far away from her, maybe sixty meters. It was hard to see much detail.

I heard the crackle of police radios, and I heard Graham saying, "Here's your liaison, gentlemen. Now maybe we can get started on our investigation. Peter?"

I turned to the Japanese men by the elevator. I didn't know which I should talk to; there was an awkward moment until one of them stepped forward. He was about thirty-five and wore an expensive suit. The man gave a very slight bow, from the neck, just a hint. I bowed back. Then he spoke.

"*Konbanwa. Hajimemashite, Sumisu-san. Ishiguro desu. Dōzo yoroshiku.*" A formal greeting, although perfunctory. No wasted time. His name was Ishiguro. He already knew my name.

I said, "*Hajimemashite. Watashi wa Sumisu desu. Dōzo yoroshiku.*" How do you do. Glad to meet you. The usual.

"*Watashi no meishi desu. Dōzo.*" He gave me his business card. He was quick in his movements, brusque.

"*Dōmo arigatō gozaimasu.*" I accepted his card with both hands, which wasn't really necessary, but taking Connor's advice, I wanted to do the most formal thing. Next I gave him my card. The ritual required us both to look at each other's cards, and to make some minor comment, or to ask a question like "Is this your office telephone number?"

Ishiguro took my card with one hand and said, "Is this your home phone, Detective?" I was surprised. He spoke the kind of unaccented English you can only learn by living here for a long time, starting when you're young. He must have gone to school here. One of the thousands of Japanese who studied in America in the seventies. When they were sending 150,000 students a year to America, to learn about our country. And we were sending 200 American students a year to Japan.

"That's my number at the bottom, yes," I said.

Ishiguro slipped my card into his shirt pocket. I started to make a polite comment about his card, but he interrupted me. "Look, Detective. I think we can dispense with the formalities. The only reason there's a problem here tonight is that your colleague is unreasonable."

"My colleague?"

Ishiguro gave a head jerk. "The fat one there. Graham. His demands are unreasonable, and we strongly object to his intention to carry out an investigation tonight."

I said, "Why is that, Mr. Ishiguro?"

"You have no probable cause to conduct one."

"Why do you say that?"

Ishiguro snorted. "I would think it's obvious, even to you."

I stayed cool. Five years as a detective, and then a year in the press section had taught me to stay cool.

I said, "No, sir, I'm afraid it's not obvious."

He looked at me disdainfully. "The fact is, Lieutenant, you have no reason to connect this girl's death to the party we're holding downstairs."

"It looks like she's wearing a party dress—"

He interrupted me rudely. "My guess is you'll probably discover that she has died of an accidental drug overdose. And therefore her death has nothing to do with our party. Wouldn't you agree?"

I took a deep breath. "No, sir, I wouldn't agree. Not without an investigation." I took another breath. "Mr. Ishiguro, I appreciate your concerns, but—"

"I wonder if you do," Ishiguro said, interrupting me again. "I insist that you appreciate the position of the Nakamoto company tonight. This is a very significant evening for us, a very *public* evening. We are naturally distressed by the prospect that our function might be marred by unfounded allegations of a woman's death, especially this, a woman of no importance . . ."

"A woman of no importance?"

Ishiguro made a dismissing wave. He seemed to be tired of talking to me. "It's obvious, just look at her. She's no better than a common prostitute. I can't imagine how she came to be in this building at all. And for this reason, I strongly protest the intention of Detective Graham to interrogate the guests at the reception downstairs. That's entirely unreasonable. We have many senators, congressmen, and officials of Los Angeles among our guests. Surely you agree that such prominent people will find it awkward—"

I said, "Just a minute. Detective Graham told you he was going to interrogate everybody at the reception?"

"That is what he said to me. Yes."

Now, at last, I began to understand why I'd been called. Graham didn't like the Japanese and he had threatened to spoil their evening. Of course it was never going to happen. There was no way Graham was going to interrogate United States senators, let alone the district attorney or the mayor. Not if he expected to come to work tomorrow. But the Japanese annoyed him, and Graham had decided to annoy them back.

I said to Ishiguro, "We can set up a registration desk downstairs, and your guests can sign out as they leave."

"I am afraid that will be difficult," Ishiguro began, "because surely you will admit—"

"Mr. Ishiguro, that's what we're going to do."

"But what you ask is extremely difficult—"

"Mr. Ishiguro."

"You see, for us this is going to cause—"

"Mr. Ishiguro, I'm sorry. I've just told you what police procedure is going to be."

He stiffened. There was a pause. He wiped some sweat from his upper lip and said, "I am disappointed, Lieutenant, not to have greater cooperation from you."

"Cooperation?" That was when I started to get pissed off. "Mr. Ishiguro, you've got a dead woman in there, and it is our job to investigate what happened to—"

"But you must acknowledge our special circumstances—"

Then I heard Graham say, "Aw, Christ, *what is this*?"

Looking over my shoulder, I saw a short, bookish Japanese man twenty meters beyond the yellow tape. He was taking pictures of the crime scene. The camera he held was so small it was nearly concealed in the palm of his hand. But he wasn't concealing the fact that he had crossed the tape barrier to take his pictures. As I watched, he moved slowly back toward us, raising his hands for a moment to snap a picture, then blinking behind his wire-frame spectacles as he selected his next shot. He was deliberate in his movements.

Graham went up to the tape and said, "For Christ's sake, get out of there. This is a crime scene. You can't take pictures in there." The man didn't respond. He kept moving backward. Graham turned away. "Who is this guy?"

Ishiguro said, "This is our employee, Mr. Tanaka. He works for Nakamoto Security."

I couldn't believe what I was seeing. The Japanese had their own employee wandering around inside the yellow tapes, contaminating the crime scene. It was outrageous. "Get him out of there," I said.

"He is taking pictures."

"He can't do that."

Ishiguro said, "But this is for our corporate use."

I said, "I don't care, Mr. Ishiguro. He can't be inside the yellow tape, and he can't take pictures. Get him out of there. And I want his film, please."

"Very well." Ishiguro said something quickly in Japanese. I turned, just in time to see Tanaka slip under the yellow tape, and disappear among the blue-suited men clustered by the elevator. Behind their heads, I saw the elevator doors open and close.

Son of a bitch. I was getting angry. "Mr. Ishiguro, you are now obstructing an official police investigation."

Ishiguro said calmly, "You must try to understand our position, Detective Smith. Of course we have complete confidence in the Los Angeles Police Department, but we must be able to undertake our own private inquiry, and for that we must have—"

Their own private inquiry? The *son of a bitch.* I suddenly couldn't speak. I clenched my teeth, seeing red. I was furious. I wanted to arrest Ishiguro. I wanted to spin him around, shove him up against the wall, and snap the cuffs around his fucking wrists and—

"Perhaps I can be of assistance, Lieutenant," a voice behind me said.

I turned. It was John Connor, smiling cheerfully.

I stepped aside.

Connor faced Ishiguro, bowed slightly, and presented his card. He spoke rapidly. *"Totsuzen shitsurei desuga, jikoshōkai wo shitemo yoroshii desuka. Watashi wa John Connor to mōshimasu. Meishi o dōzo. Dōzo yoroshiku."*

"John Connor?" Ishiguro said. *"The* John Connor? *Omeni kakarete kōei desu. Watashi wa Ishiguro desu. Dōzo yoroshiku."* He was saying he was honored to meet him.

"Watashi no meishi desu. Dōzo." A graceful thank you.

But once the formalities were completed, the conversation went so quickly I caught only an occasional word. I was obliged to appear interested, watching and nodding, when in fact I had no idea what they were talking about. Once I heard Connor refer to me as *wakaimono*, which I knew meant his protégé or apprentice. Several times, he looked at me severely, and shook his head like a regretful father. It seemed he was apologizing for me. I also heard him refer to Graham as *bushitsuke*, a disagreeable man.

But these apologies had their effect. Ishiguro calmed down, dropping his shoulders. He began to relax. He even smiled. Finally he said, "Then you will not check identification of our guests?"

"Absolutely not," Connor said. "Your honored guests are free to come and go as they wish."

I started to protest. Connor shot me a look.

"Identification is unnecessary," Connor continued, speaking formally, "because I am sure that no guest of the Nakamoto Corporation could ever be involved in such an unfortunate incident."

"Fucking A," Graham said, under his breath.

Ishiguro was beaming. But I was furious. Connor had contradicted me. He had made me look like a fool. And on top of that, he wasn't following police procedure—we could all be in trouble for that later on. Angrily, I shoved my hands in my pockets and looked away.

"I am grateful for your delicate handling of this situation, Captain Connor," Ishiguro said.

"I have done nothing at all," Connor replied, making another formal bow. "But I hope you will now agree it is appropriate to clear the floor, so the police may begin their investigation."

Ishiguro blinked. "Clear the floor?"

"Yes," Connor said, taking out a notebook. "And please assist me to know the names of the gentlemen standing behind you, as you ask them to leave."

"I am sorry?"

"The names of the gentlemen behind you, please."

"May I ask why?"

Connor's face darkened, and he barked a short phrase in Japanese. I didn't catch the words, but Ishiguro turned bright red.

"Excuse me, Captain, but I see no reason for you to speak in this—"

And then, Connor lost his temper. Spectacularly and explosively. He moved close to Ishiguro, making sharp stabbing motions with his finger while he shouted: *"Iikagen ni shiro! Soko o doke! Kiiterunoka!"*

Ishiguro ducked and turned away, stunned by this verbal assault.

Connor leaned over him, his voice hard and sarcastic: *"Doke! Doke! Wa-karanainoka?"* He turned, and pointed furiously toward the Japanese men by the elevator. Confronted with Connor's naked anger, the Japanese looked away, and puffed anxiously on their cigarettes. But they did not leave.

"Hey, Richie," Connor said, calling to the crime unit photographer Richie Walters. "Get me some IDs of these guys, will you?"

"Sure, Captain," Richie said. He raised his camera and began moving down the line of men, firing his strobe in quick succession.

Ishiguro suddenly got excited, stepping in front of the camera, holding up his hands. "Wait a minute, wait a minute, what is this?"

But the Japanese men were already leaving, wheeling away like a school of fish from the strobe flash. In a few seconds they were gone. We had the floor to ourselves. Alone, Ishiguro looked uncomfortable.

He said something in Japanese. Apparently it was the wrong thing.

"Oh?" Connor said. "*You* are to blame here," he said to Ishiguro. "*You* are the cause of all these troubles. And *you* will see that my detectives get any assistance they need. I want to speak to the person who discovered the body, and the person who called in the original report. I want the name of every person who has been on this floor since the body was discovered. And I want the film from Tanaka's camera. *Ore wa honkida.* I will arrest you if you obstruct this investigation further."

"But I must consult my superiors—"

"*Namerunayo.*" Connor leaned close. "Don't fuck with me, Ishiguro-san. Now leave, and let us work."

"Of course, Captain," he said. With a tight, brief bow he left, his face pinched and unhappy.

Graham chuckled. "You told him off pretty good."

Connor spun. "What were you doing, telling him you were going to interrogate everybody at the party?"

"Aw, shit, I was just winding him up," Graham said. "There's no way I'm going to interrogate the mayor. Can I help it if these assholes have no sense of humor?"

"They have a sense of humor," Connor said. "And the joke is on you. Because Ishiguro had a problem, and he solved it with your help."

"*My* help?" Graham was frowning. "What're you talking about?"

"It's clear the Japanese wanted to delay the investigation," Connor said. "Your aggressive tactics gave them the perfect excuse—to call for the Special Services liaison."

"Oh, come on," Graham said. "For all they know, the liaison could have been here in five minutes."

Connor shook his head. "Don't kid yourself: they knew exactly who was on call tonight. They knew exactly how far away Smith would be, and exactly how long it would take him to get here. And they managed to delay the investigation an hour and a half. Nice work, detective."

Graham stared at Connor for a long moment. Then he turned away. "Fuck," he said. "That's a load of bullshit, and you know it. Fellas, I'm going to work. Richie? Mount up. You got thirty seconds to document before my guys come in and step on your tail. Let's go, everybody. I want to get finished before she starts to smell too bad."

And he lumbered off toward the crime scene.

❖　❖　❖

With their suitcases and evidence carts, the SID team trailed after Graham. Richie Walters led the way, shooting left and right as he worked his way forward into the atrium, then going through the door into the conference room. The walls of the conference room were smoked glass, which dimmed his flash. But I could see him inside, circling the body. He was shooting a lot: he knew this was a big case.

I stayed behind with Connor. I said, "I thought you told me it was bad form to lose your temper with the Japanese."

"It is," Connor said.

"Then why did you lose yours?"

"Unfortunately," he said, "it was the only way to assist Ishiguro."

"To *assist* Ishiguro?"

"Yes. I did all that for Ishiguro—because he had to save face in front of his boss. Ishiguro wasn't the most important man in the room. One of the Japanese standing by the elevator was the *jūyaku*, the real boss."

"I didn't notice," I said.

"It's common practice to put a lesser man in front, while the boss stays in the background, where he is free to observe progress. Just as I did with you, *kōhai*."

"Ishiguro's boss was watching all the time?"

"Yes. And Ishiguro clearly had orders not to allow the investigation to begin. I needed to start the investigation. But I had to do it in such a way that he would not look incompetent. So I played the out-of-control *gaijin*. Now he owes me a favor. Which is good, because I may need his help later on."

"He owes you a favor?" I said, having trouble with this idea. Connor had just screamed at Ishiguro—thoroughly humiliating him, as far as I was concerned.

Connor sighed. "Even if you don't understand what happened, believe me: Ishiguro understands very well. He had a problem, and I helped him."

I still didn't really understand, and I started to say more, but Connor held up his hand. "I think we better take a look at the scene, before Graham and his men screw things up any more than they already have."

It'd been almost two years since I worked the detective division, and it felt good to be around a homicide again. It brought back memories: the nighttime tension, the adrenaline rush of bad coffee in paper cups, and all the teams working around you—it's a kind of crazy energy, circling the center where somebody is lying, dead. Every homicide crime scene has that same energy, and that finality at the center. When you look at the dead person, there is a kind of obviousness, and at the same time there is an impossible mystery. Even in the simplest domestic brawl, where the woman finally decided to shoot the guy, you'd look at her, all covered in scars and cigarette burns, and you had to ask, why tonight? What was it about tonight? It's always clear what you are seeing, and there's always something that doesn't add up. Both things at once.

And at a homicide you have the sense of being right down to the basic truths of existence, the smells and the defecation and the bloating. Usually somebody's crying, so you're listening to that. And the usual bullshit stops; somebody died, and it's an unavoidable fact, like a rock in the road that makes all the traffic go around it. And in that grim and real setting, this camaraderie springs up, because you're working late with people you know, and actually know very well because you see them all the time. L.A. has four homicides a day; there's another one every six hours. And every detective at the crime scene already has ten homicides dragging on his backlog, which makes this new one an intolerable burden, so he and everybody else is hoping to solve it on the spot, to get it out of the way. There is that kind of finality and tension and energy all mixed together.

And after you do it for a few years, you get so you like it. And to my surprise, as I entered the conference room, I realized that I missed it.

The conference room was elegant: black table, black high-backed leather chairs, the lights of the nighttime skyscrapers beyond the glass walls. Inside the room, the technicians talked quietly, as they moved around the body of the dead girl.

She had blond hair cut short. Blue eyes, full mouth. She looked about twenty-five. Tall, with a long-limbed, athletic look. Her dress was black and sheer.

Graham was well into his examination; he was down at the end of the table, squinting at the girl's black patent high heels, a penlight in one hand, his notebook in another.

Kelly, the coroner's assistant, was taping the girl's hands in paper bags to protect them. Connor stopped him. "Just a minute." Connor looked at one hand, inspecting the wrist, peering closely under the fingernails. He sniffed under one nail. Then he flicked the fingers rapidly, one after another.

"Don't bother," Graham said laconically. "There's no rigor mortis yet, and no detritus under the nails, no skin or cloth fibers. In fact, I'd say there aren't many signs of a struggle at all."

Kelly slipped the bag over the hand. Connor said to him, "You have a time of death?"

"I'm working on it." Kelly lifted the girl's buttocks to place the rectal probe. "The axillary thermocouples are already in place. We'll know in a minute."

Connor touched the fabric of the black dress, checked the label. Helen, part of the SID team, said, "It's a Yamamoto."

"I see that," Connor said.

"What's a Yamamoto?" I said.

Helen said, "Very expensive Japanese designer. This little black nothing is at least five thousand dollars. That's assuming she bought it used. New, it's maybe fifteen thousand."

"Is it traceable?" Connor asked her.

"Maybe. Depends on whether she bought it here, or in Europe, or Tokyo. It'll take a couple of days to check."

Connor immediately lost interest. "Never mind. That'll be too late."

He produced a small, fiber-optic penlight, which he used to inspect the girl's scalp and hair. Then he looked quickly at each ear, giving a little murmur of surprise at the right ear. I peered over his shoulder, and saw a drop of dried blood at the pierced hole for her earring. I must have been crowding Connor, because he glanced up at me. "Excuse me, *kōhai*."

I stepped back. "Sorry."

Next, Connor sniffed the girl's lips, opened and closed her jaw rapidly, and poked around inside her mouth, using his penlight as a probe. Then he turned her head from side to side on the table, making her look left and right. He spent some time feeling gently along her neck, almost caressing it with his fingers.

And then, quite abruptly, he stepped away from the body and said, "All right, I'm finished."

And he walked out of the boardroom.

Graham looked up. "He never was worth a damn at a crime scene."

I said, "Why do you say that? I hear he's a great detective."

"Oh, hell," Graham said. "You can see for yourself. He doesn't even know what to do. Doesn't know procedure. Connor's no detective. Connor has *connections*. That's how he solved all those cases he's so famous for. You remember the Arakawa honeymoon shootings? No? I guess it was before your time, Petey-san. When was that Arakawa case, Kelly?"

"Seventy-six," Kelly said.

"Right, seventy-six. Big fucking case that year. Mr. and Mrs. Arakawa, a young couple visiting Los Angeles on their honeymoon, are standing on the curb in East L.A. when they get gunned down from a passing car. Drive-by gang-style shooting. Worse, at autopsy it turns out Mrs. Arakawa was pregnant. The press has a field day: L.A.P.D. can't handle gang violence, is the way the story goes. Letters and money come from all over the city. Everyone is upset about what happened to this fresh young couple. And of course the detectives assigned to the case don't discover shit. I mean, a case involving murdered Japanese nationals: they're getting *nowhere*.

"So, after a week, Connor is called in. And he solves it in one day. A fucking miracle of detection. I mean, it's a *week later*. The physical evidence is long gone, the bodies of the honeymooners are back in Osaka, the street corner where it happened is piled high in wilted flowers. But Connor is able to show that the youthful Mr. Arakawa is actually quite a bad boy in Osaka. He shows that the street-corner gangland shooting is actually a *yakuza* killing contracted in Japan to take place in America. And he shows that the nasty husband is the innocent bystander: they were really gunning for the wife, knowing she was pregnant, because it's *her* father they wanted to teach a lesson. So. Connor turns it all around. Pretty fucking amazing, huh?"

"And you think he did it all with his Japanese connections?"

"You tell me," Graham said. "All I know is, pretty soon after that, he goes to Japan for a year."

"Doing what?"

"I heard he worked as a security guy for a grateful Japanese company. They took care of him, is what it amounted to. He did a job for them, and they paid off. Anyway, that's the way I figure it. Nobody really knows. But the man is not a detective. Christ: just look at him now."

Out in the atrium, Connor was staring up at the high ceiling in a dreamy, reflective way. He looked first in one direction, and then another. He seemed to be trying to make up his mind. Suddenly, he walked briskly toward the elevators, as if he were leaving. Then without warning, he turned on his heel, and walked back to the center of the room, and stopped. Next, he began to inspect the leaves on the potted palm trees scattered around the room.

Graham shook his head. "What is this, gardening? I'm telling you, he's a strange guy. You know he's gone to Japan more than once. He always comes back. It never works out for him. Japan is like a woman that he can't live with, and can't live without, you know? Myself, I don't fucking get it. I like America. At least, what's left of it."

He turned to the SID team, which was moving outward from the body. "You guys find those panties for me yet?"

"Not yet, Tom."

"We're looking, Tom."

I said, "What panties?"

Graham lifted the girl's skirt. "Your friend John couldn't be bothered to finish his examination, but I'd say there's something significant here. I'd say that's seminal fluid oozing out of the vagina, she's not wearing panties, and there's a red line at the groin where they were ripped off. External genitals are red and raw. It's pretty clear she had forcible intercourse before she was killed. So I'm asking the boys to find the panties."

One of the SID team said, "Maybe she wasn't wearing any."

Graham said, "She was wearing them, all right."

I turned back to Kelly. "What about drugs?"

He shrugged. "We'll get lab values on all fluids. But to the eye, she looks clean. Very clean." I noticed that Kelly was distinctly uneasy, now.

Graham saw it, too. "For Christ's sake, what are you hangdog about, Kelly? We keeping you from a late-night date, or what?"

"No," Kelly said, "but to tell you the truth, not only is there no evidence of a struggle, or of drugs—I don't see any evidence that she was murdered at all."

Graham said, "No evidence she was murdered? Are you kidding?"

Kelly said, "The girl has throat injuries that suggest she may have been into one of the sexual bondage syndromes. She has signs beneath the makeup that she's been tied up before, repeatedly."

"So?"

"So, technically speaking, maybe she wasn't murdered. Maybe she experienced sudden death from natural causes."

"Aw, Christ. Come on."

"It's quite possible this is a case of what we call death from inhibition. Instantaneous physiological death."

"Meaning what?"

He shrugged. "The person just dies."

"For no reason at all?"

"Well, not exactly. There's usually minor trauma involving the heart or nerves. But the trauma isn't sufficient to cause death. I had one case where a ten-year-old kid got hit in the chest with a baseball—not very hard—and fell down dead in the school yard. Nobody within twenty meters of him. Another case, a woman had a minor car accident, banged into the steering wheel with her chest, not very hard, and while she was opening the car door to get out, she dropped dead. It seems to happen where there is neck or chest injury, which may irritate the nerves running to the heart. So, yeah, Tom. Technically, sudden death is a distinct possibility. And since having sex is not a felony, it wouldn't be murder."

Graham squinted. "So you're saying maybe *nobody* killed her?"

Kelly shrugged. He picked up his clipboard. "I'm not putting any of this down. I'm listing the cause of death as asphyxiation secondary to manual strangulation. Because the odds are, she was strangled. But you should file it away in the back of your mind that maybe she wasn't. Maybe she just popped off."

"Fine," Graham said. "We'll file it. Under medical examiner's fantasies. Meanwhile, any of you guys got an ID on her?"

The SID team, still searching the room, murmured no.

Kelly said, "I think I got a time of death." He checked his temperature probes and read off a chart. "I register a core of ninety-six point nine. In this ambient room temperature, that's consistent with up to three hours post-mortem."

"Up to three hours? That's great. Listen Kelly, we already knew she died *sometime* tonight."

"It's the best I can do." Kelly shook his head. "Unfortunately, the cooling curves don't discriminate well for under three hours. All I can say is death occurred sometime within three hours. But my impression is that this girl has been dead a while. Frankly, I would say it's close to three hours."

Graham turned to the SID team. "Anybody find the panties yet?"

"Not so far, Lieutenant."

Graham looked around the room and said, "No purse, no panties."

I said, "You think somebody cleaned up here?"

"I don't know," he said. "But doesn't a girl who's coming to a party in a fifteen-thousand-dollar dress usually carry a purse?" Then Graham looked past my shoulder and smiled: "Well, what do you know, Petey-san? One of your admirers to see you."

Striding toward me was Ellen Farley, the mayor's press secretary. Farley was thirty-five, dark blond hair cropped close to her head, perfectly groomed as always. She had been a newscaster when she was younger, but had worked for the mayor's office for many years. Ellen Farley was smart, fast on her feet, and she had one of the great bodies, which as far as anyone knew she retained for her own exclusive use.

I liked her enough to have done a couple of favors for her when I was in the L.A.P.D. press office. Since the mayor and the chief of police hated each other, requests from the mayor's office sometimes passed from Ellen to me, and I handled them. Mostly small things: delaying the release of a report until the weekend, so it'd run on Saturday. Or announcing that charges in a case hadn't been brought yet, even though they had. I did it because Farley was a straight shooter, who always spoke her mind. And it looked like she was going to speak her mind now.

"Listen, Pete," she said. "I don't know what's going on here, but the mayor's been hearing some pretty strong complaints from a Mr. Ishiguro—"

"I can imagine—"

"And the mayor asked me to remind you that there is no excuse for officials of this city to be rude to foreign nationals."

Graham said loudly, "Especially when they make such large campaign contributions."

"Foreign nationals can't contribute to American political campaigns," Farley said. "You know that." She lowered her voice. "This is a sensitive case, Pete. I want you to be careful. You know the Japanese have a special concern about how they are treated in America."

"Okay, fine."

She looked through the glass walls of the conference room, toward the atrium. "Is that John Connor?"

"Yes."

"I thought he was retired. What's he doing here?"

"Helping me on the case."

Farley frowned. "You know the Japanese have mixed feelings about him. They have a term for it. For somebody who is a Japan lover and goes to the other extreme, and turns into a basher."

"Connor isn't a basher."

"Ishiguro felt roughly treated."

"Ishiguro was telling us what to do," I said. "And we have a murdered girl here, which everybody seems to be forgetting—"

"Come on, Pete," she said, "nobody's trying to tell you how to do your job. All I'm saying is you have to take into account the special—"

She stopped.

She was looking at the body.

"Ellen?" I said. "Do you know her?"

"No." She turned away.

"You sure?"

I could see she was rattled.

Graham said, "You saw her downstairs earlier?"

"I don't—maybe. I think so. Listen, fellas, I've got to get back."

"Ellen. Come on."

"I don't know who she is, Pete. You know I'd tell you if I did. Just keep it cordial with the Japanese. That's all the mayor wanted me to say. I've got to go now."

She hurried back toward the elevators. I watched her leave, feeling uneasy.

Graham came over and stood beside me. "She's got a great ass," he said. "But she ain't leveling, buddy, even with you."

I said, "What do you mean, even with me?"

"Everybody knows you and Farley were an item."

"What are you talking about?"

Graham punched me on the shoulder. "Come on. You're divorced now. Nobody gives a shit."

I said, "It's not true, Tom."

"You can do what you want. Handsome guy like you."

"I'm telling you, it's not true."

"Okay, fine." He held up his hands. "My mistake."

I watched Farley at the other end of the atrium, ducking under the tape. She pressed the elevator button, and waited for it to come, tapping her foot impatiently.

I said, "You really think she knows who the girl is?"

"Damn right she does," Graham said. "You know why the mayor likes her. She stands by his side and whispers everybody's name to him. People she hasn't seen for years. Husbands, wives, children, everyone. Farley knows who this girl is."

"Then why didn't she tell us?"

"Fuck," Graham said. "Must be important to somebody. She took off like a shot, didn't she? I tell you, we better figure out who this dead girl is. Because I fucking hate being the last one in town to know."

Connor was across the room, waving to us.

"What does he want now?" Graham said. "Waving like that. What's he got in his hand?"

"Looks like a purse," I said.

"Cheryl Lynn Austin," Connor said, reading. "Born Midland, Texas, graduate of Texas State. Twenty-three years old. Got an apartment in Westwood, but hasn't been here long enough to change her Texas driver's license."

The contents of the purse were spread out on a desk. We pushed them around with pencils.

"Where'd you find this purse?" I asked. It was a small, dark, beaded clutch with a pearl clasp. A vintage forties purse. Expensive.

"It was in the potted palm near the conference room." Connor unzipped a tiny compartment. A tight roll of crisp hundred-dollar bills tumbled onto the table. "Very nice. Miss Austin is well taken care of."

I said, "No car keys?"

"No."

"So she came with somebody."

"And evidently intended to leave with somebody, too. Taxis can't break a hundred-dollar bill."

There was also a gold American Express Card. Lipstick and a compact. A pack of Mild Seven Menthol cigarettes, a Japanese brand. A card for the Daimatsu Night Club in Tokyo. Four small blue pills. That was about it.

Using his pencil, Connor upended the beaded purse. Small green flecks spilled out onto the table. "Know what that is?"

"No," I said. Graham looked at it with a magnifying glass.

Connor said, "It's *wasabi*-covered peanuts."

Wasabi is green horseradish served in Japanese restaurants. I had never heard of *wasabi*-covered peanuts.

"I don't know if they're sold outside Japan."

Graham grunted. "I've seen enough. So what do you think now, John? Is Ishiguro going to get those witnesses you asked for?"

"I wouldn't expect them soon," Connor said.

"Fucking right," Graham said. "We won't see those witnesses until day after tomorrow, after their lawyers have briefed them on exactly what to say." He stepped away from the table. "You realize why they're delaying us. A Japanese killed this girl. That's what we're dealing with."

"It's possible," Connor said.

"Hey, buddy. More than possible. We're *here*. This is their building. And that girl is just the type they go for. The American beauty long-stemmed rose. You know all those little guys want to fuck a volleyball player."

Connor shrugged. "Possibly."

"Come on," Graham said. "You know those guys eat shit all day long at home. Crammed into subways, working in big companies. Can't say what they think. Then they come over here, away from the constraints of home, and suddenly they're rich and free. They can do whatever they want. And sometimes one of them goes a little crazy. Tell me I'm wrong."

Connor looked at Graham for a long time. Finally he said, "So as you see it, Tom, a Japanese killer decided to dispatch this girl on the Nakamoto boardroom conference table?"

"Right."

"As a symbolic act?"

Graham shrugged. "Christ, who knows? We're not talking normality here. But I'll tell you one thing. I'm going to get the fucker who did this, if it's the last goddamned thing I do."

The elevator descended rapidly. Connor leaned against the glass. "There are many reasons to dislike the Japanese," he said, "but Graham knows none of them." He sighed. "You know what they say about us?"

"What?"

"They say Americans are too eager to make theories. They say we don't spend enough time observing the world, and so we don't know how things actually *are*."

"Is that a Zen idea?"

"No," he laughed. "Just an observation. Ask a computer salesman what he thinks of his American counterparts, and he'll tell you that. Everyone in Japan who deals with Americans thinks it. And when you look at Graham, you realize they're right. Graham has no real knowledge, no first-hand experience. He just has a collection of prejudices and media fantasies. He doesn't know anything about the Japanese—and it never occurs to him to find out."

I said, "Then you think he's wrong? The girl wasn't killed by a Japanese?"

"I didn't say that, *kōhai*," Connor replied. "It's very possible Graham is right. But at the moment—"

The doors opened and we saw the party, heard the band playing "Moonlight Serenade." Two party-going couples stepped into the elevator. They looked like real estate people: the men silver-haired and distinguished looking, the women pretty and slightly tacky. One woman said, "She's smaller than I thought."

"Yes, tiny. And that . . . was that her boyfriend?"

"I guess. Wasn't he the one in the video with her?"

"I think that was him."

One of the men said, "You think she had her boobs done?"

"Hasn't everybody?"

The other woman giggled. "Except me, of course."

"Right, Christine."

"But I'm thinking about it. Did you see Emily?"

"Oh, she did hers so *big*."

"Well, Jane started it, blame her. Now everyone wants them big."

The men turned and looked out the window. "Hell of a building," one said. "Detailing is fantastic. Must have cost a fortune. You doing much with the Japanese now, Ron?"

"About twenty percent," the other man said. "That's way down from last year. It's made me work on my golf game, because they always want to play golf."

"Twenty percent of your business?"

"Yeah. They're buying up Orange County now."

"Of course. They already own Los Angeles," one of the women said, laughing.

"Well, just about. They have the Arco building over there," the man said, pointing out the window. "I guess by now they have seventy, seventy-five percent of downtown Los Angeles."

"And more in Hawaii."

"Hell, they *own* Hawaii—ninety percent of Honolulu, a hundred percent of the Kona coast. Putting up golf courses like mad."

One woman said, "Will this party be on *ET* tomorrow? They had enough cameras here."

"Let's remember to watch."

The elevator said, "*Mōsugu de gozaimasu.*"

We came to the garage floor, and the people got off. Connor watched them go, and shook his head. "In no other country in the world," he said, "would you hear people calmly discussing the fact that their cities and states were sold to foreigners."

"Discussing?" I said. "They're the ones doing the selling."

"Yes. Americans are eager to sell. It amazes the Japanese. They think we're committing economic suicide. And of course they're right." As he spoke, Connor pressed a button on the elevator panel marked EMER-GENCY ONLY.

A soft pinging alarm sounded.

"What'd you do that for?"

Connor looked at a video camera mounted in the corner of the ceiling and waved cheerfully. A voice on the intercom said, "Good evening, officers. Can I help you?"

"Yes," Connor said. "Am I speaking to building security?"

"That's right, sir. Is something wrong with your elevator?"

"Where are you located?"

"We're on the lobby level, southeast corner, behind the elevators."

"Thank you very much," Connor said. He pushed the button for the lobby.

The security office of the Nakamoto Tower was a small room, perhaps five meters by seven. It was dominated by three large, flat video panels, each divided into a dozen smaller monitor views. At the moment, most of these were black rectangles. But one row showed images from the lobby and the garage; another row showed the party in progress. And a third row showed the police teams up on the forty-sixth floor.

Jerome Phillips was the guard on duty. He was a black man in his mid-forties. His gray Nakamoto Security uniform was soaked around the collar, and dark under the armpits. He asked us to leave the door open as we entered. He appeared noticeably uneasy to have us there. I sensed he was hiding something, but Connor approached him in a friendly way. We showed our badges and shook hands. Connor managed to convey the idea that we were all security professionals, having a little chat together. "Must be a busy night for you, Mr. Phillips."

"Yeah, sure. The party and everything."

"And crowded, in this little room."

He wiped sweat from his forehead. "Boy, you got that right. All of them packed in here. Jesus."

I said, "All of who?"

Connor looked at me and said, "After the Japanese left the forty-sixth floor, they came down here and watched us on the monitors. Isn't that right, Mr. Phillips?"

Phillips nodded. "Not all of 'em, but quite a few. Down here, smoking their damn cigarettes, staring and puffing and passing around faxes."

"Faxes?"

"Oh, yeah, every few minutes, somebody'd bring in another fax. You know, in Japanese writing. They'd all pass it around, make comments. Then one of 'em would leave to send a fax back. And the rest would stay to watch you guys up on the floor."

Connor said, "And listen, too?"

Phillips shook his head. "No. We don't have audio feeds."

"I'm surprised," Connor said. "This equipment seems so up-to-date."

"Up-to-date? Hell, it's the most advanced in the world. These people, I tell you one thing. These people do it right. They have the best fire alarm and fire prevention system. The best earthquake system. And of course the best electronic security system: best cameras, detectors, everything."

"I can see that," Connor said. "That's why I was surprised they don't have audio."

"No. No audio. They do high-resolution video only. Don't ask me why. Something to do with the cameras and how they're hooked up, is all I know."

On the flat panels I saw five different views of the forty-sixth floor, as seen from different cameras. Apparently the Japanese had installed cameras all over the floor. I remembered how Connor had walked around the atrium, staring up at the ceiling. He must have spotted the cameras then.

Now I watched Graham in the conference room, directing the teams. He was smoking a cigarette, which was completely against regulations at a crime scene. I saw Helen stretch and yawn. Meanwhile, Kelly was getting ready to move the girl's body off the table onto a gurney, before zipping it into the bag, and he was—

Then it hit me.

They had cameras up there.

Five different cameras.

Covering every part of the floor.

I said, "Oh my God" and I spun around, very excited. I was about to say something when Connor smiled at me in an easy way, and placed his hand on my shoulder. He squeezed my shoulder—hard.

"Lieutenant," he said.

The pain was incredible. I tried not to wince. "Yes, Captain?"

"I wonder if you'd mind if I asked Mr. Phillips one or two questions."

"No, Captain. Go right ahead."

"Perhaps you'd take notes."

"Good idea, Captain."

He released my shoulder. I got out my notepad.

Connor sat on the edge of the table and said, "Have you been with Nakamoto Security long, Mr. Phillips?"

"Yes, sir. About six years now. I started over in their La Habra plant, and when I hurt my leg—in a car accident—and couldn't walk so good, they moved me to security. In the plant. Because I wouldn't have to walk around, you see. Then when they opened the Torrance plant, they moved me over there. My wife got a job in the Torrance plant, too. They do Toyota subassemblies. Then, when this building opened, they brought me here, to work nights."

"I see. Six years altogether."

"Yes, sir."

"You must like it."

"Well, I tell you, it's a secure job. That's something in America. I know they don't think much of black folks, but they always treated me okay. And hell, before this I worked for GM in Van Nuys, and that's . . . you know, that's *gone*."

"Yes," Connor said sympathetically.

"That place," Phillips said, shaking his head at the memory. "Christ. The management assholes they used to send down to the floor. You couldn't believe it. M.B. fucking A., out of Detroit, little weenies didn't know *shit*. They didn't know how the line worked. They didn't know a tool from a die. But they'd still order the foremen around. They're all pulling in two hundred fucking thousand a year and they didn't know shit. And nothing ever worked right. The cars were all a piece of shit. But here," he said, tapping the counter. "Here, I got a problem, or something doesn't work, I tell somebody. And they come right down, and they know the system—how it works—and we go over the problem together, and it gets *fixed*. Right away. Problems get fixed here. That's the difference. I tell you: these people *pay attention*."

"So you like it here."

"They always treated me okay," Phillips said, nodding.

That didn't exactly strike me as a glowing endorsement. I had the feeling this guy wasn't committed to his employers and a few questions could drive the wedge. All we had to do was encourage the break.

"Loyalty is important," Connor said, nodding sympathetically.

"It is to them," he said. "They expect you to show all this enthusiasm for the company. So you know, I always come in fifteen or twenty minutes early, and stay fifteen or twenty minutes after the shift is over. They like you to put in the extra time. I did the same at Van Nuys, but nobody ever noticed."

"And when is your shift?"

"I work nine to seven."

"And tonight? What time did you come on duty?"

"Quarter to nine. Like I said, I come in fifteen minutes early."

The original call had been recorded about eight-thirty. So if this man came at a quarter to nine, he would have arrived almost fifteen minutes too late to see the murder. "Who was on duty before you?"

"Well, usually it's Ted Cole. But I don't know if he worked tonight."

"Why is that?"

The guard wiped his forehead with his sleeve, and looked away.

"Why is that, Mr. Phillips?" I said, with a little more force.

The guard blinked and frowned, saying nothing.

Connor said quietly, "Because Ted Cole wasn't here when Mr. Phillips arrived tonight, was he, Mr. Phillips?"

The guard shook his head. "No, he wasn't."

I started to ask another question, but Connor raised his hand. "I imagine, Mr. Phillips, you must have been pretty surprised when you came in this room, at a quarter to nine."

"You damn right I was," Phillips said.

"What did you do when you saw the situation?"

"Well. Right away, I said to the guy, 'Can I help you?' Very polite but still firm. I mean, this *is* the security room. And I don't know who this guy is, I've never seen him before. And the guy is tense. *Very* tense. He says to me, 'Get out of my way.' Real pushy, like he owns the world. And he shoves past me, taking his briefcase with him.

"I say, 'Excuse me, sir, I'll have to see some identification.' He don't answer me, he just keeps going. Out the lobby and down the stairs."

"You didn't try and stop him?"

"No, sir. I didn't."

"Because he was Japanese?"

"You got that right. But I called up to central security—it's up on the ninth floor—to say I found a man in the room. And they say, 'Don't worry, everything is fine.' But I can hear they're tense, too. Everybody is tense. And then I see on the monitor . . . the dead girl. So that's the first I knew what it was about."

Connor said, "The man you saw. Can you describe him?"

The guard shrugged. "Thirty, thirty-five. Medium height. Dark blue suit like they all wear. Actually he was more hip than most of them. He had this tie with triangles on it. Oh—and a scar on his hand, like a burn or something."

"Which hand?"

"The left hand. I noticed it when he was closing the briefcase."

"Could you see inside the briefcase?"

"No."

"But he was closing it when you came in the room?"

"Yes."

"Was it your impression he took something from this room?"

"I really couldn't say, sir."

Phillips's evasiveness began to annoy me. I said, "What do you think he took?"

Connor shot me a look.

The guard went bland: "I really don't know, sir."

Connor said, "Of course you don't. There's no way you could know what was in somebody else's briefcase. By the way, do you make recordings from the security cameras here?"

"Yes, we do."

"Could you show me how you do that?"

"Sure thing." The guard got up from the desk and opened a door at the far end of the room. We followed him into a second small room, almost a closet, stacked floor to ceiling with small metal boxes, each with stenciled notations in Japanese *kanji* script, and numbers in English. Each with a glowing red light, and an LED counter, with numbers running forward.

Phillips said, "These are our recorders. They lay down signals from all the cameras in the building. They're eight-millimeter, high-definition video." He held up a small cassette, like an audio cassette. "Each one of these records eight hours. We change over at nine p.m., so that's the first thing I do when I come on duty. I pop out the old ones, and switch over to the fresh ones."

"And did you change cassettes tonight, at nine o'clock?"

"Yes, sir. Just like always."

"And what do you do with the tapes you remove?"

"Keep 'em in the trays down here," he said, bending to show us several long, thin drawers. "We keep everything off the cameras for seventy-two hours. That's three days. So we keep nine sets of tapes all together. And we just rotate each set through, once every three days. Get me?"

Connor hesitated. "Perhaps I'd better write this down." He produced a small pad and a pen. "Now, each tape lasts eight hours, so you have nine different sets . . . ."

"Right, right."

Connor wrote for a moment, then shook his pen irritably. "This damn pen. It's out of ink. You have a wastebasket?"

Phillips pointed to the corner. "Over there."

"Thank you."

Connor threw the pen away. I gave him mine. He resumed his notes. "You were saying, Mr. Phillips, that you have nine sets . . ."

"Right. Each set is numbered with letters, from A to I. Now when I come in at nine, I eject the tapes and see whatever letter is already in there, and put in the next one. Like tonight, I took out set C, so I put in set D, which is what's recording now."

"I see," Connor said. "And then you put tape set C in one of the drawers here?"

"Right." He pulled open a drawer. "This one here."

Connor said. "May I?" He glanced at the neatly labeled row of tapes. Then he quickly opened the other drawers, and looked at the other stacks of tapes. Except for the different letters, all the drawers looked identical.

"I think I understand now," Connor said. "What you actually do is use nine sets in rotation."

"Exactly."

"So each set gets used once every three days."

"Right."

"And how long has the security office been using this system?"

"The building's new, but we've been going, oh, maybe two months now."

"I must say it's a very well-organized system," Connor said appreciatively. "Thank you for explaining it to us. I have only a couple of other questions."

"Sure."

"First of all, these counters here—" Connor said, pointing to the LED counters on the video recorders. "They seem to show the elapsed times since the tapes began recording. Is that right? Because it's now almost eleven o'clock, and you put in the tapes at nine, and the top recorder says 1:55:30 and the next recorder says 1:55:10, and so on."

"Yes, that's right. I put the tapes in one right after another. It takes a few seconds between tapes."

"I see. These all show almost two hours. But I notice that one recorder down here shows an elapsed time of only thirty minutes. Does that mean it's broken?"

"Huh," Phillips said, frowning. "I guess maybe it is. 'Cause I changed the tapes all one after another, like I said. But these recorders are the latest technology. Sometimes there are glitches. Or we had some power problems. Could be that."

"Yes. Quite possibly," Connor said. "Can you tell me which camera is hooked to this recorder?"

"Yes, of course." Phillips read the number off the recorder, and went out to the main room with the monitor screens. "It's camera four-six slash six," he said. "This view here." He tapped the screen.

It was an atrium camera, and it showed an overall view of the forty-sixth floor.

"But you see," Phillips said, "the beauty of the system is, even if one recorder screws up, there are still other cameras on that floor, and the video recorders on the others seem to be working okay."

"Yes, they do," Connor said. "By the way, can you tell me why there are so many cameras on the forty-sixth floor?"

"You didn't hear it from me," Phillips said. "But you know how they like efficiency. The word is, they are going to *kaizen* the office workers."

"So basically these cameras have been installed to observe workers during the day, and help them improve their efficiency?"

"That's what I heard."

"Well, I think that's it," Connor said. "Oh, one more question. Do you have an address for Ted Cole?"

Phillips shook his head. "No, I don't."

"Have you ever been out with him, socialized with him?"

"I have, but not much. He's an odd guy."

"Ever been to his apartment?"

"No. He's kind of secretive. I think he lives with his mother or something. We usually go to this bar, the Palomino, over by the airport. He likes it there."

Connor nodded. "And one last question: where is the nearest pay phone?"

"Out in the lobby, and around to your right, by the restrooms. But you're welcome to use the phone here."

Connor shook the guard's hand warmly. "Mr. Phillips, I appreciate your taking the time to tálk to us."

"No problem."

I gave the guard my card. "If you think of anything later that could help us, Mr. Phillips, don't hesitate to call me." And I left.

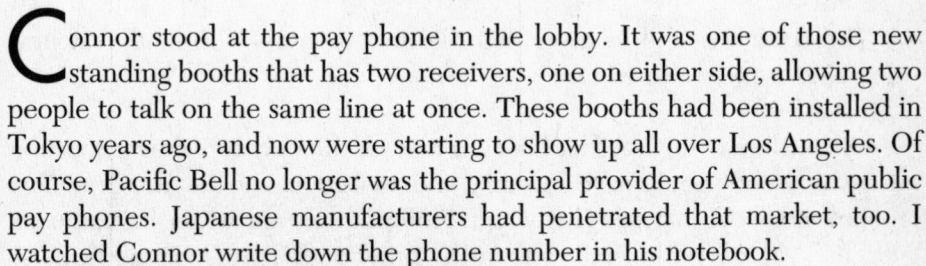

Connor stood at the pay phone in the lobby. It was one of those new standing booths that has two receivers, one on either side, allowing two people to talk on the same line at once. These booths had been installed in Tokyo years ago, and now were starting to show up all over Los Angeles. Of course, Pacific Bell no longer was the principal provider of American public pay phones. Japanese manufacturers had penetrated that market, too. I watched Connor write down the phone number in his notebook.

"What are you doing?"

"We have two separate questions to answer tonight. One is how the girl came to be killed on an office floor. But we also need to find out who placed the original call, notifying us of the murder."

"And you think the call might have been placed from this phone?"

"Possibly."

He closed his notebook, and glanced at his watch. "It's late. We better get going."

"I think we're making a big mistake here."

"Why is that?" Connor asked.

"I don't know if we should leave the tapes in that security room. What if somebody switches them while we're gone?"

"They've already been switched," Connor said.

"How do you know?"

"I gave up a perfectly good pen to find out," he said. "Now come on." He started walking toward the stairs leading down to the garage. I followed him.

"You see," Connor said, "when Phillips first explained that simple system of rotation, it was immediately clear to me that there might have been a switch. The question was how to prove it."

His voice echoed in the concrete stairwell. Connor continued down, taking the steps two at a time. I hurried to keep up.

Connor said, "If somebody switched the tapes, how would they go about it? They would be working hastily, under pressure. They'd be terrified of making a mistake. They certainly wouldn't want to leave any incriminating tapes behind. So probably they'd switch an entire set, and replace it. But replace it with what? They can't just put in the next set. Since there are only nine sets of tapes all together, it would be too easy for someone to notice that one set was missing, and the total was now eight. There would be an obvious empty drawer. No, they would have to replace the set they were taking away with an entirely new set. Twenty brand-new tapes. And that meant I ought to check the trash."

"That's why you threw your pen away?"

"Yes. I didn't want Phillips to know what I was doing."

"And?"

"The trash was full of crumpled plastic wrappers. The kind that new videotapes come wrapped in."

"I see."

"Once I knew the tapes had been replaced, the only remaining question was, which set? So I played dumb, and looked in all the drawers. You probably noticed that set C, the set Phillips removed when he came on duty, had slightly whiter labels than the other sets. It was subtle, because the office has only been active two months, but you could tell."

"I see." Somebody had come into the security room, taken out twenty fresh tapes, unwrapped them, written new labels, and popped them into the video machines, replacing the original tapes that had recorded the murder.

I said, "If you ask me, Phillips knows more about this than he was telling us."

"Maybe," Connor said, "but we have more important things to do. Anyway, there's a limit to what he knows. The murder was phoned in about eight-thirty. Phillips arrived at quarter to nine. So he never saw the murder. We can assume the previous guard, Cole, did. But by a quarter of nine, Cole was gone, and an unknown Japanese man was in the security room, closing up a briefcase."

"You think he's the one who switched the tapes?"

Connor nodded. "Very possibly. In fact, I wouldn't be surprised if this man was the killer himself. I hope to find that out at Miss Austin's apartment." He threw open the door, and we went into the garage.

A line of party guests waited for valets to bring their cars. I saw Ishiguro chatting up Mayor Thomas and his wife. Connor steered me toward them. Standing alongside the mayor, Ishiguro was so cordial he was almost obsequious. He gave us a big smile. "Ah, gentlemen. Is your investigation proceeding satisfactorily? Is there anything more I can do to help?"

I didn't get really angry until that moment: until I saw the way he toadied up in front of the mayor. It made me so mad I began to turn red. But Connor took it in stride.

"Thank you, Ishiguro-san," he said, with a slight bow. "The investigation is going well."

"You're receiving all the help you requested?" Ishiguro said.

"Oh, yes," Connor said. "Everyone has been very cooperative."

"Good, good. I'm glad." Ishiguro glanced at the mayor, and smiled at him, too. He was all smiles, it seemed.

"But," Connor said, "there is just one thing."

"Just name it. If there is anything we can do . . ."

"The security tapes seem to have been removed."

"Security tapes?" Ishiguro frowned, clearly caught off guard.

"Yes," Connor said. "Recordings from the security cameras."

"I don't know anything about that," Ishiguro said. "But let me assure you, if any tapes exist, they are yours to examine."

"Thank you," Connor said. "Unfortunately, it seems the crucial tapes have been removed from the Nakamoto security office."

"Removed? Gentlemen, I believe there must be some mistake."

The mayor was watching this exchange closely.

Connor said, "Perhaps, but I don't think so. It would be reassuring, Mr. Ishiguro, if you were to look into this matter yourself."

"I certainly will," Ishiguro said. "But I must say again. I can't imagine, Captain Connor, that any tapes are missing."

"Thank you for checking, Mr. Ishiguro," Connor said.

"Not at all, Captain," he said, still smiling. "It is my pleasure to assist you in whatever way I can."

"The son of a bitch," I said. We were driving west on the Santa Monica freeway. "The little prick looked us right in the eye and *lied*."

"It's annoying," Connor said. "But you see, Ishiguro takes a different view. Now that he is beside the mayor, he sees himself in another context, with another set of obligations and requirements for his behavior. Since he is sensitive to context, he's able to act differently, with no reference to his earlier behavior. To us, he seems like a different person. But Ishiguro feels he's just being appropriate."

"What burns me is he acted so confident."

"Of course he did," Connor said. "And he would be quite surprised to learn that you're angry with him. You consider him immoral. He considers you naive. Because for a Japanese, consistent behavior is not possible. A Japanese becomes a different person around people of different rank. He becomes a different person when he moves through different rooms of his own house."

"Yeah," I said. "That's fine, but the fact is he's a lying son of a bitch."

Connor looked at me. "Would you talk that way to your mother?"

"Of course not."

"So you change according to context, too," Connor said. "The fact is we all do. It's just that Americans believe there is some core of individuality that doesn't change from one moment to the next. And the Japanese believe context rules everything."

"It sounds to me," I said, "like an excuse for lying."

"He doesn't see it as lying."

"But that's what it *is*."

Connor shrugged. "Only from your point of view, *kōhai*. Not from his."

"The hell."

"Look, it's your choice. You can understand the Japanese and deal with them as they are, or you can get pissed off. But our problem in this country is that we don't deal with the Japanese the way they really are." The car hit a deep pothole, bouncing so hard that the car phone fell off the receiver. Connor picked it up off the floor, and put it back on the hook.

Up ahead, I saw the exit for Bundy. I moved into the right lane. "One thing I'm not clear about," I said. "Why do you think the man with the briefcase in the security room might be the killer?"

"It's because of the time sequence. You see, the murder was reported at eight thirty-two. Less than fifteen minutes later, at eight forty-five, a

Japanese man was down there switching the tapes, arranging a cover-up. That's a very fast response. Much too fast for a Japanese company."

"Why is that?"

"Japanese organizations are actually very slow to respond in a crisis. Their decision-making relies on precedents, and when a situation is unprecedented, people are uncertain how to behave. You remember the faxes? I am sure faxes have been flying back and forth to Nakamoto's Tokyo headquarters all night. Undoubtedly the company is still trying to decide what to do. A Japanese organization simply cannot move fast in a new situation."

"But an individual acting alone can?"

"Yes. Exactly."

I said, "And that's why you think the man with the briefcase may be the killer."

Connor nodded. "Yes. Either the killer, or someone closely connected with the killer. But we should learn more at Miss Austin's apartment. I believe I see it up ahead, on the right."

The Imperial Arms was an apartment building on a tree-lined street a kilometer from Westwood Village. Its fake Tudor beams needed a paint job, and the whole building had a run-down appearance. But that was not unusual in this middle-class section of apartments inhabited by graduate students and young families. In fact, the chief characteristic of the Imperial Arms seemed to be its anonymity: you could drive by the building every day and never notice it.

"Perfect," Connor said, as we walked up the steps to the entrance. "It's just what they like."

"What who likes?"

We came into the lobby, which had been renovated in the most bland California style: pastel wallpaper with a flower print, overstuffed couches, cheap ceramic lamps, and a chrome coffee table. The only thing to distinguish it from a hundred other apartment lobbies was the security desk in the corner, where a heavyset Japanese doorman looked up from his comic book with a distinctly unfriendly manner. "Help you?"

Connor showed his badge. He asked where Cheryl Austin's apartment was.

"I announce you," the doorman said, reaching for the phone.

"Don't bother."

"No. I announce. Maybe she have company now."

"I'm sure she doesn't," Connor said. "*Kore wa keisatsu no shigoto da.*" He was saying we were on official police business.

The doorman gave a tense bow. "*Kyugo shitu.*" He handed Connor a key.

We went through a second glass door, and down a carpeted corridor. There were small lacquer tables at each end of the corridor, and in its simplicity, the interior was surprisingly elegant.

"Typically Japanese," Connor said, with a smile.

I thought: a run-down, fake Tudor apartment building in Westwood? Typically Japanese? From a room to the left, I heard faint rap music: the latest Hammer hit.

"It's because the outside gives no clue to the inside," Connor explained. "That's a fundamental principle of Japanese thinking. The public facade is unrevealing—in architecture, the human face, everything. It's always been that way. You look at old samurai houses in Takayama or Kyoto. You can't tell anything from the outside."

"This is a Japanese building?"

"Of course. Why else would a Japanese national who hardly speaks English be the doorman? And he is a *yakuza*. You probably noticed the tattoo."

I hadn't. The *yakuza* were Japanese gangsters. I didn't know there were *yakuza* here in America, and said so.

"You must understand," Connor said, "there is a shadow world—here in Los Angeles, in Honolulu, in New York. Most of the time you're never aware of it. We live in our regular American world, walking on our American streets, and we never notice that right alongside our world is a second world. Very discreet, very private. Perhaps in New York you will see Japanese businessmen walking through an unmarked door, and catch a glimpse of a club behind. Perhaps you will hear of a small sushi bar in Los Angeles that charges twelve hundred dollars a person, Tokyo prices. But they are not listed in the guidebooks. They are not a part of our American world. They are part of the shadow world, available only to the Japanese."

"And this place?"

"This is a *bettaku*. A love residence where mistresses are kept. And here is Miss Austin's apartment."

Connor unlocked the door with the key the doorman had given him. We went inside.

It was a two-bedroom unit, furnished with expensive oversized rental pieces in pastel pink and green. The oil paintings on the walls had been rented, too; a label on the side of one frame said Breuner's Rents. The kitchen counter was bare, except for a bowl of fruit. The refrigerator contained only yogurt and cans of Diet Coke. The couches in the living room didn't look as if anybody had ever sat on them. On the coffee table was a picture book of Hollywood star portraits and a vase of dried flowers. Empty ashtrays scattered around.

One of the bedrooms had been converted to a den, with a couch and a television, and an exercise bike in the corner. Everything was brand-new. The television still had a sticker that said DIGITAL TUNING FEATURE diagonally across one corner. The handlebars of the exercise bike were covered in plastic wrap.

In the master bedroom, I finally found some human clutter. One mirrored closet door stood open, and three expensive party dresses were thrown across the bed. Evidently she had been trying to decide what to wear. On the dresser top were bottles of perfume, a diamond necklace, a gold Rolex, framed photographs, and an ashtray with stubbed-out Mild Seven Menthol cigarettes. The top dresser drawer, containing panties and undergarments, was partially open. I saw her passport stuck in the corner, and thumbed through it. There was one visa for Saudi Arabia, one for Indonesia, and three entry stamps for Japan.

The stereo in the corner was still turned on, an ejected tape in the player. I pushed it in and Jerry Lee Lewis sang, "You shake my nerves and you rattle my brain, too much love drives a man insane. . . ." Texas music, too old for a young girl like this. But maybe she liked golden oldies.

I turned back to the dresser. Several framed color enlargements showed Cheryl Austin smiling in front of Asian backgrounds—the red gates of a shrine, a formal garden, a street with gray skyscrapers, a train station. The pictures seemed to be taken in Japan. In most of the pictures Cheryl was alone, but in a few she was accompanied by an older Japanese man with glasses and a receding hairline. A final shot showed her in what looked like the American West. Cheryl was standing near a dusty pickup truck, smiling beside a frail, grandmotherly woman in sunglasses. The older woman wasn't smiling and looked uncomfortable.

Tucked in beside the dresser were several large paper rolls, standing on end. I opened one. It was a poster showing Cheryl in a bikini, smiling and holding up a bottle of Asahi beer. All the writing on the poster was in Japanese.

I went into the bathroom.

I saw a pair of jeans kicked in the corner. A white sweater tossed on the countertop. A wet towel on a hook by the shower stall. Beads of water inside the stall. Electric hair-curlers unplugged by the counter. Stuck in the mirror frame, photos of Cheryl standing with another Japanese man on the Malibu pier. This man was in his midthirties, and handsome. In one photograph, he had draped his arm familiarly over her shoulder. I could clearly see the scar on his hand.

"Bingo," I said.

Connor came into the room. "Find something?"

"Our man with the scar."

"Good." Connor studied the picture carefully. I looked back at the clutter of the bathroom. The stuff around the sink. "You know," I said, "something bothers me about this place."

"What's that?"

"I know she hasn't lived here long. And I know everything is rented . . . but still . . . I can't get over the feeling that this place has a contrived look. I can't quite put my finger on why."

Connor smiled. "Very good, Lieutenant. It does have a contrived look. And there's a reason for it."

He handed me a Polaroid photo. It showed the bathroom we were standing in. The jeans kicked in the corner. The towel hanging. The curlers on the counter. But it was taken with one of those ultra-wide-angle cameras that distort everything. The SID teams sometimes used them for evidence.

"Where did you get this?"

"From the trash bin in the hall, by the elevators."

"So it must have been taken earlier tonight."

"Yes. Notice anything different about the room?"

I examined the Polaroid carefully. "No, it looks the same . . . wait a minute. Those pictures stuck in her mirror. They aren't in the Polaroid. Those pictures have been added."

"Exactly." Connor walked back into the bedroom. He picked up one of the framed pictures on the dresser. "Now look at this one," he said. "Miss Austin and a Japanese friend in Shinjuku Station in Tokyo. She was probably drawn to the Kabukichō section—or perhaps she was just shopping. Notice the right-hand edge of the picture. See the narrow strip that's lighter in color?"

"Yes." And I understood what that strip meant: there had been another picture on top of this one. The edge of this picture had stuck out, and was sun-faded. "The overlying picture has been removed."

"Yes," Connor said.

"The apartment has been searched."

"Yes," Connor said. "A very thorough job. They came in earlier tonight, took Polaroids, searched the rooms, and then put things back the way they were. But it's impossible to do that exactly. The Japanese say artlessness is the most difficult art. And these men can't help themselves, they're obsessive. So they leave the picture frames a little too squared-off on the counter, and the perfume bottles a little too carefully cluttered. Everything is a little forced. Your eye can see it even if your brain doesn't register it."

I said, "But why search the room? What pictures did they remove? Her with the killer?"

"That's not clear," Connor said. "Evidently her association with Japan, and with Japanese men, was not objectionable. But there was something they had to get right away, and it can only be—"

Then, from the living room, a tentative voice said, "Lynn? Honey? You here?"

She was silhouetted in the doorway, looking in. Barefooted, wearing shorts and a tank top. I couldn't see her face well, but she was obviously what my old partner Anderson would call a snake charmer.

Connor showed his badge. She said her name was Julia Young. She had a Southern accent, and a slight slur to her speech. Connor turned on the light and we could see her better. She was a beautiful girl. She came into the room hesitantly.

"I heard the music—is she here? Is Cheryl Lynn okay? I know she went to that party tonight."

"I haven't heard anything," Connor said, with a quick glance at me. "Do you know Cheryl Lynn?"

"Well, sure. I live right across the hall, in number eight. Why is everybody in her room?"

"Everybody?"

"Well, you two. And the two Japanese guys."

"When were they here?"

"I don't know. Maybe half an hour ago. Is it something about Chery-lynn?"

I said, "Did you get a look at the men, Miss Young?" I was thinking she might have been looking out of the peephole of her door.

"Well, I *guess*. I said hello to them."

"How's that?"

"I know one of them pretty well. Eddie."

"Eddie?"

"Eddie Sakamura. We all know Eddie. Fast Eddie."

I said, "Can you describe him?"

She gave me a funny look. "He's the guy in the pictures—the young guy with the scar on his hand. I thought everybody knew Eddie Sakamura. He's in the newspaper all the time. Charities and stuff. He's a big party guy."

I said, "Do you have any idea how I could find him?"

Connor said, "Eddie Sakamura is part owner of a Polynesian restaurant in Beverly Hills called Bora Bora. He hangs out there."

"That's him," Julia said. "That place is like his office. I can't stand it myself, it's too noisy. But Eddie's just running around, chasing those big blondes. He loves to look up to a girl."

She leaned against a table, and pushed her full brown hair back from her face seductively. She looked at me and gave a little pout. "You two guys partners?"

"Yes," I said.

"He showed me his badge. But you didn't show me yours."

I took out my wallet. She looked at it. "Peter," she said, reading. "My very first boyfriend was named Peter. But he wasn't as handsome as you." She smiled at me.

Connor cleared his throat and said, "Have you been in Cherylynn's apartment before?"

"Well, I *guess*. I live right across the way. But she hasn't been in town much lately. Seems like she's always traveling."

"Traveling where?"

"All over. New York, Washington, Seattle, Chicago . . . all over. She has this boyfriend who travels a lot. She meets him. Actually I think she just meets him when his wife isn't around."

"This boyfriend is married?"

"Well, there's something in the way. You know. Obstructing."

"Do you know who he is?"

"No. She once said he'd never come to her apartment. He's some big important guy. Real rich. They send the jet for her, and off she goes. Whoever he is, he drives Eddie crazy. But Eddie is the jealous type, you know. Got to be *iro otoko* to all the girls. The sexy lover."

Connor said, "Is Cheryl's relationship a secret? With this boyfriend?"

"I don't know. I never thought it was. It's just real intense. She's madly in love with the guy."

"She's madly in love?"

"You can't imagine. I've seen her drop everything to run and meet him. One night she comes over, gives me two tickets to the Springsteen concert, but she's all excited because she's going to *Detroit*. She's got her little carry-on in her hand. She's got her little nice-girl dress on. Because he just called ten minutes ago and said, 'Meet me.' Her face all bright, she looks about five years old. I don't know why she can't figure it out."

"Figure what out?"

"This guy is just using her."

"Why do you say that?"

"Cherylynn is beautiful, and real sophisticated-looking. She's worked all over the world as a model, mostly in Asia. But deep down she's a small-town girl. I mean, Midland is an oil town, there's lots of money, but it's still a small town. And Cherylynn wants the ring on the finger and the kids and the dog in the yard. And this guy isn't going to do it. She hasn't figured it out."

I said, "But you don't know who this man is?"

"No, I don't." A sly look crossed her face. She shifted her body, dropping one shoulder so her breasts thrust forward. "But you're not really here because of some old boyfriend, are you?"

Connor nodded. "Not really, no."

Julia smiled in a knowing way. "It's Eddie, isn't it?"

"Umm," Connor said.

"I knew it," she said. "I knew he'd get in trouble sooner or later. We all talked about it, all the girls here in the Arms." She made a vague gesture. "Because he's just going too fast. Fast Eddie. You wouldn't think he was Japanese. He's so flashy."

Connor said, "He's from Osaka?"

"His father's a big industrialist there, with Daimatsu. He's a nice old guy. When he comes over to visit, sometimes he sees one of the girls on the second floor. And Eddie. Eddie was supposed to get educated here for a few years, then go home to work for the *kaisha*, the company. But he won't go home. He loves it here. Why not? He's got everything. He buys a new Ferrari every time he bangs up the old one. He's got more money than God. He's lived here long enough, he's just like an American. Handsome. Sexy.

And with all the drugs. You know, real party animal. What's in Osaka for him?"

I said, "But you said you always knew . . ."

"That he'd get in trouble? Sure. Because of that crazy side. That *edge*." She shrugged. "A lot of them have it. These guys come over from Tokyo, and even if they have a *shōkai*, an introduction, you still have to be careful. They think nothing of dropping ten or twenty thousand in a night. It's like a tip for them. Leave it on the dresser. But then, what they want to do—at least, some of them . . ."

She drifted into silence. Her eyes had a vacant, unfocused look. I didn't say anything, I just waited. Connor was looking at her, nodding sympathetically.

Abruptly, she began to speak again, as if unaware of the pause. "And to them," she said, "their wishes, their desires, it's just as natural as leaving the tip. It's completely natural to them. I mean, I don't mind a little golden shower or whatever, handcuffs, you know. Maybe a little spanking if I like the guy. But I won't let anybody cut me. I don't care how much money. None of those things with knives or swords . . . But they can be . . . A lot of them, they are so polite, so correct, but then they get turned on, they have this . . . this *way* . . ." She broke off, shaking her head. "They're strange people."

Connor glanced at his watch. "Miss Young, you've been very helpful. We may need to speak to you again. Lieutenant Smith will take your phone number—"

"Yes, of course."

I flipped open my pad.

Connor said, "I'm going to have a word with the doorman."

"Shinichi," she said.

Connor left. I took down Julia's number. She licked her lips as she watched me write. Then she said, "You can tell me. Did he kill her?"

"Who?"

"Eddie. Did he kill Cherylynn?"

She was a pretty girl but I could see the excitement in her eyes. She was looking at me with a steady gaze. Her eyes were shining. It was creepy. I said, "Why do you ask?"

"Because. He was always threatening to. Like this afternoon, he threatened her."

I said, "Eddie was here this afternoon?"

"Sure." She shrugged. "He's here all the time. He came to see her this afternoon, real worked up. They put extra soundproofing to the walls in this building when they took it over. But even so, you could hear them scream at each other in her apartment. Him and Cherylynn. She'd have on her Jerry Lee Lewis, the one she played day and night until you just about went crazy, and they'd be screaming and throwing things. He'd always say, 'I'll kill you, I'll kill you, you bitch.' So. Did he?"

"I don't know."

"But she's dead?" Her eyes still shining.

"Yes."

"It had to happen," she said. She seemed completely calm. "We all knew it. It was just a matter of time. If you want, call me. If you need more information."

"Yes. I will." I gave her my card. "And if you think of anything else, you can call me at this number."

She slipped it into the hip pocket of her shorts, twisting her body. "I like talking to you, Peter."

"Yes. Okay."

I walked down the corridor. When I got to the end I looked back. She was standing in her doorway, waving good-bye.

Connor was using the phone in the lobby while the doorman stared sullenly at him, as if he wanted to stop him, but couldn't think of a reason why.

"That's right," Connor was saying. "All the outgoing calls from that phone between eight and ten p.m. That's right." He listened for a moment. "Well, I don't care if your data isn't organized that way, just get it for me. How long will it take? Tomorrow? Don't be ridiculous. What do you think this is? I need it within two hours. I'll call you back. Yes. Fuck you, too." He hung up. "Let's go, *kōhai.*"

We walked outside to the car.

I said, "Checking your contacts?"

"Contacts?" He looked puzzled. "Oh. Graham said something to you about my 'contacts.' I don't have any special informants. He just thinks I do."

"He mentioned the Arakawa case."

Connor sighed. "That old thing." We walked toward the car. "You want to know that story? It's simple. Two Japanese nationals get killed. The department puts detectives on the case who can't speak Japanese. Finally, after a week, they give the case to me."

"And what did you do?"

"The Arakawas were staying at the New Otani Hotel. I got the phone records of the calls they made to Japan. I called those numbers, and spoke to some people in Osaka. Then I called Osaka and talked to the police there. Again, in Japanese. They were surprised to hear we didn't know the whole story."

"I see."

"Not quite," Connor said. "Because the police department here was very embarrassed. The press had gone out on a limb, criticizing the department. All sorts of people had sent flowers. There had been a big show of sympathy for what turned out to be gangsters. A lot of people were embarrassed. So the whole thing became my fault. I had done something underhanded to solve the case. Pissed me off, I can tell you."

"That's why you went to Japan?"

"No. That's another story."

We came to the car. I looked back at the Imperial Arms, and saw Julia Young standing at the window, staring down at us. "She's seductive," I said.

"The Japanese call women like that *shirigaru onna*. They say she has a light ass." He opened the car door, and got in. "But she's on drugs. We can't trust anything she told us. Even so, there's starting to be a pattern I don't like." He glanced at his watch, and shook his head. "Damn. We're taking too long. We'd better go to the Palomino, to see Mr. Cole."

I started driving south, toward the airport. Connor sat back in his seat and folded his arms across his chest. He stared at his feet, looking unhappy.

"Why do you say there's a pattern you don't like?"

Connor said, "The wrappers in the waste basket. The Polaroid in the trash. Those things shouldn't have been left behind."

"You said yourself, they're in a hurry."

"Maybe. But you know the Japanese think American police are incompetent. This sloppiness is a sign of their disdain."

"Well, we're not incompetent."

Connor shook his head. "Compared to the Japanese, we *are* incompetent. In Japan, every criminal gets caught. For major crimes, convictions run ninety-nine percent. So any criminal in Japan knows from the outset he is going to get caught. But here, the conviction rate is more like seventeen percent. Not even one in five. So a criminal in the States knows he probably *isn't* going to get caught—and if he's caught, he won't be convicted, thanks to all his legal safeguards. And you know every study of police effectiveness shows that American detectives either solve the case in the first six hours, or they never solve it at all."

"So what are you saying?"

"I'm saying that a crime occurred here with the expectation that it won't be solved. And I want to solve it, *kōhai*."

Connor was silent for the next ten minutes. He sat very still, with his arms folded and his chin sunk on his chest. His breathing was deep and regular. I might have thought he had fallen asleep, except his eyes were open.

I just drove the car, and listened to him breathe.

Finally, he said: "Ishiguro."

"What about him?"

"If we knew what made Ishiguro behave as he did, we'd understand this case."

"I don't understand."

"It's hard for an American to see him clearly," Connor said. "Because in America, you think a certain amount of error is normal. You expect the plane to be late. You expect the mail to be undelivered. You expect the washing machine to break down. You expect things to go wrong all the time.

"But Japan is different. Everything *works* in Japan. In a Tokyo train station, you can stand at a marked spot on the platform and when the train stops, the doors will open right in front of you. Trains are on time. Bags are not lost. Connections are not missed. Deadlines are met. Things happen as planned. The Japanese are educated, prepared, and motivated. They get things done. There's no screwing around."

"Uh-huh . . ."

"And tonight was a very big night for the Nakamoto Corporation. You can be sure they planned everything down to the smallest detail. They have the vegetarian hors d'oeuvres that Madonna likes and the photographer she prefers. Believe me: they're prepared. They have planned for every exigency. You know how they are: they sit around and discuss endless possibilities—what if there's a fire? What if there's an earthquake? A bomb scare? Power failure? Endlessly going over the most unlikely events. It's obsessive, but when the final night arrives, they've thought of everything and they're in complete control. It's very bad form not to be in control. Okay?"

"Okay."

"But there is our friend Ishiguro, the official representative of Nakamoto, standing in front of a dead girl, and he's clearly not in control. He's *yōshiki nō*, doing Western-style confrontation, but he isn't comfortable—

I'm sure you noticed the sweat on his lip. And his hand is damp; he keeps wiping it on his trousers. He is *rikutsuppoi*, too argumentative. He's talking too much.

"In short, he's behaving as if he doesn't really know what to do, as if he doesn't even know who this girl is—which he certainly does, since he knows everybody invited to that party—and pretending he doesn't know who killed her. When he almost certainly knows that, too."

The car bounced in a pothole, and jolted back up. "Wait a minute. Ishiguro knows who killed the girl?"

"I'm sure of it. And he's not the only one. At least three people must know who killed her, at this point. Didn't you say you used to be in press relations?"

"Yes. Last year."

"You keep any contacts in TV news?"

"A few," I said. "They might be rusty. Why?"

"I want to look at some tape that was shot tonight."

"Just look? Not subpoena?"

"Right. Just look."

"That shouldn't be a problem," I said. I was thinking I could call Jennifer Lewis at KNBC, or Bob Arthur at KCBS. Probably Bob.

Connor said, "It has to be somebody you can approach personally. Otherwise the stations won't help us. You noticed there were no TV crews at the crime scene tonight. At most crime scenes, you have to fight your way past the cameras just to get to the tape. But tonight, no TV crews, no reporters. Nothing."

I shrugged. "We were on land lines. The press couldn't monitor radio transmissions."

"They were already there," Connor said, "covering the party with Tom Cruise and Madonna. And then a girl gets murdered on the floor above. So where were the TV crews?"

I said, "Captain, I don't buy it."

One of the things I learned as a press officer is that there aren't any conspiracies. The press is too diverse, and in a sense too disorganized. In fact, on the rare occasions when we needed an embargo—like a kidnapping with ransom negotiations in progress—we had a hell of a time getting cooperation. "The paper closes early. The TV crews have to make the eleven o'clock news. They probably went back to edit their stories."

"I disagree. I think the Japanese expressed concern about their *kigyō image*, their company image, and the press cooperated with no coverage. Trust me, *kōhai*: the pressure is being applied."

"I can't believe that."

"Take my word for it," Connor said. "The pressure is on."

Just then, the car phone rang.

"God damn it, Peter," a familiar rough voice said. "What the fuck's going on with that homicide investigation?" It was the chief. It sounded like he had been drinking.

"How do you mean, Chief?"

Connor looked at me, and punched the speaker phone button so he could hear.

The chief said: "You guys harassing the Japanese? We going to have another set of racial allegations against the department here?"

"No sir," I said. "Absolutely not. I don't know what you've heard—"

"I heard that dumb fuck Graham was making insults as usual," the chief said.

"Well, I wouldn't exactly say insults, Chief—"

"Look, Peter. Don't shit me. I already reamed out Fred Hoffmann for sending Graham in the first place. I want that racist turd off the case. We've all got to get along with the Japanese from now on. It's the way the world is. You hearing me, Peter?"

"Yes, sir."

"Now about John Connor. You got him with you, is that right?"

"Yes, sir."

"Why did you bring him into this?"

I thought: why did I bring him in? Fred Hoffmann must have decided to say that Connor was my idea, and not his own.

"I'm sorry," I said. "But I—"

"I understand," the chief said. "You probably thought you couldn't handle the case yourself. Wanted some help. But I'm afraid you bought more trouble than help. Because the Japanese don't like Connor. And I got to tell you. I go way back with John. We entered the academy together back in fifty-nine. He's always been a loner and a troublemaker. You know, anybody who goes to live in some foreign country, it's because he can't fit in here at home. I don't want him screwing up this investigation now."

"Chief—"

"This is how I see it, Peter. You got a homicide here, wrap it up and get it over with. Do it quick and do it neat. I'm looking to you and you alone. You hearing me?"

"Yes, sir."

"The connection is good?"

"Yes, sir," I said.

"Wrap it up, Pete," the chief said. "I don't want anybody else calling me on this."

"Yes, sir."

"Finish it by tomorrow latest. That's it." And he hung up.

I put the phone back in the cradle.

"Yes," Connor said. "I'd say pressure is being applied."

I drove south on the 405 freeway, toward the airport. It was foggier here. Connor stared out the window.

"In a Japanese organization, you'd never get a call like that. The chief just hung you out to dry. He takes no responsibility—it's all your problem. And he's blaming you for things that have nothing to do with you, like Graham, and me." Connor shook his head. "The Japanese don't do that. The Japanese have a saying: fix the problem, not the blame. In American organizations it's all about *who* fucked up. Whose head will roll. In Japanese organizations it's about *what*'s fucked up, and how to fix it. Nobody gets blamed. Their way is better."

Connor was silent, staring out the window. We were driving past Slauson, the Marina freeway a dark curve arcing above us in the fog.

I said, "The chief was in the bag, that's all."

"Yes. And uninformed, as usual. But even so, it sounds like we'd better have this case solved before he gets out of bed tomorrow."

"Can we do that?"

"Yes. If Ishiguro delivers those tapes."

The phone rang again. I answered it.

It was Ishiguro.

I handed the phone to Connor.

I could hear Ishiguro faintly through the receiver. He sounded tense, speaking rapidly. "*A, moshi moshi, Connor-san desuka? Keibi no heyani denwa shitan desuga ne. Daremo denain desuyo.*"

Connor cupped his hand over the phone and translated. "He called the security guard but no one was there."

"*Sorede, chuōkeibishitsu ni renraku shite, hito wo okutte moraimashite, issho ni tēpu o kakunin shite kimashita.*"

"Then he called the main security office and asked them to come down with him to check the tapes."

"*Tēpu wa subete rekōdā no naka ni arimasu. Nakunattemo torikaer-aretemo imasen. Subete daijōbu desu.*"

"The tapes are all in the recorders. No tapes are missing or switched." Connor frowned and replied. "*Iya, tēpu wa surikaerarete iru hazu nanda. Tēpu o sagase!*"

"*Dakara, daijōbu nandesu, Connor-san. Dōshiro to iun desuka?*"

"He insists everything is in order."

Connor said, "*Tēpu o sagase!*" To me, he said, "I told him I wanted the damn tapes."

"*Daijōbuda to itterudeshou. Dōshite sonnaini tēpu ni kodawarun desuka?*"

"*Ore niwa wakatte irunda. Tēpu wa nakunatte iru.* I know more than you think, Mr. Ishiguro. *Mōichido iu, tēpu o sagasunda!*"

Connor banged the phone in the cradle, and sat back, snorting angrily. "Bastards. They're taking the position that there are no missing tapes."

"What does that mean?" I said.

"They've decided to play hardball." Connor stared out the window at the traffic, and tapped his teeth with his finger. "They'd never do it unless they felt they had a strong position. An unassailable position. Which means . . ."

Connor drifted off into his private thoughts. I saw his face intermittently reflected in the glass under passing street lamps. Finally he said, "No, no, no," as if he were talking to someone.

"No, what?"

"It can't be Graham." He shook his head. "Graham is too risky—too many ghosts from the past. And it's not me, either. I'm old news. So it must be you, Peter."

I said, "What are you talking about?"

"Something has happened," Connor said, "to make Ishiguro think he has leverage. And I'd guess it's something to do with you."

"Me?"

"Yeah. It's almost certainly something personal. You have any problems in your past?"

"Like what?"

"Any priors, arrests, internal affairs investigations, allegations of ques-tionable conduct like drinking or homosexuality or chasing women? Any drug rehab program, problems with partners, problems with superiors. Any-thing personal or professional. Anything."

I shrugged. "Jeez, I don't think so."

Connor just waited, looking at me. Finally he said, "They think they have something, Peter."

"I'm divorced. I'm a single parent. I have a daughter, Michelle. She's two years old."

"Yes . . ."

"I lead a quiet life. I take care of my kid. I'm responsible."

"And your wife?"

"My ex-wife is a lawyer in the D.A.'s office."

"When did you get divorced?"

"Two years ago."

"Before the child was born?"

"Just after."

"Why did you get divorced?"

"Christ. Why does anybody get divorced."

Connor said nothing.

"We were only married a year. She was young when we met. Twenty-four. She had these fantasies about things. We met in court. She thought I was a rough, tough detective facing danger every day. She liked that I had a gun. All that. So we had this affair. Then when she got pregnant she didn't want to have an abortion. She wanted to get married instead. It was some romantic idea she had. She didn't really think it through. But the pregnancy was hard, and it was too late to abort, and pretty soon she decided she didn't like living with me because my apartment was small, and I didn't make enough money, and I lived in Culver City instead of Brentwood. And by the time the baby was finally born, it was like she was completely disillusioned. She said she had made a mistake. She wanted to pursue her career. She didn't want to be married to a cop. She didn't want to raise a kid. She said she was sorry, but it was all a mistake. And she left."

Connor was listening with his eyes closed. "Yes . . ."

"I don't see why all this matters. She left two years ago. And after that, I couldn't—I didn't want to work detective hours any more, because now I had to raise the kid, so I took the tests and transferred to Special Services, and I worked the press office. No problems there. Everything went fine. Then last year this Asian liaison job came up, and it paid better. Another couple hundred a month. So I applied for that."

"Uh-huh."

"I mean, I can really use the money. I have extra expenses now, like Michelle's day care. You know what day care costs for two-year-olds? And I have full-time housekeeping, and Lauren doesn't make her child-support payments more than half the time. She says she can't manage on her salary, but she just bought a new BMW, so I don't know. I mean, what am I going to do, take her to court? She works for the fucking D.A."

Connor was silent. Up ahead, I saw the airplanes coming down over the freeway. We were approaching the airport.

"Anyway," I said. "I was glad when the liaison job came along. Because it works out better for the hours, and for the money. And that's how I got to be here. In this car with you. That's it."

"*Kōhai*," he said quietly. "We're in this together. Just tell me. What is the problem?"

"There isn't any problem."

"*Kōhai*."

"There isn't."

"*Kōhai* . . ."

"Hey, John," I said, "let me tell you something. When you apply for Special Services liaison, five different committees go over your record. To get a liaison job, you have to be *clean*. The committees went over my record. And they found nothing substantial."

Connor nodded. "But they found *something*."

"Christ," I said, "I was a detective for five years. You can't work that long without a few complaints. You know that."

"And what were the complaints against you?"

I shook my head. "Nothing. Little stuff. I arrested a guy my first year, he accused me of undue force. That charge was dropped after inquiry. I arrested a woman for armed robbery, she claimed I planted a gram on her. Charge dropped; it was her gram. Murder suspect claimed I beat and kicked him during questioning. But other officers were present at all times. A drunken woman on a domestic violence call later claimed I molested her child. She dropped the charge. Teenage gang leader arrested for murder said I made a homosexual pass at him. Charge withdrawn. That's it."

If you're a cop you know that complaints like these are background noise, like traffic on the street. There's nothing you can do about them. You're in an adversarial environment, accusing people of crimes all the time. They accuse you back. That's just the way it works. The department never pays any attention unless there's a pattern or repetition. If a guy has three or four complaints of undue force over a couple of years, then he gets an inquiry. Or a string of racial complaints, he gets an inquiry. But otherwise, as the assistant chief Jim Olson always says, being a cop is a job for the thick-skinned.

Connor didn't say anything for a long time. He frowned, thinking it over. Finally he said, "What about the divorce? Problems there?"

"Nothing unusual."

"You and your ex are on speaking terms?"

"Yes. We're okay. Not great. But okay."

He was still frowning. Still looking for something. "And you left the detective division two years ago?"

"Yes."

"Why?"

"I already told you."

"You said that you couldn't work the hours."

"That was most of it, yeah."

"That, and what else?"

I shrugged. "After the divorce, I just didn't want to work homicide any more. I felt like—I don't know. Disillusioned. I had this little infant and my wife had moved out. She was going on with her life, dating some hotshot attorney. I was left holding the kid. I just felt flat. I didn't want to be a detective any more."

"You seek counseling at that time? Therapy?"

"No."

"Trouble with drugs or alcohol?"

"No."

"Other women?"

"Some."

"During the marriage?"

I hesitated.

"Farley? In the mayor's office?"

"No. That was later."

"But there *was* somebody during the marriage."

"Yes. But she lives in Phoenix now. Her husband got transferred."

"She was in the department?"

I shrugged.

Connor sat back in his seat. "Okay, *kōhai*," he said. "If this is all there is, you're fine." He looked at me.

"That's all."

"But I have to warn you," he said. "I've been through this kind of thing before, with the Japanese. When the Japanese play hardball, they can make things unpleasant. *Really* unpleasant."

"You trying to scare me?"

"No. Just telling you the way things are."

"Fuck the Japanese," I said. "I've got nothing to hide."

"Fine. Now I think you better call your friends at the network, and tell them we'll be over, after our next stop."

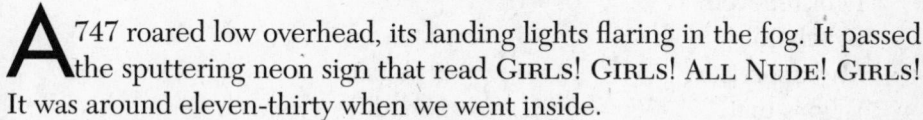

A 747 roared low overhead, its landing lights flaring in the fog. It passed the sputtering neon sign that read GIRLS! GIRLS! ALL NUDE! GIRLS! It was around eleven-thirty when we went inside.

To call the Club Palomino a strip joint was to flatter it. It was a converted bowling alley with cactus and horses painted on the walls. It seemed smaller inside than it appeared from the outside. A woman in a silver tassled G-string who looked close to forty danced listlessly in orange light. She seemed as bored as the customers hunched over tiny pink tables. Topless waitresses moved through the smoky air. The tape-recorded music had a loud hiss.

A guy just inside the door said, "Twelve bucks. Two drink minimum." Connor flipped his badge. The guy said, "Okay, fine."

Connor looked around and said, "I didn't know Japanese came here." I saw three businessmen in blue suits, sitting at a corner table.

"Hardly ever," the bouncer said. "They like the Star Strip downtown. More glitz, more tits. You ask me, those guys got lost from their tour."

Connor nodded, "I'm looking for Ted Cole."

"At the bar. Guy with the glasses."

Ted Cole was sitting at the bar. His windbreaker covered his Naka-moto Security uniform. He stared at us dully when we came up and sat beside him.

The bartender came over. Connor said, "Two Buds."

"No Bud. Asahi okay?"

"Okay."

Connor flipped his badge. Cole shook his head and turned away from us. He looked studiously at the stripper.

"I don't know anything."

Connor said, "About what?"

"About anything. I'm minding my own business. I'm off duty." He was a little drunk.

Connor said, "When did you get off duty?"

"I got off early tonight."

"Why is that?"

"Stomach trouble. I got an ulcer, it acts up sometimes. So I got off early."

"What time?"

"I got off at eight-fifteen at the latest."

"Do you punch a time clock?"

"No. We don't do that. No time clock."

"And who took over for you?"

"I got relieved."

"By whom?"

"My supervisor."

"Who is that?"

"I don't know him. Japanese guy. Never seen him before."

"He's your supervisor, and you never saw him before?"

"New guy. Japanese. I don't know him. What do you want from me, anyway?"

"Just to ask a few questions," Connor said.

"I got nothing to hide," Cole said.

One of the Japanese men sitting at the table came up to the bar. He stood near us and said to the bartender, "What kind of cigarettes you got?"

"Marlboro," the bartender said.

"What else?"

"Maybe Kools. I have to check. But I know we got Marlboro. You want Marlboro?"

Ted Cole stared at the Japanese man. The Japanese seemed not to notice him as he stood at the bar. "Kent?" the Japanese said. "You got any Kent lights?"

"No. No Kent."

"Okay then, Marlboro," the Japanese man said. "Marlboro is okay." He turned and smiled at us. "This is Marlboro country, right?"

"That's right," Connor said.

Cole picked up his beer and sipped it. We were all silent. The Japanese man beat the bar with his hands, in time to the music. "Great place," he said. "Lot of atmosphere."

I wondered what he was talking about. This place was a dump.

The Japanese slid onto the bar stool next to us. Cole studied his beer bottle as if he'd never seen one before. He turned it in his hands, making rings on the bar top.

The bartender brought cigarettes, and the Japanese man tossed a five-dollar bill on the table. "Keep the change." He tore open the pack, and took out a cigarette. He smiled at us.

Connor took out his lighter to light the man's cigarette. As the man leaned over the flame, he said, "*Doko kaisha ittenno?*"

The man blinked. "Sorry?"

"*Wakannē no?*" Connor said. "*Doko kaisha ittenno?*"

The man smiled, and slipped off the bar stool. "*Soro soro ikanakutewa. Shitsurei shimasu.*" He gave a little wave, and he went back to his friends across the room.

"*Dewa mata,*" Connor said. He moved around to sit on the stool where the Japanese man had been sitting.

Cole said, "What was that all about?"

"I just asked him what company he worked for," Connor said. "But he didn't want to talk. I guess he wanted to get back to his friends." Connor ran his hands under the bar, feeling. "Feels clean."

Connor turned back to Cole and said, "Now then, Mr. Cole. You were telling me that a supervisor took over for you. At what time was that?"

"Eight-fifteen."

"And you didn't know him?"

"No."

"And before that time, while you were on duty, were you taping from the video cameras?"

"Sure. The security office always tapes from the cameras."

"And did the supervisor remove the tapes?"

"Remove them? I don't think so. The tapes are still there, as far as I know."

He looked at us in a puzzled way.

"You fellows are interested in the tapes?"

"Yes," Connor said.

"Because I never paid much attention to the tapes. I was interested in the cameras."

"How's that?"

"They were getting the building ready for the big party, and there were lots of last-minute details. But you still had to wonder why they pulled so many security cameras off other parts of the building and put them up on that floor."

I said, "They what?"

"Those cameras weren't on the forty-sixth floor yesterday morning," Cole said. "They were scattered all around the building. Somebody moved them during the day. They're easy to move, you know, because there's no wires attached."

"The cameras have no wires?"

"No. It's all cellular transmission inside the building itself. Built that way. That's why they don't have audio: they can't transmit full bandwidth on cellular. So they just send an image. But they can move those cameras around to suit their purposes. See whatever they want to see. You didn't know that?"

"No," I said.

"I'm surprised nobody told you. It's one of the features of the building they're most proud of." Cole drank his beer. "Only question I have is why somebody would take five cameras and install them on the floor *above* the party. 'Cause there's no security reason. You can lock off the elevators above a certain floor. So for security, you'd want your cameras on the floors below the party. Not above."

"But the elevators weren't locked off."

"No. I thought that was kind of unusual, myself." He looked at the Japanese across the room. "I got to be going soon," he said.

"Well," Connor said. "You've been very helpful, Mr. Cole. We may want to question you again—"

"I'll write down my phone number for you," Cole said, scribbling on a bar napkin.

"And your address?"

"Yeah, right. But actually, I'm going out of town for a few days. My mother's been feeling sick, and she asked me to take her down there to Mexico for a few days. Probably go this weekend."

"Long trip?"

"Week or so. I got vacation days coming up, it seems like a good time to take it."

"Sure," Connor said. "I can see how it would. Thanks again for your help." He shook hands with Cole, and punched him lightly on the shoulder. "And you take care of *your* health."

"Oh, I will."

"Stop drinking, and have a safe drive home." He paused. "Or wherever you may decide to go tonight, instead."

Cole nodded. "I think you're right. That's not a bad idea."

"I know I'm right."

Cole shook my hand. Connor was heading out the door. Cole said, "I don't know why you guys are bothering."

"With the tapes?"

"With the Japanese. What can you do? They're ahead of us every step of the way. And they have the big guys in their pocket. We can't beat 'em now. You two guys'll never beat 'em. They're just too good."

Outside, beneath the crackling neon sign, Connor said, "Come on, time is wasting."

We got in the car. He handed me the bar napkin. On it was scrawled in block letters:

THEY STOLE THE TAPES

"Let's get going," Connor said.

I started the car.

The eleven o'clock news was finished for the night, and the newsroom was nearly deserted. Connor and I went down the hall to the sound stage where the *Action News* set was still lit up.

On the set, the evening broadcast was being replayed with the sound off. The anchorman pointed to the monitor. "I'm not stupid, Bobby. I watch these things. She did the lead-in and the wrap-up the last three nights." He sat back in his chair and crossed his arms. "I'm waiting to hear what you have to say, Bobby."

My friend Bob Arthur, the heavyset, tired producer of the eleven o'clock news, sipped a tumbler of straight scotch as big as his fist. He said, "Jim, it just worked out that way."

"Worked out that way my ass," the anchorman said.

The anchorwoman was a gorgeous redhead with a killer figure. She was taking a long time to shuffle through her notes, making sure she stayed to overhear the conversation between Bob and her coanchor.

"Look," the anchorman said. "It's in my contract. Half the lead-ins and half the wraps. It's contractual."

"But Jim," the producer said. "The lead tonight was Paris fashions and the Nakamoto party. That's human interest stuff."

"It should have been the serial killer."

Bob sighed. "His arraignment was postponed. Anyway, the public is tired of serial killers."

The anchorman looked incredulous. "The public is tired of serial killers? Now, where'd you get that?"

"You can read it yourself in the focus groups, Jim. Serial killers are over-exposed. Our audience is worried about the economy. They don't want any more serial killers."

"Our audience is worried about the economy so we lead off with Nakamoto and Paris fashions?"

"That's right, Jim," Bob Arthur said. "In hard times, you do star parties. That's what people want to see: fashion and fantasy."

The anchor looked sullen. "I'm a journalist, I'm here to do hard news, not fashion."

"Right, Jim," the producer said. "That's why Liz did the intros tonight. We want to keep your image hard news."

"When Teddy Roosevelt led this country out of the Great Depression, he didn't do it with fashion and fantasy."

"Franklin Roosevelt."

"Whatever. You know what I'm saying. If people are worried, let's *do* the economy. Let's *do* the balance of payments or whatever it is."

"Right, Jim. But this is the eleven o'clock news in the local market, and people don't want to hear—"

"And that's what's wrong with America," the anchorman pronounced, stabbing the air with his finger. "People don't want to hear the real news."

"Right, Jim. You're absolutely right." He put his arm over the anchorman's shoulder. "Get some rest, okay? We'll talk tomorrow."

That seemed to be a signal of some kind, because the anchorwoman finished with her notes and strode off.

"I'm a journalist," the anchor said. "I just want to do the job I was trained for."

"Right, Jim. More tomorrow. Have a good night."

"Stupid dickhead," Bob Arthur said, leading us down a corridor. "Teddy Roosevelt. Jesus. They're not journalists. They're actors. And they count their lines, like all actors." He sighed, and took another drink of scotch. "Now tell me again, what do you guys want to see?"

"Tape from the Nakamoto opening."

"You mean the air tapes? The story we ran tonight?"

"No, we want to see the original footage from the camera."

"The field tapes. Jeez. I hope we still have them. They may have been bulked."

"Bulked?"

"Bulk degaussed. Erased. We shoot forty cassettes a day here. Most of them get erased right away. We used to save field tapes for a week, but we're cutting costs, you know."

On one side of the newsroom were shelves of stacked Betamax cartridges. Bob ran his finger along the boxes. "Nakamoto . . . Nakamoto . . . No, I don't see them." A woman went past. "Cindy, is Rick still here?"

"No, he's gone home. You need something?"

"The Nakamoto field tapes. They aren't on the shelf."

"Check Don's room. He cut it."

"Okay." Bob led us across the newsroom to the editing bays on the far side. He opened a door, and we entered a small, messy room with two monitors, several tape decks, and an editing console. Tapes in boxes were scattered around the floor. Bob rummaged through them. "Okay, you guys are in luck. Camera originals. There's a lot of it. I'll get Jenny to run you through them. She's our best spotter. She knows everybody." He stuck his head out the door. "Jenny? Jenny!"

"Okay, let's see," Jenny Gonzales said, a few minutes later. She was a bespectacled, heavyset woman in her forties. She scanned the editor's notes and frowned. "It doesn't matter how many times I tell them, they just will not put things in proper . . . Finally. Here we are. Four tapes. Two limo driveups. Two roving inside, at the party. What do you want to see?"

Connor said, "Start with the driveups." He glanced at his watch. "Is there any way to do this fast? We're in a hurry."

"Fast as you want. I'm used to it. Let's see it at high speed."

She hit a button. At high speed, we saw the limousines pulling up, the doors jumping open, the people getting out, jerkily walking away.

"Looking for anyone in particular? Because I see somebody marked footages for celebrities during the edit."

"We're not looking for a celebrity," I said.

"Too bad. It's probably all we shot." We watched the tape. Jenny said, "There's Senator Kennedy. He's lost some weight, hasn't he. Oops, gone. And Senator Morton. Looking very fit. No surprise. That creepy assistant of his. He makes my teeth shiver. Senator Rowe, without his wife, as usual. There's Tom Hanks. I don't know this Japanese guy."

Connor said, "Hiroshi Masukawa, vice-president of Mitsui."

"There you go. Senator Chalmers, hair transplant looking good. Congressman Levine. Congressman Daniels. Sober for a change. You know, I'm surprised Nakamoto got so many of these Washington people to attend."

"Why do you say that?"

"Well, when you get down to it, it's just the opening of some new building. An ordinary corporate bash. It's on the West Coast. And Nakamoto is pretty controversial right at the moment. Barbra Streisand. I don't know who the guy is with her."

"Nakamoto is controversial? Why?"

"Because of the MicroCon sale."

I said, "What's MicroCon?"

"MicroCon is an American company that makes computer equipment. A Japanese company named Akai Ceramics is trying to buy it. There's opposition to the sale in Congress, because of worries about America losing technology to Japan."

I said, "And what does this have to do with Nakamoto?"

"Nakamoto's the parent company of Akai." The first tape finished, and popped out. "Nothing there you wanted?"

"No. Let's go on."

"Right." She slid the second tape in. "Anyway, I'm surprised how many of these senators and congressmen felt it was acceptable to show up here tonight. Okay, here we go. More driveups. Roger Hillerman, under secretary of state for Pacific affairs. That's his assistant with him. Kenichi Aikou, consul general of Japan, here in L.A. Richard Meier, architect. Works for Getty. Don't know her. Some Japanese . . ."

Connor said, "Hisashi Koyama, vice-president of Honda U.S."

"Oh, yeah," Jenny said. "He's been here about three years now. Probably going home soon. That's Edna Morris, she heads the U.S. delegation to the GATT talks. You know, General Agreement on Tariffs and Trade. I can't believe she showed up here, it's an obvious conflict of interest. But there she is, all smiling and relaxed. Chuck Norris. Eddie Sakamura. Sort of a local playboy. Don't know the girl with him. Tom Cruise, with his Australian wife. And Madonna, of course."

On the accelerated tape, the strobes flashed almost continuously as Madonna stepped from her limousine and preened. "Want to slow it down? You interested in this?"

Connor said, "Not tonight."

"Well, we probably have a lot on her," Jenny said. She pushed the very high-speed fast-forward and the image streaked gray. When she punched back, Madonna was wiggling toward the elevator, leaning on the arm of a slender Hispanic boy with a mustache. The image blurred as the camera swung back toward the street. Then it stabilized again.

"There's Daniel Okimoto. Expert on Japanese industrial policy. That's Arnold, with Maria. And behind them is Steve Martin, with Arata Isozaki, the architect who designed the Museum—"

Connor said, "Wait."

She punched the console button. The picture froze. Jenny seemed surprised. "You're interested in Isozaki?"

"No. Back up, please."

The tape ran backward, the frames flicking and blurring as the camera panned off Steve Martin, and went back to record the next arrival from the limousines. But for a moment in the pan, the camera swung past a group of people who had already gotten out of their limousines, and were walking up the carpeted sidewalk.

Connor said, "There."

The image froze. Slightly blurred, I saw a tall blonde in a black cocktail dress walking forward alongside a handsome man in a dark suit.

"Huh," Jenny said. "You interested in him, or her?"

"Her."

"Let me think," Jenny said, frowning. "I've seen her at parties with the Washington types for about nine months now. She's this year's Kelly Emberg. The athletic modelly kind. But sophisticated, sort of a Tatiana look-alike. Her name is . . . Austin. Cindy Austin, Carrie Austin . . . Cheryl Austin. That's it."

I said, "You know anything else about her?"

Jenny shook her head. "Listen, I think getting a name is pretty good. These girls show up all the time. You see a new one everywhere for six months, a year, and then they're gone. God knows where they go. Who can keep track of them?"

"And the man with her?"

"Richard Levitt. Plastic surgeon. Does a lot of big stars."

"What's he doing here?"

She shrugged. "He's around. Like a lot of these guys, he's a companion to the stars in their time of need. If his patients are getting divorced or whatever, he escorts the woman. When he's not taking out clients, he takes out models like her. They certainly look good together."

On the monitor, Cheryl and her escort walked toward us in intermittent jerks: one frame every thirty seconds. Stepping slow. I noticed they never looked at each other. She seemed tense, expectant.

Jenny Gonzales said, "So. Plastic surgeon and a model. Can I ask what's the big deal about these two? Because at an evening like this, they're just, you know, party favors."

Connor said, "She was killed tonight."

"Oh, *she's* the one? Interesting."

I said, "You've heard about the murder?"

"Oh, sure."

"Was it on the news?"

"No, didn't make the eleven o'clock," Jenny said. "And it probably won't be on tomorrow. I can't see it myself. It's not really a story."

"Why is that?" I asked, glancing at Connor.

"Well, what's the peg?"

"I don't follow you."

"Nakamoto would say, it's only news because it happened at their opening. They'd take the position that any reporting of it is a smear on them. But in a way they're right. I mean, if this girl got killed on the freeway, it wouldn't make the news. If she got killed in a convenience store robbery, it wouldn't make the news. We have two or three of those every night. So the fact that she gets killed at a party . . . who cares? It's still not news. She's young and pretty, but she's not special. It's not as if she has a series or anything."

Connor glanced at his watch. "Shall we look at the other tapes?"

"The footage from the party? Sure. You looking for this particular girl?"

"Right."

"Okay, here we go." Jenny put in the third tape.

We saw scenes from the party on the forty-fifth floor: the swing band, people dancing beneath the hanging decorations. We strained for a glimpse of the girl in the crowd. Jenny said, "In Japan, we wouldn't have to do this by eye. The Japanese have pretty sophisticated video-recognition software now. They have a program where you identify an image, say a face, and it'll automatically search tape for you, and find every instance of that face. Find it in a crowd, or wherever it appears. Has the ability to see a single view of a three-dimensional object, and then to recognize the same object in other views. It's supposed to be pretty nifty. But slow."

"I'm surprised the station hasn't got it."

"Oh, it's not for sale here. The most advanced Japanese video equipment isn't available in this country. They keep us three to five years behind. Which is their privilege. It's their technology, they can do what they want. But it'd sure be useful in a case like this."

The party images were streaming past, a frenetic blur.

Suddenly, she locked the image.

"There. Background camera left. Your Austin girl's talking to Eddie Sakamura. Of course he'd know her. Sakamura knows all the models. Normal speed here?"

"Please," Connor said, staring at the screen.

The camera made a slow pan around the room. Cheryl Austin remained in view for most of the shot. Laughing with Eddie Sakamura, throwing her head back, resting her hand on his arm, happy to be with him. Eddie clowned for her, his face mobile. He seemed to enjoy making her laugh. But from time to time, her eyes flicked away, glancing around the room. As if she was waiting for something to happen. Or for someone to arrive.

At one point, Sakamura became aware he did not have her full attention.

He grabbed her arm and pulled her roughly toward him. She turned her face away from him. He leaned close to her and said something angrily. Then a bald man stepped forward, very close to the camera. The light flared on his face, washing out his features, and his head blocked our view of Eddie and the girl. Then the camera panned left, and we lost them.

"Damn."

"Again?" Jenny backed it up, and we ran it once more.

I said, "Eddie's obviously not happy with her."

"I'd say."

Connor frowned. "It's so difficult to know what we are seeing. Do you have sound for this?"

Jenny said, "Sure, but it's probably walla." She punched buttons and ran it again. The track was continuous cocktail party din. Only for brief moments did we hear an isolated phrase.

At one point, Cheryl Austin looked at Eddie Sakamura and said, ". . . can't help if it's important to you I get . . ."

His reply to her was garbled, but later, he said clearly to her, "Don't understand . . . all about the Saturday meeting . . ."

And in the last few seconds of the pan, when he pulled her to him, he snarled a phrase like ". . . be a fool . . . no cheapie . . ."

I said, "Did he say 'No cheapie'? "

"Something like that," Connor said.

Jenny said, "Want to run it again?"

"No," Connor said. "There's nothing more to be learned here. Go forward."

"Right," Jenny said.

The image accelerated, the party-goers becoming frenetic, laughing and raising glasses for quick sips. And then I said, "Wait."

Back to normal speed. A blond woman in an Armani silk suit shaking hands with the bald-headed man we had seen a few moments before.

"What is it?" Jenny said, looking at me.

"That's his wife," Connor said.

The woman leaned forward to kiss the bald man lightly on the mouth. Then she stepped back and made some comment about the suit he was wearing.

"She's a lawyer in the D.A.'s office," Jenny said. "Lauren Davis. She's assisted on a couple of big cases. The Sunset Strangler, the Kellerman shooting. She's very ambitious. Smart and well connected. They say she has a future if she stays in the office. It must be true, because Wyland doesn't ever let her get air time. As you see, she makes a good appearance, but he keeps her away from the microphones. The bald guy she's talking to is John

McKenna, with Regis McKenna in San Francisco. The company that does the publicity for most high-tech firms."

I said, "We can go forward."

Jenny pushed the button. "She really your wife, or is your partner kidding?"

"No, she's really my wife. Was."

"You're divorced now?"

"Yeah."

Jenny looked at me, and started to say something. Then she decided not to, and looked back at the screen. On the monitor, the party continued at high speed.

I found myself thinking of Lauren. When I knew her, she was bright and ambitious, but she really didn't understand very much. She had grown up privileged, she had gone to Ivy League schools, and had the privileged person's deep belief that whatever she happened to think was probably true. Certainly good enough to live by. Nothing needed to be checked against reality.

She was young, that was part of it. She was still feeling the world, learning how it worked. She was enthusiastic, and she could be impassioned in expounding her beliefs. But of course her beliefs were always changing, depending on whom she had talked to last. She was very impressionable. She tried on ideas the way some women try on hats. She was always informed on the latest trend. I found it youthful and charming for a while, until it began to annoy me.

Because she didn't have any core, any real substance. She was like a television set: she just played the latest show. Whatever it was. She never questioned it.

In the end, Lauren's great talent was to conform. She was expert at watching the TV, the newspaper, the boss—whatever she saw as the source of authority—and figuring out what direction the winds were blowing. And positioning herself so she was where she ought to be. I wasn't surprised she was getting ahead. Her values, like her clothes, were always smart and up-to-date—

". . . to you, Lieutenant, but it's getting late . . . Lieutenant?"

I blinked, and came back. Jenny was talking to me. She pointed to the screen, where a frozen image showed Cheryl Austin in her black dress, standing with two older men in suits.

I looked over at Connor, but he had turned away, and was talking on the telephone.

"Lieutenant? This of interest to you?"

"Yes, sure. Who are they?"

Jenny started the tape. It ran at normal speed.

"Senator John Morton and Senator Stephen Rowe. They're both on the Senate Finance Committee. The one that's been having hearings about this MicroCon sale."

On the screen, Cheryl laughed and nodded. In motion, she was remarkably beautiful, an interesting mixture of innocence and sexuality. At moments, her face appeared knowing and almost hard. She appeared to know both men, but not well. She did not come close to either of them, or touch them except to shake hands. For their part, the senators seemed acutely aware of the camera, and maintained a friendly, if somewhat formal demeanor.

"Our country's going to hell, and on a Thursday night, United States senators are standing around chatting with models," Jenny said. "No wonder we're in trouble. And these are important guys. They're talking about Morton as a presidential candidate in the next election."

I said, "What do you know about them personally?"

"They're both married. Well. Rowe's semi-separated. His wife stays home in Virginia. He gets around. Tends to drink too much."

I looked at Rowe on the monitor. He was the same man who had gotten on the elevator with us earlier in the evening. And he had been drunk then, almost falling down. But he wasn't drunk now.

"And Morton?"

"Supposedly he's Mr. Clean. Ex-athlete, fitness nut. Eats health food. Family man. Morton's big area is science and technology. The environment. American competitiveness, American values. All that. But he can't be that clean, I've heard he has a young girlfriend."

"Is that right?"

She shrugged. "The story is, his staffers are trying to break it off. But who knows what's true."

The tape ejected and Jenny pushed in the next one. "This is the last, fellas."

Connor hung up the phone and said, "Forget the tape." He stood. "We've got to go, *kōhai*."

"Why?"

"I've been talking to the phone company about the calls made from the pay phone in the lobby of the Nakamoto building between eight and ten."

"And?"

"No calls were made during those hours."

I knew that Connor thought that someone had gone out of the security room and called from the pay phone—Cole, or one of the Japanese. Now his hopes of following a promising lead by tracing the call were dashed. "That's too bad," I said.

"Too bad?" Connor said, surprised. "It's extremely helpful. It narrows things down considerably. Miss Gonzales, do you have any tapes of people leaving the party?"

"Leaving? No. Once the guests arrived, all the crews went upstairs to shoot the actual party. Then they brought the tape back here to make the deadline, while the party was still going on."

"Fine. Then I believe we're finished here. Thanks for your help. Your knowledge is remarkable. *Kōhai*, let's go."

Driving again. This time to an address in Beverly Hills. By now it was after one in the morning, and I was tired. I said, "Why does the pay phone in the lobby matter so much?"

"Because," Connor said, "our whole conception of this case revolves around whether someone made a call from that phone, or not. The real question now is, which company in Japan has locked horns with Nakamoto?"

"Which company in Japan?" I said.

"Yes. It is clearly a corporation belonging to a different *keiretsu*," Connor said.

I said, "*Keiretsu*?"

"The Japanese structure their businesses in large organizations they call *keiretsu*. There are six major ones in Japan, and they're huge. For example, the Mitsubishi *keiretsu* consists of seven hundred separate companies that work together, or have interrelated financing, or interrelated agreements of various sorts. Big structures like that don't exist in America because they violate our antitrust laws. But they are the norm in Japan. We tend to think of corporations as standing alone. To see it the Japanese way, you'd have to imagine, say, an association of IBM and Citibank and Ford and Exxon, all having secret agreements among themselves to cooperate, and to share financing or research. That means a Japanese corporation never stands alone—it's always acting in partnership with hundreds of other companies. And in competition with the companies of other *keiretsu*.

"So when you think about what Nakamoto Corporation is doing, you have to ask what the Nakamoto *keiretsu* is doing, back in Japan. And what companies in other *keiretsu* oppose it. Because this murder is embarrassing to Nakamoto. It could even be seen as an attack against Nakamoto."

"An attack?"

"Think about it. Nakamoto plans a great, star-studded opening night for their building. They want it to go perfectly. For some reason, a guest at the party gets strangled. And the question is—who called it in?"

"Who reported the murder?"

"Right. Because after all, Nakamoto controls that environment completely: it's their party, their building. And it would be a simple matter for them to wait until eleven o'clock, after the party was over and the guests had left, to report the murder. If I were preoccupied with appearances, with the nuances of public face, that's the way I'd do it. Because anything else is potentially dangerous to the corporate image of Nakamoto."

"Okay."

"But the report wasn't delayed," Connor said. "On the contrary, somebody called it in at eight thirty-two, just as the party was getting under way. Thus putting the whole evening at risk. And our question has always been: who called it in?"

I said, "You told Ishiguro to find the person who called. And he hasn't done it yet."

"Correct. Because he can't."

"He doesn't know who called it in?"

"Correct."

"You don't think anybody from the Nakamoto Corporation made the call?"

"Correct."

"An enemy of Nakamoto called?"

"Almost certainly."

I said, "So how do we find out who called the report in?"

Connor laughed. "That's why I checked the lobby phone. It's crucial to that question."

"Why is it crucial?"

"Suppose you work for a competing corporation, and you want to know what's going on inside Nakamoto. You can't find out, because Japanese corporations hire their executives for life. The executives feel they are part of a family. And they'd never betray their own family. So Nakamoto Corporation presents an impenetrable mask to the rest of the world, which makes even the smallest details meaningful: which executives are in town from Japan, who is meeting with whom, comings and goings, and so on. And you might be able to learn those details, if you strike up a relationship with an American security guard who sits in front of monitors all day. Particularly if that guard has been subjected to Japanese prejudice against blacks."

"Go on," I said.

"The Japanese often try to bribe local security officers from rival firms. The Japanese are honorable people, but their tradition allows such behavior. All's fair in love and war, and the Japanese see business as war. Bribery is fine, if you can manage it."

"Okay."

"Now, in the first few seconds after the murder, we can be certain of only two people who knew a girl had been killed. One is the killer himself. The other is the security guard, Ted Cole, who watched it on the monitors."

"Wait a minute. Ted Cole watched it on the monitors? He knows who the killer is?"

"Obviously."

"He said he left at eight-fifteen."

"He was lying."

"But if you knew that, then why didn't we—"

"He'll never tell *us*," Connor said. "The same way Phillips won't tell us. That's why I didn't arrest Cole, bring him down for questioning. In the end it would be a waste of time—and time is of the essence here. We know he won't tell us. My question is, *did he tell anyone else?*"

I began to see what he was driving at. "You mean, did he walk out of the security office to the lobby pay phone, and call somebody to tell them that a murder had occurred?"

"Correct. Because he wouldn't use the phone in his office. He'd use the pay phone, and call somebody—an enemy of Nakamoto, a competing corporation. Somebody."

I said, "But now we know that no calls were made from that phone."

"Correct," Connor said.

"So your whole line of reasoning collapses."

"Not at all. It is clarified. If Cole didn't notify anybody, then who phoned in the murder? Clearly, the source can only be the murderer himself."

I felt a chill.

"He called it in to embarrass Nakamoto?"

"Presumably," Connor said.

"Then where did he call from?"

"That's not clear yet. I assume from somewhere inside the building. And there are a few other confusing details that we have not begun to consider."

"Such as?"

The car phone rang. Connor answered it, and handed the receiver to me. "It's for you."

"No, no," Mrs. Ascenio said. "The baby is fine. I checked on her a few minutes ago. She is fine. Lieutenant, I wanted you to know Mrs. Davis called." That was how she referred to my ex-wife.

"When?"

"I think ten minutes ago."

"Did she leave a number?"

"No. She say she can't be reached tonight. But she want you to know: something has come up, and maybe she go out of town. So she say maybe she don't take the baby this weekend."

I sighed. "Okay."

"She say she call you tomorrow and let you know for sure."

"Okay."

I wasn't surprised. It was typical Lauren. Last-minute changes. You could never make plans involving Lauren because she was always changing her mind. Probably this latest change meant that she had a new boyfriend and she might go away with him. She wouldn't know until tomorrow.

I used to think all this unpredictability was bad for Michelle, that it would make her insecure. But kids are practical. Michelle seems to understand that's the way her mother is, and she doesn't get upset.

I'm the one who gets upset.

Mrs. Ascenio said, "You coming back soon, Lieutenant?"

"No. It looks like I'll be out all night. Can you stay?"

"Yes, but I have to leave by nine in the morning. You want I pull out the couch?"

I had a couch bed in the living room. She used it when she stayed over. "Yes, sure."

"Okay, good-bye, Lieutenant."

"Good-bye, Mrs. Ascenio."

Connor said, "Anything wrong?" I was surprised to hear tension in his voice.

"No. Just my ex pulling her usual shit. She's not sure she'll take the baby this weekend. Why?"

Connor shrugged. "Just asking."

I didn't think that was all there was to it. I said, "What did you mean earlier, when you said that this case could turn ugly?"

"It may not," Connor said. "Our best solution is to wrap it up in the next few hours. And I think we can. Here's the restaurant up ahead on the left."

I saw the neon sign. Bora Bora.

"This is the restaurant owned by Sakamura?"

"Yes. Actually he's just a part owner. Don't let the valet take the car. Park it in the red. We may need to leave quickly."

The Bora Bora was this week's hot L.A. restaurant. The decor was a jumble of Polynesian masks and shields. Lime green wooden outriggers jutted out over the bar like teeth. Above the open kitchen, a Prince video played ghostlike on an enormous five-meter screen. The menu was Pacific Rim; the noise deafening; the clientele movie-industry hopeful. Everyone was dressed in black.

Connor smiled. "It looks like Trader Vic's after a bomb went off, doesn't it? Stop staring. Don't they let you out enough?"

"No, they don't," I said. Connor turned to speak to the Eurasian hostess. I looked at the bar, where two women kissed briefly on the lips. Farther down, a Japanese man in a leather bomber jacket had his arm around a huge blonde. They were both listening to a man with thinning hair and a pugnacious manner whom I recognized as the director of—

"Come on," Connor said to me. "Let's go."

"What?"

"Eddie's not here."

"Where is he?"

"At a party in the hills. Let's go."

The address was on a winding road in the hills above Sunset Boulevard. We would have had a good view of the city up here, but the mist had closed in. As we approached, the street was lined on both sides with luxury cars: mostly Lexus sedans, with a few Mercedes convertibles and Bentleys. The parking attendants looked surprised as we pulled up in our Chevy sedan, and headed up to the house.

Like other residences on the street, the house was surrounded by a three-meter wall, the driveway closed off with a remote-controlled steel gate. There was a security camera mounted above the gate, and another at the path leading up to the house itself. A private security guard stood by the path and checked our badges.

I said, "Whose house is this?"

Ten years ago, the only people in Los Angeles who maintained such elaborate security were either Mafioso, or stars like Stallone whose violent roles attracted violent attention. But lately it seemed everybody in wealthy residential areas had security. It was expected, almost fashionable. We walked up steps through a cactus garden toward the house, which was modern, concrete, and fortresslike. Loud music played.

"This house belongs to the man who owns Maxim Noir." He must have seen my blank look. "It's an expensive clothing store famous for its snotty salespeople. Jack Nicholson and Cher shop there."

"Jack Nicholson and Cher," I said, shaking my head. "How do you know about it?"

"Many Japanese shop at Maxim Noir now. It's like most expensive American stores—it'd go out of business without visitors from Tokyo. It's dependent on the Japanese."

As we approached the front door a large man in a sport coat appeared. He had a clipboard with names. "I'm sorry. It's by invitation only, gentlemen."

Connor flashed his badge. "We'd like to speak to one of your guests," he said.

"Which guest is that, sir?"

"Mr. Sakamura."

He didn't look happy. "Wait here, please."

From the entryway, we could see into the living room. It was crowded with party-goers, who at a quick glance seemed to be many of the same people who had been at the Nakamoto reception. As in the restaurant, almost everyone was wearing black. But the room itself caught my attention: it was stark white, entirely unadorned. No pictures on the wall. No furniture. Just bare white walls and a bare carpet. The guests looked uncomfortable. They were holding cocktail napkins and drinks, looking around for someplace to put them.

A couple passed us on their way to the dining room. "Rod always knows what to do," she said.

"Yes," he said. "So elegantly minimalist. The *detail* in executing that room. I don't know how he ever got that paint job. It's abso*lute*ly perfect. Not a brush stroke, not a blemish. A perfect surface."

"Well, it has to be," she said. "It's integral to his whole conception."

"It's really quite daring," the man said.

"Daring?" I said. "What are they talking about? It's just an empty room."

Connor smiled. "I call it *faux zen*. Style without substance."

I scanned the crowd.

"Senator Morton's here." He was standing in the corner, holding forth. Looking very much like a presidential candidate.

"So he is."

The guard hadn't returned, so we stepped a few feet into the room. As I approached Senator Morton, I heard him say, "Yes, I can tell you exactly why I'm disturbed about the extent of Japanese ownership of American industry. If we lose the ability to make our own products, we lose control over our destiny. It's that simple. For example, back in 1987 we learned that Toshiba sold the Russians critical technology that allowed the Soviets to silence their submarine propellers. Russian nuclear subs now sit right off the coast and we can't track them, because they got technology from Japan. Congress was furious, and the American people were up in arms. And rightly so, it was outrageous. Congress planned economic retaliation against Toshiba. But the lobbyists for American companies pleaded their case for them, because American companies like Hewlett-Packard and Compaq were dependent on Toshiba for computer parts. They couldn't stand a boycott because they had no other source of supply. The fact was, we couldn't afford to retaliate. They could sell vital technology to our enemy, and there wasn't a damned thing we could do about it. That's the problem. We're now dependent on Japan—and I believe America shouldn't be dependent on any nation."

Somebody asked a question, and Morton nodded. "Yes, it's true that our industry is not doing well. Real wages in this country are now at 1962 levels. The purchasing power of American workers is back where it was thirty-odd years ago. And that matters, even to the well-to-do folks that I see in this room, because it means American consumers don't have the money to see movies, or buy cars, or clothing, or whatever you people have to sell. The truth is, our nation is sliding badly."

A woman asked another question I couldn't hear, and Morton said, "Yes, I said 1962 levels. I know it's hard to believe, but think back to the fifties, when American workers could own a house, raise a family, and send the kids to college, all on a single paycheck. Now both parents work and most people still can't afford a house. The dollar buys less, everything is more expensive. People struggle just to hold on to what they have. They can't get ahead."

I found myself nodding as I listened. About a month before, I had gone looking for a house, hoping to get a backyard for Michelle. But housing prices were just impossible in L.A. I was never going to be able to afford one, unless I remarried. Maybe not even then, considering—

I felt a sharp jab in the ribs. I turned around and saw the doorman. He jerked his head toward the front door. "Back, fella."

I was angry. I glanced at Connor, but he just quietly moved back to the entrance.

In the entryway, the doorman said, "I checked. There's no Mr. Saka-mura here."

"Mr. Sakamura," Connor said, "is the Japanese gentleman standing at the back of the room, to your right. Talking to the redhead."

The doorman shook his head. "I'm sorry, fellas. Unless you have a search warrant, I'll have to ask you to leave."

"There isn't a problem here," Connor said. "Mr. Sakamura is a friend of mine. I know he'd like to talk to me."

"I'm sorry. Do you have a search warrant?"

"No," Connor said.

"Then you're trespassing. And I'm asking you to leave."

Connor just stood there.

The doorman stepped back and planted his feet wide. He said, "I think you should know I'm a black belt."

"Are you really?" Connor said.

"So is Jeff," the doorman said, as a second man appeared.

"Jeff," Connor said. "Are you the one who'll be driving your friend here to the hospital?"

Jeff laughed meanly. "Hey. You know, I like humor. It's funny. Okay, Mr. Wise Guy. You're in the wrong place. You've had it explained. Move out. *Now*." He poked Connor in the chest with a stubby finger.

Connor said quietly, "That's assault."

Jeff said, "Hey. Fuck you, buddy. I told you you're in the wrong place—"

Connor did something very fast, and Jeff was suddenly down on the floor, moaning in pain. Jeff rolled away, coming to rest against a pair of black trousers. Looking up, I saw that the man wearing the trousers was dressed entirely in black: black shirt, black tie, black satin jacket. He had white hair and a dramatic Hollywood manner. "I'm Rod Dwyer. This is my home. What seems to be the problem?"

Connor introduced us politely and showed his badge. "We're here on official business. We asked to speak to one of your guests, Mr. Sakamura, who is the man standing over there in the corner."

"And this man?" Dwyer asked, pointing to Jeff, who was gasping and coughing on the floor.

Connor said calmly, "He assaulted me."

"I didn't fucking assault him!" Jeff said, sitting up on his elbow, coughing.

Dwyer said, "Did you *touch* him?"

Jeff was silent, glowering.

Dwyer turned back to us. "I'm sorry this happened. These men are new. I don't know what they were thinking of. Can I get you a drink?"

"Thanks, we're on duty," Connor said.

"Let me ask Mr. Sakamura to come over and talk to you. Your name again?"

"Connor."

Dwyer walked away. The first man helped Jeff to his feet. As Jeff limped away, he muttered, "Fucking assholes."

I said, "Remember when police were respected?"

But Connor was shaking his head, looking down at the floor. "I am very ashamed," he said.

"Why?"

He wouldn't explain further.

"Hey, John! John Connor! *Hisashiburi dana!* Long time no see! How they hanging, guy? Hey!" He punched Connor in the shoulder.

Up close, Eddie Sakamura wasn't so handsome. His complexion was gray, with pock-marked skin, and he smelled like day-old scotch. His movements were edgy, hyperactive, and he spoke quickly. Fast Eddie was not a man at peace.

Connor said, "I'm pretty good, Eddie. How about you? How you doing?"

"Hey, can't complain, Captain. One or two things only. Got a five-oh-one, drunk driving, try to beat that, but you know, with my record, it's getting hard. Hey! Life goes on! What're you doing here? Pretty wild place, huh? Latest thing: no furniture! Rod sets new style. Great! Nobody can sit down any more!" He laughed. "New style! Great!"

I had the feeling he was on drugs. He was too manic. I got a good look at the scar on his left hand. It was purple-red, roughly four centimeters by three. It appeared to be an old burn.

Connor lowered his voice and said, "Actually, Eddie, we're here about the *yakkaigoto* at Nakamoto tonight."

"Ah, yes," Eddie said, lowering his voice, too. "No surprise she came to a bad end. That's one *henntai.*"

"She was perverted? Why do you say that?"

Eddie said, "Want to step outside? Like to smoke cigarette and Rod doesn't allow smoking in the house."

"Okay, Eddie."

We went outside and stood by the edge of the cactus garden. Eddie lit a Mild Seven Menthol. "Hey, Captain, I don't know what you heard already so far. But that girl. She fucked some of the people in there. She fucked Rod. Some of the other people. So. We can talk easier out here, okay with you?"

"Sure."

"I know that girl real well. Real well. You know I'm *hipparidako*, hey? I can't help it. Popular guy! She's all over me. All the time."

"I know that, Eddie. But you say she had problems?"

"Big problems, amigo. Grande problemos. I tell you. She was a sick girl, this girl. She got off on pain."

"World's full of 'em, Eddie."

He sucked on his cigarette. "Hey, no," he said. "I'm talking something else. I'm talking, how she gets off. When you hurt her real bad she comes. She's always asking, more, more. Do it more. Squeeze harder."

Connor said, "Her neck?"

"Yeah. Her neck. Right. Squeeze her neck. Yeah. You heard? And sometimes a plastic bag. You know, drycleaning bag? Put it over her head and clamp it, hold it around her neck while you fuck her and she sucks the plastic against her mouth and turns blue in the face. Claws at your back. Gasp and wheeze. Christ Almighty. Don't care for that, myself. But I'm telling you, this girl has a pussy. I mean she gets off, it's wild ride. You remember afterwards. I'm telling you. But for me, too much. Always on the edge, you know? Always a risk. Always pushing the edge. Maybe this time. Maybe this is the last time. You know what I'm saying?" He flicked his cigarette away. It sputtered among the cactus thorns. "Sometimes it's exciting. Like Russian roulette. Then I couldn't take it, Captain. Seriously. I couldn't. And you know me, I like a wild time."

I decided that Eddie Sakamura gave me the creeps. I tried to make notes while he talked, but his words were tumbling out, and I couldn't keep up. He lit another cigarette, his hands shaking. He kept talking fast, swinging the glowing tip in the air for emphasis.

"And I mean, this girl, it's a *problem*," Eddie said. "Okay, pretty girl. She's pretty. But sometimes she can't go out, looks too bad. Sometimes, she needs lot of makeup, because neck is sensitive skin, man. And hers is bruised. Ring around the collar. Bad. You saw that, maybe. You see her dead, Captain?"

"Yeah, I saw her."

"So then . . ." he hesitated. He seemed to step back, reconsider something. He flicked ash from the cigarette. "So. Was she strangled, or what?"

"Yes, Eddie. She was strangled."

He inhaled. "Yeah. Figures."

"Did you see her, Eddie?"

"Me? No. What are you talking about? How could I see her, Captain?" He exhaled, blowing smoke into the night.

"Eddie. Look at me."

Eddie turned toward Connor.

"Look in my eyes. Now tell me. Did you see the body?"

"No. Captain, come on." Eddie gave a nervous little laugh, and looked away. He flicked the cigarette so it tumbled in the air, dripping sparks. "What is this? Third degree? No. I didn't see the body."

"Eddie."

"I swear to you, Captain."

"Eddie. How are you involved in this?"

"Me? Shit. Not me, Captain. I know the girl, sure. I see her sometimes. I fuck her, sure. What the hell. She's little weird, but she's fun. A fun girl. Great pussy. That's it, man. That's all of it." He looked around, lit another cigarette. "This's a nice cactus garden, huh? Xeriscape, they call it. It's the latest thing. Los Angeles goes back to desert life. It's *hayatterunosa*: very fashionable."

"Eddie."

"Come on, Captain. Give me break here. We know each other long time."

"Sure, Eddie. But I have some problems. What about the security tapes?"

Eddie looked blank, innocent. "Security tapes?"

"A man with a scar on his hand and a tie with triangles on it came into the Nakamoto security office and took the security videotapes."

"*Fuck*. What security office? What're you doing, Captain?"

"Eddie."

"Who said that to you? That's not *true*, man. Take the security tapes? I never did thing like that. What're you, crazy?" He twisted his tie, looked at the label. "This is Polo tie, Captain. Ralph Lauren. Polo. Lot of these ties, bet you."

"Eddie. What about the Imperial Arms?"

"What about it?"

"You go there tonight?"

"No."

"You clean up Cheryl's room?"

"*What?*" Eddie appeared shocked. "*What?* No. Clean up her room? Where you getting all this shit, Captain?"

"The girl across the hall . . . Julia Young," Connor said. "She told us she saw you tonight, with another man. In Cheryl's room at the Imperial Arms."

Eddie threw his arms in the air. "Jesus. Captain. You listen. That girl wouldn't know, she saw me last night or last month, man. That girl is a fucking hophead. You look between her toes you find the marks. You look under her tongue. Look on her pussylips. You find 'em. That's a dream girl, man. She doesn't know when things happen. *Man.* You come here, give me this. I don't like this." Eddie tossed his cigarette away, and immediately lit another. "I don't like this one bit. You don't see what's going on?"

"No," Connor said. "Tell me, Eddie. What's going on?"

"This shit's not true, man. None of this true." He puffed rapidly. "You know what this is about? It's not about some fucking girl, man. It's about Saturday meetings. The *Doyou kai, Connor-san.* The secret meetings. That's what it's about."

Connor snapped, "*Sonna bakana.*"

"No *bakana, Connor-san.* Not bullshit."

"What does a girl from Texas know about *Doyou kai?*"

"She knows something. *Hontō nanda.* And she likes to cause trouble, this girl. She likes to make turmoil."

"Eddie, I think maybe you better come in with us."

"Fine. Perfect. You do their job for them. For the *kuromaku.*" He spun to Connor. "Shit, Captain. Come on. You know how it works. This girl killed at Nakamoto. You know my family, my father, is Daimatsu. Now in Osaka they will read that a girl is killed at Nakamoto and I am arrested in connection. His son."

"Detained."

"Detained. Whatever. You know what that will mean. *Taihennakoto ni naru zo.* My father resign, his company must make apologies to Nakamoto. Perhaps reparations. Give some advantage in business. It is powerful *ōsawagi ni naruzo.* You will do this, if you take me into your custody." He flicked his cigarette away. "Hey. You think I did this murder, you arrest me. Fine. But you are just covering your ass, you maybe do a lot of damage to me. Captain: you know this."

Connor said nothing for a long time. There was a long silence. They walked around the garden, in circles.

Finally, Eddie said, "*Na, Connor-san. Tanomuyo . . .*" His voice sounded pleading. It seemed like he was asking for a break.

Connor sighed. "You got your passport, Eddie?"

"Yeah, sure. Always."

"Let's have it."

"Yeah, sure. Okay, Captain. Here goes."

Connor glanced at it, handed it to me. I slipped it in my pocket.

"Okay, Eddie. But this better not be *murina koto*. Or you'll be declared persona non grata, Eddie. And I will personally put you on the next plane for Osaka. *Wakattaka?*"

"Captain, you protect the honor of my family. *On ni kiru yo.*" And he bowed formally, both hands at his sides.

Connor bowed back.

I just stared. I couldn't believe what I was seeing. Connor was going to let him go. I thought he was crazy to allow it.

I handed Eddie my business card and gave my usual speech about how he could call me later if he thought of anything. Eddie shrugged and slipped the card into his shirt pocket, as he lit another cigarette. I didn't count: he was dealing with Connor.

Eddie started back toward the house, paused. "I have this redhead here, very interesting," he said. "When I leave the party, I go to my house in the hills. You need me, I will be there. Good night, Captain. Good night, Lieutenant."

"Good night, Eddie."

We went back down the steps.

"I hope you know what you are doing," I said.

"So do I," Connor said.

" 'Cause he seems guilty as hell to me."

"Maybe."

"If you ask me, it'd be better to take him in. Safer."

"Maybe."

"Want to go back and get him?"

"No." He shook his head. "My *dai rokkan* says no."

I knew that word: it meant sixth sense. The Japanese were big on intuition. I said, "Yeah, well, I hope you're right."

We continued down the steps in the darkness.

"Anyway," Connor said. "I owe him."

"For what?"

"There was a time, a few years ago, when I needed some information. You remember the *fugu* poisoning business? No? Well anyway, no one in the community would tell me. They stonewalled me. And I needed to know. It was . . . it was important. Eddie told me. He was scared to do it, because he didn't want anyone to know. But he did it. I probably owe my life to him."

We came to the bottom of the stairs.

"And did he remind you of that?"

"He would never remind me. It is my job to remember."

I said, "That's fine, Captain. All that obligation stuff is fine and noble. And I'm all for interracial harmony. But meanwhile, it's possible that he killed her, stole the tapes, and cleaned up the apartment. Eddie Sakamura looks like a blown-out speedball to me. He acts like a suspect. And we're just walking away. Letting him go."

"Right."

We kept walking. I thought it over and got more worried. I said, "You know, officially this is my investigation."

"Officially, it's Graham's investigation."

"Yeah, okay. But we're going to look stupid if it turns out he did it."

Connor sighed, as if he was losing patience. "Okay. Let's go over it the way you think it might have happened. Eddie kills the girl, right?"

"Right."

"He can see her any time but he decides to fuck her on the boardroom table, and he kills her. Then he goes down to the lobby, and pretends to be a Nakamoto executive—even though the last thing Eddie Sakamura looks like is an executive. But let's say he passes himself off. He manages to dismiss the guard. He takes the tapes. He walks out just as Phillips comes in. Then he goes to Cheryl's apartment to clean that up, but somehow he adds a picture of himself, stuck in Cheryl's mirror. Next he stops by the Bora Bora and tells everybody he's going to a party in Hollywood. Where we find him, in a room without furniture, calmly chatting up a redhead. Is that how the evening lays out to you?"

I said nothing. It didn't make much sense, when he put it that way. On the other hand . . .

"I just hope he didn't do it."

"So do I."

We came down to the street level. The valet ran to get our car.

"You know," I said, "the blunt way he talks about things, like putting the bag over her head, it's creepy."

"Oh, that doesn't mean anything," Connor said. "Remember, Japan has never accepted Freud or Christianity. They've never been guilty or embarrassed about sex. No problem with homosexuality, no problem with kinky sex. Just matter-of-fact. Some people like it a certain way, so some people do it that way, what the hell. The Japanese can't understand why we get so worked up about a straightforward bodily function. They think we're a little screwed up on the subject of sex. And they have a point." Connor glanced at his watch.

A security car pulled up. The uniformed guard leaned out. "Hey, is there a problem at the party up there?"

"Like what?"

"Couple of guys get in a fight? Some kind of fight? We had a report phoned in."

"I don't know," Connor said. "Maybe you better go up and check."

The guard climbed out of his car, hefted a big gut, and started up the stairs. Connor looked back at the high walls. "You know we have more private security than police, now? Everyone's building walls and hiring guards. But in Japan, you can walk into a park at midnight and sit on a bench and nothing will happen to you. You're completely safe, day or night. You can go anywhere. You won't be robbed or beaten or killed. You're not always looking behind you, not always worrying. You don't need walls or bodyguards. Your safety is the safety of the whole society. You're free. It's a wonderful feeling. Here, everybody has to lock themselves up. Lock the door. Lock the car. People who spend their whole lives locked up are in prison. It's crazy. It kills the spirit. But it's been so long now that Americans have forgotten what it's like to really feel *safe*. Anyway. Here's our car. Let's get down to the division."

We had started driving down the street when the DHD operator called. "Lieutenant Smith," she said, "we have a request for Special Services."

"I'm pretty busy," I said. "Can the backup take it?"

"Lieutenant Smith, we have patrol officers requesting Special Services for a vee dig in area nineteen."

She was telling me there was a problem with a visiting dignitary. "I understand," I said, "but I've already rolled out on a case. Give it to the backup."

"But this is on Sunset Plaza Drive," she said. "Aren't you located—"

"Yes," I said. Now I understood why she was insistent. The call was only a few blocks away. "Okay," I said. "What's the problem?"

"It's a vee dig DUI. Reported in as G-level plus one. Last name is Rowe."

"Okay," I said. "We're going." I hung up the phone, and turned the car around.

"Interesting," Connor said. "G-level plus one is American government?"

"Yes," I said.

"It's Senator Rowe?"

"Sounds like it," I said. "Driving under the influence."

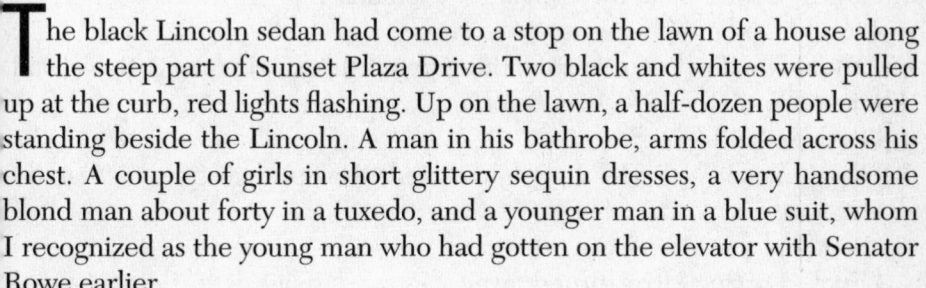

The black Lincoln sedan had come to a stop on the lawn of a house along the steep part of Sunset Plaza Drive. Two black and whites were pulled up at the curb, red lights flashing. Up on the lawn, a half-dozen people were standing beside the Lincoln. A man in his bathrobe, arms folded across his chest. A couple of girls in short glittery sequin dresses, a very handsome blond man about forty in a tuxedo, and a younger man in a blue suit, whom I recognized as the young man who had gotten on the elevator with Senator Rowe earlier.

The patrolmen had the video camera out, shining the bright light on Senator Rowe. He was propping himself up against the front fender of the Lincoln, holding his arm up to cover his face against the light. He was swearing loudly as Connor and I walked up.

The man in the bathrobe came toward us and said, "I want to know who's going to pay for this."

"Just a minute, sir." I kept walking.

"He can't just ruin my lawn like this. It has to be paid for."

"Just give me a minute, sir."

"Scared the hell out of my wife, too, and she has cancer."

I said, "Sir, please give me a minute, and then I'll talk to you."

"Cancer of the *ear*," he said emphatically. "The *ear*."

"Yes, sir. All right, sir." I continued toward the Lincoln, and the bright light.

As I passed the aide, he fell into step beside me and said, "I can explain everything, Detective." He was about thirty, with the bland good looks of a congressional staffer. "I'm sure I can resolve everything."

"Just a minute," I said. "Let me talk to the senator."

"The senator's not feeling well," the aide said. "He's very tired." He stepped in front of me. I just walked around him. He hurried to catch up. "It's jet lag, that's the problem. The senator has jet lag."

"I have to talk to him," I said, stepping into the bright light. Rowe was still holding up his arm. I said, "Senator Rowe?"

"Turn that fucking thing *off,* for fuck's sake," Rowe said. He was heavily intoxicated; his speech so slurred it was difficult to understand him.

"Senator Rowe," I said, "I'm afraid I'll have to ask you to—"

"Fuck you and the horse you rode in on."

"Senator Rowe," I said.

"Turn that fucking camera off."

I looked back to the patrolman and signaled to him. He reluctantly turned the camera off. The light went out.

"Jesus *Christ,*" Rowe said, finally dropping his arm. He looked at me with bleary eyes. "What the fuck is going on here."

I introduced myself.

"Then why don't you *do* something about this *fucking zoo,*" Rowe said. "I'm just driving to my *fucking hotel.*"

"I understand that, Senator."

"Don't know . . ." He waved his hand, a sloppy gesture. "What the fucking *problem* is around here."

"Senator, you were driving this car?"

"Fuck. Driving." He turned away. "Jerry? Explain it to them. Christ's sake."

The aide came up immediately. "I'm sorry about all this," he said smoothly. "The senator isn't feeling at all well. We just came back from Tokyo yesterday evening. Jet lag. He's not himself. He's tired."

"Who was driving the car?" I said.

"I was," the aide said. "Absolutely."

One of the girls giggled.

"No, he wasn't," the man in the bathrobe shouted, from the other side of the car. *"He* was driving it. And he couldn't get out of the car without falling down."

"Christ, fucking zoo," Senator Rowe said, rubbing his head.

"Detective," the aide said, "I was driving the car and these two women here will testify that I was." He gestured to the girls in party dresses. Giving them a look.

"That's a goddamn lie," the man in the bathrobe said.

"No, that's correct," the handsome man in the tuxedo said, speaking for the first time. He had a suntan and a relaxed manner, like he was used to having his orders obeyed. Probably a Wall Street guy. He didn't introduce himself.

"I was driving the car," the aide said.

"All gone to shit," Rowe muttered. "Want to go to my hotel."

"Was anyone hurt here?" I said.

"Nobody was hurt," the aide said. "Everybody is fine."

I asked the patrolmen behind me, "You got a one-ten to file?" That was the report of property damage for vehicular accident.

"We don't need to," a patrolman said to me. "Single car, and the amount doesn't qualify." You only had to fill it out if the damage was more than two hundred dollars. "All we got is a five-oh-one. If you want to run with that."

I didn't. One of the things you learned about in Special Services was SAR, situational appropriate response. SAR meant that in the case of elected officials and celebrities, you let it go unless somebody was going to press charges. In practice, that meant that you didn't make an arrest short of a felony.

I said to the aide, "You get the property owner's name and address, so you can deal with the damage to the lawn."

"He already got my name and address," the man in the bathrobe said. "But I want to know what's going to be *done*."

"I told him we'd repair any damage," the aide said. "I assured him we would. He seems to be—"

"Damn it, look: her planting is *ruined*. And she has *cancer* of the *ear*."

"Just a minute, sir." I said to the aide, "Who's going to drive the car now?"

"I am," the aide said.

"He is," Senator Rowe said, nodding. "Jerry. Drive the car."

I said to the aide, "All right. I want you to take a Breathalyzer—"

"Sure, yes—"

"And I want to see your driver's license."

"Of course."

The aide blew into the Breathalyzer and handed me his driver's license. It was a Texas license. Gerrold D. Hardin, thirty-four years old. Address in Austin, Texas. I wrote down the details, and gave it back.

"All right, Mr. Hardin. I'm going to release the senator into your custody tonight."

"Thank you, Lieutenant. I appreciate it."

The man in the bathrobe said, "You're going to *let him go*?"

"Just a minute, sir." I said to Hardin, "I want you to give this man your business card, and stay in contact with him. I expect the damage to his yard to be resolved to his satisfaction."

"Absolutely. Of course. Yes." Hardin reached into his pocket for a card. He brought out something white in his hand, like a handkerchief. He stuffed it hastily back in his pocket, and then walked over to give his card to the man in the bathrobe.

"You're going to have to replace all her begonias."

"Fine, sir," Hardin said.

"*All* of 'em."

"Yes. That's fine, sir."

Senator Rowe pushed off the front fender, standing unsteadily in the night. "Fucking begonias," he said. "Christ, what a fucking night this is. You got a wife?"

"No," I said.

"I do," Rowe said. "Fucking begonias. Fuck."

"This way, Senator," Hardin said. He helped Rowe into the passenger seat. The girls climbed into the back seat, on either side of the handsome Wall Street guy. Hardin got behind the wheel and asked Rowe for the keys. I looked away to watch the black and whites as they pulled away from the curb. When I turned back, Hardin rolled down the window and looked at me. "Thank you for this."

"Drive safely, Mr. Hardin," I said.

He backed the car off the lawn, driving over a flower bed.

"*And* the irises," the man in the bathrobe shouted, as the car pulled away down the road. He looked at me. "I'm telling you, the other man was driving, and he was drunk."

I said, "Here's my card. If things don't turn out right, call me."

He looked at the card, shaking his head, and went back into his house. Connor and I got back into the car. We drove down the hill.

Connor said, "You got information on the aide?"

"Yes," I said.

"What was in his pocket?"

"I'd say it was a pair of women's panties."

"So would I," Connor said.

Of course there was nothing we could do. Personally, I would have liked to spin the smug bastard around, push him up against the car and search him, right there. But we both knew our hands were tied: we had no probable cause to search Hardin, or to arrest him. He was a young man driving with two young women in the back seat, either of whom might be without her panties, and a drunken United States senator in the front seat. The only sensible thing to do was to let them all go.

But it seemed like an evening of letting people go.

The phone rang. I pushed the speaker button. "Lieutenant Smith."

"Hey, buddy." It was Graham. "I'm over here at the morgue, and guess what? I have some Japanese bugging me to attend the autopsy. Wants to sit in and observe, if you can believe that shit. He's all bent out of shape because we started the autopsy without him. But the lab work is starting to come back. It is not looking good for Nippon Central. I'd say we have a Japanese perp. So: you coming here or what?"

I looked at Connor. He nodded.

"We're heading there now," I said.

The fastest way to the morgue was through the emergency room at County General Hospital. As we went through, a black man covered in blood was sitting up on his gurney, screaming "Kill the pope! Kill the pope! Fuck him!" in a drug-crazed frenzy. A half-dozen attendants were trying to push him down. He had gunshot wounds in his shoulder and hand. The floors and walls of the emergency room were spattered with blood. An orderly went down the hall, cleaning it up with a mop. The hallways were lined with black and Hispanic people. Some of them held children in their laps. Everyone looked away from the bloody mop. From somewhere down the corridor, we heard more screams.

We got onto the elevator. It was quiet.

Connor said, "A homicide every twenty minutes. A rape every seven minutes. A child murdered every four hours. No other country tolerates these levels of violence."

The doors opened. Compared to the emergency room, the basement corridors of the county morgue were positively tranquil. There was a strong odor of formaldehyde. We went to the desk, where the thin, angular diener, Harry Landon, was bent over some papers, eating a ham sandwich. He didn't look up. "Hey, guys."

"Hey, Harry."

"What you here for? Austin prep?"

"Yeah."

"They started about half an hour ago. Guess there's a big rush on her, huh?"

"How's that?"

"The chief called Dr. Tim out of bed and told him to do it pronto. Pissed him off pretty good. You know how particular Dr. Tim is." The diener smiled. "And they called in a lot of lab people, too. Who ever heard of pushing a full workup in the middle of the night? I mean, you know what this is going to cost in overtime?"

I said, "And what about Graham?"

"He's around here someplace. He had some Japanese guy chasing after him. Dogging him like a shadow. Then every half hour, the Japanese asks me can he use the phone, and he makes a call. Speaks Japanese a while. Then he goes back to bothering Graham. He says he wants to see the autopsy, if you can believe that. Keeps pushing, pushing. But anyway, the Japanese makes his last call about ten minutes ago, and suddenly a big change comes over him. I was here at the desk. I saw it on his face. He goes *mojo mojo* like he can't believe his ears. And then he *runs* out of here. I mean it: *runs*."

"And where's the autopsy?"

"Room two."

"Thanks, Harry."

"Close the *door*."

"Hi, Tim," I said, as we came into the autopsy room. Tim Yoshimura, known to everyone as Dr. Tim, was leaning over the stainless-steel table. Even though it was one-forty in the morning, he was as usual immaculate. Everything was in place. His hair was neatly combed. His tie was perfectly knotted. The pens were lined up in the pocket of his starched lab coat.

"Did you *hear* me?"

"I'm closing it, Tim." The door had a pneumatic self-closing mechanism, but apparently that wasn't fast enough for Dr. Tim.

"It's only because I don't want that Japanese individual looking in."

"He's gone, Tim."

"Oh, is he? But he may be back. He's been unbelievably persistent and irritating. The Japanese can be a real pain in the ass."

I said, "Sounds funny coming from you, Tim."

"Oh, I'm not Japanese," he said seriously. "I'm Japanese-American, which means in their eyes I'm *gaijin*. If I go to Japan, they treat me like any other foreigner. It doesn't matter how I look, I was born in Torrance—and that's the end of it." He glanced over his shoulder. "Who's that with you? Not John Connor? Haven't seen you in ages, John."

"Hi, Tim." Connor and I approached the table. I could see the dissection was already well advanced, that the Y-shaped incision had been made, and the first organs removed and placed neatly on stainless-steel trays.

"Now maybe *somebody* can tell me, what is the big deal about this case?" Tim said. "Graham is so pissed off he won't say anything. He went next door to the lab to see the first of the results. But I still want to know why I got called out of bed to do this one. Mark's on duty, but he is apparently not senior enough to do it. And of course the M.E. is out of town at a conference in San Francisco. Now that he has that new girlfriend he is always out of town. So I get called. I can't remember the last time I got called out of bed."

"You can't?" I said. Dr. Tim was precise in all ways, including his memory.

"The last time was January three years ago. But that was to *cover*. Most of the staff was out with the flu, and the cases were backing up. Finally one night we ran out of lockers. They had these bodies lying around on the floor in bags. Stacked up in piles. Something had to be done. The smell was terrible. But no, I can't remember being called out just because a case was politically *tense*. Like this one."

Connor said, "We're not sure why it is tense, either."

"Maybe you better find out. Because there's a lot of pressure here. The M.E. calls me from San Francisco, and he keeps saying, 'Do it now, do it tonight, and get it done.' I say, 'Okay, Bill.' Then he says, 'Listen, Tim. Do this one right. Go slow, take lots of pictures and lots of notes. Document your ass off. Shoot with two cameras. Because I got a feeling that anybody who has anything to do with this case could get into deep shit.' So. It's natural to wonder what the big deal is."

Connor said, "What time was that call to you?"

"About ten-thirty, eleven."

"The M.E. say who called him?"

"No. But it's usually only one of two people: the chief of police or the mayor."

Tim looked at the liver, pulling apart the lobes, then placed it on a steel tray. The assistant was taking flash pictures of each organ and then setting it aside.

"So? What've you found?"

"Frankly, the most interesting findings so far are external," Dr. Tim said. "She had heavy makeup on her neck, to cover a pattern of multiple contusions. Bruises of different ages. Without a spectroscopic curve for the hemoglobin breakdown products at the bruise sites, I'd still say these bruises are of variable age, up to two weeks old. Perhaps older. Consistent with a pattern of repeated, chronic cervical trauma. I don't think there's any question: we're looking at a case of sexual asphyxia."

"She's a gasper?"

"Yeah. She is."

Kelly thought so. For once Kelly was right.

"It's more common in men, but it is certainly reported in women. The syndrome is the individual is sexually aroused only by the hypoxia of near-strangulation. These individuals ask their sexual partners to strangle them, or put a plastic bag over their head. When they're alone, they sometimes tie a cord around their neck, and hang themselves while they masturbate. Since the effect requires that they are strangled almost to the point of passing out, it's easy to make a mistake and go too far. They do, all the time."

"And in this case?"

Tim shrugged. "Well. She has physical findings consistent with a sexual asphyxia syndrome of long standing. And she has ejaculate in her vagina and abrasions on her external vaginal labia, consistent with a forced sexual episode on the same night of her death."

Connor said, "You're sure the vaginal abrasions occurred before death?"

"Oh, yes. They are definitely antemortem injuries. There's no question she had forced sex sometime before she died."

"Are you saying she was raped?"

"No. I wouldn't go that far. As you see, the abrasions are not severe, and there are no associated injuries to other parts of her body. In fact, there are no signs of physical struggle at all. So I would consider the findings consistent with premature vaginal entry with insufficient lubrication of the external labia."

I said, "You're saying she wasn't wet."

Tim looked pained. "Well. In crude layman's terms."

"How long before death did these abrasions occur?"

"It could be as much as an hour or two. It wasn't near the actual time of death. You can tell that from the extravasation and swelling of the affected areas. If death occurs soon after the injury, blood flow stops, and therefore the swelling is limited or absent. In this case, as you see, swelling is quite pronounced."

"And the sperm?"

"Samples have gone to the lab. Along with all her usual fluids." He shrugged. "Have to wait and see. Now, are you two going to fill me in? Because it looks to me like this little girl was going to get in trouble, sooner or later. I mean, she's *cute,* but she's screwed up. So . . . what is the big deal? Why am I out of bed in the middle of the night to do a careful, documented post on some little gasper?"

I said, "Beats me."

"Come on. Fair is fair," Dr. Tim said. "I showed you mine, now you show me yours."

"Why, Tim," Connor said. "You made a joke."

"Fuck you," Tim said. "You guys owe me. Come on."

"I'm afraid Peter is telling you the truth," Connor said. "All we know is that this murder occurred at the time of a big public Japanese reception, and they are eager to get it cleared up right away."

"That makes sense," Tim said. "The last time the shit hit the fan around here, it was because of that thing involving the Japanese consulate.

Remember, the Takashima kidnapping case? Maybe you don't remember: it never made the papers. The Japanese managed to keep it *very* quiet. But anyway, a guard was killed under odd circumstances, and for two days, they put a hell of a pressure on our office. I was amazed what they could do. We had Senator Rowe calling us in person, telling us what to do. The governor calling in person. Everybody calling us. You'd think it was the president's kid. I mean, these people have *influence*."

"Of course they do. They've paid handsomely for it," Graham said, coming into the room.

"Close the *door*," Tim said.

"But this time, all their fucking influence won't help," Graham said. "Because this time, we have them by the short and curlies. We have a murder: and based on the lab results so far, we can say without question that the murderer was Japanese."

The pathology lab next door was a large room lit by even banks of fluorescent lights. Rows of microscopes, neatly laid out. But late at night, only two technicians were working in the big space. And Graham was standing beside them, gloating.

"Look for yourself. Pubic hair comb-through reveals male pubic hair, moderate curl, ovoid cross section, almost certainly Asian in origin. The first semen analysis is blood type: AB, relatively rare among Caucasians, but much more common among Asians. The first analysis of protein in the seminal fluid comes up negative for the genetic marker for . . . what's it called?"

"Ethanol dehydrogenase," the technician said.

"Right. Ethanol dehydrogenase. It's an enzyme. Missing in Japanese. And missing in this seminal fluid. And there's the Diego factor, which is a blood-group protein. So. We have more tests coming, but it seems clear that this girl had forced sex with a Japanese man before she was killed by him."

"It's clear you've found evidence of Japanese semen in her vagina," Connor said. "That's all."

"Christ," Graham said. "Japanese semen, Japanese pubic hair, Japanese blood factors. We are talking a Japanese perp here."

He had set out some pictures from the crime scene, showing Cheryl lying on the boardroom table. He started to pace back and forth in front of them.

"I know where you guys have been, and I know you've been wasting your time," Graham said. "You went for videotapes: but they're gone, right? Then you went to her apartment: but it was cleaned up before you ever got there. Which is exactly what you'd expect if the perp is Japanese. It lays right out, plain as can be."

Graham pointed to the pictures. "There's our girl. Cheryl Austin from Texas. She's cute. Fresh. Good figure. She's an actress, sort of. She does a few commercials. Maybe a Nissan commercial. Whatever. She meets some people. Makes some contacts. Gets on some lists. You with me?"

"Yes," I said to Graham. Connor was staring intently at the pictures.

"One way or another, our Cheryl's doing well enough to be wearing a black Yamamoto gown when she gets invited to the grand opening of the Nakamoto Tower. She comes with some guy, maybe a friend or a hair-dresser. A beard. Maybe she knows other people at the party, and maybe not. But in the course of the evening, somebody big and powerful suggests they slip away for a while. She agrees to go upstairs. Why not? This girl likes adventure. She likes danger. She's cruising for a bruising. So she goes upstairs—maybe with the other guy, maybe separately. But anyway, they meet upstairs, and they look around for a place to do it. A place that's exciting. And they decide—him, probably, *he* decides—to do it right on the fucking boardroom table. So they start doing it, they're whanging away but things get out of hand. Her loverboy gets a little too worked up, or else he's kinky, and . . . he squeezes her neck a little too hard. And she's dead. You with me so far?"

"Yes . . ."

"So now loverboy has a problem. He's come upstairs to fuck a girl, but unfortunately he's killed her. So what does he do? What *can* he do? He goes back down, rejoins the party, and since he is a big samurai cocksman, he tells one of his underlings that he has this little problem. He has unfortu-nately snuffed out the life of a local whore. Very inconvenient for his busy schedule. So the underlings run around and clean up the boss's mess. They clean up incriminating evidence from the floor upstairs. They remove the videotapes. They go to her apartment and remove evidence there. Which is all fine, except it takes time. So somebody has to stall the police. And that's where their smoothie suckass lawyer Ishiguro comes in. He delays us a good hour and a half. So. How does that sound?"

There was a silence when he had finished. I waited for Connor to speak.

"Well," Connor said, at last. "My hat is off to you, Tom. That sequence of events sounds correct in many respects."

"You're damned right it does." Graham puffed up. "Damn fucking right."

The telephone rang. The lab technician said, "Is there a Captain Connor here?"

Connor went to answer the phone. Graham said to me, "I'm telling you. A Jap killed this girl, and we are going to find him and fucking flay him. *Flay* him."

I said, "Why do you have it in for them, anyway?"

Graham gave me a sullen look. He said, "What are you talking about?"

"I'm talking about how you hate the Japanese."

"Hey, listen," Graham said. "Let's get something straight, Petey-san. I don't hate anybody. I do my job. Black man, white man, Japanese man, it makes no difference to me."

"Okay, Tom." It was late at night. I didn't want to argue.

"No, hell. You fucking think I'm prejudiced."

"Let's just drop it, Tom."

"No, hell. We're not going to drop it. Not now. Let me tell you something, Petey-san. You got yourself this fucking liaison job, isn't that right?"

"That's right, Tom."

"And how come you applied for it? Because of your great love of Japanese culture?"

"Well, at the time, I was working in the press office—"

"No, no, cut the shit. You applied for it," Graham said, "because there was an extra stipend, isn't that right? Two, three thousand a year. An educational stipend. It comes into the department from the Japan-America Amity Foundation. And the department allows it as an educational stipend, paid to members of the force so that they can further their education in Japanese language and culture. So. How're those studies going, Petey-san?"

"I'm studying."

"How often?"

"One night a week."

"One night a week. And if you miss classes, do you lose your stipend?"

"No."

"Fucking right you don't. In fact, it doesn't make any difference if you go to classes at all. The fact is, buddy, you got yourself a bribe. You got three thousand dollars in your pocket and it comes right from the land of the rising sun. Of course, it's not that much. Nobody can buy you for three grand, right? Of course not."

"Hey, Tom—"

"But the thing is, they aren't buying you. They're just *influencing* you. They just want you to think twice. To tend to look favorably upon them. And why not? It's human nature. They've made your life a little better. They contribute to your well-being. Your family. Your little girl. They scratch your back, so why shouldn't you scratch theirs? Isn't that about it, Petey-san?"

"No, it isn't," I said. I was getting angry.

"Yes, it is," Graham said. "Because that's how influence works. It's deniable. You say it isn't there. You tell yourself it isn't there—but it is. The only way you can be clean is to be *clean,* man. If you got no stake in it, if you got no income from it, then you can talk. Otherwise, man, they pay you and I say, they *own* you."

"Just a fucking minute—"

"So don't you talk to me about *hating,* man. This country is in a war and some people understand it, and some other people are siding with the enemy. Just like in World War II, some people were paid by Germany to promote Nazi propaganda. New York newspapers published editorials right out of the mouth of Adolf Hitler. Sometimes the people didn't even know it. But they did it. That's how it is in a war, man. And *you* are a fucking collaborator."

I was grateful when, at that moment, Connor came back to where we were standing. Graham and I were about to square off when Connor said calmly, "Now, just so I understand, Tom. According to your scenario, after the girl was murdered, what happened to the tapes?"

"Oh, hell, those tapes are *gone,*" Graham said. "You're never going to see those tapes again."

"Well, it's interesting. Because that call was the division headquarters. It seems Mr. Ishiguro is there. And he's brought a box of videotapes with him, for me to look at."

Connor and I drove over. Graham took his own car. I said, "Why did you say the Japanese would never touch Graham?"

"Graham's uncle," Connor said. "He was a prisoner of war during World War II. He was taken to Tokyo, where he disappeared. Graham's father went over after the war to find out what happened to him. There were unpleasant questions about what happened. You probably know that some American servicemen were killed in terminal medical experiments in Japan. There were stories about the Japanese feeding their livers to subordinates as a joke, things like that."

"No, I didn't know," I said.

"I think everybody would prefer to forget that time," Connor said, "and move on. And probably correctly. It's a different country now. What was Graham going on about?"

"My stipend as a liaison officer."

Connor said, "You told me it was fifty a week."

"It's a little more than that."

"How much more?"

"About a hundred dollars a week. Fifty-five hundred a year. But that's to cover classes, and books, and commuting expenses, baby-sitters, everything."

"So you get five grand," Connor said. "So what?"

"Graham was saying I was influenced by it. That the Japanese had bought me."

Connor said, "Well, they certainly try to do that. And they're extremely subtle."

"They tried it with you?"

"Oh, sure." He paused. "And often I accepted. Giving gifts to ensure that you will be seen favorably is something the Japanese do by instinct. And it's not so different from what we do, when we invite the boss over for dinner. Goodwill is goodwill. But we don't invite the boss over for dinner when we're up for a promotion. The proper thing to do is to invite the boss early in the relationship, when nothing is at stake. Then it's just goodwill. The same with the Japanese. They believe you should give the gift early, because then it is not a bribe. It is a gift. A way of making a relationship with you before there is any pressure on the relationship."

"And you think that's okay?"

"I think it's the way the world works."

"Do you think it's corrupting?"

Connor looked at me and said, "Do you?"

I took a long time to answer. "Yes. I think maybe so."

He started to laugh. "Well, that's a relief," he said. "Because otherwise, the Japanese would have wasted all their money on you."

"What's so funny?"

"Your confusion, *kōhai*."

"Graham thinks it's a war."

Connor said, "Well, that's true. We are definitely at war with Japan. But let's see what surprises Mr. Ishiguro has for us in the latest skirmish."

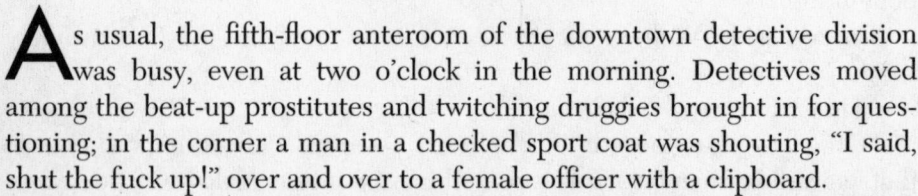

As usual, the fifth-floor anteroom of the downtown detective division was busy, even at two o'clock in the morning. Detectives moved among the beat-up prostitutes and twitching druggies brought in for questioning; in the corner a man in a checked sport coat was shouting, "I said, shut the fuck up!" over and over to a female officer with a clipboard.

In all the swirl and noise, Masao Ishiguro looked distinctly out of place. Wearing his blue pinstripe suit, he sat in the corner with his head bowed and his knees pressed together. He had a cardboard box balanced on his knees.

When he saw us, he jumped to his feet. He bowed deeply, placing his hands flat on his thighs, a sign of additional respect. He held the bow for several seconds. Then he immediately bowed again, and this time he waited, bent over, staring at the floor, until Connor spoke to him in Japanese. Ishiguro's reply, also in Japanese, was quiet and deferential. He kept looking at the floor.

Tom Graham pulled me over by the water cooler. "Holy Christ," he said. "It looks like we got a fucking *confession* happening here."

"Yeah, maybe," I said. I wasn't convinced. I'd seen Ishiguro change his demeanor before.

I watched Connor as he talked to Ishiguro. The Japanese man remained hangdog. He kept looking at the floor.

"I never would have figured him," Graham said. "Not in a million years. Never him."

"How is that?"

"Are you kidding? To kill the girl, and then to stay in the room, and order us around. What fucking nerves of steel. But look at him now: Christ, he's almost *crying.*"

It was true: tears seemed to be welling up in Ishiguro's eyes. Connor took the box and turned away, crossing the room to us. He gave me the box. "Deal with this. I'm going to take a statement from Ishiguro."

"So," Graham said. "Did he confess?"

"To what?"

"The murder."

"Hell, no," Connor said. "What makes you think that?"

"Well, he's over there bowing and scraping—"

"That's just *sumimasen*," Connor said. "I wouldn't take it too seriously."

"He's practically crying," Graham said.

"Only because he thinks it'll help him."

"He didn't confess?"

"No. But he discovered that the tapes had been removed, after all. That means he made a serious mistake, with his public blustering in front of the mayor. Now he could be accused of concealing evidence. He could be disbarred. His corporation could be disgraced. Ishiguro is in big trouble, and he knows it."

I said, "And that's why he's so humble?"

"Yes. In Japan, if you screw up, the best thing is to go to the authorities and make a big show of how sorry you are, and how bad you feel, and how you will never do it again. It's pro forma, but the authorities will be impressed by how you've learned your lesson. That's *sumimasen:* apology without end. It's the Japanese version of throwing yourself on the mercy of the court. It's understood to be the best way to get leniency. And that's all Ishiguro is doing."

"You mean it's an act," Graham said, his eyes hardening.

"Yes and no. It's difficult to explain. Look. Review the tapes. Ishiguro says he brought one of the VCRs, because the tapes are recorded in an unusual format, and he was afraid we wouldn't be able to play them. Okay?"

I opened the cardboard box. I saw twenty small eight-millimeter cartridges, like audio cassette cartridges. And I saw a small box, the size of a Walkman, which was the VCR. It had cables to hook to a TV.

"Okay," I said. "Let's have a look."

The first of the tapes that showed the forty-sixth floor was a view from the atrium camera, high up, looking down. The tape showed people working on the floor, in what looked like an ordinary office day. We fast-forwarded through that. Shadows of sunlight coming through the windows swung in hot arcs across the floor, and then disappeared. Gradually, the light on the floor softened and dimmed, as daylight came to an end. One by one, desk lights came on. The workers moved more slowly now. Eventually they began to depart, leaving their desks one by one. As the population thinned, we noticed something else. Now the camera moved occasionally, panning one or another of the workers as they passed beneath. Yet at other times, the camera would not pan. Eventually we realized the camera must be equipped for automatic focusing and tracking. If there was a lot of movement in the frame—several people going in different directions—then the camera did not move. But if the frame was mostly empty, the camera would fix on a single person walking through, and track him.

"Funny system," Graham said.

"It probably makes sense for a security camera," I said. "They'd be much more concerned about a single person on the floor than a crowd."

As we watched, the night lights came on. The desks were all empty. Now the tape began to flicker rapidly, almost like a strobe.

"Something wrong with this tape?" Graham said, suspiciously. "They fucked around with it?"

"I don't know. No, wait. It's not that. Look at the clock."

On the far wall, we could see the office clock. The minute hands were sweeping smoothly from seven-thirty toward eight o'clock.

"It's time lapse," I said.

"What is it, taking snapshots?"

I nodded. "Probably, when the system doesn't detect anybody for a while, it begins to take single frames every ten or twenty seconds, until—"

"Hey. What's that?"

The flickering had stopped. The camera had begun to pan to the right, across the deserted floor. But there was nobody in the frame. Just empty desks, and occasional night lights, which flared in the video.

"Maybe they have a wide sensor," I said. "That looks beyond the borders of the image itself. Either that, or it's being moved manually. By a guard, somewhere. Maybe down in the security room."

The panning image came to rest on the elevator doors. The doors were at the far right, in deep shadow, beneath a kind of ceiling overhang that blocked our view.

"Jeez, dark under there. Is someone there?"

"I can't see anything," I said.

The image began to swim in and out of focus.

"What's happening now?" Graham said.

"Looks like the automatic focus is having trouble. Maybe it can't decide what to focus on. Maybe the overhang is bothering the logic circuits. My video camera at home does the same thing. The focus gets screwed up when it can't tell what I am shooting."

"So is the camera trying to focus on something? Because I can't see anything. It just looks black under there."

"No, look. There's someone there. You can see pale legs. Very faint."

"Christ," Graham said, "that's our girl. Standing by the elevator. No, wait. Now she's moving."

A moment later, Cheryl Austin stepped from beneath the ceiling overhang, and we saw her clearly for the first time.

She was beautiful and assured. She moved unhesitatingly into the room. She was direct, purposeful in her movements, with none of the awkward, shuffling sloppiness of the young.

"Jesus, she's good-looking," Graham said.

Cheryl Austin was tall and slender; her short blond hair made her seem even taller. Her carriage was erect. She turned slowly, surveying the room as if she owned it.

"I can't believe we're seeing this," Graham said.

I knew what he meant. This was a girl who had been killed just a few hours before. Now we were seeing her on a videotape, walking around just minutes before her death.

On the monitor, Cheryl picked up a paperweight on one of the desks, turned it in her hand, put it back. She opened her purse, closed it again. She glanced at her watch.

"Starting to fidget."

"She doesn't like to be kept waiting," Graham said. "And I bet she doesn't have much practice at it, either. Not a girl like that."

She began to tap on the desk with her fingers in a distinct rhythm. It seemed familiar to me. She bobbed her head to the rhythm. Graham squinted at the screen, "Is she talking? Is she saying something?"

"It looks like it," I said. We could barely see her mouth moving. And then I suddenly put it together, her movements, everything. I realized I could sync her lips. "I chew my nails and I twiddle my thumbs. I'm real nervous but it sure is fun. Oh baby, you drive me crazy . . ."

"Jesus," Graham said. "You're right. How'd you know that?"

"Goodness, gracious, great balls of—"

Cheryl stopped singing. She turned toward the elevators.

"Ah. Here we go."

Cheryl walked toward the elevators. Just as she stepped beneath the overhang, she threw her arms around the man who had arrived. They embraced and kissed warmly. But the man remained beneath the overhang. We could see his arms around Cheryl, but we could not see his face.

"Shit," Graham said.

"Don't worry," I said. "We'll see him in a minute. If not this camera, another camera. But I think we can say this is not somebody she just met. This is somebody she already knows."

"Not unless she's *real* friendly. Yeah, look. This guy isn't wasting any time."

The man's hands slid up the black dress, raising her skirt. He squeezed her buttocks. Cheryl Austin pressed against his body. Their clinch was intense, passionate. Together they moved deeper into the room, turning slowly. Now the man's back was to us. Her skirt was bunched around her waist. She reached down to rub his crotch. The couple half walked, half stumbled to the nearest desk. The man bent her back against the desk and suddenly she protested, pushing him away.

"Ah, ah. Not so fast," Graham said. "Our girl has standards, after all."

I wondered if that was it. Cheryl seemed to have led him on, then changed her mind. I noticed that she had changed moods almost instantaneously. It made me wonder if she had been acting all along, if her passion was faked. Certainly the man did not seem particularly surprised by her sudden change. Sitting up on the desk, she kept pushing at him, almost angrily. The man stepped away. His back was still to us. We couldn't see his face. As soon as he had stepped back, she changed again: smiling, kittenish now. With slow movements, she got off the desk and adjusted her skirt, twisting her body provocatively as she looked around. We could see his ear and the side of his face, just enough to see that his jaw was moving. He was talking to her. She smiled at him, and came forward, slid her arms around his neck. Then they began kissing again, their hands moving over each other. Walking slowly through the office, toward the conference room.

"So. Did she choose the conference room?"

"Hard to say."

"Shit, I still can't see his face."

By now they were near the center of the room, and the camera was shooting almost directly down. All we saw was the top of his head.

I said, "Does he look Japanese to you?"

"Fuck. Who can tell. How many other cameras were in that room?"

"Four others."

"Well. His face can't be blocked in all four. We'll nail his ass."

I said, "You know, Tom, this guy looks pretty big. He looks taller than she is. And she was a tall girl."

"Who can tell, in this angle? I can't tell anything except he has a suit on. Okay. There they go, toward the conference room."

As they approached the room, she suddenly began to struggle.

"Oops," Graham said. "She's unhappy again. Moody young thing, isn't she?"

The man gripped her tightly and she spun, trying to twist free. He half carried her, half dragged her to the room. At the doorway, she spun a final time, grabbed the door frame, struggling.

"She lose the purse there?"

"Probably. I can't see clearly."

The conference room was located directly opposite the camera, so we had a view of the entire room. But the interior of the conference room was very dark, so the two people were silhouetted against the lights of the sky-scrapers through the outer glass windows. The man lifted her up in his arms and set her down on the table, rolled her onto her back. She became pas-sive, liquid, as he slid her skirt up her hips. She seemed to be accepting, moving to meet him, and then he made a quick movement between their bodies, and suddenly something flew away.

"There go the panties."

It looked as if they landed on the floor. But it was hard to tell for sure. If they were panties, they were black, or some other dark color. So much, I thought, for Senator Rowe.

"The panties were gone by the time we got there," Graham said, staring at the monitor. "Fucking withholding of evidence, pure and simple." He rubbed his hands together. "You got any Nakamoto stock, buddy, I'd sell it. 'Cause it isn't going to be worth shit by tomorrow afternoon."

On the screen, she was still welcoming him, and he was fumbling with his zipper, when suddenly she tried to sit up, and slapped him hard on the face.

Graham said, "There we go. A little *spice*."

The man grabbed her hands, and tried to kiss her, but she resisted him, turning her face away. He pushed her back on the table. He leaned his weight on her body, holding her there. Her bare legs kicked and churned.

The two silhouettes merged and separated. It was difficult to determine exactly what was happening. It looked as if Cheryl kept trying to sit up, and the man kept shoving her back. He held her down, one hand on her upper chest, while her legs kicked at him, and her body twisted on the table. He still held her on the table, but the whole scene was more arduous than arousing. As it continued, I had trouble with the image I was seeing. Was this a genuine rape? Or was she play-acting? After all, she kept kicking and struggling, but she wasn't succeeding in pushing him away. The man might be stronger than she was, but I had the feeling that she could have kicked him back if she had really wanted to. And sometimes it looked as if her arms were locked around his neck, instead of trying to push him away. But it was difficult to know for sure when we were seeing—

"Uh-oh. Trouble."

The man stopped his rhythmic pumping. Beneath him, Cheryl went limp. Her arms slid away from his shoulders, dropped back on the table. Her legs fell slack on either side of him.

Graham said, "Is that it? Did it just happen?"

"I can't tell."

The man patted her cheek, then shook her more vigorously. He seemed to be talking to her. He remained there for a while, maybe thirty seconds, and then he slipped away from her body. She stayed on the table. He walked around her. He was moving slowly, as if he could not believe it.

Then he looked off to the left, as if he had heard a sound. He stood frozen for a moment, and then he seemed to make up his mind. He went into action, moving around the room, looking in a methodical way. He picked up something from the floor.

"The panties."

"He took 'em himself," Graham said. "Shit."

Now the man moved around the girl, and bent briefly over her body on the far side.

"What's he doing there?"

"I don't know. I can't see."

"Shit."

The man straightened and moved away from the conference room, back into the atrium. He was no longer silhouetted. There was a chance we could identify him. But he was looking back into the conference room. Back at the dead girl.

"Hey, buddy," Graham said, talking to the image on the monitor. "Look over here, buddy. Come on. Just for a minute."

On the screen, the man continued to look at the dead girl as he took several more steps into the atrium. Then he began to walk quickly away to the left.

"He's not going back to the elevators," I said.

"No. But I can't see his *face*."

"Where is he going?"

"There's a stairwell at the far end," Graham said. "Fire exit."

"Why is he going there, instead of the elevator?"

"Who knows? I just want to see his face. Just once."

But now the man was to the far left of our camera, and even though he was no longer turned away, we could see only his left ear and cheekbone. He walked quickly. Soon he would be gone from our view, beneath the ceiling overhang at the far end of the room.

"Ah, shit. This angle's no good. Let's look at another tape."

"Just a minute," I said.

Our man was moving toward a dark passageway that must lead to the staircase. But as he went, he passed a decorative gilt-frame mirror hanging on the wall, right by the passage. He passed it just as he went under the overhang, into final darkness.

"There!"

"How do you stop this thing?"

I was pressing buttons on the player frantically. I finally found the one that stopped it. We went back. Then forward again.

Again, the man moved purposefully toward the dark passage, with long, quick strides. He moved past the mirror, and for an instant—a single video frame—we could see his face reflected in the mirror—see it clearly—and I pressed the button to freeze the frame—

"Bingo," I said.

"A fucking Jap," Graham said. "Just like I told you."

Frozen in the mirror was the face of the killer as he strode toward the stairwell. I had no trouble recognizing the tense features of Eddie Sakamura.

This one is mine," Graham said. "It's my case. I'm going to go bring the bastard in."

"Sure," Connor said.

"I mean," Graham said, "I'd rather go alone."

"Of course," Connor said. "It's your case, Tom. Do whatever you think best."

Connor wrote down Eddie Sakamura's address for him.

"It's not that I don't appreciate your help," Graham said. "But I'd rather handle it myself. Now, just so I have my facts straight: you guys talked to this guy earlier tonight, and you didn't bring him in?"

"That's right."

"Well, don't worry about it," Graham said. "I'll bury that in the report. It won't come back to you, I promise you." Graham was in a magnanimous mood, pleased at the prospect of arresting Sakamura. He glanced at his watch. "Fucking A. Less than six hours since the original call, and we already have the murderer. Not bad."

"We don't have the murderer quite yet," Connor said. "I'd bring him in right away, if I were you."

"I'm leaving now," Graham said.

"Oh, and Tom," Connor said, as Graham headed toward the door.

"Eddie Sakamura is a strange guy, but he's not known to be violent. I doubt very much that he's armed. He probably doesn't even own a gun. He went home from the party with a redhead. He's probably in bed with her now. I think it would be advisable to bring him in alive."

"Hey," Graham said. "What is it with you two?"

"Just a suggestion," Connor said.

"You really think I'm going to shoot this little shithead?"

"You'll go out there with a couple of black and whites for backup, won't you?" Connor said. "The patrolmen might be excitable. I'm just giving you the background."

"Hey. Thanks for your fucking support," Graham said, and he left. He was so broad, he had to turn slightly sideways to go through the door.

I watched him go. "Why are you letting him do this alone?"

Connor shrugged. "It's his case."

"But you've been aggressive all night in pursuing his case. Why stop now?"

Connor said. "Let Graham have the glory. After all, what has it got to do with us? I'm a cop on extended leave. And you're just a corrupt liaison officer." He pointed to the videotape. "You want to run that for me, before you give me a ride home?"

"Sure." I rewound the tape.

"I was thinking we could get a cup of coffee, too," Connor said. "They make a good one in the SID labs. At least, they used to."

I said, "You want me to get coffee while you look at the tape?"

"That would be nice, *kōhai*," Connor said.

"Sure." I started the tape for him, and turned to leave.

"Oh, and *kōhai*. While you're down there, ask the night duty officer what facilities the department has for videotapes. Because all these need to be duplicated. And we may need hard copies of individual frames. Especially if there's trouble about Sakamura's arrest as Japan-bashing by the department. We may need to release a picture. To defend ourselves."

It was a good point. "Okay," I said. "I'll check."

"And I take mine black with one sugar." He turned to look at the monitor.

The scientific investigation division, or SID, was in the basement of Parker Center. It was after two in the morning when I got there, and most of the sections were closed down. SID was pretty much a nine-to-five operation. Of course, the teams worked at night collecting evidence from crime scenes, but the evidence was then stored in lockers, either downtown or at one of the divisions, until the next morning.

I went to the coffee machine, in the little cafeteria next to Latent Prints. All around the room were signs reading DID YOU WASH YOUR HANDS? THIS MEANS YOU and DON'T EXPOSE FELLOW OFFICERS TO RISK. WASH YOUR HANDS. The reason was that the SID teams used poisons, especially Criminalistics. There was so much mercury, arsenic, and chromium floating around that in the old days, officers had sometimes gotten sick by drinking from a Styrofoam cup that another lab worker had merely touched.

But these days people were more careful; I got two cups of coffee and went back to the night-duty desk. Jackie Levine was on duty, with her feet up on the desk. She was a heavyset woman wearing toreador pants and an orange wig. Despite her bizarre appearance, she was widely acknowledged to be the best print lifter in the department. She was reading *Modern Bride* magazine. I said, "You going to do it again, Jackie?"

"Hell, no," she said. "My daughter."

"Who's she marrying?"

"Let's talk about something happy," she said. "One of those coffees for me?"

"Sorry," I said. "But I have a question for you. Who handles videotape evidence here?"

"Videotape evidence?"

"Like tape from surveillance cameras. Who analyzes it, makes hard copies, all that?"

"Well, we don't get much call for that," Jackie said. "Electronics used to do it here, but I think they gave it up. Nowadays, video either goes to Valley or Medlar Hall." She sat forward, thumbed through a directory. "If you want, you can talk to Bill Harrelson over at Medlar. But if it's anything special, I think we farm it out to JPL or the Advanced Imaging Lab at U.S.C. You want the contact numbers, or you want to go through Harrelson?"

Something in her tone told me what to do. "Maybe I'll take the contact numbers."

"Yeah, I would."

I wrote the numbers down and went back up to the division. Connor had finished the tape and was running it back and forth at the point where Sakamura's face appeared in the mirror.

"Well?" I said.

"That's Eddie, all right." He appeared calm, almost indifferent. He took the coffee from me and sipped it. "Terrible."

"Yeah, I know."

"It used to be better." Connor set the cup aside, turned off the video recorder, stood, and stretched. "Well, I think we've done a good evening's work. What do you say we get some sleep? I have a big golf game in the morning at Sunset Hills."

"Okay," I said. I packed the tapes back in the cardboard box, and set the VCR carefully in the box, too.

Connor said, "What're you going to do with those tapes?"

"I'll put 'em in the evidence locker."

Connor said, "These are the originals. And we don't have duplicates."

"I know, but I can't get dupes made until tomorrow."

"Exactly my point. Why don't you keep them with you?"

"Take them home?" There were all sorts of departmental injunctions about taking evidence home. It was against the rules, to put it mildly.

He shrugged. "I wouldn't leave this to chance. Take the tapes with you, and then you can arrange the duplication yourself, tomorrow."

I stuck them under my arm. I said, "You don't think anybody at the department would—"

"Of course not," Connor said. "But this evidence is crucial and we wouldn't want anybody to walk by the evidence locker with a big magnet while we were asleep, would we?"

So in the end I took the tapes. As we went out the door, we passed Ishiguro, still sitting there, contrite. Connor said something quickly to him in Japanese. Ishiguro jumped to his feet, bowed quickly, and scurried out of the office.

"Is he really so scared?"

"Yes," Connor said.

Ishiguro moved quickly down the hall ahead of us, head bent low. He seemed almost a caricature of a mousy, frightened man.

"Why?" I said. "He's lived here long enough to know that any case we might have against him for withholding evidence is not strong. And we have even less of a case against Nakamoto."

"That's not the point," Connor said. "He's not worried about legalities. He's worried about scandal. Because that's what would happen if we were in Japan."

We came around the corner. Ishiguro was standing by the banks of elevators, waiting. We waited, too. There was an awkward moment. The first elevator came, and Ishiguro stepped away for us to get on. The doors closed on him bowing to us in the lobby. The elevator started down.

Connor said, "In Japan, he and his company could be finished forever."

"Why?"

"Because in Japan, scandal is the most common way of revising the pecking order. Of getting rid of a powerful opponent. It's a routine procedure over there. You uncover a vulnerability, and you leak it to the press, or to government investigators. A scandal inevitably follows, and the person or organization is ruined. That's how the Recruit scandal brought down Takeshita as prime minister. Or the financial scandals brought down Prime Minister Tanaka in the seventies. It's the same way the Japanese screwed General Electric a couple of years ago."

"They screwed General Electric?"

"In the Yokogawa scandal. You heard of it? No? Well, it's classic Japanese maneuvering. A few years ago, General Electric made the best scanning equipment in the world for hospitals. GE formed a subsidiary, Yokogawa Medical, to market this equipment in Japan. And GE did business the Japanese way: cutting costs below competitors to get market share, providing excellent service and support, entertaining customers—giving potential buyers air tickets and traveler's checks. We'd call it bribes, but it's standard business procedure in Japan. Yokogawa quickly became the market leader, ahead of Japanese companies like Toshiba. The Japanese companies didn't like that and complained about unfairness. And one day government agents raided Yokogawa's offices and found evidence of the bribes. They arrested several Yokogawa employees, and blackened the company name in scandal. It didn't hurt GE sales in Japan very much. It didn't matter that other Japanese companies also offer bribes. For some reason, it was the non-Japanese company that got caught. Amazing, how that happens."

I said, "Is it really that bad?"

"The Japanese can be tough," Connor said. "They say 'business is war,' and they mean it. You know how Japan is always telling us that their markets are open. Well, in the old days, if a Japanese bought an American car, he got audited by the government. So pretty soon, nobody bought an American car. The officials shrug: what can they do? Their market is open: they can't help it if nobody wants an American car. The obstructions are endless. Every imported car has to be individually tested on the dock to make sure it complies with exhaust-emission laws. Foreign drugs can only be tested in Japanese laboratories on Japanese nationals. Foreign skis were once banned because Japanese snow was said to be wetter than European and American snow. That's the way they treat other countries, so it's not surprising they worry about getting a taste of their own medicine."

"Then Ishiguro is waiting for some scandal? Because that's what would happen in Japan?"

"Yes. He's afraid that Nakamoto will be finished in a single stroke. But I doubt that it will. Chances are, it'll be business as usual in Los Angeles tomorrow."

❋   ❋   ❋

I drove Connor back to his apartment. As he climbed out of the car I said, "Well, it's been interesting, Captain. Thanks for spending the time with me."

"You're welcome," Connor said. "Call me any time, if you need help in the future."

"I hope your golf game isn't too early tomorrow."

"Actually, it's at seven, but at my age I don't need much sleep. I'll be playing at the Sunset Hills."

"Isn't it a Japanese course?" The purchase of the Sunset Hills Country Club was one of the more recent outrages in L.A. The West Los Angeles golf course was bought for a huge cash price: two hundred million dollars in 1990. At the time, the new Japanese owners said no changes would be made. But now, the American membership was slowly being reduced by a simple procedure: whenever an American retired, his place was offered to a Japanese. Sunset Hills memberships were sold in Tokyo for a million dollars each, where they were considered a bargain; there was a long waiting list.

"Well," Connor said, "I'm playing with some Japanese."

"You do that often?"

"The Japanese are avid golfers, as you know. I try to play twice a week. Sometimes you hear things of interest. Good night, *kōhai*."

"Good night, Captain."

I drove home.

I was pulling onto the Santa Monica freeway when the phone rang. It was the DHD operator. "Lieutenant, we have a Special Services call. Officers in the field request assistance of the liaison."

I sighed. "Okay." She gave me the mobile number.

"Hey, buddy."

It was Graham. I said, "Hi, Tom."

"You alone yet?"

"Yeah. I'm heading home. Why?"

"I was thinking," Graham said. "Maybe we should have the Japanese liaison on hand for this bust."

"I thought you wanted to do it alone."

"Yeah, well, maybe you want to come over and help out with this bust. Just so everything is done by the book."

I said, "Is this a CYA?" I meant cover your ass.

"Hey. You going to help me out, or not?"

"Sure, Tom. I'm on my way."

"We'll wait for you."

Eddie Sakamura lived in a small house on one of those narrow twisting streets high in the Hollywood hills above the 101 freeway. It was 2:45 a.m. when I came around a curve and saw the two black and whites with their lights off, and Graham's tan sedan, parked to one side. Graham was standing with the patrolmen, smoking a cigarette. I had to go back a dozen meters to find a place to park. Then I walked over to them.

We looked up at Eddie's house, built over a garage at street level. It was one of those two-bedroom white stucco houses from the 1940s. The lights were on, and we heard Frank Sinatra singing. Graham said, "He's not alone. He's got some broads up there."

I said, "How do you want to handle it?"

Graham said, "We leave the boys here. I told 'em no shooting, don't worry. You and I go up and make the bust."

Steep stairs ran up from the garage to the house.

"Okay. You take the front and I'll take the back?"

"Hell, no," Graham said. "I want you with me, buddy. He's not dangerous, right?"

I saw the silhouette of a woman pass one of the windows. She looked naked. "Shouldn't be," I said.

"Okay then, let's do it."

We started up the stairs single file. Frank Sinatra was singing "My Way." We heard the laughter of women. It sounded like more than one. "Christ, I hope they got some fucking drugs out."

I thought the chances of that were pretty good. We reached the top of the stairs, ducking to avoid being seen through the windows.

The front door was Spanish, heavy and solid. Graham paused. I moved a few steps toward the back of the house, where I saw the greenish glow of pool lights. There was probably a back door going out to the pool. I was trying to see where it was.

Graham tapped my shoulder. I came back. He gently turned the handle

465

of the front door. It was unlocked. Graham took out his revolver and looked at me. I took out my gun.

He paused, held up three fingers. Count of three.

Graham kicked the front door open and went in low, shouting "Hold it, police! Hold it right there!" Before I got into the living room, I could hear the women screaming.

There were two of them, completely naked, running around the room and shrieking at the top of their lungs, "Eddie! Eddie!" Eddie wasn't there. Graham was shouting, "Where is he? Where is Eddie Sakamura?" The redhead grabbed a pillow from the couch to cover herself, and screamed, "Get out of here, you fucker!" and then she threw the pillow at Graham. The other girl, a blonde, ran squealing into the bedroom. We followed her, and the redhead threw another pillow at us.

In the bedroom, the blonde fell on the floor and howled in pain. Graham leaned over her with his gun. "Don't shoot me!" she cried. "I didn't do anything!"

Graham grabbed her by the ankle. There was all this twisting bare flesh. The girl was hysterical. "Where is Eddie?" Graham said. "Where is he?"

"*In a meeting!*" the girl squealed.

"Where?"

"*In a meeting!*" And flailing around, she kicked Graham in the nuts with her other leg.

"Aw, Christ," Graham said, letting the girl go. He coughed and sat down hard. I went back to the living room. The redhead had her high heels on but nothing else.

I said, "Where is he?"

"You bastards," she said. "You fucking bastards."

I went past her toward a door at the far end of the room. It was locked. The redhead ran up and began to hit me on the back with her fists. "Leave him alone! Leave him alone!" I was trying to open the locked door while she pounded on me. I thought I heard voices from the other side of the door.

In the next moment Graham's big bulk slammed into the door and the wood splintered. The door opened. I saw the kitchen, lit by the green light of the pool outside. The room was empty. The back door was open.

"*Shit.*"

By now the redhead had jumped on my back, and locked her legs around my waist. She was pulling my hair, screaming obscenities. I spun around in circles, trying to throw her off me. It was one of those strange moments where in the middle of all the chaos I was thinking, *be careful, don't hurt her,* because it would look bad for a pretty young girl to end up with a broken arm or cracked ribs, it would mean police brutality even though right now she was tearing my hair out by the roots. She bit my ear and I felt pain. I slammed myself back against the wall, and I heard her grunt as the breath was knocked out of her. She let go.

Out the window, I saw a dark figure running down the stairs. Graham saw it, too.

"Fuck," he said. He ran. I ran, too. But the girl must have tripped me because I fell over, landing hard. When I got to my feet I heard the sirens of the black and whites and their engines starting up.

Then I was back outside, running down the steps. I was maybe ten meters behind Graham, about thirty feet, when Eddie's Ferrari backed out of the garage, ground the gears, and roared down the street.

The black and whites immediately took up pursuit. Graham ran for his sedan. He had pulled out to follow while I was still running for my own car, parked farther down the road. As his car flashed past me, I could see his face, grim and angry.

I got into my car and followed.

You can't drive fast in the hills and talk on the phone. I didn't even try. I estimated I was half a kilometer behind Graham, and he was some distance behind the two patrol cars. When I got to the bottom of the hill, the 101 overpass, I saw the flashing lights going down the freeway. I had to back up and pull around to the entrance below Mulholland, and then I joined traffic heading south.

When the traffic began to slow up, I stuck my flasher on the roof, and pulled into the right-hand breakdown lane.

I got to the concrete embankment about thirty seconds after the Ferrari hit it flat out at a hundred and sixty kilometers an hour. I guess the gas tank had exploded on impact, and the flames were jumping fifteen meters into the air. The heat was tremendous. It looked like the trees up on the hill might catch on fire. You couldn't get anywhere near the twisted wreck of the car.

The first of the fire trucks pulled up, with three more black and whites. There were sirens and flashing lights everywhere.

I backed up my car to make room for the trucks, then walked over to Graham. He smoked a cigarette as the firemen began to spray the wreck with foam.

"Christ," Graham said. "What a fucking cockup."

"Why didn't the backup patrolmen stop him when he was in the garage?"

"Because," Graham said, "I told them not to shoot at him. And we weren't there. They were trying to decide what to do when the guy drove away." He shook his head. "This is going to look like shit in the report."

I said, "Still, it's probably better you didn't shoot him."

"Maybe." He ground out his cigarette.

By now, the firemen had gotten the fire out. The Ferrari was a smoking hulk crumpled against the concrete. There was a harsh smell in the air.

"Well," Graham said. "No point staying around here. I'll go back to the house. See if those girls are still there."

"You need me for anything else?"

"No. You might as well go. Tomorrow is another day. Shit, it'll be paper-work until we drop." He looked at me. He hesitated. "We in sync about this? About what happened?"

"Hell, yes," I said.

"No way to handle it differently," he said. "Far as I can see."

"No," I said. "Just one of those things."

"Okay, buddy. See you tomorrow."

"Good night, Tom."

We got into our cars.

I drove home.

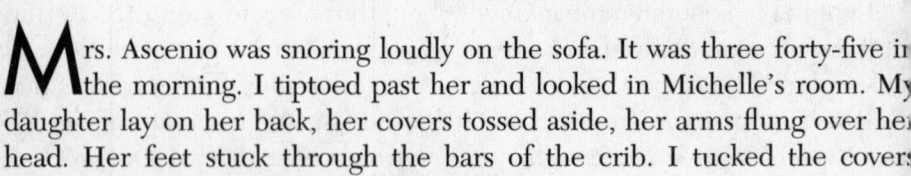

Mrs. Ascenio was snoring loudly on the sofa. It was three forty-five in the morning. I tiptoed past her and looked in Michelle's room. My daughter lay on her back, her covers tossed aside, her arms flung over her head. Her feet stuck through the bars of the crib. I tucked the covers around her and went into my own room.

The television was still on. I turned it off. I pulled off my tie and sat down on the bed to remove my shoes. I suddenly realized how tired I was. I took off my coat and trousers and threw them onto the television set. I lay down on my back and thought I should take off my shirt. It felt sweaty and grimy on my body. I closed my eyes for a moment and let my head sink back into the pillow. Then I felt a pinching, and something tugging at my eyelids. I heard a chirping sound and thought in a moment of horror that birds were pecking at my eyes.

I heard a voice saying, "Open your eyes, Daddy. Open your eyes." And

I realized that it was my daughter, trying to pull my eyelids up with small fingers.

"Yuuuh," I said. I glimpsed daylight, rolled away, and buried my face in the pillow.

"Daddy? Open your eyes. Open your eyes, Daddy."

I said, "Daddy was out late last night. Daddy is tired."

She paid no attention. "Daddy, open your eyes. Open your eyes. Daddy? Open your eyes, Daddy."

I knew that she would continue saying the same thing, over and over, until I lost my mind, or opened my eyes. I rolled onto my back and coughed. "Daddy is still tired, Shelly. Go see what Mrs. Ascenio is doing."

"Daddy, open your eyes."

"Can't you let Daddy sleep a while? Daddy wants to sleep a little longer this morning."

"It's morning now, Daddy. Open your eyes. Open your eyes."

I opened my eyes. She was right.

It was morning.

What the hell.

SECOND DAY

Eat your pancakes."

"I don't want any more."

"Just one more bite, Shelly." Sunlight streamed through the kitchen window. I yawned. It was seven o'clock in the morning.

"Is Mommy coming today?"

"Don't change the subject. Come on, Shel. One more bite. Please?"

We were sitting at her kid-size table in the corner of the kitchen. Sometimes I can get her to eat at the little table when she won't eat at the big table. But I wasn't having much luck today. Michelle stared at me.

"Is Mommy coming?"

"I think so. I'm not sure." I didn't want to disappoint her. "We're waiting to hear."

"Is Mommy going out of town again?"

I said, "Maybe." I wondered what "going out of town" meant to a two-year-old, what sort of image she would have of it.

"Is she going with Uncle Rick?"

Who is Uncle Rick? I held the fork in front of her face. "I don't know, Shel. Come on, open up. One more bite."

"He has a new car," Michelle said, nodding solemnly, the way she did whenever she was informing me of important news.

"Is that right?"

"Uh-huh. Black one."

"I see. What kind of car is it?"

"Sades."

"A Sades?"

"No. *Sades.*"

"You mean Mercedes?"

"Uh-huh. Black one."

"That's nice," I said.

"When is Mommy coming?"

"One more bite, Shel."

She opened her mouth, and I moved the fork toward her. At the last moment she turned her head aside, pursing her lips. "No, Daddy."

"All right," I said. "I give up."

"I'm not hungry, Daddy."

"I can see that."

Mrs. Ascenio was cleaning up the kitchen before she went back to her own apartment. There was another fifteen minutes before my housekeeper Elaine came to take Michelle to day care. I still had to get her dressed. I was putting her pancakes in the sink when the phone rang. It was Ellen Farley, the mayor's press aide.

"Are you watching?"

"Watching what?"

"The news. Channel seven. They're doing the car crash right now."

"They are?"

"Call me back," she said.

I went into the bedroom and turned on the television. A voice was saying, "—reported a high-speed chase on the Hollywood freeway southbound, which ended when the suspect drove his Ferrari sportscar into the Vine Street overpass, not far from the Hollywood Bowl. Observers say the car hit the concrete embankment at more than a hundred miles an hour, instantly bursting into flames. Fire trucks were called to the scene but there were no survivors. The driver's body was so badly burned that his glasses melted. The officer in charge of the pursuit, Detective Thomas Graham, said that the driver, Mr. Edward Sakamura, was wanted in connection with the alleged murder of a woman at a downtown location. But today, friends of Mr. Sakamura expressed disbelief at this charge, and claimed that police strong-arm tactics panicked the suspect and caused him to flee. There are complaints that the incident was racially motivated. It is not clear whether police intended to charge Mr. Sakamura with the murder, and observers noted that this was the third high-speed pursuit on the 101 freeway in the last two weeks. Questions of police judgment in these pursuits have arisen after a Compton woman was killed in a high-speed pursuit last January. Neither Detective Graham nor his assistant Lieutenant Peter Smith was available to be interviewed, and we are waiting to hear if the officers will be disciplined or suspended by the department."

Jesus.

"Daddy . . ."

"Just a minute, Shel."

The image showed the crumpled, smoking wreckage being loaded onto a flatbed truck for removal from the side of the highway. There was a black smear on the concrete where the car had struck the wall.

The station cut back to the studio, where the anchorwoman faced the camera and said, "In other developments, KNBC has learned that two police officers interviewed Mr. Sakamura earlier in the evening in connection with the case, but did not arrest him at that time. Captain John Connor and Lieutenant Smith may face disciplinary review by the department, with questions being raised of possible procedural violations. However, the good news is there are no longer delays for traffic moving southbound on the 101. Now over to you, Bob."

I stared numbly at the TV. *Disciplinary review?*

The phone rang. It was Ellen Farley again. "You get all that?"

"Yeah, I did. I can't believe it. What's it about, Ellen?"

"None of this is coming from the mayor's office, if that's what you're asking. But the Japanese community has been unhappy with Graham before. They think he's a racist. It looks like he played right into their hands."

"I was there. Graham acted correctly."

"Yeah, I know you were there, Pete. Frankly, it's unfortunate. I don't want to see you tarred by the same brush."

I said, "Graham acted correctly."

"Are you listening, Pete?"

"What about this suspension and disciplinary review?"

"That's the first I heard of it," Ellen said. "But that would be internally generated. It's coming from your own department. By the way, is it true? Did you and Connor see Sakamura last night?"

"Yes."

"And you didn't arrest him?"

"No. We didn't have probable cause to arrest him when we talked to him. Later on, we did."

Ellen said, "Do you really think he could have done this murder?"

"I know he did. We have it on tape."

"On tape? Are you serious?"

"Yeah. We have the murder on videotape from one of the Nakamoto security cameras."

She was silent for a while. I said, "Ellen?"

"Look," Ellen said. "Off the record, okay?"

"Sure."

"I don't know what's going on here, Pete. There's more than I understand."

"Why didn't you tell me who the girl was, last night?"

"I'm sorry about that. I had a lot to take care of."

"Ellen."

A silence. Then: "Pete, this girl got around. She knew a lot of people."

"Did she know the mayor?"

Silence.

"How well did she know him?"

"Listen," Ellen said. "Let's just say she was a pretty girl and she knew a lot of people in this town. Personally, I thought she was unbalanced, but she was good-looking and she had a hell of an effect on men. You had to see it to believe it. Now there's a lot of irons in the fire. You saw the *Times* today?"

"No."

"Take a look. If you ask me, you want to be very correct, the next couple of days. Dot your *i*'s and cross your *t*'s. Do everything by the book. And watch your back, okay?"

"Okay. Thanks, Ellen."

"Don't thank me. I didn't call." Then her voice got softer. "Take care of yourself, Peter."

I heard a dial tone.

"Daddy?"

"Just a minute, Shel."

"Can I watch cartoons?"

"Sure, honey."

I found her a station with some cartoons and walked into the living room. I opened the front door and picked up the *Times* from the mat. It took me a while to find the story on the last page of the Metro section.

CHARGES OF POLICE RACISM CLOUD JAPANESE FETE

I skimmed the first paragraph. Japanese officials of the Nakamoto corporation complained about "callous and insensitive" police behavior, which they said detracted from a star-studded opening night at their new skyscraper on Figueroa. At least one Nakamoto official expressed the view that the police actions were "racially motivated." A spokesperson said: "We do not believe the Los Angeles Police Department would behave in this fashion if a Japanese corporation were not involved. We feel strongly that the actions of the police reflect a double standard for treatment of Japanese at the hands of American officials." Mr. Hiroshi Ogura, chairman of the board of Nakamoto, was present at the party, which drew such celebrities as Madonna and Tom Cruise, but he could not be reached for comment on the incident. A spokesman said, "Mr. Ogura is deeply disturbed that official hostility should mar this gathering. He very much regrets the unpleasantness that occurred."

According to observers, Mayor Thomas sent a staff member to deal with the police, but with little result. The police did not modify their behavior, despite the presence of the special Japanese liaison officer, Lieutenant Peter Smith, whose job is to defuse racially sensitive situations. . . .

And so on.

You had to read four paragraphs before you discovered that a murder had occurred. That particular detail seemed to be almost irrelevant.

I looked back at the lead. The story was from the City News Service, which meant there was no byline.

I felt angry enough to call my old contact at the *Times,* Kenny Shubik. Ken was the leading Metro reporter. He had been at the paper forever, and he knew everything that was going on. Since it was still eight in the morning, I called him at home.

"Ken. Pete Smith."

"Oh, hi," he said. "Glad you got my message."

In the background, I heard what sounded like a teenage girl: "Oh, *come on,* Dad. Why can't I go?"

Ken said, "Jennifer, let me talk here for a minute."

"What message?" I said.

Ken said, "I called you last night, because I thought you ought to know right away. He's obviously working off a tip. But do you have any idea what's behind it?"

"Behind what?" I said. I didn't know what he was talking about. "I'm sorry, Ken, I didn't get your message."

"Really?" he said. "I called you about eleven-thirty last night. The DHD dispatcher said you had rolled out on a case but you had a car phone. I told her it was important, and for you to call me at home if necessary. Because I felt sure you'd want to know."

In the background, the girl said, "Dad, *come on,* I have to decide what to *wear.*"

"Jennifer, damn it," he said. "Chill out." To me he said, "You have a daughter, don't you?"

"Yeah," I said. "But she's only two."

"Just wait," Ken said. "Look, Pete. You really didn't get my message?"

"No," I said. "I'm calling about something else: the story in this morning's paper."

"What story?"

"The Nakamoto coverage on page eight. The one about 'callous and racist police' at the opening."

"Jeez, I didn't think we had a Nakamoto story yesterday. I know Jodie was doing the party, but that won't run until tomorrow. You know, Japan draws the glitterati. Jeff didn't have anything on the scheds in Metro yesterday."

Jeff was the Metro editor. I said, "There's a story in the paper this morning about the murder."

"What murder?" he said. His voice sounded odd.

"There was a murder at Nakamoto last night. About eight-thirty. One of the guests was killed."

Ken was silent at the other end of the line. Putting things together. Finally he said, "Were you involved?"

"Homicide called me in as Japanese liaison."

"Hmmm," Ken said. "Listen. Let me get to my desk and see what I can find out. Let's talk in an hour. And give me your numbers so I can call you direct."

"Okay."

He cleared his throat. "Listen, Pete," he said. "Just between us. Do you have any problems?"

"Like what?"

"Like a morals problem, or a problem with your bank account. Discrepancy about reported income . . . anything I should know about? As your friend?"

"No," I said.

"I don't need the details. But if there's something that isn't quite right. . . . "

"Nothing, Ken."

" 'Cause if I have to go to bat for you, I don't want to discover I have stepped in shit."

"Ken. What's going on?"

"I don't want to go into detail right now. But offhand I would say somebody is trying to fuck you in the ass," Ken said.

The girl said, "*Dad*dy, that's dis*gus*ting."

"Well, you're not supposed to be listening. Pete?"

"Yeah," I said. "I'm here."

"Call me in an hour," Ken said.

"You're a pal," I said. "I owe you."

"Fucking right you do," Ken said.

He hung up.

I looked around the apartment. Everything still looked the same. Morning sunlight was still streaming into the room. Michelle was sitting in her favorite chair, watching cartoons and sucking her thumb. But somehow everything felt different. It was creepy. It was like the world had tilted.

But I had things to do. It was also getting late; I had to get her dressed before Elaine came to take her to day care. I told her that. She started to cry. So I turned off the television set, and she threw herself on the floor and began to kick and scream. "No, Daddy! Car*toons,* Daddy!"

I picked her up and slung her underarm to the bedroom to get her changed. She was screaming at the top of her lungs. The phone rang again. This time it was the division dispatcher.

"Morning, Lieutenant. I have your uncleared messages."

"Let me get a pencil," I said. I put Michelle down. She cried even louder. I said, "Can you go pick out which shoes you want to wear today?"

"Sounds like you got a murder there," the dispatcher said.

"She doesn't want to get dressed for school."

Michelle was tugging at my leg. "No, Daddy. No school, Daddy."

"Yes, school," I said firmly. She bawled. "Go ahead," I said to the dispatcher.

"Okay, eleven forty-one last night, you had a call from a Ken Subotik or Subotnick, *L.A. Times,* he said please call him. Message reads 'The Weasel is checking up on you.' He said you would know what that meant. You can call him at home. You have the number?"

"Yes."

"Okay. One forty-two a.m. this morning, you had a call from a Mr. Eddie Saka—looks like Sakamura. He said it's urgent, please call him at home, 555-8434. It's about the missing tape. Okay?"

Shit.

I said, "What time was that call?"

"One forty-two a.m. The call was forwarded to County General and I guess their switchboard couldn't locate you. You were at the morgue or something?"

"Yeah."

"Sorry, Lieutenant, but once you're out of your car, we have to go through intermediates."

"Okay. Anything else?"

"Then at six forty-three a.m., Captain Connor left a beeper number for you to call. He said he's playing golf this morning."

"Okay."

"And at seven-ten, we had a call from Robert Woodson, who is with Senator Morton's office. Senator Morton wants to meet you and Captain Connor at one o'clock today at the Los Angeles Country Club. He asked that you call and confirm that you will attend the meeting with the senator. I tried to reach you but your phone was busy. Will you call the senator?"

I said I would call the senator. I told the dispatcher to page Connor for me at the golf course, and have him call me in the car.

I heard the front door unlock. Elaine came in. "Good morning," she said. "I'm afraid Shelly isn't dressed yet."

"That's okay," she said. "I'll do it. What time is Mrs. Davis coming to pick her up?"

"We're waiting to hear."

Elaine had been through this routine many times before. "Come on, Michelle. Let's pick your clothes for today. Time to get ready for school."

I looked at my watch, and was on my way to get another cup of coffee when the phone rang. "Lieutenant Peter Smith, please."

It was the assistant chief, Jim Olson.

"Hi, Jim."

"Morning, Pete." He sounded friendly. But Jim Olson never called anybody before ten o'clock in the morning unless there was a big problem. Olson said, "Looks like we got ourselves a rattlesnake by the tail. You see the papers today?"

"Yeah, I did."

"You happen to catch the morning news?"

"Some of it."

"The chief's been calling me for damage control. I wanted to get where you stand before I make a recommendation. Okay?"

"Okay."

"I just got off the phone with Tom Graham. He admits last night was a prime screwup. Nobody is covered in glory."

"I'm afraid not."

"Couple of naked broads impeded two able-bodied police officers and prevented apprehension of the suspect? Is that about it?"

It sounded ridiculous. I said, "You had to be there, Jim."

"Uh-huh," he said. "Well, one good thing so far. I've been checking if correct pursuit procedures were followed. Apparently they were. We have recordings off the computers, and we have voice recordings off the radio, and it's all strictly by the book. Thank God. Nobody even swears. We can release those records to the media if this thing gets any worse. So we're covered there. But it's very unfortunate that Sakamura is dead."

"Yes."

"Graham went back to get the girls, but the house was deserted. The girls were gone."

"I see."

"In all the rush, nobody got the names of the girls?"

"No, I'm afraid not."

"That means we have no witnesses to the events in the house. So we're a little vulnerable."

"Uh-huh."

"They're cutting Sakamura's body out of the wreck this morning to ship what's left to the morgue. Graham tells me as far as he's concerned, the case is wrapped up. I gather there are videotapes that show Sakamura killed the girl. Graham says he is ready to file his concluding five-seven-nine report. Is that how you see it? The case closed?"

"I guess so, Chief. Sure."

"Then we can shut this fucker down," the chief said. "The Japanese community finds the Nakamoto inquiry irritating and offensive. They don't want it to continue any longer than necessary. So if we can call it a day, it would help."

"It's okay with me," I said. "Let's call it a day."

"Well that's good, Pete," the chief said. "I'm going to speak to the chief, see if we can head off any disciplinary action."

"Thanks, Jim."

"Try not to worry. Myself, I don't see a disciplinary issue. As long as we have videos that show Sakamura did it."

"Yeah, we do."

"About those videos," he said. "I've had Marty looking in the evidence locker. He can't seem to find 'em."

I took a deep breath and said, "No, I have them."

"You didn't log them in the evidence locker last night?"

"No. I wanted to get copies made."

He coughed. "Pete. It'd be better if you had followed procedure on that."

"I wanted to get copies made," I said.

"Tell you what," Jim said, "get your copies made, and get the originals onto my desk by ten o'clock. Okay?"

"Okay."

"It can take that long to locate the material from the evidence locker. You know how it is."

He was saying he would cover for me. "Thanks, Jim."

"Don't thank me, because I didn't do anything," he said. "Far as I know, procedure has been followed."

"Right."

"But just between you and me: get it done right away. I can hold the fort for a couple of hours. But something's going on down here. I don't know exactly where it's coming from. So don't push it, okay?"

"Okay, Jim. I'm on my way now."

I hung up the phone, and went to get copies made.

Pasadena looked like a city at the bottom of a glass of sour milk. The Jet Propulsion Laboratory, on the outskirts of town, was nestled in the foothills near the Rose Bowl. But even at eight-thirty in the morning, you couldn't see the mountains through the yellow-white haze.

I tucked the box of tapes under my arm, showed my badge, signed the guard's clipboard, and swore I was an American citizen. The guard sent me to the main building, across an inner courtyard.

For decades, the Jet Propulsion Laboratory had served as the command center for American spacecraft that photographed Jupiter and the rings of Saturn, and sent pictures back to earth as video images. JPL was the place where modern video-image processing had been invented. If anybody could copy these tapes, they could.

Mary Jane Kelleher, the press secretary, took me up to the third floor. We walked down a lime green corridor, past several doors that opened into empty offices. I mentioned it.

"It's true," she said, nodding. "We've been losing some good people, Peter."

"Where are they going?" I said.

"Mostly to industry. We always lost a few to IBM in Armonk, or Bell Labs in New Jersey. But those labs don't have the best equipment or funding any more. Now it's the Japanese research labs like Hitachi in Long Beach, Sanyo in Torrance, Canon in Inglewood. They're hiring a lot of American researchers now."

"Is JPL concerned about it?"

"Sure," she said. "Everybody knows the best way to transfer technology is inside somebody's head. But what can you do?" She shrugged. "Researchers want to do research. And America doesn't do so much R and D any more. Budgets are tighter. So it's better to work for the Japanese. They pay well, and they genuinely respect research. If you need a piece of equipment, you get it. Anyway, that's what my friends tell me. Here we are."

She took me into a laboratory crammed with video equipment. Black boxes stacked on metal shelves and on metal tables; cables snaking across the floor; a variety of monitors and display screens. In the center of all this was a bearded man in his midthirties named Kevin Howzer. He had an image on his monitor of a gear mechanism, in shifting rainbow colors. The desk was littered with Coke cans and candy wrappers; he had been up all night, working.

"Kevin, this is Lieutenant Smith from the L.A.P.D. He's got some unusual videotapes he needs copied."

"Just copied?" Howzer sounded disappointed. "You don't want anything *done* to them?"

"No, Kevin," she said. "He doesn't."

"No problem."

I showed Howzer one of the cassettes. He turned it over in his hand, and shrugged. "Looks like a standard eight-millimeter cart. What's on it?"

"High-definition Japanese TV."

"You mean it's an HD signal?"

"I guess so."

"Shouldn't be a problem. You got a playback I can use?"

"Yes." I took the playback machine out of the box and handed it to him.

"Jeez, they make things nice, don't they? Beautiful unit." Kevin examined the controls in front. "Yeah, that's high-definition all right. I can handle it." He turned the box around and peered at the plugs on the back. Then he frowned. He swung his desk light over and opened the plastic flap on the cassette, exposing the tape. It had a faint silver tinge. "Huh. Do these tapes involve anything legal?"

"Actually, they do."

He handed it back to me. "Sorry. I can't copy it."

"Why not?"

"See the silver color? That's evaporated metal tape. Very high density. I'll bet the format has real-time compression and decompression coming out of the box. I can't make you a copy, because I can't match the formats, which means I can't lay down the signal in an equivalent way that is guaranteed readable. I can make you a copy, but I can't be sure the copy is exact because I can't match formats. So if you have any legal issues—and I assume you do—you're going to have to take it somewhere else to get it copied."

"Like where?"

"This could be the new proprietary D-four format. If it is, the only place that can copy it is Hamaguchi."

"Hamaguchi?"

"The research lab in Glendale, owned by Kawakami Industries. They have every piece of video equipment known to man over there."

I said, "Do you think they'd help me?"

"To make copies? Sure. I know one of the lab directors, Jim Donaldson. I can call over there for you, if you like."

"That would be great."

"No problem."

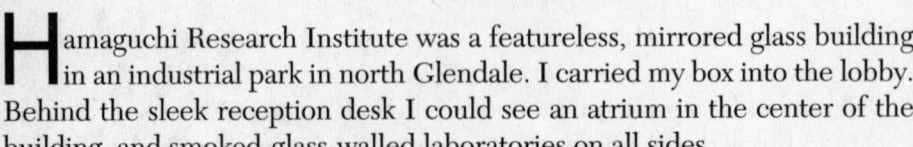

Hamaguchi Research Institute was a featureless, mirrored glass building in an industrial park in north Glendale. I carried my box into the lobby. Behind the sleek reception desk I could see an atrium in the center of the building, and smoked-glass-walled laboratories on all sides.

I asked for Dr. Jim Donaldson and took a seat in the lobby. While I was waiting, two men in suits came in, nodded familiarly to the receptionist, and sat on the couch near me. Ignoring me, they spread out glossy brochures on the coffee table.

"See here," one of them said, "this is what I was talking about. This is the shot we end with. This one closes."

I glanced over, saw a view of wildflowers and snow-capped mountains. The first man tapped the photos.

"I mean, that's the Rockies, my friend. It's real Americana. Trust me, that's what sells them. And it's a hell of a parcel."

"How big did you say it is?"

"It's a hundred and thirty thousand acres. The biggest remaining piece of Montana that's still available. Twenty by ten kilometers of prime ranch acreage fronting on the Rockies. It's the size of a national park. It's got grandeur. It's got dimension, scope. It's very high quality. Perfect for a Japanese consortium."

"And they talked price?"

"Not yet. But the ranchers, you know, they're in a tough situation. It's legal now for foreigners to export beef to Tokyo, and beef in Japan is something like twenty, twenty-two dollars a kilo. But nobody in Japan will buy American beef. If Americans send beef, it will rot on the docks. But if they sell their ranch to the Japanese, then the beef can be exported. Because the Japanese will buy from a Japanese-owned ranch. The Japanese will do business with other Japanese. And ranches all around Montana and Wyoming have been sold. The remaining ranchers see Japanese cowboys riding on the range. They see the other ranches putting in improvements, rebuilding barns, adding modern equipment, all that. Because the other ranches can get high prices in Japan. So the American owners, they're not stupid. They see the writing on the wall. They know they can't compete. So they sell."

"But then what do the Americans do?"

"Stay and work for the Japanese. It's not a problem. The Japanese need someone to teach them how to ranch. And everybody on the ranch gets a raise. The Japanese are sensitive to American feelings. They're sensitive people."

The second man said, "I know, but I don't like it. I don't like the whole thing."

"That's fine, Ted. What do you want to do, write your congressman? They're all working for the Japanese, anyway. Hell, the Japanese are running these ranches with American government subsidies." The first man twisted a gold chain at his wrist. He leaned close to his companion. "Look, Ted. Let's not get all moral here. Because I can't afford it. And neither can you. We are talking a four-percent overall and a five-year payout on a seven hundred mil purchase. Let's make sure we keep that in sight, okay? You personally are looking at two point four million in the first year alone. And it's a five-year payout. Right?"

"I know. It just bothers me."

"Well, Ted. I don't think you'll be bothered when this deal closes. But there's a couple of details we need to handle . . ." At that point, they seemed to realize I was listening. They stood up and moved out of earshot. I heard the first man say something about "assurances that the State of Montana favors and approves . . ." and the second man was nodding, slowly. The first man punched him in the shoulder, cheering him up.

"Lieutenant Smith?"

A woman was standing beside my chair. "Yes?"

"I'm Kristen, Dr. Donaldson's assistant. Kevin over at JPL called about you. Something about tapes you need help with?"

"Yes. I need them copied."

"I'm sorry I wasn't here to take Kevin's call. One of the secretaries took it, and she didn't really understand the situation."

"How's that?"

"Unfortunately, Dr. Donaldson isn't here right now. He's making a speech this morning."

"I see."

"And that makes it difficult for us. With him not in the lab."

"I just want to copy some tapes. Perhaps someone else in the lab can help me," I said.

"Ordinarily yes, but I'm afraid it's impossible today."

It was the Japanese wall. Very polite, but a wall. I sighed. It was probably unrealistic to imagine a Japanese research company would help me. Even with something as neutral as copying tapes.

"I understand."

"Nobody's in the lab this morning at all. They were all working late on a rush project last night, and I guess they were here to all hours. So everybody's late coming in today. That's what the other secretary didn't understand. People are coming in late. So. I don't know what to tell you."

I made one last attempt. "As you know, my boss is the chief of police. This is the second place I've stopped at already this morning. He's really riding me to get this duplicated right away."

"I'd love to help you. I know Dr. Donaldson would be happy to. We've done special work for the police before. And I'm sure we can duplicate whatever material you have. Maybe later today. Or if you'd care to leave it with us . . ."

"I'm afraid I can't do that."

"Okay. Sure. I understand. Well, I'm sorry, Lieutenant. Perhaps you can come back later in the day?" She gave a little shrug.

I said, "Probably not. I guess it's just my bad luck that everybody had to work last night."

"Yes. It's a pretty unusual situation."

"What was it, something came up? Research problem?"

"I really don't know. We have so much video capability on site, occasionally we get a rush request for something unusual. A TV commercial that needs a special effect, or something like that. We worked on that new Michael Jackson video for Sony. Or somebody needs to restore tape that has been ruined. You know, rebuild the signal. But I don't know what came up last night. Except it must have been a lot of work. Something like twenty tapes to be worked on. And a real rush. I hear they didn't finish until after midnight."

I thought: *It can't be.*

I was trying to think what Connor would do, how he would handle it. I decided it was worth a stab in the dark. I said, "Well, I'm sure Nakamoto is grateful for all your hard work."

"Oh, they are. Because it turned out real well for them. They were happy."

I said, "You mentioned that Mr. Donaldson was giving a speech—"

"*Dr.* Donaldson, yes—"

"Where is he doing that?"

"At a corporate-training seminar at the Bonaventure Hotel. Management techniques in research. He must be pretty tired this morning. But he's always a good speaker."

"Thanks." I gave her my card. "You've been very helpful, and if there is ever anything you think of, or want to tell me, call me."

"Okay." She glanced at my card. "Thank you."

I turned to go. As I was leaving, an American in his late twenties, wearing an Armani suit and the smug look of an M.B.A. who reads the fashion magazines, came down and said to the other two men, "Gentlemen? Mr. Nakagawa will see you now."

The men leapt up, grabbing their glossy brochures and pictures, and followed the assistant as he walked in calm measured strides toward the elevator.

I went back outside, into the smog.

The sign in the hallway read WORKING TOGETHER: JAPANESE AND AMERICAN MANAGEMENT STYLES. Inside the conference room, I saw one of those twilight business seminars where men and women sit at long tables covered in gray cloth, taking notes in semigloom as a lecturer drones on at the podium.

While I was standing there, in front of a table with the name tags of latecomers, a bespectacled woman came over to me and said, "Have you registered? Did you get your packet?"

I turned slightly and flashed my badge. I said, "I would like to speak to Dr. Donaldson."

"He's our next speaker. He's on in seven or eight minutes. Can someone else help you?"

"It'll just take a moment."

She hesitated. "But there's so little time before he speaks . . ."

"Then you better get going."

She looked as if I had slapped her. I don't know what she expected. I was a police officer and I'd asked to speak to somebody. Did she think it was negotiable? I felt irritable, remembering the young fashion plate in the Armani suit. Walking in measured steps, like a person of weight and importance, as he led the real estate salesmen away. Why did that kid think he was important? He might have an M.B.A., but he was still just answering the door for his Japanese boss.

Now, I watched the woman circle the conference room, moving toward the dais where four men waited to speak. The business audience was still taking notes as the sandy-haired man at the podium said, "There *is* a place for the foreigner in a Japanese corporation. Not at the top, of course, perhaps not even in the upper echelons. But there is certainly a place. You must realize that the place you hold as a foreigner in a Japanese corporation is an important one, that you are respected, and that you have a job to do. As a foreigner, you will have some special obstacles to overcome, but you can do that. You can succeed if you remember to *know your place*."

I looked at the businessmen in their suits with their heads bowed, taking notes. I wondered what they were writing. Know your place?

The speaker continued: "Many times you hear executives say, 'I have no place in a Japanese corporation, and I had to quit.' Or you will hear people say, 'They didn't listen to me, I had no chance to get my ideas implemented, no chance for advancement.' Those people didn't understand the role of a foreigner in Japanese society. They were not able to fit in, and so they had to leave. But that is *their* problem. The Japanese are perfectly ready to accept Americans and other foreigners in their companies. Indeed, they are eager to have them. And you will be accepted: so long as you remember your place."

A woman raised her hand and said, "What about prejudice against women in Japanese corporations?"

"There is no prejudice against women," the speaker said.

"I've heard that women can't advance."

"That is simply not true."

"Then why all the lawsuits? Sumitomo Corp. just settled a big anti-discrimination suit. I read one-third of Japanese corporations have had suits brought by American employees. What about that?"

"It is perfectly understandable," the speaker said. "Any time a foreign corporation begins to do business in a new country, it is likely to make mistakes while it gets used to the habits and patterns of the country. When American corporations first went multinational in Europe in the fifties and sixties, they encountered difficulties in the countries they entered, and there were lawsuits then. So it is not remarkable that Japanese corporations also have some period of adjustment coming into America. It is necessary to be patient."

A man said with a laugh, "Is there ever a time when it's *not* necessary to be patient with Japan?" But he sounded rueful, not angry.

The others in the room continued to make notes.

"Officer? I'm Jim Donaldson. What is this about?"

I turned. Dr. Donaldson was a tall, thin man with glasses and a precise, almost prissy air. He was dressed in collegiate style, a tweed sport coat and a red tie. But he had the nerd pack of pens peeking out of his shirt pocket. I guessed he was an engineer.

"I just had a couple of questions about the Nakamoto tapes."

"The Nakamoto tapes?"

"The ones in your laboratory last night."

"My laboratory? Mr., ah—"

"Smith, Lieutenant Smith." I gave him my card.

"Lieutenant, I'm sorry, but I don't know what you're talking about. Tapes in my lab last night?"

"Kristen, your secretary, said everybody in the lab was working late on some tapes."

"Yes. That's true. Most of my staff."

"And the tapes came from Nakamoto."

"From *Nakamoto*?" He shook his head. "Who told you that?"

"She did."

"I assure you, Lieutenant, the tapes were not from Nakamoto."

"I heard there were twenty tapes."

"Yes, at least twenty. I'm not sure of the exact number. But they were from McCann-Erickson. An ad campaign for Asahi beer. We had to do a logo transformation on every ad in the campaign. Now that Asahi beer is the number one beer in America."

"But the question of Nakamoto—"

"Lieutenant," he said impatiently, glancing at the podium, "let me explain something. I work for Hamaguchi Research Labs. Hamaguchi is owned by Kawakami Industries. A competitor of Nakamoto. Competition among the Japanese corporations is very intense. *Very* intense. Take my word for it: my lab didn't do any work on any Nakamoto tapes last night. Such a thing would never happen, under any circumstances. If my secretary said it did, she's mistaken. It's absolutely out of the realm of possibility. Now, I have to give a speech. Is there anything else?"

"No," I said. "Thanks."

There was scattered applause as the speaker on the podium finished. I turned and left the room.

❖ ❖ ❖

I was driving away from the Bonaventure when Connor called in from the golf course. He sounded annoyed. "I got your page. I had to interrupt my game. This better be good."

I told him about the one o'clock appointment with Senator Morton.

"All right," he said. "Pick me up here at ten-thirty. Anything else?"

I told him about my trips to JPL and Hamaguchi, then my conversation with Donaldson.

Connor sighed. "That was a waste of time."

"Why?"

"Because Hamaguchi is funded by Kawakami, and they're in competition with Nakamoto. There is no way they would do anything to help Nakamoto."

"That's what Donaldson told me," I said.

"Where are you going now?"

"To the U.S.C. video labs. I'm still trying to get the tapes copied."

Connor paused. "Anything else I should know?"

"No."

"Fine. See you at ten-thirty."

"Why so early?"

"Ten-thirty," he said, and hung up.

As soon as I hung up, the phone rang. "You were supposed to call me." It was Ken Shubik at the *Times*. He sounded sulky.

"Sorry. I got tied up. Can we talk now?"

"Sure."

"You got information for me?"

"Listen." He paused. "Are you anywhere around here?"

"About five blocks from you."

"Then come by for a cup of coffee."

"You don't want to talk on the phone?"

"Well . . ."

"Come on, Ken. You always want to talk on the phone." Shubik was like all the *Times* reporters, he sat at his desk in front of his computer and wore a headset and talked on the phone all day long. It was his preferred way of doing things. He had all his stuff in front of him, he could type his notes into the computer as he talked. When I was a press officer, my office had been at police headquarters in Parker Center, two blocks from the Times building. And still a reporter like Ken would rather talk to me on the phone than see me in person.

"Come on by, Pete."

That was clear enough.

Ken didn't want to talk on the phone.

"Okay, fine," I said. "See you in ten minutes."

The *Los Angeles Times* is the most profitable newspaper in America. The newsroom takes up one entire floor of the Times building, and thus the area of a city block. The space has been skillfully subdivided, so you are never confronted by how large it actually is, and how many hundreds of people work there. But still it seems you walk for days past reporters sitting at clusters of modular workstations, with their glowing computer screens, their blinking telephones, and their tacked-up pictures of the kids.

Ken's workstation was in Metro, on the east side of the building. I found him standing by his desk, pacing. Waiting for me. He took me by the elbow.

"Coffee," he said. "Let's get coffee."

"What is it?" I said. "You don't want to be seen with me?"

"No. Shit. I want to avoid the Weasel. He's down hustling that new girl in Foreign. She doesn't know any better yet." Ken nodded toward the far end of the newsroom. There, by the windows, I saw the familiar figure of Willy Wilhelm, known to everyone as Weasel Wilhelm. Willy's narrow, ferretlike face was at this moment composed into a mask of smiling attentiveness as he joked with a blond girl sitting before a terminal.

"Very cute."

"Yeah. A little big in the rear. She's Dutch," Ken said. "She's only been here a week. She hasn't heard about him."

Most organizations had a person like the Weasel: somebody who is more ambitious than scrupulous, somebody who finds a way to make himself useful to the powers that be, while being roundly hated by everyone else. That was the case with Weasel Wilhelm.

Like most dishonest people, the Weasel believed the worst about everybody. He could always be counted on to portray events in their most unflattering light, insisting that anything less was a cover-up. He had a nose for human weakness and a taste for melodrama. He cared nothing for the truth of any situation, and he considered a balanced appraisal weak. As far as the

Weasel was concerned, the underlying truth was always strong stuff. And that was what he dealt in.

The other reporters at the *Times* despised him.

Ken and I went into the central hallway. I followed him toward the coffee machines, but he led me into the library. In the middle of the floor the *Times* had a library that was larger and better equipped than many college facilities.

"So, what is it about Wilhelm?" I said.

"He was in here last night," Ken said. "I came by after the theater to pick up some notes I needed for a morning interview I was doing from home. And I saw the Weasel in the library. Maybe eleven o'clock at night. You know how ambitious the little turd is. I could see it in his face. He had the scent of blood. So naturally, you want to know about what."

"Naturally," I said. The Weasel was an accomplished backstabber. A year earlier, he had managed to get the editor of the Sunday Calendar fired. Only at the last minute did he fail to land the job himself.

Ken said, "So I whisper to Lilly, the night librarian. 'What is it? What's the Weasel up to?' She says, 'He's checking police reports on some cop.' So that's a relief, I think. But then I begin to wonder. I mean, I'm still the senior Metro reporter. I still do a story out of Parker Center a couple of times a month. What does he know that I don't? For all I know, this should be my story. So I say to Lilly, what's the name of this cop?"

"Let me guess," I said.

"That's right," Ken said. "Peter J. Smith."

"What time was this?"

"About eleven."

"Great," I said.

"I thought you'd want to know," Ken said.

"I do."

"So I said to Lilly—this is last night—I said, 'Lilly, what kind of stuff is he pulling?' And he's pulling everything, all the old clips from the morgue and apparently he's got a source inside Parker who's going to leak him internal affairs records. Some kind of a hearing about child molestation. Charge brought a couple of years ago."

"Ah, shit," I said.

"That true?" Ken said.

"There was a hearing," I said. "But it was bullshit."

Ken looked at me. "Fill me in."

"It was three years back," I said. "I was still working detective. My partner and I answered a domestic violence call in Ladera Heights. His panic couple, fighting. Both very drunk. Woman wants me to arrest her hus band, and when I refuse to, says he's sexually abusing her baby. I go look at the baby. The baby looks okay. I still refuse to arrest the husband. The woman is pissed. The next day she comes in and accuses *me* of sexual molestation. There's a preliminary hearing. Charges dismissed as without merit."

"Okay," Ken said. "Now, you got any travel that's questionable?"

I frowned. "Travel?"

"The Weasel was trying to locate travel records last night. Airplane trips, junkets, padded expenses . . ."

I shook my head. "It doesn't ring a bell."

"Yeah, I figured he must be wrong about that one. You're a single parent, you're not going on any junkets."

"No way."

"Good."

We were walking deeper into the library. We came to a corner where we could see out to the Metro section of the newsroom through glass walls. I saw the Weasel still talking to the girl, chatting her up. I said, "What I don't understand, Ken, is why me? I mean, I got no heat on me at all. No controversy. I haven't been a working detective for three years. I'm not even a press officer any more. I'm liaison. I mean, what I do is political. So why is a *Times* reporter gunning for me?"

"At eleven o'clock on a Thursday night, you mean?" Ken said. He was staring at me like I was an idiot. Like there was drool coming down my chin.

I said, "You think the Japanese are doing this?"

"I think the Weasel does jobs for people. He is a scumbag for hire. He does jobs for the studios, record companies, brokerage houses, even the Realtors. He's a *consultant*. The Weasel now drives a Mercedes 500sl, you know."

"Oh, yeah?"

"Pretty good on a reporter's salary, wouldn't you say?"

"Yeah, I would."

"So. You got on the wrong side of somebody? You do that last night?"

"Maybe."

"Because somebody called the Weasel to track you down."

I said, "I can't believe this."

"Believe it," Ken said. "The only thing that worries me is the Weasel's source inside Parker Center. Somebody in the department's leaking him internal affairs stuff. You okay inside your own department?"

"As far as I know."

"Good. Because the Weasel is up to his usual tricks. This morning I talked to Roger Bascomb, our in-house counsel."

"And?"

"Guess who called him all hot and bothered with a question last night? The Weasel. And you want to guess what the question was?"

I said nothing.

"The question was, does serving as a police press-officer make an individual a public personality? As in, a public personality who can't sue for libel?"

I said, "Jesus."

"Right."

"And the answer?"

"Who cares about the answer? You know how this works. All the Weasel has to do is call a few people and say, 'Hi, this is Bill Wilhelm over here at the *L.A. Times*. We're going with a story tomorrow that says Lieutenant Peter Smith is a child molester, do you have any comment on that?' A few well-placed calls, and the story doesn't even have to run. The editors can kill it but the damage is already done."

I said nothing. I knew what Ken was telling me was true. I had seen it happen more than once.

I said, "What can I do?"

Ken laughed. "You could arrange one of your famous incidents of L.A. police brutality."

"That's not funny."

"Nobody at this paper would cover it, I can promise you that. You could fucking kill him. And if somebody made a home video? Hey, people here would *pay* to see it on video."

"Ken."

Ken sighed. "I can dream. Okay. There's one thing. Last year, after Wilhelm was involved in the, ah, change of management over in Calendar, I got an anonymous package in the mail. So did a few other people. Nobody did anything about it at the time. It's pretty dirty pool. You interested?"

"Yeah."

Ken took a small manila envelope from the inside pocket of his sport coat. It had one of those strings that you wrap back and forth to close it. Inside was a series of photos, printed in a strip. It showed Willy Wilhelm engaged in an intimate act with a dark-haired man. His head buried in his lap.

"You can't see the Weasel's face too well in all the angles," Ken said. "But it's him, all right. Action snap of the reporter entertaining his source. Having a drink with him, so to speak."

"Who is the guy?"

"It took us a while. His name is Barry Borman. He's the regional head of sales for Kaisei Electronics in southern California."

"What can I do with this?"

"Give me your card," Ken said. "I'll clip it to the envelope, and have it delivered to the Weasel."

I shook my head. "I don't think so."

"It'd sure make him think twice."

"No," I said. "It's not for me."

Ken shrugged. "Yeah. It might not work, anyway. Even if we squeeze the Weasel's nuts, the Japanese probably have other ways. I still haven't been able to find out how that story ran last night. All I hear is, 'Orders from the top, orders from the top.' Whatever that means. It could mean anything."

"Somebody must have written it."

"I tell you, I can't find out. But you know, the Japanese have a powerful influence at the paper. It's more than just the ads they take. It's more than their relentless PR machine drumming out of Washington, or the local lobbying and the campaign contributions to political figures and organizations. It's the sum of all those things and more. And it's starting to be insidious. I mean, you can be sitting around in a staff meeting discussing some article that we might run, and you suddenly realize, nobody wants to *offend* them. It isn't a question of whether a story is right or wrong, news or not news. And it isn't a one-to-one equation, like 'We can't say that or they'll pull their ads.' It's more subtle than that. Sometimes I look at my editors, and I can tell they won't go with certain stories because they are afraid. They don't even know what they are afraid of. They're just afraid."

"So much for a free press."

"Hey," Ken said. "This is not the time for sophomore bullshit. You know how it works. The American press reports the prevailing opinion. The prevailing opinion is the opinion of the group in power. The Japanese are now in power. The press reports the prevailing opinion as usual. No surprises. Just take care."

"I will."

"And don't hesitate to call, if you decide you want to arrange mail service."

I wanted to talk to Connor. I was beginning to understand why Connor had been worried, and why he had wanted to conclude the investigation quickly. Because a well-mounted campaign of innuendo is a fearsome thing. A skillful practitioner—and the Weasel was skillful—would arrange it so that a new story came out, day after day, even when nothing happened. You got headlines like GRAND JURY UNDECIDED ON POLICEMAN'S GUILT when in fact the grand jury hadn't met yet. But people saw the headlines, day after day, and drew their own conclusions.

The truth was, there was always a way to spin it. At the end of the innuendo campaign, if your subject was found blameless, you could still mount a headline like GRAND JURY FAILS TO FIND POLICEMAN GUILTY or DISTRICT ATTORNEY UNWILLING TO PROSECUTE ACCUSED COP. Headlines like that were as bad as a conviction.

And there was no way to bounce back from weeks of negative press. Everybody remembered the accusation. Nobody remembered the exoneration. That was human nature. Once you were accused, it was tough to get back to normal.

It was getting creepy, and I had a lot of bad feelings. I was a little preoccupied, pulling into the parking lot next to the physics department at U.S.C., when the phone rang again. It was assistant chief Olson.

"Peter."

"Yes, sir."

"It's almost ten o'clock. I thought you'd be down here putting the tapes on my desk. You promised them to me."

"I've been having trouble getting the tapes copied."

"Is that what you've been doing?"

"Sure. Why?"

"Because from the calls I get, it sounds like you aren't dropping this investigation," Jim Olson said. "In the last hour, you've been out asking questions at a Japanese research institute. Then you've interrogated a scientist who works for a Japanese research institute. You're hanging around some Japanese seminar. Let's get it straight, Peter. Is the investigation over, or not?"

"It's over," I said. "I'm just trying to get the tapes copied."

"Make sure that's all it is," he said.

"Right, Jim."

"For the good of the whole department—and the individuals in it—I want this thing behind us."

"Right, Jim."

"I don't want to lose control of this situation."

"I understand."

"I hope you do," he said. "Get the copies made, and get your ass down here." And he hung up.

I parked the car, and went into the physics building.

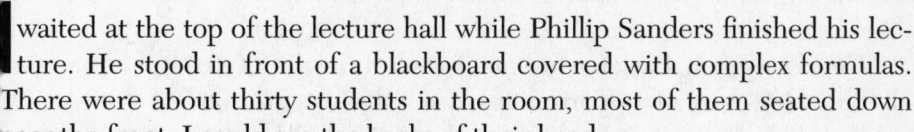

I waited at the top of the lecture hall while Phillip Sanders finished his lecture. He stood in front of a blackboard covered with complex formulas. There were about thirty students in the room, most of them seated down near the front. I could see the backs of their heads.

Dr. Sanders was about forty years old, one of those energetic types, in constant motion, pacing back and forth, tapping the equations on the blackboard in short emphatic jabs with his chalk as he pointed to the "signal covariant ratio determination" and the "factorial delta bandwidth noise." I couldn't even guess what subject he was teaching. Finally I concluded it must be electrical engineering.

When the bell rang on the hour, the class stood and packed up their bags. I was startled: nearly everyone in the class was Asian, both men and women. Those that weren't Asian were Indian or Pakistani. Out of thirty students only three were white.

"That's right," Sanders said to me later, as we walked down the hallway toward his laboratory. "A class like Physics 101 doesn't attract Americans. It's been that way for years. Industry can't find them, either. We would be up shit creek if we didn't have the Asians and Indians who come here to get doctorates in math and engineering, and then work for American companies."

We continued down some stairs, and turned left. We were in a basement passageway. Sanders walked quickly.

"But the trouble is, it's changing," he continued. "My Asian students are starting to go home. Koreans are going back to Korea. Taiwanese the same. Even Indians are returning home. The standard of living is going up in their countries, and there's more opportunity back home now. Some of these foreign countries have large numbers of well-trained people." He led me briskly down a flight of stairs. "Do you know what city has the highest number of Ph.D.'s per capita in the world?"

"Boston?"

"Seoul, Korea. Think about *that* as we rocket into the twenty-first century."

Now we were going down another corridor. Then briefly outside, into sunlight, down a covered walkway, and back into another building. Sanders kept glancing back over his shoulder, as if he was afraid of losing me. But he never stopped talking.

"And with foreign students going home, we don't have enough engineers to do American research. To create new American technology. It's a simple balance sheet. Not enough trained people. Even big companies like IBM are starting to have trouble. Trained people simply don't exist. Watch the door."

The door swung back toward me. I went through. I said, "But if there are all these high-tech job opportunities, won't they begin to attract students?"

"Not like investment banking. Or law." Sanders laughed. "America may lack engineers and scientists, but we lead the world in the production of lawyers. America has half the lawyers in the entire world. Think of that." He shook his head.

"We have four percent of the world population. We have eighteen percent of the world economy. But we have fifty percent of the lawyers. And thirty-five thousand more every year, pouring out of the schools. That's where our productivity's directed. That's where our national focus is. Half our TV shows are about lawyers. America has become Land of Lawyers. Everybody suing. Everybody disputing. Everybody in court. After all, three quarters of a million American lawyers have to do *something*. They have to make their three hundred thousand a year. Other countries think we're crazy."

He unlocked a door. I saw a sign that said ADVANCED IMAGING LABORATORY in hand-painted lettering, and an arrow. Sanders led me down a long basement hallway.

"Even our brightest kids are badly educated. The best American kids now rank twelfth in the world, after the industrialized countries of Asia and Europe. And that's our top students. At the bottom, it's worse. One-third of high school graduates can't read a bus schedule. They're illiterate."

We came to the end of the hallway, and turned right. "And the kids I see are lazy. Nobody wants to work. I teach physics. It takes years to master. But all the kids want to dress like Charlie Sheen and make a million dollars before they're twenty-eight. The only way you can make that kind of money is in law, investment banking, Wall Street. Places where the game is paper profits, something for nothing. But that's what the kids want to do, these days."

"Maybe at U.S.C."

"Trust me. Everywhere. They all watch television."

He swung another door open. Still another corridor. This one smelled moldy, damp.

"I know, I know. I'm old-fashioned," Sanders said. "I still believe that every human being stands for something. You stand for something. I stand for something. Just being on this planet, wearing the clothes we wear, doing the work we do, we each stand for something. And in this little corner of the world," he said, "we stand for cutting the crap. We analyze network news and see where they have been fucking around with the tape. We analyze TV commercials and show where the tricks are—"

Sanders suddenly stopped.

"What's the matter?"

"Wasn't there someone else?" he said. "Didn't you come here with someone else?"

"No. Just me."

"Oh, good." Sanders continued on at his same breakneck pace. "I always worry about losing people down here. Ah, okay. Here we are. The lab. Good. This door is just where I left it."

With a flourish, he threw the door open. I stared at the room, shocked.

"I know it doesn't look like much," Sanders said.

That, I thought, was a serious understatement.

I was looking at a basement space with rusty pipes and fittings hanging down from the ceiling. The green linoleum on the floor curled up in several places to expose concrete beneath. Arranged around the room were battered wooden tables, each heaped with equipment, and drooping wires down the sides. At each table, a student sat facing monitors. In several places, water plinked into buckets on the floor. Sanders said, "The only space we could get was here in the basement, and we don't have the money to put in little amenities like a ceiling. Never mind, doesn't matter. Just watch your head."

He moved forward into the room. I am about a hundred and eighty centimeters tall, not quite six feet, and I had to crouch to enter the room. From somewhere in the ceiling above, I heard a harsh rasping sizzle.

"Skaters," Sanders explained.

"Sorry?"

"We're underneath the ice rink. You get used to it. Actually, it's not bad now. When they have hockey practice in the afternoon, then it's a bit noisy."

We moved deeper into the room. I felt like I was in a submarine. I glanced at the students at their workstations. They were all intent on their work; nobody looked up as we passed. Sanders said, "What kind of tape do you want to duplicate?"

"Eight-millimeter Japanese. Security tape. It might be difficult."

"Difficult? I doubt that very much," Sanders said. "You know, back in my youth, I wrote most of the early video image-enhancement algorithms. You know, despeckling and inversion and edge tracing. That stuff. The Sanders algorithms were the ones everybody used. I was a graduate student at Cal Tech then. I worked at JPL in my spare time. No, no, we can do it."

I handed him a tape. He looked at it. "Cute little bugger."

I said, "What happened? To all your algorithms?"

"There was no commercial use for them," he said. "Back in the eighties, American companies like RCA and GE got out of commercial electronics entirely. My image enhancement programs didn't have much use in America." He shrugged. "So I tried to sell them to Sony, in Japan."

"And?"

"The Japanese had already patented the products. In Japan."

"You mean they already had the algorithms?"

"No. They just had patents. In Japan, patenting is a form of war. The Japanese patent like crazy. And they have a strange system. It takes eight years to get a patent in Japan, but your application is made public after eighteen months, after which royalties are moot. And of course Japan doesn't have reciprocal licensing agreements with America. It's one of the ways they keep their edge.

"Anyway, when I got to Japan I found Sony and Hitachi had some related patents and they had done what is called 'patent flooding.' Meaning they covered possible related uses. They didn't have the rights to use my algorithms—but I discovered I didn't have the rights, either. Because they had already patented the *use* of my invention." He shrugged. "It's complicated to explain. Anyway, that's ancient history. By now the Japanese have devised *much* more complicated video software, far surpassing anything we have. They're years ahead of us now. But we struggle along in this lab. Ah. Just the person we need. Dan. Are you busy?"

A young woman looked up from the computer console. Large eyes, horn-rim glasses, dark hair. Her face was partially blocked by the ceiling pipes.

"You're not Dan," Sanders said, sounding surprised. "Where's Dan, Theresa?"

"Picking up a midterm," Theresa said. "I'm just helping run the real-time progressions. They're finishing now." I had the impression that she was older than the other students. It was hard to say why, exactly. It certainly wasn't her clothes: she wore a bright colored headband and a U2 T-shirt under a jeans jacket. But she had a calm quality that made her seem older.

"Can you switch to something else?" Sanders said, walking around the able to look at the monitor. "Because we have a rush job here. We have to help out the police." I followed Sanders, ducking pipes.

"Sure, I guess," the woman said. She started to shut down units on the desk. Her back was turned to me, and then finally I could see her. She was dark, exotic-looking, almost Eurasian. In fact she was beautiful, drop-dead beautiful. She looked like one of those high cheek-boned models in magazines. And for a moment I was confused, because this woman was too beautiful to be working in some basement electronics laboratory. It didn't make sense.

"Say hello to Theresa Asakuma," he said. "The only Japanese graduate student working here."

"Hi," I said. I blushed. I felt stupid. I felt that information was coming at me too fast. And all things considered, I would rather not have a Japanese handling these tapes. But her first name wasn't Japanese, and she didn't look Japanese, she looked Eurasian or perhaps part Japanese, so exotic, maybe she was even—

"Good morning, Lieutenant," she said. She extended her left hand, the wrong hand, for me to shake. She held it out to me sideways, the way someone does when their right hand is injured.

I shook hands with her. "Hello, Miss Asakuma."

"Theresa."

"Okay."

"Isn't she beautiful?" Sanders said, acting as if he took credit for it. "Just beautiful."

"Yes," I said. "Actually, I'm surprised you're not a model."

There was an awkward moment. I couldn't tell why. She turned quickly away.

"It never interested me," she said.

And Sanders immediately jumped in and said, "Theresa, Lieutenant Smith needs us to copy some tapes. *These* tapes."

Sanders held one out to her. She took it in her left hand and held it to the light. Her right hand remained bent at the elbow, pressed to her waist. Then I saw that her right arm was withered, ending in a fleshy stump protruding beyond the sleeve of her jeans jacket. It looked like the arm of a thalidomide baby.

"Quite interesting," she said, squinting at the tape. "Eight-millimeter high density. Maybe it's the proprietary digital format we've been hearing about. The one that includes real-time image enhancement."

"I'm sorry, I don't know," I said. I was feeling foolish for having said anything about being a model. I dug into my box and brought out the playback machine.

Theresa immediately took a screwdriver and removed the top. She bent over the innards. I saw a green circuit board, a black motor, and three small crystal cylinders. "Yes. It's the new setup. Very slick. Dr. Sanders, look they're doing it with just three heads. The board must generate component RGB, because over here—you think this is compression circuitry?"

"Probably digital to analog converter," Sanders said. "Very neat. So small." He turned to me, holding up the box. "You know how the Japanese can make things this way and we can't? They *kaizen* 'em. A process of deliberate, patient, continual refinements. Each year the products get a little better, a little smaller, a little cheaper. Americans don't think that way. Americans are always looking for the quantum leap, the big advance forward. Americans try to hit a home run—to knock it out of the park—and then sit back. The Japanese just hit singles all day long, and they never sit back. So with something like this, you're looking at an expression of philosophy as much as anything."

He talked like this for a while, pivoting the cylinders, admiring it. Finally I said, "Can you copy the tapes?"

"Sure," Theresa said. "From the converter, we can run a signal out of this machine and lay it down on whatever media you like. You want three quarter? Optical master? VHS?"

"VHS," I said.

"That's easy," she said.

"But will it be an accurate copy? The people at JPL said they couldn't guarantee the copy would be accurate."

"Oh, hell, JPL," Sanders said. "They just talk like that because they work for the government. We get things *done* here. Right Theresa?"

But Theresa wasn't listening. I watched her plugging cables and wires, moving swiftly with her good hand, using her stump to stabilize and hold the box. Like many disabled people, her movements were so fluid it was hardly noticeable that her right hand was missing. Soon she had the small playback machine hooked to a second recorder, and several different monitors.

"What're all these?"

"To check the signal."

"You mean for playback?"

"No. The big monitor there will show the image. The others let me look at the signal characteristics, and the data map: how the image has been laid down on the tape."

I said, "You need to do that?"

"No. I just want to snoop. I'm curious about how they've set up this high density format."

Sanders said to me, "What is the actual source material?"

"It's from an office security camera."

"And this tape is original?"

"I think so. Why?"

"Well, if it's original material we want to be extra careful with it," Sanders said. He was talking to Theresa, instructing her. "We don't want to set up any feedback loops scrambling the media surface. Or signal leaks off the heads that will compromise the integrity of the data stream."

"Don't worry," she said. "I got it handled." She pointed to her setup. "See that? It'll warn of an impedance shift. And I'm monitoring the central processor too."

"Okay," Sanders said. He was beaming like a proud parent.

"How long will this take?" I said.

"Not long. We can lay down the signal at very high speed. The rate limit is a function of the playback device, and it seems to have a fast-forward scan. So, maybe two or three minutes per tape."

I glanced at my watch. "I have a ten-thirty appointment I can't be late for, and I don't want to leave these . . ."

"You need all of them done?"

"Actually, just five are critical."

"Then let's do those first."

We ran the first few seconds of each tape, one after another, looking for the five that came from the cameras on the forty-sixth floor. As each tape started, I saw the camera image on the central monitor of Theresa's table. On the side monitors, signal traces bounced and jiggled like an intensive care unit. I mentioned it.

"That's just about right," she said. "Intensive care for video." She ejected one tape, stuck in another, and started it up. "Oops. Did you say this material was original? It's not. These tapes are copies."

"How do you know?"

"Because we got a windup signature." Theresa bent over the equipment, staring at the signal traces, making fine adjustments with her knobs and dials.

"I think that's what you got, yes," Sanders said. He turned to me. "You see, with video it's difficult to detect a copy in the image itself. The older analog video shows some degradation in successive generations, but in a digital system like this, there is no difference at all. Each copy is literally identical to the master."

"Then how can you say the tapes are copies?"

"Theresa isn't looking at the picture," Sanders said. "She's looking at the signal. Even though we can't detect a copy from the image, sometimes we can determine the image came from another video playback, instead of a camera."

I shook my head. "How?"

Theresa said, "It has to do with how the signal is laid down in the first half-second of taping. If the recording video is started before the playback video, there is sometimes a slight fluctuation in the signal output as the playback machine starts up. It's a mechanical function: the playback motors can't get up to speed instantaneously. There are electronic circuits in the playback machine to minimize the effect, but there's always an interval of getting up to speed."

"And that's what you detected?"

She nodded. "It's called a windup signature."

Sanders said, "And that never happens if the signal is coming direct from a camera, because a camera has no moving parts. A camera is instantaneously up to speed at all times."

I frowned. "So these tapes are copies."

"Is that bad?" Sanders said.

"I don't know. If they were copied, they might also be changed, right?"

"In theory, yes," Sanders said. "In practice, we'd have to look carefully. And it would be very hard to know for certain. These tapes come from a Japanese company?"

"Yes."

"Nakamoto?"

I nodded. "Yes."

"Frankly I'm not surprised they gave you copies," Sanders said. "The Japanese are extremely cautious. They're not very trusting of outsiders. And Japanese corporations in America feel the way we would feel doing business in Nigeria: they think they're surrounded by savages."

"Hey," Theresa said.

"Sorry," Sanders said, "but you know what I mean. The Japanese feel they have to put up with us. With our ineptitude, our slowness, our stupidity, our incompetence. That makes them self-protective. So if these tapes have any legal significance, the last thing they'd do is turn the originals over to a barbarian policeman like you. No, no, they'd give you a copy and keep the original in case they need it for their defense. Fully confident that with your inferior American video technology, you'd never be able to detect that it was a copy, anyway."

I frowned. "How long would it take to make copies?"

"Not long," Sanders said, shaking his head. "The way Theresa is scanning now, five minutes a tape. I imagine the Japanese can do it much faster. Say, two minutes a tape."

"In that case, they had plenty of time to make copies last night."

As we talked, Theresa was continuing to shuffle the tapes, looking at the first portions of each. As each image came up, she'd glance at me. I would shake my head. I was seeing all the different security cameras. Finally, the first of the tapes from the forty-sixth floor appeared, the familiar office image I had seen before.

"That's one."

"Okay. Here we go. Laying it onto VHS." Theresa started the first copy. She ran the tape forward at high speed, the images streaky and quick. On the side monitors, the signals bounced and jittered nervously.

She said, "Does this have something to do with the murder last night?"

"Yes. You know about that?"

She shrugged. "I saw it on the news. The killer died in a car crash?"

"That's right," I said.

She was turned away. The three-quarter profile of her face was strikingly beautiful, the high curve of her cheekbone. I thought of what a playboy Eddie Sakamura was known to be. I said, "Did you know him?"

"No," she said. After a moment she added, "He was Japanese."

Another moment of awkwardness descended on our little group. There was something that both Theresa and Sanders seemed to know that I did not. But I didn't know how to ask. So I watched the video.

Once again, I saw the sunlight moving across the floor. Then the room lights came up as the office personnel thinned. Now the floor was empty. And then, at high speed, Cheryl Austin appeared, followed by the man. They kissed passionately.

"Ah ha," Sanders said. "Is this it?"

"Yes."

He frowned as he watched the action progress. "You mean the murder is *recorded?*"

"Yes," I said. "On multiple cameras."

"You're kidding."

Sanders fell silent, watching events proceed. With the streaky high-speed image, it was difficult to see more than the basic events. The two people moving to the conference room. The sudden struggle. Forcing her back on the table. Stepping away suddenly. Leaving the room in haste.

Nobody spoke. We all watched the tape.

I glanced at Theresa. Her face was blank. The image was reflected in her glasses.

Eddie passed the mirror, and went into the dark passageway. The tape ran on for a few more seconds, and then the cassette popped out.

"That's one. You say there are multiple cameras? How many all together?"

"Five, I think," I said.

She marked the first cassette with a stick-on label. She started the second tape in the machine, and began another high-speed duplication.

I said, "These copies are exact?"

"Oh, yes."

"So they're legal?"

Sanders frowned. "Legal in what sense?"

"Well, as evidence, in a court of law—"

"Oh, no," Sanders said. "These tapes would never be admissible in a court of law."

"But if they're exact copies—"

"It's nothing to do with that. All forms of photographic evidence including video, are no longer admissible in court."

"I haven't heard that," I said.

"It hasn't happened yet," Sanders said. "The case law isn't entirely clear. But it's coming. All photographs are suspect these days. Because now, with digital systems, they can be changed perfectly. *Perfectly*. And that's something new. Remember years ago, how the Russians would remove politicians from photographs of their May Day line ups? It was always a crude cut-and-paste job—and you could always see that something had been done. There was a funny space between the shoulders of the remaining people. Or a discoloration on the back wall. Or you could see the brushstrokes of the retoucher who tried to smooth over the damage. But anyway, you could see it—fairly easily. You could *see* the picture had been altered. The whole business was laughable."

"I remember," I said.

"Photographs always had integrity precisely because they were impossible to change. So we considered photographs to represent reality. But for several years now, computers have allowed us to make seamless alterations of photographic images. A few years back the *National Geographic* moved the Great Pyramid of Egypt on a cover photo. The editors didn't like where the pyramid was, and they thought it would compose better if it was moved. So they just altered the photograph and moved it. Nobody could tell. But if you go back to Egypt with a camera and try to duplicate that picture, you'll find you can't. Because there is no place in the real world where the pyramids line up that way. The photograph no longer represents reality. But you can't tell. Minor example."

"And someone could do the same thing to this tape?"

"In theory, any video can be changed."

On the monitor, I watched the murder occurring a second time. This camera was from the far end of the room. It didn't show the actual murder very well, but afterward, Sakamura was clearly visible as he walked toward the camera.

I said, "The image could be changed how?"

Sanders laughed. "These days, you can make any damn change you want."

"Could you change the identity of the murderer?"

"Technically, yes," Sanders said. "Mapping a face onto a complex moving object is now possible. Technically possible. But as a practical matter, it'd be a bitch to do."

I said nothing. But it was just as well. Sakamura was our leading suspect and he was dead; the chief wanted the case finished. So did I.

"Of course," Sanders said, "the Japanese have all sorts of fancy video algorithms for surface mapping and three-dimensional transformations. They can do things that we can't begin to imagine." He drummed his fingers on the table again. "What is the timetable of these tapes? What's their history?"

I said, "The murder happened at eight-thirty last night, as shown on the clock. We were told the tapes were removed from the security office around eight forty-five p.m. We asked for them, and there was some back-and-forth with the Japanese."

"As always. And when did you finally take possession?"

"They were delivered to division headquarters around one-thirty a.m."

"Okay," Sanders said. "That means they had the tapes from eight forty-five to one-thirty."

"Right. A little less than five hours."

Sanders frowned. "Five tapes, with five different camera angles, to change in five hours?" Sanders shook his head. "No way. It just can't be done, Lieutenant."

"Yeah," Theresa said. "It's impossible. Even for them. It's just too many pixels to change."

I said, "You're sure about that."

"Well," Theresa said, "the only way it could be done that fast is with an automated program, and even the most sophisticated programs need you to polish the details by hand. Things like bad blur can give it all away."

"Bad blur?" I said. I found I liked asking her questions. I liked looking at her face.

"Bad motion blur," Sanders said. "Video runs at thirty frames a second.

You can think of each frame of video as a picture that's shot at a shutter speed of one-thirtieth of a second. Which is very slow—much slower than pocket cameras. If you film a runner at a thirtieth of a second, the legs are just streaks. Blurs.

"That's called motion blur. And if you alter it by a mechanical process, it starts to look wrong. The image appears too sharp, too crisp. Edges look odd. It's back to the Russians: you can see it's been changed. For realistic motion, you need the right amount of blur."

"I see."

Theresa said, "And there's the color shift."

"Right," Sanders said. "Inside the blur itself, there is a color shift. For example, look there on the monitor. The man is wearing a blue suit, and his coat is swinging out as he spins the girl around the room. Now. If you take a frame of that action, and blow it up to its pixels, you will find that the coat is navy, but the blur is progressive shades of lighter blue, until at the edge it seems almost transparent—you can't tell from a single frame exactly where the coat ends and the background begins."

I could vaguely imagine it. "Okay . . ."

"If the edge colors don't blend smoothly, you will notice it immediately. It can take hours to clean up a few seconds of tape, as in a commercial. But if you don't do it, you will see it like *that*." He snapped his fingers.

"So even though they duplicated the tapes, they couldn't have altered them?"

"Not in five hours," Sanders said. "They just didn't have time."

"Then we are seeing what actually happened."

"No doubt about it," Sanders said. "But we'll poke around with this image, anyway, after you go. Theresa wants to fiddle with it, I know she does. So do I. Check in with us later today. We'll tell you if there's anything funny. But basically, it can't be done. And it wasn't done here."

As I pulled into the parking circle at the Sunset Hills Country Club, I saw Connor standing in front of the big stucco clubhouse. He bowed to the three Japanese golfers standing with him, and they bowed back. Then he shook hands with them all, tossed the clubs into the back seat, and got into my car.

"You're late, *kōhai*."

"Sorry. It's only a few minutes. I was held up at U.S.C."

"Your lateness inconvenienced everyone. As a matter of politeness, they felt obliged to keep me company in front of the club while I waited for you. Men of their position are not comfortable standing around. They are busy. But they felt obligated and could not leave me there. You embarrassed me very much. And you reflected poorly on the department."

"I'm sorry. I didn't realize."

"Start to realize, *kōhai*. You're not alone in the world."

I put the car in gear, and drove out. I looked at the Japanese in the rearview mirror. They were waving as we left. They did not appear unhappy, or in a rush to leave. "Who were you playing with?"

"Aoki-san is the head of Tokio Marine in Vancouver. Hanada-san is a vice-president of Mitsui Bank in London. And Kenichi Asaka runs all of Toyota's Southeast Asian plants from K.L. to Singapore. He's based in Bangkok."

"What are they doing here?"

"They're on vacation," Connor said. "A short holiday in the States for golf. They find it pleasant to relax in a slower-paced country like ours."

I drove up the winding drive to Sunset Boulevard, and stopped to wait for the light. "Where to?"

"The Four Seasons Hotel."

I turned right, heading toward Beverly Hills. "And why are these men playing golf with you?"

"Oh, we go way back," he said. "A few favors here and there, over the years. I'm nobody important. But relationships must be maintained. A phone call, a small gift, a game when you're in town. Because you never know when you will need your network. Relationships are your source of information, your safety valve, and your early warning system. In the Japanese way of seeing the world."

"Who asked for this game?"

"Hanada-san was already intending to play. I just joined him. I'm quite a good golfer, you know."

"Why did you want to play?"

"Because I wanted to know more about the Saturday meetings," Connor said.

I remembered the Saturday meetings. On the video we had seen at the newsroom, Sakamura had grabbed Cheryl Austin and said: You don't understand, this is all about the Saturday meetings.

"And did they tell you?"

Connor nodded. "Apparently they began a long time ago," he said. "Nineteen eighty or so. First they were held in the Century Plaza, and later in the Sheraton, and finally in the Biltmore."

Connor stared out the window. The car jounced over the potholes on Sunset Boulevard.

"For several years, the meetings were a regular event. Prominent Japanese industrialists who happened to be in town would attend an ongoing discussion of what should be done about America. Of how the American economy should be managed."

"*What*?"

"Yes."

"That's outrageous!"

"Why?" Connor said.

"*Why*? Because this is *our* country. You can't have a bunch of foreigners sitting around in secret meetings and deciding how to manage it!"

"The Japanese don't see it that way," Connor said.

"I'm sure they don't! I'm sure they think they have a goddamn right!"

Connor shrugged. "As a matter of fact, that's exactly what they think. And the Japanese believe they have earned the right to decide—"

"*Christ*—"

"Because they have invested heavily in our economy. They have lent us a lot of money, Peter: a *lot* of money. Hundreds of billions of dollars. For most of the last fifteen years, the United States has run a billion dollars of trade deficit a *week* with Japan. That's a billion dollars every week that they must do something with. A torrent of money roaring toward them. They don't especially want so many dollars. What can they do with all their excess billions?

"They decided to lend the money back to us. Our government was running a budget deficit, year after year. We weren't paying for our own programs. So the Japanese financed our budget deficit. They invested in us. And they lent their money, based on certain assurances from our government. Washington assured the Japanese that we would set our house in order. We would cut our deficit. We would improve education, rebuild our infrastructure, even raise taxes if necessary. In short, we would clean up our act. Because only then does an investment in America make sense."

"Uh-huh," I said.

"But we did none of those things. We let the deficit get worse, and we devalued the dollar. We cut its value in half in 1985. You know what that did to Japanese investments in America? It fucked them. Whatever they invested in 1984 now paid half its previous return."

I vaguely remembered something about this. I said, "I thought we did that to help our trade deficit, to boost exports."

"We did, but it didn't work. Our trade balance with Japan got worse. Normally, if you devalue your currency by half, the cost of everything imported doubles. But the Japanese slashed prices on their VCRs and copiers, and held their market share. Remember, business is war.

"All we really accomplished was to make American land and American companies cheap for the Japanese to buy, because the yen was now twice as strong as it had been. We made the biggest banks in the world all Japanese. And we made America a poor country."

"What does this have to do with the Saturday meetings?"

"Well," Connor said, "suppose you have an uncle who is a drunk. He says if you lend him money he'll stop drinking. But he doesn't stop drinking. And you'd like to get your money. You want to salvage what you can from your bad investment. Also, you know that your uncle, being a drunk, is likely to get loaded and hurt somebody. Your uncle is out of control. So something has to be done. And the family sits down together to decide what to do about their problem uncle. That's what the Japanese decided to do."

"Uh-huh." Connor must have heard the skepticism in my voice.

"Look," he said. "Get this conspiracy stuff out of your head. Do you want to take over Japan? Do you want to run their country? Of course not. No sensible country wants to take over another country. Do business, yes. Have a relationship, yes. But not *take over*. Nobody wants the responsibility. Nobody wants to be bothered. Just like with the drunken uncle—you only have those meetings when you're forced to. It's a last resort."

"So that's how the Japanese see it?"

"They see billions and billions of their dollars, *kōhai*. Invested in a country that's in deep trouble. That's filled with strange individualistic people who talk constantly. Who confront each other constantly. Who argue all the time. People who aren't well educated, who don't know much about the world, who get their information from television. People who don't work very hard, who tolerate violence and drug use, and who don't seem to object to it. The Japanese have billions of dollars in this peculiar land and they would like a decent return on their investment. And even though the American economy is collapsing—it will soon be third in the world after Japan and Europe—it's still important to try and hold it together. Which is all they're trying to do."

"That's it?" I said. "They're just doing the good work of saving America?"

"Somebody needs to do it," Connor said. "We can't go on this way."

"We'll manage."

"That's what the English always said." He shook his head. "But now England is poor. And America is becoming poor, too."

"Why is it becoming poor?" I said, speaking louder than I intended.

"The Japanese say it's because America has become a land without substance. We let our manufacturing go. We don't make things any- more. When you manufacture products, you add value to raw materials, and you literally create wealth. But America has stopped doing that. Ameri- cans make money now by paper manipulation, which the Japanese say is bound to catch up to us because paper profits don't reflect real wealth. They think our fascination with Wall Street and junk bonds is crazy."

"And therefore the Japanese ought to manage us?"

"They think *someone* ought to manage us. They'd prefer we do it ourselves."

"Jesus."

Connor shifted in his seat. "Save your outrage, *kōhai*. Because according to Hanada-san, the Saturday meetings stopped in 1991."

"Oh?"

"Yes. That was when the Japanese decided not to worry about whether America would clean up its act. They saw advantages in the present situa- tion: America is asleep, and inexpensive to buy."

"So there aren't Saturday meetings any more?"

"There are occasional ones. Because of *nichibei kankei*: the ongoing Japanese-American relationship. The economies of the two countries are interlocked by now. Neither country can pull out, even if they wanted to. But the meetings are no longer important. They are basically social func- tions. So what Sakamura said to Cheryl Austin is wrong. And her death had nothing to do with the Saturday meetings."

"What does it have to do with?"

"My friends seemed to think it was personal. A *chijou no motsure*, a crime of passion. Involving a beautiful, *irokichigai* woman and a jealous man."

"And you believe them?"

"Well, the thing is, they were unanimous. All three of these business- men. Of course Japanese are reluctant to express disagreement among themselves, even on the golf course of an underdeveloped peasant country. But I have learned that unanimity toward a *gaijin* may cover a multitude of sins."

"You think they were lying?"

"Not exactly." Connor shook his head. "But I had the impression they were telling me something by not telling me. This morning was a game of *hara no saguriai*. My friends were not forthcoming."

Connor described his golf game. There had been long silences all morning. Everyone in the foursome was polite and considerate, but spoken comments were rare and reserved. Most of the time, the men walked over the course in complete silence.

"And you had gone there for information?" I said. "How could you stand it?"

"Oh, I was getting information." But as he explained it, it was all unspoken. Basically, the Japanese have an understanding based on centuries of shared culture, and they are able to communicate feelings without words. It's the closeness that exists in America between a parent and child—a child often understands everything, just from a parent's glance. But Americans don't rely on unspoken communication as a general rule, and the Japanese do. It is as if all Japanese are members of the same family, and they can communicate without words. To a Japanese, silences have meaning.

"It's nothing mystical or wonderful," Connor said. "For the most part it is because the Japanese are so hemmed in by rules and conventions, they end up unable to say anything at all. For politeness, to save face, the other person is obliged to read the situation, the context, and the subtle signs of body posture and unstated feeling. Because the first person feels he can't actually put anything into words. Any speaking at all would be indelicate. So the point must be gotten across in other ways."

I said, "And that's how your morning was spent? Not talking?"

Connor shook his head. He felt he had quite clear communication with the Japanese golfers, and wasn't troubled by the silences at all.

"Because I was asking them to talk about other Japanese—members of their family—I had to frame my questions with great delicacy. Just as I would if I were asking whether your sister was in jail or any subject that was painful or awkward for you. I would be attentive to how long it took you to answer, and the pauses between your statements, the tone of your voice— all sorts of things. Beyond the literal communication. Okay?"

"Okay."

"It means you get the feeling by an intuition."

"And what was the intuition you got?"

"They said, 'We are mindful that you have performed services for us in the past. We feel a desire to help you now. But this murder is a Japanese matter and thus we are unable to tell you everything that we might like to. From our reticence, you may draw useful conclusions about the underlying issue.' That's what they said to me."

"And what is the underlying issue?"

"Well," Connor said. "They mentioned MicroCon several times."

"That high-tech company?"

"Yes. The one that's being sold. Apparently it's a small company in Silicon Valley that makes specialized computer machinery. And there are political problems about the sale. They referred to those problems several times."

"So this murder has something to do with MicroCon?"

"I think so." He shifted in his chair. "By the way, what did you learn at U.S.C. about the tapes?"

"For one thing, that they were duplicated."

Connor nodded. "I assumed that," he said.

"You did?"

"Ishiguro would never give us the originals. The Japanese think everybody who is not Japanese is a barbarian. They mean it, literally: *barbarian*. Stinking, vulgar, stupid barbarian. They're polite about it, because they know you can't help the misfortune of not being born Japanese. But they still think it."

I nodded. That was more or less what Sanders had said, too.

"The other thing," Connor said, "is that the Japanese are extremely successful, but they are not daring. They are plotters and plodders. So they're not going to give us the originals because they don't want to take any chances. Now. What else did you learn about the tapes?"

"What makes you think there was something else?" I said.

"When you looked at the tapes," he said, "I'm sure you noticed an important detail that—"

And then we were interrupted by the telephone.

"Captain Connor," said a cheerful voice, over the speaker phone. "This is Jerry Orr. Over at Sunset Hills Country Club? You left without taking the papers with you."

"The papers?"

"The application," Orr said. "You need to fill it out, Captain. Of course it's just routine. I can assure you, there won't be any problem with it, considering who your sponsors are."

"My sponsors," Connor said.

"Yes, sir," Orr said. "And congratulations. As you know, it's almost impossible to obtain a membership at Sunset these days. But Mr. Hanada's company had already bought a corporate membership some time ago, and they have decided to put it in your name. I must say, it's a very nice gesture from your friends."

"Yes, it is," Connor said, frowning.

I was looking at him.

"They know how fond you are of playing golf here," Orr said. "You know the terms, of course. Hanada will purchase the membership over five years, but after that time, it'll be transferred to your name. So when you retire from club membership, you're free to sell it. Now: will you be picking up the paperwork here, or should I send it to your home?"

Connor said, "Mr. Orr, please convey my heartfelt appreciation to Mr. Hanada for his very great generosity. I hardly know what to say. But I will have to call you back about this."

"That's fine. You just let us know where to send it."

"I'll call you back," Connor said.

He pushed the button to end the call, and stared forward, frowning. There was a long silence.

I said, "How much is a membership at that club worth?"

"Seven fifty. Maybe a million."

I said, "Pretty nice gift from your friends." I was thinking again of Graham, and the way Graham had always implied that Connor was in the pocket of the Japanese. There didn't seem to be much doubt of it now.

Connor was shaking his head. "I don't get it."

"What's not to get?" I said. "Jesus, Captain. Seems pretty straightforward to me."

"No, I don't get it," Connor said.

And then the phone rang again. This time, it was for me.

"Lieutenant Smith? It's Louise Gerber. I'm *so* glad I was able to reach you."

I didn't recognize her name. I said, "Yes?"

"Since tomorrow is Saturday, I was wondering if you had any time to look at a house."

Then I remembered who she was. A month earlier I had gone out with a broker to look at houses. Michelle is getting older, and I wanted to get her out of an apartment. To get her a backyard if I could. It was pretty discouraging. Even with a real estate slump, the smallest houses were four and five hundred thousand. I couldn't possibly qualify for that, on my salary.

"This is a very special situation," she said, "and I thought of you and your little girl. It's a small house in Palms—very small—but it's a corner lot and it has a charming backyard. Flowers and a lovely lawn. The asking is three hundred. But the reason I thought of you is that the seller is willing to take back all the paper on it. I think you could get it for very little down. Do you want to see it?"

I said, "Who is the seller?"

"I don't really know. It's a special situation. The house is owned by an elderly woman who has gone into a nursing home and her son who lives in Topeka intends to sell it, but he wants an income flow instead of an outright sale. The property's not formally listed yet, but I know the seller is motivated. If you could get in tomorrow, you might be able to do something. And the backyard is charming. I can just see your little girl there."

Now Connor was looking at me. I said, "Miss Gerber, I'd have to know more about it. Who the seller is, and so on."

She sounded surprised. "Gee, I thought you'd jump at it. A situation like this doesn't come along very often. Don't you want to look at it?"

Connor was looking at me, nodding. He mouthed, say yes.

"I'll have to get back to you about this," I said.

"All right, Lieutenant," she said. She sounded reluctant. "Please let me know."

"I will."

I hung up.

"What the hell is going on?" I said. Because there wasn't any way to get around it. Between us, we had just been offered a lot of money. A *lot* of money.

Connor shook his head. "I don't know."

"Is it to do with MicroCon?"

"I don't know. I thought MicroCon was a small company. This doesn't make sense." He looked very uneasy. "What exactly *is* MicroCon?"

I said, "I think I know who to ask."

"MicroCon?" Ron Levine said, lighting a big cigar. "Sure, I can tell you about MicroCon. It's an ugly story."

We were sitting in the newsroom of American Financial Network, a cable news operation located near the airport. Through the window of Ron's office, I could see the white satellite dishes on the roof of the adjacent garage. Ron puffed on his cigar and grinned at us. He had been a financial reporter at the *Times* before taking an on-camera job here. AFN was one of the few television operations where the on-camera people weren't scripted; they had to know what they were talking about, and Ron did.

"MicroCon," he said, "was formed five years ago by a consortium of American computer manufacturers. The company was intended to develop the next generation of X-ray lithography machines for computer chips. At the time MicroCon started up, there were no American manufacturers of lithography machines—they'd all been put out of business in the eighties, under intense competition from the Japanese. MicroCon developed new technology, and has been building machines for American companies. Okay?"

"Okay," I said.

"Two years ago, MicroCon was sold to Darley-Higgins, a management company in Georgia. Darley's other operations were foundering; the company decided to sell MicroCon to raise cash. They found a buyer in Akai Ceramics, an Osaka company that already made lithography machines in Japan. Akai had plenty of cash, and was willing to acquire the American company for a high price. Then Congress moved to stop the sale."

"Why?"

"The decline of American business is starting to disturb even Congress. We've lost too many basic industries to Japan—steel and shipbuilding in the sixties, television and computer chips in the seventies, machine tools in the eighties. One day somebody wakes up and realizes these industries are vital for American defense. We've lost the ability to make components essential to our national security. We're entirely dependent on Japan to supply them. So Congress starts to worry. But I hear the sale is going through, anyway. Why? Do you guys have something to do with the sale?"

"In a sense," Connor said.

"Lucky you," Ron said, puffing on his cigar. "If you're involved in a sale to the Japanese, it's like striking oil. Everybody gets rich. You two are looking at some pretty big gifts, I imagine."

Connor nodded. "Very big."

"I'm sure," Ron said. "They'll take care of you: buy you a house or a car, get you cheap financing, something like that."

I said, "Why would they do that?"

Ron laughed. "Why would they eat sushi? It's the way they conduct business."

Connor said, "But isn't MicroCon a small sale?"

"Yeah, pretty small. The company's worth a hundred million. Akai's buying it for a hundred and fifty. On top of that, they probably have another twenty million in incentives to the current corporate officers, maybe ten million in legal, ten million in consultant fees spread around Washington, and ten million in miscellaneous gifts for people like you. So call it two hundred million, in total."

I said, "Two hundred million for a hundred-million company? Why are they paying more than it's worth?"

"They're not," Ron said. "As far as they're concerned, they're getting a bargain."

"Why?"

"Because," Ron said, "if you own the machines that are used to make something, like computer chips, you own the downstream industries that depend on those machines. MicroCon will give them control over the American computer industry. And as usual, we're allowing it to happen. Just the way we lost our television industry, and our machine-tool industry."

"What happened to the TV industry?" I said.

He glanced at his watch. "After World War II, America was the world's leading manufacturer of televisions. Twenty-seven American companies like Zenith, RCA, GE, and Emerson had a solid technological lead over foreign manufacturers. American companies were successful around the world, except in Japan. They couldn't penetrate the closed Japanese market. They were told if they wanted to sell in Japan, they had to license their technology to Japanese companies. And they did, reluctantly, under pressure from the American government, which wanted to keep Japan as a friendly ally against Russia. Okay?"

"Okay . . ."

"Now, licensing is a bad idea. It means Japan gets our technology for their own use, and we lose Japan as an export market. Pretty soon Japan begins to make cheap black-and-white TVs and exports them to America— something we can't do in Japan, right? By 1972, sixty percent of American black-and-white sales are imports. By 1976, one hundred percent are imports. We've lost the black-and-white market. American workers don't make those sets any more. Those jobs are gone from America.

"We say it doesn't matter: our companies have moved on to color. But the Japanese government starts an intensive program to develop a color-television industry. Once again, Japan licenses American technology, refines it in their protected markets, and floods us with exports. Once again, exports drive out American companies. Exactly the same story. By 1980 only three American companies still make color TVs. By 1987, there's only one, Zenith."

"But Japanese sets were better and cheaper," I said.

"They may have been better," Ron said, "but they were only cheaper because they were sold below production cost, to wipe out American competitors. That's called dumping. It's illegal under both American and international law."

"Then why didn't we stop it?"

"Good question. Especially since dumping was only one of many illegal Japanese marketing techniques. They also fixed prices: they had something called the Tenth-Day Group. Japanese managers met every ten days in a Tokyo hotel to set prices in America. We protested, but the meetings continued. They also pushed distribution of their products by collusive arrangements. The Japanese allegedly paid millions in kickbacks to American distributors like Sears. They engaged in massive customs fraud. And they destroyed the American industry, which could not compete.

"Of course, our companies protested, and sued for relief—there were dozens of cases of dumping, fraud, and antitrust brought against Japanese companies in federal court. Dumping cases are usually resolved within a year. But our government provided no help—and the Japanese are skilled foot-draggers. They paid American lobbyists millions to plead their case. By the time the suits came to trial twelve years later, the battle was over in the marketplace. And of course all during this time, American companies could never fight back in Japan. They couldn't even get a foot in the door in Japan."

"You're saying the Japanese took over the television industry illegally?"

Ron shrugged. "They couldn't have done it without our help," he said. "Our government was coddling Japan, which they saw as a tiny emerging country. And American industry was perceived as not needing government help. There's always been a strain of antibusiness sentiment in America. But our government never seemed to realize, it's just not the same here. When Sony develops the Walkman, we don't say, 'Nice product. Now you have to license it to GE and sell it through an American company.' If they seek distribution, we don't tell them, 'I'm sorry, but American stores all have preexisting arrangements with American suppliers. You'll have to distribute through an American company here.' If they seek patents, we don't say, 'Patents take eight years to be awarded, during which time your application will be publicly available so that our companies can read what you've invented and copy it free of charge, so that by the time we issue a patent our companies will already have their own version of your technology.'

"We don't do any of those things. Japan does all of them. Their markets are closed. Our markets are wide open. It's not a level playing field. In fact, it's not a playing field at all. It's a one-way street.

"And by now we have a defeatist business climate in this country. American companies got their asses handed to them in black-and-white television. They got their asses handed to them in color television. The U.S. government refused to help our companies fight illegal Japanese trade practices. So when Ampex invented the VCR, they didn't even try to make a commercial product. They just licensed the technology to Japan and moved on. And pretty soon you find that American companies don't do research. Why develop new technology if your own government is so hostile to your efforts that you won't be able to bring it to market?"

"But isn't American business weak and badly managed?"

"That's the standard line," Ron said. "As promoted by the Japanese and their American spokesmen. It's only with a few episodes that people ever glimpsed how outrageous the Japanese really were. Like the Houdaille case. You know that one? Houdaille was a machine-tool company that claimed its patents and licenses were being violated by companies in Japan. A federal judge sent Houdaille's lawyer to Japan to gather evidence. But the Japanese refused to issue him a visa."

"You're kidding."

"What do they care?" Ron said. "They know we'll never retaliate. When the Houdaille case came before the Reagan administration, it did nothing. So Houdaille got out of machine tools. Because nobody can compete against dumped products—that's the whole point of doing it."

"Don't you lose money if you dump?"

"For a while, yes. But you're selling millions of units, so you can refine your production lines, and get your costs down. A couple of years later, you really can make the products for a lower cost. Meanwhile you've wiped out the competition and you control the market. You see, the Japanese think strategically—they're in for the long haul, for how things will look fifty years from now. An American company has to show a profit every three months or the CEO and the officers will be out on the street. But the Japanese don't care about short-term profits at all. They want market share. Business is like warfare to them. Gaining ground. Wiping out the competition. Getting control of a market. That's what they've been doing for the last thirty years.

"So the Japanese dumped steel, televisions, consumer electronics, computer chips, machine tools—and nobody stopped them. And we lost those industries. Japanese companies and the Japanese government target specific industries, which they take over. Industry after industry, year after year. While we sit around and spout off about free trade. But free trade is meaningless unless there is also fair trade. And the Japanese don't believe in fair trade at all. You know, there's a reason the Japanese love Reagan. They cleaned up during his presidency. In the name of free trade, he spread our legs real wide."

"Why don't Americans understand this?" I said.

Connor laughed. "Why do they eat hamburgers? It's the way they are, *kōhai*."

From the newsroom, a woman called, "Somebody named Connor here? Call for you from the Four Seasons Hotel."

Connor glanced at his watch and stood up. "Excuse me." He walked out into the newsroom. Through the glass I saw him talking on the phone, making notes.

"You realize," Ron said, "it's all still going on. Why is a Japanese camera cheaper in New York than in Tokyo? You ship it halfway around the world, pay import duty and distribution costs, and it's still cheaper? How is that possible? Japanese tourists buy their own products here because they're cheaper. Meanwhile, American products in Japan cost seventy percent more than here. Why doesn't the American government get tough? I don't know. Part of the answer is up there."

He pointed to the monitor in his office; a distinguished-looking man was talking above a running tickertape. The sound was turned low. "You see that guy? That's David Rawlings. Professor of business at Stanford. Specialist in the Pacific Rim. He's a typical—turn that up, will you? He might be talking about MicroCon."

I turned the knob on the set. I heard Rawlings say: " . . . think American attitudes are completely irrational. After all, Japanese companies are providing jobs for Americans, while American companies are moving jobs offshore, taking them away from their own people. The Japanese can't understand what the complaints are about."

Ron sighed. "Typical bullshit," he said.

On the screen, Professor Rawlings was saying, "I think the American people are rather ungrateful for the help our country is getting from foreign investors."

Ron laughed. "Rawlings is part of the group we call the Chrysanthemum Kissers. Academic experts who deliver the Japanese propaganda line. They don't really have a choice, because they need access to Japan to work, and if they start to sound critical, their contacts in Japan dry up. Doors are closed to them. And in America, the Japanese will whisper in certain ears that the offending person is not to be trusted, or that their views are 'out of date.' Or worse—that they're racist. Anybody who criticizes Japan is a racist. Pretty soon these academics begin to lose speaking engagements and consulting jobs. They know that's happened to their colleagues who step out of line. And they don't make the same mistake."

Connor came back into the room. He said, "Is there anything illegal about this MicroCon sale?"

"Sure," Ron said. "Depending on what Washington decides to do. Akai Ceramics already has sixty percent of the American market. MicroCon will give it a virtual monopoly. If Akai were an American company, the government would block the sale on antitrust grounds. But since Akai is not an American company, the sale isn't scrutinized closely. In the end, it'll probably be allowed."

"You mean a Japanese company can have a monopoly in America but an American company can't?"

"That's the usual outcome these days," Ron said. "But American laws often promote the sale of our companies to foreigners. Like Matsushita buying Universal Studios. Universal's been for sale for years. Several American companies tried to buy it, but couldn't. Westinghouse tried in 1980. No deal: violates antitrust. RCA tried. No deal: violates conflict of interest. But when Matsushita came in, there were no laws against it at all. Recently our laws changed. Under present law, RCA could buy Universal. But back then, no. MicroCon is just the latest example of crazy American regulations."

I said, "But what do American computer companies say about the MicroCon sale?"

Ron said, "American companies don't like the sale. But they don't oppose it, either."

"Why not?"

"Because American companies feel over-regulated by the government already. Forty percent of all American exports are covered by security regulations. Our government doesn't allow our computer companies to sell to Eastern Europe. The cold war is over but the regulations still exist. Meanwhile the Japanese and Germans are selling products like mad. So the Americans want less regulation. And they see any attempt to block the MicroCon sale as government interference."

I said, "It still doesn't make sense to me."

"I agree," Ron said. "The American companies are going to get killed in the next few years. Because if Japan is the sole source of chip-making machines, they're in a position to withhold the machines from American companies."

"Would they do that?"

"They've done it before," Ron said. "Ion implanters and other machines. But the American companies can't get together. They squabble among themselves. And meanwhile the Japanese are buying high-tech companies at the rate of about one every ten days. For the last six years. We're being disemboweled. But our government doesn't pay attention, because we have something called CFIUS—the Committee on Foreign Investment in the United States—that monitors the sale of high-tech companies. Except CFIUS never does anything. Of the last five hundred sales, only one was blocked. Company after company gets sold, and nobody in Washington says boo. Finally, Senator Morton makes a stink, and says 'Wait a minute here.' But nobody's listening to him."

"The sale is going through anyway?"

"That's what I heard today. The Japanese PR machine is hard at work, cranking out favorable publicity. And they are tenacious. They are on top of everything. I mean everything—"

There was a knock at the door, and a blond woman stuck her head in. "Sorry to disturb you, Ron," she said, "but Keith just got a call from the Los Angeles representative for NHK, Japanese national television. He wants to know why our reporter is bashing Japan."

Ron frowned. "Bashing Japan? What's he talking about?"

"He claims our reporter said on air, 'The damn Japanese are taking over this country.' "

"Come on," Ron said. "Nobody would say that—on air. Who's supposed to have said that?"

"Lenny. In New York. Over the backhaul," the woman said.

Ron shifted in his chair. "Uh-oh," he said. "Did you check the tapes?"

"Yeah," she said. "They're tracing the download now in the main control room. But I assume it's true."

"Hell."

I said, "What's the backhaul?"

"Our satellite feed. We pick up segments from New York and Washington every day, and replay them. There's always about a minute before and after that isn't aired. We cut it out, but the raw transmission can be picked up by anybody with a private dish who wants to hunt for our signal. And people do. We warn the talent to be careful what they do in front of a camera. But last year, Louise unbuttoned her blouse and miked herself— and we got calls from all over the country."

Ron's phone rang. He listened for a moment, and said, "Okay. I understand," and hung up. "They checked the tape. Lenny was talking on camera before the feed, and he said to Louise, 'The goddamn Japanese are going to own this country if we don't wise up.' It wasn't on air, but he did say it." He shook his head ruefully. "The NHK guy knows we didn't run it?"

"Yeah. But he's saying it can be picked up and he's protesting on that basis."

"Hell," Ron said. "So they even monitor our backhaul. Jesus. What does Keith want to do?"

"Keith says he's tired of warning New York talent. He wants you to handle it."

"Does he want me to call the NHK guy?"

"He says use your judgment, but we have a deal with NHK for the half-hour show we send them every day and he doesn't want that risked. He thinks you should apologize."

Ron sighed. "Now I have to apologize for what wasn't even on air. God *damn* it." He looked at us. "Guys, I have to go. Was there anything else?"

"No," I said. "Good luck."

"Listen," Ron said. "We all need good luck. You know NHK is starting Global News Network with a billion dollars in capitalization. They're going to take on Ted Turner's CNN around the world. And if past history is any guide . . ." He shrugged. "Kiss the American media good-bye."

As we were leaving, I heard Ron say on the phone, "Mr. Akasaka? Ron Levine, over here at AFN. Yes, sir. Yes, Mr. Akasaka. Sir, I wanted to express my concern and deep apologies about what our reporter said over the satellite—"

We closed the door, and left.

"Where now?" I said.

The Four Seasons Hotel is favored by stars and politicians, and it has a graceful entrance, but we were parked around the corner by the service entrance. A large dairy truck was pulled up to a loading dock, and kitchen staff was unloading cartons of milk. We had been waiting here for five minutes. Connor glanced at his watch.

I said, "Why are we here?"

"We're complying with the Supreme Court, *kōhai*."

At the loading dock, a woman in a business suit came out, looked around, and waved. Connor waved back. She disappeared again. Connor got out his billfold and took out a couple of twenties.

"One of the first things I learned as a detective," Connor said, "is that hotel staff can be extremely helpful. Particularly since the police have so many restrictions these days. We can't go into a hotel room without a warrant. If we did, whatever we found in a search would be inadmissible, right?"

"Right."

"But the maids can go in. Valet and housekeeping and room service can go in."

"Uh-huh."

"So I've learned to maintain contacts at all the big hotels." He opened the door. "I'll only be a moment."

He walked to the loading dock and waited. I tapped the steering wheel with my hands. The words came into my head:

I changed my mind, this love is fine.
Goodness, gracious, great balls of fire.

On the loading dock, a maid in uniform came out, and talked to Connor briefly. He took notes. She held something golden in the palm of her hand. He didn't touch it, he just looked at it, and nodded. She slipped it back in her pocket. Then he gave her money. She went away.

You shake my nerves and you rattle my brain.
Too much love drives a man insane.
You broke my will, but what a thrill—

A valet came out onto the loading dock, carrying a man's blue suit on a hanger. Connor asked a question, and the valet looked at his watch before he answered. Then Connor crouched down and peered closely at the lower edges of the suit coat. He opened the jacket and examined the trousers on the hanger.

The valet took away the first suit, and brought a second one out onto the dock. This one was a blue pinstripe suit. Connor repeated his inspection. He seemed to find something on the coat, and scraped it carefully into a small glassine bag. Then he paid the valet and walked back to the car.

I said, "Checking Senator Rowe?"

"Checking a number of things," he said. "But, yes, Senator Rowe."

"Rowe's aide had white panties in his pocket last night. But Cheryl was wearing black panties."

"That's true," Connor said. "But I think we are making progress."

"What've you got in the bag?"

He took the little glassine bag out, and held it to the light. I saw small dark strands through the plastic. "Carpet fibers, I think. Dark, like the carpet at the Nakamoto conference room. Have to check with the lab to be sure. Meanwhile, we have another problem to solve. Start the car."

"Where are we going?"

"Darley-Higgins. The company that owns MicroCon."

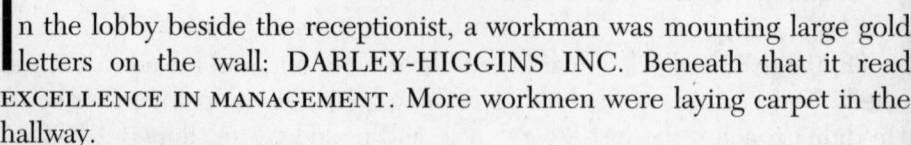

In the lobby beside the receptionist, a workman was mounting large gold letters on the wall: DARLEY-HIGGINS INC. Beneath that it read EXCELLENCE IN MANAGEMENT. More workmen were laying carpet in the hallway.

We showed our badges and asked to see the head of Darley-Higgins, Arthur Greiman.

The receptionist had a Southern accent and an upturned nose. "Mr. Greiman is in meetings all day. Is he expecting you?"

"We're here about the MicroCon sale."

"Then you want Mr. Enders, our vice-president for publicity. He speaks to people about MicroCon."

"All right," Connor said.

We sat down on a couch in the reception area. On a couch across the room sat a pretty woman in a tight skirt. She had a roll of blueprints under her arm. The workmen continued to hammer. I said, "I thought the company was in financial trouble. Why're they redecorating?"

Connor shrugged.

The secretary answered the phone, routing the calls. "Darley-Higgins, one moment, please. Darley-Higgins . . . Oh, please hold, Senator . . . Darley-Higgins, yes, thank you . . ."

I picked up a brochure from the coffee table. It was the annual report of Darley-Higgins Management Group, with offices in Atlanta, Dallas, Seattle, San Francisco, and Los Angeles. I found a picture of Arthur Greiman. He looked happy and self-satisfied. The report included an essay signed by him entitled, "A Commitment to Excellence."

The secretary said to us, "Mr. Enders will be right with you."

"Thank you," Connor said.

A moment later, two men in business suits walked out into the hallway. The woman with the blueprints stood. She said, "Hello, Mr. Greiman."

"Hello, Beverly," the older man said. "I'll be with you in a minute."

Connor stood up, too. The secretary immediately said, "Mr. Greiman, these men—"

"Just a minute," Greiman said. He turned to the man with him, who was younger, in his early thirties. "Just make sure you get it straight with Roger," Greiman said.

The younger man was shaking his head. "He won't like it."

"I know he won't. But tell him anyway. Six million four in direct compensation for the CEO is the minimum."

"But Arthur—"

"Just tell him."

"I will, Arthur," the younger man said, smoothing his tie. He lowered his voice. "But the board may balk at raising you above six when company earnings are down so much—"

"We're not talking about *earnings*," Greiman said. "We're talking about compensation. It has nothing to do with earnings. The board has to match current compensation levels for chief executives. If Roger can't bring the board into line on this, I'm going to cancel the March meeting and ask for changes. You tell him *that*."

"Okay, I will, Arthur, but—"

"Just do it. Call me tonight."

"Right, Arthur."

They shook hands. The younger man walked off unhappily. The receptionist said, "Mr. Greiman, these gentlemen—"

Greiman turned to us. Connor said, "Mr. Greiman, we'd like to speak to you for a minute about MicroCon." And he turned slightly aside, and showed his badge.

Greiman exploded in rage. "Oh, for Christ's sake. Not *again*. This is goddamned *harassment*."

"Harassment?"

"What would you call it? I've had senatorial staffers here, I've had the F.B.I. here. Now I have the L.A. police? We're not criminals. We own a company and we have the right to sell it. Where is Louis?"

The receptionist said, "Mr. Enders is coming."

Connor said calmly, "Mr. Greiman, I'm sorry to disturb you. We have only one question. It'll just take a minute."

Greiman glowered. "What's your question?"

"How many bidders were there for MicroCon?"

"That's none of your business," he said. "Anyway, our agreement with Akai stipulates that we can't discuss the sale publicly in any way."

Connor said, "Was there more than one bidder?"

"Look, you have questions, you talk to Enders. I'm busy." He turned to the woman with blueprints. "Beverly? What have you got for me?"

"I have a revised layout for the boardroom, Mr. Greiman, and tile samples for the washroom. A very nice gray I think you'll like."

"Good, good." He led her down the hallway away from us.

Connor watched them go, and then abruptly turned toward the elevator. "Come on, *kōhai*. Let's get some fresh air."

Why does it matter if there were other bidders?" I said, when we were back in the car.

"It goes back to the original question we had," Connor said. "Who wants to embarrass Nakamoto? We know the sale of MicroCon has strategic significance. That's why Congress is upset. But that almost certainly means other parties are upset, too."

"In Japan?"

"Exactly."

"Who will know that?"

"Akai."

The Japanese receptionist tittered when she saw Connor's badge. Connor said, "We would like to see Mr. Yoshida." Yoshida was the head of the company.

"One moment, please." She got up and hurried away, almost running.

Akai Ceramics was located on the fifth floor of a bland office-block in El Segundo. The decor was spare and industrial-looking. From the reception area, we could see into a large space, which was not partitioned: lots of metal desks and people at the phones. The soft click of word processors.

I looked at the office. "Pretty bare."

"All business," Connor said, nodding. "In Japan, ostentation is frowned on. It means you are not serious. When old Mr. Matsushita was the head of the third biggest company in Japan, he still took the regular commercial jet between his head offices in Osaka and Tokyo. He was the head of a fifty-billion-dollar company. But no private jets for him."

As we waited, I looked at the people working at the desks. A handful were Japanese. Most were Caucasian. Everyone wore blue suits. There were almost no women.

"In Japan," Connor said, "if a company is doing poorly, the first thing that happens is the executives cut their own salaries. They feel responsible for the success of the company, and they expect their own fortunes to rise and fall as the company succeeds or fails."

The woman came back, and sat at her desk without speaking. Almost immediately, a Japanese man wearing a blue suit came toward us. He had gray hair, horn-rimmed glasses, and a solemn manner. He said, "Good morning. I am Mr. Yoshida."

Connor made the introductions. We all bowed and exchanged business cards. Mr. Yoshida took each card with both hands, bowing each time, formally. We did the same. I noticed that Connor did not speak Japanese to him.

Yoshida led us to his office. It had windows looking toward the airport. The furnishings were austere.

"Would you like coffee, or tea?"

"No, thank you," Connor said. "We are here in an official capacity."

"I understand." He gestured for us to sit down.

"We would like to talk to you about the purchase of MicroCon."

"Ah, yes. A troubling matter. But I am not aware that it should involve the police."

"Perhaps it doesn't," Connor said. "Can you tell us about the sale, or is the agreement sealed?"

Mr. Yoshida looked surprised. "Sealed? Not at all. It is all very open, and has been from the beginning. We were approached by Mr. Kobayashi, representing Darley-Higgins in Tokyo, in September of last year. That was the first we learned the company was for sale. Frankly, we were surprised that it would be offered. We began negotiations in early October. The negotiating teams had the basis of a rough agreement by mid-November. We proceeded to the final stage of negotiations. But then the Congress raised objections, on November sixteenth."

Connor said, "You said you were surprised that the company would be offered for sale?"

"Yes. Certainly."

"Why is that?"

Mr. Yoshida spread his hands on his desk and spoke slowly. "We understood that MicroCon was a government-owned company. It had been financed in part by funds from the American government. Thirteen percent of capitalization, if I remember. In Japan, that would make it a government-owned company. So naturally we were cautious to enter into negotiations.

We do not want to offend. But we received assurance from our representatives in Washington there would be no objection to the purchase."

"I see."

"But now there are difficulties, as we feared. I think now we make a cause for Americans. In Washington, some people are upset. We do not wish this."

"You didn't expect Washington would make objections?"

Mr. Yoshida gave a diffident shrug. "The two countries are different. In Japan we know what to expect. Here, there is always an individual who may have another opinion, and speak it. But Akai Ceramics does not wish a high profile. It is awkward now."

Connor nodded sympathetically. "It sounds as if you want to withdraw."

"Many in the home office criticize me, for not knowing what would happen. But I tell them, it is impossible to know. Washington has no firm policy. It changes every day, according to the politics." He smiled and added. "Or, I would say, that is how it seems to us."

"But you expect the sale to go forward?"

"This I cannot say. Perhaps the criticism from Washington will be too much. And you know the Tokyo government wants to be friends with America. They give pressure on business, not to make purchases that will upset America. Rockefeller Center and Universal Studios, these purchases that make criticism for us. We are told to be *yōjinbukai*. It means . . ."

"Discreet," Connor said.

"Careful. Yes. Wary." He looked at Connor. "You speak Japanese?"

"A little."

Yoshida nodded. For a moment he seemed to consider switching to Japanese, but did not. "We wish to have friendly relations," he said. "These criticisms of us, we feel they are not fair. The Darley-Higgins company has many financial difficulties. Perhaps bad management, perhaps some other reason. I cannot say. But that is not our fault. We are not responsible for that. And we did not seek MicroCon. It was offered to us. Now we are criticized for trying to help." He sighed.

Outside, a big jet took off from the airport. The windows rattled.

Connor said, "And the other bidders for MicroCon? When did they drop out?"

Mr. Yoshida frowned. "There were no other bidders. The company was privately offered. Darley-Higgins did not wish to make known their financial difficulties. So we cooperated with them. But now . . . the press makes many distortions about us. We feel very . . . *kizu tsuita*. Wounded?"

"Yes."

He shrugged. "That is how we feel. I hope you understand my poor English."

There was a pause. In fact, for the next minute or so, nobody said anything. Connor sat facing Yoshida. I sat beside Connor. Another jet took off, and the windows vibrated again. Still nobody spoke. Yoshida gave a long sigh. Connor nodded. Yoshida shifted in his chair, and folded his hands over his belly. Connor sighed, and grunted. Yoshida sighed. Both men seemed to be entirely focused. Something was taking place, but I was not clear what. I decided it must be this unspoken intuition.

Finally, Yoshida said, "Captain, I wish no misunderstanding. Akai Ceramics is an honorable company. We have no part in any . . . complications that have occurred. Our position is difficult. But I will assist you in whatever way I can."

Connor said, "I am grateful."

"Not at all."

Then Yoshida stood up. Connor stood up. I stood up. We all bowed, and then we all shook hands.

"Please do not hesitate to contact me again, if I can be of assistance."

"Thank you," Connor said.

Yoshida led us to the door to his office. We bowed again, and he opened the door.

Outside was a fresh-faced American man in his forties. I recognized him at once. He was the blond man who had been in the car with Senator Rowe the night before. The man who hadn't introduced himself.

"Ah, Richmond-san," Yoshida said. "Very good luck you are here. These gentlemen are just asking about MicroCon *baishū*." He turned to us. "Perhaps you will like to talk to Mr. Richmond. His English is much better than mine. He can give you many more details you may wish to know."

Bob Richmond. Myers, Lawson, and Richmond." His handshake was firm. He was suntanned, and looked as though he played a lot of tennis. He smiled cheerfully. "Small world, isn't it?"

Connor and I introduced ourselves. I said, "Did Senator Rowe get back all right?"

"Oh yes," Richmond said. "Thanks for your help." He smiled. "I hate to think how he's feeling this morning. But I guess it's not the first time." He shifted back and forth on the balls of his feet, like a tennis player waiting for a serve. He looked slightly concerned. "I must say, you two are the last people I ever expected to see here. Is there anything I should know about? I represent Akai in the MicroCon negotiations."

"No," Connor said mildly. "We're just getting general background."

"Is this to do with what happened at Nakamoto last night?"

Connor said, "Not really. Just background."

"If you like, we can talk in the conference room."

"Unfortunately," Connor said, "we're late for an appointment. But perhaps we can talk later."

"You bet," Richmond said. "Happy to. I'll be back in my office in about an hour." He gave us his card.

"That's fine," Connor said.

But Richmond still seemed worried. He walked with us to the elevator. "Mr. Yoshida is from the old school," he said. "I'm sure he was polite. But I can tell you he is furious about what happened with this MicroCon thing. He's taking a lot of heat from Akai Tokyo. And it's very unfair. He really was sandbagged by Washington. He got assurances there would be no objection to the sale, and then Morton pulled the rug out from under him."

Connor said, "Is that what happened?"

"No question about it," Richmond said. "I don't know what Johnny Morton's problem is, but he came right out of left field on this. We made all the proper filings. CFIUS registered no objection until long after the negotiations were concluded. You can't do business like this. I just hope John sees the light, and lets this thing go through. Because at the moment it looks pretty racist."

"Racist? Really?"

"Sure. It's exactly like the Fairchild case. Remember that one? Fujitsu tries to buy Fairchild Semiconductor in eighty-six, but Congress blocks the sale, saying it's against national security. Congress doesn't want Fairchild sold to a foreign company. Couple of years later Fairchild is going to be sold to a French company, and this time there's not a peep from Congress. Apparently, it's okay to sell to a foreign company—just not a *Japanese* company. I'd say that's racist policy, pure and simple." We came to the elevator. "Anyway, call me. I'll make myself available."

"Thank you," Connor said.

We got on the elevator. The doors closed.

"Asshole," Connor said.

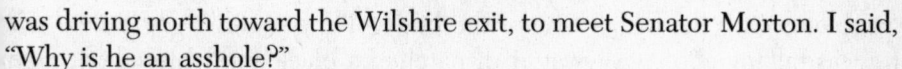

was driving north toward the Wilshire exit, to meet Senator Morton. I said, "Why is he an asshole?"

"Bob Richmond was the assistant trade negotiator for Japan under Amanda Marden until last year. He was privy to all the strategy meetings of the American government. One year later, he turns around and starts working for the Japanese. Who now pay him five hundred thousand a year plus bonuses to close this deal. And he's worth it, because he knows everything there is to know."

"Is that legal?"

"Sure. It's standard procedure. They all do it. If Richmond worked for a high-tech company like Microsoft, he'd have to sign an agreement that he wouldn't work for a competing company for five years. Because you shouldn't be able to peddle trade secrets to the opposition. But our government has easier rules."

"Why is he an asshole?"

"This racist stuff." Connor snorted. "He knows better. Richmond knows exactly what happened with the Fairchild sale. And it had nothing to do with racism."

"No?"

"And there's another thing Richmond knows: the Japanese are the most racist people on earth."

"They are?"

"Absolutely. In fact, when the Japanese diplomats—"

The car phone rang. I pushed the speaker button and said, "Lieutenant Smith."

Over the speaker, a man said, "Jesus, *finally*. Where the hell have you guys been? I want to get to sleep."

I recognized the voice: Fred Hoffmann, the watch commander from the night before.

Connor said, "Thanks for getting back to us, Fred."

"What is it you wanted?"

"Well, I'm curious," Connor said, "about the Nakamoto calls you got last night."

"You and everybody else in this town," Hoffmann said. "I got half the department on my ass about this. Jim Olson is practically camping on my desk, going through the paperwork. Even though it was all routine at the time."

"If you'd just review what happened . . ."

"Sure. First thing, I got the transmittal from metro. That was the original phone-in. Metro wasn't sure what it meant, because the caller had an Asian accent and sounded confused. Or maybe on drugs. He kept talking about 'problems with the disposition of the body.' They couldn't get it clear what he was talking about. Anyway, I dispatched a black and white about eight thirty. Then when they confirmed a homicide, I assigned Tom Graham and Roddy Merino—for which I got all *kinds* of shit later."

"Uh-huh."

"But what the hell, they were up on the roster next. You know we're supposed to stay in strict rotation for detective assignments. To avoid the appearance of special treatment. That's policy. I was just following it."

"Uh-huh."

"Anyway. Then Graham calls in at nine o'clock, and reports there's trouble at the scene, and there is a request for the Special Services liaison. Again, I check the list. Pete Smith is the SSO on call. So I give Graham his number at home. And I guess he called you, Pete."

"Yes," I said. "He did."

"All right," Connor said. "What happened after that?"

"About two minutes after Graham calls, maybe nine oh-five, I get a call from somebody with an accent. I would say it sounds like an Asian accent but I don't know for sure. And the guy says that on behalf of Nakamoto he is requesting Captain Connor be assigned to the case."

"The caller didn't identify himself?"

"Sure he did. I made him identify himself. And I wrote down the name Koichi Nishi."

"And he was from Nakamoto?"

"That's what he said," Hoffmann said. "I'm just sitting there, working the phone, what the hell do I know. I mean, this morning Nakamoto is formally protesting the fact that Connor was assigned to the case and saying they have nobody named Koichi Nishi employed by them. They're claiming it's all a fabrication. But let me tell you, somebody called me. I'm not making it up."

"I'm sure you're not," Connor said. "You say the caller had an accent?"

"Yeah. His English was pretty good, you know, almost hip, but there was a definite accent. The only thing I thought was funny was that he seemed to know a hell of a lot about you."

"Oh?"

"Yeah. First thing he says to me, do I know your phone number or should he give it to me. I say I know the number. I'm thinking, I don't need some Japanese to tell me the phone numbers of people on the force. Then he says, you know, Captain Connor doesn't always answer his phone. Be sure to send somebody down there to pick him up."

"Interesting," Connor said.

"So I called Pete Smith, and told him to swing by and pick you up. And that's all I knew. I mean, this is all in the context of some political problem they're having at Nakamoto. I knew Graham was unhappy. I figured other people were unhappy, too. And everybody knows Connor has special relationships with the community, so I put it through. And now there is all this shit coming down. Fucking beats me."

"Tell me about the shit," Connor said.

"It starts maybe eleven o'clock last night, when the chief called me about Graham. Why did I assign Graham. I tell him why. But he's still not happy. Then right at the end of my watch, maybe five a.m., there is the business about how Connor got brought in. How did it happen, why did it happen. And now there's a story in the *Times* and this whole thing about racism by the police. I don't know which way to turn here. I keep explaining I did the routine thing. By the book. Nobody is buying that. But it's true."

"I'm sure it is," Connor said. "Just one more thing, Fred. Did you ever listen to the original metro call?"

"Damn right I did. I heard it about an hour ago. Why?"

"Did the voice that called in sound like Mr. Nishi?"

Hoffmann laughed. "Christ. Who knows, Captain. Maybe. You're asking me if one Asian voice sounds like another Asian voice I heard earlier. Honestly, I don't know. The original voice on the call sounded pretty confused. Maybe in shock. Maybe on drugs. I'm not sure. All I know is, whoever Mr. Nishi actually was, he knew a hell of a lot about you."

"Well, that's very helpful. Get some rest." Connor thanked him, and hung up. I pulled off the freeway and headed down Wilshire, to our meeting with Senator Morton.

Okay, Senator, now look this way, please . . . a little more . . . that's it, that's *very* strong, very *masculine*, I like it a lot. Yes, bloody good. Now I will need three minutes, please." The director, a tense man wearing a bomber jacket and a baseball cap, climbed down off the camera and barked orders in a British accent. "Jerry, get a scrim there, the sun is too bright. And can we do something about his eyes? I need a little fill in the eyes, please. Ellen? You see the shine on his right shoulder. Flag it, love. Pull the collar smooth. The microphone is visible on his tie. And I can't see the gray in his hair. Bring it up. And straighten out the carpeting on the ground so he doesn't trip when he walks, people. Please. Come on now. We're losing our lovely light."

Connor and I were standing to one side, with a cute production assistant named Debbie who held a clipboard across her breasts and said meaningfully, "The director is Edgar Lynn."

"Should we recognize that name?" Connor said.

"He's the *most* expensive and *most* sought-after commercial director in the world. He is a *great* artist. Edgar did the *fantastic* Apple 1984 commercial, and . . . oh, lots of others. And he has directed famous movies, too. Edgar is *just* the *best*." She paused. "And not too crazy. Really."

Across from the camera, Senator John Morton stood patiently while four people fussed with his tie, his jacket, his hair, his makeup. Morton was wearing a suit. He was standing under a tree with the rolling golf course and the skyscrapers of Beverly Hills in the background. The production crew had laid down a strip of carpet for him to walk on as he approached the camera.

I said, "And how is the senator?"

Debbie nodded. "Pretty good. I think he has a shot."

Connor said, "You mean a chance for the presidency?"

"Yeah. Especially if Edgar can do his magic. I mean, let's face it, Senator Morton is not exactly *Mel Gibson*, you know what I mean? He's got a big nose, and he's a little bald, and those freckles are a *problem* because they

536

photograph so prominently. They distract you from his eyes. And the eyes are what sell a candidate."

"The eyes," Connor said.

"Oh, yeah. People get elected on their eyes." She shrugged, as if it was common knowledge. "But if the senator puts himself in Edgar's hands . . . Edgar is a great artist. He can make it happen."

Edgar Lynn walked past us, huddled with the cameraman. "Christ, clean up the luggage under his eyes," Lynn said. "And get the chin. Firm that chin with a hard inky low and up."

"Okay," the cameraman said.

The production assistant excused herself and we waited, watching. Senator Morton was still some distance away, being worked over by the makeup and wardrobe people.

"Mr. Connor? Mr. Smith?" I turned. A young man in a blue pinstripe suit was standing beside us. He looked like a Senate staffer: well turned-out, attentive, polite. "I'm Bob Woodson. With the senator's office. Thank you for coming."

"You're welcome," Connor said.

"I know the senator is eager to talk to you," Woodson said. "I'm sorry, this seems to be running a little late. We were supposed to finish shooting by one." He glanced at his watch. "Now, I guess it may be quite a while. But I know the senator wants to talk to you."

Connor said, "Do you know what about?"

Someone shouted, "Run-through! Run-through for sound and camera, please!"

The cluster around Senator Morton vanished, and Woodson turned his attention to the camera.

Edgar Lynn was back looking through the lens. "There still isn't enough gray. Ellen? You will have to add gray to his hair. It isn't reading now."

Woodson said, "I hope he doesn't make him look too old."

Debbie, the production assistant, said, "It's just for the shot. It isn't reading for the shot, so we add some gray. See, Ellen is just putting it at the temples. It'll make him distinguished."

"I don't want him old. Especially when he's tired, he sometimes looks old."

"Don't worry," the assistant said.

"All right now," Lynn said. "That's enough for now. Senator? Shall we try a run-through?"

Senator Morton said, "Where does this begin?"

"Line?"

A script girl said, " 'Perhaps like me . . .' "

Morton said, "Then we've already done the first part?"

Edgar Lynn said, "That's right, love. We start here with your turn to the camera, and you give us a very strong, very direct *masculine* look, and begin 'Perhaps like me.' Right?"

"Okay," Morton said.

"Remember. Think *masculine*. Think *strong*. Think *in control*."

Morton said, "Can we shoot it?"

Woodson said, "Lynn's going to piss him off."

Edgar Lynn said, "All right. Shoot the rehearsal. Here we go."

Senator Morton walked toward the camera. "Perhaps like me," he said, "you're concerned about the erosion of our national position in recent years. America is still the greatest military power, but our security depends on our ability to defend ourselves militarily *and* economically. And it is economically that America has fallen behind. How far behind? Well, under the last two administrations, America has gone from the greatest creditor nation to the greatest debtor nation the world has ever seen. Our industries have fallen behind the rest of the world. Our workers are less educated than workers in other countries. Our investors demand short-term gain and cripple our industries' ability to plan for the future. And as a result, our standard of living is declining rapidly. The outlook for our children is bleak."

Connor murmured, "Somebody is actually saying it."

"And in this time of national crisis," Morton continued, "many Americans have another concern, as well. As our economic power fades, we are vulnerable to a new kind of invasion. Many Americans fear that we may become an economic colony of Japan, or Europe. But especially Japan. Many Americans feel that the Japanese are taking over our industries, our recreation lands, and even our cities." He gestured to the golf course with skyscrapers in the background.

"And in doing so, some fear that Japan now has the power to shape and determine the future of America."

Morton paused, beneath the tree. He gave the appearance of thinking.

"How justified are these fears for the American future? How much should we be concerned? There are some who will tell you foreign investment is a blessing, that it helps our nation. Others take the opposite view, and feel we are selling our precious birthright. Which view is correct? Which should—which is—which—oh, *fuck!* What's the line again?"

"Cut, cut," Edgar Lynn called. "Take five, everybody. I need to clean up a few things, and then we can do it for real. Very good, Senator. I liked it."

The script girl said, "'Which should we believe for the future of America,' Senator."

He repeated, "Which should we believe for the future of . . ." He shook his head. "No wonder I can't remember it. Let's change that line. Margie? Let's change that line, please. Never mind, bring me a script, I'll change it myself."

And the crowd of makeup and wardrobe people descended on him again, touching him up and fluffing him down.

Woodson said, "Wait here, I'll try and get you a few minutes with him."

We stood beside a humming trailer, with power cables coming out of it. As soon as Morton approached us, two aides came running up, brandishing thick books of computer printout. "John, you better look at this."

"John, you better consider this."

Morton said, "What is it?"

"John, this is the latest Gallup and Fielding."

"John, this is the cross-referenced analysis by voter age-brackets."

"And?"

"Bottom line, John, the president is *right*."

"Don't tell me that. I'm running *against* the president."

"But John, he's right about the C-word. You can't say the C-word in your television ad."

"I can't say 'conservation'?"

"You can't say it, John."

"It's death, John."

"The figures show it."

"You want us to run over the figures, John?"

"No," Morton said. He glanced at Connor and me. "I'll be right with you," he said, with a smile.

"But look here, John."

"It's very clear, John. Conservation means diminution of life-style. People are already experiencing diminution of life-style. They don't want any more of it."

"But that's wrong," Morton said. "That's not how it works."

"John, it's what the voters *think*."

"But they're wrong about this."

"John, you want to educate the voters, well and good."

"Yes, I do want to educate the voters. Conservation is not synonymous with diminution of life-style. It is synonymous with more wealth, power, and freedom. The idea is not to make do with less. The idea is to do all the things you are doing now—heat your house, drive your car—using less gas and oil. Let's have more efficient heaters in our houses, more efficient cars on our streets. Let's have cleaner air, better health. It can be done. Other countries have done it. Japan has done it."

"John, please."

"Not Japan."

"In the last twenty years," Morton said. "Japan cut the energy cost of finished goods by sixty percent. America has done nothing. Japan can now make goods cheaper than we can, because Japan has pushed investment in energy-efficient technology. Conservation is competitive. And we aren't being competitive—"

"Fine, John. Conservation *and* statistics. *Really* boring."

"Nobody cares, John."

"The American people care," Morton said.

"John: they absolutely don't."

"And they aren't going to listen. Look, John. We have age-regressions here, particularly among the over fifty-fives, which is the most solid voting block, and they are straight ahead on this issue. They want no decreases. No conservation. The old people of America don't want it."

"But older people have children, and grandchildren. They must care about the future."

"Older people don't give a flying fuck, John. It's right here in black and white. They think their kids don't care about them, and they're right. So they don't care about their kids. It's that simple."

"But certainly the children—"

"Children don't vote, John."

"Please, John. Listen to us."

"No conservation, John. Competitiveness, yes. Look to the future, yes. Face our problems, yes. A new spirit, yes. But no conservation. Just look at the numbers. Don't do it."

"Please."

Morton said, "I'll think about it, fellas."

The two aides seemed to realize that that was all they were going to get. They closed their printouts with a snap.

"You want us to send Margie over to rewrite?"

"No. I'm thinking about it."

"Maybe Margie should just rough out a few lines."

"No."

"Okay, John. Okay."

"You know," Morton said, as they were leaving, "some day an American politician is going to do what he thinks is right, instead of what the polls tell him. And it's going to look revolutionary."

The two aides turned back together. "John, come on. You're tired."

"It's been a long trip. We understand."

"John. Trust us on this, we have the figures. We are telling you with ninety-five percent confidence intervals how the people feel."

"I know damn well how they feel. They feel frustrated. And I know why. It's been fifteen years since they've had any *leadership*."

"John. Let's not do this one again. This is the twentieth century. Leadership is the quality of telling people what they want to hear."

They walked away.

Immediately, Woodson came up, carrying a portable phone. He started to speak, but Morton held up his hand. "Not now, Bob."

"Senator, I think you need to take this—"

"*Not now.*"

Woodson backed away. Morton glanced at his watch. "You're Mr. Connor and Mr. Smith?"

"Yes," Connor said.

"Let's walk," Morton said. He started away from the film crew, toward a hill overlooking the rolling course. It was Friday. Not many people were playing. We stood about fifty meters from the crew.

"I asked you to come," Morton said, "because I understand you're the officers in charge of the Nakamoto business."

I was about to protest that it wasn't true, that Graham was the officer in charge, when Connor said, "That's true, we are."

"I have some questions about that case. I gather it's been resolved now?"

"It seems to be."

"Is your investigation finished?"

"For all practical purposes, yes," Connor said. "The investigation is concluded."

Morton nodded. "I'm told you officers are particularly knowledgeable about the Japanese community, is that right? One of you has even lived in Japan?"

Connor gave a slight bow.

"You were the one playing golf with Hanada and Asaka today?" Morton said.

"You're well informed."

"I spoke with Mr. Hanada this morning. We have had contact in the past, on other matters." Morton turned abruptly and said, "My question is this. Is the Nakamoto business related to MicroCon?"

"How do you mean?" Connor said.

"The sale of MicroCon to the Japanese has come before the Senate Finance Committee, which I chair. We've been asked for a recommendation by staff from the Committee on Science and Technology, which must actually authorize the sale. As you know, the sale is controversial. In the past I have gone on record as opposing the sale. For a variety of reasons. You're familiar with all this?"

"Yes," Connor said.

"I still have problems about it," Morton said. "MicroCon's advanced technology was developed in part with American taxpayer money. I'm outraged that our taxpayers should pay for research that is being sold to the Japanese—who will then use it to compete against our own companies. I feel strongly we should be protecting American capacity in high-tech areas. I feel we should be protecting our intellectual resources. I feel we should be limiting foreign investment in our corporations and our universities. But I seem to be alone in this. I can't find support in the Senate or in industry. Commerce won't help me. The trade rep's worried it'll upset the rice negotiations. *Rice.* Even the Pentagon is against me on this. And I just wondered, since Nakamoto is the parent company of Akai Ceramics, whether the events of last night had any relationship to the proposed sale."

He paused. He was looking at us in an intense way. It was almost as if he expected that we would know something.

Connor said, "I'm not aware of any linkage."

"Has Nakamoto done anything unfair or improper to promote the sale?"

"Not that I am aware, no."

"And your investigation is formally concluded?"

"Yes."

"I just want to be clear. Because if I back down on my opposition to this sale, I don't want to find that I've stuck my hand in a box of snakes. One could argue that the party at Nakamoto was an attempt to win over opponents to the sale. So a change of position can be worrisome. You know in Congress they can get you coming and going, with a thing like this."

Connor said, "Are you abandoning your opposition to the sale?"

From across the lawn, an aide said, "Senator? They're ready for you, sir."

"Well." Morton shrugged. "I'm out on a limb with this thing. Nobody agrees with my position on MicroCon. Personally, I think it's another Fairchild case. But if this battle can't be won, I say, let's not fight it. Plenty of other battles to be fought, anyway." He straightened, smoothed his suit.

"Senator? When you're ready, sir." And he added, "They're concerned about the light."

"They're concerned about the light," Morton said, shaking his head.

"Don't let us keep you," Connor said.

"Anyway," Morton said. "I wanted your input. I understand you to say that last night had nothing to do with MicroCon. The people involved had nothing to do with it. I'm not going to read next month that someone was working behind the scenes, trying to promote or block the sale. Nothing like that."

"Not as far as I know," Connor said.

"Gentlemen, thank you for coming," he said. He shook both of our hands, and started away. Then he came back. "I appreciate your treating this matter as confidential. Because, you know, we have to be careful. We are at war with Japan." He smiled wryly. "Loose lips sink ships."

"Yes," Connor said. "And remember Pearl Harbor."

"Christ, that too." He shook his head. He dropped his voice, becoming one of the boys. "You know, I have colleagues who say sooner or later we're going to have to drop another bomb. They think it'll come to that." He smiled. "But I don't feel that way. Usually."

Still smiling, he headed back to the camera crew. As he walked, he collected people, first a woman with script changes, then a wardrobe man, then a sound man fiddling with his microphone and adjusting the battery pack at his waist, and the makeup woman, until finally the senator had disappeared from view, and there was just a cluster of people moving awkwardly across the lawn.

I said, "I like him."

I was driving back into Hollywood. The buildings were hazy in the smog.

"Why shouldn't you like him?" Connor said. "He's a politician. It's his job to make you like him."

"Then he's good at his job."

"Very good, I think."

Connor stared out the window silently. I had the sense that something was troubling him.

I said, "Didn't you like what he was saying in the commercial? It sounded like all the things you say."

"Yes. It did."

"Then what's the matter?"

"Nothing," Connor said. "I was just thinking about what he actually *said*."

"He mentioned Fairchild."

"Of course," Connor said. "Morton knows the real story about Fairchild, very well."

I started to ask him what it was, but he was already telling me.

"Have you ever heard of Seymour Cray? For years, he was the best designer of supercomputers in the world. Cray Research made the fastest computers in the world. The Japanese were trying to catch up with him, but they just couldn't do it. He was too brilliant. But by the mid-eighties, Japanese chip dumping had put most of Cray's domestic suppliers out of business. So Cray had to order his custom-designed chips from Japanese manufacturers. There was nobody in America to make them. And his Japanese suppliers experienced mysterious delays. At one point, it took them a *year* to deliver certain chips he had ordered—and during that time, his Japanese competitors made great strides forward. There was also a question of whether they had stolen his new technology. Cray was furious. He knew they were fucking with him. He decided that he had to form a liaison with an American manufacturer, and so he chose Fairchild Semiconductor, even though the company was financially weak, far from the best. But Cray couldn't trust the Japanese anymore. He had to make do with Fairchild. So now Fairchild was making his next generation of custom chips for him—and then he learned that Fairchild was going to be sold to Fujitsu. His big competitor. It was concern about situations like that, and the national security implications, that led Congress to block the sale to Fujitsu."

"And then?"

"Well, blocking the sale didn't solve Fairchild's financial problems. The company was still in trouble. And it eventually had to be sold. There was a rumor it was going to be bought by Bull, a French company that didn't compete in supercomputers. That sale might have been permitted by Congress. But in the end, Fairchild was sold to an American company."

"And MicroCon is another Fairchild?"

"Yes, in the sense that MicroCon will give the Japanese a monopoly on vital chip-making machinery. Once they have a monopoly, they can withhold the machines from American companies. But now I think—"

That was when the phone rang. I left it on the speakerphone.

It was Lauren. My ex-wife.

* * *

"Peter?"

I said, "Hello, Lauren."

"Peter, I am calling to inform you that I'm going to pick up Michelle early today." Her voice sounded tense, formal.

"You are? I didn't know you were picking her up at all."

"I never said that, Peter," she answered quickly. "Of course I'm picking her up."

I said, "Okay, fine. By the way, who's Rick?"

There was a pause. "Really. That is beneath you, Peter."

"Why?" I said. "I'm just curious. Michelle mentioned it this morning. She said he has a black Mercedes. Is he the new boyfriend?"

"Peter. I hardly think that is on the same level."

I said, "The same level as what?"

"Let's not play games," she said. "This is difficult enough. I'm calling to tell you I have to pick up Michelle early because I'm taking her to the doctor."

"Why? She's over her cold."

"I'm taking her for an examination, Peter."

"For what?"

"An *examination*."

"I heard you," I said. "But—"

"The physician who will examine her is Robert Strauss. He is an expert, I'm told. I have been asking people in the office who is the best person. I don't know how this is going to turn out, Peter, but I want you to know I am concerned, particularly in the light of your history."

"Lauren, what are you talking about?"

"I'm talking about child abuse," she said. "I'm talking about sexual molestation."

"What?"

"There's no getting around it, at this point. You know you've been accused of it in the past."

I felt churning nausea. Whenever a relationship goes sour, there's always some residue of resentment, some pockets of bitterness and anger—as well as lots of private things that you know about the other person, that you can use against them. If you choose to do that. Lauren never had.

"Lauren, you know that abuse charge was trumped up. You know everything about that. We were married at the time."

"I only know what you told me." Her voice sounded distant now, moralistic, a little sarcastic. Her prosecutor's voice.

"Lauren, for Christ's sake. This is ridiculous. What's going on?"

"It is not ridiculous. I have my responsibilities as a mother."

"Well, for God's sake, you've never been particularly worried about your responsibilities as a mother before. And now you—"

"It's true that I have a demanding career," she said, in an icy tone, "but there has never been any question that my daughter comes first. And I deeply, *deeply* regret if my past behavior in any way contributed to this unpleasant circumstance now." I had the feeling that she wasn't talking to me. She was rehearsing. Trying out the words to see how they would sound before a judge. "Clearly, Peter, if there is child abuse, Michelle cannot continue to live with you. Or even to see you."

I felt pain in my chest. A wrenching.

"What are you talking about? Who told you there was child abuse?"

"Peter, I don't think it's appropriate for me to comment at this point in time."

"Was it Wilhelm? Who called you, Lauren?"

"Peter, there's no point in going into this. I'm officially notifying you that I'm going to pick Michelle up at four p.m. I want her ready to go at four this afternoon."

"Lauren—"

"I have my secretary, Miss Wilson, listening on the line and making stenographic notes of our conversation. I'm giving you formal notice of my intention to pick up my daughter and take her for a physical examination. Do you have any questions about my decision?"

"No."

"Four o'clock, then. Thank you for your cooperation. And let me add on a personal note, Peter, I'm truly sorry that it has come to this."

And she hung up.

I had been involved in sex abuse cases when I was a detective. I knew how it worked. The fact is, you usually can't determine anything from a physical exam. It's always equivocal. And if a kid is questioned by a psychologist who hammers her with questions, the kid will eventually start to go along, and make up answers to please the psychologist. Normal procedure requires the psychologist to videotape the kids, to prove that the questioning wasn't leading. But the situation is almost always unclear when it finally comes before a judge. And the judge must therefore rule conservatively. Which means, if there is a possibility of abuse, to keep the child away from the accused parent. Or at least, not allow unsupervised visitation. No overnight visits. Or perhaps not even—

"That's enough," Connor said, sitting beside me in the car. "Come back now."

"Sorry," I said. "But it's upsetting."

"I'm sure. Now: what haven't you told me?"

"About what?"

"The molestation charge."

"Nothing. There's nothing to it."

"*Kōhai*," he said quietly. "I can't help you if you won't tell me."

"It had nothing to do with sexual molestation," I said. "It was something else entirely. It was about money."

Connor said nothing. He just waited. Looking at me.

"Ah, hell," I said.

And I told him.

You have these times in your life when you believe you know what you're doing, but you really don't. Later on, you can look back, and you see you weren't acting right at all. You drifted into something, and you were completely screwed up. But at the time, you thought everything was fine.

What happened to me was, I was in love. Lauren was one of those patrician-acting girls, lean and graceful and understated. She looked like she grew up with horses. And she was younger than me, and beautiful.

I always knew it wouldn't work between us, but I was trying to make it work anyway. We had gotten married and had begun living together and she was starting to be dissatisfied. Dissatisfied with my apartment, where it was located, how much money we had. All of that. She was throwing up, which didn't help. She had crackers in the car, crackers by the bed, crackers everywhere. She was so miserable and so unhappy that I tried to please her in little ways. Get her things. Bring her things. Cook her meals. Do little domestic things. It wasn't my usual way, but I was in love. I was drifting into this habit of pleasing her. Trying to please her.

And there was constant pressure. More this, more that. More money. More, more.

We also had a specific problem. Her health insurance through the D.A.'s office didn't cover pregnancy and neither did mine. After we got married, we couldn't get coverage in time to pay for the baby. It was going to cost eight thousand dollars and we had to come up with it. Neither of us had the money. Lauren's father was a doctor in Virginia but she didn't want to ask him for the money because he disapproved of her marrying me in the first place. My family doesn't have any money. So. There wasn't any money. She worked for the D.A. I worked for the department. She had a lot of debts on her MasterCard and owed money on her car. We had to come up with eight thousand dollars. It's hanging over our heads. How we are going to do this. And it gets to be an unspoken thing, at least from her. That I should handle it.

So one night in August I'm out on a domestic violence call in Ladera Heights. Hispanic couple. They've been drinking and going at it pretty good, she's got a split lip and he's got a black eye, and their kid's screaming in the next room, but pretty soon we calm them down and we can see that nobody is seriously injured, so we're about to leave. And the wife sees we're about to leave. At that point she starts yelling that the husband has been fooling with the daughter. Physically abusing the daughter. When the husband hears this, he looks really pissed, and I think it's bullshit, the wife is just doing something to harass him. But the wife insists we check the daughter, so I go into the kid's room and the kid is about nine months old and screaming red in the face, and I pull the covers back to check for bruises and there I see a kilo of white brick. Under the covers with the kid.

So.

I don't know, it's one of those situations, they're married so she'd have to testify against her husband, there's no probable cause, the search is invalid, on and on. If he's got a halfway decent lawyer he can beat this, no problem. So I go out and call the guy in. I know I can't do anything. All I'm thinking is that if his kid ever got this brick in her mouth, chewed on it, it would kill her. I want to talk to him about that. I figure I'll fuck him over a little. Scare him a little.

So now it's him and me in the kid's room. The wife is still out in the living room with my partner, and suddenly the guy pulls out an envelope two centimeters thick. He cracks it open. I see hundred-dollar bills. An inch thick of hundred-dollar bills. And he says, "Thanks for your help, officer."

There's got to be ten thousand dollars in that envelope. Maybe more. I don't know. The guy holds out the envelope and looks at me. Expecting me to take it.

I say something lame about how it's dangerous to hide shit in a kid's bed. Right away, the guy picks up the brick, puts it on the floor, kicks it out of sight under the bed. Then he says, "You are right. Thank you, officer. I would hate something happens to my daughter." And he holds out the envelope.

So.

Everything is in turmoil. The wife is outside screaming at my partner. The kid is in here screaming at us. The guy is holding the envelope. He smiles and nods. Like, go ahead and take it. It's yours. And I think . . . I don't know what I thought.

Next thing I know, I'm out in the living room and I say everything is fine with the kid, and now the woman starts to scream in her drunken way that *I* abused her child—now it's me, not the husband—and that I am in a conspiracy with the husband, that we are both child abusers. My partner figures she's crazy drunk and we leave, and that's it. My partner says, "You were in that room a while." And I say, "I had to check the kid." And that's it. Except the next day she comes in and makes a formal complaint that I abused her child. She's hung over and she has a record, but even so it's a serious charge and it goes through the system as far as the preliminary, where it gets thrown out as entirely without merit.

That's it.

That's what happened.

That's the whole story.

"And the money?" Connor said.

"I went to Vegas for the weekend. I won big. I paid taxes on thirteen thousand in unearned income that year."

"Whose idea was that?"

"Lauren. She told me how to handle it."

"So she knows what happened?"

"Sure."

"And the department investigation? Did the preliminary board issue a report?"

"I don't think it got that far. They just heard it orally and dismissed it. There's probably a notation in the file, but not an actual report."

"All right," Connor said. "Now tell me the rest."

So I told him about Ken Shubik, and the *Times,* and the Weasel. Connor listened silently, frowning. As I talked, he began to suck air through his teeth, which was the Japanese way of expressing disapproval.

"*Kōhai,*" he said, when I finished, "you are making my life extremely difficult. And certainly you make me appear foolish when I should not. Why didn't you tell me this earlier?"

"Because it has nothing to do with you."

"*Kōhai.*" He was shaking his head. "*Kōhai . . .*"

I was thinking about my daughter again. About the possibility—just the possibility—that I would not be able to see her—that I would not be able to—

"Look," Connor said, "I told you it could be unpleasant. Take my word for it. It can get much more unpleasant than this. This is only the beginning. It can get *nasty*. We must proceed quickly and try to wrap everything up."

"I thought everything *was* wrapped up."

Connor sighed, and shook his head. "It's not," he said. "And now we must resolve everything before you meet your wife at four o'clock. So let's make sure we are done by then."

"Christ, I'd say it's pretty fucking wrapped up," Graham said. He was walking around Sakamura's house in the Hollywood hills. The last of the SID teams was packing up cases to leave.

"I don't know why the chief has such a bug up his ass on this," Graham said. "The SID boys have been doing most of their work right here, on the spot, because he's in such a rush. But thank God: everything ties up perfect. Sakamura is our boy. We combed his bed for pubic hair—it matches the pubic hair found on the girl. We got dried saliva off his toothbrush. It matches blood type and genetic markers for the sperm inside the dead girl. Matchup is ninety-seven percent sure. It's his come inside her, and his pubic hair on her body. He fucked her and then he killed her. And when we came to arrest him, he panicked, made a break for it, and died as a result. Where is Connor?"

"Outside," I said.

Through the windows, I could see Connor standing down by the garage, talking to policemen in a black-and-white patrol car. Connor was pointing up and down the street; they were answering questions.

"What's he doing down there?" Graham said.

I said I didn't know.

"Damn, I don't understand him. You can tell him the answer to his question is no."

"What question?"

"He called me an hour ago," Graham said. "Said he wanted to know how many pairs of reading glasses we found here. We checked. The answer is, no reading glasses. Lots of sunglasses. Couple of pairs of women's sunglasses. But that's it. I don't know why he cared. Strange man, isn't he? What the hell is he doing now?"

We watched as Connor paced back and forth around the squad car, then pointed up and down the road again. One man was in the car, talking on the radio. "Do you understand him?" Graham said.

"No, I don't."

"He's probably trying to track down the girls," Graham said. "Christ, I wish we had gotten the ID on that redhead. Especially now it's turned out this way. She must have fucked him, too. We could have gotten some sperm from her, and made an exact match with all the factors. And I look like a horse's ass, letting the girls get away. But shit, who knew it was going to go that way. It was all so fast. Naked girls up here, prancing around. A guy gets a little confused. It's natural. Shit, they were good-looking, weren't they?"

I said they were.

"And there's nothing left of Sakamura," Graham said. "I talked to the PEO boys an hour ago. They're downtown, cutting the corpse out of the car, but I guess he's burned beyond identification. The M.E.'s office is going to try, but good luck." He stared unhappily out the window. "You know what? We did the best we could with this fucking case," he said. "And I think we did pretty good. We got the right guy. We did it fast, no fuss no muss. But all I hear now is a lot of Japan-bashing. Fuck. You can't win."

"Uh-huh," I said.

"And *Christ* they have juice now," Graham said. "The heat on my ass is terrific. I got the chief calling me, wanting this thing wrapped up. I got some reporter at the *Times* investigating me, hauling out some old shit about a questionable use of force on a Hispanic back in 1978. Nothing to it. But this reporter, he's trying to show I've always been a racist. And what is the background of his story? That last night was a 'racist' incident. So I am now an example of racism rearing its ugly head again. I tell you. The Japanese are masters of the smear job. It's fucking scary."

"I know," I said.

"They getting to you, too?"

I nodded.

"For what?"

"Child abuse."

"Christ," Graham said. "And you got a daughter."

"Yes."

"Doesn't it piss you off? Innuendo and smear tactics, Petey-san. Nothing to do with reality. But try and tell that to a reporter."

"Who is it?" I asked. "The reporter talking to you."

"Linda Jensen, I think she said."

I nodded. Linda Jensen was the Weasel's protégé. Somebody once said that Linda didn't fuck her way to the top. She fucked other people's reputations to the top. She had been a gossip columnist in Washington before graduating to the big time in Los Angeles.

"I don't know," Graham said, shifting his bulk. "Personally, I think it's not worth it. They're turning this country into another Japan. You've already got people afraid to speak. Afraid to say anything against them. People just won't talk about what's happening."

"It would help if the government passed a few laws."

Graham laughed. "The government. They *own* the government. You know what they spend in Washington every year? Four hundred million fucking dollars a year. That's enough to pay the campaign costs of everybody in the United States Senate *and* the House of Representatives. That is a lot of fucking money. Now you tell me. Would they spend all that money, year after year, if it wasn't paying off for them? Of course they wouldn't. Shit. The end of America, buddy. Hey. Looks like your boss wants you."

I looked out the window. Connor was waving to me.

I said, "I better go."

"Good luck," Graham said. "Listen. I may take a couple of weeks off."

"Yeah? When?"

"Maybe later today," Graham said. "The chief mentioned it. He said as long as the fucking *Times* is on my ass, maybe I should. I'm thinking of a week in Phoenix. I got family there. Anyway, I wanted you to know, I might be going."

"Okay, sure," I said.

Connor was still waving to me. He seemed impatient. I hurried down to see him. As I came down the steps, I saw a black Mercedes sedan pull up, and a familiar figure emerge.

It was Weasel Wilhelm.

By the time I got down there, the Weasel had his notepad and tape recorder out. A cigarette hung from the corner of his mouth. "Lieutenant Smith," he said. "I wonder if I could talk to you."

"I'm pretty busy," I said.

"Come on," Connor called to me. "Time's a'wasting." He was holding the door open for me.

I started toward Connor. The Weasel fell in step with me. He held a tiny black microphone toward my face. "I'm taping, I hope you don't mind. After the Malcolm case, we have to be extra careful. I wonder if you would comment on racial slurs allegedly made by your associate Detective Graham during last night's Nakamoto investigation?"

"No," I said. I kept walking.

"We've been told he referred to them as 'fucking Japs.' "

"I have no comment," I said.

"He also called them 'little Nips.' Do you think that kind of talk is appropriate to an officer on duty?"

"Sorry. I don't have a comment, Willy."

He held the microphone up to my face as we walked. It was annoying. I wanted to slap it away, but I didn't. "Lieutenant Smith, we're preparing a story on you and we have some questions about the Martinez case. Do you remember that one? It was a couple of years back."

I kept walking. "I'm pretty busy now, Willy," I said.

"The Martinez case resulted in accusations of child abuse brought by Sylvia Morelia, the mother of Maria Martinez. There was an internal affairs investigation. I wondered if you had any comment."

"No comment."

"I've already talked to your partner at that time, Ted Anderson. I wondered if you had any comment on that."

"Sorry. I don't."

"Then you aren't going to respond to these serious allegations against you?"

"The only one I know that's making allegations is you, Willy."

"Actually, that's not entirely accurate," he said, smiling at me. "I'm told the D.A.'s office has started an investigation."

I said nothing. I wondered if it was true.

"Under the circumstances, Lieutenant, do you think the court made a mistake in granting you custody of your young daughter?"

All I said was, "Sorry. No comment, Willy." I tried to sound confident. I was starting to sweat.

Connor said, "Come on, come on. No time." I got into the car. Connor said to Wilhelm, "Son, I'm sorry, but we're busy. Got to go." He slammed the car door. I started the engine. "Let's go," Connor said.

Willy stuck his head in the window. "Do you think that Captain Connor's Japan-bashing represents another example of the department's lack of judgment in racially sensitive cases?"

"See you, Willy." I rolled up the window, and started driving down the hill.

"A little faster wouldn't bother me," Connor said.

"Sure," I said. I stepped on the gas.

In the rearview mirror, I saw the Weasel running for his Mercedes. I took the turn faster, tires squealing. "How did that lowlife know where to find us? He monitoring the radio?"

"We haven't been on the radio," Connor said. "You know I'm careful about the radio. But maybe the patrol car phoned in something when we arrived. Maybe we have a bug in this car. Maybe he just figured we'd turn up here. He's a scumbag. And he's connected to the Japanese. He's their plant at the *Times*. Usually the Japanese are a little more classy about who they associate with. But I guess he'll do everything they want done. Nice car, huh?"

"I notice it's not Japanese."

"Can't be obvious," Connor said. "He following us?"

"No. I think we lost him. Where are we going now?"

"U.S.C. Sanders has had enough time screwing around by now."

We drove down the street, down the hill, toward the 101 freeway. "By the way," I said. "What was all that about the reading glasses?"

"Just a small point to be verified. No reading glasses were found, right?"

"Right. Just sunglasses."

"That's what I thought," Connor said.

"And Graham says he's leaving town. Today. He's going to Phoenix."

"Uh-huh." He looked at me. "You want to leave town, too?"

"No," I said.

"Okay," Connor said.

I got down the hill and onto the 101 going south. In the old days it would be ten minutes to U.S.C. Now it was more like thirty minutes. Especially now, right at midday. But there weren't any fast times, anymore. Traffic was always bad. The smog was always bad. I drove through haze.

"You think I'm being foolish?" I said. "You think I should pick up my kid and run, too?"

"It's one way to handle it." He sighed. "The Japanese are masters of indirect action. It's their instinctual way to proceed. If someone in Japan is unhappy with you, they never tell you to your face. They tell your friend, your associate, your boss. In such a way that the word gets back. The Japanese have all these ways of indirect communication. That's why they socialize so much, play so much golf, go drinking in *karaoke* bars. They need these extra channels of communication because they can't come out and say what's on their minds. It's tremendously inefficient, when you think about it. Wasteful of time and energy and money. But since they cannot confront—because confrontation is almost like death, it makes them sweat and panic—they have no other choice. Japan is the land of the end run. They never go up the middle."

"Yeah, but . . ."

"So behavior that seems sneaky and cowardly to Americans is just standard operating procedure to Japanese. It doesn't mean anything special. They're just letting you know that powerful people are displeased."

"Letting me know? That I could end up in court over my daughter? My relationship with my kid could be ruined? My own reputation could be ruined?"

"Well, yes. Those are normal penalties. The threat of social disgrace is the usual way you're expected to know of displeasure."

"Well, I think I know it, now," I said. "I think I get the fucking picture."

"It's not personal," Connor said. "It's just the way they proceed."

"Yeah, right. They're spreading a lie."

"In a sense."

"No, not in a sense. It's a fucking lie."

Connor sighed. "It took me a long time to understand," he said, "that Japanese behavior is based on the values of a farm village. You hear a lot about samurai and feudalism, but deep down, the Japanese are farmers. And if you lived in a farm village and you displeased the other villagers, you were banished. And that meant you died, because no other village would take in a troublemaker. So. Displease the group and you die. That's the way they see it.

"It means the Japanese are exquisitely sensitive to the group. More than anything, they are attuned to getting along with the group. It means not standing out, not taking a chance, not being too individualistic. It also means not necessarily insisting on the truth. The Japanese have very little faith in truth. It strikes them as cold and abstract. It's like a mother whose son is accused of a crime. She doesn't care much about the truth. She cares more about her son. The same with the Japanese. To the Japanese, the important thing is relationships between people. That's the real truth. The factual truth is unimportant."

"Yeah, fine," I said. "But why are they pushing now? What's the difference? This murder is solved, right?"

"No, it's not," Connor said.

"It's not?"

"No. That's why we have all the pressure. Obviously, somebody badly *wants* it to be over. They want us to give it up."

"If they are squeezing me and squeezing Graham—how come they're not squeezing you?"

"They are," Connor said.

"How?"

"By making me responsible for what happens to you."

"How are they making you responsible? I don't see that."

"I know you don't. But they do. Believe me. They do."

I looked at the line of cars creeping forward, blending into the haze of downtown. We passed electronic billboards for Hitachi (#1 IN COMPUTERS IN AMERICA), for Canon (AMERICA'S COPY LEADER), and Honda (NUMBER ONE RATED CAR IN AMERICA!). Like most of the new Japanese ads, they were bright enough to run in the daytime. The billboards cost thirty thousand dollars a day to rent; most American companies couldn't afford them.

Connor said, "The point is the Japanese know they can make it very uncomfortable. By raising the dust around you, they are telling me, 'handle it.' Because they think I can get this thing done. Finish it off."

"Can you?"

"Sure. You want to finish it off now? Then we can go have a beer, and enjoy some Japanese truth. Or do you want to get to the bottom of why Cheryl Austin was killed?"

"I want to get to the bottom."

"Me, too," Connor said. "So let's do it, *kōhai*. I think Sanders's lab will have interesting information for us. The tapes are the key, now."

Phillip Sanders was spinning like a top. "The lab is shut down," he said. He threw up his hands in frustration. "And there's nothing I can do about it. *Nothing.*"

Connor said, "When did it happen?"

"An hour ago. Buildings and Grounds came by and told everybody in the lab to leave, and they locked it up. Just like that. There's a big padlock on the front door, now."

I said, "And the reason was?"

"A report that structural weakness in the ceiling has made the basement unsafe and will invalidate the university's insurance if the skating rink comes crashing down on us. Some talk about how student safety comes first. Anyway, they closed the lab, pending an investigation and report by a structural engineer."

"And when will that happen?"

He gestured to the phone. "I'm waiting to hear. Maybe some time next week. Maybe not until next month."

"Next *month*."

"Yeah. Exactly." Sanders ran his hand through his wild hair. "I went all the way to the dean on this one. But the dean's office doesn't know. It's coming from high up in the university. Up where the board of governors knows rich donors who make contributions in multi-million-dollar chunks. The order came from the highest levels." Sanders laughed. "These days, it doesn't leave much mystery."

I said, "Meaning what?"

"You realize Japan is deeply into the structure of American universities, particularly in technical departments. It's happened everywhere. Japanese companies now endow twenty-five professorships at M.I.T., far more than any other nation. Because they know—after all the bullshit stops—that they can't innovate as well as we can. Since they need innovation, they do the obvious thing. They buy it."

"From American universities."

"Sure. Listen, at the University of California at Irvine, there's two floors of a research building that you can't get into unless you have a Japanese passport. They're doing research for Hitachi there. An American university closed to Americans." Sanders swung around, waving his arms. "And around here, if something happens that they don't like, it's just a phone call from somebody to the president of the university, and what can he do? He can't afford to piss the Japanese off. So whatever they want, they get. And if they want the lab closed, it's closed."

I said, "What about the tapes?"

"Everything is locked in there. They made us leave everything."

"Really?"

"They were in a hell of a rush. It was gestapo stuff. Pushing and prodding us to get out. You can't imagine the panic at an American university if it thinks it may lose some funding." He sighed. "I don't know. Maybe Theresa managed to take some tapes with her. You could ask her."

"Where is she?"

"I think she went ice skating."

I frowned. "Ice skating?"

"That's what she said she was going to do. So you could check over there."

And he looked right at Connor. In a particularly meaningful way.

✥   ✥   ✥

Theresa Asakuma wasn't ice skating. There were thirty little kids in the rink, with a young teacher trying in vain to control them. They looked like fourth graders. Their laughter and yells echoed in the high ceiling of the rink.

The building was almost deserted, the bleachers empty. A handful of fraternity boys sat up in one corner, looking down and punching each other on the shoulder. On our side, up high, near the ceiling, a janitor mopped. A couple of adults who looked like parents stood at the railing, down near the ice. Opposite us, a man was reading a newspaper.

I didn't see Theresa Asakuma anywhere.

Connor sighed. Wearily, he sat on the wooden bleachers and leaned back. He crossed his legs, taking his ease. I stood there, watching him. "What are you doing? She's obviously not here."

"Have a seat."

"But you're always in such a rush."

"Have a seat. Enjoy life."

I sat down next to him. We watched the kids skating around the perimeter of the ice. The teacher was shouting, "Alexander? Alexander! I've told you before. No hitting! Don't you hit her!"

I leaned back against the bleachers. I tried to relax. Connor watched the kids and chuckled. He appeared entirely at ease, without a care in the world.

I said, "Do you think Sanders is right? The Japanese squeezed the university?"

"Sure," Connor said.

"And all that business about Japan buying into American technology? Buying professorships at M.I.T.?"

"It's not illegal. They're supporting scholarship. A noble ideal."

I frowned. "So you think it's okay?"

"No," he said. "I don't think it's okay at all. If you give up control of your own institutions you give up everything. And generally, whoever pays for an institution controls it. If the Japanese are willing to put up the money—and if the American government and American industry aren't—then the Japanese will control American education. You know they already *own* ten American colleges. Own them outright. Bought them for the training of their young people. So that they can be assured of the ability to send young Japanese to America."

"But they already can do that. Lots of Japanese go to American universities."

"Yes. But as usual, the Japanese are planning ahead. They know in the future it may get tougher. They know that sooner or later, there will be a backlash. No matter how diplomatically they play it—and they are in the acquisition phase now, so they're playing it very diplomatically. Because the fact is, countries don't like to be dominated. They don't like to be occupied—economically or militarily. And the Japanese figure some day the Americans will wake up."

I watched the kids skating in the rink. I listened to their laughter. I thought of my daughter. I thought of the four o'clock meeting.

I said, "Why are we sitting here?"

"Because," he said.

So we sat there. The teacher was rounding the kids up now, leading them off the ice. "Skates off here. Skates off here, please. That means you too, Alexander! Alexander!"

"You know," Connor said, "if you wanted to buy a Japanese company, you couldn't do it. The people in the company would consider it shameful to be taken over by foreigners. It would be a disgrace. They would never allow it."

"I thought you could. I thought the Japanese had liberalized their rules."

Connor smiled. *"Technically.* Yes. Technically, you can buy a Japanese company. But as a practical matter, you can't. Because if you want to take over a company, you first have to approach its bank. And get the agreement of the bank. That's what is necessary, in order to proceed. And the bank doesn't agree."

"I thought General Motors owns Isuzu."

"GM owns a third of Isuzu. Not a controlling interest. And yes, there are isolated instances. But overall, foreign investment in Japan has declined by half in the last ten years. One company after another finds the Japanese market just too tough. They get tired of the bullshit, the hassles, the collusion, the rigged markets, the *dangō*, the secret agreements to keep them out. They get tired of the government regulations. The run around. And eventually they give up. They just . . . give up. Most other countries have given up: Germans, Italians, French. Everybody's getting tired of trying to do business in Japan. Because no matter what they tell you, Japan is closed. A few years ago, T. Boone Pickens bought one-fourth of the stock of a Japanese company, but he couldn't get on the board of directors. Japan is *closed."*

"So what are we supposed to do?"

"The same thing the Europeans are doing," Connor said. "Reciprocity. Tit for tat. One of yours for one of mine. Everybody in the world has the same problem with Japan. It's just a question of what solution works best. The European solution is pretty direct. Works well, at least so far."

On the rink, some teenage girls began to do warmups and a few tentative leaps. Now the schoolteacher was leading her charges along the corridor past us. As she went by, she said, "Is one of you Lieutenant Smith?"

"Yes, ma'am," I said.

One kid said, "Do you have a gun?"

The teacher said, "That woman asked me to tell you that what you're looking for is in the men's locker room."

"It is?" I said.

The kid said, "Can I see it?"

The teacher said, "You know, the Oriental woman? I think she was Oriental."

"Yes," Connor said. "Thank you."

"I want to see the gun."

Another kid said, "Quiet, stupid. Don't you know anything? They're *undercover*."

"I want to see the gun."

Connor and I started walking away. The kids trailed after us, still asking to see our guns. Across the rink, the man with the newspaper looked up curiously. He watched us leave.

"Nothing like an inconspicuous exit," Connor said.

The men's locker room was deserted. I started going through the green metal lockers, one after another, looking for the tapes. Connor didn't bother. I heard him call to me, "Back here."

He was in the rear by the showers. "You found the tapes?"

"No."

He was holding open a door.

We went down a flight of concrete stairs to a landing. There were two doors. One opened onto a below-grade truck entrance. The other went into a dark hallway with wooden beams. "This way," Connor said.

We went down this hallway, crouched over. We were underneath the rink again. We passed throbbing stainless-steel machinery, and then came to a series of doors.

"Do you know where we're going?" I said.

One of the doors was ajar. He pushed it open. The room lights were out, but I could see that we were in the lab. Off in a corner, I saw a faint monitor glow.

We walked toward it.

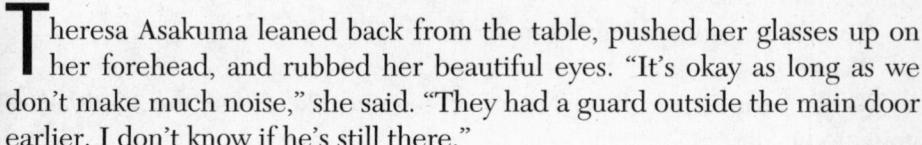

Theresa Asakuma leaned back from the table, pushed her glasses up on her forehead, and rubbed her beautiful eyes. "It's okay as long as we don't make much noise," she said. "They had a guard outside the main door earlier. I don't know if he's still there."

"A guard?"

"Yeah. They were serious about shutting down the lab. It was spectacular, like a drug bust. It really surprised the Americans."

"And you?"

"I don't have the same expectations about this country."

Connor pointed to the monitor in front of her. It showed a freeze-frame image of the couple, embracing as they moved toward the conference room. The same image, seen from other camera angles, was reproduced on other monitors on the desk. Some of the monitors had superimposed red lines, radiating out from the night lights. "What have you learned from the tapes?"

Theresa pointed to the main screen. "I'm not certain," she said. "To be completely certain, I would have to run 3-D modeling sequences to match the dimensions of the room and keep track of all the light sources, and the shadows cast by all the sources. I haven't done that, and I probably can't with the equipment in this room. It would probably require an overnight run on a mini. Maybe I could get time next week from the astrophysics department. The way things are going, maybe not. But in the meantime, I have a strong feeling."

"Which is?"

"The shadows don't match."

In the darkness, Connor nodded slowly. As if that made sense to him.

I said, "Which shadows don't match?"

She pointed to the screen. "As these people move around the floor, the shadows they cast don't line up exactly. They're in the wrong place, or the wrong shape. Often it's subtle. But I think it is there."

"And the fact that the shadows don't match means . . ."

She shrugged. "I'd say the tapes have been altered, Lieutenant."

There was a silence. "Altered how?"

"I'm not sure how much has been done. But it seems clear that there was another person in that room, at least part of the time."

"Another person? You mean a third person?"

"Yes. Someone watching. And that third person has been systematically erased."

"No *shit*," I said.

It was making my head spin. I looked at Connor. He was staring intently at the monitors. He seemed completely unsurprised. I said, "Did you already know this?"

"I suspected something of the sort."

"Why?"

"Well, early in the investigation it seemed likely that the tapes were going to be altered."

"Why?" I said.

Connor smiled. "Details, *kōhai*. Those little things we forget." He glanced at Theresa, as if he was reluctant to talk too much in front of her.

I said, "No, I want to hear this. When did you first know the tapes were altered?"

"In the Nakamoto security room."

"Why?"

"Because of the missing tape."

"What missing tape?" I said. He had mentioned it before.

"Think back," Connor said. "In the security room, the guard told us that he changed the tapes when he came on duty, around nine o'clock."

"Yes . . ."

"And the tape recorders all had timers, showing an elapsed time of about two hours. Each recorder started about ten or fifteen seconds later than the previous one. Because that was the time interval it took him to change each tape."

"Right . . ." I remembered all that.

"And I pointed out to him one tape recorder that didn't fit the sequence. Its tape was only running for half an hour. So I asked if it was broken."

"And the guard seemed to think it was."

"Yes. That's what he said. I was letting him off the hook. Actually, he knew perfectly well it was not broken."

"It wasn't?"

"No. It was one of the few mistakes that the Japanese have made. But they only made it because they were stuck—they couldn't get around it. They couldn't beat their own technology."

I leaned back against the wall. I looked apologetically at Theresa. She looked beautiful in the semidarkness of the monitors. "I'm sorry. I'm lost."

"That's because you are rejecting the obvious explanation, *kōhai*. Think back. If you saw a line of tape recorders, each one running a few seconds later than the one before, and you saw one recorder way out of sequence, what would you think?"

"That someone had changed the tape in that one recorder at a later time."

"Yes. And that's exactly what happened."

"One tape was switched later?"

"Yes."

I frowned. "But why? All of the tapes were replaced at nine o'clock. So none of the replacements showed the murder, anyway."

"Correct," Connor said.

"Then why switch one tape after that?"

"Good question. It's puzzling. I couldn't make sense of it for a long time. But now I know," Connor said. "You have to remember the timing. The tapes were all changed at nine. Then one tape was changed again at ten-fifteen. The obvious assumption was that something important happened between nine o'clock and ten-fifteen, that it was recorded on the tape, and the tape was therefore taken away for some reason. I asked myself: what could this important event be?"

I thought back. I frowned. I couldn't think of anything.

Theresa began to smile and nod, as if something had just amused her. I said, "You know?"

"I can guess," she said, smiling.

"Well," I said. "I'm glad everyone seems to know the answer except me. Because I can't think of anything important being recorded on that tape. By nine o'clock, the yellow barrier was up, isolating the crime scene. The girl's body was on the other side of the room. There were a lot of Japanese standing by the elevators, and Graham was calling me on the phone for help. But nobody actually began an investigation until I got there at about ten. Then we had a lot of back and forth with Ishiguro. I don't think anybody crossed the tape until almost ten-thirty. Say ten-fifteen at the earliest. So if somebody looked at a recording, all it would show is a deserted room, and a girl lying on the table. That's all."

Connor said, "Very good. Except you have forgotten something."

Theresa said, "Did anybody cross the room? Anybody at all?"

"No," I said. "We had the yellow barrier up. Nobody was allowed on the other side of the tape. In fact—"

And then I remembered. "Wait a minute! There was somebody! That little guy with the camera," I said. "He was on the other side of the barrier, taking pictures."

"That's right," Connor said.

"What little guy?" she said.

"A Japanese guy. He was taking pictures. We asked Ishiguro about him. He said his name was, ah . . ."

"Mr. Tanaka," Connor said.

"That's right, Mr. Tanaka. And you asked Ishiguro for the film from his camera." I frowned. "But we never got it."

"No," Connor said. "And frankly, I never thought we would."

Theresa said, "This man was taking pictures?"

"I doubt that he was actually taking pictures," Connor said. "Perhaps he was, because he was using one of those little Canons—"

"The ones that shoot video stills, instead of film?"

"Right. Would there be any use for those, in retouching?"

"There might be," she said. "The images might be used for texture mapping. They'd go in fast, because they were already digitized."

Connor nodded. "Then perhaps he was taking pictures, after all. But it was clear to me that his picture-taking was just an excuse to allow him to walk on the other side of the yellow line."

"Ah," Theresa said, nodding.

I said, "How do you know that?"

"Think back," Connor said.

I had been standing facing Ishiguro when Graham yelled: Aw, Christ, what is this? And I looked back over my shoulder and saw a short Japanese man about ten meters beyond the yellow tape. The man's back was turned to me. He was taking pictures of the crime scene. The camera was very small. It fitted into the palm of his hand.

"Do you remember how he moved?" Connor said. "He moved in a distinctive way."

I tried to recall it. I couldn't.

Graham had gone forward to the tape, saying: For Christ's sake, you can't be in there. This is a goddamned crime scene. You can't take pictures! And there was a general uproar. Graham was yelling at Tanaka, but he continued to be entirely focused on his work, shooting the camera and backing toward us. Despite all the yelling, Tanaka didn't do what a normal person would do—turn around and walk toward the tape. Instead, he backed up to the yellow stripe and, still turned away, ducked his head and went under it.

I said, "He never turned around. He backed up all the way."

"Correct. That is the first mystery. Why would he back up? Now, I think, we know."

"We do?"

Theresa said, "He was repeating the walk of the girl and the killer in reverse, so it would be laid down on videotape and he would have a good record of where the shadows in the room were."

"That's right," Connor said.

I remembered that when I protested, Ishiguro had said to me: This is our employee. He works for Nakamoto Security.

And I had said: This is outrageous. He can't take pictures.

And Ishiguro had explained: But this is for our corporate use.

And meanwhile the man had disappeared in the crowd, slipping through the knot of men at the elevator.

But this is for our corporate use.

"Damn it!" I said. "So Tanaka left us, went downstairs, and removed a single tape, because that tape had a record of his own walk across the room, and the shadows he cast?"

"Correct."

"And he needed that tape to make changes in the original tapes?"

"Correct."

I was finally beginning to understand. "But now, even if we can figure out how the tapes were altered, they won't stand up in a court of law, is that right?"

"That's right," Theresa said. "Any good lawyer will make sure they're inadmissible."

"So the only way to go forward is to get a witness who can testify to what was done. Sakamura might know, but he's dead. So we're stuck unless we can somehow get our hands on Mr. Tanaka. I think we better get him in custody right away."

"I doubt that will ever happen," Connor said.

"Why not? You think they'll keep him from us?"

"No, I don't think they have to. It is very likely that Mr. Tanaka is already dead."

C onnor immediately turned to Theresa. "Are you good at your job?"

"Yes," she said.

"Very good?"

"I think so."

"We have little time left. Work with Peter. See what you can extract from the tape. *Gambatte:* try very hard. Trust me that your efforts will be rewarded. In the meantime, I have some calls to make."

I said, "You're leaving?"

"Yes. I'll need the car."

I gave him the keys. "Where are you going?"

"I'm not your *wife.*"

"I'm just asking," I said.

"Don't worry about it. I need to see some people." He turned to go.

"But why do you say Tanaka is dead?"

"Well, perhaps he's not. We'll discuss it when there is more time. Right now, we have a lot to finish before four o'clock. That is our true deadline. I think you have surprises in store for you, *kōhai.* Just call it my *chokkan,* my intuition. Okay? You have trouble, or something unexpected, call me on the car phone. Good luck. Now work with this lovely lady. *Urayamashii ne!* "

And he left. We heard the rear door close.

I said to Theresa, "What did he say?"

"He said he envies you." She smiled in the darkness. "Let's begin."

She pressed buttons on the equipment in rapid succession. The tape rolled back to the beginning of the sequence.

I said, "How are we going to do this?"

"There are three basic approaches to learn how video has been doctored. The first is blur and color edges. The second is shadow lines. We can try to work with those elements, but I've been doing that for the last two hours, and I haven't gotten very far."

"And the third method?"

"Reflected elements. I haven't looked at them yet."

I shook my head.

"Basically, reflected elements—REs—are portions of the scene that are reflected within the image itself. Like when Sakamura walks out of the room, and his face is reflected in the mirror. There are almost certainly other reflections in that room. A desk lamp may be chrome, and it may show the people, distorted, as they pass. The walls of the conference room are glass. We may be able to pull a reflection off the glass. A silver paperweight on a desk, with a reflection in it. A glass vase of flowers. A plastic container. Anything shiny enough to make a reflection."

I watched her reset the tapes, and prepare to run forward. Her one good hand moved quickly from one machine to the next as she talked. It was odd to stand next to a woman so beautiful, who was so unselfconscious of her beauty.

"In most images, there is something reflective," Theresa said. "Outside, there are car bumpers, wet streets, glass windowpanes. And inside a room there are picture frames, mirrors, silver candlesticks, chrome table-legs. . . . There's always something."

"But won't they fix the reflections, too?"

"If they have time, yes. Because now there are computer programs to map an image onto any shape. You can map a picture onto a complicated, twisted surface. But it takes time. So. Let's hope they had no time."

She started the tapes forward. The first portion was dark, as Cheryl Austin first appeared by the elevators. I looked at Theresa. I said, "How do you feel about this?"

"What do you mean?"

"Helping us. The police."

"You mean, because I am Japanese?" She glanced at me, and smiled. It was an odd, crooked smile. "I have no illusions about Japanese. Do you know where Sako is?"

"No."

"It is a city—a town, really—in the north. In Hokkaido. A provincial place. There is an American airfield there. I was born in Sako. My father was a *kokujin* mechanic. You know that word, *kokujin*? *Niguro*. A black man. My mother worked in a noodle shop where the air force personnel went. They married, but my father died in an accident when I was two years old. There was a small pension for the widow. So we had some money. But my grandfather took most of it, because he insisted he had been disgraced by my birth. I was *ainoko* and *niguro*. They are not nice words, what he called me. But my mother wanted to stay there, to stay in Japan. So I grew up in Sako. In this . . . *place* . . ."

I heard the bitterness in her voice.

"You know what the *burakumin* are?" she said. "No? I am not surprised. In Japan, the land where everyone is supposedly equal, no one speaks of *burakumin*. But before a marriage, a young man's family will check the family history of the bride, to be sure there are no *burakumin* in the past. The bride's family will do the same. And if there is any doubt, the marriage will not occur. The *burakumin* are the untouchables of Japan. The outcasts, the lowest of the low. They are the descendants of tanners and leather workers, which in Buddhism is unclean."

"I see."

"And I was lower than *burakumin*, because I was deformed. To the Japanese, deformity is shameful. Not sad, or a burden. *Shameful*. It means you have done something wrong. Deformity shames you, and your family, and your community. The people around you wish you were dead. And if you are half black, the *ainoko* of an American big nose . . ." She shook her head. "Children are cruel. And this was a provincial place, a country town."

She watched the tape go forward.

"So I am glad to be here. You Americans do not know in what grace your land exists. What freedom you enjoy in your hearts. You cannot imagine the harshness of life in Japan, if you are excluded from the group. But I know it very well. And I do not mind if the Japanese suffer a little now, from my efforts with my *one good hand*."

She glared at me. The intensity turned her face to a mask. "Does that answer your question, Lieutenant?"

"Yes," I said. "It does."

"When I come to America, I think the Americans are very foolish about the Japanese—but never mind. Here is the sequence now. You watch the top two monitors. I will watch the bottom three. Look carefully for objects that reflect. Look closely. Here it comes."

I watched the monitors in the darkness.

Theresa Asakuma was feeling bitter about the Japanese, but so was I. The incident with Weasel Wilhelm had made me angry. Angry the way somebody who's scared can be angry. One sentence he had said kept coming back to my mind, again and again.

Under the circumstances, don't you think the court made a mistake in granting you custody of your young daughter?

I never wanted custody. In all the turmoil of the divorce, of Lauren moving out, packing up, this is yours, this is mine—in all that, the last thing I wanted was custody of a seven-month-old baby. Shelly was just starting to move around the living room, holding onto the furniture. She would say "Mama." Her first word. But Lauren didn't want the responsibility and kept saying, "I can't handle it, Peter. I just can't handle it." So I took custody. What else could I do?

But now it was almost two years later. I had changed my life. I had changed my job, my schedule. She was *my* daughter now. And the thought of giving her up was like twisting a knife in my stomach.

Under the circumstances, Lieutenant, don't you think . . .

On the monitor, I watched as Cheryl Austin waited in the darkness for the arrival of her lover. I watched the way she looked around the room.

The court made a mistake . . .

No, I thought, the court didn't make a mistake. Lauren couldn't handle it, and had never been able to handle it. Half the time, she skipped on her weekends. She was too busy to see her own daughter. Once after a weekend she returned Michelle to me. Michelle was crying. Lauren said, "I just don't know what to do with her." I checked. Her diapers were wet and she had a painful rash. Michelle always gets a rash when her diapers aren't changed promptly.

Lauren hadn't changed her diapers often enough during the weekend. So I changed her, and there were streaks of shit in Michelle's vagina. She hadn't cleaned her own daughter properly.

Don't you think the court made a mistake?

No, I didn't.

Under the circumstances, don't you think—

"Fuck it," I said.

Theresa stabbed a button, stopped the tapes. The images froze on the monitors all around us. "What is it?" she said. "What did you see?"

"Nothing."

She looked at me.

"I'm sorry. I was thinking of something else."

"Don't."

She started the tape again.

On multiple monitors, the man embraced Cheryl Austin. Images from the different cameras were coordinated in an eerie way. It was as if we could see all sides of the event—front and back, top and sides. It was like a moving architectural blueprint.

And it felt creepy, to watch.

My two monitors showed the view from the far end of the room, and from high above, looking straight down. Cheryl and her lover were small in one monitor, and in the other one, I saw only the tops of their heads. But I watched.

Standing alongside me, Theresa Asakuma breathed slowly, regularly. In and out. I glanced at her.

"Pay attention."

I looked back.

The lovers were in a passionate embrace. The man pressed Cheryl back against a desk. In my top view, I could see her face, looking straight up as she lay back. Beside her, a framed picture on the desk fell over.

"There," I said.

Theresa stopped the tape.

"What?" she said.

"There." I pointed to the framed picture. It lay flat, facing upward. Reflected in the glass, we could see the outline of the man's head as he bent over Cheryl. It was very dark. Just a silhouette.

"Can you get an image from that?" I said.

"I don't know. Let's try."

Her hand moved swiftly across the controls, touching them briefly. "The video image is digital," she said. "It's in the computer now. We'll see what we can do with it." The image began to jump, growing larger in increments as she zoomed in on the picture frame. The image moved past Cheryl's frozen, grainy face, her head thrown back in an instant of passion. Moved down from her shoulder, toward the frame.

As the picture enlarged, it became more grainy. It began to decompose into a pattern of dots, like a newspaper photo held too close to your face. Then the dots themselves enlarged, formed edges, turned into small blocks of gray. Pretty soon I couldn't tell what we were looking at.

"Is this going to work?"

"I doubt it. But there's the edge of the frame, and there's the face."

I was glad she could see it. I couldn't.

"Let's sharpen."

She pressed buttons. Computer menus dropped down, flashed back. The image became crisper. Grittier. But I could see the frame. And the outline of the head.

"Sharpen again."

She did that.

"All right. Now we can adjust our grayscale . . ."

The face in the frame began to emerge from the gloom.

It was chilling.

Enlarged so much, the grain was severe—each pupil of the eyes was a single black spot—and we really couldn't see who it was. The man's eyes were open, and his mouth was twisted, distorted in passion, or arousal, or hate. But we couldn't really tell.

Not really.

"Is that a Japanese face?"

She shook her head. "There's not enough detail in the original."

"You can't bring it out?"

"I'll work on it later. But I think, no. It won't ever be there. Let's go on."

The images snapped back into full movement. Cheryl suddenly shoved the man away, pushing his chest with the flat of her hand. The face disappeared from the picture frame.

We were back to the original five views.

The couple broke and she complained, pushing him repeatedly. Her face looked angry. Now that I had seen the man's face reflected in the frame, I wondered if she had become frightened of what she saw. But it was impossible to tell.

The lovers stood in the deserted room, discussed where to go. She was looking around. He nodded his head. She pointed toward the conference room. He seemed to agree or accept.

They kissed, clinched again. There was a familiarity in the way they joined and parted, joined again.

Theresa saw it, too. "She knows him."

"Yes. I'd say."

Still kissing, the couple moved awkwardly toward the conference room. At this point my monitors were no longer very useful. The far camera showed the whole room, and the couple moving laterally across it, from right to left. But the figures were tiny, and difficult to see. They were moving between the desks, heading toward—

"Wait," I said. "What was that?"

She went back, frame by frame.

"There," I said.

I pointed to the image. "See that? What's that?"

As the couple moved across the room, the camera tracked past a large Japanese calligraphy scroll hanging on the wall near the elevator. The scroll was encased in glass. For a brief moment, there was a glint of light in the glass. That was what had caught my eye.

A glint of light.

Theresa frowned. "It's not a reflection from the couple," she said.

"No."

"Let's look."

She began zooming again. The image jumped toward the hanging scroll, growing grittier with each step. The glint enlarged, broke in two fragments. There was a fuzzy spot of light in one corner. And a vertical slit of light, running almost the length of the picture.

"Let's rock it," she said.

She began to make the image go forward and back, one frame at a time. Flipping from one to the other. In one frame, the vertical slit was missing. In the next frame, it was there. The vertical bar lasted for the next ten frames. Then it was gone, never to reappear. But the fuzzy spot in the corner was always present.

"Hmmm."

She pushed in on the spot. Under ever-increasing magnification, it disintegrated until it looked like a cluster of stars from an astronomy picture. But it seemed to have some kind of internal organization. I could almost imagine an **X** shape to it. I said so.

"Yes," she said. "Let's sharpen."

She did that. The computers worked on the data. The fuzzy cluster resolved itself. Now it looked like Roman numerals.

⌠⏐Ӿ⌠⏐

"What the hell is that?" I said.

She kept working. "Edge trace," she said. The outline of the Roman numerals appeared more clearly.

⌠⏐Ӿ⌡

Theresa continued to try and resolve it. As she worked, in some ways the image seemed to get better, and in some ways, less clear. But eventually we could recognize it.

TIXƎ

"It's the reflection of an exit sign," she said. "There's an exit at the far end of the room opposite the elevators, is that right?"

"Yes," I said.

"It's being reflected in the glass of the scroll. That's all it is." She flipped to the next frame. "But this vertical bar of light. That's interesting. See? It appears, and is gone." She ran it back and forth several times.

And then I figured it out.

"There's a fire exit back there," I said. "And a staircase going downstairs. That must be the reflection of the light from the stairwell as someone opens the door and closes it again."

"You mean someone came into the room," she said. "From the back stairs?"

"Yes."

"Interesting. Let's try and see who it is."

She ran the tapes forward. At this high magnification, the grainy image spattered and popped like fireworks on the screen. It was as if the smallest components of the image had a life of their own, their dance independent of the image they assembled to make. But it was exhausting to watch. I rubbed my eyes. "Jesus."

"Okay. *There.*"

I looked up. She had frozen the image. I couldn't see anything but erratic black-and-white dots. There seemed to be a pattern but I couldn't tell what it was. It reminded me of the sonograms when Lauren was pregnant. The doctor would say, The head is here, that's the baby's stomach there. . . . But I couldn't see anything. It was just abstract. My daughter still in the womb.

The doctor had said, See? She wiggled her fingers. See? Her heart is beating.

I had seen that. I had seen the heart beating. The little heart and the little ribs.

Under the circumstances, Lieutenant, don't you think—

"See?" Theresa said. "That's his shoulder. That's the outline of the head. Now he is moving forward—see him getting larger?—and now he is standing in that far passageway, looking around the corner. He is cautious. You can see the profile of his nose for a moment as he turns to look. See that? I know it's hard. Watch carefully. Now he is looking at them. He is watching them."

And suddenly, I could see it. The spots seemed to fall into place. I saw a silhouetted man standing in the hallway by the far exit.

He was watching.

Across the room, the lovers were wrapped up in their kiss. They didn't notice the new arrival.

But someone was watching them. It gave me a chill.

"Can you see who he is?"

She shook her head. "Impossible. We are at the limits of everything. I cannot even resolve eyes, a mouth. Nothing."

"Then let's go on."

✿　✿　✿

The tapes snapped back, full speed. I was jarred by the sudden return to normal size and normal movement. I watched as the lovers, kissing passionately, continued to cross the room.

"So now they are being watched," Theresa said. "Interesting. What kind of a girl is this?"

I said, "I believe the term is *torigaru onnai*."

She said, "She is light in her bird? *Tori* what?"

"Never mind. I mean she is a loose woman."

Theresa shook her head. "Men always say things like that. To me, it looks like she loves him, but she is troubled in her mind."

The lovers were approaching the conference room, and Cheryl suddenly twisted away, attempting to break free from the man.

"If she loves him, she's got a strange way of showing it," I said.

"She senses something is wrong."

"Why?"

"I don't know. Perhaps she hears something. The other man. I don't know."

Whatever the reason, Cheryl was struggling with the lover, who now had both arms around her waist and was almost dragging her into the conference room. Cheryl twisted once more at the door, as the man tried to pull her in.

"A good chance here," Theresa said.

The tape froze again.

All the walls of the conference room were glass. Through the outer walls, the lights of the city were visible. But the inner walls, facing the atrium, were dark enough to act as a black mirror. Since Cheryl and her lover were near the inner glass walls, their images were reflected in the glass as they struggled.

Theresa ran the tape forward, frame by frame, looking for an image that might hold up. From time to time, she zoomed in, probed the pixels, zoomed back out. It was difficult. The two people were moving quickly, and they were often blurred. And the lights from the skyscrapers outside sometimes obscured otherwise good images.

It was frustrating.

It was slow.

Stop. Zoom in. Slide around in the image, trying to locate a section that had enough detail. Give up. Go forward again. Stop again.

Finally, Theresa sighed. "It's not working. That glass is murder."

"Then let's keep going."

I saw Cheryl grab the door frame, trying to keep from being pulled into the conference room. The man finally pulled her free, she slid backward with a look of terror on her face, and then she swung her arms back to hit the man. Her purse went flying. Then they were both inside the room. Silhouettes moving quickly, turning.

The man shoved her back against the table, and Cheryl appeared in the camera that aimed straight down on the conference room. Her short blond hair contrasted with the dark wood of the table. Her mood changed again, she stopped struggling for a minute. She had a look of expectation. Excitement. She licked her lips. Her eyes followed the man as he leaned over her. He slid her skirt up her hips.

She smiled, pouted, whispered in his ear.

He pulled her panties away, a quick jerk.

She smiled at him. It was a tense smile, half-aroused, half-pleading.

She was excited by her own fear.

His hands caressed her throat.

Standing in the darkened laboratory, with the hiss of skaters on the ice above, we watched the final violent act, again and again. It played on five monitors, different angles, as her pale legs went up, onto his shoulders, and he crouched over her, hands fumbling at his trousers. With repetition, I noticed small things not seen before. The way she slid down the table to meet him, wiggling her hips. The way his back arched at the moment of penetration. The change in her smile, catlike, knowing. Calculating. How she urged him on, saying something. Her hands around his back, caressing. The sudden change in mood, the flash of anger in her eyes, the abrupt slap. The way she fought him, first to arouse him, and then later, struggling in a different way, because then something was wrong. The way her eyes bulged, and she had a look of real desperation. Her hands pushing his arms, shoving his coat sleeves up, revealing the tiny metallic sparkle of cuff links. The glint of her watch. Her arm falling back, palm open. Five fingers pale against the black of the table. Then a tremor, the fingers twitching, and stillness.

His slowness to understand something was wrong. The way he went rigid for a moment, then took her head in his hand, moved it back and forth, trying to arouse her, before he finally pulled away. Even looking at his back, you could almost feel his horror. He remained slow, as if in a trance. Pacing around the room in aimless half steps, first this way, then that. Trying to recover his wits, to decide what to do.

Each time I saw the sequence repeated, I felt a different way. The first few times, there was a tension, a voyeuristic sensation, itself almost sexual. And then later, I felt progressively more detached, more analytical. As if I was drifting away, moving back from the monitor. And finally, the entire sequence seemed to break down before my eyes, the bodies losing their human identities altogether, becoming abstractions, elements of design, shifting and moving in dark space.

Theresa said, "This girl is sick."

"It looks that way."

"She is not a victim. Not this one."

"Maybe not."

We watched it again. But I no longer knew why we were watching. Finally I said, "Let's go forward, Theresa."

We had been running the sequence to a certain point on the tape counter, and then going back to run again. So we had seen a part of the tape again and again, but we hadn't gone farther. Almost immediately as we went forward, something remarkable happened. The man stopped pacing and looked sharply off to one side—as if he had seen something, or heard something.

"The other man?" I said.

"Perhaps." She pointed to the monitors. "This is the area in the tapes where the shadows do not seem to match up. Now, we know why."

"Something was erased?"

She ran the tape backward. On the side monitor view, we could see the man look up, in the direction of the exit. He gave every appearance that he had seen someone. But he did not appear frightened or guilty.

She zoomed in. The man was just a silhouette. "You can't see anything, can you?"

"Profile."

"What about it?"

"I am looking at the jaw line. Yes. See? The jaw is moving. He is talking."

"Talking to the other man?"

"Or to himself. But he is certainly looking off. And now see? He has sudden new energy."

The man was moving around the conference room. His behavior purposeful. I remembered how confusing this part had been, when I saw it the night before at the police station. But with five cameras, it was clear. We could see exactly what he was doing. He picked up the panties from the floor.

And then he bent over the dead girl, and removed her watch.

"No kidding," I said. "He took her watch."

I could only think of one reason why: the watch must have an inscription. The man put the panties and the watch in his pocket, and was turning to go, when the image froze again. Theresa had stopped it.

"What is it?" I said.

She pointed to one of the five monitors. "There," she said.

She was looking at the side view, from the overall camera. It showed the conference room as seen from the atrium. I saw the silhouette of the girl on the table, and the man inside the conference room.

"Yeah? So?"

"*There*," she said, pointing. "They forgot to erase that one." In the corner of the screen, I saw a ghostly form. The angle and the lighting were just right to enable us to see him. It was a man.

The third man.

He had come forward, and now was standing in the middle of the atrium, looking toward the killer, inside the conference room. The image of the third man was complete, reflected in the glass. But it was faint.

"Can you get that? Can you make it out?"

"I can try," she said.

The zooms began. She punched in, saw the image decompose. She sharpened it, heightened contrast. The image streaked, and went dull, flat. She coaxed it back, reconstituted it. She moved closer, enlarging it. It was tantalizing. We could almost make an identification.

Almost, but not quite.

"Frame advance," she said.

Now, one by one, the frames clicked ahead. The image of the man was alternately sharper, blurred, sharp.

And then at last, we saw the waiting man clearly.

"No *shit*," I said.

"You know who he is?"

"Yes," I said. "It's Eddie Sakamura."

After that, we made swift progress. We knew, without a doubt, that the tapes had been altered and the identity of the killer had been changed. We watched as the killer came out of the room, and moved toward the exit, with a regretful look back at the dead girl.

I said, "How could they change the killer's face in just a few hours?"

"They have very sophisticated mapping software," she said. "It's by far the most advanced in the world. The Japanese are becoming much better in software. Soon they will surpass the Americans in that, as they already have in computers."

"So they did it with better software?"

"Even with the best software it would be daring to try it. And the Japanese are not daring. So I suspect this particular job was not so hard. Because the killer spends most of his time kissing the girl, or in shadow, so you can't see his face. I am guessing they had the idea very late, as an after-thought, to make a change of identity. Because they saw that they only had to change this part coming up. . . . There, where he passes the mirror."

In the mirror, I saw the face of Eddie Sakamura, clearly. His hand brushing the wall, showing the scar.

"You see," she said, "if they changed that, the rest of the tape could pass. In all the cameras. It was a golden opportunity, and they took it. That is what I think."

On the monitors, Eddie Sakamura went past the mirror, into shadow. She ran it back. "Let's look."

She put up the reflection in the mirror, and step-zoomed in to the face until it broke into blocks. "Ah," she said. "You see the pixels. You see the regularity. Someone has done some retouching here. Here, on the cheek-bone, where there is a shadow beneath his eye. Normally you get some irregularity at the edge between two gray scales. Here, the line is cleaned up. It has been repaired. And let me see—"

The image spun laterally.

"Yes. Here, too."

More blocks. I couldn't tell what she was looking at. "What is it?"

"His right hand. Where the scar is. You see, the scar has been added, you can tell from the way the pixels configure."

I couldn't see it, but I took her word for it. "Then who was the actual killer?"

She shook her head. "It will be difficult to determine. We have searched the reflections and we have not found it. There is a final procedure which I did not try, because it is the easiest of all, but it is also the easiest to change. That is to search the shadow detail."

"Shadow detail?"

"Yes. We can try to do image intensification in the black areas of the picture, in the shadows and the silhouettes. There may be a place where there is enough ambient light to enable us to derive a recognizable face. We can try."

She didn't sound enthusiastic about the prospects.

"You don't think it will work?"

She shrugged. "No. But we might as well try. It is all that is left."

"Okay," I said. "Let's do it."

She started to run the tape in reverse, walking Eddie Sakamura backward from the mirror toward the conference room. "Wait a minute," I said. "What happens after the mirror? We haven't looked at that part."

"I looked earlier. He goes under an overhang, and moves away, toward the staircase."

"Let's see it anyway."

"All right."

The tape ran forward. Quickly, Eddie Sakamura went toward the exit. His face flashed in the mirror as he went past it. The more often I saw it, the more fake that moment looked. It even seemed as if a small delay, a tiny pause, had been added to his movement. To help us make the identification.

Now the killer walked on, into a dark passage leading toward the staircase, which was somewhere around the corner, out of view. The far wall was light, so he was silhouetted. But there was no detail visible in the silhouette. He was entirely dark.

"No," she said. "I remember this part. Nothing here. Too dark. *Kuronbō.* What they used to call me. Black person."

"I thought you said you could do shadow detail."

"I can, but not here. Anyway, I am sure this part has been retouched. They know we will examine the section of tape on either side of the mirror. They know we will go in with pixel microscopes and scan every frame. So they will have fixed that area carefully. And they will blacken the shadows on this person."

"Okay, but even so—"

"Hey!" she said suddenly. "What was that?"

The image froze.

I saw the outline of the killer, walking away toward the white wall in the background, the exit sign above his head.

"Looks like a silhouette."

"Yes, but something is wrong."

She ran the tape backward, slowly.

As I watched, I said, "*Machigai no umi oshete kudasaii.*" It was a phrase I had learned from one of my early classes.

She smiled in the darkness. "I must help you with your Japanese, Lieutenant. Are you asking me if there has been a mistake?"

"Yes."

"The word is *umu,* not *umi. Umi* is ocean. *Umu* means you are asking yes or no about something. And yes, I believe there may have been a mistake."

The tape continued backward, the silhouette of the killer coming back toward us. She sucked in her breath, in surprise.

"There *is* a mistake. I cannot believe it. Do you see it now?"

"No," I said.

She ran the tape forward for me. I watched as the man walked away in silhouette.

"There, do you see it now?"

"No, I'm sorry."

She was becoming irritable. "Pay attention. Look at the shoulder. Watch the shoulder of the man. See how it rises and falls with each step, in a rhythmic way, and then suddenly . . . There! You see it?"

I did. Finally. "The outline seemed to jump. To get bigger."

"Yes. Exactly. To jump bigger." She adjusted the controls. "Quite a lot bigger, Lieutenant. They tried to blend the jump into the up-step, to make it less conspicuous. But they did not try very hard. It is clear anyway."

"And what does that mean?"

"It means they are arrogant," she said. She sounded angry. I couldn't tell why.

So I asked her.

"Yes. Now it pisses me off," she said. She was zooming in on the image, her one hand moving quickly. "It is because they have made an obvious mistake. They expect we will be sloppy. We will not be thorough. We will not be intelligent. We will not be *Japanese.*"

"But—"

"Oh, I *hate* them." The image moved, shifted. She was concentrating on the outline of the head, now. "You know Takeshita Noboru?"

I said, "Is that a manufacturer?"

"No. Takeshita was prime minister. A few years ago, he made a joke about visiting American sailors on a Navy ship. He said America is now so poor, the Navy boys cannot afford to come ashore to enjoy Japan. Everything is too expensive for them. He said they could only remain on their ship and give each other AIDS. Big joke in Japan."

"He said that?"

She nodded. "If I was American, and someone said that to me, I would take this ship away, and tell Japan to go fuck itself, pay for its own defense. You didn't know Takeshita said this?"

"No . . ."

"American news." She shook her head. "Such nothing."

She was furious, working quickly. Her fingers slipped on the controls, the image jumped back, lost definition. "Shit fuck."

"Take it easy, Theresa."

"Fuck, take it easy. We're going to score now!"

She moved in on the silhouetted head, isolating it, then following it, frame by frame. I saw the image jump larger, distinctly.

"You see, that is the join," she said. "That is where the changed image goes back to the original. Here on, it's original material on the tape. This is the original man walking away from us, now."

The silhouette moved toward the far wall. She proceeded frame by frame. Then the outline began to change shape.

"Ah. Okay. Good, what I hoped for . . ."

"What is it?"

"He is taking a last look. A look back at the room. See? The head is turning. There is his nose, and now, the nose is gone again, because he has turned completely. Now he is looking back at us."

The silhouette was dense black.

"Lot of good it does us."

"Watch."

More controls.

"The detail is there," she said. "It is like dark exposure on film. The detail has been recorded, but we cannot see it yet. So. . . . Now I have enhancement. And now I will get the shadow detail. . . . Now!"

And in a sudden, shocking moment, the dark silhouette blossomed, the wall behind flaring white, making a kind of halo around the head. The dark face became lighter, and we could see the face for the first time, distinctly and clearly.

"Huh, white man." She sounded disappointed.

"My God," I said.

"You know who he is?"

"Yes," I said.

The features were twisted with tension, the lip turned up in a kind of snarl. But the identity was unmistakable.

I was looking at the face of Senator John Morton.

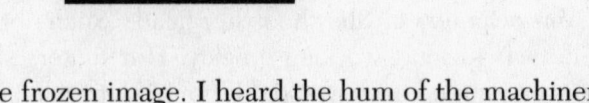

I sat back, staring at the frozen image. I heard the hum of the machinery. I heard water dripping into buckets, somewhere in the darkness of the laboratory. I heard Theresa breathing alongside me, panting like a runner who has finished a race.

I sat there and just stared at the screen. Everything fell into place, like a jigsaw puzzle that assembled itself before my eyes.

Julia Young: She has a boyfriend who travels a lot. She's always traveling. New York, Washington, Seattle . . . she meets him. She's madly in love with him.

Jenny, in the TV studio: Morton has a young girlfriend that's driving him crazy. Makes him jealous. Some young girl.

Eddie: She likes to cause trouble, this girl. She likes to make turmoil.

Jenny: I've seen this girl hanging around at parties with some of the Washington types for about six months now.

Eddie: She was a sick girl. She liked pain.

Jenny: Morton heads the Senate Finance Committee. The one that's been having hearings about this MicroCon sale.

Cole, the security guard, in the bar: They have the big guys in their pocket. They own 'em. We can't beat 'em now.

And Connor: Somebody wants this investigation to be over. They want us to give it up.

And Morton: So your investigation is formally concluded?

"Hell," I said.

She said, "Who is he?"

"He's a senator."

"Oh." She looked at the screen. "And why do they care about him?"

"He has a powerful position in Washington. And I think he has something to do with the sale of a company. Maybe other reasons, too."

She nodded.

I said, "Can we print a picture of this?"

"No. We don't have equipment for hard copies. The lab can't afford it."

"Then what can we do? I need something to take with me."

"I can take a Polaroid for you," she said. "Not great, but okay for now." She started poking around the lab, stumbling in the dark. Finally she came back with a camera. She moved close to the screen and shot several copies.

We waited for them to come out, standing in the blue light from the monitors.

"Thanks," I said. "For all your help."

"You are welcome. And I'm sorry."

"Why?"

"I know you expected it would be a Japanese man."

I realized she was speaking for herself. I didn't answer her. The pictures darkened. They were good quality, the image clear. As I slipped them in my pocket, I felt something hard there. I brought it out.

"You have a Japanese passport?" she said.

"No. It's not mine. It's Eddie's." I put it back in my pocket. "I have to go," I said. "I have to find Captain Connor."

"All right." She turned back to the monitors.

"What are you going to do?" I said.

"I will stay, and work more."

I left her, went out the back door, and made my way down the dark passageway to the outside.

Blinking in the harsh daylight, I went to a pay phone and called Connor. He was in the car.

"Where are you?" I said.

"Back at the hotel."

"What hotel?"

"The Four Seasons," Connor said. "It's Senator Morton's hotel."

"What are you doing there?" I said. "Do you know that—"

"*Kōhai*," he said. "Open line, remember? Call yourself a taxi and meet me at 1430 Westwood Boulevard. We will meet there in twenty minutes."

"But how—"

"No more questions." And he hung up.

I looked at the building at 1430 Westwood Boulevard. It had a plain brown facade, just a door with a painted number. On one side was a French bookstore. On the other side was a watch repair place.

I went up and knocked on the door. I noticed a small sign in Japanese characters beneath the numbers.

Nothing happened, so I opened the door. I found myself in an elegant, tiny sushi bar. It had only four seats for customers. Connor was alone there, sitting at the far end. He waved to me. "Say hello to Imae. The best sushi chef in Los Angeles. Imae-san, Sumisu-san."

The chef nodded and smiled. He put something on the shelf before my seat. *"Kore o dōzo, Sumisu-san."*

I sat down. *"Dōmo, Imae-san."*

"Hai."

I looked at the sushi. It was some kind of pink fish eggs, with a raw yellow egg yolk sitting on top. I thought it looked revolting.

I turned to Connor.

He said *"Kore o tabetakoto arukai?"*

I shook my head. "Sorry. You lost me."

"You'll have to work on your Japanese, for your new girlfriend."

"What new girlfriend?"

Connor said, "I thought you would thank me. I gave you all that time with her."

"You mean Theresa?"

He smiled. "You can do much worse, *kōhai*. And I gather you have, in the past. Anyway, I asked you if you knew what that was." He pointed to the sushi.

"No, I don't."

"Quail egg and salmon roe," he said. "Good protein. Energy. You need it."

I said, "Do I have to?"

Imae said, "Make you strong for girlfriend." And he laughed. He said something quickly in Japanese to Connor.

Connor replied, and the two had a good laugh.

"What's funny?" I said. But I wanted to change the subject, so I ate the first of the sushi. If you got past the slimy texture, it was actually very good.

Imae said, "Good?"

"Very good," I said. I ate the second one, and turned to Connor. "You know what we found on those tapes? It's unbelievable."

Connor held up his hand. "Please. You must learn the Japanese way to have relaxation. Everything in its place. *Oaisō onegai shimasu.*"

"Hai, Connor-san."

The sushi chef produced the bill, and Connor peeled off money. He bowed and there was a rapid exchange in Japanese.

"We're leaving now?"

"Yes," Connor said. "I've already eaten, and you, my friend, can't afford to be late."

"For what?"

"For your ex-wife, remember? We'd better go to your apartment now, and meet her."

I was driving again. Connor was staring out the window. "How did you know it was Morton?"

"I didn't," Connor said. "At least, not until this morning. But it was clear to me last night that the tape had been altered."

I thought of all the effort that Theresa and I had gone to, all the zooming and inspection and image manipulation. "You're telling me you just looked at the tape, and you could tell?"

"Yes."

"How?"

"There was one glaring error. Remember when you met Eddie at the party? He had a scar on his hand."

"Yes. It looked like an old burn scar."

"Which hand was it on?"

"Which hand?" I frowned. I thought back to the meeting. Eddie in the cactus garden at night, smoking cigarettes, flicking them away. Eddie turning, moving nervously. Holding the cigarettes. The scar had been on . . . "His left hand," I said.

"That's right," Connor said.

"But the scar appears on the tape, too," I said. "You see it clearly when he walks past the mirror. His hand touches the wall for a moment—"

I stopped.

On the tape, his *right* hand had touched the wall.

"Jesus," I said.

"Yes," Connor said. "They made a mistake. Maybe they got confused about what was a reflection and what wasn't. But I imagine they were working hastily, and they couldn't remember which hand it was, and they just added the scar anyway. Mistakes like that happen."

"So last night, you saw the scar on the wrong hand . . ."

"Yes. And I knew at once that the tape was changed," Connor said. "I had to prepare you to analyze the tape in the morning. So I sent you to SID, to get names of places that would work on the tape. And then I went home to bed."

"But you allowed us to arrest Eddie. Why? You must have known that Eddie wasn't the killer."

"Sometimes, you have to let things play out," Connor said. "It was clear we were meant to think that Eddie killed the girl. So: play it out."

"But an innocent man died," I said.

"I wouldn't call Eddie innocent," Connor said. "Eddie was in this up to his neck."

"And Senator Morton? How did you know it was Morton?"

"I didn't, until he called us in for that little meeting today. Then he gave himself away."

"How?"

"He was smooth. You have to think about what he actually said," Connor said. "Wedged in between all the bullshit, he asked us three times if our investigation was finished. And he asked us if the murder had anything to do with MicroCon. When you think about it, that's a very peculiar question."

"Why? He has contacts. Mr. Hanada. Other people. He told us that."

"No," Connor said, shaking his head. "If you take away all the bullshit, what Senator Morton told us was his train of thought: Is the investigation over? And can you connect it to MicroCon? Because I am now going to change my position on the MicroCon sale."

"Okay . . ."

"But he never explained a crucial point. Why was he changing his position on the MicroCon sale?"

"He told us why," I said. "He had no support, nobody cares."

Connor handed me a Xerox. I glanced at it. It was a page from a newspaper. I gave it back. "I'm driving. Tell me."

"This is an interview Senator Morton gave in *The Washington Post*. He repeats his stand on MicroCon. It's against the interest of national defense and American competitiveness to sell the company. Blah blah. Eroding our technology base and selling off our future to the Japanese. Blah blah. That was his position on Thursday morning. On Thursday night he attends a party in California. By Friday morning, he has a different view of MicroCon. The sale is fine with him. Now you tell me why."

"Jesus," I said. "What are we going to do?"

Because there is a thing about being a policeman. Most of the time, you feel pretty good. But at certain points, it comes back to you that you are just a cop. The truth is, you're pretty far down the ladder. And you are reluctant to take on certain kinds of people, certain kinds of power. It gets messy. It gets out of control. You can have your ass handed to you.

"What do we do?" I said again.

"One thing at a time," Connor said. "Is this your apartment building up here?"

※　※　※

The TV minivans were lined up along the street. There were several sedans with PRESS signs behind the windshield. A knot of reporters stood outside the front door to my apartment, and along the street. Among the reporters I saw Weasel Wilhelm, leaning against his car. I didn't see my ex-wife.

"Keep driving, *kōhai*," Connor said. "Go to the end of the block and turn right."

"Why?"

"I took the liberty of calling the D.A.'s office a while ago. I arranged for you to meet your wife in the park down here."

"You did?"

"I thought it would be better for everybody."

I drove around the corner. Hampton Park was adjacent to the elementary school. At this hour of the afternoon, kids were outside, playing baseball. I drove slowly along the street, looking for a parking place. I passed a sedan with two people inside. There was a man in the passenger seat, smoking a cigarette. There was a woman behind the wheel, drumming her fingers on the dashboard. It was Lauren.

I parked the car.

"I'll wait here," Connor said. "Good luck."

She always favored pale colors. She was wearing a beige suit and a cream silk blouse. Her blond hair was pulled back. No jewelry. Sexy and businesslike at the same time, her particular talent.

We walked along the sidewalk on the edge of the park, looking at the kids playing ball. Neither of us said anything. The man who had come with her waited in the car. A block away, we could see the press clustered outside my apartment.

Lauren looked at them and said, "Jesus *Christ*, Peter. I can't believe you, I really can't. This is very badly handled. This is very insensitive to my position."

I said, "Who told them?"

"Not me."

"Someone did. Someone told them you were coming at four o'clock."

"Well, it wasn't me."

"You just happened to show up with full makeup on?"

"I was in court this morning."

"Okay. Fine."

"Fuck you, Peter."

"I said, fine."

"Such a fucking detective."

She turned, and we walked back the way we had come. Moving away from the press.

She sighed. "Look," she said. "Let's try and be civil about this."

"Okay."

"I don't know how you managed to get yourself into this mess, Peter. I'm sorry, but you're going to have to give up custody. I can't permit my daughter to be raised in a suspect environment. I can't allow that. I have my position to think of. My reputation in the office."

Lauren was always preoccupied with appearances. "Why is the environment suspect?"

"Why? Child abuse is an extremely serious allegation, Peter."

"There's no child abuse."

"The allegations from your past must be dealt with."

"You know all about those allegations," I said. "You were married to me. You know everything about it."

She said stubbornly, "Michelle has to be tested."

"Fine. The exam will be negative."

"At this point, I don't really care what the exam shows. It's gone beyond that, Peter. I'm going to have to get custody. For my peace of mind."

"Oh, for Christ's sake."

"Yes, Peter."

"You don't know what it's like to raise a child. It'll take too much time away from your career."

"I have no choice, Peter. You have left me no choice." Now she sounded long suffering. Martyrdom was always one of her strong suits.

I said, "Lauren, you know the past accusations are false. You're just running with this thing because Wilhelm called you."

"He didn't call *me*. He called the assistant D.A. He called my *boss*."

"Lauren."

"I'm sorry, Peter. But you brought it on yourself."

"Lauren."

"I mean it."

"Lauren, this is very dangerous."

She laughed harshly. "Tell me. You think I don't know how dangerous this is, Peter? This could be my ass."

"What are you talking about?"

"What do you *think* I'm talking about, you son of a bitch?" she said, furiously. "I'm talking about Las Vegas."

I was silent. I didn't follow her line of thought at all.

"Look," she said. "How many times have you been to Las Vegas?"

"Just once."

"And the one time you went, you won big?"

"Lauren, you know all about that—"

"Yes, I do. Clearly I do. And what is the timing of your big winning trip to Las Vegas, and the accusations against you of child abuse? A week apart? Two weeks apart?"

So that was it. She was worried that somebody could put those two things together, that it could be traced back, somehow. And that it would implicate her.

"You should have made another trip, last year."

"I was busy."

"If you remember, Peter, I told you to go every year, for the next couple of years. Establish a pattern."

"I was busy. I had a child to raise."

"Well." She shook her head. "Now we're here."

I said, "What's the problem? They'll never figure it out."

That was when she really exploded. "Never figure it out? They've *already* figured it out. They already *know*, Peter. I'm sure they've already talked to Martinez or Hernandez or whoever that couple is."

"But they can't possibly—"

"For Christ's *sake*. How do you think somebody gets a job as Japanese liaison? How did *you* get the job, Peter?"

I frowned, thinking back. It was more than a year ago. "There was a posting of the job in the department. A list of candidates applied for it . . ."

"Yes. And then what?"

I hesitated. The truth was, I wasn't sure exactly what happened administratively. I had just applied for the job and had forgotten all about it, until it came through. I had been busy in those days. Working in the press section was a hectic job.

"I'll tell you what happens," Lauren said. "The chief of Special Services for the department makes a final determination of appropriate candidates, *in consultation with members of the Asian community.*"

"Well, that's probably true, but I don't see—"

"And do you know how long the members of the Asian community take to review the list of candidates? *Three months,* Peter. That's long enough to learn everything about the people on that list. *Everything.* They know everything from the size of your shirt collar to your financial status. And believe me, they know about the allegations of child abuse. And your trip to Las Vegas. And they can put it together. *Anybody* can put it together."

I was going to protest, when I found myself remembering what Ron said earlier in the day: Now they watch the backhaul.

She said, "You're going to stand there and tell me you don't know how all this works? That you weren't paying attention to the process? Christ, Peter, come on. You understood what was involved in that liaison job: *you wanted the money*. Just like everybody else who has anything to do with the Japanese. You know how they make their deals. There's something for everyone. You get something. The department gets something. The chief gets something. Everybody gets taken care of. And in return they get to pick exactly the kind of person they want as a liaison. They know they have a handle on you going in. And now they have a handle on me, too. All because you didn't take your goddamn trip to Las Vegas last year and establish a pattern, the way I told you to."

"So now you think you have to get custody of Michelle?"

She sighed. "At this point, we're just playing out our roles."

She glanced at her watch, and looked toward the reporters. I saw that she was impatient to get on with it, to meet the press and make the speech she had already prepared for herself. Lauren had always had a strong sense of drama.

"Are you sure what your role is, Lauren? Because it's going to get very messy around here in the next few hours. You may not want to be involved."

"I *am* involved."

"No." I took the Polaroid out of my pocket and showed it to her.

"What's this?"

"That's a video frame from the Nakamoto security tapes, taken last night. At the time of the murder of Cheryl Austin."

She frowned at the picture. "You're kidding."

"No."

"You're going with this?"

"We have to."

"You're going to arrest Senator Morton? You're *out* of your *fucking mind*."

"Maybe."

"You'll never see daylight, Peter."

"Maybe."

"They'll bury you so fast and so deep you'll never know what hit you."

"Maybe."

"You can't make this work. You know you can't. In the end, it's only going to harm Michelle."

I didn't say anything to that. I found I liked her less all the time. We walked along, her spike heels clicking on the sidewalk.

Finally she said, "Peter, if you insist on following this reckless course of action, there's nothing I can do. As your friend, I advise you not to. But if you insist, there is nothing I can do to help you."

I didn't answer. I waited and watched her. In the hard sunlight, I saw she was starting to get wrinkles. I saw the dark roots of her hair. The fleck of lipstick on her tooth. She took off her sunglasses and glanced at me, her eyes worried. Then she turned away, looking toward the press. She tapped the sunglasses in the palm of her hand.

"If this is really what's happening, Peter, I think maybe I had better hold off a day and let events take their course."

"All right."

"You understand: I'm not dropping my concerns, Peter."

"I understand."

"But I don't think the question of Michelle's custody should be mixed up in some other, crazy controversy."

"Of course not."

She put her sunglasses back on. "I feel sorry for you, Peter. I really do. At one time you had a promising future in the department. I know you've been mentioned for a position under the chief. But nothing can save you if you do this."

I smiled. "Well."

"You have anything besides photographic evidence?"

"I don't know if I should give you too many details."

"Because if you only have photographic evidence, you have no case, Peter. The D.A. won't touch it. Photographic evidence doesn't fly anymore. It's too easily doctored. The courts know it. If all you have is a picture of this guy doing the crime, it won't wash."

"We'll see."

"Peter," she said. "You are going to lose everything. Your job, your career, your child, everything. Wake up. Don't do it."

She started back toward her car. I walked with her. We didn't say anything. I waited for her to ask how Michelle was, but she never did. It wasn't surprising. She had other things to think about. Finally we arrived at her car, and she went around to the driver's side to get in.

"Lauren."

She looked at me over the top of the car.

"Let's keep it clean for the next twenty-four hours, okay? No well-placed calls to anybody."

"Don't worry," she said. "I never heard any of this. Frankly, I wish I never heard of *you*."

And she got in the car and drove off. As I watched her go, I felt my shoulders drop, and a tension leave me. It was more than the fact that I'd done what I set out to do—I had talked her out of it, at least for a while. It was more than that. There was something else, finally gone.

Connor and I went up the rear stairs of my apartment building, avoiding the press. I told him what had happened. He shrugged.

"This was a surprise to you? How the liaisons are chosen?"

"Yeah. I guess I never paid attention."

He nodded. "That's how it happens. The Japanese are very skilled at providing what they call incentives. Originally, the department had qualms about letting outsiders say anything about which officers would be chosen. But the Japanese said they simply wanted to be consulted. Their recommendations wouldn't be binding. And they pointed out that it made sense for them to have some input in the choice of liaisons."

"Uh-huh . . ."

"And just to show they were even-handed, they proposed a contribution to the officers' relief fund, to benefit the whole department."

"How much was that?"

"I think half a million. And the chief was asked to come to Tokyo and consult on criminal record-keeping systems. Three-week trip. One-week stopover in Hawaii. All first class. And lots of publicity, which the chief loves."

We got to the second-floor landing. Went up to the third.

"So," Connor said, "by the time it's all finished, it's rather difficult for the department to ignore the recommendations of the Asian community. Too much is at stake."

"I feel like quitting," I said.

"That's always an option," he said. "Anyway, you got your wife to back off?"

"My ex-wife. She got the point right away. She's a finely tuned political animal, Lauren is. But I had to tell her who the murderer was."

He shrugged. "There's not much she can do in the next couple of hours."

I said, "But what about these pictures? She says they won't stand up in court. And Sanders said the same thing: the day of photographic evidence is over. Do we have any other evidence?"

"I've been working on that," Connor said. "I think we're all right."

"How?"

Connor shrugged.

We came to the back entrance to my apartment. I unlocked the door, and we went into the kitchen. It was empty. I went down the corridor to the front hall. My apartment was quiet. The doors to the living room were closed. But there was the distinct smell of cigarette smoke.

Elaine, my housekeeper, was standing in the front hall, looking out the window at the reporters on the street below. She turned when she heard us. She looked frightened.

I said, "Is Michelle all right?"

"Yes."

"Where is she?"

"Playing in the living room."

"I want to see her."

Elaine said, "Lieutenant, there's something I have to tell you first."

"Never mind," Connor said. "We already know."

He threw open the door to the living room. And I had the biggest shock of my life.

John Morton sat in the makeup chair at the television studio, a Kleenex tucked around his collar, while the girl powdered his forehead. Standing at his side, his aide Woodson said, "This is how they recommend you handle it." He handed a fax to Morton.

"The basic through-line," Woodson said, "is that foreign investment invigorates America. America is made stronger by the influx of foreign money. America has much to learn from Japan."

"And we aren't learning it," Morton said gloomily.

"Well, the argument can be made," Woodson said. "It's a viable position and as you can see, the way Marjorie shaped it, it doesn't read as a change of position so much as a refinement of your previous view. You can skate on this one, John. I don't think it is going to be an issue."

"Is the question even going to come up?"

"I think so. I've told the reporters you are prepared to discuss a modification of your position on MicroCon. How you now favor the sale."

"Who'll ask it?"

"Probably Frank Pierce of the *Times*."

Morton nodded. "He's okay."

"Yeah. Business orientation. Should be fine. You can talk about free markets, fair trade. Lack of national security issues on this sale. All that."

The makeup girl finished, and Morton stood up from the chair.

"Senator, I'm sorry to bother you, but could I have your autograph?"

"Sure," he said.

"It's for my son."

"Sure," he said.

Woodson said, "John, we have a rough assembly of the commercial if you want to see it. It's very rough, but you might like to give comments. I've set it up for you in the next room."

"How much time have I got?"

"Nine minutes to airtime."

"Fine."

He started out the door and saw us. "Good evening, gentlemen," he said. "You need me for anything?"

"Just a short conversation, Senator," Connor said.

"I've got to look at a tape," Morton said. "Then we can talk. But I've only got a couple of minutes . . ."

"That's all right," Connor said.

We followed him into another room, which overlooked the studio below. Down there, on a beige-colored set that said NEWSMAKERS, three reporters were shuffling through their notes and being fitted with microphones. Morton sat in front of a television set, and Woodson plugged in a cassette.

We saw the commercial that was shot earlier in the day. It had a time-code running at the bottom of the frame, and it opened with Senator Morton, looking determined, walking over the golf course.

The basic message was that America had lost its economic competitiveness, and that we had to get it back.

"It's time for all of us to pull together," Morton said, on the monitor. "Everyone from our politicians in Washington, to our leaders of business and labor, to our teachers and children, to all of us in our homes. We need to pay our bills as we go, and cut the government deficit. We need to increase savings. To improve our roads and education. We need a government policy of energy conservation—for our environment, for our children's lungs, and for our global competitiveness."

The camera moved close to the senator's face, for his closing remarks.

"There are some who say that we are entering a new era of global business," he said. "They say it no longer matters where companies are located, or where things are made. That ideas of national economies are old-fashioned and out of date. To those people, I say—Japan doesn't think so. Germany doesn't think so. The most successful countries in the world today maintain strong national policies for energy conservation, for the control of imports, for promotion of exports. They nourish their industries, protecting them against unfair competition from abroad. Business and government work together to look after their own people and their jobs. And those countries are doing better than America, because those economic policies reflect the real world. Their policies work. Ours don't. We do not live in an ideal world, and until we do, America had better face the truth. We had better build our own brand of hard-nosed economic nationalism. We had better take care of Americans. Because nobody else will.

"I want to make it clear: the industrial giants of Japan and Germany are not the cause of our problems. Those countries are challenging America with new realities—and it is up to us to face those realities, and meet their economic challenge head on. If we do so, our great country will enter an era of unparalleled prosperity. But if we continue as we are, mouthing the ancient platitudes of a free market economy, disaster awaits us. The choice is ours. Join me in choosing to meet the new realities—and to make a better economic future for the American people."

The screen went blank.

Morton sat back. "When does this run?"

"It'll start in nine weeks. Test run in Chicago and the Twin Cities, associated focus groups, any modifications, then the national break in July."

"Long after MicroCon . . ."

"Oh, yes."

"Okay, good. Go with it."

Woodson took the tape, and left the room. Morton turned to us. "Well? What can I do for you?"

Connor waited until the door had closed. Then he said, "Senator, you can tell us about Cheryl Austin."

There was a pause. Morton looked at each of us. A blank expression came over his face. "Cheryl Austin?"

"Yes, Senator."

"I'm not sure that I know who—"

"Yes, Senator," Connor said. And he handed Morton a watch. It was a woman's gold Rolex.

"Where did you get this?" Morton said. His voice was low now, icy.

A woman knocked on the door. "Six minutes, Senator." She closed the door.

"Where did you get this?" he repeated.

"Don't you know?" Connor said. "You haven't even looked at the back. At the inscription."

"Where did you get this?"

"Senator, we'd like you to talk to us about her." He took a glassine bag from his pocket, and set it on the table next to Morton. It contained a pair of women's black panties.

"I have nothing to say to you gentlemen," Morton said. "Nothing at all."

Connor took a videotape from his pocket, and set it next to the senator. "This is a tape from one of five different cameras which recorded the incident on the forty-sixth floor. The tape has been altered, but it was still possible to extract an image that shows who the person with Cheryl Austin was."

"I have nothing to say," Morton said. "Tapes can be edited and changed and then changed again. It doesn't mean anything. This is all lies and baseless allegation."

"I'm sorry, Senator," Connor said.

Morton stood up and began to pace. "I want to impress upon you gentlemen the severity of the charges that you are considering. Tapes can be altered. These particular tapes have been in the custody of a Japanese corporation which, it could be argued, has a wish to exert influence over me. Whatever they may or may not show, I assure you they will not stand up to scrutiny. The public will clearly see this as an attempt to blacken the name of one of the few Americans willing to speak up against the Japanese threat. And as far as I am concerned, you two are pawns in the hands of foreign powers. You don't understand the consequences of your actions. You are making damaging allegations without proof. You have no witnesses to anything that may allegedly have happened. In fact, I would even say—"

"Senator." Connor's voice was soft but insistent. "Before you go any farther, and say anything you may regret, would you look down at the studio? There's somebody there you need to see."

"What is the meaning of this?"

"Just look, Senator. If you would, please."

Snorting angrily, Morton strode to the window and looked down at the studio. I looked too. I saw the reporters swiveling in their chairs, laughing and joking with each other as they waited to ask questions. I saw the moderator, adjusting his tie and clipping on his mike. I saw a workman wiping the shiny sign that said NEWSMAKERS. And in the corner, standing right where we had told him to stand, I saw a familiar figure with his hands in his pockets, looking up at us.

Eddie Sakamura.

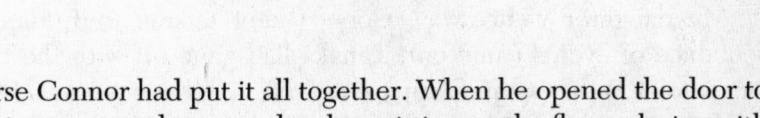

Of course Connor had put it all together. When he opened the door to my living room and saw my daughter sitting on the floor, playing with her Tinkertoys with Eddie Sakamura, he hadn't even blinked. He just said, "Hello, Eddie. I was wondering how long it'd take you to get here."

"I've been here all day," Eddie said. He sounded put out. "You guys. Never come here. I wait and wait. Have a peanut butter jelly sandwich with Shelly. You have nice girl, Lieutenant. Cute girl."

"Eddie is funny," my daughter said. "He smokes, Daddy."

"I see that," I said. I felt slow and stupid. I was still trying to understand.

My daughter came over and held her arms up. "Pick me up, Daddy." I picked her up.

"Very nice girl," Eddie said. "We made a windmill. See?" He spun the spokes of the Tinkertoy. "Works."

I said, "I thought you were dead."

"Me?" He laughed. "No. Never dead. Tanaka dead. Mess hell out of my car, too." He shrugged. "I have bad luck with Ferraris."

"So does Tanaka," Connor said.

I said, "Tanaka?"

Michelle said, "Daddy, can I watch Cinderella?"

"Not right now," I said. "Why was Tanaka in the car?"

"Panicky guy," Eddie said. "Very nervous guy. Maybe guilty, too. Must have got scared, I don't know for sure."

Connor said, "You and Tanaka took the tapes."

"Yes. Sure. Right after. Ishiguro says to Tanaka: Get the tapes. So

Tanaka gets them. Sure. But I know Tanaka, so I go along. Tanaka takes them to some lab."

Connor nodded. "And who went to the Imperial Arms?"

"I know Ishiguro sends some men, to clean up. I don't know who."

"And you went to the restaurant."

"Sure, yes. Then I went to the party. Rod's party. No problem."

"And what about the tapes, Eddie?"

"I told you. Tanaka takes them. I don't know where. He's gone. He works for Ishiguro. For Nakamoto."

"I understand," Connor said. "But he didn't take all the tapes, did he."

Eddie gave a crooked grin. "Hey."

"You kept some?"

"No. Just one. Just a mistake, you know. In my pocket." He smiled.

Michelle said, "Daddy, can I watch Disney channel?"

"Sure," I said. I put her down. "Elaine will help you."

My daughter went away. Connor kept talking to Eddie. Slowly the sequence of events came out. Tanaka had gone off with the tapes, and at some point in the evening, apparently realized that one was missing. He figured it out, Eddie said, and he came back to Eddie's house to collect the missing tape. He had interrupted Eddie with the girls. He had demanded the tape.

"I don't know for sure, but after I talk to you, I figure they set me up. We have a big argument."

"And then the police came. Graham came."

Eddie nodded slowly. "Tanaka-san shit a brick. Hey! He's unhappy Japanese man."

"So you made him tell you everything . . ."

"Oh yeah, Captain. He tells me very fast—"

"And in return you told him where the missing tape was."

"Sure. In my car. I give him the keys. So he can unlock it. He has the keys."

Tanaka had gone into the garage to get the tape. The patrolmen downstairs ordered him to halt. He started the car and drove off.

"I watch him go, John. Drives like shit."

So it had been Tanaka who was driving the car when it hit the embankment. It was Tanaka who had burned to death. Eddie explained that he hid in the shrubbery behind the swimming pool and waited until everybody left.

"Cold as shit out there," he said.

I said to Connor, "You knew all this?"

"I suspected. The reports of the crash said that the body was badly burned, and that even the glasses had melted."

Eddie said, "Hey, I don't wear glasses."

"Exactly," Connor said. "Even so, I asked Graham to check, the next day. He never found any glasses in Eddie's house. So it couldn't have been Eddie in the car. The next day, when we went to Eddie's house, I had the patrolmen check the license plates on all the cars parked on the street. Sure enough: there was a yellow Toyota sedan, a short distance up the road, registered to Akira Tanaka."

"Hey, pretty good," Eddie said. "Smart."

I said, "Where were you, all this time?"

"At Jasmine's house. Very nice house."

"Who's Jasmine?"

"Redhead number. Very nice woman. Got a Jacuzzi, too."

"But why did you come here?"

Connor said to me, "He had to. You have his passport."

"Right," Eddie said. "And me, I have your business card. You give me. Home address and phone. I need my passport, Lieutenant. I got to go now. So I come here, and wait. And holy shit, all the reporters. Cameras. Everything. So I stay low, play with Shelly." He lit a cigarette, turned nervously. "So. What do you say, Lieutenant? How about you give me my passport? *Netsutuku*. No harm done. I'm dead anyway. Okay?"

"Not just yet," Connor said.

"Come on, John."

"Eddie, you have to do a little job first."

"Hey. What job? I got to go, Captain."

"Just one job, Eddie."

Morton took a deep breath, and turned away from the studio window. I had to admire his self-control. He seemed completely calm. "It appears," he said, "that my options at this moment are somewhat reduced."

"Yes, Senator," Connor said.

He sighed. "You know it was an accident. It really was."

Connor nodded sympathetically.

"I don't know what it was about her," Morton said. "She was beautiful, of course, but it wasn't . . . it wasn't that. I only met her a short time ago. Four, five months ago. I thought she was a nice girl. Texas girl, sweet. But it was . . . one of those things. It just happened. She had this way of getting under your skin. It was crazy. Unexpected. I started to think about her all the time. I couldn't . . . she would call me, when I was on a trip. She would find out when I was on a trip, somehow. And pretty soon, I couldn't tell her to stay away. I couldn't. She always seemed to have money, always had a plane ticket. She was crazy. Sometimes, she would make me so *mad*. It was like my . . . I don't know. Demon. Everything changed when she was around. Crazy. I had to stop seeing her. And eventually I had the feeling she was paid for. Someone was paying her. Someone knew all about her. And me. So I had to stop it. Bob told. Hell, everybody in the office told me. I couldn't. Finally I did. It was over. But when I came to that reception, there she was. Shit." He shook his head. "It just happened. What a mess."

The girl stuck her head in the door. "Two minutes, Senator. They're asking for you downstairs if you're ready."

Morton said to us, "I'd like to do this first."

"Of course," Connor said.

His self-possession was extraordinary. Senator Morton conducted a televised interview with three reporters for half an hour, without a trace of tension or discomfort. He smiled, cracked jokes, bantered with the reporters. It was as if he had no problems at all.

At one point he said, "Yes, it's true that the British and the Dutch both have larger investments in America than the Japanese. But we can't ignore the reality of targeted, adversarial trade as practiced by Japan—where business and government make a planned attack on some segment of the American economy. The British and Dutch don't operate that way. We haven't lost basic industries to those countries. But we've lost many to Japan. That is a real difference—and that's the reason for concern."

He added, "And, of course, if we want to buy a Dutch or English company, we can. But we can't buy a Japanese company."

The interview continued, but nobody asked him about MicroCon. So he steered it: in reply to a question, he said, "Americans should be able to criticize Japan without being called racists or bashers. Every country has conflicts with other countries. It's inevitable. Our conflicts with Japan should be freely discussed, without these ugly epithets. My opposition to the MicroCon sale has been termed racist, but it is nothing of the sort."

Finally, one reporter asked him about the MicroCon sale. Morton hesitated, then he leaned forward across the table.

"As you know, George, I have opposed the MicroCon sale from the beginning. I still oppose it. It is time for Americans to take steps to preserve the assets of this nation. Its real assets, its financial assets, and its intellectual assets. The MicroCon sale is unwise. My opposition continues. Therefore, I am pleased to say that I have just learned Akai Ceramics has withdrawn its bid to purchase the MicroCon Corporation. I think this is the best solution all around. I applaud Akai for its sensitivity on this matter. The sale will not go forward. I am very pleased."

I said, "What? The bid was withdrawn?"

Connor said, "I guess it is now."

Morton was cheerful as the interview drew to a close. "Since I've been characterized as so critical of Japan, perhaps you'll let me express my admiration for a moment. The Japanese have a wonderful lighthearted side, and it shows up in the most unlikely places.

"You probably know that their Zen monks are expected to write a poem close to the moment of death. It's a very traditional art form, and the most famous poems are still quoted hundreds of years later. So you can imagine, there's a lot of pressure on a Zen *roshi* when he knows he's nearing death and everyone expects him to come up with a great poem. For months, it's all he can think about. But my favorite poem was written by one particular monk who got tired of all the pressure. It goes like this."

And then he quoted this poem.

> *Birth is thus,*
> *Death is thus,*
> *Poem or no poem*
> *What's the fuss?*

All the reporters started laughing. "So let's not take all this Japan business too seriously," Morton said. "That's another thing we can learn from the Japanese."

At the end of the interview, Morton shook hands with the three reporters and stepped away from the set. I saw that Ishiguro had arrived in the studio, very red-faced. He was sucking air through his teeth in the Japanese manner.

Morton said cheerfully, "Ah, Ishiguro-san. I see you have heard the news." And he slapped him on the back. Hard.

Ishiguro glowered. "I am extremely disappointed, Senator. It will not go well from this point." He was clearly furious.

"Hey," Morton said. "You know what? Tough shit."

"We had an *arrangement*," Ishiguro hissed.

"Yes, we did," Morton said. "But you didn't keep your end of it, did you?"

The senator came over to us and said, "I suppose you want me to make a statement. Let me get this makeup off, and we can go."

"All right," Connor said.

Morton walked away, toward the makeup room.

Ishiguro turned to Connor and said, *"Totemo taihenna koto ni narimashita ne."*

Connor said, "I agree. It is difficult."

Ishiguro hissed through his teeth. "Heads will roll."

"Yours first," Connor said. "*Sō omowa nakai.*"

The senator was walking toward the stairway going up to the second floor. Woodson came over to him, leaned close, and whispered something. The senator threw his arm around his shoulder. They walked arm in arm a moment. Then the senator went upstairs.

Ishiguro said bleakly, "*Konna hazuja nakatta no ni.*"

Connor shrugged. "I am afraid I have little sympathy. You attempted to break the laws of this country and now there is going to be big trouble. *Eraikoto ni naruyo, Ishiguro-san.*"

"We will see, Captain."

Ishiguro turned and gave Eddie a frosty look. Eddie shrugged and said, "Hey, I got no problems! Know what I mean, compadre? You got all problems now." And he laughed.

The floor manager, a heavyset guy wearing a headset, came over. "Is one of you Lieutenant Smith?"

I said I was.

"A Miss Asakuma is calling you. You can take it over there." He pointed to a living-room set. Couch and easy chairs, against a morning city skyline. I saw a blinking telephone by one chair.

I walked over and sat in the chair and picked up the phone. "Lieutenant Smith."

"Hi, it's Theresa," she said. I liked the way she used her first name. "Listen, I've been looking at the last part of the tape. The very end. And I think there may be a problem."

"Oh? What kind of a problem?" I didn't tell her Morton had already confessed. I looked across the stage. The senator had already gone upstairs; he was out of sight. Woodson, his aide, was pacing back and forth at the foot of the stairs, a pale, stricken look on his face. Nervously, he fingered his belt, feeling it through his suit coat.

Then I heard Connor say, "Ah, *shit!* " and he broke into a run, sprinting across the studio toward the stairs. I stood up, surprised, dropped the phone, and followed him. As Connor passed Woodson, he said "You *son of a bitch,*" and then he was taking the stairs two at a time, racing upward. I was right behind him. I heard Woodson say something like, "I *had* to."

When we got to the second floor hallway Connor shouted "Senator!" That was when we heard the single, cracking report. It wasn't loud: it sounded like a chair falling over.

But I knew that it was a gunshot.

SECOND NIGHT

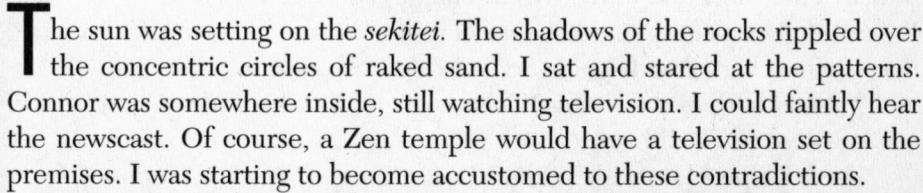

The sun was setting on the *sekitei*. The shadows of the rocks rippled over the concentric circles of raked sand. I sat and stared at the patterns. Connor was somewhere inside, still watching television. I could faintly hear the newscast. Of course, a Zen temple would have a television set on the premises. I was starting to become accustomed to these contradictions.

But I didn't want to watch TV any more. I had seen enough, in the last hour, to know how the media was going to play it. Senator Morton had been under a great deal of stress lately. His family life was troubled; his teenage son had recently been arrested for drunk driving, after an accident in which another teenager had been seriously injured. The senator's daughter was rumored to have had an abortion. Mrs. Morton was not available for comment, although reporters were standing outside the family townhouse in Arlington.

The senator's staff all agreed that the senator had been under enormous pressure lately, trying to balance family life and his own impending candidacy. The senator had not been himself; he had been moody and withdrawn, and in the words of one staffer, "He seemed to have been troubled by something personal."

While no one questioned the senator's judgment, one colleague, Senator Dowling, said that Morton had "become a bit of a fanatic about Japan lately, perhaps an indication of the strain he was under. John didn't seem to think accommodation with Japan was possible anymore, and of course we all know that we have to make an accommodation. Our two nations are now too closely bound together. Unfortunately, none of us could have known the strain he was really under. John Morton was a private man."

I sat watching the rocks in the garden turn gold, then red. An American Zen monk named Bill Harris came out and asked me if I wanted tea, or perhaps a Coke. I said no. He went away. Looking back inside, I saw flickering blue light from the tube. I couldn't see Connor.

I looked back at the rocks in the garden.

The first gunshot had not killed Senator Morton. When we kicked open the bathroom door, he was bleeding from the neck, staggering to his feet. Connor shouted "Don't!" just as Morton put the gun in his mouth and fired again. The second shot was fatal. The gun kicked out of his hands and went spinning across the tile floor of the bathroom. It came to rest near my shoes. There was a lot of blood on the walls.

Then people started screaming. I had turned back and I saw the makeup girl in the doorway, holding her hands to her face and screaming at the top of her lungs. Eventually, when the paramedics came, they sedated her.

Connor and I had stayed until the division sent Bob Kaplan and Tony Marsh. They were the detectives in charge, and we were free to go. I told Bob we'd give statements whenever he wanted them, and we left. I noticed that Ishiguro had already gone. So had Eddie Sakamura.

That had bothered Connor. "That damn Eddie," he said. "Where is he?"

"Who cares?" I said.

"There's a problem with Eddie," Connor said.

"What problem?"

"Didn't you notice how he acted around Ishiguro? He was too confident," Connor said. "*Much* too confident. He should have been frightened and he wasn't."

I shrugged. "You said it yourself, Eddie's crazy. Who knows why he does what he does." I was tired of the case, and tired of Connor's endless Japanese nuances. I said I thought Eddie had probably gone back to Japan. Or to Mexico, where he had said earlier that he wanted to go.

"I hope you're right," Connor said.

He led me toward the rear entrance to the station. Connor said he wanted to leave before the press arrived. We got into our car and left. He directed me to the Zen center. We had been there ever since. I had called Lauren but she was out of the office. I called Theresa at the lab but her line was busy. I called home, and Elaine said that Michelle was fine, and the reporters had all gone. She asked if I wanted her to stay and give Michelle dinner. I said yes, that I might be home late.

And then for the next hour, I watched television. Until I didn't want to watch any more.

It was almost dark. The sand was purple-gray. My body was stiff from sitting, and it was growing chilly. My beeper went off. I was getting a call from the division. Or perhaps it was Theresa. I got up and went inside.

On the television set, Senator Stephen Rowe was expressing sympathy for the bereaved family, and talking about the fact that Senator Morton had been overstressed. Senator Rowe pointed out that the Akai offer had not been withdrawn. The sale was, so far as Rowe knew, still going through, and there would not now be any serious opposition.

"Hmmm," Connor said.

"The sale is back on?" I said.

"It seems it was never off." Connor was obviously worried.

"You don't approve of the sale?"

"I'm worried about Eddie. He was so cocky. It's a question of what Ishiguro will do now."

"Who cares?" I was tired. The girl was dead, Morton was dead, and the sale was going forward.

Connor shook his head. "Remember the stakes," he said. "The stakes are huge. Ishiguro isn't concerned about a sordid little murder, or even the strategic purchase of some high-tech company. Ishiguro is concerned about Nakamoto's reputation in America. Nakamoto has a large corporate presence in America, and it wants it to be larger. Eddie can damage that reputation."

"How?"

He shook his head. "I don't know, for sure."

My beeper went off again. I called in. It was Frank Ellis, the watch officer at division headquarters for the evening.

"Hey, Pete," he said. "We got a call for Special Services. Sergeant Matlovsky, down at vehicle impound. He's asking for language assistance."

"What is it?" I said.

"He says he's got five Japanese nationals down there, demanding to inspect the wrecked vehicle."

I frowned. "What wrecked vehicle?"

"That Ferrari. The one in the high-speed pursuit. Apparently it's pretty ragged: the impact crushed it, and there was a fire. And the body was cut out with torches by the VHDV teams this morning. But the Japanese insist on inspecting the vehicle anyway. Matlovsky can't tell from the paperwork whether it's okay to let somebody look at it or not. You know, whether it's material to an ongoing investigation or not. And he can't speak the language to understand the Japanese. One of the Japanese claims to be related to the deceased. So, you want to go down there and handle it?"

I sighed. "Am I on tonight? I was on last night."

"Well, you're on the board. You traded nights with Allen, looks like."

I dimly remembered. I had traded nights with Jim Allen so he could take his kid to a Kings hockey game. I had agreed to it a week ago, but it seemed like something from my distant past.

"Okay," I said. "I'll handle it."

I went back to tell Connor I had to leave. He listened to the story and suddenly jumped to his feet, "Of course! Of *course!* What was I thinking of? Damn!" He pounded his hand in his fist. "Let's go, *kōhai.*"

"We're going to impound?"

"Impound? Absolutely not."

"Then what are we doing?"

"Oh, damn it, I'm a fool!" he said. He was already heading for the car.

I hurried after him.

As I pulled up in front of Eddie Sakamura's house, Connor leapt from the car, and raced up the steps. I parked and ran after him. The sky was deep blue. It was almost night.

Connor was taking the steps two at a time. "I blame myself," he said. "I should have seen it earlier. I should have understood what it meant."

"What *what* meant?" I said. I was panting a little, at the top of the steps.

Connor threw open the front door. We went inside. The living room was exactly as I had last seen it, earlier in the day, when I had stood there talking to Graham.

Connor went quickly from room to room. In the bedroom, a suitcase lay open. Armani and Byblos jackets lay on the bed, waiting to be packed. "The little idiot," Connor said. "He should never have come back here."

The pool lights were on outside. They cast a green rippling pattern on the ceiling. Connor went outside.

The body lay face down in the water, naked, floating in the center of the pool, a dark silhouette in the glowing green rectangle. Connor got a skimmer pole and pushed Eddie toward the far edge. We hauled him up onto the concrete lip.

The body was blue and cold, beginning to stiffen. He appeared unmarked.

"They would be careful about that," Connor said.

"About what?"

"About not letting anything show. But I'm sure we can find the proofs . . ." He got out his penlight and peered inside Eddie's mouth. He inspected the nipples, and the genitals. "Yes. There. See the rows of red dots? On the scrotum. And there on the side of the thigh . . ."

"Alligator clips?"

"Yes. For the electric shock coil. *Damn!*" Connor said. "Why didn't he tell me? All that time, when we were driving from your apartment to the television station to see the senator. He could have said something then. He could have told me the truth."

"About what?"

Connor didn't answer me. He was lost in his own thoughts. He sighed. "You know, in the end, we are just *gaijin*. Foreigners. Even in his desperation, we're excluded. And anyway, he probably wouldn't tell us because . . ."

He fell silent. He stared at the corpse. Finally, he slid the body back into the water. It floated out again.

"Let somebody else do the paperwork," Connor said, standing up. "We don't need to be the ones who found the body. It doesn't matter." He watched Eddie drift back to the center of the pool. The head tilted down slightly. The heels bobbed on the surface.

"I liked him," Connor said. "He did favors for me. I even met his family when I was in Japan. Some of his family. Not the father." He watched the body rotate slowly. "But Eddie was okay. And now, I want to *know*."

I was lost. I had no idea what he was talking about, but I didn't think I should say anything. Connor looked angry.

"Come on," he said finally. "We have to move fast. There's only a couple of possibilities. And once again, we have fallen behind events. But if it's the last thing I do, I want to get that son of a bitch."

"What son of a bitch?"

"Ishiguro."

We were driving back to my apartment. "You take the night off," he said.

"I'm going with you," I said.

"No. I'll do this alone, *kōhai*. It's better if you don't know."

"Know what?" I said.

We went on like this for a while. He didn't want to tell me. Finally he said, "Tanaka went to Eddie's house last night because Eddie had the tape. Presumably, the original."

"Right . . ."

"And Tanaka wanted it back. That's why they had an argument. When you and Graham came, and all hell broke loose, Eddie told Tanaka the tape was in the Ferrari. So Tanaka went down there, panicked when he saw the police, and drove the car away."

"Right."

"I always assumed the tape was destroyed in the crash, and the fire."

"Yes . . ."

"But obviously it wasn't. Because Eddie wouldn't dare be so cocky around Ishiguro unless he still had a tape. The tape would be his ace in the hole. He knew it. But he obviously didn't understand how ruthless Ishiguro would be."

"They tortured him for the tape?"

"Yes. But Eddie must have surprised them. He didn't tell them."

"How do you know?"

"Because," Connor said, "otherwise, there wouldn't be five Japanese nationals asking to inspect the wreck of a Ferrari in the middle of the night."

"So they're still looking for the tape?"

"Yes. Or evidence of the tape. They may not even know how many are missing, at this point."

I thought it over.

"What are you going to do?" I said.

"Find the tape," Connor said. "Because it matters. People are dying for that tape. If we can find the original . . ." He shook his head. "It'll put Ishiguro in deep shit. Which is just where he belongs."

I pulled up in front of my apartment building. As Elaine had said, all the reporters were gone. The street was quiet. Dark.

"I still want to go with you," I said again.

Connor shook his head. "I'm on extended leave," he said. "You're not. You've got your pension to think of. And you don't want to know exactly what I am going to do tonight."

"I can guess," I said. "You're going to retrace Eddie's steps from last night. Eddie left his house and went to stay with the redhead. Maybe he went somewhere else, too—"

"Look," Connor said. "Let's not waste more time, *kōhai*. I have some contacts and some people I can lean on. Leave it at that. If you need me, you can call me on the car phone. But don't call unless you have to. Because I'll be busy."

"But—"

"Come on, *kōhai*. Out of the car. Spend a nice night with your kid. You did a good job, but your job is finished now."

Finally, I got out of the car.

"*Sayonara*," Connor said, with an ironic wave. And he drove off.

"Daddy! Daddy!" She ran toward me, arms outstretched. "Pick me up, Daddy."

I picked her up. "Hi, Shelly."

"Daddy, can I watch *Sleeping Beauty*?"

"I don't know. Have you had dinner yet?"

"She ate two hot dogs and an ice cream cone," Elaine said. She was washing dishes in the kitchen.

"Jeez," I said. "I thought we were going to stop feeding her junk food."

"Well, it's all she would eat," Elaine said. She was irritable. It was the end of a long day with a two-year-old.

"Daddy, can I watch *Sleeping Beauty*?"

"Just a minute, Shelly, I'm talking to Elaine."

"I tried that soup," Elaine said, "but she wouldn't touch it. She wanted a hot dog."

"Daddy, can I watch Disney channel?"

"Michelle," I said.

Elaine said, "So I thought it was better that she eat something. I think she was thrown off. You know, the reporters and everything. All the excitement."

"Daddy? Can I? *Sleeping Beauty*?" She was squirming in my arms. Patting my face to get my attention.

"Okay, Shel."

"Now, Daddy?"

"Okay."

I put her down. She ran into the living room and turned on the TV, pushing the remote without hesitation. "I think she watches too much television."

"They all do," Elaine said, shrugging.

"Daddy?"

I went into the living room and plugged in the cassette. I fast-forwarded to the credits, then let it run.

"Not this part," she said impatiently.

So I fast-forwarded to the beginning of the action. Pages turning in a book.

"This part, this part," she said, tugging at my hand.

I let the tape run at normal speed. Michelle sat in the chair and started sucking her thumb. She pulled her thumb out of her mouth and patted the seat beside her. "Here, Daddy," she said.

She wanted me to sit with her.

I sighed. I looked at the room. It was a mess. Her crayons and coloring books were scattered over the floor. And the large Tinkertoy windmill.

"Let me clean up," I said. "I'll be right here, with you."

She popped her thumb back in her mouth, and turned to the screen. Her attention was total.

I cleaned up the crayons and put them back in the cardboard box. I folded up her coloring books and set them on the shelf. I was suddenly tired and sat down for a minute on the floor next to Michelle. On the screen, three fairies, red, green, and blue, were flying into the throne room of the castle.

"That's Merryweather," Michelle said, pointing. "She's the blue one."

From the kitchen, Elaine said, "Can I fix you a sandwich, Lieutenant?"

"That'd be great," I said. I found I just wanted to sit there and be with my daughter. I wanted to forget everything, at least for a while. I was grateful that Connor had dropped me off. I sat and watched the TV dumbly.

Elaine brought in a salami sandwich with lettuce and mustard. I was hungry. Elaine looked at the TV, shook her head, and went back into the kitchen. I ate my sandwich, and Michelle insisted on a few bites. She likes salami. I worry about the additives in it, but I guess it's no worse than hot dogs.

After I had the sandwich, I felt a little better. I got up to finish cleaning up the room. I picked up the Tinkertoy windmill and started taking it apart, putting the sticks back into the cardboard tube. Michelle said, "No this, no this!" in a pained voice. I thought she didn't want me to take apart the windmill, but that wasn't it at all. She was cupping her hands over her eyes. She didn't like to see Maleficent, the bad witch. I fast-forwarded past the witch, and she relaxed again.

I dismantled the Tinkertoy windmill and put everything back into the tube container. I put the metal cap on the tube and set it on the lowest shelf of the bookcase. That was where it always went. I like to keep the toys low, so Michelle can get to them herself.

The tube fell off the shelf, onto the carpet. I picked it up again. There was something on the shelf. A small gray rectangle. I knew at once what it was.

It was an eight-millimeter video cassette, with Japanese writing on the label.

Elaine said, "Lieutenant? Do you need anything else?" She had her coat on; she was ready to go.

"Hang on a minute," I said.

I went to the phone, and called the switchboard downtown. I asked them to connect me to Connor in my car. I waited impatiently. Elaine looked at me.

"Just another minute, Elaine," I said.

On the TV, the prince was singing a duet with Sleeping Beauty while birds chirped. Michelle was sucking her thumb.

The operator said, "I'm sorry, there is no answer from the car."

"Okay," I said. "Do you have a forwarding number for Captain Connor?"

A pause. "He's not on our active roster."

"I know that. But did he leave a number?"

"I don't have anything, Lieutenant."

"I'm trying to find him."

"Wait a minute." She put me on hold. I swore.

Elaine stood in the front hallway. She was waiting to go.

The operator came back on. "Lieutenant? Captain Ellis says that Captain Connor has gone."

"Gone?"

"He was here a while ago, but he's gone now."

"You mean he was *downtown*?"

"Yes, but he's gone now. I don't have a number for him. I'm sorry."

I hung up. What the hell was Connor doing downtown?

Elaine was still standing in the front hallway. "Lieutenant?"

I said, "Just a minute, Elaine."

"Lieutenant, I have a—"

"I said, *just a minute*."

I started pacing. I didn't know what to do. I was suddenly overwhelmed with fear. They had killed Eddie for the tape. They wouldn't hesitate to kill anybody else. I looked at my daughter, watching television with her thumb in her mouth. I said to Elaine, "Where's your car?"

"In the garage."

"Okay. Look. I want you to take Michelle and I want you to go—"

The phone rang. I grabbed it, hoping it was Connor. "Hello."

"Moshi moshi. Connor-san desu ka?"

"He's not here," I said. As soon as the words were out of my mouth, I cursed myself. But it was too late, the damage was done.

"Very good, Lieutenant," the voice said, heavily accented. "You have what we want, don't you?"

I said, "I don't know what you are talking about."

"I think you do, Lieutenant."

I could hear a faint hiss on the line. The call was coming from a car phone. They could be anywhere.

They could be right outside.

Damn!

I said, "Who is this?"

But I heard only a dial tone.

Elaine said, "What is it, Lieutenant?"

I was running to the window. I saw three cars double-parked in the street below. Five men getting out of them, dark silhouettes in the night.

tried to stay calm. "Elaine," I said. "I want you to take Michelle, and both of you go into my bedroom. Get under the bed. I want you to stay under there and be very quiet, no matter what happens. Do you understand?"

"No, Daddy!"

"Do it now, Elaine."

"No, Daddy! I want to watch Sleeping Beauty."

"You can watch it later." I had taken out my gun and was checking the clip. Elaine's eyes were wide.

She took Michelle. "Come on, honey."

Michelle squirmed in her arms, protesting. "No, Daddy!"

"Michelle."

She went silent, shocked at my tone. Elaine carried her into the bedroom. I loaded another clip, and put it in my jacket pocket.

I turned off the lights in the bedroom, and in Michelle's room. I looked at her crib, and the covers with little elephants sewn into it. I turned off the lights in the kitchen.

I went back into the living room. The TV was still playing. The wicked witch was instructing her raven to find Sleeping Beauty. "You are my last hope, my pet, do not fail me," she said to the bird. The bird flew away.

I stayed low. I moved toward the door. The phone rang again. I crawled back to answer it.

"Hello."

"*Kōhai.*" It was Connor's voice. I heard the static hiss of the car phone.

I said, "Where are you?"

"You have the tape?"

"Yes, I have the tape. Where are you?"

"At the airport."

"Well, *get here*. Right away. And call for backup! Jesus!"

I heard a sound on the landing, outside my door. A soft sound, like footsteps.

I hung up the phone. I was sweating.

Christ.

If Connor was at the airport, he was twenty minutes away from me. Maybe more.

Maybe more.

I was going to have to handle this on my own.

I watched the door, listening intently. But I didn't hear anything else on the landing outside.

From the bedroom, I heard my daughter say, "I want Sleeping Beauty. I want *Daddy*." I heard Elaine whispering to her. Michelle whimpered.

Then it was quiet.

The phone rang again.

"Lieutenant," the heavily accented voice said, "there is no need for backups."

Christ, they were listening to the car phone.

"We want no harm, Lieutenant. We want only one thing. Will you be so kind, to bring the tape out to us?"

"I have the tape," I said.

"We know."

I said, "You can have it."

"Good. It will be better."

I knew I was on my own. I was thinking fast. My sole idea was: Get them away from here. Get them away from my daughter.

"But not here," I said.

There was a knock at the front door. Quick, insistent rapping.

Damn!

I could feel events closing in around me. Things were happening too fast. I was crouched down on the floor, with the phone pulled down from the table above. Trying to stay below the windows.

The knock came again.

I said into the phone, "You can have the tape. But first call off your boys."

"Say again, please?"

Christ, a fucking language problem!

"Call your men away. Get them out in the street. I want to see."

"Lieutenant, we must have tape!"

"I know that," I said. "I'll give it to you." While I talked, I kept my eyes on the door. I saw the knob turning. Someone was trying to open the front door. Slowly, quietly. Then the knob was released. Something white slid under the door.

A business card.

"Lieutenant, please cooperate."

I crawled forward and picked up the card. It said: Jonathan Connor, Captain, Los Angeles Police Department.

Then I heard a whisper from the other side.

"*Kōhai.*"

I knew it was a trick. Connor said he was at the airport, so it had to be a trick—

"Perhaps I can be of assistance, *kōhai.*"

Those were the words he had used before, at the start of the case. I was confused to hear them.

"Open the fucking door, *kōhai.*"

It was Connor. I reached up and opened the door. He slipped into the room, bent over. He was dragging something blue: a Kevlar vest. I said, "I thought you were—"

He shook his head, and whispered, "Knew they must be here. Had to be. I've been waiting in the car in the alley behind the house. How many are there in front?"

"I think, five. Maybe more."

He nodded.

The accented voice on the phone said, "Lieutenant? You are there? Lieutenant?"

I held the receiver away from my ear so Connor could listen while I talked. "I'm here," I said.

On the TV, there was a loud witch's cackle.

"Lieutenant, I hear something with you."

"It's just Sleeping Beauty," I said.

"What? Sreeping Booty?" the voice said, puzzled. "What is this?"

"Television," I said. "It's the *television*."

Now I heard whispers at the other end of the line. The rush of a car going by on the street. It reminded me that the men were in an exposed position outside. Standing there on a residential street lined with apartment buildings on both sides. Lots of windows. People that might look out at any time. Or people walking by. The men would have to move quickly.

Perhaps they already were.

Connor was tugging at my jacket. Signaling me to undress. I slid out of my coat as I spoke into the phone.

"All right," I said. "What do you want me to do?"

"You bring tape to us."

I looked at Connor. He nodded. Yes.

"All right," I said. "But first get your people back."

"I am sorry?"

Connor made a fist. His face turned to a snarl. He wanted me to be angry. He covered the phone and whispered in my ear. A Japanese phrase.

"Pay attention!" I said. "*Yoku kike!* "

At the other end, there was a grunt. Surprise.

"*Wakatta*. The men come away. And now, you come, Lieutenant."

"Okay," I said. "I'm coming."

I hung up the phone.

Connor whispered, "Thirty seconds," and disappeared out the front door. I was still buttoning up my shirt around the vest. Kevlar is bulky and hot. Immediately I started to sweat.

I waited thirty seconds, staring at the face of my watch. Watching the hand go around. And then I went outside.

Someone had turned the lights out in the hallway. I tripped over a body. I got to my feet, and looked at a slender Asian face. It was just a kid, surprisingly young. A teenager. He was unconscious, breathing shallowly.

I moved slowly down the stairs.

There wasn't anybody on the second-floor landing. I kept going down. I heard canned laughter from a television, behind one of the doors on the second floor. A voice said, "So tell us, where did you go on this first date?"

I continued down to the ground floor. The front door of the apartment building was glass. I looked out and saw only parked cars, and a hedge. A short section of lawn in front of the building. The men and the cars were somewhere off to the left.

I waited. I took a breath. My heart was pounding. I didn't want to go out there, but all I could think was to get them away from my daughter. To move the action away from my—

I stepped out into the night.

The air was cold on my sweating face and neck.

I took two steps forward.

Now I could see the men. They stood about ten meters away, beside their cars. I counted four men. One of them waved to me, beckoning me over. I hesitated.

Where were the others?

I couldn't see anybody except the men by the cars. They waved again, beckoning me. I started toward them when suddenly a heavy thumping blow from behind knocked me flat onto my face on the wet grass.

It was a moment before I realized what had happened.

I had been shot in the back.

And then the gunfire erupted all around me. Automatic weapons. The street was lit up like lightning from the gunfire. The sound echoed off the apartment buildings on both sides of the street. Glass was shattering. I heard people shouting all around me. More gunfire. I heard the sound of ignitions, cars roaring down the street past me. Almost immediately there was the sound of police sirens and tires squealing, and the glare of searchlights. I stayed where I was, face down on the grass. I felt like I was there for about an hour. Then I realized that the shouts now were all in English.

Finally someone came and crouched over me and said, "Don't move, Lieutenant. Let me look first." I recognized Connor's voice. His hand touched my back, probing. Then he said, "Can you turn over, Lieutenant?"

I turned over.

Standing in the harsh light of the searchlights, Connor looked down at me. "They didn't penetrate," he said. "But you're going to have a hell of a sore back tomorrow."

He helped me to my feet.

I looked back to see the man who had shot me. But there was nobody there: just a few shell casings, glinting dull yellow in the green grass, by the front door.

THIRD DAY

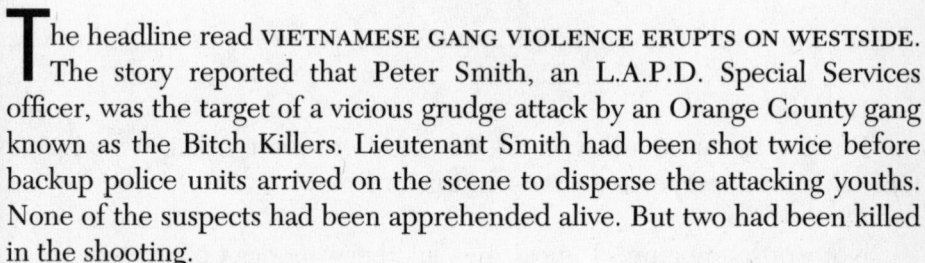

The headline read VIETNAMESE GANG VIOLENCE ERUPTS ON WESTSIDE. The story reported that Peter Smith, an L.A.P.D. Special Services officer, was the target of a vicious grudge attack by an Orange County gang known as the Bitch Killers. Lieutenant Smith had been shot twice before backup police units arrived on the scene to disperse the attacking youths. None of the suspects had been apprehended alive. But two had been killed in the shooting.

I read the papers in the bathtub, soaking my aching back. I had two large, ugly bruises on either side of my spine. It hurt to breathe.

I had sent Michelle to stay with my mother in San Diego for the weekend, until things were sorted out. Elaine had driven her down, late last night.

I continued reading.

According to the story, the Bitch Killers was thought to be the same gang that had walked up to a black two-year-old boy, Rodney Howard, and shot the child in the head while he was playing on his tricycle in the front yard of his Inglewood home a week earlier. That incident was rumored to be an initiation into the gang, and the viciousness of it had touched off a furor about whether the L.A.P.D. was able to handle gang violence in southern California.

There were a lot of reporters outside my door again, but I wasn't talking to any of them. The phone rang constantly, but I let the answering machine take it. I just sat in the tub, and tried to decide what to do.

In the middle of the morning I called Ken Shubik at the *Times*.

"I wondered when you'd check in," he said. "You must be pleased."

"About what?"

"About being alive," Ken said. "These kids are murder."

"You mean the Vietnamese kids last night?" I said. "They spoke Japanese."

"No."

"Yes, Ken."

"We didn't get that story right?"

"Not really."

"That explains it," he said.

"Explains what?"

"That was the Weasel's story. And the Weasel is in bad odor today. There's even talk of firing him. Nobody can figure it out, but something's happening around here," he said. "Somebody high in editorial all of a sudden has a bug up his ass about Japan. Anyway, we're starting a series investigating Japanese corporations in America."

"Oh, yeah?"

"Of course you'd never know it from today's paper. You see the business section?"

"No, why?"

"Darley-Higgins announced the sale of MicroCon to Akai. It's on page four of the business section. Two-centimeter story."

"That's it?"

"Not worth any more, I guess. Just another American company sold to the Japanese. I checked. Since 1987, there have been a hundred and eighty American high-tech and electronics companies bought by the Japanese. It's not news any more."

"But the paper is starting to investigate?"

"That's the word. It won't be easy, because all the emotional indicators are down. The balance of payments with Japan is dropping. Of course it only looks better because they don't export so many cars to us now. They make them here. And they've farmed out production to the little dragons, so the deficits appear in their columns, not Japan's. They've stepped up purchases of oranges and timber, to make things look better. Basically, they treat us as an underdeveloped country. They import our raw materials. But they don't buy our finished goods. They say we don't make anything they want."

"Maybe we don't, Ken."

"Tell it to the judge." He sighed. "But I don't know if the public gives a damn. That's the question. Even about the taxes."

I was feeling a little dull. "Taxes?"

"We're doing a big series on taxes. The government is finally noticing that Japanese corporations do a lot of business here, but they don't pay much tax in America. Some of them pay none, which is ridiculous. They control their profits by overpricing the Japanese subcomponents that their American assembly plants import. It's outrageous, but of course, the American government has never been too swift about penalizing Japan before. And the Japanese spend half a billion a year in Washington, to keep everybody calmed down."

"But you're going to do a tax story?"

"Yeah. And we're looking at Nakamoto. My sources keep telling me Nakamoto's going to get hit with a price-fixing suit. Price-fixing is the name of the game for Japanese companies. I pulled a list of who's settled lawsuits. Nintendo in 1991, price-fixing games. Mitsubishi that year, price-fixing TVs. Panasonic in 1989. Minolta in 1987. And you know that's just the tip of the iceberg."

"Then it's good you're doing the story," I said.

He coughed. "You want to go on record? About the Vietnamese who speak Japanese?"

"No," I said.

"We're all in this together," he said.

"I don't think it would do any good," I said.

I had lunch with Connor at a sushi bar in Culver City. As we were pulling up, someone was placing a CLOSED sign in the window. He saw Connor, and flipped it to say OPEN.

"They know me here," Connor said.

"You mean they like you?"

"It's hard to know about that."

"They want your business?"

"No," Connor said. "Probably Hiroshi would prefer to close. It won't be profitable for him to keep his people on, just for two *gaijin* customers. But I come here often. He is honoring the relationship. It doesn't really have to do with business or liking."

We got out of the car.

"Americans don't understand," he said. "Because the Japanese system is fundamentally different."

"Yeah, well, I think they're starting to understand," I said. I told him Ken Shubik's story about price-fixing.

Connor sighed. "It's a cheap shot to say the Japanese are dishonest. They're not—but they play by different rules. Americans just don't get it."

"That's fine," I said. "But price-fixing is illegal."

"In America," he said. "Yes. But it's normal procedure in Japan. Remember, *kōhai*: fundamentally different. Collusive agreements are the way things are done. The Nomura stock scandal showed that. Americans get moralistic about collusion, instead of just seeing it as a different way of doing business. Which is all it is."

We went into the sushi bar. There was a lot of bowing and greeting. Connor spoke Japanese and we sat at the bar. We didn't order.

I said, "Aren't we going to order?"

"No," Connor said. "It would be offensive. Hiroshi will decide for us what we would like."

So we sat at the bar and Hiroshi brought us dishes. I watched him cutting fish.

The phone rang. From the far end of the sushi bar, a man said, "*Connor-san, onna no hito ga matteru to ittemashita yo.*"

"*Dōmo,*" Connor said, nodding. He turned to me, and pushed back from the bar. "Guess we won't eat, after all. Time for us to go to our next appointment. You brought the tape with you?"

"Yes."

"Good."

"Where are we going?"

"To see your friend," he said. "Miss Asakuma."

We were bouncing along the potholes of the Santa Monica freeway, heading downtown. The afternoon sky was gray; it looked like rain. My back hurt. Connor was looking out the window, humming to himself.

In all the excitement, I had forgotten about Theresa's call the night before. She had said she was looking at the last part of the tape, and she thought there was a problem.

"Have you talked to her?"

"Theresa? Briefly. I gave her some advice."

"Last night, she said there was a problem with the tape."

"Oh? She didn't mention that to me."

I had the feeling he wasn't telling me the truth, but my back was throbbing and I wasn't in the mood to press him. There were times when I thought Connor had become Japanese himself. He had that reserve, that secretive manner.

I said, "You never told me why you left Japan."

"Oh, that." He sighed. "I had a job, working for a corporation. Advising on security. But it didn't work out."

"Why not?"

"Well, the job was all right. It was fine."

"Then what was it?"

He shook his head. "Most people who've lived in Japan come away with mixed feelings. In many ways, the Japanese are wonderful people. They're hardworking, intelligent, and humorous. They have real integrity. They are also the most racist people on the planet. That's why they're always accusing everybody else of racism. They're so prejudiced, they assume everybody else must be, too. And living in Japan . . . I just got tired, after a while, of the way things worked. I got tired of seeing women move to the other side of the street when they saw me walking toward them at night. I got tired of noticing that the last two seats to be occupied on the subway were the ones on either side of me. I got tired of the airline stewardesses asking Japanese passengers if they minded sitting next to a *gaijin*, assuming that I couldn't understand what they were saying because they were speaking Japanese. I got tired of the exclusion, the subtle patronizing, the jokes behind my back. I got tired of being a nigger. I just . . . got tired. I gave up."

"Sounds to me like you don't really like them."

"No," Connor said. "I do. I like them very much. But I'm not Japanese, and they never let me forget it." He sighed again. "I have many Japanese friends who work in America, and it's hard for them, too. The differences cut both ways. They feel excluded. People don't sit next to them, either. But my friends always ask me to remember that they are human beings first, and Japanese second. Unfortunately, in my experience that is not always true."

"You mean, they're Japanese first."

He shrugged. "Family is family."

We drove the rest of the way in silence.

We were in a small room on the third floor of a boardinghouse for foreign students. Theresa Asakuma explained it was not her room; it belonged to a friend who was studying in Italy for a term. She had set up the small VCR and a small monitor on a table.

"I thought I should get out of the lab," she said, running the machine fast forward. "But I wanted you to see this. This is the end of one of the tapes you brought me. It begins right after the senator has left the room."

She slowed the tape, and I saw the wide view of the forty-sixth floor of the Nakamoto building. The floor was deserted. The pale body of Cheryl Austin lay on the dark conference table.

The tape continued to roll.

Nothing happened. It was a static scene.

I said, "What are we looking at?"

"Just wait."

The tape continued. Still nothing happened.

And then I saw, clearly, the girl's leg twitch.

"What was *that*?"

"A spasm?"

"I'm not sure."

Now the girl's arm, outlined against the dark wood, moved. There was no question about it. The fingers closed and opened.

"She's still alive!"

Theresa nodded. "That's the way it looks. Now watch the clock."

The clock on the wall said 8:36. I watched it. Nothing happened. The tape ran for two more minutes.

Connor sighed.

"The clock isn't moving."

"No," she said. "I first noticed the grain pattern, on a close scan. The pixels were jumping back and forth."

"Meaning what?"

"We call it rock and roll. It's the usual way to disguise a freeze-frame. A normal freeze is visible to the eye, because the smallest units of the image are suddenly static. Whereas in a regular picture, there's always some small movement, even if it's just random. So what you do is you rock and roll, cycling three seconds of image over and over. It gives a little movement, makes the freeze less obvious."

"You're saying the tape was frozen at eight thirty-six?"

"Yes. And the girl was apparently still alive at that time. I don't know for sure. But maybe."

Connor nodded. "So that's why the original tape is so important."

"What original tape?" she said.

I produced the tape I had found in my apartment the night before.

"Run it," Connor said.

❖　❖　❖

In crisp color, we saw the forty-sixth floor. It was from the side camera, with a good view of the conference room. And it was one of the original tapes: we saw the murder, and we saw Morton leave the girl behind on the table.

The tape ran on. We watched the girl.

"Can you see the wall clock?"

"Not in this angle."

"How much time do you think has gone by?"

Theresa shook her head. "It's time lapse. I can't say. A few minutes."

Then, the girl moved on the table. Her hand twitched, and then her head moved. She was alive. There was no question about it.

And in the glass of the conference room, we saw the shape of a man. He walked forward, appearing from the right. He entered the room, looking back once to make sure he was alone. It was Ishiguro. Very deliberately, he walked to the edge of the table, placed his hands on the girl's neck, and strangled her.

"Jesus."

It seemed to take a long time. The girl struggled toward the end. Ishiguro held her down, long after she had stopped moving.

"He's not taking any chances."

"No," Connor said. "He's not."

Finally, Ishiguro stepped back from the body, shot his cuffs, straightened his suit jacket.

"All right," Connor said. "You can stop the tape now. I've seen enough."

We were back outside. Weak sunlight filtered through the smoggy haze. Cars roared by, bouncing in the potholes. The houses along the street looked cheap to me, in disrepair.

We got in our car.

"What now?" I said.

He handed me the car phone. "Call downtown," he said, "and tell them we have a tape that shows Ishiguro did the murder. Tell them we're going to Nakamoto now, to arrest Ishiguro."

"I thought you didn't like car phones."

"Just do it," Connor said. "We're about finished, anyway."

So I did it. I told the dispatcher what our plan was, where we were going. They asked if we wanted backup. Connor shook his head, so I said we didn't need backup.

I hung up the phone.

"Now what?"

"Let's go to Nakamoto."

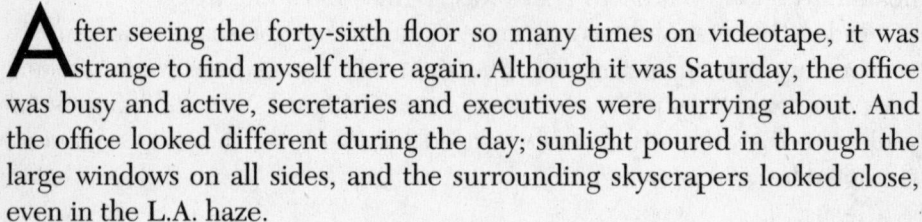

After seeing the forty-sixth floor so many times on videotape, it was strange to find myself there again. Although it was Saturday, the office was busy and active, secretaries and executives were hurrying about. And the office looked different during the day; sunlight poured in through the large windows on all sides, and the surrounding skyscrapers looked close, even in the L.A. haze.

Looking up, I saw that the surveillance cameras had been removed from the walls. To the right, the conference room where Cheryl Austin had died was being remodeled. The black furniture was gone. Workmen were installing a blond wood table and new beige chairs. The room looked completely different.

On the other side of the atrium, a meeting was being held in the large conference room. Sunlight streamed in through the glass walls on forty people sitting on both sides of a long table covered in green felt. Japanese on one side, Americans on the other. Everyone had a neat stack of documents in front of them. Prominent among the Americans, I noticed the lawyer, Bob Richmond.

Standing beside me, Connor sighed.

"What is it?"

"The Saturday meeting, *kōhai.*"

"You mean *that's* the Saturday meeting Eddie was talking about?"

Connor nodded. "The meeting to conclude the MicroCon sale."

There was a receptionist seated near the elevators. She watched us staring for a moment, then said politely, "Can I help you, gentlemen?"

"Thank you," Connor said. "But we're waiting for someone."

I frowned. From where we were standing, I could clearly see Ishiguro inside the conference room, seated near the center of the table on the Japanese side, smoking a cigarette. The man to his right leaned over to whisper something to him; Ishiguro nodded and smiled.

I glanced over at Connor.

"Just wait," Connor said.

Several minutes passed, and then a young Japanese aide hurried across the atrium and entered the conference room. Once inside, he moved more slowly, circling the table unobtrusively until he was standing behind the chair of a distinguished, gray-haired man seated toward the far end of the table. The aide bent and whispered something to the older man.

"Iwabuchi," Connor said.

"Who is he?"

"Head of Nakamoto America. Based in New York."

Iwabuchi nodded to the young aide, and got up from the table. The aide pulled his chair out for him. Iwabuchi moved down the line of Japanese negotiators. As he passed one man, he brushed him lightly on the shoulder. Iwabuchi continued to the end of the table, then opened the glass doors and walked outside, onto a terrace beyond the conference room.

A moment later, the second man stood to leave.

"Moriyama," Connor said. "Head of the Los Angeles office."

Moriyama also went outside onto the terrace. The two men stood in the sun and smoked cigarettes. The aide joined them, speaking quickly, his head bobbing. The senior men listened intently, then turned away. The aide remained standing there.

After a moment, Moriyama turned back to the aide and said something. The aide bowed quickly and returned to the conference room. He moved to the seat of another man, dark-haired with a mustache, and whispered in his ear.

"Shirai," Connor said. "Head of finance."

Shirai stood up, but did not go onto the terrace. Instead, he opened the inner door, crossed the atrium, and disappeared into an office on the far side of the floor.

In the conference room, the aide went to still a fourth man, whom I recognized as Yoshida, the head of Akai Ceramics. Yoshida also slipped out of the room, going into the atrium.

"What's going on?" I said.

"They're distancing themselves," Connor said. "They don't want to be there when it happens."

I looked back at the terrace, and saw the two Japanese men outside moving casually along the length of the terrace, toward a door at the far end.

I said, "What are we waiting for?"

"Patience, *kōhai.*"

The young aide departed. The meeting in the conference room proceeded. But in the atrium, Yoshida pulled the young aide over and whispered something.

The aide returned to the conference room.

"Hmmm," Connor said.

This time the aide went to the American side of the table, and whispered something to Richmond. I couldn't see Richmond's face, because his back was to us, but his body jerked. He twisted and leaned back to whisper something to the aide. The aide nodded and left.

Richmond remained seated at the table, shaking his head slowly. He bent over his notes.

And then he passed a slip of paper across the table to Ishiguro.

"That's our cue," Connor said. He turned to the receptionist, showed her his badge, and we walked quickly across the atrium toward the conference room.

A young American in a pinstripe suit was standing in front of the table and saying, "Now, if you will direct your attention to Rider C, the summary statement of assets and—"

Connor came into the room first. I was right after him.

Ishiguro looked up, showing no surprise. "Good afternoon, gentlemen." His face was a mask.

Richmond said smoothly, "Gentlemen, if this can wait, we're in the middle of something rather complicated here—"

Connor interrupted him. "Mr. Ishiguro, you are under arrest for the murder of Cheryl Lynn Austin," and then he read him his Miranda rights, while Ishiguro stared fixedly at him. The others in the room were entirely silent. Nobody moved at the long table. It was like a still life.

Ishiguro remained seated. "This is an absurdity."

"Mr. Ishiguro," Connor said, "would you please stand?"

Richmond said softly, "I hope you guys know what you are doing."

Ishiguro said, "I know my rights, gentlemen."

Connor said, "Mr. Ishiguro, would you please stand?"

Ishiguro did not move. The smoke from his cigarette curled up in front of him.

There was a long silence.

Then Connor said to me, "Show them the tape."

One wall of the conference room consisted of video equipment. I found a playback machine like the one I had used, and plugged the tape in. But no image came up on the big central monitor. I tried pushing various buttons, but couldn't get a picture.

From a rear corner, a Japanese secretary who had been taking notes hurried up to help me. Bowing apologetically, she pushed the proper buttons, bowed again, and returned to her place.

"Thank you," I said.

On the screen, the image came up. Even in the bright sunlight, it was clear. It was right at the moment we had seen in Theresa's room. The moment where Ishiguro approaches the girl and holds the struggling body down.

Richmond said, "What is this?"

"It's a fake," Ishiguro said. "It's a fraud."

Connor said, "This is a tape taken by Nakamoto security cameras on the forty-sixth floor Thursday night."

Ishiguro said, "It's not legal. It's a fraud."

But nobody was listening. Everybody was looking at the monitor. Richmond's mouth was open. "Jesus," he said.

On the tape, it seemed to take a long time for the girl to die.

Ishiguro was glaring at Connor. "This is nothing but a sensational publicity stunt," he said. "It is a fabrication. It means *nothing*."

"Jesus Christ," Richmond said, staring at the screen.

Ishiguro said, "It has no legal basis. It is not admissible. It will never stand up. This is just a disruption—"

He broke off. For the first time, he had looked down to the other end of the table. And he saw that Iwabuchi's chair was empty.

He looked the other way. His eyes darted around the room.

Moriyama's chair was empty.

Shirai's chair.

Yoshida's chair.

Ishiguro's eyes twitched. He looked at Connor in astonishment. Then he nodded, gave a guttural grunt, and stood. Everyone else was staring at the screen.

He walked up to Connor. "I'm not going to watch this, Captain. When you are through with your charade, you will find me outside." He lit a cigarette, squinting at Connor. "Then we will talk. *Kicchiirito na*." He opened the door and walked onto the terrace. He left the door open behind him.

I started to follow him out, but Connor caught my eye. He shook his head fractionally. I remained where I was.

I could see Ishiguro outside, standing at the railing. He smoked his cigarette and turned his face to the sun. Then he glanced back at us and shook his head pityingly. He leaned against the railing, and put his foot on it.

In the conference room, the tape continued. One of the American lawyers, a woman, stood up, snapped her briefcase shut, and walked out of the room. Nobody else moved.

And finally, the tape ended.

I popped it out of the machine.

There was silence in the room. A slight wind ruffled the papers of the people at the long table.

I looked out at the terrace.

It was empty.

By the time we got out to the railing, we could hear the sirens faintly, on the street below.

Down on ground level, the air was dusty and we heard the deafening sound of jackhammers. Nakamoto was building an annex next door, and construction was in full swing. A line of big cement trucks was pulled up along the curb. I pushed my way through the cluster of Japanese men in blue suits, and broke through to look down into the pit.

Ishiguro had landed in a wet concrete pouring. His body lay sideways, just the head and one arm sticking above the soft concrete surface. Blood ran in spreading fingers across the gray surface. Workmen in blue hardhats were trying to fish him out, using bamboo poles and ropes. They weren't having much success. Finally a workman in thigh-high rubber boots waded in to pull the body out. But it proved more difficult than he expected. He had to call for help.

Our people were already there, Fred Perry and Bob Wolfe. Wolfe saw me and walked up the hill. He had his notebook out. He shouted over the din of the jackhammers. "You know anything about this, Pete?"

"Yeah," I said.

"Got a name?"

"Masao Ishiguro."

Wolfe squinted. "Spell that?"

I started to try to spell it, talking over the sound of the construction. Finally I just reached in my pocket and fished out his card. I gave it to Wolfe.

"This is him?"

"Yeah."

"Where'd you get it?"

"Long story," I said. "But he's wanted for murder."

Wolfe nodded. "Let me get the body out and we'll talk."

"Fine."

Eventually, they used the construction crane to pull him out. Ishiguro's body, sagging and heavy with concrete, was lifted into the air, and swung past me, over my head.

Bits of cement dripped down on me, and spattered on the sign at my feet. The sign was for the Nakamoto Construction Company, and it said in bold letters: BUILDING FOR A NEW TOMORROW. And underneath, PLEASE EXCUSE THE INCONVENIENCE.

It took another hour to get everything settled at the site. And the chief wanted our reports by the end of the day, so afterward we had to go down to Parker to do the paperwork.

It was four o'clock before we went across the street to the coffee shop next to Antonio's bail bond shop. Just to get away from the office. I said, "Why did Ishiguro kill the girl in the first place?"

Connor sighed. "It's not clear. The best I can understand it is this. Eddie was working for his father's *kaisha* all along. One of the things he did was supply girls for visiting dignitaries. He'd been doing that for years. It was easy—he was a party guy; he knew the girls; the congressmen wanted to meet the girls, and he got a chance to make friends with the congressmen. But in Cheryl he had a special opportunity, because Senator Morton, head of the Finance Committee, was attracted to her. Morton was smart enough to break off the affair, but Eddie kept sending her in private jets to meet him unexpectedly, keeping the thing alive. Eddie liked her, too: he had sex with her that afternoon. And it was Eddie who arranged for her to come to the party at Nakamoto, knowing that Morton would be there. Eddie was pushing Morton to block the sale, so Eddie was preoccupied with the Saturday meeting. By the way, on the news-station tape you thought he said 'no cheapie' to Cheryl. He was saying *nichibei*. The Japanese-American relationship.

"But I think Eddie just intended for Cheryl to meet Morton. I doubt he had any idea about the forty-sixth floor. He certainly didn't expect her to go up there with Morton. The idea of going there must have been suggested during the party by someone from Nakamoto. The company left the floor accessible for a very simple reason: there's a bedroom suite up there that executives sometimes use. Somewhere in the back."

I said, "How did you know that?"

Connor smiled. "Hanada-san mentioned he had once used it. Apparently it's quite luxurious."

"So you *do* have contacts."

"I have a few. I imagine Nakamoto was probably just being accommodating, too. They may have installed cameras up there with the idea of blackmail, but I'm told there were no cameras in the bedroom suite. And the fact that they had a camera right in the conference room suggests to me that Phillips was right—the cameras were placed to *kaizen* the office workers. Certainly they couldn't have expected the sexual encounter to occur where it did.

"Anyway, when Eddie saw Cheryl going off with Morton to another part of the Nakamoto building, it must have alarmed the hell out of him. So he followed them. He witnessed the murder, which I believe was probably accidental. And Eddie then helped out his friend Morton, calling him over, getting him out of there. Eddie went back to the party with Morton."

"What about the tapes?"

"Ah. You remember we talked about bribery. One of Eddie's bribes was to a low-level security officer named Tanaka. I believe Eddie supplied him with drugs. Anyway, Eddie had known him for a couple of years. And when Ishiguro ordered Tanaka to pull the tapes, Tanaka told Eddie."

"And Eddie went down and got the tapes himself."

"Yes. Together with Tanaka."

"But Phillips said Eddie was alone."

"Phillips lied, because he knew Tanaka. That's also why he didn't make more of a fuss—Tanaka said it was all right. But when Phillips told us the story, he left Tanaka out."

"And then?"

"Ishiguro sent a couple of guys to clean out Cheryl's apartment. Tanaka took the tapes someplace to get them copied. Eddie went to the party in the hills."

"But Eddie kept one."

"Yes."

I thought it over. "But when we talked to Eddie at the party, he told a completely different story."

Connor nodded. "He lied."

"Even to you, his friend?"

Connor shrugged. "He thought he could get away with it."

"What about Ishiguro? Why did he kill the girl?"

"To get Morton in his pocket. And it worked—they got Morton to change his position on MicroCon. For a while there, Morton was going to allow the sale to go forward."

"Ishiguro would kill her for that? For some corporate sale?"

"No, I don't think it was calculated at all. Ishiguro was high-strung, under great pressure. He felt he had to prove himself to his superiors. He had much at stake—so much, that he behaved differently from an ordinary Japanese under these circumstances. And in a moment of extreme pressure, he killed the girl, yes. As he said, she was a woman of no importance."

"Jesus."

"But I think there's more to it than that. Morton was very ambivalent about the Japanese. I had the sense there was a lot of resentment—those jokes about dropping the bomb, all that. And having sex on the boardroom table. It's . . . disrespectful, wouldn't you say? It must have infuriated Ishiguro."

"And who called in the murder?"

"Eddie."

"Why?"

"To embarrass Nakamoto. Eddie got Morton safely back to the party, and then called in. Probably from a phone somewhere at the party. When he called, he didn't know about the security cameras yet. Then Tanaka told him about them, and Eddie started to worry that Ishiguro might set him up. So he called back."

"And he asked for his friend John Connor."

"Yes."

I said, "So Eddie was Koichi Nishi?"

Connor nodded. "His little joke. Koichi Nishi is the name of a character in a famous Japanese movie about corporate corruption."

Connor finished his coffee and pushed away from the counter.

"And Ishiguro? Why did the Japanese abandon him?"

"Ishiguro had played it too fast and loose. He acted too independently Thursday night. They don't like that. Nakamoto would have sent him back pretty soon. He was destined to spend the rest of his life in Japan in a *madogiwa-zoku*. A window seat. Somebody who's bypassed by corporate decisions, and stares out the window all day. In a way, it's a life sentence."

I thought it over. "So when you used the car phone, calling the station, telling them what you planned . . . who was listening?"

"Hard to say." Connor shrugged. "But I liked Eddie. I owed him one. I didn't want to see Ishiguro go home."

Back in the office there was an elderly woman waiting for me. She was dressed in black and she introduced herself as Cheryl Austin's grandmother. Cheryl's parents died in a car crash when she was four, and she had raised the little girl afterward. She wanted to thank me for my help in the investigation. She talked about what Cheryl had been like, as a little girl. How she had grown up in Texas.

"Of course, she was pretty," she said, "and the boys surely did like her.

Always a bunch of them hanging around, you couldn't shake them off with a stick." She paused. "Of course, I never thought she was entirely right in the head. But she wanted to keep those boys around. And she liked them to fight over her, too. I remember she was seven or eight, she'd get those kids brawling in the dust, and she'd clap her hands and watch them go at it. By the time she was teenage, she was real good at it. Knew just what to do. It wasn't real nice to see. No, something was wrong in the head. She could be mean. And that song, she always played it, day and night. About lose my mind, I'd think."

"Jerry Lee Lewis?"

"Of course, I knew why. That was her Daddy's favorite song. When she was just a little bit of a thing, he'd drive her to town in his convertible, with his arm around her, and the radio making that awful racket. She'd have her best sundress on. She was such a pretty thing when she was a child. The image of her mother."

Then the woman started to cry, thinking about that. I got her a Kleenex. Tried to be sympathetic.

And pretty soon she wanted to know what had happened. How Cheryl had died.

I didn't know what to say to her.

As I was coming out of the ground-floor entrance to Parker Center, walking out by the fountains, a Japanese man in a suit stopped me. He was about forty, with dark hair and a mustache. He greeted me formally, and gave me his card. It took a moment to realize that this was Mr. Shirai, the head of finance for Nakamoto.

"I wanted to see you in person, Sumisu-san, to express to you how much my company regrets the behavior of Mr. Ishiguro. His actions were not proper and he acted without authority. Nakamoto is an honorable company and we do not violate the law. I want to assure you that he does not represent our company, or what we stand for in doing business. In this country, the work of Mr. Ishiguro put him in contact with many investment bankers, and men who make leveraged buy-outs. Frankly, I believe he was too long in America. He adopted many bad habits here."

So there it was, an apology and an insult in the same moment. I didn't know what to say to him, either.

Finally, I said, "Mr. Shirai, there was the offer of financing, for a small house . . ."

"Oh, yes?"

"Yes. Perhaps you didn't hear of it."

"Actually, I believe I have heard something of that."

I said, "I was wondering what you intended to do about that offer now."

There was a long silence.

Just the splash of the fountains off to my right.

Shirai squinted at me in the hazy afternoon light, trying to decide how to play it.

Finally he said, "Sumisu-san, the offer is improper. It is of course withdrawn."

"Thank you, Mr. Shirai," I said.

Connor and I drove back to my apartment. Neither of us talked. I was driving on the Santa Monica freeway. The signs overhead had been spray-painted by gangs. I was aware of how uneven and bumpy the roadway was. To the right, the skyscrapers around Westwood stood hazy in smog. The landscape looked poor and decrepit.

Finally I said, "So is that all this was? Just competition between Nakamoto and some other Japanese company? Over MicroCon? Or what?"

Connor shrugged. "Multiple purposes, probably. The Japanese think in those ways. And to them, America is now only an arena for their competition. That much is true. We're just not very important, in their eyes."

We came to my street. There was a time when I thought it was pleasant, a little tree-lined street of apartments, with a playground at the end of the block for my daughter. Now I wasn't feeling that way. The air was bad, and the street seemed dirty, unpleasant.

I parked the car. Connor got out, shook my hand. "Don't be discouraged."

"I am."

"Don't be. It's very serious. But it can all change. It's changed before. It can change again."

"I guess."

"What are you going to do now?" he asked.

"I don't know," I said. "I feel like going somewhere else. But there's nowhere to go."

He nodded. "Leave the department?"

"Probably. Certainly leave Special Services. It's too . . . unclear for me."

He nodded. "Take care, *kōhai*. Thanks for your help."

"You, too, *sempai*."

I was tired. I climbed the stairs to my apartment and went inside. It was quiet, with my daughter gone. I got a can of Coke from the refrigerator and walked into the living room, but my back hurt when I sat in the chair. I got up again, and turned on the television. I couldn't watch it. I thought of how

Connor said everybody in America focused on the unimportant things. It was like the situation with Japan: if you sell the country to Japan, then they will own it, whether you like it or not. And people who own things do what they want with them. That's how it works.

I walked into my bedroom and changed my clothes. On the bedside table, I saw the pictures from my daughter's birthday that I had been sorting when all this started. The pictures that didn't look like her, that didn't fit the reality anymore. I listened to the tinny laughter from the television in the other room. I used to think things were basically all right. But they're not all right.

I walked into my daughter's room. I looked at her crib, and her covers with the elephants sewn on it. I thought of the way she slept, so trustingly, lying on her back, her arms thrown over her head. I thought of the way she trusted me to make her world for her now. And I thought of the world that she would grow into. And as I started to make her bed, I felt uneasy in my heart.

Transcript of: March 15 (99)

INT: All right, Pete, I think that about does it for us. Unless you have anything else.

SUBJ: No. I'm done.

INT: I understand you resigned from the Special Services.

SUBJ: That's right.

INT: And you made a written recommendation to Chief Olson that the Asian liaison program be changed. You said the connection with the Japan-America Amity Foundation should be severed?

SUBJ: Yes.

INT: Why is that?

SUBJ: If the department wants specially trained officers, we should pay to train them. I just think it's healthier.

INT: Healthier?

SUBJ: Yes. It's time for us to take control of our country again. It's time for us to start paying our own way.

INT: Have you had a response from the Chief?

SUBJ: Not yet. I'm still waiting.

If you don't want Japan to buy it, don't sell it.

Akio Morita

Afterword

"People deny reality. They fight against real feelings caused by real circumstances. They build mental worlds of shoulds, oughts, and might-have-beens. Real changes begin with real appraisal and acceptance of what is. Then realistic action is possible."

These are the words of David Reynolds, an American exponent of Japanese Morita psychotherapy. He is speaking of personal behavior, but his comments are applicable to the economic behavior of nations, as well.

Sooner or later, the United States must come to grips with the fact that Japan has become the leading industrial nation in the world. The Japanese have the longest lifespan. They have the highest employment, the highest literacy, the smallest gap between rich and poor. Their manufactured products have the highest quality. They have the best food. The fact is that a country the size of Montana, with half our population, will soon have an economy equal to ours.

But they haven't succeeded by doing things our way. Japan is not a Western industrial state; it is organized quite differently. And the Japanese have invented a new kind of trade—adversarial trade, trade like war, trade intended to wipe out the competition—which America has failed to understand for several decades. The United States keeps insisting the Japanese do things our way. But increasingly, their response is to ask, why should *we* change? We're doing better than you are. And indeed they are.

What should the American response be? It is absurd to blame Japan for successful behavior, or to suggest that they slow down. The Japanese consider such American reactions childish whining, and they are right. It is more appropriate for the United States to wake up, to see Japan clearly, and to act realistically.

In the end, that will mean major changes in the United States, but it is inevitably the task of the weaker partner to adjust to the demands of a relationship. And the United States is now without question the weaker partner in any economic discussion with Japan.

A century ago, when Admiral Perry's American fleet opened the nation, Japan was a feudal society. The Japanese realized they had to change, and they did. Starting in the 1860s, they brought in thousands of Western specialists to advise them on how to change their government and their industries. The entire society underwent a revolution. There was a second convulsion, equally dramatic, after World War II.

But in both cases, the Japanese faced the challenge squarely, and met it. They didn't say, let the Americans buy our land and our institutions and hope they will teach us to do things better. Not at all. The Japanese invited thousands of experts to visit—and then sent them home again. We would do well to take the same approach. The Japanese are not our saviors. They are our competitors. We should not forget it.

Acknowledgments

For advice and assistance during my research, I am grateful to Nina Easton, James Flanigan, Ken Reich, and David Shaw, all of the *Los Angeles Times*; Steve Clemons of the Japan America Society of Southern California; Senator Al Gore; Jim Wilson of the Jet Propulsion Laboratory; Kevin O'Connor of Hewlett-Packard; Lieutenant Fred Nixon of the Los Angeles Police Department; Ron Insana of CNBC/FNN; and Keith Manasco. For suggestions and corrections of the manuscript at various points, I am indebted to Mike Backes, Douglas Crichton, James Fallows, Karel van Wolferen, and Sonny Mehta. Valery Wright shepherded the manuscript through seemingly endless revisions, Shinoi Osuka and later Sumi Adachi Sovak assisted ably with the Japanese text, and Roger McPeek gave me his understanding of video technology and future security systems.

The subject of Japanese-American relations is highly controversial. I wish to state clearly that the views expressed in this novel are my own, and are not to be attributed to any of the individuals listed above.

Bibliography

This novel questions the conventional premise that direct foreign investment in American high technology is by definition good, and therefore should be allowed to continue without restraint or limitation. I suggest things are not so simple.

Although this book is fiction, my approach to Japan's economic behavior, and America's inadequate response to it, follows a well-established body of expert opinion, much of it listed in the bibliography. Indeed, in preparing this novel, I have drawn heavily from a number of the sources below.

I hope readers will be provoked to read further from more knowledgeable authors. I have listed the principal texts in rough order of readability and pertinence to the issues raised in this novel.

PRINCIPAL SOURCES

Clyde V. Prestowitz, Jr., *Trading Places: How We Are Giving Our Future to Japan and How to Reclaim It* (New York: BasicBooks, 1989).

James Fallows, *More Like Us: Putting America's Native Strengths and Traditional Values to Work to Overcome the Asian Challenge* (Boston: Houghton Mifflin, 1989).

———, "Containing Japan," *The Atlantic*, May 1989, pp. 40–54.

———, "Getting Along with Japan," *The Atlantic*, December 1989, pp. 53–64.

Peter F. Drucker, *The New Realities* (New York: Harper & Row, 1989).

Ezra F. Vogel, *Japan as Number One: Lessons for America* (Cambridge, Mass.: Harvard University Press, 1979).

Karel van Wolferen, *The Enigma of Japanese Power* (New York: Alfred A. Knopf, 1989).

Chalmers Johnson, *MITI and the Japanese Miracle* (Stanford: Stanford University Press, 1982).

Michael T. Jacobs, *Short-Term America: The Causes and Cures of Our Business Myopia* (Boston: Harvard Business School Press, 1991).

Robert Kuttner, *The End of Laissez-Faire: National Purpose and the Global Economy after the Cold War* (New York: Alfred A. Knopf, 1991).

Michael L. Dertouzos, Richard K. Lester, and Robert M. Solow, *Made in America: Regaining the Productive Edge*, The Report of the M.I.T. Commission on Industrial Productivity (Cambridge, Mass.: M.I.T. Press, 1989).

Pat Choate, *Agents of Influence* (New York: Alfred A. Knopf, 1990).

Dorinne K. Kondo, *Crafting Selves: Power, Gender and Discourses of Identity in a Japanese Workplace* (Chicago: University of Chicago Press, 1990).

Kenichi Ohmae, *Fact and Friction: Kenichi Ohmae on U.S.-Japan Relations* (Tokyo: *The Japan Times*, Ltd., 1990).

Donald M. Spero, "Patent Protection or Piracy—A CEO Views Japan," *Harvard Business Review*, September–October 1990, pp. 58–67.

OTHER SOURCES

Daniel E. Bob and SRI International, *Japanese Companies in American Communities: Cooperation, Conflict and the Role of Corporate Citizenship* (New York: Japan Society, 1990).

Bryan Burrough and John Helyar, *Barbarians at the Gate: The Fall of RJR Nabisco* (New York: Harper & Row, 1990).

Alfred D. Chandler, Jr., *Scale and Scope: The Dynamics of Industrial Capitalism* (Cambridge, Mass.: Belknap Press of Harvard University Press, 1990).

Ronald Dore, *Taking Japan Seriously: A Confucian Perspective on Leading Economic Issues* (Stanford: Stanford University Press, 1987).

David Halberstam, *The Next Century* (New York: William Morrow and Co., 1991).

Kichiro Hayashi, editor, *The U.S.-Japanese Economic Relationship: Can It Be Improved?* (New York: New York University Press, 1989).

Kanji Ishizumi, *Acquiring Japanese Companies* (Tokyo: *The Japan Times*, Ltd., 1988).

Gary Katzenstein, *Funny Business: An Outsider's Year in Japan* (New York: Prentice Hall Press, 1989).

Maryann Keller, *Rude Awakening: The Rise, Fall and Struggle for Recovery of General Motors* (New York: William Morrow and Co., 1989).

Paul Kennedy, *The Rise and Fall of the Great Powers* (New York: Random House, 1987).

W. Carl Kester, *Japanese Takeovers: The Global Contest for Corporate Control* (Cambridge, Mass.: Harvard Business School Press, 1991).

Philip Kotler, Liam Fahey, and S. Jatusripitak, *The New Competition: What Theory Z Didn't Tell You About Marketing* (New Jersey: Prentice Hall, 1985).

Paul Krugman, *The Age of Diminished Expectations: U.S. Economic Policy in the 1990's* (Cambridge, Mass.: M.I.T. Press, 1990).

Takie Sugiyama Lebra, *Japanese Patterns of Behavior* (Honolulu: University of Hawaii Press, 1976).

Michael Lewis, *Liar's Poker* (New York: Penguin Books, 1989).

Charles A. Moore, *The Japanese Mind: Essentials of Japanese Philosophy and Culture* (Honolulu: University of Hawaii Press, 1967).

Kenichi Ohmae, *The Borderless World: Power and Strategy in the Interlinked Economy* (New York: Harper Business, 1990).

Daniel I. Okimoto, *Between MITI and the Market: Japanese Industrial Policy for High Technology* (Stanford: Stanford University Press, 1989).

L. Craig Parker, Jr., *The Japanese Police System Today: An American Perspective* (New York: Kodansha, 1987).

Michael E. Porter, *The Competitive Advantage of Nations* (New York: Free Press, 1990).

Jim Powell, *The Gnomes of Tokyo: The Positive Impact of Foreign Investment in North America* (New York: American Management Association, 1989).

Clyde V. Prestowitz, Jr., Alan Tonelson, and Robert W. Jerome, "The Last Gasp of GATTism," *Harvard Business Review*, March–April 1991, pp. 130–38.

Michael Random, *Japan: Strategy of the Unseen* (Wellingborough, England: Thorsons Publishing Group, 1987).

Donald Richie, *The Films of Akira Kurosawa* (Berkeley: University of California Press, 1970).

Robert M. Stern, *Trade and Investment Relations Among the United States, Canada, and Japan* (Chicago: University of Chicago Press, 1989).

Sheridan M. Tatsuno, *Created in Japan: From Imitators to World-Class Innovators* (New York: Harper & Row, 1990).

Peter Trasker, *The Japanese: Portrait of a Nation* (New York: New American Library, 1987).

Thomas R. Zengage and C. Tait Ratcliffe, *The Japanese Century: Challenge and Response* (Hong Kong: Longman Group [Far East] Ltd., 1988).

About the Author

MICHAEL CRICHTON is admired for his technothriller novels and adventure-filled screenplays. His novels, most of them *New York Times* bestsellers, include *The Lost World, Jurassic Park, Sphere, Congo, Eaters of the Dead, The Great Train Robbery, The Terminal Man, The Andromeda Strain,* and the two novels in this collection, *Disclosure* and *Rising Sun.* He has also authored four nonfiction works: *Five Patients, Jasper Johns, Electronic Life,* and *Travels.*

Born in Chicago in 1942, Michael Crichton was educated at Harvard College and the Harvard Medical School. In 1969, he was a postdoctoral fellow at the Salk Institute in LaJolla, California, and in 1988 was Visiting Writer at the Massachusetts Institute of Technology.